HEARTS O

THE AMULET

RONDA LEE

You are now entering The Old Maple Forest

AmErica House
Baltimore

First printing

http://www.heartsofdarkness-theseries.com

Cover art by: Ronda Lee
Back cover photo by: Deena Festa

ISBN: 1-58851-491-9
PUBLISHED BY AMERICA HOUSE BOOK PUBLISHERS
www.publishamerica.com
Baltimore

Printed in the United States of America

Dedicated To

The loving memory of Phil Stern who I will never be able to forget – 'Papa Stern... he really loved you a lot...'

My Editor Kim Brown who always found time in her busy schedule for me and made me her top priority. Without her there would be no Hearts of Darkness.

My on-line friend Jon Jones (JJ) who was with me chapter by chapter and motivated me to finish and continue on with the series.

Acknowledgement

Chrissy Vivianni - who knew the book before the book
Eric White - a creative, patient and dear friend

My on-line chatters who always asked 'how's the book coming?'
Bill "Knight" Macleod
Silver Shadow
Kevin "KCWhisper"
Jon Jones "JJ"
Joe "Sagman"
Run21
& Many, Many More

My family for sticking by me in another hard time

Everyone I worked with or for in radio and gave me some of the happiest days of my life - Thank you!!

Lisa and the Hope Alliance, Inc (a non profit rescue in New Haven, Connecticut dedicated to finding homes for abused and homeless cats). Proceeds from this book's sales will be donated to make sure the organization continues to run. I believe in your cause. (http://hopealliance.hypermart.net)

Mike at Chaotic Creations for making my 'Amulet'
(http://www.firescale.com)

Chapter 1

Fear gripped the woman as she took refuge behind an old metal dumpster in a dark, narrow alley. She had but only a moment. What to do? Her hands fluttered like dying moths from her trembling mouth to her heaving chest. She froze suddenly as a sound came from her left - loud, heavy, ominous. With a stifled cry, she dropped to the filthy ground, crouched awkwardly on her hands and knees. Shaking in horror, she crept like a hunted animal away from the relative safety of the large metal container - she had to make it out of the alley - she had to make it, so much depended on her. Her labored breathing filled her ears as she gasped for breath, struggling to fill her burning lungs. The night air was thick and heavy with humidity – and something else. Something rancid – evil. Sara knew she must not stop – *could* not stop. She had to live. She had to let Kala know!

There is simply no preparation for the news of a death. We all learn at a young age that everything is born, lives an amount of time and then passes on. Rarely do any of us get out of our teenage years without experiencing the loss of someone elderly within the family – by this time you know death is very finalizing and everything good goes to Heaven, everything bad goes to Hell. The reality of death is something mortals don't want to think about. We act as if we can somehow escape our own death when the doorway opens up and that bright white light shines upon us. If there is a way to live forever, no one I know of has found it yet. Besides, who wants to live forever at the ripe old age of ninety? It's not like you can wear a bikini at the beach then, anyways. If there is a way to go on living – to never die – show me *now* before my first wrinkle.

I had just lost someone I deeply loved, which further proves the fact that humans die. We are not supernatural – not even Sara, who raised me virtually as her own and would have sacrificed all she had for me. Suddenly, Sara was no longer available by phone, for dinner or to give me a shoulder to cry on. I knew this bereavement would take time. It became my experience that struggling through a loved one's death with all the tears and tissues was at first selfish – you go through the 'what I am going to do without them?' The loneliness of each hour that passed without her was nearly unbearable. Wondering how I was ever going to make it through the rest of my own life without her left me feeling as if I just couldn't. I was ready to die. I had had enough. Why live? Help me find a really good reason.

It's all about how *we* feel in their passing. I finally decided when I could cry no more tears, that death is all about love. I can always express love and continue to love Sara, no matter where she is. Love is how you feel on the inside and as long as you can feel it, it's a foundation to rebuild on – things will be okay eventually.

My relationship with Sara was unusual and so was her death. Sara was not my mother, not an aunt or a sister – no blood relation whatsoever. She was a friend and sometimes a genuinely devoted friendship can be more fulfilling in life, and in death, than any family member can ever hope to be.

Sara's death was totally unexpected. Not that expected deaths are easily taken – but murder on the other hand is a whole new experience to go through. An unexpected phone call in the heart of the night – that loud drumming ring in the darkest of hours that already tells you something is wrong; the tension as a stranger's voice tells you someone you know is 'gone' – that's something that remains seared deep within you forever. The blank voice on the phone – just words – they didn't know who Sara was, what she meant to me. Their job was to relay only the devastating information with no time or inclination to answer my questions at all. Through my tears and frustrations I begged for details of her death. All the voice offered was "she did not suffer". Even now when the phone rings late at night I hear that anonymous voice telling me about Sara's death.

After she died, I tried to get information about what had happened. Sara had no immediate family, so the authorities were understandably tight-lipped about the circumstances. I did not know where to go or who to talk to. Everyone who knew Sara, including me, was trapped in confusion. There was very little information released to the newspapers about her demise, or the circumstances surrounding it. Her death was labeled "suspicious" and was being investigated, so perhaps there were good reasons for tight lips. Finally, in despair, I contacted the Detective who was working on Sara's case, hoping for the tiniest of details. The arrangements for Sara's body had not been made yet – this was beginning to sicken me, thinking about Sara tucked away in a body bag somewhere; something needed to be done.

My initial meeting with the Detective who was the primary investigator in Sara's death was delayed by his schedule. I sat for several hours in the lobby of a crowded police station, not wanting to leave, not wanting to miss my chance to put to rest all the crazy thoughts I had as to how Sara died. Every horror movie I had ever seen, every twisted plot, every murder weapon covered in crimson blood clouded my mind. It had to end. I knew the truth might be more than I could bear, but even that would be better than my wild imaginings. I naively hoped the police would at least share their findings.

You'd think that Sara was my lover with the way I was rambling on about her. The fact is, she was my best friend. More than that, Sara was everything to me. Sara was the mother I never really had; Sara was a friend and supported every decision I ever made – even the stupid ones. Sara was a teacher of the world to me – and Sara was a witch. My relationship with Sara was complete and very rewarding. I would do anything for her and she for me. There was a time in my life when all I wanted to do was 'find that perfect someone', settle down, get married and feel needed. Sara had a different objective for me. Sara wanted to make sure I was happy with *me* first – then if I wanted to complete my life with the man of my dreams – and have kids – great, but she wanted me to be happy with who I was first. She called me 'special' and there was something about the way she looked at me, and the soft reverent tone in her voice that was very convincing. I was 'special'.

Sara met me when I was young and struggling with a less than happy relationship with my mother. My parent's marriage had fallen apart, I was in my mid teens, and my mother was having a hard enough time taking care of herself, let alone me. I had to mature and take on responsibilities quicker than most. It was then that I met Sara at a bookstore she owned, and became 'store' property after that. Sara picked up where my mother left off. Having no children of her own, she told me I was practice for the time that she might. Anyone looking for me before or after school knew where to find me – with Sara. The fact that Sara was a witch never bothered me. When she first told me I laughed; I thought she was calling herself a 'bitch' and was changing the word to something more G-rated for my young and impressionable ears. But after handing me a few books to read in my free time about Druid and Celtic cultures, and assisting me in some school science projects with her knowledge of earth and elements, I realized she meant *witch* all along. I wanted to be just like her.

Sara was very highly respected in her community, a community that included others like her. People who did not like her though, thought she was evil, a nutcase. 'Satanic Sara' I would hear others call her – but she didn't seem to mind; they were just ignorant to what she was. Sara was amazed, and a little hurt, by those people who had known her and liked her for many years, but then avoided her when they found out she was Wiccan. Like all of a sudden the fact that she was Wiccan for thirty years had changed her overnight! Sara had a hard time believing that modern society could be so narrow-minded.

Sara was Sara – a.k.a. Auburn Starr to her Coven, and to the patrons of her bookstore she called "Spellbound." She had long, wavy, natural auburn hair, and wondrous lapis blue eyes that reflected light like Caribbean waters. Her eyebrows, high and thin on her intelligent forehead, complimented her creamy complexion. Sara looked much younger than she was, with a childlike nose and freckles to match. She was very attractive and dated regularly; men loved her.

Sara owned Spellbound with another witch; an older woman with silvering gray locks named Addy Baker, known to most as Dove; just plain Dove. Sara and Addy had grown up together and even attended college together, and some time later opened up Spellbound, which was the largest and oldest occult bookstore in the state, I might add. Addy married, but Sara never did and neither one had children. Addy always wanted them, but was never fortunate enough to bear any. But Sara had me, a big grown up kid, perfect in every way, so she would say.

I worked at Spellbound too, a few times a week to help them out. I enjoyed my time there. I would clean or dust, tag merchandise, assist them in any way that I could. But I had a life away from Sara and Spellbound. I worked days at a radio station as a disc jockey, and enjoyed my career. I had worked hard to get where I was in such a short amount of time, but I sometimes wondered if Sara's spells might have helped too.

While it might not be apparent, radio is a very male oriented business. It means a great deal for a woman to get somewhere in broadcasting without climbing the ladder of success on her back. First of all, a woman's life expectancy in the business is very short, mostly due to the sexist attitude behind the smiles of the men who run the stations. Even though radio is a non-visual medium, if you are the woman behind the microphone you had better look as good as you sound, or better. If you don't have boobs and butt men would die for, your career will be even shorter. The first signs of fat, gray, or droop and you're working on AM radio. Luckily, I'm still young and firm enough to get by, and as long as dye comes in a bottle, I'm good to go. Maybe even a spell or two could hold me over between having my roots done. All in all I was proud of myself. Proud of who I was for the first time in my life. But I could never forget Sara, since she was my greatest influence in her life – and in her death.

It wasn't until Tuesday evening when I met with Detective Drake at the 23:00 hour Diner to talk to him regarding the suspicious death of my friend. I sat in an orange vinyl booth, located in the very back of the restaurant, in the corner by the rest rooms. I watched the waitresses wander in and out of the kitchen, listening to the clanking of dinnerware and the clatter of pots and pans. There was an elderly man sipping coffee at the counter; he seemed familiar to me. I remembered him on occasions sitting in the park, reading a book on a bench in the afternoons when I would pass by to get home. I didn't know him by name, just by face. Someone's grandfather for sure.

When the waitress passed my table she inquired about ordering. I asked for a Diet Coke. The Diner seemed kind of empty for the time of night, but diner people aren't your normal type of people anyway; mostly they're insomniacs, or unhappily married, maybe lonely or old, or addicted to a substance. I found myself looking at each face in the restaurant trying to imagine what their problem was. Were they on drugs? Were they unemployed? Perhaps they were sex maniacs; it had to be one of those things. I wondered what those same people saw in me when they looked at my face, and watched me drink my Diet Coke through one of those bendy straws you can hardly find any more. I wondered.

My musing didn't last too long before a man in his mid-thirties began to head in my direction; he was either going towards the bathroom or coming to see me – it was a 50/50 chance. Just short of my booth, he began to speak. "I'm Detective Jeffery Drake. Are you Kala?" He came to a full stop directly in front of me – wide shoulders, thin waist, buff body – cute.

I pushed my Diet Coke with bendy straw off to the side and looked up casually. "Yes I am," I answered.

He slid in to the booth and looked squarely at me. "I want to apologize for missing our last meeting," he began. "Things have been crazy all over town." He sighed as if overwhelmed.

I smiled. "I'm sure it has been." I sipped my soda and surreptitiously admired his handsome features. He was a man who was well put together, which is to say not only fairly muscular but markedly so. His hair was relatively long for someone in law enforcement, but was a nice shade of caramel blond with natural streaks of light brown. His face was youthful, but the unshaven five-o-clock shadow he sported made him ruggedly good looking.

"I'm really sorry about your friend," he said sympathetically, while fidgeting with the wrapper from my straw. He seemed uncomfortable, his fingers twisting the paper, his brown eyes moving evasively around the diner.

"Thank you. But that's why I need to speak to you," I said earnestly. "Sara was my best friend. I'm lost without her. I need to know what happened; I need to know! Please!" My eyes implored his. I nervously awaited his response, sipping my soda again and dunking my straw up and down between the crushed ice.

"I can't say much. I hope you understand," the detective admonished me.

The waitress approached the booth again, this time to check with my visitor to see what he needed. The order was coffee and it was instantly delivered with milk and sugar on the side.

"Just what I need – more caffeine," he laughed lightly.

"We all get our fix in difference ways," I said, pulling my dark hair away from my face.

"Your friend," he began. "I really can't go into much. I'm still investigating the case. I hope to know more soon, but things have slowed down." He sipped his black coffee.

"I understand. I just keep thinking about her, wondering what happened. How was she killed; please tell me, you don't have to go into detail," I pleaded, sitting still and straight, waiting for the brutal truth.

He spun his coffee cup around slowly, concentrating on the design painted on the porcelain and picking at a small chip on the side. "I can't. I'm sorry. I came here tonight because you have been calling so much and leaving so many messages. All I can say is that the circumstances are unusual, but not overly gruesome. I have been working homicides for ten years and I have seen a lot of dead bodies. I can easily say a death is not gruesome, and mean it. However, in the past ten years, the homicides I investigate seem to be getting a little more on the abnormal side."

"Abnormal? In what way? How?" I asked quickly.

"There isn't just one odd piece; it's all out of the ordinary. She was a witch, right?"

"Yes, why? What does that have to do with anything?" My forehead wrinkled in thought, trying to follow him.

"Just trying to piece it all together. That's my job," he said. "Our office contacted Addy Baker today; she'll be making your friend's final arrangements."

"Oh. I haven't spoken to her today." I shocked myself as I realized this. I had been trying to see her or at least talk to her daily since Sara's death. Addy had taken it as hard as I had.

"When I can talk about your friend Sara, I will call you and Addy right away. I promise." He slugged the rest of his coffee down.

"Please. It's very important to us." I felt short of breath, holding my feelings back.

Drake stood up, threw a few dollars on the table, and said his good bye, leaving the diner with me knowing little more than before. Was Sara's death some sort of X-File episode? Where was Mulder and Scully when you needed them?

After my meeting with Detective Drake, I drove to Spellbound to check on Addy. I wanted to see how she was doing and talk to her about Sara's arrangements. It was just starting to get dark as I found a parking space on the street near the storefront. The shop was lit up and conducting business as usual. I gave myself several minutes of silence in the car, summoning the energy to go in and confront my losses again. Sara would not be here, at least, not in body. This shop would always be a constant reminder of all I had, and all I had lost. I knew there were a lot of good memories here, but right now all I felt was hurt and dismay. I wanted to move on, but Sara's mysterious death would not allow me to start the process. I felt as if somehow I had to find the reason and the meaning behind it all, because then and only then could I live my life as I was supposed to. Whatever fate had in store for me, I could then accept.

"Hi there Addy," I said as I walked into the shop. The few customers inside mirrored my friendly smile; they were regulars used to the comings and goings of Sara's friends.

Addy forced a smile in return. "Hello," she said. "I've been waiting to see you." I walked behind the glass counter and hugged her. She stiffly hugged me back. I could tell by the grief in her eyes that stress had taken its toll.

"I would have been here sooner but I finally got a chance to talk to one of the detectives investigating the case," I whispered in her ear as I pulled away.

Her eyes widened at my news. "And?" She took a step back and sat on a tall wooden stool near the cash register.

I crossed my arms, and bobbed my head. "Well, they aren't saying much. This detective – Drake – either didn't have much information, or wasn't willing to share what he had."

I could see tears welling in Addy's eyes. I didn't want to see her cry. I didn't want to cry anymore. "I spoke to him too," she said. "To make arrangements."

I nodded. "He did say that when I was with him," I confessed. "Oh Addy, I just need to know what happened to her! I need to know!"

Addy's eyes wandered for a moment, trying to gain a little composure. "I know you do. So do I, I think. I'm not sure if I can handle it. She's gone and whether we know how it happened, or never know, it won't change the fact that she is not here."

She was right, but there was something about the *never knowing* that was too empty for me to stomach. "If we never know, we may never be able to find out who did it. Can you live with that?" I asked her.

"Live? Well, I'm finding that hard enough right now. I can't even think past tomorrow. And now Keith and I need to make plans for Sara." Keith is Addy's husband.

"I'll do whatever I can to help you and Keith out. We are in this together.

We loved Sara and that will never change. It's not about who loved her more, or who should do more for her now," I said, touching her arm gently. I didn't want Addy to think I was making light of all the hard things she had to do and this was surely one of those things.

"Sara never really had a will," Addy began. "I can only act on what she may have said in our conversations, or what I may have overheard, or what I feel she may have wanted." A few tears trickled down her pale cheeks.

Having to make arrangements for someone's personal effects is a hard thing to do, especially when they never stated in writing what they would want done. Addy was right though; we could only do what we felt was right, or act on what we knew she believed in. One thing we both knew for certain was that Sara wanted to be cremated. As far as what to do after that, neither Addy nor I were sure.

"Where do you think Sara would want to be?" I asked rather wistfully – I was thinking in terms of eternity.

"Her ashes," Addy replied, knowing what I was referring to. "I would think one of the Coven's sacred areas, where we often met. I had thought maybe the Old Maple Forest, where the natural altar stands. There is a lot of good energy there."

I agreed, having been there for meetings myself in the past. It was a place that felt different to me spiritually, more than any other place I had been in. The energy was strong, but peculiar. I was never very good at looking deep within myself to try and discover what gave me the odd feelings. I had tried, but never trusted my instincts. I constantly questioned how I felt. Sara would always tell me, 'Listen to that little voice inside you, it's there for a reason'. Well, I must be deaf, 'cause I never heard it.

The old Maple Forest is one of those places to visit when you feel a little daring, I guess. There are rumors of people who have taken pictures while in that forest, and found other images on the film after it was developed. Images other than what the person had taken a photograph of, things like little orbs of light, or strange shadows. I had never seen any pictures myself, but I had experienced the feeling of being watched. I never felt threatened, but the feeling was obvious and no one was ever there. And still I recall other stories of ominous pockets in the Old Maple Forest where the quiet was almost deafening – no sigh of wind, no sounds of birds or animals. People would just be walking along and stumble into this black hole, so to speak, of nothingness. In this black hole you could yell and scream to your heart's content and never be heard; someone ten feet outside of this void could see you, but not hear you. Again, I had never experienced this, but the stories always fascinated me. Perhaps it was these fables, caught in my imagination that caused my pulse to race and my heart to flutter when I returned time and again to the Old Maple Forest with Sara's Coven. Maybe it was those distractions that would not allow me to truly feel any goodness there like Sara did. Or perhaps all the stories are just that – fiction with not an ounce of truth to it, something someone made up when they discovered a clan of witches held masses there.

"If you can think of a better place, please let me know," Addy implored.

"No, you are right. It was a special place to Sara. I think it would be fine," I replied.

"I would like to scatter her ashes with just the Coven present. No wake. I don't think Sara would mind that," Addy said softly. She began to braid her gray hair.

"I agree with you. When should we do this?" I asked, sitting on the carpeted floor out of the view of patrons.

Addy sighed. "Soon. Friday I suppose."

"Okay."

We were silent for a moment while Addy helped a customer with his order; brown bagged it and sent the Wiccan gentleman on his way. I heard him offer his condolences before he left.

Addy took her seat again on the stool. "There is one other thing. Actually, it has nothing to do with what we were talking about."

"What's that?" I asked, looking up in her direction.

Addy looked a little stronger as she leaned under the counter and removed a red file folder. She handed it to me. "Open it."

I reached up for the folder, and opened it. I was not positive what I was looking at for sure – some invoices for stationary, a sign, and a lease. "What is this?" I asked, still thumbing through the paperwork.

"You know how much Sara loved art work. All kinds of art work."

"Yeah, crappy stuff too," I added with a little smile.

"She liked what she liked," Addy said, though the thought made her chuckle slightly. "Sara decided within the last few weeks that in addition to Spellbound she wanted to open an art gallery."

I was a little surprised. "Really? She never mentioned it."

"Well, I think she wanted to get everything in order before she told anyone about it. I found out about the gallery quite by accident. I took a phone call from a real estate agent regarding some storefront property Sara was interested in. Of course, I thought right off the bat that she was unhappy with Spellbound's present location and never thought to consult *me* as to where I might like to relocate. When I confronted her, I think she felt obligated to explain what she was doing." Addy recalled her conversation.

"Wow, I'm surprised. I mean, I know she loved art; I just didn't think she'd go that far. A gallery..." I set the file folder on the floor next to me and crossed my legs, leaning back on my elbows.

"Sara had told me that she wanted to give local artists a chance to display their work so they could maybe sell something and make some money doing something they loved. That is so like Sara. I supported her in starting up the gallery." Addy paused to tie up her braid, and then continued. "She bought a store, she had it painted, carpeted, fixtures installed, got a sign made up and was ready to open in less than thirty days. She was going to start recruiting talent to come into the gallery some time next week. It's all in the file." Addy motioned with a slight nod to the red folder.

"What are we going to do with it now?" I asked, picking the folder back up and now reading each sheet of paper in more detail.

"Sara was the primary person on all the legal paperwork filed, and I was the secondary name, but I would like for you to take it over. I think you and Sara would have spent a lot of time together there, had it all worked out right," Addy smiled encouragingly.

I thought a moment and rubbed my forehead. "I know less than nothing about art," I stammered.

"Art is in the eye of the beholder. You said it yourself when you said Sara liked crap. What is crap to you is art to someone else," Addy argued.

"So I just look for stuff that looks like shit and plaster the whole gallery with it?" I asked half joking, but felt I would probably do just that.

"No... no... you use your judgment; use your little voice."

Not the voice thing again, I thought to myself. "I don't know the first thing about running a business. I work days at the radio station. Where do I find time to run an art gallery?" I asked her quickly.

"Kala, it will be *your* place. I will help you; you can have special hours, make it totally exclusive. By appointment only, like only on weekends. We can make this work. It will be good for you too."

"All right. We can give it a shot," I sighed, defeated. I guess I owed Addy this much, now that Spellbound was entirely her responsibility. Why leave her with an art gallery, too? "What is the name of this art gallery?" I asked.

"The sign is going up tomorrow. She was going to call it 'Out of the Shadows'. I believe she even called the newspaper and was going have a little piece written explaining how someone could have his or her work put on exhibit. I'll see if I can find out more about that tomorrow. Between the two of us we can get this off the ground." She smiled supportively.

"Okay, we'll take it one day at a time," I surrendered, being as optimistic as possible. I got up from the floor, brushing the dust off my black jeans. "I'll stop by tomorrow afternoon."

"By then I will have Sara's ashes," Addy said quietly, and she lowered her head as the sadness returned.

I hesitated before speaking. "Addy, one day at a time. We *will* get through this. We will."

She nodded, but we both knew it would be many days before the sadness subsided.

I left the store and headed home. It was very dark now, and the streets in town were rather quiet, not like they normally are during the busy daylight hours. It made for a quick but quiet ride home. Once I got home I let myself in and noticed I had several messages on my answering machine. I was not surprised; probably someone at the radio station telling me I had forgotten to do something before I left, or asking me to pop in early to cut a spot. Maybe I forgot to sign a meter-reading log, but whatever it was, it would not end the world, or at least not the one I was living in. I hit 'play' on the machine and walked into the kitchen to grab a Diet Coke from the fridge. Message one was a hang up, followed by message two which was the same, and number three. "This is annoying," I said aloud as I approached the machine to listen to the final message, if there really was one.

"Hey Kala," the voice began cheerfully. "It's Drew. I'm in the neighborhood – want to meet up? I can bring over a six or something. Call me in the car. Bye."

Drew was a real nice guy, several years younger than I was, in his last year of college. He was interning at the radio station and I usually saw him 2-3 times a week. He was very outgoing and likeable, but it was obvious that he wanted to date me exclusively. We had gone out many times for drinks, pizza, and Happy Hour type stuff, both alone and with others, so I don't think it was a 'look who I'm dating' kind of thing. I think he really liked me. This was possibly because I treated him like an equal and not like the glorified gopher most people felt he was. Interns are usually non-paid station possessions who do thankless tasks, make total assholes of themselves on the air because someone tells them to and are constantly on the road grabbing pizzas for the staff. I felt he was there to learn a job, so I made him work, and he respected me for that. In some offices, people might get the wrong idea about Drew and me, thinking that our relationship could lead to sexual harassment; but it was all done in dirty fun and we always laughed and got along, joking that both of us could file suit legitimately and win. We had serious talks, too. Because I went the extra mile to get to know Drew, I knew he had a girlfriend. I knew she wasn't his 'perfect girl'; their relationship was just something set up by his filthy rich parents, and some business associates his father knew. I felt bad for him; I thought his parents were using him. I mean, give the guy a break; he was in college, he had good grades, he applied himself and as far as I knew, never really caused them any problems, so why? Why do it? So Drew tried to make himself as busy as possible to avoid seeing his girlfriend, or even his parents, most of the time claiming he didn't need the stress and the questions. I think that's why he liked to see me so often; he can tell his folks or his girlfriend he's working and not really lie, because he's spending time with someone he works with. Usually our conversations start off very business like, all radio, music, events, and then branch off into anything and everything from there.

I paced the rug in the living room, pondering if I wanted to bother having Drew come over, knowing I had to work the next day. I sipped my soda, wanting to relax in a hot bath and maybe even cry a little before I got into bed for the night. There was a knock on the door, which disrupted my thoughts.

"Who is it?" I asked loudly, approaching the doorway.

"It's me... Drew," the familiar voice answered. "I come in peace. I bring beer."

I smiled as I opened the door. "I just got in."

"I know. The last time I drove by your place your car wasn't here. I've been stalking you." Drew walked by me, a six-pack of long-necked bottles in his hand. "I'll put these in the fridge."

I shut the door behind him; he had helped me decide what I was going to do tonight. I could not turn him away now.

"Want a beer?" Drew called from the kitchen area.

"Not yet. I'll finish my soda. Thanks." I fell exhausted onto the couch and threw my legs up on the coffee table.

Drew returned to the living room holding his beer and sat down next to me on the couch. "Rough day," he sighed. " I feel like I don't know when I slept last." He stretched out and put his feet up near mine.

"Then why aren't you home in bed?" I questioned him, playing with the tab on the can of soda.

He shrugged, sipping his beer. "Not ready to sleep, I guess. I need to unwind first. I had a three hour exam this afternoon. I'm kind of' coming down off that."

Drew was a nice looking guy, not someone who would stand out in a crowd as being a Calvin Klein model, but better than average. He had short, brown hair, and usually sported some sort of facial hair; the five o'clock shadow one week, or a goatee the next. His eyes were gray with little brown specks; I know this because one afternoon we had a contest to see who could out-stare the other. He won. Drew's body was long and lanky, although he had a nice build for someone of his size. He was one of those guys who could eat and eat and never gain any weight. This was obvious because I knew most of his diet consisted of pizza and beer, and if I were eating that most of the week I'd have to be rolled out of my home.

"I for one will be glad when the weekend is here," I admitted, glancing in his direction, waiting to hear about his plans.

"Don't even talk about the weekend," he scowled. "Maybe someone will hold me hostage at gun point between now and then."

"That doesn't sound good. What's going on this weekend that's got you in a tizzy?" I turned to face him, knowing it had to be a parental thing – always rocky.

He began to rub his forehead. "Ahhh, just this big event at some club at home. A big dinner, black tie, best behavior kind of' thing with Mom and Dad. Girlfriend will be there too. So that will ruin Saturday, and then on Sunday I'm sure Jennifer will have something horrible planned." Drew rolled his eyes and finished the last of his beer, following it up with a burp.

"Sometimes we have to do things we don't want to do. Trust me, life is full of those little joys."

"I'm getting another beer. Want one?" he asked, pulling himself off the couch and turning to wait for my answer. "Come on! Drink with me!"

"Yeah, okay, just one," I gave in, not one to refuse a second invitation.

He took my empty soda can and went into the kitchen, returning with two open beer bottles. He sat a little closer to me this time, placing the beer in my hands, and easing himself deep into the cushions of the couch. "Talk to me."

"About?" I asked obtusely. Please, not Sara I thought.

"You know what. Talk to me." He ran his fingers through his hair, pulling it off his forehead.

By now, I knew he meant Sara. "There's nothing much to say. I still don't know how she was killed and the police won't talk. It hurts too much to think about." My nose began to feel funny, tingly, a sign I wanted to cry.

"How is Addy doing?" Drew asked. He leaned over and rubbed my shoulder gently.

"Better than I thought. She has known Sara forever. I mean, they grew up together, went to school together, opened the store together; it has to be horrible for her. I know how I feel, so it must be even worse, if that's possible." Tears began to build up in my eyes as my vision blurred, just waiting to overflow and run down my face.

"I'm so sorry. I know how close you all are; I feel very badly. I wish I could take some of the pain away." He touched my hair and stroked it tenderly.

"You have enough pain, don't you?" I tried to joke with him, rubbing the tears off my face with the back of my hand.

"Yeah, but it's all localized in my ass. Besides, I'm your friend; friends help out that way." He continued to work his fingers through my hair, towards the back of my head, and to my neck.

"Well, I wish you could help too, but I have to get through this my way."

"If you want to talk, I'd be glad to listen. You listen to me bitch and moan all the time about school, parents, my girlfriend, being treated like shit by everyone but you at the station. It would be an honor to actually hear someone talk to me about something serious, instead of 'you forgot to super-size my fries'."

I tried to smile – he was funny – but I couldn't.

Drew pulled me to him and hugged me. I really wished that he hadn't because I didn't want to cry in front of anyone. I hated to cry, and I hated it even more when someone was watching. I buried my head into his chest, trying to wait out the storm. He held me tight and kissed my hair, rocking me like an infant.

"It's okay," he soothed. "I know you hurt."

And I did, very badly. My body ached because I was in so much pain over Sara's death. I wanted to feel better, I wanted to stop crying, but the more I thought of stopping the more I cried. Drew patiently rocked and caressed me until my sobbing subsided. He willing retrieved a box of tissues from the bathroom and passed them two at a time to me, until my nose and eyes were dry. He continued to hold me close, relaxed deep in the cushions. His lanky body took up the entire length of the couch; his strong arms cradled my head to his chest. I clung to his warmth like a life raft, my hand clutching a fistful of Champion T-shirt and a used tissue. Silently, Drew kissed my check. After awhile, I stirred slightly. "Just wanted to make sure you were awake," he whispered.

I nodded. I had been thinking. "Sara is being cremated," I sighed.

Drew took a moment before responding. "Does that bother you?"

"I don't know. If it were my body, it'd be okay," I whispered into his chest.

"Do you think it's okay with Sara?" Drew asked quietly. He knew Sara only through me and never met her in person.

"Uh huh," I replied.

"Then that's all that matters." He squeezed my arm and drew me closer yet to him. I felt him reach behind us and take his beer off the table. I heard the cool liquid pass quickly down his throat; I felt the muscles in his neck contract with each swallow. He positioned the chilled glass bottle against my flushed cheek. "Want a sip?"

I shook my head 'no', even though the cool sensation felt good.

He took one more drink, and placed the bottle back on the table, settling back into our modest nest he'd made. We lay in silence again, until Drew spoke. "Can I kiss you?"

My eyes, which were closed and restful, flickered open. I tipped my head back and looked at him through eyes puffed with tears. "What?"

He held my head gently and bent forward close to my face. I could feel his lips press against mine, soft and warm. It wasn't intended to be a passionate kiss; it was simple and loving, but safe. He held my hand and played with my fingers as he said, "I really should get going before I fall asleep here."

"It is getting late," I mumbled. I struggled to sit up, and got a friendly shove from Drew who was getting up behind me. I stood up under my own power and navigated myself around the coffee table, feeling Drew close behind. I walked to the door and politely thanked him for stopping by.

"Any time; I like being in the neighborhood. It gives me a nice place to relax and a clean bathroom to use." He touched the side of my face and brought me closer so that he could give me another kiss, this time, a bit softer, warmer and with a hint of passion.

"Good night," I half smiled.

"Night." Drew raised his eyebrows playfully as if I was missing something by allowing him to leave. "Bye," he smirked and was out the door and bounding down the cement stairs to his car.

Chapter 2

Sara's funeral was scheduled for Friday night. Addy and I had spent most of the day weeping at Sara's place, cleaning up, packing boxes and trying to find the perfect item that reminded us of Sara that we could use as a memento at the funeral that evening. It's an important part of a Wiccan funeral to have a meaningful item present when saying good-bye to the deceased. As Addy suggested, the funeral would be held at the Old Maple Forest with just the Coven and myself attending. Sara had been the Priestess of the Coven at the time of her death, and it was voted unanimously that Addy take her place. So, it was Addy who had the honor of handling the arrangements for the funeral. None of us had ever been to a Wiccan ceremony before, and, Addy confessed, neither had she. No Wiccan she knew of had died. Addy was concerned that she would not be able to complete the ceremony, but I told her not to worry about screwing it up because I didn't think anyone would notice, and Sara would probably find it funny if she did.

The Coven met at the entrance to the forest. The sun was not ready to set, but the trees were so large and thick with foliage that it appeared much later than it actually was. We were all dressed in black, a traditional color for funerals no matter what your religion or belief. Just a short walk into the forest, then a sharp turn down a path to the left, and we came towards what Sara referred to as the natural altar. The natural altar was something she had stumbled across many years ago while hiking. It was a small cleared area that housed two immense tree trunks; their perfectly flat, smooth tops reaching just about the ideal height for a table, or in this case, an altar. Directly next to one stump was the smaller one, shorter, but still smooth and flat. Addy draped the larger stump with a royal blue cloth; it was now her altar. The smaller stump she covered with a black cloth. She placed all her essential tools on the blue altar; a deep red crystal challis, followed by a brushed silver urn that held Sara's ashes, and a staff made of mahogany that Sara had made. This elegant staff was the item we chose to display to say good-bye to Sara. It was something that she had made herself, back when she was very much alive and young, passionate about learning, and about being Wiccan.

During the actual ceremony my mind began to drift, not because I was disinterested in what Addy had to say, but because this was in reality the end, and maybe I was not ready for that yet. I stood silent, wanting to be somewhere else. I remained motionless for so long that I wasn't sure I could even feel my body anymore. There was the distinct sensation of truly *not* being there. Although it was odd, it was welcomed. I felt I could just *hover* there until this was over, and then manage to snap out of it to walk back to my car. That would work. My only problem with staying in this state was that I didn't. My sensation of contentment vanished when I was touched on the shoulder. I turned my head to the right to see who wanted my attention at this moment in time; given the fact Addy was still conducting her sermon. There was no one next to me. I turned completely around and still found no one. The person closest to me was holding a heavy book, and I knew she was not responsible for the tap that I distinctly felt. My stomach flipped a few times as I began to remember the stories about the Old Maple Forest that I had heard. I was not going to dismiss the touch I felt as anything but a touch. I felt it; I knew what I felt; I felt a hand, a hand with weight and fingers. Sara?

When the ceremony was over, Sara's ashes were scattered near the natural altar. In many ways I felt good; I felt good that it was over, good that her spirit was free, but uneasy that the only thing that was left to the person I knew was now being carried away in the breeze, and on the bottom of people's shoes. Everyone said their good-byes to Addy and me and left. I remained behind to help Addy pick up the ceremonial items.

"It's getting pretty dark," I pointed out as I folded up the blue cloth and placed it into a canvas sack – this was not what I wanted to say but it seemed like a good start.

Addy looked around. "Yes it is. Thanks for helping me."

"No problem," I replied. "Addy, something weird happened to me during the funeral." I stopped working and waited to explain further.

"I figured that. I caught a glimpse of something behind you once," Addy told me as she picked up her bag. Her manner was as if this *something* behind me that touched me was an insect or a bird – something typical. "Come on, let's go." She began to walk out of the forest.

"You *saw* something?" I felt goose bumps all over my body. I clutched the bag I had been packing up to my chest and trotted to catch up to Addy.

"It was something. A spirit perhaps," she explained unemotionally, walking towards the parking lot, not even glancing in my direction.

"Why didn't you say something to me then?" I asked flabbergasted, my heart racing. I felt violated.

"What would you have me do? Stop in the middle of a funeral to shoo away a dead person's soul? Kala, I was performing a funeral. Think of what I was doing. It is possible I evoked a few spirits. And of course, there are those stories about the forest, which have been around for as long as I can remember. I think you are making too much of it. You are fine."

I kept walking, wanting to leave now more than ever. "Too much? I'm making too much of it? Sorry... stuff like this gives me the creeps."

"What if it was Sara?" Addy asked as she reached her two-door Cherokee.

"I thought about that; that would be okay. That would be great. But I just want to be asked before I'm touched, I guess." I needed a bath now. I felt crawly.

"Can't have everything," Addy sighed. "Don't worry, you're okay."

I nodded. I was.

Addy opened up the passenger door to her car and put her bag on the floor, then took the bag I had been carrying and did the same. "Go get some sleep; I'd like to meet you at the art gallery tomorrow." Addy seemed very business-like all of a sudden – perhaps her way of putting Sara behind her now.

"Are you sure? Is it too soon?" I asked, taking my keys from my pocket.

"No. Sara wants us to get on with things," she smiled briefly as she walked around the Jeep to the driver's side.

"Did you hear from Sara?" I asked her quickly. There was something about the tone in her voice that sounded like a first hand account of Sara's sentiments. If Sara could figure out a way to visit us from the other side I knew she would.

"No, I didn't, but I did feel something, not here, but on my way here tonight. I felt Sara encouraging me to help you get started. She really wants this to get off the ground. It will make her happy."

"You felt that?" I asked enviously. I wondered why I had not felt anything, at least, nothing that made me sure it was Sara. I wanted to feel Sara.

"Yes, she's watching us. Be good. I'll meet you in the afternoon at the gallery."

"Okay, I'll be there."

I had a very hard time sleeping. I felt funny, uncomfortable, even edgy, and no matter what I did, or how cozy I tried to make myself, I could not fall asleep. I was wide-awake; my inner clock telling me it was day, not the middle of the night. I watched TV for an hour, and then tried to read, but soon three a.m. rolled around and I still could not sleep. Even after a warm bath and a cup of decaf tea, I was wide-awake. I desperately wanted to sleep; I wanted to rest my brain, but my body would not release it. Finally I dozed off, only to be jarred awake a few hours later by the phone's insistent ringing. It was Drew, checking up on me to see how I was. He was calling from his parent's place, getting ready for a hellish weekend of big toothy smiles, party hats, and his best Sunday clothes. He said he had been thinking of me, and just needed to call to set his mind at ease. I thought that was very sweet of him. He said he missed me at work, and wanted to take me to lunch on Monday – his treat.

On my arrival at the gallery the sign hanging over the shop window proclaimed, "Out Of The Shadows." I didn't think much of the name on paper but on a big piece of wood it was rather catchy considering what was to be displayed inside this store when everything was up and running. The front door was made of old wood, adorned with a glass window at the top that let people see in without appearing overly nosey – it was wide open right now, held with a heavy iron block. As I walked in, I noticed several easels set up along the wall, empty arms ready to hold oils, watercolors, all types of art for display. There was track lighting mounted throughout the room, the fixtures aimed at multiple levels of platforms against the walls and in the middle of the gallery, set to display sculptures or larger pieces of work.

I could hear Addy's voice, and another, coming from the back of the store, out of sight. I had a few moments to admire what Sara had wanted to do with this place; it looked old, though everything was new. The floor was done in a unique stone pattern; it resembled something from a storybook, perhaps the same stone path that Hansel and Gretel walked down. The red velvet covering the walls had an elaborate pattern etched in it. Here and there were wrought iron sconces holding tall white pillar candles; each sconce had its own snuffer attached, meaning, I presumed, they were totally functional. Facing the street was a very large display window, allowing pedestrians a chance to admire the artwork. It wasn't one large plate of glass like you'd find in a newer store, but probably ten or twelve small panes, held firmly in a wooden framework. Above the window was a long, wrought iron pole, supporting yards and yards of red and gold velvet, tied in graceful drapes that flowed from one side to the other, ending up in puddles of texture on the faux stone floor. A cauldron sat solidly in the window, holding a sign that said 'Opening Soon.' I liked the cauldron, and decided it would stay and become part of the gallery. Above me, suspended from a bronze canopy, hung a very unusual lighting fixture. It resembled a wagon wheel, complete with wooden spokes. There were lights suspended from each spoke by chains of different lengths, which made the high ceilings feel a little closer. Taking it all in, I got the feeling that Sara had been shooting for a Medieval European theme, which I liked.

I could hear footsteps approaching from the back room, along with Addy's voice conversing with another. She saw me and smiled. "I'm glad you were able to make it."

"I told you that I would be here."

"Kala, let me introduce Melinda Banks. She's the interior decorator who was helping Sara with 'Out of the Shadows'."

I shook the woman's hand. Melinda was one of those 'Stevie Nicks' type people – very gothic and witchy in the way the public perceives witches to be. I figured she was probably Sara and Addy's age. She wore a laced up corset over a white blouse, a flowing blue skirt, and brown leather-like shoes. Her long, dark, wavy hair, shot through with gray, hung wildly in her face; it reminded me of a spider web – her face, the prey caught in the tangled center.

"I'm very sorry about Sara. We became close during the last month that she and I were working on the gallery," Melinda spoke softly. "Sara would be very happy that you have decided to take this on."

"It will be very new to me." I took a deep breath, already somewhat overwhelmed. I looked around again.

"Do you like the place?" Addy asked brightly.

"I think it looks wonderful. I can certainly see Sara's influence," I smiled. I meant that too – I could see Sara not just working here, but living in here.

"Oh yes, she knew exactly what she wanted," Melinda smiled back. "It was such a joy to work with her."

The three of us walked around the gallery from front to back, talking about the work in progress, and what still needed to be done. Melinda said that she would make herself available to help with the actual exhibitions, if I needed it. She also told me that Sara had hired a media group to do newspaper ads, press releases, and other marketing tasks over the first few months to encourage business. I felt like most of the immediate pressure was off Addy and me; all we had to do was make some phone calls, meet with the prospective artists, of which there was a list of about a hundred, then eventually see the work that would go up in the gallery.

Addy gave me the keys to the gallery, stating it was all mine now and asked that I lock up before I left – she and Melinda were leaving. It was time for me to get acquainted with this new part of my life. How I was ever going to make this all happen I had no idea. I puttered around in the back room of the shop before I left, stacking some boxes and moving fixtures about. I was surveying my work, my hands on my hips, when I heard the front door open. I wasn't sure who it was – I wasn't open for business and did not expect Addy or Melinda to return. I stopped what I was doing and headed out to the front, finding a tall, attractive gentleman gazing raptly around the gallery, taking it all in like a child.

"Hi, can I help you?" I asked, making my way towards him.

He turned abruptly, startled. “Hi.” he managed to say, his eyes wide on me.

“We really aren’t open yet. Still setting up.” I swept my hand around and stated the obvious.

The man said nothing but just stared at me as I spoke.

I introduced myself. “I’m Kala. I own the gallery.”

“I’m Victor. I read about this place,” he finally spoke up.

“Are you an artist?” I asked with a smile, hoping to hear a positive response – if he were he’d be coming back.

“Yes. Yes I am. I also teach some art classes at the community college up the street,” he volunteered and pointed outside.

Victor was a nice looking man – possibly the nicest I had ever seen. Tall, well over six feet, long dark hair tied in a fashionable ponytail. He was clean-shaven, wearing a gray T-shirt and faded blue jeans. As I looked in his brown eyes, I guessed him to be in his early thirties.

“Great. Maybe we could work together sometime, maybe with your students,” I boldly suggested. I was new to this gallery thing and could use at least one person behind me who knew something about art. Who better than a self-proclaimed artist who also taught his talent?

“You aren’t the original owner of this place, are you?” he asked, looking around.

“No. No, I’m not. It’s a long story,” I admitted.

“I read about it. I’m sorry. I suppose she was a close friend of yours,” Victor said sympathetically, apparently knowing something about Sara and her death.

“Yes,” I replied tersely.

“I’m sorry. I didn’t mean to stir up any emotions,” he apologized. “I just felt compelled to stop by. I live close to here and walk by almost every night.”

“It’s all right,” I smiled.

“I’d really like to show you some of my work if you are interested,” he said with enthusiasm. “I can’t really bring them down here, but you could stop by my studio; it’s actually my home, but it sounds more professional if I call it a studio.” He handed me his business card.

I took it, turning it in my hand as I answered my handsome friend. “Maybe...” I said coyly, and looked at him through my lashes, smiling shyly. This was exciting. I felt a little warm.

“It’s a passion of mine now, painting, I mean,” Victor explained. “I’d really like to be able to show it off. Who knows, maybe sell it, make a few dollars, and get my name around; that would be nice.” He smiled as he talked about his hobby.

I put his card into my shirt pocket. "We are still getting ready right now. Soon I'll be contacting artists and finishing the displays."

"Okay. Well, it was nice meeting you," Victor said. "I'll let you get back to work."

"All right. Thanks for stopping by."

He was gone. But not forgotten. I hoped I'd see him again. I was sure that I would – the little voice inside me told me and I heard it for the very first time.

Chapter 3

Over the next few weeks, things got very busy in my life. I worked all day at the radio station, then spent hours at the art gallery making and returning phone calls, filling appointments, as well as meeting with artists and getting their work on display. By the end of the month I was exhausted. So was Addy. But, our hard work paid off, for half the studio was occupied by local artist's hand-made treasures, in all shapes and forms, which would soon be on display for the public to view, critique, and buy.

One evening I was once again working late at the gallery. It must have been after eight when I heard a gentle tap on the pane of glass in the front door. I looked up from the desk, peering to see who it might be. As I recognized the face, a delicious warmth ran through my body, thrilling and unexpected. Victor. I stopped what I was doing and unlocked the door. "This is a surprise," I said, as I pulled the door towards me and allowed him to enter.

"Like I said, I pass by here almost every night. I just left class, and I was on my way home." He walked by me, a white bag of Chinese takeout in his hand. He was dressed in a nice button down shirt, black jeans and black soccer style shoes. Handsome, just like I remembered him.

"On your way home with dinner; good for you." I shut the door and re-locked it behind him.

He turned around to face me, the tantalizing odor of food accompanying his words. "Actually, I thought you might want to join me. I brought enough for two, because I know you've been working here late for weeks now. I thought you might want to eat before midnight," he smiled teasingly.

I returned the smile. "It's been a rough few weeks." I leaned against the desk where I had been working. "But things are coming together."

Victor looked around the gallery, eyeing some substantial metal statuary, and taking in the changes. The gallery looked much different from when he'd been in before. "Yeah. I see you're getting work in here. Good."

"I was going to call you, to see what you had to put on display. I've just been very busy," I sighed.

"Well," Victor began, looking at the bag of food he was carrying. "We could talk over dinner. It's a nice night out, with a full moon. The park is across the street; we could walk over there. What do you say?"

I was hungry, and I loved Chinese. "What's in the bag?" I asked, as my stomach rumbled audibly.

"Kung Pao Chicken, and Pork Lo Mein. I even have two cans of chilled Diet Coke, and if you're good, I'll split my spring roll with you."

"Oh my; you really know how to treat a gal," I laughed. "All right. Let's eat." I walked to the front door, unlocked it and pulled it open. "To our table?"

"I'm right behind you."

We walked across an empty Main Street to the small park. It was part of the community college's property; you could see some of the campus. We sat down at a round cement picnic table, complete with stone bench, located under a metal Victorian street lamp. The night was still and warm, but not too hot. It had been humid most of the day, but with the fall of night things weren't so sticky. The skyline still showed a faint tinge of burnt orange, remnants of a sunset that darkness was quickly overwhelming. Against this backdrop I could see the cityscape, all its tall buildings creeping into the sky, dark objects with pinpoints of light serving as outlines. The moon was large, looming overhead as if watching us, chaperoning perhaps. Even though the full moon was a beautiful sight, so clear and luminous, it was the crescent moon that I preferred. I loved the shape, its mystery enhanced by not being able to see the entire sphere. Once, I saw a Harvest Moon, rich in ivory color, looking so close to earth that I felt if I had gotten in my car and driven to the end of the street, I could drive right onto its surface. I have never seen a sight like it again.

I sat across from Victor and helped him unpack the bag of food, and divvy out napkins, plastic forks and sodas.

"It was nice of you to think of me," I said aloud, as I dug into the chicken dish. "I would have had cold pizza, or something like that, at home."

"Cold pizza, hmmm, that makes a great breakfast," Victor added, winding lo mein noodles around his fork.

"Ever wonder why they haven't come out with pizza flavored cereal yet?"

"Always."

"I think it would be a great idea," I smiled.

"Sometimes I get tired of having dinner alone," Victor confessed. "Thanks for saying yes."

"You couldn't possibly eat all this yourself; what was I supposed to do?"

"Oh," he smirked, and laughed. "You don't know my appetite. I don't bite off more that I can chew, so to speak."

"Growing boy," I smiled back. "Drink a gallon of milk at one sitting, too?"

"With my pizza-flavored cereal," he replied.

We smiled at each other. Such a fine-looking guy, I thought. Why was he not married? Was there something wrong with him? Why was he with me?

At the end of dinner, we went for a short walk around the park. We talked about the gallery, and about our lives. Victor told me that it had taken him a long time, with a lot of heartache, to figure out what he wanted to do in life. Being an artist was what made him happy, and he was willing to risk disapproval from those around him to attain that goal. He would do what was needed. Victor was an artist at heart. He became a painter, and a teacher of art. That was what made him happy. It didn't make him filthy rich, but he could live his life the way he wanted and still pay his bills. It was also honest work, which was important to him. I told Victor I would gladly look at his work and see if it could be displayed at the gallery. I could not imagine why it would not be, but in all rights I needed to see what I was getting myself into.

"What do you paint?" I asked, walking next to him, our strides slow and easy.

He hesitated before answering. "Hard to explain. Perhaps the best way to describe it to you would be to say I paint history, or past events."

"Oh, do you like history?" I asked. Victor seemed to be very intelligent; I thought it was something he studied.

"I know a lot about it," he replied. "So I paint it. I paint what I know, or what stirs me. If there is no emotion, there is no painting."

"What type of history do you paint? Specific times in history? Events?" I inquired.

We came upon a stone bench in front of a small pond; he sat first and I took a seat next to him. "Yes to both."

"I think that's interesting. Anything you are fond of painting?" I asked, sitting back and crossing my legs.

"I guess there is," he replied distantly, as if he were not comfortable talking about his work any longer. He gazed distractedly out over the water and fidgeted with some threads on the button-down shirt he was wearing.

"Oh. Well, I guess I'll see for myself soon," I suggested.

"Do you really want to?" He sounded surprised and turned to look at me.

"Of course. Why would I not want to see your work? It doesn't sound like anything I have yet in the gallery, or like anything I know I will be getting. I'm curious to see what your work looks like," I answered.

"All right. But you might have to acquire a taste for what I do."

"You of all people should know that to be true in all aspects of art," I chuckled. "I do not judge anyone's work. It's not my job. I can't even draw."

"I'm sure you could draw. Have you tried?" Victor asked, as if talking to a child or first-time student.

"When I was in school, many years ago. I just didn't do well."

Victor stood up and reached for my hand. "C'mon." I placed my hand in his and he helped me to my feet. We continued to walk, heading back towards the gallery. "Why don't you come by the school tomorrow night, just for an hour. I have a few pieces of work there I can show you. I don't have a class, so maybe I can show you a few basics about painting then."

I thought for a moment, responsibilities weighing heavily on my mind. I had a Battle of the Bands promotion to do for the radio station, the gallery's opening was imminent, and in many ways I was still grieving over Sara. I sighed.

"I know you are busy. Just an hour or so. Give yourself a break from all the work," Victor encouraged me.

We crossed the street and reached the front door of the gallery. I put my key in the lock, pausing indecisively.

"I'll pick you up here around seven. It's a short walk to my classroom." He smiled with his big brown eyes and placed his hand on my shoulder. "C'mon."

"Ok, for a little while," I caved in. I was never any good at standing my ground.

He nodded in approval. "Good. I'll be here at seven."

"I'll be here."

"I guess I'll head home so you can get back to work. Take care."

"I will. See you tomorrow night."

I opened the gallery, shut and re-locked the door behind me. It had been a nice evening out, something I had not done with anyone else but Drew for a while now. Victor seemed very pleasant, and his story of struggle and indecision, deciding that he finally wanted to become an artist, made him seem genuine to me. His feelings, and his desire to teach others what he loved, appeared to come from his heart. I was rather curious though, about what it was that he painted. History. History is such a wide topic; I mean, yesterday is history now, so I could not even begin to imagine what he painted. War? The rise and fall of civilizations? Mankind? It was a mystery. Hopefully, I would know more tomorrow night. Whatever it was that he did paint, I could tell he was emotionally involved with the subject.

I left the gallery about a half an hour later, and drove home. I had been driving my car with the top down for several days, and decided to leave it down, despite the late hour. The moon was as striking as it had been earlier with my handsome companion and it made me think of him again. I wondered what Victor was really like, what kind of boy friend he would make, and what his family was like. I thought about his age, and what his body looked like fresh from a shower. I wondered how different he was from Drew, since he was the only other man I knew to compare him to. I was rather anxious to meet up with him again, even though I really didn't have the time for it. An hour or so out of my evening might be good for me, I thought, just as Victor advised.

Pulling into my driveway, I decided I was too tired to put the top up on the car and anyway, I was a firm believer that if someone wanted to break into my car, the top being up would not stop him. I left it down. I never left anything of value in it, so my losses would not be great. I checked the time before shutting the car off; it was going on eleven and I was dragging. I needed sleep badly. I also needed to be at work early in the morning; the 'Battle of the Bands' promotion was on the agenda.

Every year the station ran the same end of summer concert. Last year I was not part of it; this year I was. Although I usually loved to be part of station functions, lately, with my life in an uproar, the fewer projects I involved myself in the better. Unfortunately, I had a contract with the station and if they said I was part of an event, then I was part of an event. I collected all my belongings from the front seat of the car and slammed the door shut. I fumbled for my keys as I walked up the stairs to the condo, and paused briefly, selecting the key that would allow me access to home. Suddenly, I was overcome by two strange sensations. I had the distinct feeling that there was someone behind me, watching me, and simultaneously my 'little voice' jolted me. I did not hear what the little voice said, because the feeling of being stalked was so intense that it was literally louder than the voice; the emotion I felt was so strong that it deafened me to *my* little voice.

I struggled to climb one more stair. A haunting power pulled at me, pleaded with me to face it, turn around and confront it. My little voice, which paled in comparison to the psychic pull I was feeling, encouraged me to keep going. I was almost to the door, holding the silver key out and aiming for the lock on the front door. As I turned the key and heard the deadbolt tumble open, the weight of the unknown entity behind me vanished. Immediately, I felt normal, sane, as if the experience had never occurred. I continued into the house and locked the door behind me. I had never experienced such an overwhelming emotional, psychological and physical sensation at the same time. It had been like walking in water, that feeling of using extra energy to get where you want to go. Was I just over-tired? I hadn't imagined it. Is this what happens when you are ready to have a nervous breakdown? Maybe I just needed a hot bath.

After calming my shaky nerves with a beer, I played my messages back on the answering machine. Drew had left two, one wondering how I was, even though he had seen me earlier in the day, and the other to see if I wanted to grab a late dinner. It was too late to return his call, and I knew I'd be seeing him first thing at the station, so I didn't bother to return his calls. I booted up my computer and answered some emails while I ran a tub of hot water. I tossed in a menthol bath bomb, which always seemed to clear my head. I lit a few candles, turned off the lights and climbed into my bath. It felt so nice to finally relax after the hectic day. The only downside was I knew I'd have to drag myself out eventually.

I slept pretty peacefully during the night, only waking up once, but I'm not sure why. When the alarm went off, I felt refreshed enough to get up right away and get ready for my meeting and start my day. As I was getting dressed I mentally went through all the things I wanted to accomplish during the day. I remembered that tonight, I'd be meeting up with Victor again, and I smiled at the thought. I kept trying to remind myself that I was thirty, not thirteen, but it didn't seem to work.

On my way out the door, I grabbed my tote bag full of radio station paperwork and accessories, and headed off to work. I stood on the front step locking my front door, remembering for a moment what I had felt the night before; it was hard to fully recollect how strong the feeling of being watched was, but I refused to dismiss it. Just because I could not recapture the emotions that coursed through me as I stood in the dark, with only the moon as a witness to what I experienced, did not mean it did not happen. It angered me that I could not remember. Not that I wanted to feel that way again; I just wanted to remember, to be able to analyze, rationalize, find an explanation, but I could not. My car was where I had left it the night before, untouched except for the light mist of dew on the hood. I placed my bag on the floor behind the driver's seat and slid behind the wheel. With my sunglasses snugly on my face, I turned the engine over, popped my GodSmack CD in and backed out of my driveway. As I shifted into drive, I noticed a pendant swinging from my rearview mirror. The pendant wasn't mine, and had not been there when I parked the car. I stopped and unwound the pendant's silver chain off the mirror, holding it in my hand. It was a pentagram, and although I had owned several over the years, many given as gifts, this one was definitely not mine. It was Sara's. I remembered it vividly. It was an antique that she had purchased at an estate sale when I was fifteen. She had dragged me along with her one Sunday, going from sale to sale, and I remember we'd bought it that day.

Bewildered, I put it in my pocket and continued to work. I thought intently on the way to the station. I had not remembered packing it when Addy and I were cleaning out Sara's place. Addy never mentioned having it.

I never mentioned wanting it. But the biggest question of all, how did it get here, on my mirror? And, did this have anything to do with the feelings I had last night after I had gotten out of my car? If it had been Sara who was behind me, watching me, I doubted that I would feel such horror. Here I was, analyzing and picking apart an entirely wonderful mystery, thinking there must be a feasible answer. What if it was Sara who was my little voice? Was she warning me? I was feeling really freaked out now. How would I ever come home tonight in the dark? I needed to talk to Addy at some point today; she would help, she would put my mind at rest – I hoped.

But with a full day ahead of me, my musings on the nocturnal mysteries facing me had to be shelved for now. I arrived at the station a few minutes early for the meeting. I met Drew in the hallway. With a smile and a flourish, he took my bag and handed me a Dunkin Donuts Hazelnut coffee just the way I liked it, cream and sweet n' low. "You must have gotten home late last night again," Drew spoke, as we walked into the conference room together.

I sat down in a high back swivel chair and sipped my coffee, "Yeah, eleven or so." I took my notebook out of my bag. "Thanks for the coffee."

"Always welcome," he smiled. "Working late at the gallery again?"

"Yeah, it'll be worth it when I'm done, though. I think." I rubbed my forehead. I could feel a headache approaching.

"Oh yeah. It will be." Drew patted me on the back. "This Battle of the Bands concert is gonna be killer. You're going to do great!" He was trying to be as encouraging as possible.

"If I don't have a breakdown before then," I managed a laugh, even though I wasn't sure if I was joking.

"Not you," he shook his head. "You are one of the strongest people I have ever met." Drew relaxed back into his chair and crossed his legs.

I thought that was an odd comment, but he sounded so sure of himself. "What makes you so sure?" I asked curiously.

"Of what?" He was puzzled.

"That I'm so strong. What makes you think that?" I asked.

He shrugged. "I'm not sure. I mean you come off confident, even when you aren't. You have that way about you; it's a personality thing. You have it." Drew struggled for the right words.

I frowned, not sure what he meant.

Drew uncrossed his legs and looked at me earnestly. "Well, it's like this. You know how most kids will test their parents, because they know they can get away with *some* stuff, and they keep testing and pushing to see how far they can go. And then one day, your Mom has had it up to here with you and she punishes you, and you act like – right Mom, whatever. And you figure in a day all will be okay, but then she threatens to tell your *Dad*, and then you're like 'oh shit' because you know this is one guy you just don't piss off. You don't mess with Dad because if he says he's gonna do something, chances are he already has and you are the last to know. That's what you are; you are that person, the one who is strong, who can be feared, who means what they say and we have *no idea* just what you are capable of doing when you put your mind to it. You are the worst person of all when it comes to that kind of stuff. Other than that, you're a pussy cat."

I furrowed my brow and laughed a bit. "Wow; I guess that means I could whip your butt."

"Honey, I'm crazy about you; I'd let you whip my butt anytime," he whispered with a lascivious leer.

I shut up quickly, smiling to myself. Despite the powerful persona Drew had made me out to be, the thought of literally whipping someone's butt did not exactly thrill me. Finishing our donuts, we went on to the meeting.

Chapter 4

After a very long meeting, four hours on the air, a quick lunch and 2 sixty-second spots, I was ready to leave the radio station. Unfortunately, Drew began asking me what I was doing for the evening, and hinting about getting together. Trying to explain to Drew that I was busy, and he wasn't invited, was like telling a child there was no Santa Claus; the disappointment was evident in his eyes. In many ways Drew was immature, his cushy upbringing as a rich, only child contributing to his attitude. Well, adult life was a little different. I never thought I'd need to explain to another adult that, besides work, I had other responsibilities to deal with. Every night did not revolve around a six-pack of beer, the ball game and chatting on the computer. It wasn't that I didn't care about him – he was very dear to me – but I felt like my life was being shuffled like a deck of cards and I was stuck playing whatever game the dealer decided. For the longest time I was playing 'go fish'; now I was playing 'crazy eights' and tomorrow could be 'solitaire'.

My first stop after I left work was to Spellbound to visit Addy. My experience from last night still bothered me. Call it supernatural, or paranormal, or whatever, but the more I thought about what had happened last night, the more the hair on the back of my neck stood on end. Not to mention the fact that I had in my pocket a piece of jewelry belonging to a dead friend, that just magically appeared without explanation.

The shop was empty of customers when I arrived. Addy was sitting at the counter having lunch. She waved as I walked in, chewing her vegetarian entrée. "Hi, how's it going?" I asked, shutting the door behind me.

"All right. How is the gallery coming?" she asked, tapping a napkin to her lips.

"Okay, I'm amazed to say. I'm going to look at some more paintings tonight. Prospective talent I recently met, and he's cute," I smiled. I stood in front of Addy, the glass counter between us.

"Excellent. I took a few messages for you. They're on the bulletin board in the back room." Addy packed up her half-eaten lunch and piled it into the small garbage can next to the door.

"Addy, there is a reason why I came by so early this afternoon. I need to talk to you about some weird stuff that's been happening." I got serious all of a sudden. "I'm not sure what to make of it."

"Tell me," she ordered, and sat on her wooden stool, assuming the 'I know everything stance,' arms crossed, face stern. "What's going on?"

I paused a moment, thinking before I started my story. "Last night, when I got home, *something* was there. I mean, I didn't see anything, but that was because I didn't look. I felt it. I mean, *I felt it.* I was so scared." I thought back briefly, remembering how difficult it was for me not to succumb to the power behind me. "But this inner voice refused to let me acknowledge my fear; it forced me into my condo. It was like someone, or something, had this rope around me dragging me in two different directions. I know there was someone or something behind me. It was *bad.* It had bad intent. I can't describe it any better than that." I nervously shifted my weight from foot to foot, feeling the anxiety I had the night before, only this time in broad daylight.

Addy did not respond immediately. She looked at the floor as she contemplated what I'd told her. I watched her raise an eyebrow as if she was having a conversation with herself, a possibly debate of sorts. "You know," she began. "Death is a traumatic experience for someone to have to go through. Sara is probably the closest person to you who has ever died. Death is a very spiritual thing, not just for the soul that goes onward, but for the people who are left behind to deal with the death. There is this struggle with anger, the need for acceptance, and the need to believe that there is another life, and that people continue to live. I have heard of some cases, where the death of a loved one can make someone more 'spiritual', and when I say that, I mean spiritual in an inner way, not necessarily a religious way; it makes you more aware. It makes you more open to the 'other side,' more vulnerable to good and bad spirits. It's a desire within you to want something better for the person who died, and that you believe that this special place really does exist and in this special place are very special people. The night of Sara's funeral; you experienced something paranormal; I sensed something as well. Last night again, well, I think that maybe Sara's death has caused you to experience spiritual growth. It may be manifesting now. Some believe there is a doorway from this world to the next; it opens from time to time. During these times is when you may experience some supernatural influences. This power that you have, this ability to sense feelings and changes, may have always been within you. Don't fight it."

I bit my bottom lip as I listened to what she had to say. "My inner voice spoke to me last night; it was so overwhelming," I sighed, trying to remember. "It was two very different experiences."

"Yes. Yes, I know," Addy nodded her head; she understood what I was trying to convey.

"It scares me," I confessed. "These are not good feelings, like when someone or something loves you. It's horrible."

"Those may be the emotions you have now; it might not always be that way. You will need to work on controlling and channeling them," Addy interjected.

"But that's not all. This morning, this was on the rearview mirror of my car." As I spoke I pulled the chain and pendant from my pocket, holding it up for her to see.

Addy's eyes flickered with surprise. "This was in your car?"

"Yes. And I did not put it there," I quickly added.

"Detective Drake spoke to me about that necklace," she awkwardly stated. "According to him, Sara was wearing that necklace the night of her death. He told me that it was in the crime photos and the people who brought her in that night remembered seeing it, but it disappeared before the autopsy. He apologized to me for its loss, but had no explanation." It was difficult for Addy to talk about Sara's death as bluntly as the officers had.

"But, even if it had been lost, how would someone know to return it to me?" I was puzzled.

"The detective told me that if it was found, they would bring it by the store. They would not know to bring it to you. This is strange," Addy agreed. "Maybe we should give Detective Drake a call. I haven't heard from him in a few days."

"If you think that's best."

"Well, if he didn't find it and his department didn't find it, then the person who did knew who Sara was, or knew that you were close enough to her to give it to you," Addy rambled on as she picked up the telephone and began to dial.

I was worried more about the fact that someone knew where I lived.

While Addy was on the phone trying to contact Detective Drake, I went into the back room to read the messages for me on the bulletin board. There were four, all from people who were interested in meeting me to talk about the gallery. One message was from Victor. Seeing his name made my heart skip a little; actually I think it stopped just for a split second. The note asked if I would meet him on campus at seven tonight, at The McKenzie building, room 3.

Addy was off the phone when I rejoined her at the counter. She told me that Drake was out of the office, but she'd left a message for him to call her as soon as possible. Somehow nothing was making me feel any better about being alone tonight, in the dark. I felt like I was three again, afraid of what loomed in the shadows. Perhaps I was on to something. Maybe parents don't know what they are talking about when they shush their children and ridicule their fears of monsters in the dark. Maybe there really was something under my bed. Tonight, I would be too chicken to look.

I waited around for the rest of the hour to see if Drake would call Addy back. He didn't. Figures. He probably didn't care about solving Sara's death. It wasn't like solving every murder was his job; as long as he met his quota he collected a check. I guess the hard ones just didn't get solved. Too bad for the friends and family who wanted closure; it wasn't cost-efficient or something bureaucratic like that. Maybe I was too cynical, but it seemed like, if you're going to get murdered, try to have a witness around, or at least live long enough to tell the cops who did it. Cynical or not, the sun was only going to be up another few hours, and I was still holding the necklace of Sara's, a constant reminder of a murderer on the loose.

I spent the evening at the gallery, trying to catch up. Addy had said that if Drake called, she would have him call me, too. I returned a few calls of my own, making some tentative appointments with students from the college to bring their metal art pieces for viewing. I had visions of cookware – forks, spoons and knives – in my mind. I figured that I could just as well be presented a kitchen as a statue or something to exhibit.

Just about the time I was getting ready to drive over to the campus, (I could have walked, but I thought I'd feel defenseless without my wheels) I saw Detective Drake standing outside on the sidewalk. I saw him before he saw me, and my fears seemed to diminish in his authoritative presence. When he finally did see me, he pointed at me. "I need to speak to you. Have a minute?" he said, although it sounded more like an order than a request.

I sat against the storefront window and crossed my arms. " I guess." I was not going to give him the satisfaction of knowing I did.

"I spoke to Addy. I wanted to see you," he began, bracing his arm against a lamppost. "You have something."

I nodded.

"Can I see it?" He put his hand out.

"What do you have for me?" I asked, negotiating. My arms were still crossed over my chest.

He looked irritated. "Is it your birthday?"

"Nope."

"Then what do you want from me?" he inquired, putting his hands into his pockets, appearing slightly angered with my attitude.

"Well now," I thought aloud. "Hmmm, it's been weeks since we buried Sara and I have not heard from you. I stopped leaving messages for you like you asked. I haven't made a big deal about you losing things. Her file must still be somewhere on your desk, right? Or, did you lose that too?" I shot back sarcastically, and it was a direct hit.

He flushed in anger. "Listen, I'm working on it. I have done everything but hire a fortune teller."

"So hire one," I told him. "Or do you not believe in that sort of stuff?" My hands clenched in disgust.

"You have to just trust me. We are doing everything we can."

"Whatever." I turned around to lock the door of the shop.

"I need to see the necklace," he stated, as he came up behind me. I could feel the timbre of his voice through the base of my neck, deep and stern.

"Or you'll shoot me?" I asked, turning around and pulling the necklace from my pocket, holding it up for him to examine. I pushed a section of hair behind my ear that had started to annoy me in the evening breeze.

"Having a bad day?" he asked, as he removed the antique from my palm.

"Don't worry about it," I snapped.

Drake studied the necklace, then took an enlarged photo from his jacket pocket. The photo appeared to be of a woman's neck, wearing the same pendant as Sara's. "How did you get this?" he asked.

I grimaced as I recalled the events earlier today. "It was hanging off my rearview mirror this morning when I got in my car to go to work."

"What time was that? Was your car locked?" he asked, staring directly at me. I knew I was being questioned in an official capacity.

"About nine, and no."

"Where is your car?" he asked, looking around.

I walked the twenty feet it would take to show him, stopping short of my black convertible. I presented the automobile to him with a flourish, as if I was one of Bob Barker's Beauties in the Showcase Showdown.

He approached the driver's side and looked in. "The top was up?"

"No."

"You left the top down all night?" he asked, as if I were a careless teenager.

"Yes. I was tired and it was getting late," I said defensively. I took my car keys and spun the key ring around my finger.

"What time did you get in last night?"

"It was almost eleven," I replied. I was getting impatient. I had to meet Victor.

"Did you notice anyone in the parking lot last night? Someone you didn't know? A car?" Drake asked, handing me back the necklace.

I took the necklace and impulsively decided to wear it. I felt Sara would approve. "No," I answered quickly, even though it felt like a lie.

"Thanks for your time. I'll be in touch," Drake said as he put the photo back into his jacket pocket.

"That's it?" I asked. "You have no idea who took it off Sara's body? You have no idea how it got in my car? Or even when it was lost? Is this LA?" My anger mounted.

I must have hit a sore spot because Drake quickly approached and stood nose to nose with me. "I don't know what your problem is today, but I won't be spoken to like this. I am doing everything I can with what little I have to solve this god-forsaken case!"

"Then it's not enough. And how safe do you think I feel? Someone knows where I live, and that person knew Sara or something about her, enough to know it was her necklace and I was her friend and this is my car," I said hotly, stepping back from Drake and opening my car door. "Who knows, maybe you can solve my murder next," I spat at him.

"Don't even go there," he answered, grabbing the door away from me. I sat in the driver's seat, looking stonily forward. "I'll have an officer check on you tonight. Okay?"

"I don't want anyone poking around my place. I'll be fine." I looked up at him.

"It would make me feel better."

"Fine." I was done arguing with the man for now. I had been a bitch and felt I'd gotten my point across. He knew I was angry about the way the case was being handled. That was my goal.

"Take it slow. I can still give you a ticket," he teased, trying to soften our parting as he shut my door.

I started the car and put it in reverse. "I will." I only would because it was a two-minute drive.

Chapter 5

I found the building Victor had told me about in his message. It appeared to consist of student classrooms that had probably started out to be temporary, but had now been used for so long they'd turned permanent. Room number 3 was at the end of a long hall, the floor looking worn and in need of polish. The door was open and I could see Victor sitting at a large wooden desk near the middle of the room. The desk was past its prime by some twenty years, and had been painted many times over. There were several layers of paint wearing through, though presently it was yellow. Victor was sorting through a pile of papers; his attention focused on his task. He looked so scholarly; I hesitated to interrupt him. Finally, I cleared my throat to get his attention. He glanced up quickly, and smiled when he saw it was me. "Hey. Glad you could make it." He slid the papers into a drawer in his desk and stood. "C'mon in. This is my classroom." He smiled proudly, extending his arms in the emptiness.

I looked around the room, noticing the sense of orderliness despite dozens of easels, jars of paint, boxes of brushes and rolls upon rolls of paper towels. "Big class," I observed, as I walked closer to him. In the back of the room some completed art projects stood against the wall. Some were only half-done and others had hardly been started. The walls in the classroom had been painted by students, and consisted of continuous murals on all four sides, all different genre. Two large plate glass windows overlooked the lower side of the campus near the parking lot. Looking out, I could see the street lamps were getting ready to power up and had started their bursts of flickering.

Victor studied me as I approached him, getting close but not too close for people who had just recently met. Although close would be just fine for me. "Something wrong?" he asked, sitting down on his desktop, making himself comfortable, his legs dangling over the front.

I shrugged.

"What?" He patted the section of desk next to him, letting me know I could sit next to him if I wanted. I hopped up, my arm brushing his deliberately. "Do you want to talk? Or would you like to paint?" he asked.

I lowered my head. "I 'm late because the detective who's on Sara's case came by. Sara was my friend; the one who was murdered; the original owner of the gallery," I sighed.

"Any news?" Victor asked.

"No. I don't think things look well. We will probably never know.

Basically, it sucks," I answered, my voice dropping to a sad monotone. I clasped my hands together in front of me as my thumbs flicked up and down, and I began to play with my rings, a sure sign that I was nervous.

"Don't give up yet, something could break. It really hasn't been that long, even though I know it feels long."

"You are probably right. It's hard looking at things from where I am."

Victor went silent, and then I noticed him looking at me again, at my neck, at my necklace. Our eyes met. I felt a spasm in the pit of my stomach; maybe it was just his good looks that hit me hard at that split second, his dark sexy eyes and strong facial features, or maybe it was something else. I tried to dismiss it immediately. "Where did you get that necklace? It looks old," he observed. He reached out and touched the pendant between his fingers. "What's it made out of?"

I lowered my eyes and watched him handle the object against my chest. "It was Sara's. She was wearing it the night she died. I have no idea what it is made of. I don't think they make anything like it now," I answered him.

"I guess not; it seems very unusual. It's probably worth quite a bit to the right person. But I'm sure it's worth more to you in sentimental value." He slid off the desk, and turned to face me. "Enough with the small talk; I do have a few things to show you here." We were getting down to business.

"Okay," I smiled, and stood next to him.

Victor directed me to the back of the classroom, to a door in the corner. The door was black metal, scratched and dented. The silver plated doorknob was barely attached and hung to one side. Victor pulled the door open and flicked on the overhead light. The 50-watt light bulb hanging from a swaying white cord threw dim shadows. This was a closet, a storage facility for what looked like a hundred paintings of all different sizes. The closet felt like a cubbyhole, long but narrow, made even more so by all the canvases that were stacked six deep against the walls. Victor walked in first, stopping after three steps. He bent forward and began to separate the canvases. I stayed where I was, close to the door, where I felt like I could breathe; this little place was too small for me. Finally Victor stood up with a painting in his right hand. It was not very big, about twenty inches across. He motioned to me he was coming out with it, so I backed out of the closet, giving him room to exit.

"I know it's horrible in there, but I really don't have time to go through it," Victor said in embarrassment.

"Are all of those yours?" I asked.

"No. Students' work over the years. I inherited the collection, just as I am sure teachers before me did," he laughed. "It's hard. It's all art, so how do you throw it away?"

"You're right; that would be hard. And, I guess it's not stuff you take home and put on your refrigerator," I added.

He chuckled in agreement as he walked by me.

Close to the center of the room where the light was brighter stood an empty easel, waiting to hold a painting. I hoped I would genuinely like Victor's work, and not have to smile and pretend that I did. I could not imagine being a parent and having to force myself to look at my child's finger painting of six smeared colors, and be able to see the family dog. Talk about interpretation! When Victor finally revealed his painting to me, I was pleasantly surprised to find it quite interesting. Interesting. Yes, it was history. Yes, it was good. Did it only appeal to certain people? Well, most likely. It was different.

"What do you think?" he asked, his lack of confidence apparent. He adjusted the painting on the easel and took several steps back, trying to see it from my viewpoint.

"What made you decide to paint that scene?" I asked out of pure curiosity. I walked closer to it.

"You don't like it," his voice fell, dismay in his tone.

"No. Actually I do. But it's very dark," I added.

His painting depicted a time some three hundred years ago in American history. Belief in witchcraft then was rampant, and people accused of sorcery were put to death by drowning, pressing or being burned alive. The scene he'd painted was done in dark, somber tones of green, brown, blues, grays and blacks. It graphically illustrated women, obviously alleged witches, tied to a tall wooden pole with thick rope. They were surrounded by burning sticks, hay and other debris, the billowing smoke and tongues of flame just beginning to devour them as the local villagers watched with avid glee. Sad.

"I didn't know what you would think, with your Wiccan background," Victor apologized.

"It happened. It's history," I responded. "It wasn't right, but neither was what happened to the Jews or to the slaves; you can only wonder if society will ever learn."

"Don't count on it. Anything different is never accepted – gays and lesbians for example," Victor interjected, approaching his painting and looking intently at it.

"You're right. I guess we are a hopeless race of humans," I agreed. "We will probably never be anything more than that."

"Working here on campus I see a lot, and being in the art community means I see even more. People here aren't afraid to let you see their differences, whether you are ready to accept them or not. They exist, and they make you deal with them."

"Maybe that's good. Maybe they don't have a problem; maybe it's everyone else," I suggested, looking up at him. A long silence came upon us again. I had forgotten how much taller he was than me. It felt good to have someone big and strong next to me. I wondered what it would feel like to have his arms holding me. How safe I would feel. My mind drifted a bit. "Well, I don't see why you can't put some of your work on display at the gallery. We should set up a time for you to come by. I'll get some space ready for you," I offered, ending the quiet.

"Great! I'm really happy that you like it. I was worried," Victor sounded relieved. "Not all my work is this dark. But there are a lot of dark spots in history."

I nodded, knowing what he meant.

Victor took my hand in his and pulled me towards an island of easels near the front of the classroom. "And, as I promised you," his voice sang, as he steered me around a group of chairs "I want to see what you can do, and then I'll show you some basics in painting. You might be good and not even know it." I lagged behind, speechless. I really didn't feel in a creative mood. I was sure I'd be a disappointment to him. I stood woodenly where Victor put me, two feet in front of a towering canvas, with several opened tubes of paint. He handed me a brush and brought my arm up level to the canvas. "Go ahead."

I dropped my arm to my side and looked at him. "For real?"

He looked confused. "Yes. Try."

I stood in silence and glared at the white wall in front of me. It was white. What did he want me to do?

"Make it another color," Victor instructed. He moved closer behind me. My eyes followed him without moving my head. I felt his body graze my backside. It stirred me. I swallowed hard in anticipation and remained motionless, waiting to see what method of teaching he would try next. "Paint. Make at least a stroke," he bargained in a low whispering tone. Warmth coursed through me. I started to raise my arm; it was difficult, and I didn't want to make a mistake. Victor put his arm around me and placed his hand over mine. I held the brush as he held my hand firmly, as if helping a first grader write his ABC's. My arm, my hand, did not want to move with his; it was like I fought his direction, or was trying to work in a mirror; everything was backwards or wrong.

"It's okay," he spoke softly. The air expelled with his speech flowed through my hair, his breath a soft caress against my neck. Finally I gave in, allowing him to guide me as I made a long stroke, a bluish mark on the perfectly white canvas; it was tainted with my paint now. "See, it's not so hard." He took his hand off mine, leaving my arm and hand trembling in muscle spasms. Victor placed his hand on my lower back; I could feel him rub my shirt up and down in small but gentle motions. "You try." He backed away and gave me some space.

"I can't," I mumbled, bringing my hand back down.

"Just try. I'm not grading you. I'm going to leave the room for a few minutes. Take your time. Have fun."

I watched him leave the room and turn left down the hall. I was alone. I was alone with a big white canvas with a blue mark on it. Now what? If he came back and that was all there was, just one lonely blue mark, well, I was sure he'd be let down. I glanced out the window and down into the parking lot. The streetlights were on, and night had replaced the day. It was dark. Immediately fear rose in me, taking over my entire body. I thought about being alone later on tonight, in the dark. Just the mere thought of walking from my car to my front door made me hold my breath, caused my chest to tighten. I did not want to be irrational, but it was difficult to be any other way. I looked at the blue streak on the canvas again. This time, instead of seeing just a blue streak, I saw the long, thin, bony finger of a daemon pointing at me. I reached up carefully, my paintbrush loaded with more blue paint, and gave the daemon three more fingers; he wasn't human so I didn't give him a thumb. Now, I was looking at a hand, the hand of my daemon friend, with bluish gray fragile skin that latched onto the decaying bones beneath. I added claws to his fingers because he was beast-like and would use them to dig shallow graves for his prey.

When I closed my eyes I could see the beast's arm floating in the darkness, attached to nothingness, the remnants of some sort of primitive fabric barely covering his limb. I began to fill more of my beast in, his tattered smock-like garments surging out of my paintbrush in earthlike tones. I could not visualize what this daemon's face would be like. Something so horrible I could not even think it up. Something so terrifying it would make me gasp. I closed my eyes again, seeing the daemon, noticing that it remained beast-like, but carried itself more like a zombie than an animal, standing just short of upright. I started to feel like I was producing a Scooby Doo episode, painting this hideous creature that would be after Shaggy and the gang, only I was pretty sure it would take more than a few Scooby Snacks to get me to face this thing on my own. I blindly began to paint a face. I had no idea where my brush was taking me; it felt enchanted, like if I had let the brush go it would have just kept on painting without me. The face started out long, shaped like a pear, only thinner. Its mouth was a narrow slit, with no lips and no visible teeth. The cheekbones were prominent, protruding out and up, close to its eyes, with pieces of corroded bone splitting through and making the sockets extremely deep. There were two coal-shaped objects embedded in the sockets, serving as eyes. The shreds of skin that covered its drawn face were layered, covering perforations and resembling human scabs. The forehead was high but weak, and looked as if it had been broken and mended many times over. Only a few sparse white hairs decorated the daemon's head, with more hairs poking through where its ears might have been if it had any.

My arm was tense from holding the brush so tightly, but I think I was afraid to let go, that I might sever the connection that let me paint this nasty creature. This was not a project I completed on my own; something helped me assemble this picture; something fed me the energy and the talent I needed to finish it. How would I explain this painting to Victor? What kind of person would paint such a thing? I'm sure he expected a flower, or a piece of fruit – not a demonic-looking dead thing that dug its way out of the earth at night to feed upon the fear of innocent people.

I stepped away from my picture and laid the brush down on a nearby table covered with paper towels. Somehow, I knew I was finished. Out of the corner of my eye I saw Victor, poised in the doorway, arms crossed as he leaned against the frame, seemingly enjoying watching me paint from afar. I nervously rolled my eyes in his direction, not wanting to show him what his new student had produced. I took the painting off the easel and flipped it around, leaning it against the heating unit on the floor so that no one could see it. I stood between the canvas and the door so that anyone who came forward would have to go through me first to see what I had done.

Victor uncrossed his arms and put his hands on his hips. "Okay, let's see it."

"No, it's not meant for anyone's eyes," I stammered. "It's a mistake!"

Victor began to walk in my direction and I defensively leaned against the heater, my legs spread in a wide stance, protecting my representation of horror. "I was gone five minutes. How much could you have done, and how bad can it be?" he asked, laughing. "You are taking this too seriously. You were supposed to have fun with it."

"Well I didn't," I shot back, keeping him at arm's length. All of a sudden the man I wanted close to me I now wanted very far away.

Victor was startled by my reaction. "Kala, what's wrong? I don't care if it's bad."

"It's not bad," I corrected him.

"Well, that's great. I'm glad you did well. Why won't you let me see it?" he asked, trying to maneuver around me.

"Because I didn't mean to paint it," I tried to explain.

"Sometimes that happens; you try to paint a ship and it looks like a torpedo. It's okay," he reasoned with me.

"I mean," I fumbled for words. I didn't know how to explain it to him. That somehow I had a possessed paintbrush? I moved away from the canvas and let Victor see my creation.

Before he picked up the painting he placed both hands on my shoulders and squeezed gently. "You're the one with the gallery, remember that." He ran his fingers through my hair and pushed it away from my face. Without bending over he picked up the large canvas and turned it around, putting it up onto the easel for a better look. His face showed no immediate reaction or emotion. He gazed at the painting and took a step or two to the right, then put an arm around my shoulder and brought me over to him. "Tell me about this," he asked, pointing at my blue daemon.

I shrugged.

"It's good."

I looked over at him; he still had his eyes on the painting.

"I know a little about painting dark images, and you seem to have captured the grim detail in this zombie creature. It looks like something from 'Tales from the Crypt'," Victor analyzed out loud.

I still said nothing.

"Honestly, I did not expect something like this. I thought I'd come back and see a few shapes; I'm pleasantly surprised that you exceeded my expectations. In the few minutes I was gone I didn't think that you could gather so much detail. But you did." His arm remained around me as he led me by the sleeve and put me between him and the painting. "Talk to me about it."

"It's a daemon," I replied flatly. "A blue daemon."

"Yes."

"That's it."

"You said that you didn't mean to paint it. What did you mean to paint?" Victor put both hands on my shoulders and began to massage them, trying to get me to loosen up.

I sighed. "The blue streak looked like a finger, that's how it all started."

"That's a great piece of imagination," he commented. "Most of my work starts the same way, one mark becomes another and so on. It's normal. Some of my pictures take on qualities similar to yours as well. If I had come back in here and seen a bowl of fruit, I would have felt you were painting something to try and please me, that you would think I would expect you to come up with something like that. I'm very happy that you found this instead."

I turned around, stunned. "You are?"

"Of course. I knew you were talented. You just had to prove it to yourself. You can probably do a ton of other things you don't know about either, all because you haven't tried," Victor lectured, not quite in the tone of a parent, but more in the tone of someone very worldly.

I felt a little better about the daemon picture, but not about the daemon itself. It was like all of a sudden I *knew* what had been following me last night, what the source of the power was that had been behind me. It had been the daemon – the Blue Daemon. There was no doubt in my mind; it was so instinctive that I did not even have to ask myself 'what' it was; I just *knew*. I was all knowing. I even began to think I *knew* more about the daemon than I humanly should. I *knew* that he used his claws to gain access to the night; digging himself out of a burrow it called home, deep in the earth. I also *knew* he used those same claws to dig shallow graves for the victims he methodically picked out over the centuries of his existence. I even *knew* that the method for choosing his victims was not done by the daemon because it had no brain, it had no conscience, and it had no way to reason. Another power, a higher power, a more self-serving power, was responsible. But what I didn't know was, why? Why did I know all this? And why was this daemon searching for me? Who sent the daemon?

Victor and I chatted, a little less about my daemon picture and a little more about his work, since, after all, he was the artist, not me. We decided that we would get together Saturday evening to arrange his work and get it up on display, and that his job between now and then was to find a few paintings that he wanted to put in the gallery. A task he seemed to think would be easy even though he claimed his studio was overflowing with paintings that he'd done over the years. He locked up his classroom, leaving my blue daemon behind, and walked me out to my car.

"It was good getting together," I smiled, as we stood next to my car in the warm summer night. The sky was dark and clear and the brilliant stars made the heavens look like a giant bolt of psychedelic polka dot fabric.

"Guess I'll be seeing you on Saturday," he stated.

"Where is your car?" I asked, looking around the vacant lot.

"I walk; I don't live that far away," he answered.

"Can I give you a lift?" I asked. I felt bad that he walked to and from the campus.

"I have a car. I just prefer to walk. Especially on nights like this," he spoke, looking up. "You live close to here, right?"

"Yeah, over at Rye Condos," I replied.

"Why don't I ride back there with you, and I'll walk home from there. It's only a few blocks to my place. That way I will know you got home all right."

He seemed like such a gentleman, and since I was pretty scared to be alone, I thought it was a wonderful idea. "Yeah, that's fine." I was eager to take him up on his offer.

It was a brief drive from the campus to the condo. I left the top down and Victor seemed to enjoy the night sky and the warm air rushing through his hair, all perks from riding in a convertible. He removed the elastic from his ponytail, allowing it to flow freely. When we reached my condo, he neatly gathered it back into place and tied it. I parked the car in front of my unit and raised the top, securing it with two clamps at the windshield, and rolled up the windows. Tonight I was going all out; I was even going to lock it. I turned the engine off and sat next to Victor for a moment, not sure if I should invite him in, or allow him to leave right away. It was still relatively early and I could have used the company.

"Would you like to come in for a little while?" I asked, turning to face him.

"I'd love to, but I promised my friend downstairs that I would do something for him tonight," Victor replied as he graciously declined the offer.

"Oh." I pulled the keys from the ignition. "I understand."

"Trust me, I'd rather be with you than running speaker wire for his new stereo any day," he confessed.

I laughed. "At least I rank higher than speaker wire." It struck me as funny.

"Much higher."

Victor leaned over and turned my face towards his. He kissed me lightly on the lips. A first kiss with someone new is always special; it's uncharted land, a new experience, a new sensation. But, to receive a first kiss when you least expect it, instead of waiting for it, anticipating it is even better. I had forgotten to breathe before the kiss started because I was caught off guard. I pulled away only for a second for a gulp of air before I returned his kiss. His lips were soft and warm and wet enough to glide over mine without worrying about the slobber factor. I felt his fingers slide across my cheek and into my thick dark hair; he played with a handful and tipped my head farther to the side, our kisses getting more involved and heated. I positioned my hand on his thigh, closer to his knee than his crotch. I had not deliberately aimed to put my hand anywhere except to prop myself up from sliding further into my seat. In the past, all the men that I had an interest in were lousy kissers, but Victor had a certain touch and a certain style that turned me into Jell-O. Victor released his handful of my hair and allowed his hand to trail down my body, stopping at my waist. He stopped kissing me long enough to whisper, "I should get going." Then he kissed me one more time for good measure.

"Really?" I asked, disappointed things had to end right then.

"Yeah. But I look forward to seeing you on Saturday night," he smiled, rubbing my leg softly, warmly.

"It's a date," I said, returning his smile.

"Yes, let's consider it a date."

Victor walked me up the stairs to my front door. I stopped before putting my key into the lock to see if I felt the presence of anyone or anything other than Victor, but I did not. I gave Victor a quick kiss, said good night and let myself in.

Chapter 6

As a child, I slept so heavily I would've missed an army invasion, and I continued this habit as an adult. I could nap anytime; yet still grab a good eight hours sleep without missing a beat. I thought I was never one for dreaming, yet in my childhood I remember my mother and grandmother conversing in low tones about the horrendous nightmares I experienced. I never recalled those nightmares, and my mother would dismiss my questions, saying they didn't matter, just forget them. As best as I can remember, my nights were uneventful, even during the time my brother disappeared.

I was fifteen when Kevin, my older brother by some ten years, left our home, never to return. I don't remember much about that time, only that my mother never cried, and refused to talk about him. I believe the police were involved, but even that was kept from me.

Considering what I had gone through these past weeks, I suppose I shouldn't have been surprised that I finally experienced a dream I remembered. Unfortunately, it was a dream of the worst kind, and of course I would remember it in excruciating detail. Waking from my dream was almost worse than the nightmare itself, sitting bolt upright in my bed, soaked in cold sweat and completely disoriented.

As my dream began, I remember feeling cold, seeing my breath puff out in little clouds; I was outdoors but I was not sure where I was. Nothing looked familiar to me. I did not even *feel* familiar to me. I was hosting a body that was not mine – or was it? I could feel and touch, but I was not *me*. I looked down at myself and saw that I was wearing a long gray wool coat, which explained why I felt itchy; I am allergic to wool and avoid it at all costs. I was wearing these funny black granny boots, obvious antiques to my twentieth century eyes. I touched my face. My cheeks felt hot as if I was running a fever, and I realized I was not feeling well either, so I must have been sick. My hair was long, pulled back and tied with twine, and I wore a funny little black felt hat. I hoped I didn't see anyone I knew dressed the way I was.

I remember thinking in my dream-state that I needed to get home, wherever home was. The road in front of me was unpaved, covered in packed snow except where wheels had churned dirty ruts. I walked clumsily down the street, heading in the direction I thought was home. Two large brown and white horses pulled a carriage by me, driven by a man dressed in black, heading in the direction I had been returning from. I looked up and down the street, which was now vacant, and noticed a Candy Shoppe, a Pub and a General Store, their tall narrow buildings standing side by side, closed for the night. It was like I was back in time, the 1800's perhaps. I was not good with history anyway, but this was not a time I found myself familiar with. I kept walking on the slippery street, heading out of town, occasionally glancing nervously around me. I felt like I was being followed. This was all too familiar, like déjà vu'. I had been in this situation before; I knew this feeling of being watched, not knowing by who or what, or where it was. I could not walk any faster for fear I would slip and fall. My lungs began to hurt as I continued to breathe in the cold winter air. I coughed and my chest ached with pain; yes, I was sick. The stars twinkled softly in the clear night sky as the moon lit up the snow, guiding me as well as a flashlight. I began to feel frustrated with my intuitions and emotions. I wanted to cry out to whatever was following me to stop, leave me alone! I would not tolerate it. As my fear grew, my anger mounted. I would put a stop to this! How dare it! I did not care how brave or stupid I was to confront my feelings; I just remember thinking, *I can take care of you.*

I saw a small red house on the corner, and knew it was *my house.* I breathed a sigh of relief that I was almost home. But, I was not safe yet.

Desperately I called into the night, demanding yet pleading, "Who are you?" in a voice that scared me. It didn't even sound like me. It wasn't me. I spun around. I did not want to confront my fear like this but I had to, whether I wanted to or not. I was not acting alone; I shared this ill body with someone, but who?

I heard breathing. Not mine. I heard the rustle of birds in flight. No birds. I glared into a nearby tree, seeing something. "I'm warning you. Leave me alone!" I yelled. My lungs began to hurt again. "I may not know who you are, but I know what you are." I had no idea what I was saying; words tumbled out of my mouth of their own volition. Something reached out and touched my hair; it was playing with me now. I spun around again and looked up into a nearby tree. Nothing. I started to walk towards the house again, knowing I was still being followed. I heard footsteps behind me. I took two more steps, then quickly turned around, hoping to catch a glimpse of whatever it was.

The next thing I knew I was laying in the snow on my back, under a big oak tree. The tree's gnarly, leafless limbs spread crookedly in every direction, creaking in the cold winter breeze. Through the branches I could see the black sky, spattered with stars; the crescent moon cradled in the velvety darkness. *How pretty,* I thought. Why was I lying down in the snow? I was cold. I tried to get up, to get on my feet, but my arms and legs would not respond to my commands. I tried to move my fingers and was able to gather up some snow, but it was so hard to do even that. I was becoming so sleepy. A horrible ringing began in my ears, gradually increasing in volume. I realized someone was trying to talk to me, but the sound that filled my head almost drowned out the voice. I could not see the owner of the voice, but I tried to whisper for help; I wasn't sure if anything audible came out of my mouth. My vision began to fade and I blinked quickly, trying to clear it, but it soon failed. I could not see the moon or the sky or even the branches of the tree directly overhead. I only saw darkness, my head filled with the deafening high-pitched tone.

I felt the pressure of someone or something climb on top of me, hot breath on my now cold face. I was paralyzed in fear. I was blind and too weak to move my arms and legs. I lay there vulnerable to whoever or whatever was crouched over me. For the first time I anticipated death, my own; it was happening. I had lost all my senses; my body was slowly shutting down. If this was death it could not happen fast enough. I could feel nothing physical anymore – no pain, no cold – yet still remained mentally aware of my circumstances. I knew I was almost dead; I had to do something! I fought with all the strength I had to leave my body, struggling mightily in my mental prison. Suddenly, like a cork shot from a bottle of champagne, I was free, rising to the top like a torrent of bubbles. I realized I was looking down at myself, but I was not alone; a dark figure in a long coat lay over me. The snow surrounding this tableau was stained crimson from the blood that had spilt from my lifeless body. I did not know who the man was, but somehow I knew he was not completely human. I tried to lower myself to see the face of my killer but instead I floated higher and higher, and no matter how hard I kicked my legs I kept ascending. Suddenly, with a start, I woke up.

Exhausted from my nightmare, I sat in bed for a moment, collecting my wits. I threw the covers back and staggered into the bathroom. Leaning on the basin, I turned the faucet, preparing to throw cold water on my face to jolt myself back to reality. As my haggard face looked back at me from the mirror, I noticed a rash on my neck and chest. I pressed a cold washcloth on it, easing the itchy feeling. As I stood there, I remembered the wool coat from my dream. How strange, I thought; was the dream so real I could have an allergic reaction to a fabric? Troubled, I returned to bed.

I slept lightly the rest of the night, not deep enough to dream again, but at least restful enough where I could begin my day not feeling like a zombie. I had a lot to do anyway, so lack of sleep was not going to be an excuse. I anticipated my evening with Victor, wondering what it would be like. Maybe I could squeeze a nap in later to make sure I lasted through the night.

While I was having my morning coffee out on the deck, enjoying the sun, I thought about talking to Addy about the strange events happening to me. I wondered what she would think about the painting and the dream. I missed Sara at this moment; she always had explanations for everything, or would find one. I respected Addy's opinions, but I did not share the same closeness with her as I had with Sara. In many ways, I felt like I was using Addy's expertise, not sharing as friends would. I had never turned to her in the past, but with Sara gone, I had no choice. I hoped Addy didn't mind, didn't view me as one more troublesome problem on top of all her others, but there was no one else I could really confide in. My mother wanted nothing to do with me; it had been nearly two years since I had last seen her, even though she lived just an hour away. My relationship with Drew was not ready for such a test, and Victor and I hardly knew each other, although I thought him to be very open-minded. I did not expect our first date to tread into such areas, but stranger things have happened. I finally decided not to talk to Addy about the daemon and my dream, at least for now; she had enough on her mind already and I was not sure I knew how to disclose what had been happening to me anyway.

I spent most of the day cleaning; a once a month going over was all my tidy place usually required. I always tried to clean up after myself so things never got out of hand. By early afternoon, I had completed my chores and decided to run out to the grocery store. The sunshine that had warmed me earlier in the day was gone, replaced by dark gray clouds rolling in – rain, no doubt. By the time I got out of the store with two bags of necessities, the sky had opened up and the rain was just plummeting to the pavement. Rain is supposed to smell clean and fresh, but city rain smells really odd, as if it takes on the odors of the dirty asphalt streets, making it heavy and sour. I remembered the big yard I used to play in as a child; after it rained the grass was so fragrant, especially if it was freshly cut; the smell filled your nostrils as if heaven sent. I missed that; maybe someday I would have that again.

The rain did not let up and I got soaked bringing in just the two bags of groceries. The raindrops were not drops, but bullets sent by attacking clouds; soon the thunder and lightening began, and then the power went out. Could the day get much more fun? I just hoped that the power would come back on before I had to get ready for my date with Victor.

By dinnertime I had given up on the fact that I would have artificial lighting any time soon. I drove down to the gallery, hoping that it would have electricity, but every traffic light was out on my way there and the block was dark. I let myself into the gallery. There was still enough daylight to walk around without the fear of running into any art and damaging it. I lit each sconce on the wall until they all flickered with a golden flame. The gallery looked very romantic; now I hoped the power would not return before Victor got here.

Using a flashlight, I got the ladder and a toolbox I had set aside in the back room to put up Victor's paintings. I had saved space on the wall near my desk for his work, enough room I figured for at least three or four pieces.

I had not been in the gallery more than an hour when a car pulled up in front of the shop and parked. I watched from my desk as Victor sprinted through the heavy rain to the door of the gallery and knocked. I got up nervously and looked down at what I was wearing, feeling that I should have changed before I got here. Too late now, jeans and a short-sleeved sweater would have to do. I unbolted the door and pulled it open. A very wet Victor staggered in.

"It's something out there," I laughed, shutting the door behind him.

Victor turned around to face me. His long hair was drenched and plastered down flat on his head; he combed his fingers through it without much success. "I tried to call you at home and when I couldn't reach you there I figured you must be here."

"No power?" I asked, crossing my arms and leaning back against the wall.

"Nope. I think it's out all over the city," Victor stated. He peeled off his jean jacket and draped it over the doorknob to dry. "I should have brought a change of clothes. I can't believe how it's coming down."

"Did you want to pass on tonight?" I asked, hoping that he did not want to.

"I'm all set. I have the paintings in the car. I didn't know if we'd have enough light in here to work, but I think the candles will be fine. They look good, too," he commented, dropping his voice an octave.

"Yeah, they do."

"I guess I'm going to get wet again," Victor sighed with a painful look on his face. "All my stuff is in the car."

"You could wait a while and see if it lets up," I suggested.

"Or, I can go now and get it over with," he added.

I nodded. Those were his options.

Victor took a deep breath, "I'll bite the bullet. I'll go now."

"How many paintings do you have?" I asked.

"Three. I think I can get them all at once."

Victor raced back out to his car and removed the canvases quickly from the front seat, slammed the car door and sprinted back to the wide-open doorway of the gallery, trying to shelter the canvasses as he ran.

"It's so nasty out there," Victor said, and began trying to tame his hair again. He bent over and let his hair hang, shaking the excess water from it, and separating the strands so they would dry quicker. I found this tremendously sexy. A man with great hair is a perfect turn on for me.

"I'm jealous," I said, as I opened the toolbox and took out a hammer.

"Of what? Me?" Victor chuckled. He leisurely walked in my direction as if he had no clue.

"Yeah. You have the nicest hair. Every girl you ever dated must have hated you for it," I smiled. "Women work like dogs to have nice hair, and guys do nothing."

"It took years for it to look like this," he protested. "And I do appreciate what I have."

I rolled my eyes as if I only half believed that statement and knew he was only trying to make me feel good.

Victor and I worked on where his paintings would hang, and in what order he wanted them displayed. He would not even show me which paintings he had chosen to display until the nail holes were made. Finally, he let me have my first look at his work. The first painting depicted an Irish Castle, set out on a bluff, overlooking a rocky shoreline. The colors were nice – muted, but not drab and dark like the one I had seen a day before. The second painting was of a woman who looked like a sorceress. She was holding a crystal ball, and was surrounded by fairies. The painting was dark, but had nice bright contrasts of purples, reds, and golds. The last painting I actually liked more than the rest; it depicted a full moon shining over a harbor filled with tall-masted sailing ships, and it looked very realistic to me.

"You do very nice work," I complimented him, as I adjusted the last picture on the wall.

"Thanks. It was harder than I thought choosing which of my paintings to display here," he confessed.

I turned to face him. "I'm sure it was, if you have as many as you say you do."

"Is it the light in here or are you tired?" Victor asked, studying my face.

I thought a moment. Last night's dream couldn't have taken that much of a toll on me. "I feel okay. I had a pretty weird dream last night, but I slept," I explained, putting some extra nails into the toolbox.

"Oh. Sometimes dreams can really wear you out. I'm fascinated by people's dreams. Want to talk about it?" he asked, leaning up against the aluminum ladder.

"Why? It was as weird as the painting I did for you. Do you really want to hear ramblings from Miss Blue Daemon lady?" I asked sarcastically, sliding the toolbox onto my desk.

"I do if it affected you that much. Was the Blue Daemon in it?" he questioned.

"It was right up his alley. But no, I don't think so," I answered.

"It was a nightmare then," he speculated out loud. "Not reoccurring, I hope?"

It had not occurred to me that I might have the dream again until he said that. I shuddered involuntarily, hoping that was not the case. "Not yet."

"That's good. Sometimes talking about it puts it in perspective."

I nodded in agreement; talking about anything usually helps.

"But if you don't want to talk about it, that's fine too."

I looked around the gallery; the candles were still burning and the power had not yet come back on. "It's just creepy talking about it now, with no power and all." I admitted to part of my fear. "Let me put the ladder away and we can talk some more."

Victor stood away from the ladder. "Do you want me to put it away for you?" he asked, ever the gentleman.

"I can do it," I replied, holding the flashlight and dragging the ladder with me towards the back room.

In the back, away from the glow of the candles, it was a little darker than I had anticipated. I tried to maneuver the flashlight while sliding the ladder back where I found it. Suddenly, there was a loud clap of thunder that startled me badly; I dropped the flashlight and caught my hand in the ladder, pinching it deeply.

"Are you okay back there?" Victor called. "Need some help?"

"I dropped the flashlight," I called back. I was pissed, and felt stupid that I was stuck, unable to bend over to get the flashlight with my hand pinched in the ladder.

I heard him enter the back room. "Are you okay?" he repeated.

"My hand is pinched in the ladder and I can't reach the flashlight," I admitted through gritted teeth.

Victor picked up the flashlight and moved over to me, shining the light on the ladder and finding where my hand was trapped. "Oh, I see." He placed the flashlight under his arm and gently opened the ladder enough so that I could free my hand. He pushed the ladder against the wall. "Let me see your hand."

He took my hand, turning it gently so that he could see where and what part of my hand had been caught. The meaty part of my thumb was pinched and broken open, bleeding slightly and already turning a bruised color.

"It's okay." I said, pulling my hand away. "It's just a little cut."

Victor took my hand back firmly and looked at it again. "You should at least clean it up or something. You have a first-aid kit here?"

"I'm fine. I have some Band-Aids at my desk," I replied. "I should have just left the ladder until tomorrow."

"Or I could have taken it for you," Victor apologized.

With flashlight in hand, Victor guided me to the front of the shop where my desk was. I sat down in my chair, opened the top drawer and took out a few Band-Aids.

"I'll live," I sighed. "If this is the worse thing that ever happens to me; I think I did good."

"You're just going to toss a Band-Aid on it? Aren't you worried about an infection or something?" Victor asked with some concern. "People still get infections, right?"

I opened the top draw of the desk again and pawed around, finding the remnants of what might have been a first aid kit. "Here are some alcohol pads, and gauze."

"Can we play doctor?" Victor teased, shining the flashlight in my face.

"Who's the doctor?" I asked, shielding my eyes.

"Me."

"I hope your malpractice insurance is paid up."

Victor set the flashlight down on the desk and opened an alcohol pad, then gestured for my hand. I sheepishly allowed Victor to clean it up. His touch was firm, yet gentle, and he did not stop until the wound was clean. The slice was larger than I thought, but I did not feel I would require stitches. I pulled my hand back so that I could take a closer look at it.

"I think I'll be fine," I glanced up at Dr. Victor who was opening another alcohol pad.

"Let's see if we can stop the bleeding," he suggested, retrieving my hand and holding the pad over the open area, applying a generous amount of pressure. I let him do his job. Finally he let my hand go and tossed the pad into the garbage. He then kneeled down in front of me and took a Band-Aid off the top of my desk. My heart skipped a beat as I watched him get down on one knee like a knight, or prince, and take my hand.

"So?" I asked, waiting to see what my prognosis was.

He kissed my palm. I felt his warm breath against my skin as his firm lips pressed deeply onto the still slightly bleeding cut. I thought I felt the nudge of his tongue. "You will live another day."

Two Band-Aids later Victor and I decided that we would go back to my place and see if power had been restored. The rain had ended and the skies were clearing. The possibility of finding a place that delivered pizza was looking good.

Chapter 7

Victor followed me back to my place and parked in the spot designated for guests. I was lucky enough to have a condo with ample parking, and never had the trouble some complexes had with a shortage of owner and guest parking spaces. I shut my car door, leaned against the driver's side fender, and waited for Victor to park his late model Grand Prix into his chosen spot. The electricity was back on, evident by all the outdoor lighting mounted in the trees, shining like super novas in the night. I waited for Victor as he locked up his car.

I had that feeling again. The same one I had the night before Sara's necklace appeared in my car, and the same one from last night's dream. I was being watched. The hair on the back of my neck stood upright, and a ghostly chill ran down my spine and through my arms as if I had been plugged in for recharging. My hands got hot and tingly as if each nerve and sensory receptor was running on overload. I rubbed my palms against my thighs, trying to counteract the intense sensation; they felt like they were on fire. I looked around me anxiously to see if I could make out anything lurking – my Blue Daemon friend perhaps – but saw nothing. I only *knew* something was out there. My gut instinct, my sixth sense, was on red alert. I became agitated; what was watching me; why couldn't I see it? What was preventing me from seeing what I feared? And a better question, what would I do if I did see it?

As Victor approached, I remained preoccupied with wanting to know who or what was watching me. "Something wrong?" Victor asked casually, pushing his sleeves up past his elbows and stuffing his car keys into his front pocket.

I did not reply at first. I wiggled my fingers, trying to work out the tingles, and continued peering around. "Ummm, I'm fine," I answered distractedly.

He placed a guiding arm around me and we headed towards my condo. I climbed two stairs, but then turned around quickly, startling Victor; something was very close behind. I could hear it breathing; it was not me, and it was not Victor. But could Victor hear it? Was I going mad?

"What's wrong? Do you hear something?" Victor asked in concern, grabbing my arm to get my attention.

"I think so." It was the first time I had openly admitted it. I stood very silent and tucked some hair around my ear, giving myself a clear audio path to whatever might be out there.

"What? Where?" he asked, looking out over the well lit, half-vacant parking lot. "Is it between the cars? Maybe it's a raccoon."

"No," I replied. I knew it was not a small timid animal. The sensation I had been feeling rapidly diminished and was gone. "It's nothing." I knew whatever it was had left. Whether it had left on its own, due to the fact it knew I knew it was there, or because of my male companion, whatever the reason, it was gone.

We went inside, into the living room, and I offered Victor a seat on the couch, asking if I could get him a soda or a beer. Victor decided on the beer. I came back from the kitchen with two bottles of beers and the yellow pages to find a pizza restaurant.

"I don't mind driving down the street to pick up a pizza," Victor offered, sitting on the edge of the couch as he took his beer. "I'm out of cigarettes and I need fuel for my car; I can do it all at the same time."

I leaned back on the couch, flipping through all the yellow pages of pizza restaurants. "You smoke, huh?" I raised an eyebrow to project a 'you know better than that' look.

His smile took on a boyish grin as if he had heard the speech before. "I'm a very light smoker. I only smoke at night."

"I can usually tell a smoker right off the bat," I announced, getting up to get the cordless phone. "I have a great nose for that stuff." I took the phone off the receiver and sat next to Victor with the phone book wide open.

"You can, huh?" He was amused with my smug self-assurance.

"Yeah." I put my nose right to the sleeve of his denim shirt and breathed in deep, smelling nothing but his cologne. "I don't smell smoke."

"That's good. Says something for my personal hygiene."

"Usually you can tell when you kiss someone whether they're a smoker or not," I smirked, remembering the kiss from last night.

His eyes sparkled with amusement. "Oh yeah. I guess you would."

"Okay, let's talk food," I declared. I didn't want Victor to think I had a one-track mind. "What do you want on your pizza?"

"No mushrooms. You can have anything else you want," Victor bargained, rolling the bottle of beer between his hands.

"Sounds good. I'm not a fan of mushrooms either. How about plain old cheese and pepperoni?"

"Works for me."

I placed the order at a pizza place downtown, all of a two-minute drive away. The pizza place was also right next door to a 24-hour gas station/mini mart so Victor could one-stop shop.

That settled, I went into the kitchen for plates and utensils as Victor headed out the door. Feeling rather like an old married couple, I told him that while he was gone I would channel-surf and find a good Saturday night movie, or pick up one on pay-per-view. He smiled agreeably and left.

Victor removed his car keys from his pocket and walked down to his car. He stopped short of the driver's side door, turned to look behind him to make sure that Kala was not watching, and quickly turned off into a thick stand of trees that bordered the parking lot and the main road. Victor's vision was superb at night, and he had no need of artificial light to make his way in total darkness. His hearing and sense of smell were as keen as any nocturnal hunters' – maybe even better. And Victor was hunting. He had felt what Kala felt earlier in the parking lot. He'd felt the eyes of something uninvited, unimaginable, watching. Victor's senses were a hundred times stronger than Kala's. He was surprised that Kala could even mildly pick up a telekinetic signal, or sense something that truly didn't belong to this world. The fact that she could left him with a feeling of admiration, but also caused him some trepidation that she had such hidden powers. What else lay dormant in her, waiting to be aroused?

"Where are you?" Victor called out. "I know you are here." His eyes scanned back and forth, looking for any signs of life or movement.

The night did not give him a clue. Silence.

"She knows! She doesn't know what you are, but she knows what you look like," Victor growled, his displeasure evident. He continued his one-sided conversation, obviously familiar with his unseen prey. The presence Kala had sensed was, unbeknownst to her, what she would recognize as her 'Blue Daemon'.

"Don't make me find you. You know I will," he warned. It had been a long time, but Victor was familiar with the Blue Daemon and knew how serious a matter it was that the creature was here. There were very few reasons that Victor knew of for daemons to be hurled into this mortal world from theirs. He knew that daemons did not normally do their deeds without direction; they did the bidding of *one.* The night Victor saw Kala's painting of the Blue Daemon he was deeply shocked, although he did not let her know. He felt responsible in a way for the Blue Daemon taking form on her canvas. As soon as he'd seen it, he knew there was an immediate need to protect her from the evil that was beginning to surround her.

Suddenly, from behind a thicket of dense brush, rose the awesome presence of a menacing beast, its tall, skeletal body glowing with a bluish gray hue. The rotting skin on the mobile corpse was scarcely fastened to the brittle bones by tattered shreds of muscle. The creature bore a keen resemblance to the painting Kala had done, the one she referred to as the

Blue Daemon.

"Why protect her?" the beast roared. "Kill her!" Its jaw clicked on bony hinges as it flailed its limbs in anger.

"I am not here to kill her. I won't let that happen," Victor argued, protecting the unsuspecting Kala. "Who sent you?" As he spoke, Victor crept in the direction of the Blue Daemon. "How many of you are there?" he demanded, refusing to back down from the daemon. He had met many in his day and would not let this race of evildoers intimidate him any longer.

"Can't say," the Blue Daemon replied. "You and I have killed together before. Why not now? Easy kill."

"That was a mistake and you know it!" Victor was infuriated with the Daemon's accusation. How dare it bring up such a painful past! "That was a very long time ago."

"No mistake." the daemon shot back.

Victor ignored the creature's words. "I am willing to let you live," he ordered, "if you leave now, and never come back to harm Kala. If you come back, I will find you and kill you. Go back to whoever summoned you and tell them I will do the same to them." He approached the beast forcefully, his aggressive demeanor causing the daemon to step defensively back.

"There is a job to do!" the Blue Daemon barked. "How does *she* know about me?"

"I don't know. But she knows you are here. She knows what you look like. She must be very strong," Victor replied. "Leave now!"

"I will come back," the daemon warned. "I have to."

"Then I will kill you. You know I can."

Eyeing each other balefully, Victor and the Blue Daemon parted ways; each knowing the other had a job to do. One to kill, the other to protect. Victor thought to himself about Kala, her untapped power apparent in the psychic disturbances around her. He was not sure how he would keep her safe, but he would die trying.

"I hope he didn't get lost," I thought to myself, sitting alone in the living room. I had kicked off my shoes to get comfortable, and was relaxing on the couch, clicking away through all the movie channels trying to find something of interest to watch while we dined on the city's best pizza. I finally settled on a movie that was a favorite of mine, hoping that Victor would like it as well. I lit a few candles on the coffee table, closed the blinds, and dimmed the light, waiting for Victor to come back with our dinner. Just about the time I thought I smelled pizza, there was a knock at the door, and I sprang up off the couch. I peeked out the spy hole in the door and, upon seeing my handsome dinner date, unlocked the door and let him in.

"Sorry it took so long," Victor immediately apologized. "It was busy everywhere."

I was just happy he had returned. "No problem. The movie just started. Put the pizza in the living room."

Victor held the pizza flat, and stepped into the living room. "Wow, candles for pizza. What do you do for Thanksgiving dinner?" he joked, setting the pizza on the coffee table and parking himself back on the couch.

"I don't," I answered quickly. "I'm no cook." I sat on the floor, stretching my legs under the coffee table and opening the cover of the box, revealing dinner. "I swear I smelled this before I even knew you were out there." I handed Victor a plate and napkin, allowing him to help himself. I served myself several slices, careful to scoop up all the toppings that dropped back in the box.

"Is this movie what I think it is?" Victor asked, taking an enormous bite of oozing pizza.

"Interview with a Vampire," I answered enthusiastically. "I haven't seen this in a long time. It was great when it came out." I sipped my beer, washing my mouth and throat clean.

"Oh."

"Have you ever seen it?" I asked, turning to converse directly with him.

He wiped his mouth with a napkin. "When it first came out. I think everyone saw it."

"If you don't want to watch it, I can find something else." He did not seem to feel the same enthusiasm I did for the movie.

"No. It's okay."

We each ate our limit on pizza and I put the leftovers in the refrigerator. I returned with two more beers and took a seat next to Victor, who had slipped his shoes off and put his feet up on the table. He balanced his beer on his flat stomach, holding it lightly with one hand to keep it from tipping.

"So, what do you like so much about this movie?" Victor asked curiously.

I sipped my beer and thought a moment. "Well, a lot. I like the costumes, they're great, and the time period it's set in. I like the struggle between the characters, and this dilemma of living forever, but the need to change to survive," I explained. "I take it you don't like the movie." I faced him, waiting for his response.

"I don't like it or dislike it. It's okay," he said distantly.

"I'm an Anne Rice fan. Maybe that's why I like the movie as well as I do," I confessed.

"The Vampire Chronicles," Victor acknowledged, looking at me with a knowing smile.

"Yes. I read them all over the last ten years or so. Have you ever read any of her stuff?" I asked.

"My neighbor downstairs reads a lot, and I know he's read her books. We have talked about her work from time to time," Victor told me. "I know she's very popular; I've see a lot of her books floating around campus. What do you think about the whole Vampire thing? Some people take her work very seriously," Victor probed, digging deeper into the subject.

"What do you mean? Like do I believe Lestat is really living in Miami?" I laughed, tucking a leg underneath me, and sinking deeper into the cushions of the couch for comfort.

"No, more like; do you believe that Vampires exist?" Victor asked.

I was taken back by the question, but I knew from being around Spellbound for as many years as I had that people believed in many things; things that could be explained, or had no explanation; things like Werewolves, Aliens, Bigfoot and Vampires. I was careful how I phrased my answer. " Well, I know Witches exist – not the stereotypical black pointy-hat, broom-flying kind – but actual Wiccans that live peacefully in our society. As far as Vampires," I stopped, careful to gather my thoughts. "I won't say I absolutely don't believe in them; I try to never close my mind to anything. But I would have to say that 90% of me thinks that if Vampires did exist in society, *we* as a society would know it. There would be pictures or evidence, something that supported the fact that Vampires were alive, so to speak." I downed my beer, feeling confident in the answer I had given him.

Victor nodded in approval. "What do you think Vampires would look like?"

"Hmmm." I thought about all the ones I had read about. "It would be nice to think of them looking as Anne Rice portrays them: angelic in some ways, strong features, beautiful long hair, nice teeth..." I smiled, teasing him.

"So, nothing to fear," Victor made his assumption out loud.

"Not true. They are depicted as killing machines. I think their striking good looks are probably traps. You know, like a spider web, lure your pray in and it never gets out," I clarified, glancing at the TV to see what part of the movie I was missing.

"Makes perfect sense." Victor stretched out his arms and legs until I heard his joints snap. "That feels so good," he moaned blissfully. "I have a hard time staying comfortable if I sit for any long period of time."

"You can stretch out if you want. I can sit on the floor." I began to get off the couch to allow him the extra room he needed.

He placed a restraining hand on my leg. "No, don't get up. You can stay.

I like sitting with you." He stopped me from getting up. "You don't have to sit so far away either, you know."

I smiled inside.

Victor lay back with his legs and feet extended onto the table and put his arm up on the back of the couch, making room for me to get close to him and settle in under his arm. This was much nicer.

We sat close to each other, silent for much of the rest of the movie, until Victor asked, "Ever wonder what it would be like to be a Vampire?"

I placed my hand on his thigh, the soft cotton of his jeans feeling cool and smooth under my fingers. "You mean to live forever?"

"I mean the whole lifestyle. Outliving everyone, seeing the world evolve, having time to travel to any place you wanted over and over again..."

"Killing people for food," I interjected.

"Everyone needs to eat," he retorted quickly. "What about beef, chicken and pork? Fish? Seafood? All raised to be consumed."

"So you mean to tell me that if Vampires existed they should harvest humans to eat? Put us on little farms or hold us in little pens until they're hungry and then drain us of our blood?" I asked incredulously.

"Is there a difference between what humans do for food versus what a Vampire might do?" Victor asked, perhaps playing devil's advocate.

I sighed and shook my head. "Never mind, it really doesn't matter now does it?" I tilted my head up to look at him.

"I guess not," he agreed. I felt him lower his arm around my shoulders and play with the sleeve of my sweater companionably.

"It's all the Aliens' fault," I blurted out. "When in doubt I blame the Aliens. They are probably responsible for Vampires. They brought them here, from a galaxy far, far away."

This made Victor chuckle. "Now that's a new twist if I ever heard one! Aliens. Now I have heard it all. Instead of Devil worshipers, Vampires were dumped off by Aliens." He smiled and pulled me closer to him, pleased at my answer. "You're cute."

I giggled because he appreciated my humor.

When the movie was over, I switched to the cartoon network and we watched old Scooby Doo classics; the ones I loved as a child. "If there is something else on TV you'd like to watch, you could put it on." I offered him the remote when I could find nothing other than cartoons.

"I'm not a big TV person," Victor admitted. "But I would like another beer." He held up his empty bottle of beer and peered through the colored glass. "I'm out."

I took my bottle off the coffee table and collected his as I got up. "I probably should have carded you before I served you earlier," I joked. "How do I know you are old enough to drink? I could be getting myself in trouble."

Victor removed the tie that confined his hair, and combed his fingers through it; loosening his dark locks so that they cascaded around his face and shoulders. He looked up at me from his seat on the couch. "Are you serious?"

I left him with an evil laugh as I walked into the kitchen, putting the empty bottles into the sink and taking two more from the top shelf of the refrigerator.

"You can't be serious." I heard him call from the living room.

I had a broad grin on my face when I returned and gave Victor his beer. I fell back into place next to him. "Just how old are you?" I asked curiously. I turned his face toward mine. "I know you're over twenty one."

"I'm older than you," he replied.

"Oh, and how old would that make you?" I brushed his hair away from his face. "I'd say thirty two," I guessed aloud.

"Hmmmm, good guess."

"What month were you born?" I asked. "We may not even be compatible."

"May. You?" he asked, holding my hand against his chest. I felt the buttons of his denim shirt rise and fall with his breath.

"July. I'm a Leo," I replied. I enjoyed the warmth of his hand over mine.

"Really. Did I miss your birthday?" he frowned, looking down and turning my hand inward, glancing at the two Band-Aids he applied earlier in the night.

"No. It's Wednesday. But don't tell anyone! I'm going to be thirty quietly," I warned.

His eyes lit up. "Well, that's reason for a small celebration. Can I at least take you out, or do you have plans already?" he asked.

"No plans. I'd love to go out," I smiled brightly. I put my hand back against his chest, fiddling with the buttons down the front of his shirt.

"I know the perfect place, but it will be a surprise," he offered.

"I can hardly wait," I said happily. I felt all funny inside, as if I could hardly contain myself from bursting out like a small child and demanding to know where he would take me. I suppose all that would have to wait for now.

We cuddled on the couch during two episodes of Scooby Doo, and then he brought up something we had talked about earlier in the evening that I had forgotten to finish.

"So, what was that dream about last night?" he asked softly, when the commercials started.

"Oh," I sighed. "It was just strange, that's all."

He caressed my arm and hugged me close to him. "Well, tell me, anyway."

I thought back to my dream, searching for a way to explain it. "I don't know where the dream was, what place or even what time. I think it was a long time ago, like horse and buggy time. I felt like I was being watched and the next thing I knew..." I stopped what I was saying for a moment, recalling how I had looked, dead in a puddle of red snow. "I was dead. I felt myself die. It was bizarre." I rested my head against his chest. I wondered how his bare chest would look, strong, muscular, smooth-skinned or thick with hair.

"Really. That is weird. Did you know it was a dream while it was happening?" Victor asked, nudging my head to see my face.

"I don't know. I guess I knew. I wasn't really in any pain. But I was sick; it was all my chest," I recalled. "A man killed me; I remember that. I could not see his face." I struggled, trying to remember more details, but couldn't.

"Hmmm. If you ever have a dream like that again, try telling yourself it's only a dream and then you can wake yourself up. Or so I've heard. Worth a try, " he suggested kindly. "Do you dream often?"

"No. Not at all, until last night," I admitted.

"Maybe you'll have a good dream tonight." He kissed my forehead and brushed his fingers through my hair.

I glanced up at him and smiled. He was so handsome I could hardly stand it. His hair was loose and free about his face. How could this man be single? Why had some beautiful woman not caught him yet, gifting him with even more beautiful children? His eyes were the color and softness of melted chocolate, their gaze inviting me to devour him whole. I reached up nervously and touched his clean-shaven face, his smooth youthful skin. My fingertips softly grazed his full lips, feeling his warm breath as he exhaled. I allowed my fingers to trail down his neck, slowing down and flexing my fingers to take in the feel of his denim shirt against his firm chest. My hands were extremely sensitive; I could almost feel things before I touched them, and I wanted to continue touching him. I wanted to kiss him again. I wanted to melt under the heat of his breath, and feel his hands explore me in the comfort of my home and not my car. Victor leaned into me and kissed my lips briefly while he ran his hand down the outside of my leg. He pulled his face away just enough so that he could look into my eyes. "You are something else," he grinned appreciatively.

I laughed lightly. "Oh?"

He kissed my lips softly, but in a way that said 'goodbye'.

"What's wrong?" I asked him, my fingers intertwined in his soft hair.

"I can't stay. It's getting late," he confessed.

His words hit me like a bucket of cold water. All of a sudden I felt like I had two heads and I was the most unattractive creature he had ever had a date with. “Oh. Okay,” I managed to force out. I pulled away from him and gathered the empty beer bottles.

“It’s not that I don’t want to stick around. I just can’t,” he tried to explain, sensing my distress. He captured my hand and forced me to stay next to him. “It’s not right to start something that I can’t finish, at least, not tonight.”

I lowered my eyes. His excuse did not make me feel any better. “I understand,” I said stonily. I stood up and took the empty beer bottles into the kitchen; I rinsed them out, tipped them upside down and dried my hands off with a kitchen towel. I had not heard Victor walk into the kitchen behind me; I turned around and was startled by his presence. I jumped back, bumping up against the counter. He took the towel out of my hands and laid it on the stone counter next to me. Victor eased me against the sink and put his arms around me gently, but with some deliberation, and kissed me. I felt his tongue enter my mouth and tangle with mine. Again, I had been surprised by him, by the manner in which he had approached me, and now how he kissed me. His mouth tasted good to me, balmy and wet, not the mouth of a smoker. I thought for a split second as I felt his tongue discovering the inside of my mouth. The pressure of his body against mine was strong. I ran my hands up his stomach and dug my fingers into his clothes, wanting to feel more of him next to me. I kissed the side of his face and ran my lips and tongue down his jaw line and then to his neck.

“Oh boy,” he mumbled, pushing himself off me, just far enough to break free from my kisses. “I really do need to go,” he confessed once again. “But it’s not that I don’t find you a turn on, because I do.”

I smiled in understanding. I felt better that he was trying to make me feel better.

“But I’ll be seeing you on Wednesday to celebrate your birthday,” he smiled.

“Oh yeah. I look forward to that.”

“Me, too.”

Chapter 8

Victor arrived at his place a few minutes after he had left Kala's. He thought about her the entire way home, and as he parked his car, and was still preoccupied as he walked up the driveway and into the foyer of the split-level home he shared with Nathan. Victor and Nathan had shared this home for several years, and took good care of it. The house was a Victorian, located in the historic section of town; it had a small fenced-in yard, with a wrap-around porch. There was a large, old-fashioned wooden swing hanging from the porch roof; Victor loved to sit and gently swing late into the night.

Once inside the house, Victor decided to visit with his friend. He'd been avoiding him recently because of Kala. Without knocking, Victor let himself into his friend's half of the divided Victorian. The living room was dark, with heavy drapes drawn over the tall windows. The only light came from a mahogany table where a gooseneck lamp was poised over a hard-covered book. A man sat at the table, reading. He was middle-aged, average in size, with short black hair. He turned the page and continued reading, as if Victor's presence had not even registered. Victor pulled out a leather wingback chair opposite him and sat down, not saying a word, until finally the man looked up in irritation. "Well," he said flatly, closing his book and leaning back in his own chair. "You saw her, again." Nathan frowned, clearly referring to Victor's date with Kala.

"Nathan," Victor began. "I know it's *her*. There is no question in my mind. Kala is the *one*." Victor leaned forward in some excitement.

Nathan remained silent, obviously contemplating Victor's announcement. His slim body, clothed in a button down black shirt and black pants, looked regal in the lamplight. He did not have to say much to Victor; they had known each other a very long time, and could read each other's thoughts. Nathan pulled a cigarette and a gold lighter out of his shirt pocket; after lighting the cigarette he tossed the lighter onto the table and took a long drag off his cigarette, exhaling out his nose. "How do you know it's her?"

"I tasted her blood. Only *I* would know if it were her or not," Victor responded in a tone that allowed no argument. He sat on the edge of his chair, ready for Nathan's rebuke.

"Isn't that what got you into trouble the first time? Just a taste?" Nathan asked, moving a ceramic ashtray closer, then tapping his ash in it. "That's how it all began, over two hundred years ago. One woman's hold over you."

Victor nodded; Nathan was correct. "Yes. But I was so young and stupid then. I have learned my lesson. You know that I have." Victor's eyes implored Nathan's once again for forgiveness. "I would not hurt her. Ever. Not again."

"Then you know what we have to do," Nathan stated. "At all costs..."

"I understand. But we do have a problem," Victor interrupted. "I have seen the Blue Daemon. Kala knows about the Blue Daemon, too."

Nathan's eyes widened in amazement. "The Blue Daemon. Who sent for it? How does Kala know about the Blue Daemon?"

Victor was not sure how to answer. "I spoke to the Blue Daemon; it would not say how many were called upon, or who they were summoned by, just that it had a job."

"How does Kala know about the Blue Daemon?" Nathan asked, rolling his cigarette around in the ashtray. "They never allow themselves to be seen, and certainly not by their prey."

"I think Kala has abilities we are not aware of yet. Her powers have been suppressed for so long that I think they are just all surfacing now. She has the ability to sense things like telekinetic energy. I'm not sure what else," Victor tried to explain.

"I hope all these powers and abilities don't all come out at once; that won't be good for anyone. She'll probably totally lose control unless someone can help her keep her head, and that's more than you or I can handle. It will also delay any plans our people have to proceed with the Book of Jorn," Nathan considered out loud. "Kala's friend Sara was a very effective buffer between Kala and our people; she blocked all signals we sent, and didn't allow any of Kala's abilities to surface. It has never been so evident until now."

"I agree. I'll keep an eye on her, while you poke around and see if you can find out where the Blue Daemon came from. I warned him if he returned, I'd kill him."

Nathan smiled. "Well, that is very dedicated of you. But we absolutely have to find the source, the one who sent the Blue Daemon, or this will never stop." Nathan took one last drag on his cigarette and put it out.

"I'll be seeing Kala for sure on Wednesday, but I will try and keep tabs on her until then."

Nathan straightened in his chair, placing his folded hands on the book he had been reading. "Just for the record; I don't like Kala. I don't care who she is supposed to be. I don't like her. And the only reason I am helping you is because it will get us out of the hot water we have been in for the last two centuries."

Victor lowered his eyes. "I know, Nathan. Kala has no idea who I am, or what our people are like, and what we have gone through. She just thinks this Blue Daemon stuff is some ghoulish nightmare. Kala has no clue as to what is happening to her."

"What do you think will happen when she does find out? When she finds out that she was born to be an Emissary to a race of people who dwell in the night, who live but do not die? Do you think she will be easy to sway if all these powers surface? I have lived long enough to see an Emissary put into power and the literal Hell it was to get her there. I don't look forward to it. The only thing I do look forward to is having my status given back to me once Kala has assumed her role. That much I deserve," Nathan said heatedly.

"Yes Nathan, you do deserve that. If I could have found a way two hundred years ago for you to have it back, I would have. I am doing all I can now to give that back to you," Victor pointed out. "But we can not rush into this; too many bad things can happen."

"You're right, we can't rush into making Kala something she is not yet ready to be. But, that does not stop us from informing the High Counsel of what you have found. It will give them time to prepare for her, and notify our people that the Emissary is on the way. I will make a call this evening. Get the ball rolling."

Victor stood up from his chair. "I understand," he said, expressionless.

"Oh, and I'm sensing something," Nathan said, looking up at Victor as he stepped back from his chair. "You care about Kala, and not in the way you would like me to believe."

Victor shrugged, "It's been two hundred years; I miss her."

"Just don't let it cloud your judgment. If you fail this time, I don't know what *they* will do to us," Nathan warned. "So don't just think about yourself."

"I won't," Victor replied. "But I have a responsibility to myself, and to Kala as well. I will do what's best for all of us."

Victor spent the rest of the evening alone and inspired. He stood in his loft with a heavy tarp under his feet, protecting the floor from spattered paint. His blinds were open, revealing the city he lived in. He could see a lot from this huge window. The night sparkled with stars; airplanes droned past on their flight paths, and the office buildings never seemed to go dark. He loved this view, so high above the city; he could even see the mountain range several hundred miles away. Victor opened a smaller window across the room to get some fresh air. He took a deep breath to clear his mind, and began pacing the tarp, clean paintbrush in hand, his head lowered in reflection. He had not been able to put Kala out of his mind. She had no idea what was happening around her, and Victor could not tell her. It was a process that would have to unfold day by day, and not be forced. In the past, the High Counsel had to handle each future Emissary with care, to coax and direct them in the right direction. Some Emissaries were almost mad with their untamed powers, their energy so great that many of Victor's people had lost their lives trying to channel them towards an even greater power – the Sovereign. Once the Emissary and the Sovereign were joined, their powers balanced and their reign could begin. This was the government of Victor's people. A people born through death, and living forever in the shadow of darkness. Respect and privilege came with age; the older you were, the higher on the counsel you moved, unless you were born of the purest blood; a descendent from one of the first of Victor's kind. These individuals were few, but they had a strong hold in the High Counsel. The birth of a pure being had only happened twice during the last two hundred years that Victor could recall. The only way to ever be Sovereign was to sit back and wait, watching hundreds of years go by, for a chance to be selected into the hierarchy by the High Counsel, or to be pure in blood. An Emissary was a human female; from the moment of her birth it was known, written in the Book of Jorn, when she would serve her role. There were fewer Emissaries born in the past five hundred years than there were those with the purest blood.

The Book of Jorn was the writings that foretold the fate of Victor's people. It chronicled the history of his ancestors, and what they held to be true. Jorn was the first of his kind, and no one was sure where he came from. No one was even sure today where he was, and if he continued to live, or had gone dormant as so many of the very old ones do for many years at a time. The Book of Jorn contained passages covering each event in a person's life; their life is already known, it is known prior to their mortal life, and after their birth into the world of the living dead. Each Sovereign, each Emissary, every trader, every hero and all catastrophic events are indexed. You lived your life according to the Book; it could not be re-written. Your role had been chosen for you, your path all lined out. Life in the Book of Jorn was perfect – or was it?

Finally Victor stopped his contemplation and approached the canvas he had positioned on a wooden easel. He opened several tubes of paint, squeezing colors randomly over his acrylic blotter. Victor held his blotter like it was an infant, cradling it in his left arm. He placed his favorite paintbrush in his right hand and began to mark up the white canvas in shades of blue and black; his inspiration had finally struck and he'd probably be painting until he could paint no longer, or until the sun threatened to rise.

I put my head on the pillow just shy of one in the morning, and was soon sleeping peacefully. At some point – I'm not sure how long it was – I shivered with cold and realized that I was once again dreaming. Once again I was back on the streets of the old-fashioned city, wearing my long gray coat that I could hardly tolerate against my skin. I wasn't sure what aggravated me more: the constant irritating itch from the wool, or the horrible pains in my lungs and chest from breathing in the frigid, raw air. Here I was again on the slippery, snow-covered street, filled with this aching need to get *home*. I recalled Victor's words to me, suggesting that I tell myself I was in a dream to try and wake myself up. It seemed logical, at least worth a try. "You are dreaming!" I harshly told myself, as I began to walk in the same direction I had the night before, the one that led to home, but also to my death. I knew I was dreaming, but I could not get myself to stop. I would not stop walking. I had no control over anything that I did. It seemed I was in the dream for the duration. Everything was the same – the slippery roads, the man in the buggy, the sense of being followed. I continued to be as brazen as I had been the night before, facing my fear and calling out in the night for it. The closer I got to my little red home on the corner, the harder my heart pounded, as the specter of death hovered menacingly. I pulled myself back, like a horse being reined, trying to prevent myself from walking into imminent death, but I just kept walking. It was a horrible frustration. "Stop! Stop!" I yelled soundlessly at myself. Finally, I did stop, but only for a moment. I felt my hair being tugged, but when I turned around I found nothing. The next thing I saw was the crescent moon overhead, and the branches of the large oak tree swaying in the wind. I was lying in the snow, on my back, glimpsing the last few moments of life I would ever know. I already knew what would happen, and I could not bear to feel my systems shut down again. The deafening tone had started in my head, and it pierced through my brain like a spike. I had not remembered it feeling like this last night; I was feeling pain, an unspeakable pain that over took me in one vast wave. My eyes were open wide, my nervous system in shock, and the night faded away until I saw no more, but continued to hear the shrilling tone. The voice from the night before was close again; I thought for a moment it was a man's voice, but my pain was too excruciating for me to let it register. The weight of another body mounted mine, which was the cue that it was time for my soul to leave my body. I wanted to exit so badly, to be rid of the pain that paralyzed me. But I also had a burning desire to know who, or what, took my life, so I mentally struggled as I felt myself lift from my dying body. I fought hard to stay, but I had very little strength left. I began to rise out of my body, streaming upwards. I thought I could visualize my killer's face, maybe see even the slightest unique detail, before the pain overtook me. Suddenly, I realized that I was no longer in pain, and that the ringing in my ears was not hurting anymore. The ringing I heard was the sound of the telephone on my nightstand. My dream had ended. How long had the phone been ringing? I fumbled for it. “Hello?” My voice was panicked from the nightmare; my nerves still jangled from the abrupt awakening.

There was silence on the other end. No answer.

“Hello?” I said again, trying to catch my breath. Was there someone there or had I missed them?

Still no reply.

I hung up and sat in bed alone, feeling beat up. I closed my eyes and tried to relax. I placed my hand on my chest and could feel my heart still thumping with fear. I also felt the flare-up of the rash caused by the wool coat on my neck and chest. I tried to ignore the itch, telling myself it was only a dream.

I picked up the phone and began to dial a number – Victor, I had seen it only once on the card he gave me, but never forgot it. I hoped he would not be upset with me for calling this late at night. The phone rang twice before he picked up. “Hello.” I heard him say, voice slightly muffled.

“Victor, it’s me,” I blurted out. I was still trying to compose myself. I walked nervously to the kitchen to get a soda to drink.

“Hi.” He seemed perplexed by my late phone call.

“I’m so sorry to be calling you. I’m not one of those psycho, fatal attraction women; I swear it!”

“Of course you aren’t,” Victor tried to comfort me. “Is something wrong?”

I opened the refrigerator and took my last can of Diet Coke. “It happened again,” I said in a pitiful voice.

“What happened?” Victor asked, although he already knew what she was referring to. His was the phone call that woke her from her nightmare; his was the voice that did not reply on the other end. He had been tuned into her all night long, keeping a mental check on her – babysitting her. Victor was all too aware of what Kala had seen in her dreams.

“The nightmare,” I cried. I had not meant to cry. I was just so confused and distraught by the event.

“Please don’t cry,” Victor begged. “It won’t help you calm down.”

I crawled back into bed and pulled the covers around me. “It was so real! I even have an allergic reaction from the wool coat I was wearing in my dream.”

“Wow, that sounds very real,” Victor lowered his voice to try and console me. “Same dream?”

"Yeah, except I was in so much pain tonight. Not like last night," I sighed heavily, wiping tears from my cheeks.

"Pain? From what?"

" I don't know. It was this horrible pain in my head. Not like a headache. Something else." I tried to recall. "I can't compare it to anything."

"Are you still in pain?" he asked.

"I feel like I've survived a car wreck," I replied, taking a sip of my soda.

"I'll hold while you go get yourself some aspirin and climb into bed; then we'll talk some more. Okay?" he offered. "I've been painting and I've got to clean up, but I'll wait."

I put the phone on the bed and went into the bathroom, took some pain medication out of the cabinet, then took a cool washcloth and blotted my face, chest and neck. I pulled my hair back and wiped the back of my neck dry near my hairline. Glancing into the mirror, I spotted something unusual on the side of my neck, near my ear, an area not affected by the rash, two small marks, which hurt when I pressed them. The marks looked like bites from an insect, or maybe sting marks from a wasp or bee, or maybe even some pimples that had not fully developed yet. I was not sure. I took my washcloth and pills back to bed, crawled under the covers and washed my medication down with some soda.

I picked up the phone. "Are you there?" I asked.

"Yes. Just washing out my brushes." I could hear water running into a sink in the background. "Feeling better?"

"A little," I replied, though I was lying.

"Put some Neosporin on your rash if you have it; it will fight the itch for you," he suggested.

"Thanks Dr. Victor," I replied, trying to put up a brave front. I held up my hand with the two Band-Aids, the one Victor had performed first aid on at the Gallery. I tugged at the plastic strips and pulled each bandage off. My hand looked well healed, especially considering the deep cut I had sustained. "The cut on my hand is almost gone!" I exclaimed in surprise.

"You must heal quickly," he said. Victor's 'special' kiss had jumpstarted Kala's own natural healing ability.

"Is the Neosporin good for bites?" I asked, placing the washcloth on the side of my neck.

"Bites?" he echoed in a higher pitched voice. "What kind of bites?"

"I don't know. It's on my neck. It's not like a rash; it's not raised. There are two marks that look red; they're kind of sore too," I explained, touching them.

"Neosporin can't hurt. I suppose it could be a bug, maybe a spider or something," Victor said reassuringly, although he was quite sure they were not.

"Bed bugs," I added.

He laughed a little. "Yes."

I felt better hearing his voice and I began to loosen up. I sank back into my pillows. "What were you painting?" I inquired, changing the subject.

"Oh, nothing. It didn't work out. Just ended up making a mess," Victor chuckled. "Happens to the best of us."

"Mmmm."

"You going to be okay?" he asked.

"I hope so," I answered.

"You can call me whenever you need to, okay? I mean that," Victor insisted.

"I will. I want the dreams to go away," I mumbled, wanting to go back to sleep, but knowing I couldn't.

"Listen to my voice. I want you to relax, get some sleep. You need to sleep. You need your energy. I will call you sometime tomorrow and check up on you, okay?"

"Hmmm," I agreed. "I'll try to sleep."

"Good; if you need me, call."

"I will."

"Good night Kala," Victor whispered as he hung up. "Sleep well."

Chapter 9

I slept surprisingly well after my conversation with Victor, waking up on my own at almost nine in the morning. My rash was gone, and the marks on my neck had vanished, although my body was still a little stiff. I took a few more aspirins with my morning coffee and skimmed through the Sunday paper on the living room floor.

Shortly before noon I received a call from Drew, who I had not heard from in several days. He asked if I wanted to go to a baseball game with him. He explained that his Dad had the tickets and could not go, and had given them to him. The seats were good; the weather was perfect, so I told Drew yes; I'd love to go.

I took a quick shower, threw on a pair of bike shorts, added a tank top, sneakers and a radio station cap, and met Drew out on the front steps thirty minutes before game time. The traffic was a little heavier than expected and we could hear the Star Spangled Banner being sung as we walked from the car to the entrance of the park. Drew sent me to our seats on the third base line while he waited in the beer line.

"Great seats," I remarked to Drew when he arrived with two large beers and two slices of pizza.

He quickly took his seat next to mine. "Dad has had these seats forever. He hardly ever just gives them away." He took a sip of his beer, flipped his baseball cap around backwards and leaned back in his chair, devouring his lunch. This was the first time I had seen Drew in shorts. He looked rather odd with his long, pale skinny legs, thick with dark hair. I tried not to stare, but the guy needed to get some sun and maybe beef up by doing some weights. His upper body was actually rather attractive, though slightly built. He wore a black muscle shirt, and sported a tattoo of a serpent on his right shoulder. I loved tattoos; the workmanship involved rivaled many a work of art.

By the fifth inning I remembered something critical regarding the sun and me – sunscreen. My shoulders felt tight and hot, and I knew just about then that by the game's end I would be severely burnt. Why it was so difficult for me to remember to put sunscreen on, or bring a bottle with me, was beyond me. It was never important until I tried to sleep the night after getting too much sun, then swearing I would never forget again. And then forgetting.

During the seventh inning stretch Drew and I were on beer number six and my sunburn didn't feel too bad. Of course, I think the alcohol helped to deaden any nerves that might have been experiencing pain.

"Wow! Look at you!" Drew gasped. "Boy, do you burn!" He reached over and slid the strap of my tank top off my shoulder just enough to show what my skin color was prior to being fried. "Jeez, your legs too!"

I glanced down. "Yeah. I'll pay later," I sighed. And I knew that I would.

"Hey, is that new?" Drew asked, reaching over to touch the pendant around my neck, the one that belonged to Sara.

I had forgotten it was on. It had already become part of me. "Actually, it's an antique. It was Sara's," I replied.

He admired it. "What's it made out of?" he asked, turning it in all different directions. "It's kind of red, and blackish. It's shiny, like a liquid or something."

"I don't know what it's made out of. Victor wanted to know that too." I looked down at it. I had not seen it in bright sunlight and it did look at little red.

"Who is Victor?" Drew asked, suddenly probing.

"Oh, he's just one of the artists who is displaying some work at the Gallery," I replied. "You should stop by and see some of the pieces on exhibit. I'm having this fancy cocktail party at the end of the month for the newspapers, the artists, and some city officials."

"Oh brother. You're getting snazzy like my parents," he rolled his eyes in disgust.

"Now, come on! I'm one of the most down to earth people you know," I argued and slapped him on the arm. "Don't pull that with me."

"Kidding!" he laughed. "Don't hurt me. I'm fragile." He giggled like a girl.

"Remember I could whip your butt," I pointed at him with mock authority.

"Oh baby! Whip me!" he laughed.

The game went into extra innings, so by the time Drew took me home it was nearly six and my skin tone was that of 'My Little Pony' – very pink. Normally, I would have invited him in, but I must have looked so pathetic he didn't even ask if he could stay for a while. He just told me he hoped that I felt better. I gave him a friendly kiss goodbye and told him I'd see him at the station in the morning.

The air conditioner had been on the entire time that I was away at the game. It felt so good on the flaming skin on my body, the cool sensation like an aloe balm. I made myself comfortable on the couch, putting my head back and breathing deep. I opened my eyes just enough to be able to see the answering machine across the room had a flashing red light, which meant someone had left me a message. "Oh, I wish I had the energy to get that," I said out loud, thinking it could have been Victor who left me a message. But I felt too comfortable to get up, and stretched my legs out, feeling the tightness of my skin with movement, and the tingling sting that would probably get worse before it got better. "Machine will have to wait," I sighed, and shut my eyes.

I heard a mechanical click and then a voice. My answering machine had started by itself! I opened my eyes, shocked out of my state of relaxation. The voice on the machine was Addy, asking me how my plans for the cocktail party at the gallery were going, and to give her a call or stop by and see her at the shop on Monday. I sat up straight on the couch, adrenaline making me feel as if someone had stapled a board to my back. I blinked my eyes several times to try and clear my head. "That was weird," I whispered. I don't know why I whispered; it wasn't like I was afraid someone would hear me.

Once the eerie feeling left me, I got up and walked to the kitchen to see what I had to drink, knowing all my Diet Coke was gone. I had a few beers left from the last time Drew was over, and decided it was an emergency worth tapping into his supply. I'm sure he'd understand, although another beer was the last thing I needed. I felt a little dehydrated and I knew alcohol would just make it worse, but I could not convince myself to drink a tall glass of water. I took my cold beer to my bedroom, pulled the shades down over the windows and climbed onto my queen-sized bed, feeling the smooth, cool fabric of my comforter under my backside. How good that would feel over my naked skin, I thought. A chill went through my feverish body. I kicked off my sneakers, hearing them tumble to the floor. I propped a second pillow under my head and cracked open my beer, taking a long swallow. I lay in the dark, silent.

Shortly after sunset Nathan walked up to the second floor of the Victorian to talk to Victor. He hardly ever found himself on the second floor. Although he cared for Victor, he did not necessarily think that what he did in his spare time was necessary and thought perhaps he could find better things to do than paint pictures. Nathan entered the loft to find Victor still at rest; he was laying on a futon in the back corner of a spare room, clutching a cordless phone to his chest.

"Getting up?" Nathan called from the doorway. His arms were crossed.

Victor stirred slightly and looked around. "Nathan. What are you doing up here?" he asked, his voice soft and sleepy.

"I made some phone calls last night while you were up here pacing the floor and painting," he told Victor. "Get up so we can talk." Nathan uncrossed his arms and walked back to the loft, taking a seat in a wicker and rattan rocker in front of the large window whose blinds were still closed.

Victor combed his hair back quickly, tied it away from his face, and walked on legs still heavy with sleep to meet Nathan near the window. He pulled back the blinds, revealing a beautiful lavender and purple sky. Victor sat on the hardwood floor near Nathan. "What did you find out?" he asked, placing the cordless phone on the windowsill.

Nathan rocked rhythmically in his chair and rested his arms on the rattan. "I spoke to Sheldon and Phillip last evening. They are on the High Counsel. They were both surprised to hear from me again; it has been so long." He looked down at Victor accusingly.

"It has been a long time," Victor agreed.

"I explained why I was calling, and they seemed very appreciative to you and I regarding Kala. They had almost given up on the hope that the Emissary would ever come. But they have had continued faith in The Book of Jorn." Nathan made clear his approval of their dedication. "Sheldon and Phillip will tell our Sovereign of the good news, and will be calling us tonight to set up a meeting."

"What is the meeting for?" Victor asked, confused. "It's too early for the High Counsel to take her."

"Victor, it has been a long time since we have been able to socialize with others like us in higher political power. I'm not questioning anything right now," Nathan stated.

"Who is our Sovereign anyway?" Victor asked.

"You don't know? Who is the President of the United States?" Nathan asked quickly, leaning forward in his chair.

"Clinton," Victor answered without pause.

"You can tell me the name of the humans' President, but you can not tell me who Sovereigns our people?" Nathan was flabbergasted by Victor's priorities.

"Hey, I'm sorry. But I try not to overly involve myself with a group of people who felt the need to banish me from our society," Victor snapped. He stood up and walked away from Nathan, not wanting to be in his company any longer.

"You killed our last Emissary! Not something to easily clear yourself of! And through my association with you, I was banished," Nathan hotly pointed out.

"I have paid for that mistake for nearly two hundred years. Almost three human life times! Do you know what I would not have given to be human and *die* to get away from you, and everyone else like you and me?"

"You are strong-willed because of it and if all goes well you might find yourself somewhere in the High Counsel, too." Nathan tried to entice Victor.

"I don't care about a seat on the counsel. You know that. I just want to live as I have been. Pick up a new hobby every ten years or so. Explore. I have no yearning to sit at a black marble table, in a high back leather chair, and dictate to a nation of dead people like me. Our society is so divided. Half of us want to be rebels with no law or ruler, and the other half won't take a shit unless it's in the Book of Jorn. We are pretty messed up." Victor pulled his shirt off over his hand and rolled it up in ball around his hand. "Have you heard anything about the Blue Daemon?"

"The High Counsel is checking on any known radicals who might know something, or be involved in it in any way. If the people involved are discovered, they will be tried and executed."

"I'm taking a shower. Let me know if you hear anything," Victor said expressionlessly. If he had to, he would take care of things himself, he thought, as he watched Nathan leave.

I had decided that I would stay in tonight. I was feeling a little under the weather when I woke from my nap, and anyway, I needed to get some laundry done. It was after eight when the phone rang. I was matching socks.

"Hello?"

"Kala, it's me, Victor." His warm voice was soothing to my ears.

"Hey, how are you?" I asked, tossing socks into my basket.

"I'm doing okay. I wanted to see how you were after last night."

"Burnt," I replied, looking down at my arms.

"Mentally?" he asked.

"No. I went to a baseball game this afternoon. I forgot to wear sunscreen. I'm pretty burnt," I explained. "They won though." As if that made it worthwhile.

"That's good I guess. Just keep putting lotion on. Nothing will really make you feel any better until it starts to heal," Victor informed me. Such a wealth of medical information!

"I wish it would heal as fast as the cut on my hand. I swear to you; it's healed completely. It's the weirdest thing that has ever happened – almost," I told him.

"Almost?" he asked, waiting for the rest of the story.

"Yeah. This afternoon, I got home from the game; I'm all tired and burnt. I flop down on the couch to relax and I see that my message light on my answering machine is flashing. Well, I was just too tired to get up and I remember thinking I wish I knew who tried to call, and the next thing I knew, my machine clicked on and it was playing my message back. Creepy, huh?"

I said, putting my laundry basket on the floor so I could lie on the couch.

"Yeah, weird," Victor agreed, although he privately thought perhaps that her telekinetic powers might have more to do with it. "So, what are you up to tonight?"

"Oh, I just finished some laundry. I should really run out to the store. Get a few things, like soda and aloe or something for my burn. But I'm not feeling too motivated," I yawned, making myself comfortable. "What are you doing?"

He huffed. "I don't know. I really hate to stick around here. My friend downstairs needs an attitude adjustment."

"You can drop by here if you're bored. I don't have anything to offer you, but my company and cable TV. But you are welcome," I invited.

"What more could a guy ask for?" Victor chuckled. "If you are willing to grace me with such things, the least I can do is stop at the store for you and get what you need."

"You don't have to. I'm just being lazy," I laughed. "But if you want something other than beer, you better stop for yourself."

"Tell me what you need. I'll be over in a little while," he instructed.

I gave Victor a short list of Diet Coke, chips and something for my sunburn. He seemed to think he could handle it.

I didn't move a muscle and lay motionless on the couch until I heard the rap of someone at my front door. I forced myself into action and headed to answer it. "Who is it?" I asked, reaching for the doorknob.

"Me."

I pulled the chain on the door, unlocked the deadbolt and pulled it open. Victor stood on the front step with a brown paper bag in his arms. He looked at my face and winced. "You look horrible."

"Well thank you so much," I replied, allowing him to enter.

Once inside he turned around to look at me again. "You do burn easy." He bent over and kissed me gently on the lips. "I didn't mean you looked horrible," he smiled.

I shut the door and locked it. "Thanks."

I put the soda in the fridge and gave Victor one of the last beers. He sat on the couch digging into the bag of wavy chips I had requested. He held up the tube of lotion he'd bought for my sunburn and began reading the label.

I set my glass of Diet Coke on the coffee table and munched a few chips. "What does it say?"

"Well, this seemed to be the best thing to get you at the time for your sunburn. But now I wonder if you won't be sicker later with sun poisoning." He reached over and felt my face. "Do you feel cold or hot?"

"I get the chills every so often," I answered.

"Could be sun poisoning. Hope this will at least take the sting out of the burn for you." He tried to be optimistic.

"You don't look like you burn too easy. You have nice dark skin," I complimented him.

"Oh, I burn pretty well, thanks," he smiled, opening the tube of lotion. "Let me see an arm."

I stuck out an appendage. He filled his hand with a generous layer of lotion and cautiously applied it to my arm. I cringed. The lightest amount of pressure made my entire body hurt. I just bit my bottom lip and did not complain; I knew I had brought this on myself. Next time maybe I would remember sunscreen.

"So sorry," he smiled sympathetically. "I don't enjoy bringing you pain."

"It's okay," I replied. He seemed to be a caring person. If I had not had sunburn, having him apply lotion to me would be pretty damn erotic. Too bad I could not enjoy it that way.

I let him put the lotion on the rest of the sunburned areas. It did not feel better right away, and I had to sit still like a stone statue until I was dry enough to move around. Victor grabbed a hand towel from the bathroom and wiped his hands clean, then took his seat next to me again. I moved a little closer and gingerly leaned against him. He placed his arm tenderly around my body. "Let me know if you need more lotion," he whispered in my ear, and kissed my check.

We caught the tail end of prime time TV, and polished off a bag of chips. When the news came on, Victor thought it best that he leave and give me a chance to try and get some sleep; he knew I had to work in the morning, and with my burn I would probably have a hard time getting comfortable.

"Do you have to leave?" I asked him, lowering my eyes. I did not want to sleep. The truth was I did not want to dream.

He looked directly at me. "I can't stay all night. I know that dream is bugging you." He seemed sympathetic, but I knew he could not do anything. "But if you need me, you can call. I don't care what time is it. I enjoy hearing from you."

I smiled, thinking it was sweet, but not liking the pretenses for having to make a late night call to him in the first place. "Maybe I could take some sleeping pills. Think that would help?"

"No, I don't. I think you should put your head on a pillow and go to sleep," he replied sternly.

"Easy for you to say. You haven't died two nights in a row, or woke up with a horrible pain in your skull and a creepy rash on your chest and bites on your neck and..."

"You're right, I haven't," Victor interrupted me. " I am not trying to downplay what is happening to you. I have never had nightmares myself, but I think it's something that should go away. You know they are not real." He held my pink face in his hands.

"If they are not real, why do I feel pain? Why do I wake up with a rash? Why did I have funny bites?" I quickly asked.

He sighed. "I don't know. But, depriving yourself of sleep is not good either. Please, try to sleep."

I nodded. After all this was not Victor's problem; this was mine. I walked Victor to the door and we kissed good night.

Before I went to bed I found a blue candle and a white candle and performed some candle magic – the blue for sleep and the white for healing. I did not know if this would make a difference, but I asked Sara to *please* help me.

I fell asleep on my own, no pills or alcohol. I recall lying in bed on my side watching the flickering candles, and thinking about Sara. She would have spent the entire night with me if I had asked, when she was alive. But she wasn't, so the best I could do was imagine her being with me. And that's why I am not sure if I was dreaming or if it actually did happen, but I saw Sara, just as I remembered her. She sat next to me on the bed and touched me. If I had been sleeping, it woke me; if I had not been paying attention, she got it. I was startled at first because even though the room was dark I saw her very clearly. It was her long red hair that I saw first.

"Sara," I whispered, sitting up. I let the covers I had been clutching tumble around me.

She smiled and said nothing.

"Sara, I miss you." I began to cry. I reached out to touch her. She appeared quite solid and, as I moved my hand closer to her bluish dress, I felt a surge of energy. I was not sure if the energy was pulling my hand closer or pushing it away, maybe both. "Sara," I said again.

"Listen to me," she spoke without moving her lips. I knew it was her voice. "You must protect yourself."

"From what?" I asked, allowing my tears to flow unchecked.

"I left you all the answers," she replied. "You must believe in yourself. You are strong."

"What answers?" I asked helplessly. I did not understand. I wanted her to sit down with me over a cup of tea and explain every detail of her death; who killed her and what this new mystery was that she was speaking of. "Sara, who killed you?"

"You have the power to change it," she continued on. "Believe that you can. Listen to your inner voice. It is always right." Sara hovered over the foot of the bed.

I moved in her direction. "Sara, please. I'm very scared. These dreams," I sobbed frantically, trying to stand, to be closer to her.

Sara reminded me of a Goddess, someone I had read about, her long hair flowing around her in a flaming halo, her dress clinging softly in layers of nearly transparent fabric. She raised her hand to stop me, her skin smooth and white like ivory; coolness surrounded her gleaming body. "The answers await you. The past can't hurt you. Change the forthcoming; only you can."

"Sara. Please stay. Tell me more," I pleaded while I stood in her presence. "I need you."

The next thing I knew I was sitting up in bed, as awake as if I'd had four espressos. The candles were still burning, but were almost gone; it was the middle of the night and still very dark outside. I turned the light on and jumped out of bed, walking completely around the bed, looking for any signs that Sara had been in my room. I saw nothing, but remembered her visit vividly. She had come to see me and she looked alive and beautiful. I was left feeling a tremendous sense of relief about the after-life, but was as equally confused about why I had to protect myself, and having to find the answers that she'd left behind. Answers to what? What was I supposed to change?

Chapter 10

I had gotten through the night. The realization hit me when my alarm woke me up at seven. I could see the sun shining from beneath my shades. I had not had any dreams that I could remember, only the immediate recollection of seeing Sara and hearing her words, which still continued to play again and again in my head. I tried not to over analyze what took place last night, for fear I'd drive myself crazy. I began to think seriously about telling Addy what had happened. I felt she deserved to know that her best friend of so many years came to see me; I just wasn't sure how much to tell her. Maybe that wasn't as important as Addy just knowing that Sara came to me; maybe that's all Addy would need to know.

I began to get ready for work, scrambling around the condo, getting my belongings together. I nearly stumbled over Sara's box of miscellaneous items that I had started to go through on the living room floor. I pushed the box closer to the wall with my foot, safely out of the way. I stopped abruptly and turned around to look down into the box. The box, I thought to myself. Sara's stuff. Could my answers be in that box? But answers to what? How did I know what I was looking for? I would have to make time tonight, no matter what, to go through Sara's box, to read every scrap of paper and figure out what the Hell was going on.

I found a parking space on the top floor of the garage and took the elevator to the sixth floor where the radio station was. When the doors opened I caught the backside of Drew sprinting by.

"Hey you," I called, exiting the elevator and slinging my tote bag of radio essentials over my shoulder, wincing as the strap stuck to my sun burned skin.

He spun around. "Morning," he smiled. Drew looked his usual cheerful self, but appeared to have slept in his clothes from the day before, his shirt full of wrinkles, his hair poking in every direction, and his face had not seen a razor in several days. "How are you feeling?" He approached me and offered to take the tote bag.

"Better. Just sore." I rolled my eyes, thinking I was still sorer than better.

"Maybe next time you'll remember sunscreen," Drew poked my arm.

"Doubt it, but there is always the chance," I smiled.

We walked past the receptionist desk that was cluttered with Monday morning paperwork. Sue, a tall blond who was all of twenty, had been our receptionist and resident station bimbo for about a year. It was obvious that she'd been hired for her good looks and easy sexual habits, not because of her office skills. I never stopped to see if I had any phone messages with her, because "that wasn't her job." I didn't much care for her. It wasn't because she was pretty, and it wasn't because she always had a great looking guy at her side, it was more the fact that she felt she deserved to be treated like a Queen Bee in a hive of predominately male worker bees. Her expectations were far too high and I cut her down every chance that I got. Sue buzzed us through a security door that led back to where the studios were without even giving us a second look.

"How did you sleep last night?" Drew asked, putting an arm around me.

"What?" I asked, instantly on guard. I immediately thought about Sara. How did he know about Sara? I stopped and faced him.

He was taken back by the tone in my voice. "I mean, how did you sleep? You were really burnt last night after the game," he said slowly, making sure I understood his question.

"Oh," I replied quickly, and felt slightly foolish. "Fine, I guess." I continued to walk down the long hallway to the on air studios.

"Is something wrong?" Drew asked, tagging behind. "You're acting like something is not right."

"I'm fine. I was thinking about something else," I answered, which was the truth. "My mind is a little preoccupied."

The glowing 'on air' light was lit outside the studio door. Drew and I waited patiently for the DJ who was on the air to finish talking before we just barged in. No one ever gave me that much respect when I was on the air, but I ran my show a little differently. If you were in my studio during my show you usually ended up on the air in some sort of capacity, or talking about the topic of my choosing. Having company walk in and out of the studio all day made the show go by faster, and the breaks between songs more interesting. My highlight of the day was asking the listeners to help me decide what I was going to have for lunch, then calling a restaurant live and placing my order. This simple task sometimes turned into quite an event, especially if someone ethnic answered the phone to take my order – Chinese, Mexican, Thai; that made for great entertainment. If the delivery person were a sport, I'd put him on the air too.

Once the 'on air' light went out, Drew and I pushed the studio door open. The DJ at the console turned around.

"Hi there, Kala," the morning man said. He sat firmly on his tall swivel stool, sorting through his notes.

"Morning," I smiled.

Bryan worked the morning shift, which ran from 6-10; he had been with the station for as long as I could remember, even when I was a listener and not employed by the station. His ex-wife also worked for the station; she was in sales and was a pleasant lady, at least until she found out he was messing around with the Sue. Then she dumped, divorced and took him for most of his monthly paycheck. 'Infidelity does not pay,' that was what the T-shirt read that his ex sent him the day the divorce was final. The T-shirt had been pinned to the wall of the studio for several months and used as a dartboard, with several darts stuck in it at all times. Darts in the 'on air' studio was a favorite past time, until one day there was not enough shirt to pin to the wall and it was thrown out. No more darts.

I did not care much for Bryan. He had that 'morning man' attitude that many DJ's seem to get no matter what shift they work. The attitude that reeks of 'do you know who I am?' and 'I am better than you are because...' and 'you should want to be just like me'. It was enough to make common folks sick, and people who worked with him want to walk in the other direction when they saw him coming. Truthfully, he wasn't as good as he thought he was, or he would have moved on to a bigger and better market by now – Chicago, New York, LA – but he hadn't. That just told me he was too comfortable in his position at the station, and comfy turns into lazy really fast.

"Hey, Drew, take some of these calls, the phones are ringing off the hook," Bryan commanded, pointing to the series of flickering and flashing studio lines on the phone system.

"What are you doing that is so important that you can't talk to your listeners?" I asked, taking my tote bag from Drew and placing it on a spare chair.

"I don't *have* to take calls," Bryan huffed, as if he was too good to push a few buttons and say hello.

"Then neither does Drew," I shot back. I pulled my headphones out of my bag and waited for Bryan to start a fight; he was good at that.

"That's what interns are for, phone calls, lunch, coffee, pulling music and spots," he sarcastically attempted to tell me off.

"Not this one. Drew is my intern. Not yours. I have him doing more important things." I stood my ground from the other side of the console.

Drew said nothing and stood next to me, since my confrontations with Bryan were a common occurrence.

Today he did not want to play any games. "Your last song is in. All yours," Bryan mumbled, pulling his headphones out of the jack on the board, pushing his stool in and walking out the studio door.

Drew and I looked at one another, surprised the conversation had not gotten as heated as they had in the past.

"That's not like him," Drew said, raising an eyebrow in puzzlement. "Maybe his ex got his car now, too."

"Yeah, that was too easy of a win," I agreed.

"Maybe this will turn into some sort of bad WWF wrestling match. You'll leave the studio to use the lady's room, and he'll come running out of the kitchen with a steel chair and slam it across your back. Then I'll have to run down the hallway with a patch cord or something, and wrap it around his neck, and haul him to the floor, and put a submission hold..."

I interrupted him. "You have a very active imagination this morning."

When I got off the air in the afternoon, I spent a short time in production with Drew. He helped me dub some spots and cut a few commercials. I wanted to get out of work as soon as I could so I could stop and see Addy, run into the gallery for a bit and get home by dinnertime to go through the rest of Sara's belongings.

Drew walked me out to the garage and wanted to know if we could get together this evening to eat, or grab a few drinks. I tried to explain I had a lot to do, which I don't think he bought. The fact was I did have things to do, and I don't know why he continued to try and make me feel guilty, and why I allowed it. I had some issues that I needed to resolve, the sooner the better for me.

I decided as I got into the car that letting Addy know about my experience last night might not be a good idea. I was not sure how much to tell her, since I knew that she might try to pressure me into telling her what Sara said to me. If she did ask, I would either tell her the truth or make something up that was believable. My experience last night felt tremendously personal and the thought of telling Addy everything that occurred seemed wrong in a way. I told myself that only telling Addy half the story did not make telling the story a lie, but a Reader's Digest version.

Because of the time of day, I was able to park my car out in front of Spellbound. The middle of the afternoon was a slow time for many shops downtown, and parking was never an issue. I could see Addy in conversation on the phone from the storefront window. I walked into the shop, hearing the jingle of the bell hitting the glass door as I let it close behind me. Addy saw me and waved. I approached the counter and leaned on the scratched glass surface. Addy said her good-byes to whomever she was speaking to, excusing herself because she had a customer.

"How have you been? Haven't seen you in a while," Addy scolded.

"Yeah. I'm sorry. I've been busy," I apologized.

"How are things going? How's the gallery?" Addy asked curiously, leaning her elbows on the counter next to me.

"Not bad. The invitations to the cocktail party have gone out in the mail. I have to call a caterer today to confirm, and I have a pretty full gallery of art," I recited off the top of my head. "And, I guess I'll need to buy something to wear to this event."

"Very good. Things are coming together," Addy smiled. She appeared pleased with my effort. "Got a date for the party yet?" she questioned me with brightness in her eyes.

I laughed out loud. I had not thought about bringing a date. "Well, not really."

"What about that guy, the one you told me about? Some guy that you thought was hot," Addy teased. "Him."

I recalled the conversation, and I knew she was referring to Victor. I smiled. "We've seen each other a few times. He's one of the artists who has some work on display; hopefully he will be at the party. I'd like him to show up."

"Well, ask him to attend. Tell him you'd like him to be your date," Addy encouraged me.

I nodded. "I'll mention it next time I talk to him."

"Anything else going on? Looks like you got some sun," she observed, as she sat high upon her wooden stool.

I stood up straight and looked down at my arms. "Yeah. I went to a game yesterday with Drew. It looks worse now than it feels."

"Well, the game part sounds like fun. I see you are wearing Sara's necklace," Addy pointed out.

"Yeah. I haven't taken it off since the day I found it in the car," I replied. I began to think about my adventure last night, and Sara. "Actually, I wanted to talk to you about Sara."

Addy tilted her head questioningly. "About?"

I sighed, not knowing how to start. It wasn't that I didn't think Addy would believe me; I knew she would, and that was the problem. I stared at Addy for a moment before I started my story. "Last night, I saw Sara."

"What?"

"She came to me last night. I don't think I was dreaming. It was too real for it to be a dream," I reminisced. I tapped my fingers on the counter top nervously, thinking about how Sara looked, so perfect. "She looked lovely," I smiled.

"Tell me," Addy instructed. I had her complete attention.

"I was sleeping and she was just there; she was radiant; her long red hair was so beautiful. She had on this bluish dress that was fluid and light. Addy, she looked like a Goddess, I swear. A beautiful Goddess." I was breathless just thinking about her again

Addy's mouth curled up in a smile. "What else?"

"I tried to touch her but couldn't; there was so much energy around her! It felt like trying to push two positive ends of a magnet together; that weird kind of barrier, an invisible power." I thought back. "And her skin was like ivory! She looked like a porcelain statue. The closer to her I got, the cooler the air felt."

"Hmmm," was all that Addy could manage to say.

"Do you believe me?" I asked, taking a step backwards. I felt as if she doubted me.

"Oh yes," she replied quickly. "Did Sara say anything? Was there a purpose for her to visit you?"

I quickly had to decide what I would tell her. Do I tell her what Sara said; do I make up something, or do I say nothing? My little voice made me say, "No. Nothing."

"Usually, from what I have heard and read, when you are visited by a spirit, the spirit is usually on a mission. There is always a reason for a spirit to return, even if it's to put someone's mind at ease if there has been great sorrow due to the person's death. There is always a reason," Addy tried to explain. "She said nothing to you?"

I shook my head no.

Addy leaned against the wall behind her. "I know it seemed very real to you, but maybe it was a dream. It was a nice dream though. You said she looked like a Goddess."

"Yes," I replied and smiled.

"Dreams can *feel* very real," Addy added.

"Oh, I know!" I promptly replied. No one knew more than I did that dreams could feel very, very real.

Addy offered several books to me from the shop that talked about spirits, mediums and other paranormal events that were similar to my experience with Sara. Addy thought they would help me determine for myself whether Sara actually came to see me, or whether I was just dreaming. I declined taking the books home right away because I told her I just didn't have the time now to spend investigating, but would think about stopping by soon to take her up on her offer.

By the time I left Spellbound I had myself worried. Sara had come to see me and *did* speak to me, and *did* have a message for me. I must admit it was a little cryptic, but she did apparently have a message for me. Was Sara on a mission? If she was, it must be important. What did I have to do with all this? It made finding out what was in Sara's box of stuff a priority. But would I even know if I found something vital in her belongings? I would have to wait to see.

I picked up my mail at the gallery and returned a few phone calls, confirming the cocktail party reception with the caterer for the end of the month. It seemed as though the gallery opening was going to go smoothly if everything stayed on track. I just wished my whole life were on track. The only other thing I needed to find time to do was buy something classy and sophisticated to wear to the party. Working in radio reduced my wardrobe to basically jeans and T-shirts, and my lack of a social life allowed me to live life in a casual mode. Maybe shopping for a dress would be fun, even though I did not have Sara with me to tell me how beautiful and stunning I looked as I tried on every dress in my size in the store.

It was after sunset when Victor and Nathan found themselves together on the front porch of the Victorian. Victor sat on the railing smoking a cigarette, and Nathan sat on the swing rocking back and forth with a mixed drink. Victor had not been looking forward to having any more conversations with his friend; they had not seen eye to eye on many issues lately, most of them dealing with his new relationship with Kala. It was Victor who claimed the porch first, and refused to leave, since Nathan arrived after him. Victor also refused to speak, verbally or telekinetically. This tactic usually angered Nathan; he would accuse Victor of being childish, even though Victor was technically Nathan's child. It was Nathan who had sired Victor into the night, and had remained his companion ever since. Many times in the preceding two centuries Victor felt that it was time to move on and fly out of Nathan's nest, to make his own decisions, to mingle with those who were not totally like him if he chose.

Taking a job at the college was a topic they constantly fought over. Nathan could not understand why Victor would openly associate with humans. In Nathan's eyes humans were a lower species. Humans were born to die, and in Nathan's extended lifetime countless human beings had died in his arms, their life drained in order to feed his. Humans were animals, nothing more, nothing less. Humans were weak and puny. Victor was never able to fully grasp how Nathan came up with his analogies. After all, Nathan was not a pureblood; he too had died to be born again. Maybe because so many years had gone by, he had forgotten what it was like to be human. Even Victor's memories had faded with time. Accepting a job at the college became a constant reminder to Victor as to what human life was all about.

At first Victor was bitter; he did not fit in with his own people due to a horrible mistake that he felt he would never be forgiven for, and he did not fit in with the humans that surrounded him at the college because he was not technically human. Victor felt very much alone. In recent years his relationship with Nathan suffered, the strain from his identity crisis creating a burden almost more than their friendship could bear. One day though, Victor decided to stop brooding over who he was. He could not change. He would not apologize any more for what had happened, and what he had become. The people who knew him at the college liked him for himself; the people he spent time with knew all they needed to know, for now or forever. Victor would outlive these people and take his secret with him; he *could* have friends. Maybe Nathan's anger toward Victor and his association with humans was not anger, but jealousy. Nathan would never admit it, and Victor never pressed the subject. It pleased Victor to know that he could walk from his home to the campus and be part of society, without drawing attention. Victor could stop and buy a newspaper, or a coffee, and have a conversation with a clerk, or waitress, and continue on his way. He'd found a way to be somewhat human and in that he found a level of happiness.

"Sheldon and Phillip will be stopping by later," Nathan stated, crossing his legs and leaning back on the swing. Nathan spoke first out of frustration with the silence.

Victor took a long pull off his cigarette before speaking. "Why are they coming by here?" He flicked his ashes over the banister, exhaling as he spoke.

"I spoke to the two of them last night and they wanted to talk, but you were not here," Nathan explained. "So, we thought it best that they come by here so we all can talk."

"Did you tell them where I was last night?" Victor asked, propping himself against the porch.

"No. I didn't have to. They pretty much know all," Nathan's voice was light, yet his words stung like a slap in the face.

"So they are coming by to tell me not to see her anymore. I just can't stop..."

"I don't know what we will be talking about exactly. Don't forget we are still not forgiven. I am not being treated any better than you right now. I know no more than you do at this moment," Nathan openly admitted.

"I'll be in my studio when they get here," Victor snapped. He slid off the railing and walked into the house, leaving Nathan by himself in the early evening glow.

I sat on the floor of my living room, surrounded by knick-knacks, books, journals, notes, trinkets, you name it. I decided instead of going through Sara's box from top to bottom, I would empty the entire contents out and force myself to pick up and hold each item before either putting it back into the box or investigating it further. I had been putting this job off, but it had become more essential than ever to start finding answers to questions, even though I did not fully understand them.

The colored candles I immediately placed back into the box, knowing there was no hardcore secret to reveal in candle magic. There were many small pouches made of beautiful fabrics like velvet and silk, tied with gold cords and filled with herbs, crystals, and quartz. This was also no great mystery to me, since these were used in many rituals and spells. Some of the herbs, crystals and quartz I recognized, others I did not, but I was sure I would find one of Sara's books that would help sort that out. Next, I found a wooden tarot card box that had Sara's Wiccan name engraved on the lid. I opened it up to find only tarot cards; no great secret answered in there either.

Finally, I decided to start picking up some of Sara's books that looked as if they had gotten much use over the years. I scooted myself closer to the couch and began to look through a stack of soft covered books that looked ratty. The top one had a black matte finished cover with no title, and many of the pages had been dog-eared. I began to check each page and shortly realized that the book was just basic Wiccan reading with information on the sabbats, some spells, and a listing of astrological signs. This was not worth looking into any longer, so I set it aside. The next book was her Book of Shadows. I knew that she'd had one at the shop, in the back room, but I hadn't seen this particular one before. Usually, witches only had one, so finding it made me feel like I had found something a little out of the ordinary. It had a gold hardcover and a black binding, with a gold tasseled bookmark. The book itself was not new. I was no expert on books, but the paper did not feel like it was made recently; it wasn't white or ivory, but more yellow tinged. It had an odd odor, as if it had been boxed away for a very long time. The binding felt like it was leather, not cloth, or something synthetic. It looked like it had been used a few times, but not nearly as much as the one I had seen her with many times at the shop. To my eye, the book did not look any different than the other one she had, but I decided that I would read it more in depth while I lay in bed later on, and truly find out for myself.

By the time I had finished going through the box, the items I had set aside to investigate further turned out to be Sara's 'Book of Shadows', a large envelope of notes and pieces of paper, and a journal which I had not known she kept. Other than that, the box contained memories – not answers to mysteries. I was not sure that I wanted to find anything in what I had set aside to look at. I did not want to find anything out of the ordinary; I wanted Sara's visit to me to be simply that, a visit. I wanted to see her, not be the subject of some mission that she, and her death, may have been a part of. It made me sick to my stomach to think that I was involved in something that was serious enough to cast the spirit of my best friend at me. I tried to lead an uncomplicated life, so why all of a sudden did I feel like complication had taken it over.

Victor stood in his loft studio, trying to resume the painting he had started the other evening; the one that Kala had inspired. Tonight Victor held the paintbrush; it remained dry as he paced slowly in front of his canvas. His mind was filled with turmoil. Usually he could block out thoughts and sounds and banter at will, but tonight he felt himself treading in a sea of clamor. He could not clear his mind and it was quite frustrating to him. This usually only happened when he needed to feed, and it had been a long time. His agitation level had been growing over the past few nights, especially as the nights grew longer, and he had been feeling weaker, requiring more rest than normal, at least for him. Victor resigned himself to the fact that very soon he would need the blood of a human to maintain the level of existence he had grown used to over the centuries. This had to be done before he escorted Kala to her birthday dinner; he did not want to risk hurting her physically or mentally. Even though Victor was not feeling precisely like himself, his sharp telekinetic powers were still at full strength and he knew when company from the High Counsel had arrived at the house. His keen sense of smell identified each one before they exited the large black car they arrived in. Through the small window Victor had opened earlier he could smell not just the two men Nathan said would be coming, but a third. Knowing company was here, Victor gave up trying to paint, not that he was accomplishing anything anyway.

Victor waited for their guests to get settled in Nathan's company before he made his own entrance. Meeting these people from the High Counsel in Nathan's presence was something Victor struggled with on the inside, not wanting any involvement what so ever from this point on. He had found Kala quite by accident, and that was it. His job was done. If all went right Nathan would have his pride and political standing given back to him, two hundred years of bitching and blame would stop, and finally Victor could get on with his life, perhaps alone and without Nathan.

Victor let out a very human sigh as he opened the door to Nathan's place and let himself in. The room was dark as it always was, since Nathan adhered to the old standard about elders wanting darkness and not liking the light at all, which made Victor feel alienated. His whole world revolved around color. But tonight the room also contained a pureblood, which made the dark room more somber than normal. Victor was the only one not clothed entirely in black. How inappropriately dressed he felt in his blue jeans and simple white T-shirt – a bad seed for sure.

Nathan sat poised regally on the arm of his leather couch, holding a glass of red wine, while two young looking men dressed in expensive suits sat next to him with their glasses full. The taller of the two men was blond and handsome with some facial hair on a strong-featured face. His hair was combed back straight, fairly stylish. The other man, a thick-haired brunette, was much shorter but looked as if he had an extremely strong body by the way his clothes fit him. He was not overly handsome, and wore a mustache to try and disguise his youth. Victor could sense that the blond was the one with pure blood - he also carried himself differently, the brunette a companion. The man Victor was not familiar with sat in a winged back chair across from Nathan and appeared to be about Nathan's age, a little older, he guessed. The man looked serious and stern, and did not resemble the other two at all – hair, dark and thin. He was dressed formally, but in good taste.

"Have a seat, Victor," Nathan suggested, pointing to a chair next to the serious one.

Victor glanced quickly at him, then sat down. He leaned forward, resting his elbows on his thighs, clasping his hands together, trying to make this awkward meeting as casual as possible. After all, he lived here too.

"It is so good of you all to come this evening," Nathan spoke.

"With good reason," the blond boldly smiled.

"Victor, I'd like you to meet Sheldon and Phillip," Nathan said, placing a hand on both men's shoulders, identifying Sheldon as the blond and Phillip as the brunette.

Victor nodded politely in their direction, still not knowing who the other man was.

"This is Stuart," Nathan stated, gesturing to the man next to Victor.

"Hello; are you part of High Counsel, too?" Victor asked, sitting back in his chair.

"No. No I'm not," the man quietly responded, crossing his legs and clutching the arms of his chair. "But it is an honor to be here."

"I didn't think you were," Victor replied, looking away from him.

"You must have very acute senses," Sheldon smiled at Victor in an admiring way.

"I have ways of knowing what I know," Victor replied, leaving his secret hidden.

"Stuart has a very significant role in all of this," Phillip stated, looking at Sheldon.

"Stuart will be a key player in making sure all this goes smoothly," Sheldon confirmed out loud.

"Smooth is good right now," Nathan smiled, trying to keep the mood in the room upbeat.

"Agreed," Sheldon raised his drink in acknowledgement.

"Okay, so what's it all about?" Victor asked, trying to get to the point. "What do you need of me?"

A silence fell over the room and Nathan shot Victor a glare of disapproval for being outspoken and speaking out of order.

"Well," Sheldon stood and walked about the room, ignoring Victor's bad manners. "We are aware of what happened some two hundred years ago between you, Victor, and Nerissa, who would have been our last Emissary. We also knew that in time, another Emissary would be born and would take power next to a Sovereign. It seems that day will happen sooner than later. It is the High Counsel's position to make sure that this happens, no matter what." Sheldon looked directly at Victor as he finished his sentence.

"You aren't doing a great job. Someone has sent at least one Blue Daemon after your selected Emissary. A Blue Daemon I've had to confront once already," Victor pointed out sarcastically.

Sheldon shrugged. "So we have heard. We are making sure that Kala is safe until we find out who is betraying her, and our people."

"How are you making sure she is safe?" Victor asked.

"Currently we have rotating shifts of highly skilled telepathic missionaries on guard from dusk until dawn. They have been hired to protect her at all costs," Phillip explained. "I hired them myself; her safety is extremely important to the High Counsel."

Victor nodded. "I hope they are good. I know from past experience the Blue Daemons are not a force to be taken lightly."

"We know you have crossed paths with them in the past," Sheldon said condescendingly. "I hope that is something you can put behind you?"

"Of course. I am not going to be put on trial again for what I did two hundred years ago. I was tried and sentenced then. I have done my time. I learned my lesson. If this is what tonight is going to be like, I'm just going to leave." Victor stood up in anger, his eyes blazing like red orbs; a sign that he'd reached his boiling point and everyone should back off.

"No. That's not what tonight is. Tonight we're are here to make sure Kala is safe, and to make sure her reign as Emissary happens as efficiently as possible," Sheldon said cautiously. "I did not mean to upset you. Please sit."

Victor breathed deeply, allowing his anger to pass through him. He abruptly sat in the chair, upright and tense.

Sheldon continued to pace the room. "Actually Victor, I kind of like the idea of you seeing Kala as often as you have been. I mean, you must feel a level of responsibility to Nathan and your people to make sure that this time around our Emissary fulfills her role. It's like the High Counsel has an insider working for them, knowing you are involved. And you said yourself that you'd learned your lesson the last time, so I highly doubt that you would jeopardize Kala's safety in any way." Sheldon had a broad smile on his face. "See where I'm going with this?"

Victor's anger began to over take him again. He hated the idea of being a pawn for the High Counsel. He spent time with Kala not just because of who she was born to be, but because he cared for who she really was: a lovely, giving, female human who was warm to hold and to kiss. "I won't work for you. Making sure she is safe is something I have to do for *her*, not for you."

"That's fine, however it gets done," Phillip said. "One insider is enough."

"Who is your insider?" Victor questioned.

"Stuart," Sheldon replied, sitting back on the couch and taking a sip of his wine.

Victor looked at him. "How do you fit into all this?" He had been confused by his presence all night.

"I am Kala's father," Stuart answered. "Her mother was very human though. I, of course, am not."

"So what does that make Kala?" Nathan asked. He'd remained silent, just absorbing the conversation up to this point.

"Human, but with many levels of unique structures that are important to us," Sheldon explained. "We have had problems for years trying to reach Kala telepathically. It took awhile but eventually we found Sara, whom I'm sure you know by name, or one way or another. Sara was a very powerful medium between our people and Kala. She refused to let our signal reach her. She refused to work with us, so in the end she was given an ultimatum. Sara claimed she was doing *her* job and it wasn't to allow our people to take Kala to be Emissary. Sara's choice was either to continue living as she had been but allow the Book of Jorn's passages to continue, become one of us and see Kala as we do, our future Emissary, or die. Sara chose death because she claimed she could still continue to work her magic that way. And there must be some truth to that, because we are still having trouble reaching Kala, but we will keep trying."

Victor shook his head, feeling as if his society of people were characters in a soap opera. "If you have missionaries stationed for her safety, and you know where she lives, and you have her father here, what do you need any of us for? Go get her," Victor pointed out. "Why all this garbage?"

"It's not time yet," Sheldon spoke softly. "There are phases, or stages, that Kala must reach in her own time, on her own terms; the best we can do is to place people in her life who can help speed up the process. We may have Kala's father in the room with us now, but Kala has not seen him in over fifteen years. There is an amount of persuading we can do, and we can make specific scenarios happen, but Kala is human. It will take time. There is a level she must reach to be Emissary. Our schedule to get her there is behind because of Sara, but hopefully with that hurdle gone we can pick up some time."

"And if she does not want to be Emissary?" Victor asked, leaning forward. "Then you do what?"

Phillip sighed loudly. "It has happened before. But we have our ways. That is not your problem."

"How long could all this take?" Nathan asked curiously. "I mean, we have brought Kala to you; when can our privileges be reinstated?"

"I know this has been particularly hard on you," Sheldon looked at Nathan and touched his arm. "You have been loyal to Victor for a long time even when your people would not stand by you. You do deserve to have your privileges restored and I will speak to Teague about them soon."

Victor left the others to continue their chatting, knowing he could contribute nothing more to their cause, and that he would continuing seeing Kala for his personal reasons and not for any of the reasons Sheldon or Phillip wanted him to have. He felt no loyalty to the High Counsel, and in many ways did not care if his civil liberties were given back to him or not; he had lived without them for many years and figured he could continue to do the same for many to come.

I sat in bed with my reading lamp on, sipping a cup of hot tea and trying to make heads or tails out of Sara's belongings. I had skimmed through her Book of Shadows and read many of her recipes for spells and incantations that were made for numerous reasons. Each page was labeled for a specific reason. I noticed many spells for protection that lead me to believe Sara had not felt safe for a long time; each spell seemed to get bigger and, at least visually on paper, stronger than the last. I began to wonder about the satchels of herbs, crystals and quartz I had found earlier, and thought that maybe they were also used for protection. I would not know for sure until I could figure out what each was used for. I set the book down on my lap and opened an envelope that I had just peeked into previously. I emptied it out and began to read each scrap of paper. Nothing meant anything to me until I found a small note that had the words ‘Blue Daemon’ on it. My heart stopped and then began to race. I saw my version of the Blue Daemon in my head; the one I had painted for Victor. What did Sara know of a Blue Daemon? Was her Blue Daemon mine? I flipped the paper over and saw an incantation with the words:

‘To rid yourself of a Blue Daemon’ – you must have and believe in the power of the Amulet. While in the presence of the Daemon you must say these exact words!

In a spirit that is pure,
I practice a craft that which is mine,
I call on those beyond the veil,
To cast you back to darkness,
and behind the gates of Hell.
In a spirit that is pure,
I ask the powers to take you back,
And free me from your harm,
Go away – be gone.

I guess Sara must have encountered the Blue Daemon herself. The thought made me shiver. Imagine having to find the strength to be able to say that incantation with the Blue Daemon breathing down my neck. To see that horrible disfigured face. What if the spell didn’t work? I’d probably be so paralyzed with fear I’d never be able to out run it.

I reread the incantation again. The very first line said ‘You must have and believe in the power of the Amulet’. At the bottom of the incantation was a sketch of the very pendant I had been wearing; the one that was Sara’s. I was wearing an Amulet. Just how much power did I have around my neck? I wondered if it came with a User’s Manual.

Chapter 11

I had slept through another night without any dreams. I wanted to believe they would never return, but knew I was being foolishly hopeful. When I awoke, I had decided to call in sick to work, which I had never done since taking the job at the radio station. I had taken a few days off when Sara died, but that was willingly given to me. My bedroom floor was covered with information about Sara that I had not gotten a chance to go through from the night before, and I felt I deserved to give myself the time to go through it.

I made my phone call to the General Manager and gave him the bad news; I would not be in today. He took the news better than I had expected and told me to feel better soon. He voiced his concern about a promo that needed to be done immediately for the station's 'Battle of the Bands' concert. Apparently, the station was running behind schedule, and, since I was the host, I needed to voice the on-air promo. I told him if there was any way I could get in there before midnight I would.

I took my time getting my day started. I had coffee, threw in a load of laundry, took a shower, got dressed and then decided that it was a good time to restart what I had been working on the night before, examining the envelope of notes Sara left behind.

I must admit it all seemed like gibberish – the note and the listings of herbs, crystals, stones and teas. I wondered why she just didn't put them in her Book of Shadows, why she left them loose on colored papers of all different sizes. I came across recipes for teas that helped you dream, enhance your psychic powers and give you courage. I saw suggestions as to what stones and crystals should be carried together to keep evil away, and protect yourself. I found incantations that, among casting Blue Daemons back to where they came from, would keep evil spirits away, as well as the 'un-dead'. Each spell referred back to the Amulet, and instructed one to believe in the power of the Amulet. As I rummaged through all these items, the evidence began to mount that Sara's life wasn't as rosy as she had led me to believe. The Sara I knew was a prim and proper Wiccan; a practitioner of the whitest of white magic; someone who focused on spells that helped people in a variety of ways – perhaps start a business venture, restore good health, or find love. She never spoke of anything or anyone evil, but there must have been some sort of presence that made her produce these concoctions, spells and sachets of crystals, herbs, teas and stones.

I picked up each sack that I'd already looked at, this time cataloguing the ingredients of each one. I was intrigued to discover that a common theme ran through them – that of repelling evil. They were designed to make the wearer spiritually stronger to keep evil at a safe distance. There were sachets that repelled negative energy, protected, fended off bad luck, and evil spirits, or even increased your psychic development and clairvoyance skills. I placed each cloth sack on my bed and labeled them. I thought that if I knew what each one did, perhaps I could make use of them in times I felt less than safe.

I had hoped I would find more information on the Amulet I had been wearing, but had come up empty so far. Addy had seen me wearing it, but had never offered any comment as to what its use was, or its power. I was sure if it had significant strength she would have mentioned something, especially since each spell that Sara wrote began with 'Believe in the power of the Amulet' and emphasized how important it was that it be worn during the entire spell. How could I believe so strongly in something I knew nothing about? Give me something to read! Oh wait a minute; this is where my *faith* is supposed to come in.

Faith was a toughie for me. If I could not see it, feel it or touch it, then it did not exist. Although my senses lately were telling me otherwise, it was my thirty-year-old skeptical self, taught by public school and science classes, that pulled me in another direction, always looking for facts and explanations. This was why I never fully practiced witchcraft with Sara, even when her spells came true. I'd be like, 'okay, how did you do that?' looking for an earthly reason when there was none. I had tried spells in the past, which always failed, though Sara said this was due to my lack of belief and faith. I would try several versions of the same spell, but they all had the same result – nothing. I guess that's why the only magic I ever did was candle magic, simple, color-coded, no screwing up, though I'm not saying that it worked either. Although, since the night I burned my blue and white candles, I had not had a dream. And, oddly enough, that same night I burned those very candles, the night I wanted Sara with me so desperately to protect me, was the night Sara came to me. Had I stumbled onto something? Can wanting something so badly give you a level of belief, actually make you believe? My faith must not be too far behind.

I sat out on the deck with some lunch and the journal that was done in Sara's own handwriting. Before I even had a chance to open the book the phone rang. I picked up the cordless and answered. "Hello."

"Kala?" A male voice spoke on the other end.

"Yes," I replied, mentally cataloguing all the men I knew, trying to match a face with the voice. I leaned back in my chair and put my feet up on the railing.

"It's Detective Drake," the voice announced. "I tried to get a hold of you at the radio station but they said you were not in today." His voice seemed more personable than it had been in past conversations.

"I'm home today," I confirmed and took a sip of my drink. "Do you have any news for me?" My heart fluttered with anticipation.

"No, I'm sorry I don't. I wanted to let you know that I have had some officers patrolling your area and things have been very quiet."

"Well, thanks for sending them around." I felt obligated to express some sort of gratitude although I wanted to ask him why he had nothing to tell me about Sara.

"I think I will keep extra patrols in your neighborhood for a little while longer. Just to make sure," Drake offered.

"If you think it's necessary," I answered, my voice showing no emotion.

"Has everything been okay?" the detective asked, more like a friend than someone doing his civil job.

I grimaced at his personal tone. "Yeah, I guess." I was hesitant, but answered his question anyway.

"That's good. I will let you get back to your day off. I promise to call when I have news to pass on to you." This was good-bye.

"Please. I still need to know," I stated firmly. "I would rather you take the extra patrols who have been out in my neighborhood and put them on Sara's case, if you want my opinion." I didn't care if I offended him.

"Well, I don't agree. I'm doing all that I can. Understand it's not my job to leave cases unsolved. That makes great TV shows, but it's not great real life."

I paused. "I do understand. I just want the person who did it found." I could put it no more plainly than that.

"That is something we both agree on."

Our phone conversation ended with at least that understanding.

I sat for the longest time in the afternoon sun, looking at Sara's journal from the outside. I admired the green fabric cover, knowing Sara herself picked it out, probably because it was a nice shade of dark green-hunter, or forest I would say. I liked it; I would have chosen it too. I'm sure it was inexpensive, something you could pick up at any bookstore in the Mall, but it was priceless to me, without even knowing what was on the inside. The pages were leafed in gold paint and stood out boldly from the green cover. I had the hardest time opening the journal to read it. I saw her words, but like a child who accidentally picked up a book that was too advanced, the best I could do was look at the writing like the words were pretty pictures. I felt as if I was violating Sara by reading what was in her journal; what if there were things in there she hadn't wanted me to know? What if I found things out I didn't want to know? The more I thought about Sara, the more I realized those questions really didn't matter. She was gone. What if there was something important in the journal, something that would lead me to the person who killed her? How could I not read it now?

I got comfortable in my chair, ready to take the first step. Taking a deep breath, I opened the book to the very first page. It was blank. So far, so good.

The next pages read: *We all have a job we were meant to do. Sometimes we have the wrong tools to complete it, or only half the talent to finish it. The best we can do is make an effort, or not try at all and give up and quit.*

Not only do I have a nearly impossible job, but also no matter how good I am, I will not be good enough. I have found a fine line between good and evil. I never thought it so until now. Just how far can goodness go before there are evil intentions in reaching the highest peak? Is there really good or evil, or is one slightly less than the other? Who decides? Is evil always bad – can it bring good to anyone? I have decided that there is no winning side, and that eventually good and evil will both crumble, leaving only what? It won't matter because it will be more of the same. I have found so many bad people who have declared themselves as being good and doing only what is best, that apparently no one is sure anymore of right and wrong. I am only one person with a job to do. I hope I do the right things because there is so much at stake. My job seems so small when I think about what Kala will have to do after me.

Kala, if you are reading this, you know I am dead, for you have my journal that I would not have willingly given to you while I was alive. Just because I am not with you, does not mean that my job is complete. Please do not dwell on my death. Knowing how I died will not bring me back. It was fate. There will be no prosecution. My death is not meant to be solved. In many ways I met my death willingly, knowing I could do more for you from the other side.

You must find the courage and the strength to decide a fate that I never had to do. You have a strength you have not even dreamed of. The elements of the Earth are at your disposal. They will come to you. They have been waiting for your call. I know that in finding your courage you will find faith, it will guide you better than any map or any advice I could give you alive or in death. You must believe in yourself and you must have faith. You must never lose the Amulet, or your sight of all you think is morally right, because it is the foundation that will support the reunion of worlds that have been separate for a very long time.

The sad truth is, you are in this pretty much alone. There are very few people you will be able to trust. Many of those people are in your life to teach you valuable lessons that I won't prevent from happening; it is a growing experience and I must allow it to continue. I won't tell you who these people are, or when your lesson has been learned; only you can decide that. Listen to your voice within, and let it guide you through these very difficult times. Hang in there.

Evil is all around you. I do not say this to scare you now, because it has always been there. Know that you have the strength within you to make the pawns of evil shy away. Once you have the strength of the Amulet, the courage of the Amulet, and the faith of the Amulet within you, there will be very little you cannot do. Do not be afraid, not even of yourself with all the changes you will go through.

I know you must be confused. Please stop asking yourself questions to which you will not find answers. Live your life day to day and look for answers around you and within you. You are the best source of knowledge you will ever find. Listen to the voice inside you and any other voice that you may hear, for even an evil voice can give you a useful message.

In my journal I will share with you all the secrets I have learned in my years, all my spells, incantations and magic. Yes, they all work. You must have the strength, courage and faith in both me and the Amulet in order for them to work for you. Find all those things, knowing that I continue to watch over you. The largest source of your magic will come from inside you, and if you allow it the proper channels, I cannot even begin to tell you how strong, and how invincible you can become. There is no limit set by me, or any God or Goddess as to how powerful you can be; if you can think it, you can do it. Imagine it and it will happen – Auburn Starr.

My hands were sweating and shaking as I closed the book and pushed it away from me on the table. My best friend in the whole wide world had left me her journal, something she meant for me to read in the event of her death. I was choked up on the inside, my chest tight and my mouth dry. I was scared to be alone, almost paranoid, but I did not know whom I could trust. My head swam with faces of friends as I wondered which of them would do me wrong. There had to be a mistake. The people I surrounded myself with, I felt safe with; I knew these people, they were friends, extended family, welcome in my home and my life. I broke down in tears, flooded with emotions of sadness, guilt, fear and anger. Why me? I had no powers. I had no strength. What was Sara talking about? She must be wrong; she died over something that made no sense.

Wiping my eyes free of tears I gathered my things, including Sara's journal, and walked into the condo. I was afraid to set the book down; I held it clutched to my chest as if it were a teddy bear. I wanted to be protected. I didn't want bad people in my life. I didn't want to have to watch over my shoulder and make sure I wasn't being followed, or that I was alone. Holding the book, I only knew I had to read more, to hear Sara's words in my head, to try and find some sort of understanding for her death and what it was that she thought I would find myself up against.

It was much later on in the evening when I got a call from Victor. I welcomed his call, but was distant in my manner, something Victor picked up on right away.

"What's wrong?" Victor asked lightly. "You aren't upset because you are going to be thirty tomorrow, are you?" he laughed. "You're just a baby; thirty is nothing!"

I had forgotten about my milestone birthday. "Oh, no, it's not that," I said quietly.

"What's wrong then? Tell me," Victor insisted. He seemed concerned, but all I could think about was what I had read in Sara's journal earlier about not being able to trust many people. Was Victor one of them? I hated to think of him as a potential enemy; he'd had a rocky road growing up, as I did, and I could relate to him in many ways. I had a hard time thinking of him as someone I could not confide in.

"I've just spent time going through Sara's belongings; it's still hard on me. The police are no closer to finding her killer, and I'm giving up hope anyone ever will," I explained, without going into too much detail. "Listen, about tomorrow night; let's pass."

"Why? I have reservations and a gift." He seemed hurt by me bowing out of our date unexpectedly.

I sighed. "I'm just not up for it."

"Kala, I know that Sara meant a great deal to you. But I also know that there is no way she would want you sitting around. She'd want you to live each day to its fullest. Wouldn't she? Especially your birthday?" Victor pressed.

He was right. I knew that Sara would want me to have fun even if I should be off fighting evil or practicing spells. "Sara would want me to have fun," I agreed slowly.

"See, so you can't cancel your date with me. We have reservations at 8. I will pick you up at 7:30 sharp. You should wear something fairly dressy. I wouldn't mind sexy. In fact, that would be great." He chuckled at his own wit.

I laughed a little too. "So this is an upscale restaurant, and you are picturing me in a little black dress and some high heels, right?" I had a mental image of what Victor was asking for.

"You are reading my mind, how nice," Victor said, amused.

"And you see me in black nylons with the seams running down the back, holding a small evening bag that has a chain strap," I continued, adding to the image I had in my head.

"Kala," Victor said in some amazement. "Are we on the same page, or what? You can't know me that well!"

It suddenly occurred to me that the images I had in my head were not mine, but Victor's. I was somehow getting a mental picture of what Victor wanted me to look like when he picked me up for our date. I could see the way he envisioned me. It felt very odd to see myself through his eyes, and even feel some of the sensations that he felt when he thought about me. Thoughts of beautiful, soft, warm and appetizing came to me right away. As quickly as the image came, without warning the vision was gone. I tried to just laugh it off, not fully understanding what I had just seen.

"C'mon, all men are alike," I laughed. "Something in black, and the littler the better."

"No, really, how did you do that?" Victor asked quickly, not wanting to let the event pass.

"Do you really think I can read minds? Get real," I told him. "If I could, I would be rich."

"All right, maybe you can't," Victor chuckled. "But that was a pretty good parlor trick!"

"I'll let you go. I need to head into the radio station tonight for a little while; I'd like to go before it's too late," I told him, thinking about the promise I had made to my boss.

"All right. I'm going to grab a bite to eat. And I will see you at 7:30 tomorrow night," he confirmed. "Happy Birthday."

I smiled. "Thanks. See you tomorrow in my little black dress."

Before I left for the radio station I gave Drew a quick call to see if he would be interested in helping me write and produce the Battle of The Bands promo that I was on my way to do. He was eager to get out of his apartment for the evening and allow me to tap into his talents in order to get my project done. I grabbed my tote bag, and Sara's journal that I had book marked with the scrap of paper containing the spell to 'rid yourself of a blue daemon', and slid it into the bag. I felt safer knowing I had it with me. It was in my hands.

Victor was still shocked that Kala had pulled such a stunt on him – reading his mind. He was not angry, just alarmed and even a little embarrassed. He did find her attractive, and women in black were a turn on for him. As soon as he realized that she was able to pick up these thoughts, he immediately blocked her ability to proceed, fearing she could learn more. He was actually taken back that she could do it so easily, having never done it before, or so she claimed. Maybe he was weaker than he thought, since he had not fed in a while. There would be no way he could even stand in the restaurant tomorrow night with Kala at his side without succumbing to the urge to satisfy his appetite for blood. He had fasted too long this time, but he had tried to hold off as long as possible. Now, he would have to take care of his needs.

Victor usually fed quickly, basically completing a necessary task. He was not particular to man or woman, nor did he discriminate due to age or race. He never fed in the same spot more than once, and was cautious not to draw attention to the crimes that he committed in the human world he existed in. The only place he promised himself he would never kill was the college campus; he could not bring himself to kill anyone from there. Those were *his* people, and in many ways he felt like the protector, not the predator, because of that.

How the years had changed him. As a very young and immature vampire, Victor could look into the eyes of his victims, seeing the pleas for help or mercy, and not feel an iota of emotion. His presence struck fear into anyone; the kind of fear that would leave most creatures immobile, and for those lucky few who thought they could get away from him, well, that made the kill even sweeter in the end. There was no escape. He was on top of the world, immortal, handsome and young. His incessant need for blood drove him to deplete his victims of every precious ounce of red fluid they had. He would do this night after night and never get tired. Each taste, each scent made for an exciting dish.

Tonight Victor was feeding to continue to exist. There was, of course, still some enjoyment in it. The taste of blood surging down his throat with each pump of the heart would always warm his body and please his palette.

I arrived at the station before Drew. Finding a parking spot on the same floor as the radio station was nearly impossible during the day, but tonight the entire floor was just about abandoned. I had forgotten that day and night radio was so much different, a lot less hustle and bustle. What a joy it was, not fighting anyone for a parking spot. What a peaceful time to be working. I grabbed my tote bag, locked my car door and began to walk towards the security doors that led to the hallway and the radio station. My footsteps echoed against the cement walls as I breathed in the cool, damp, garage air, lightly tainted with exhaust fumes. I could hear the distant rumble of a car engine coming up the ramp and turning the corner. I turned around as the vehicle approached and saw it was Drew. I smiled and waved, deciding to wait for him at the steel doorway.

He parked his car near the center of the garage at a cement pole with a big 6 painted on it in red. "Sorry I'm late," I heard Drew call, as he got out of his car; the slamming of his heavy door repeated in echoes throughout the cavernous garage.

"I'm just getting here myself," I called back to him.

Drew dodged in and out of a few parked cars, showing off his athletic ability and jogged the rest of the way to meet me.

"Missed you today," Drew shyly smiled. "I was lost without you."

"Oh please. Get a life," I laughed. "It was probably a nice slow day for you without me."

"I like you keeping me busy," he admitted, taking my tote bag from me.

"I don't have my security tag. I don't usually need one during the day. Do you have one?" I asked him, staring at the digital mechanism with two red lights that required an authorized swipe to gain us access.

"Oh yeah, sure," he quickly replied. "I was a Boy Scout. I got you covered." He took out his wallet and removed the station issued security card with his picture on it. He held it up vertically so that he could slide the side with the black strip down between the two designated markers, turning the two red lights into one flashing green beacon. Drew opened the door and allowed me to enter first.

We got settled into Production Studio 2 with its large picture window that looked over the alley. This was not my favorite studio because the equipment was a little outdated, and the room was used a lot for overnight pizza parties with empty boxes and half-full cans of soda scattered throughout the room. It was always a mess, and every time I needed to use it, I seemed to be the one who had to clean it. Tonight it was in pretty good shape, with only a broken chair that had been beaten up recently with a microphone stand, and then flipped over on top of some very old McDonald french fries that were mashed into the carpet. Production 2 was larger than the others were, and big enough for two people to work together without running into each other, so it seemed like the one to use this evening. While I gathered up the information that was left behind for me to write the sixty-second promo, I set Drew up at the operation board to let him run the digital audio equipment. The board was rather ominous looking, with lots of levers, buttons, knobs, gauges and lights; it looked like something that could launch the space shuttle. When you get used to what every function is, and read each label to every lever, button, knob and gauge, things start to make sense. I started the copy writing and had Drew go into the on air studio to find some background music for my voice to be dubbed over.

The entire project from start to finish took about two hours. It could have been done more quickly I suppose, if I had done everything myself, but I let Drew help and it slowed me down. I still had fun, because I enjoyed Drew's humor so much the entire time. I had just finished recording my last line for Drew to splice with all the rest when suddenly, the skies opened up and we could see a barrage of rain hitting the glass window, followed by streaks of gold lightning cutting through the late evening sky. We couldn't hear the sound of thunder because the room was sound proof, but I'm sure with the way the rain was coming down, and the frequency of the strikes of lightning, it was quite loud.

Victor had been out in the night for a number of hours, stalking several people as potential meals. He was downtown, in a local bar not too far from campus, and not too far from the radio station. The bar was crowded and smoke filled, by cigar more than cigarettes. There was a local band playing at the rear of the long room, and the music made a path through the bar and out the open front door where a thick and hefty Bouncer, wearing a black tank top and shorts, stood checking ID. From Victor's view out the door, he could see the summer rain coming down in solid sheets and vigorously pounding the pavement. The roads had taken on more water than they could stand, and had begun to flood over the catch basins and onto the sidewalks. How he would hate walking home on a night like this.

Kala was a good distance away, but he could still feel her thoughts. They were pleasantly distracting him from time to time, although he made sure Kala had no idea of his impolite eavesdropping. He could sense she was tired but not totally drained, was quite happy with her male friend's company, and was starving; she had forgotten to have dinner. Victor could sympathize with her hunger pains; he had them too. But he sat at the bar with a grin on his face and a gin and tonic in his hand, enjoying his telepathic company and forgetting why he was out visiting a bar, which was a little out of character for him.

With the next clap of thunder Victor came back to his senses and felt his desire to feed again stronger than before. He focused on a woman with short brown hair who had been across from him most of the night. The woman sat alone, and had not stopped drinking since she arrived. Her pasty skin stood out against the low cut red shirt she was wearing. She appeared extremely underweight; her arms like thin rails with tiny, bony wrists, and very long lanky fingers that gripped her glass. Victor shut off telepathic connection with Kala, and began to pick up scattered images and thought patterns belonging to the woman in red. He was under the impression that perhaps she was suffering a sickness, as she kept saying in her mind how awful she felt. He was not sure what her sickness was. He did not feel she was so drunk that she could not manage her faculties, and he did not think she was overly depressed. Regardless, the woman thought herself as sick.

Victor slid off his barstool and watched the lady in red cautiously as he chose the long way around the wooden 'U' shaped bar, pushing in chairs and excusing himself through crowds of young, partying city people, until he reached the stool next to her. He took the seat and examined her surreptitiously. The woman in red played with the swizzle stick submerged in her drink and ignored her handsome, deadly company. More than a minute went by before Victor spoke to the woman. "You've been here all night."

Her eyes rolled in his direction; they appeared bloodshot and tired. "So," she mumbled, and began to fiddle with the napkin that was soaking up condensation under her glass.

"I've been here all night too," Victor offered. He knew if he could get her to look him long enough in the eye he could mesmerize her into following him outside and to her car if she had one. If not, the alley would have to do. Victor could tell she had a very weak spirit and would be easy to lure away. It was sad to think that intelligent human beings could be lured away with such primal bait, that people were that easily led astray. It was actually strong-spirited people that Victor felt challenged by; to be able to finally win the physically and mentally powerful over, and see the surprise come over them as they realized what *he* was all about. Tonight Victor was not in the mood to play games, he was hungry and it had been too long.

"I don't really want any company tonight," the woman confessed, just glancing in his direction, not even noticing his beauty.

"Why not? You have a boy friend?" Victor asked, sipping his drink and turning his body sideways to face her more directly.

"No. I just want to be alone," She spoke slowly, trying to make Victor understand that she did not want his company or anyone else's.

"If you want to be alone, why are you at a bar? This is not like being alone." He tried to provoke her into confronting him.

She sighed. "Listen. I'm meeting someone here later on." The woman was still not acknowledging his physical presence.

Victor got his first clear mental image from her; she was apparently waiting for a man who had the *drugs* she needed. This was why she felt so awful; she was addicted to drugs. Victor felt saddened for an instant, and looked down at her spindly arms resting on the scratched brass trim that edged the top of the bar; he could see some old needle tracks on the soft insides of her elbows.

"What are you into? Heroin? Cocaine? You've been here a while and now you're worried *he's* not going to show." Victor did not wait for her response. "If drugs are what you need I can get them for you." The trap had been set.

This time the woman in red met his eyes, furious with his accusations. "What do you know?"

"You've been here all night. You look like Hell, and I can see your arms," Victor replied, turning her left arm upwards to reveal the dark patches on her pale skin left behind from her deadly habit.

"That's none of your business. I'm not shooting up anymore." Her eyes filled up with tears. "I'm a professional. I work here in town. I have a good job." Her voice was rough but there was also an element of desperation. She pulled her arm back and kept it close to her body.

"Well, if it's not heroin, what is it then? Speed? Cocaine?" Victor asked, trying to figure out what her new addiction was.

She swiveled the seat on her barstool to face him, deciding to ignore his question and hit him up for his offer. "How can you get what I need? What do I have to do for it?" Resigned to the fact that her supplier was a no show, she was ready to bargain with Victor.

"What do you need?" Victor asked again. He set his drink down and crossed his arms, waiting for the prey to take the lure.

The woman's eyes met Victor's and his return glance startled her as Victor locked on her consciousness. She was very fragile and confused, focused only on feeding her habit. He could tell that she had done everything shy of selling her own soul in her quest for drugs. She was right; she was a professional, but even though she had a job working in the city she didn't have a dime to her name. The woman had even lost custody of her only child less than a year ago because she had been arrested for prostitution, and caught with drugs. Although she knew she had a substance problem she was not ready to seek help, and her family could not reason with her either. The woman had a twin sister who lived a few towns over, happily married with two of her own kids. She had temporary custody of her sister's now, at least until she cleaned up her act and proved she could be responsible not only to herself, but also to her child. She had not been able to do either. Now she would never have the chance to redeem herself at all. Her death would be a sacrifice to Victor's cause, and her child would learn to know a better life.

"Do you have a car?" Victor asked quietly, so that only the two of them could hear.

"Yes. Next door," the woman replied dazedly, her green eyes fixed in deep concentration on Victor's.

"Let's go," Victor said. He slid off his barstool and guided her around the bar to the front entry, past the Bouncer who held the door to the street open wide. Victor kindly thanked him and took hold of the scrawny elbow of the woman in red. "Let's go to your car," he suggested. The rain had let up to a steady drizzle even though the thunder and lightning continued on.

Victor and the woman quickly walked several blocks on the waterlogged sidewalks, avoiding as many bottomless puddles as they could until they reached a commuter parking lot. By the time the two of them got into her car, the rain had started to fall heavily. Her car was a late model blue four door Ford, in poor shape, with a child seat in the back and a Winnie the Pooh sun screen on the rear window. She sat in the driver's seat and instinctively placed the key into the ignition.

Victor sat on the passenger side. "Leave the car off," Victor said softly, placing a hand on her thigh. "What's your name?"

"Amanda," she replied, still looking forward.

"Amanda, look at me."

The woman turned her body rigidly to face his voice.

Victor raised his hand over Amanda's face, feeling her light breath on his palm. He used two fingers and gently closed her eyes. He did not want to be the last vision she would ever see. She should not have to watch his transformation into the hideous creature that would take her life. Victor pushed her hair back softly with his hand and rubbed her neck as he leaned down onto her body. Amanda's arms instinctively wrapped Victor's torso as his needle sharp teeth pierced her throat quickly and as painlessly as he could make it. Her tainted blood filled him; the drugs did not bother his system, although he was aware that they were there. Amanda struggled only for a few seconds; she groaned and her hands clutched at Victor's clothes briefly before her body went limp. Her body trembled under Victor's as he continued to drink from her, the warm blood satisfying his need; her heart weakened as her body began to give up its fight to live. Victor held Amanda in his arms, her body all but dead; it would happen within a moment. After, he would leave and her body would be discovered sometime in the morning commute rush.

I pushed in my chair. "Drew, the rest is up to you. Make magic happen," I yawned. "I'm going home. I have to be back here in the morning." I looked out the window again to see the falling rain in the alley; it had not let up.

"You trust me to finish?" he asked, looking up from the board, unsure of his abilities.

"Sure, all you have to do is assign the promo a number, and put it on a cart until someone tomorrow can finish putting it in rotation. You've done that dozens of times," I smiled at him, trying to give him the encouragement he needed to complete what little was left of the project. I opened the production door to get some air flowing. "Have a good night."

"Okay, you, too," Drew smiled back. "Can I walk you out?" He began to push himself away from the board.

"Uh, uh – finish! I'll be fine. My car keys are in my hand. I'm going home," I told him. "Take care." I started to walk down the hallway, swinging my keys around my finger.

"Happy birthday," Drew called out after me. "Drive carefully!"

I smiled. "Thank you. I'll expect a gift in the morning." I continued to head towards the security doors, thinking about going home and reading as much as I could of Sara's journal before I went to sleep for my last night at age twenty-nine. I put the tote bag over my shoulder as I pushed my upper body solidly against the steel door. I tried to remember quickly if I had left anything behind in the studio that I could not live without until I came back in the morning, because once that door slammed shut, that was it; I had no way to get back in. I decided that I had everything I needed and let the door shut tight behind me. The garage was just as empty as it was when I arrived hours earlier. The rain was still falling at a heavy rate interspersed with the snap of lightning touching down. Suddenly, I heard a heavy dragging noise coming from behind me. I was gripped with a paralyzing hesitation that did not allow me to move.

Victor was several blocks away, sitting under an awning at a coffee club, having a tall latte and smoking a cigarette, watching the rain. His plan for the night was to stop wherever he could on his way home to prevent a total drenching, every donut shop, every newspaper stand, every public rest room. At this rate he'd be lucky to make it back to his bed by dawn. His newly acquired strength from feeding made him feel revitalized, stable and serene. He finally felt like he could control himself.

Victor was looking forward to a pleasant evening with Kala without being distracted every time a new human scent entered the air. It was the thought of spending time with Kala that caused his telepathic connection with her to be reestablished. He wondered what she was up to. He sipped his latte as he realized the feelings he shared with her earlier were not the same ones she had now, no smiles because of friendly company, no success over accomplishing a project – just utter fear. Victor put his latte down and concentrated harder on what was frightening Kala. Even with his newly energized powers he could not cut through the interference of Kala's fright. He worried immediately but did not know what to do or how to help. Finally, in desperation, he sent a thought to her as hard as he could. '*What's wrong*?'

Unable to take a step, I turned my head around in the direction of the noise. I did a double take. My initial glance did not fully register, despite the fact that my heart felt as if it would rupture out of my chest and spill onto the floor. Maybe I did not believe what I saw. It was the Blue Daemon from my painting, standing some twenty feet in back of me. I was speechless as the hideous creature glared at me with its dark, soulless stare. The beast's face was distorted, and fractured in spots, leaving gaping holes that allowed light to filter through. The decomposing skin barely hung onto the bones that supported the daemon to stand. Its long arms dangled like a primate's with one being shorter than the other. There was an indescribable smell that permeated the air, blanketing the smell of car exhaust and the mustiness of damp cement walls. The odor was enough to make me ill. Walking death.

I was terrified to turn my back to it, and I was terrified to look the daemon straight on. I clutched my tote bag to my chest, feeling a rectangular object within press against my arms. Sara's journal. The spell! I was fear-stricken. Did I have the courage and the faith to perform a spell? I was not even certain I could speak. I had not taken the Amulet off; I touched it nervously.

The beast took two steps forward. "Kala," it barked in a hoarse voice.

My eyes widened in surprise that it spoke. More surprised it knew my name.

Another two steps the daemon took and extended its arms in true zombie fashion.

I reached into my tote bag, snagging the book and letting the bag fall to the ground. My trembling fingers struggled to pull out the loose piece of paper that I was using as a marker, the one that contained the incantation Sara wrote to 'Rid Yourself a Blue Daemon.' My hands and fingers began to tingle as I attempted to hold the paper still enough to read it aloud. I broke out in a cold sweat as my body heat continued to rise.

As perspiration dripped off my face, I gathered up all the courage and inner strength I could. I hoped Sara was with me somehow to make sure I didn't screw things up because I surely believed in *her*. "In a spirit that is pure, I practice a craft that which is mine, I call on those beyond the veil, to cast you back to darkness, and behind the gates of Hell. In a spirit that is pure, I ask the powers to take you back, and free me from your harm. Go away – be gone." I said the words as loudly and as clearly as I could; all the years of voicing commercials without any advance noticed paid off because

I did not stumble. It was a perfect read. However, the spell did not appear to work. Maybe I had not sounded convincing enough.

I took several steps backwards, still holding Sara's journal against my pounding chest, the piece of paper with the spell in my other hand. What had I done wrong? Sara said the spells worked. The creature stopped only momentarily while I was reading the spell, perhaps to listen to me make an ass out of myself, but now had taken several more steps towards me.

"Your death is fate," the beast uttered next, its jaw slipping, making speech difficult.

I dropped Sara's book at my feet and held the spell firmly to read it again. I was getting angry and felt myself being cornered, trapped. My body started to feel as if it had been charged, low voltage currents traveling up and down and in and out of me. A feeling I recalled only having once before, in my parking lot at home when I thought I was being watched from afar. My entire body felt like pins and needles. I gripped the Amulet in my right hand and held it firmly. "Damn it, work!" I thought desperately. "In a spirit that is pure, I practice a craft that which is mine, I call on those beyond the veil, to cast you back to darkness, and behind the gates of Hell. In a spirit that is pure, I ask the powers to take you back, and free me from your harm. Go away – be gone." I looked directly at the Blue Daemon and glanced down only a few times to read ahead of myself.

The Blue Daemon stopped, but did not vanish. I was not sure what the spell was supposed to do. It did not state *exactly* how you got rid of the Blue Daemon.

An incredible gust of wind swept in from the city streets over the short cement garage wall, bringing with it the torrential rains and some loose debris. I realized that this was not wind due to the storms in the area, but due to another force. The wind rocked the daemon slightly on its feet, and took a circular path like a tornado but much smaller. The twister touched down several yards behind the daemon and upon touching down broke open a patch in the solid cement floor that became a black hole, a vortex of darkness that spun wildly in a spiral motion that occasionally changed direction. Somehow I knew that I had to get the daemon to go into the black hole. I knew that it would not willingly go, and I was not going to jump in first. The beast took several larger steps at me and lunged.

I pointed at the daemon, my anger growing. "Do you know what I could do to you?" I screamed at it. I had no idea what I was capable of doing, but I had so much power building up within me that I felt I would detonate and take the entire city block with me. The Blue Daemon straightened up and drew its limbs closer to its skeletal remains of a body. "I'm warning you. I'm tired of being followed and watched. You have no business with me."

"I can not rest until you die," it intoned.

My hands began to feel like they were consumed by fiery magma; my fingers were small volcanoes ready to erupt and send waves of lava spewing in all directions. I held my hands away from me and spread my fingers apart, dropping the spell to my feet. I was unable to manipulate my hands. A combustible blast tore through my body and out my hands and fingers, directly into the path of daemon. The discharge sent the daemon tumbling closer to the spinning vortex, but not into it. The blast even propelled me back a step, but in surprise. The Blue Daemon looked up at me as it tried to regain its footing. I pointed and warned, "Don't you dare!" One finally surge of flames came from the hand that was extended at the daemon and sent it off balance, plummeting into the hole. The Blue Daemon was gone. The black swirling mass continued to spin as if chewing up the daemon and digesting it.

The wind and the rain that had accompanied the vortex began to diminish, and with that the hole slowly closed in and collapsed, disappearing, leaving only a clean area on the garage floor where it had been. I stood motionless in the same spot I had been standing, frozen by the enormity of what had just occurred. I held up my hands to examine them; they looked normal.

Victor had been watching Kala work her magic with the Blue Daemon for several minutes. He stood in the corner of the garage behind some construction equipment out of sight, enthralled as the event unfolded. He was bowled over at the power Kala had shown, and the courage to stand up to a creature he knew she feared with every fiber of her being. Her powers were surfacing rapidly.

I continued to stare down at the circular pattern etched permanently into the floor. I had not fully accepted what had happened, and allowed the entire event to play back in my head again and again – a horror movie stuck on the same twelve frames. My heart was still racing as I placed my hand over my chest. I took a deep breath and slid my hand over the Amulet, rubbing it in thought. I looked down at my feet and saw the spell under the sole of my sneaker; the edges of the paper were discolored and scorched by flames. I bent down to pick it up and blacked out.

The next thing I remember was hearing voices and feeling my body on a cold hard surface. I reached up to touch my forehead and felt a warm hand capture mine, lowering it to my side.

"Kala," a male voice spoke.

I slowly opened my eyes to see Drew and Victor hovering over me.

I tried to sit up, wincing as I did.

"Take it easy there," Drew tried to comfort me, placing his hand on my back. He brushed me off gently, knocking off the loose dust and dirt I had been lying in.

"Are you okay?" Victor asked.

I stared back, not knowing how to answer. I replied with a safe, "I think so."

"When did you eat last?" Victor asked. "I think you passed out."

I turned myself over and onto my knees, slowly pushing myself up to stand. "It's been a while."

"We need to get you home. Or maybe to a hospital. You never should have come into work tonight," Drew scolded. "You called in sick this morning and you should have stayed home." He took hold of my elbow and guided me to my car, while Victor picked up Sara's journal and the loose spell, and stuffed them into my tote bag.

"I'm fine. I can get home," I said. "I can drive. Really. Victor, what are you doing here?" I asked, confused, turning around realizing for the first he was present.

Victor handed me my bag.

"You know him?" Drew asked, pointing at Victor. "I thought he just found you here unconscious."

"I know him," I replied.

"I was out tonight," Victor began to explain. "Nathan has my car, it was pouring and I knew you were working late here; I thought I could get a ride back home. It's been raining so hard."

I took my tote bag from him. "I'll give you a lift." I was still in a fog. I turned to speak to Drew. "Victor is an artist who has some work in my gallery. We have become friends."

"I see," Drew mumbled and stared jealously in Victor's direction. "Well, good thing he was stalking you. Never know what weirdo might have found you otherwise." Drew could get very sarcastic which made great on-air talk, but not good real-time socialization skills.

Victor approached Drew in a confrontational manner, taller and physically larger.

"Please don't. I'm tired. Drop it. Both of you." I tugged on Victor's shirtsleeve to get his attention.

Drew backed down and began to walk away. "The least you could do is drive her home," Drew told Victor as he headed for his own car, taking his keys from his pocket.

I willingly gave my keys to Victor and walked around him, taking a seat on the passenger side; I had never been a passenger in my own car.

Chapter 12

We waited for Drew to leave the garage before Victor started the engine of my car. I was quiet and did not really want to talk. I think Victor was uncomfortable with the silence.

"Drew, huh?" Victor asked, putting the car in drive and heading for the exit.

"Drew," I sighed. "A little hot-headed sometimes."

"Yeah, I'd say. He's going to get himself hurt one day. He's not very big, and he can't be too smart. He's going to say something to the wrong person and that will pretty much be that."

We left the radio station garage and drove out into the dark rainy night, the mid-week city streets empty of traffic. Wipers on.

"He's good at what he does." I stood up for Drew, finally feeling someone should.

"And what would that be?" Victor questioned me.

"Radio. What did you think I meant?" I asked gruffly.

"Nothing, but doesn't doing radio take some sort of personality skills?"

"Honestly, very little. If the public likes you, they listen to you; if they hate you, sometimes they still listen just to hate you. It gives them an outlet to vent their frustrations," I replied, opening up my bag to make sure everything of value made it into the car.

"I think I got everything off the garage floor." Victor glanced over at me, looking into my bag.

I looked up. "Okay."

"Are you feeling all right? Want to stop and get something to eat?" Victor asked, peeking over at me again but still keeping an eye on the wet roads.

"I just want to go home. I have some reading to catch up on," I answered. Boy, wasn't that the truth.

"Are you *sure* you are going to be okay?" he asked, his concern not allowing the subject to die. "I'm just glad I was coming up the stairs when I did tonight at the station," he sighed.

I wondered if Victor had seen anything out of the ordinary. "Yeah, thanks. I guess I must have passed out. Weird how that happens."

Victor parked my car in front of the condo and opted to walk the rest of the way home. I told him I could drive him that little distance; I would be fine. He insisted that I go to bed and get rested up for my birthday dinner. He assured me he would only get a little wet, and would not melt.

When Victor arrived back at the Victorian, he dropped in on Nathan who was having a cigarette and reading the newspaper on the couch. Nathan's eyes lifted up briefly over his half-rimmed reading spectacles as he folded his paper in half. "Got a little wet," Nathan remarked, looking at his companion who was more than damp from head to toe. "Did you finally feed? You look better." He took one last drag off his cigarette and extinguished it in a nearby ashtray.

Victor nodded and released his long wet hair, taking the elastic off and leaving it around his wrist. "Yes. I feel much better, thanks." He closed the door behind him and stood in the middle of the room, shaking his long mane like a wet dog.

"What do I owe this visit to? Must be Kala again," Nathan guessed, already sure of the answer. He placed the newspaper on his lap, prepared to listen.

"I would really appreciate it if you would keep your sarcastic comments to yourself. You told me how you feel about Kala and I can respect that, so please just give it a rest," Victor snapped.

"What happened tonight?" Nathan asked, changing the subject and trying to be more charming to please Victor. He took off his reading glasses and gestured for Victor to take a seat next to him.

Victor sat down slowly and ran his long fingers through his head of hair, pulling it off of his face but allowing it to stay loose. "Well, I saw something tonight. One of the Blue Daemons was back. I don't think it was one of the stronger ones. This one may have been sent to just scare Kala, although it's not typical, unless the Blue Daemons plan on following up quickly to kill."

"Where did you see the Blue Daemon?" Nathan asked, crossing his legs and leaning back, his interest captured by Victor's story. Nathan's tall forehead creased in deep lines of thought. "Were you out hunting them tonight?"

"No, I wasn't out hunting them," Victor admitted. He took a moment to think about what he had seen at the parking garage, and did not know exactly how to explain it. "Kala ended up fighting the Blue Daemon herself." Victor spoke bluntly, deciding not to gloss over what he'd seen.

"How did this all happen?" Nathan asked, his face showing both frustration and confusion with Victor's inability to describe the events that led up to Kala's battle with the Blue Daemon. He set his reading glasses on a small decorative table next to him, and pulled another cigarette from his pocket, followed by his gold plated lighter. He handed a cigarette to Victor, then lit it for him.

Victor took a drag before he continued his tale. "I have been able to telepathically connect with Kala, although she is unaware of this. I felt she was in danger because I received some very disturbing feelings of fear and panic. I knew where she was so I went to help. When I got there I saw that she and the Blue Daemon were in a confrontation. I realized that Kala was performing some sort of spell, or incantation, so I hid and just watched."

"Really!" Nathan seemed quite captivated with what he was hearing. "And?"

"I've never seen anything like it," Victor recalled, shaking his head. "I have witnessed witchcraft in my time, but have never seen what I did tonight." He paused and took a deep breath before he elaborated further. "The wind picked up, forming a funnel cloud. It was powerful, so powerful it created a huge black hole in the ground, a hole that spun with dark energy."

"Where were you when all this was going on? Did Kala see you?" Nathan asked, leaning forward on the couch as he reached for an ashtray.

"I stayed as far away as I could; she couldn't see me," Victor answered with assurance.

"So, what happened next?"

"Well, the Blue Daemon attacked, and the next thing I saw was Kala holding up her hands, and shooting flaming energy from her fingertips. The Blue Daemon was knocked back into the hole, which then closed up on it and vanished." Victor held his cigarette in his hand, rolling it between his fingers.

"That's quite a story," Nathan's voice sounded bemused. He leaned back on the couch, absorbed in his thoughts, finishing his cigarette before speaking again. "Did Kala know you were there at all? I mean, if you can share her thoughts; she might be able to share yours."

"Actually, I think that's something she has the ability to do, but she doesn't know it yet. I think much of what is happening to her right now she does not fully understand, and it's scary for her."

"Until she does understand what is happening, and she has some control over her abilities, you need to be very careful and be alert," Nathan warned. "If she becomes a danger to herself the High Counsel needs to know."

"Kala is very sensible," Victor said confidently. He knocked the head off his cigarette and left it smoldering in the ashtray, then stood and walked towards the door. "I am hoping that when all the events unfold she will still be the sensible person I care about," Victor opened the door. "Nathan, I need for you to do me a favor." He turned around to face Nathan.

Nathan raised his eyebrows. "What would that be?"

"Check with your High Counsel friends again, see what they know about these Blue Daemons. They'll be back and you know it," Victor said ominously.

"I'll make a few calls. See what I can do."

Victor nodded and headed upstairs.

It was just before midnight when I finally found myself winding down. I was a wreck. When Sara wrote that I was pretty much in this all alone, she was not kidding. What I would not have given to be able to pick up the phone and call *someone* and tell them what had just happened. I'd probably find myself in a mental ward at the city hospital after confessing what I had seen and claimed to have done, but at least I'd be safe in my little padded room. A little padded room sounded really good right about now.

I climbed into bed with a cup of tea and Sara's Journal. I started to think about what she had written regarding there being a 'fine line between good and evil' and wondered just how fine of a line she was referring to. I wanted in the worst way to stay as far on the side of 'good' as possible. I felt I was cursed more than blessed with whatever this task was that I was on – the same task that had sent Sara to an early demise. I didn't understand what Sara expected me to do; if she had failed at her part, what made her think I would do any better? I had no powers, not counting the fact I'd read Sara's incantation and summoned up a vortex that eventually sucked in the Blue Daemon, and fire shot out of my hands, but that doesn't prove anything. I wasn't able to do any of that stuff myself; I knew Sara had to be behind it somehow.

I pushed a few feather pillows behind my head and got comfortable, opening up the journal again. I took a deep breath, wondering what I would uncover next.

Your mind, spirit and soul are very powerful weapons. Your mind is a treasure chest of knowledge, your spirit a tree of great strength and your soul the very essence of your being. Do not take any of these things for granted; together they form who you are. We were not meant to live forever. Although no one is quite like you, many have been in your predicament. It's in knowing this that you can understand the past and change the future. Fate is a paved road and when left with no way off it's usually a one-way ride to the end. But know that in some cases a destiny can be altered if it's in the best interest of the many. Only a select few will ever have the strength and the ability to make this happen. Although there may appear to be no way to move the mountain, you must channel all the power you can find from the mind, the spirit and the soul to discover a way around it.

You hold the power; look deep within yourself; it's there. My incantations work for you because you are strong, not because they are mine. The spells and incantations I have written could just as easily be yours. If you believe and you have the faith and the courage, anything can happen. Focus on who you are and what you want to do, the power is there. If you can think it, you can do it. Imagine it and it will happen... Auburn Starr

Lesson I: Moving an Object (please start small)

The room must be quiet, at least while you are learning to focus your energies. Make yourself as comfortable as possible. Relax your body – this is very important. Relaxing is the key. Pick a small and lightweight object in the room, not too far away from you. I would suggest perhaps something durable; an unlit candle perhaps, so if you lose your concentration and it falls it will not break. Stare at the object and fix your eyes on it, then close your eyes, but continue to see that object in your mind just as you would if you had your eyes open. See the shape of the object, the color and the size in your mind. Think about what that object would feel like in your hands; be familiar with it. Try and weigh the object in your mind, and then try and pick it up with your mind. Concentrate. When you think you have a hold on the object, open your eyes and see. If it doesn't work the first time keep trying. Once you have it down, you will pick up your own techniques and styles.

I closed the journal, exhausted, knowing that I could absorb no more of Sara's words or lessons without sleep.

I knew now that fate could be changed, maybe, but a great deal of strength was needed to accomplish it, and that somehow I was going to start moving mountains by levitating candles.

"Happy Birthday Kala; time for bed," I mumbled as I put the journal on my nightstand. I turned the light off and sank into my bed for the night. I would awaken a year older, maybe even wiser.

Victor had come home, stripped himself of his wet clothes and wrapped himself in a big blanket. He sat in his loft looking out over the city through his favorite window, rocking gently in his wicker and rattan chair. His mood was thoughtful. He reflected back on the numerous years of his life. He had lived side by side with so many people; these people lived a full and productive life, and then died, while he grew no older. And although he had something most would not, an eternal life of youth and power, Victor would never have what they did, a family, and an innocent hope for the future. He wondered from time to time if he really had a better life than most. His world revolved around the night, since his kind could not safely live in the light of day. He could not decide if being able to live for an eternity was a piece of good fortune or a horrible misery. Either way, it was a life he could share with only a few.

Victor realized his thoughts were becoming maudlin; something that only occurred when something had touched his heart. These times were few and far between; he could count on one hand how often it had happened. This time it was Kala, but he realized that no matter how much he cared for her today, it could not last and it could never be, not temporarily or eternally; he was meant to be alone. It was during times like this that he missed his human emotions the most. He thought wistfully of the life that he and Kala might have had, a life together of children and hope, growing old together through the good times and the bad. Victor would never have that life; he knew that when he decided to end the one he had, his life went from day to night. Had Victor known then what he knew now, perhaps the outcome would not be the same. More than likely, Victor's body would be long since gone, his soul free and secure behind pearly gates and his ancestors might refer to him as 'great, great, great grandfather.' But that would never happen.

Taking immortality was a decision he'd made in haste, but not for the wrong reasons. Victor's decision was not made so he could live forever, or to be young and beautiful forever, but was for the chance to love someone forever. The course of events that transpired after his gift of immortality would outline the next two hundred years of his life and banish him out of a society he hardly knew, back into a society that he hardly fit in with. He was not accepted as a vampire by his people, the night-dwellers, or as human by the people who lived and worked hard by day. Victor found himself a loner, his only friend Nathan, who himself was bitterly angry at what had happened. Victor rarely found comfort in anyone he met outside the four walls that he chose to live in. On rare occasions he would find passing friendship with others like him, vampires evicted from their society, or with others who did not care about the details that led up to his exile.

Even Victor's art suffered at the hands of his immortality. He only painted what he knew and that was darkness. He never painted a colorful field of flowers. It had been so long since he had seen a beautiful sight such as that, he doubted whether he could possibly select the colors on his palette to accomplish such a piece of work. Television never did nature justice. Everything was flat and one-dimensional. Victor had tried to use TV as a medium to help him paint, and in his frustration he tossed it down the stairs; the innards and electronics flying out with each wooden step it hit. Nathan had assumed Victor finally went mad.

The fact was, Victor grew more and more aggravated over the years at who he had become. Many of his kind did not care about who they were, and only cared about killing and stalking from dusk till dawn, never being accountable to anyone. Victor had certainly run into plenty of them; Vampires who cut their eyeteeth through the human race like a hot knife through butter. Others became deeply involved in political power struggles, and status, like Nathan, who looked down upon the human race as nothing more than cattle that grazed the streets of the city, just waiting to be plucked out for consumption. What was Victor's role in the world? The world had simply passed him by even though he had been part of it for some two hundred years. He contributed nothing, except his role in the nightmares of those who had lost their friends and family to his timeless lust for blood. Instead of helping the society in which he lived, he had become a tear in the fabric that held it together. Victor had promised himself he would not raise these issues with himself again. He was who he was, and no amount of guilt or feeling sorry could change that.

In meeting Kala, many old feelings had surfaced that he had not had in countless years. Seeing Kala for the first time in the gallery was a like a bolt from the blue. Victor had not planned to make a trip that day to the gallery, but had succumbed to an overwhelming desire to enter the shop, a desire that had no logical explanation. When Victor saw Kala, saw the way she carried herself and heard her speak, the atmosphere that encircled her reminded him in every way of someone he used to know, someone he had cared so deeply about, and had let slip away in more ways than one. Ever since then he hated to look Kala in the eyes, guilt stricken that she would somehow know this; he feared that he was so transparent, every feeling and emotion he had ever felt about her in the last two centuries would overflow, and surely be detected. He knew Kala was strong, even though she had no idea what her strengths were. She would find that sharing thoughts, and using telepathic energy would be one of the easiest things she would ever learn. Since she had already displayed signs of having this ability, he could not be comfortable in her presence, knowing that he needed to keep his guard up at all times until there was an amount of control on her side. Victor was amused at his thoughts concerning etiquette. Martha Stewart would not be up for an undertaking like this.

Chapter 13

I spent the first day of my thirtieth year of life at work. I had requested no one make a big deal out of my birthday, but, unfortunately, no one where I work takes a direct hint, or misses the chance to goof off all day for a reason, and today that reason was my birthday, and that meant reason to celebrate. At ten, it was bagels and coffee, at noon it was pizza, and at two it was cake, a birthday card and a gift certificate to an all day salon to pamper myself, and no one needed pampering more than I did as of late.

I thanked everyone for my gift and offered a 'you really shouldn't have' followed by a 'I thought I told you not to make such a big deal.' The response I got from the crowd was 'we cancelled the male strippers'. So I guess I got off easy, knowing they spared me that.

I had not seen Drew all day. He had not even called in, which was strange. Granted, Wednesday was his day off, but a day off never stopped Drew from coming into the station, even if only for a few minutes to see what was going on, plus it was my birthday. I expected him to show. I was not sure what to make of his absence. I hoped he was not home sulking over his quarrel with Victor from the evening before. He was bigger than that; at least I hoped he was. I debated whether I should try and call him at home, or wait and see if he would call me. I was concerned; he was my friend, but nothing more.

I stopped in to see Addy after work and she was happy to see me. She wished me a happy birthday and told me I didn't look a day over twenty-five. She asked what my plans were for the rest of the day and how I was going to be celebrating my birthday. I explained that Victor and I were going out for a quiet dinner tonight, but I had no idea where. She asked if this Victor was the same guy that I had shown an interest in and was hoping to attend the opening of the gallery with. I smiled and admitted he was one and the same. She wanted me to keep her updated on my progress in getting Victor to go as my date. Addy then mentioned that she had received several RSVPS' concerning the opening of Out of the Shadows and everyone was planning on coming. She speculated that the turn out would be good. That was great to hear in a nerve-wracking kind of way. I had been so involved in my own issues recently that I had forgotten that eventually the gallery would need to be opened to the public, and had put little to no thought as to how the store would be run, or what hours of operation it would have. The opening party was some ten days away, yet I needed to sit down and think realistically about what kind of time I could dedicate to the gallery. But, not today. Today was my birthday and I was going to go home and get ready to have a nice birthday dinner with a handsome man. Victor.

I got home around five to find the message light on my answering machine flashing away. I hit the play back button as I dumped my bag and mail on the table near the front door and listened to the phone calls that had come in while I was away. One call was from Melinda Banks, the interior decorator that Sara was using for the gallery; she was wondering how things were going and wanted to know if she could be of any help. The second call was a hang up and the third call was from Drew. I was glad to hear his call because I had not decided whether I should have taken the initiative to call him or wait and see if I would see him at the station in the morning. His message was simple and short: 'Please call'.

I took the phone out onto the deck with a soda and returned Drew's call. The evening was warm and the sky was clear, no threat of rain that I could see which was good considering the drenching we got the night before.

The phone rang twice before Drew answered. "Hello?"

"Drew, it's Kala. Missed you today. What's going on?" I leaned back in my chair, stretching out and crossing my legs at my ankles.

"It was my day off," he answered rather flatly, sounding a little irritated.

"I know, that's why I didn't call you earlier. I just thought that you might have popped by the station at some point today, for bagels or pizza or cake," I told him. "Missed out on some free food. No beer though."

"Oh well," he mumbled like a spoiled child who was sulking.

Drew's attitude from last night seemed to have carried over. "Listen, if you have a problem with me, spill it. Don't jerk me around."

"What was up with last night?" Drew asked before I barely finished my sentence.

"What do you mean?" I asked quickly. "I went to the station to work, remember, you were with me. I passed out in the garage on my way to my car, and came to with you and Victor standing over me. If anything else happened, you'll have to fill it in for me," I replied, deliberately leaving out my battle with the Blue Daemon, hoping in the pit of my stomach that that was not what he was referring to.

"This Victor guy. Can't you see it?" Drew asked, his voice taking on an angry scolding tone.

"I have no idea what you are referring to," I replied. "Have you been drinking?"

"No, I have not been drinking," Drew retorted. "How well do you know this guy Victor? You are a popular on air radio personality and you don't think twice about where you meet these people, and what they might want."

Drew tried to explain, but sounded rather paranoid on my behalf.

I half laughed, but tried to remain serious. "Drew, I told you how I met him. He's an artist. He teaches some classes at the college. We met at the gallery. He has some work on display. My job at the station hardly ever comes up; his passion is art." I tried to ease his fear that I was somehow being stalked. "I appreciate you looking out for me, really, but I'm fine. I'm thirty years old; I can take care of myself. Oh, and one other thing, the reason Victor knew to find me at the station last night was because I spoke to him right before I talked to you last night and he knew I was going to be at the station working. It was no secret."

There was silence on Drew's end of the phone. Finally he sighed and said, "All right. Listen." There was a long pause. "I care for you. Really. And I know that I'm younger than you, and I don't have a career yet. I'm graduating. I'm a good guy. We get along; I just don't understand women sometimes," he said peevishly, not knowing what else to add to his list of frustrations.

"Drew, I like you too. But I never thought about us *really* as dating. I don't look at you as being younger than me, or as someone who doesn't have their act together. I look at you as Drew, my friend. That's the path our relationship took. I mean, you are still dating Jennifer, and if that's not working for you, then you need to make some decisions for yourself so you can be happy."

"What is it with friendship? I mean, don't relationships start there and then work into something else?"

"Sometimes, I guess, but there is usually chemistry involved. Hard to explain," I replied, thinking about how I felt when Victor was near me.

"I'll take your word for it. And I'm sorry if I've been a jerk about Victor. It's a guy thing I guess. Macho is a disease there is no cure for. And no offense, but I just don't like him," Drew stated, being honest if nothing else.

I smiled and dismissed his comment, not letting it bother me. "It's okay. You are entitled to your opinion."

"So what are you doing for your birthday?" he asked, abandoning the topic.

"Well, you missed a good day at work, lots of food and partying, but tonight I'm going out to dinner," I replied, being vague about my plans for his sake.

"Spare me the details. I know who you are going with," he said, trying to make light of it. "Have a good time."

"Thanks. I will."

"See you in the morning."

"See you then."

After I hung up I began to nervously get ready for my date with Victor. I had very little in the line of 'nice' clothes to wear for formal gatherings, and already knew that a day of shopping for the party at the gallery was in store for me. For tonight though, I had a short black skirt and a red and black sheer fabric sleeveless shirt I could wear with it. The shirt was actually Sara's, one that I had borrowed a long time ago and had never returned. I could not find one good pair of nylons in the whole drawer and had to go without; it was a good thing my legs had some recent sun. Lastly, I had to dig around for the only pair of black pumps that I owned. I wondered how Victor would be dressed; my stomach felt funny when I thought of Victor all decked out in something other than jeans and a casual shirt. After taking a quick shower and blow drying my hair, I concluded that there must be a mighty force working for me because I was having a good hair day, and only required a shot of spray here and there to keep the style I was looking for. My skin was peeling on my shoulders from all that sun I had gotten a few days earlier, and I hoped it didn't look as bad as I thought. I took the time to apply some make-up, which I hardly ever do and sprayed some perfume, sliding my shoes on just before Victor arrived.

When the doorbell rang I quickly checked my look in the mirror, spinning around a few times to get a complete picture. I opened the door to greet Victor. "Hi there."

His mouth curled instantly in a broad grin. "You look great." And with that he walked over the threshold.

Victor placed an arm around me and tapped the door shut behind us. He gave me a tender hug with his strong arms, drawing me close to his chest and kissing me on the lips. Taking a step further inside, my backside was pressed against the cool flat surface of the wall. I returned his kiss, feeling his welcoming lips on mine. How I had been waiting for this moment all day. I laced my arms around his neck, keeping our bodies and lips romantically sealed. His long shiny hair was loose, draping softly over my arms. The light touch of his hair on my bare skin sent erotic tingles through my entire body. Realizing that he was not wearing his hair in his customary tied back fashion, my fingers became intertwined in his mane; I knew I could keep fondling and running my fingers through his hair all night long. Victor pulled away gently and our lips parted. "Happy Birthday."

I said softly, "Thanks. You know, we *could* just stay here tonight." I let my hands trace the outline of his masculine shoulders.

He laughed a little. "That sounds tempting. But we have reservations, and I have been looking forward to taking you out." He backed away just enough to touch the side of my face persuasively.

"I know; figured it was worth a shot. So, where are we going?" I asked him, still within the circle of his arms.

"Luigi's," he replied, checking his watch.

"Wow, that's a hard place to get into," I said admiringly, truly surprised. "It's pretty exclusive."

"I know Luigi personally, I called him up myself. Got us the *best* table in the restaurant," Victor beamed. "I don't know too many important people, so don't get used to the extra special treatment." He laughed at himself.

"I'm impressed," I grinned. "So, I guess we should get going and not keep Luigi waiting."

Victor and I arrived downtown at Luigi's, where a young redheaded valet in a white dress shirt, black bow tie and cumberbund addressed us with a 'sir and madam' and took our car to park. Luigi's was a five star Italian restaurant located in the Little Italy section of the city. I guess every city has at least one good restaurant, and ours was no exception. Any time someone famous came to town, whether actor or actress or musician, they always seemed to end up at Luigi's, with their picture in the newspaper or on the local news the next day.

Luigi's was located in an old historic building that had been renovated several years before. I drove by the building often and had admired the detail that was evident in the building and the grounds. No expense was spared on the business's façade: from its wrought iron fence adorned sidewalks, its lush ivy vines taking hold and scaling up the entire front side of the limestone building, flower boxes anchored under each arched window with only the most colorful and thriving foliage and plant life. The main stairway that led into the lobby was impressive and resembled something you'd see in an old cathedral with its wide landings and steps that were made only of the finest gray marble.

The original Luigi's took up only a small section of the building, which was located on the corner of St. Patrick and Franklin. Right before renovations, the owner bought the entire building, converting the full three stories into a nightclub and restaurant, and bought the empty property across the street for a parking lot for customers. I had not been in the building since it was renovated, but I remembered from a previous Christmas party that the food, and the atmosphere, was very chic.

Victor and I climbed the stairs and entered the lobby, crowded with young college students and white-collar yuppies, drinking and mingling. Some people were waiting for tables in the dining room, others were trying to get into the club and others just hung out where they could. The place was packed, and it was just Wednesday. I could hardly imagine what Luigi's looked like on the weekend with a heavy partying crowd. Didn't quite seem worth the aggravation I thought, to be shoulder to shoulder with hundreds of people waiting to catch a buzz; it seemed ludicrous.

Victor took my hand and escorted me towards a hostess who was stationed near the front of the great room. She was dressed in white; her dark hair piled loosely on top of her head, with tiny curls that tumbled over her forehead and cheeks. Her make up was thickly applied over her rough skin, heavily rouged cheeks competing with fire engine red lipstick. The woman's eyelashes had so much mascara on them that they looked like furry spider legs. She either was making a pitiful attempt to recapture her youth, or had received make up lessons from a circus clown.

"Hello, we have reservations," Victor spoke loudly to the hostess, his voice just barely audible over the crowd around us.

"Your name, sir?" the woman asked in a thick Italian accent. She opened a leather bound guest book and waited expectantly.

"Victor," he replied, still holding my hand in his and squeezed it gently to remind me that he had not forgotten I was with him.

The woman looked in her book, her finger running down the long ivory pages, finally stopping. She picked up a pen and scratched a line through Victor's name. "You are a friend of Luigi's," she smiled.

Victor nodded. "Yes."

"Come with me. We have a wonderful table for you." The woman reached for two large menus adorned with gold tassels, and ushered us up a short flight of red-carpeted stairs, framed with a shiny gold plated railing that curved upwards to the second floor. The walls were covered in fancy stenciled paper, and decorated with large, turn of the century paintings mounted in enormous ornate frames. A huge crystal chandelier suspended from the arched ceiling made elaborate sparkling images on the walls and tables. Victor and I followed the hostess through a small dining room full of elegantly decorated tables resplendent with candles, white linens, water goblets, china and gold flatware. We stopped in front of two very large French doors. The woman grabbed the 'S' shaped handles and twisted them in opposite directions, allowing the heavy glass doors to open outward and onto a garden veranda. She walked out onto the stone balcony. Victor placed his hand on my back and guided me gently forward, following her path.

We were seated at a round table that was draped with white linen; iron chairs with matching cushions were pulled out for us to sit on. A trellis of dark green ivy and roses sheltered us from the open, starry sky. White tapered candles in silver candlesticks flickered softly, illuminating the table set for two with fine china and flatware. A champagne bucket on a platform was filled with crushed ice, the top of an unopened bottle peeking out. The hostess placed the menus on the table and excused herself, stating our waiter would be with us shortly. She closed the doors behind her as she left, leaving Victor and me alone on this magnificent dining balcony, one I had never known existed.

In my delight over our surroundings, I couldn't stay seated. I walked to the edge of the balcony and looked out over the streets. The stone wall that bordered the balcony came up to my waist; I leaned over taking a deep breath and permitting myself to enjoy the evening. I glanced up, taking in the star filled night sky, and could think of no other place I'd rather be at that moment. What a wonderful birthday I was having. How thoughtful Victor was to think of such a fantastically expensive restaurant to treat me to.

I spun around. "Victor, this place is great; but it's way too expensive. You didn't have to go through the trouble to take me *here*!" I blurted out, feeling guilty that he would spend so much on me so soon in our relationship.

Victor approached me with a smile that not only curled his ample lips, but also was evident in his deep brown eyes. He handed me a glass of champagne. I took the delicate flute, holding the stem between my fingers. "I wanted to do this. It's not that often I get to take a beautiful woman to a restaurant like this who can appreciate not only me, but her surroundings as well." Victor leaned forward and kissed me on the lips as his crystal champagne glass clinked against mine. "To a stunning woman on her birthday, on a simply gorgeous night. What more could I ask for?"

I felt hot all over and knew I was blushing. Victor had used beautiful, stunning and gorgeous so many times tonight already I was thinking I'd just pass out from all the compliments. I was overwhelmed by his attention, apparently far more starved for affection than I had thought. I sipped my champagne, allowing the chill amber fluid to cool my heated emotions.

"I can't thank you enough for taking me to a place like this. I've never been to anything this elegant," I smiled broadly, feeling like a child inside.

The balcony made me think of a rain forest and how it might smell, so clean and fresh with so many perfumes mixing I could not tell one from the other. The sweet fragrance of plants, flowers and shrubbery filled the air; their lush greenery flourishing in pots, climbing the walls and ironwork, and hanging from the balcony above; a true paradise. It was hard to believe I was only a few stories up from the asphalt paved city streets.

Victor touched my face softly, and then tucked some hair behind my ear; his fingers followed the line of my jaw smoothly and continued down my neck, stopping at the pendant I had been wearing against my chest.

"Still have it on," Victor commented, sipping his champagne.

I reached up to touch the pendant myself, feeling his hand under mine instead. "Yes, probably won't ever take it off," I whispered. "Means too much to me." I let my hand remain on his, resting gently on my chest.

He nodded, understanding my unspoken sadness about Sara.

"I must say," I continued in a stronger tone. "You have been very complimentary to me tonight. I need to tell you how nice you look." I felt strange paying a compliment to a man in such a way, it was like I was coming on to him, but he was so handsome I couldn't decide what was nicer to look at, the scenery, or him.

Victor was wearing a fashionable black ribbed shirt with a dark, grayish-checked blazer that made his shoulders look broad. His black slacks were pleated at the waist, making him look lean and trim, which I had no doubt he was. His pants were hemmed at the cuff, just grazing his black Italian leather shoes. Victor's sexiest feature by far, at least to me, was his hair. Tonight he was wearing it down, allowing it to glide loosely over his shoulders as he moved. "I like your hair like that," I gestured at him with my champagne glass. "It's not a secret that I think you have great hair. Some guys don't look good in long hair, they just don't carry it well, but you can."

Victor chuckled and seemed reminiscent. "I've worn it like this forever." He leaned against the stone wall next to me, touching my arm lightly with his fingers in a playful way that sent a shiver up my spine. "Why, you have goose-bumps," he laughed. "Do I really have that effect on you?"

I laughed, rubbing my arm with my free hand, trying to smooth them away. "That's nothing. You should see what you do to me when you kiss me."

He ducked his head like a schoolboy, slightly embarrassed. "Really."

I nodded vigorously, smiling.

He shook his head. "I don't know about you." A wide grin began.

"That seems to happen a lot; you not knowing what to do with me," I teased, lowering my eyes and looking up at him through my lashes.

His grin got broader.

The doors opened and our waiter took several steps onto the terrace. He was an elderly man, dressed in a full tux. "Is there anything I can get for you?" He spoke with a heavy Italian accent.

"Not yet. Soon," Victor replied, acknowledging him politely.

The waiter understood and exited gracefully, closing the doors behind him and leaving us alone once again.

"I suppose we should look at the menu," Victor suggested, taking my arm and guiding us over to the table.

I took my seat. Victor pushed in my chair and then sat across from me. I set my champagne glass down and opened the richly designed menu while Victor did the same. I scanned several pages and realized I was unable to read anything. "Victor, it's in Italian." I peered over the top of the menu.

Victor did not seem alarmed at my statement. He shut the menu and placed it down. "Yes, I know. This is a *real* Italian restaurant."

I closed my menu. "I don't know Italian. You do?" I asked.

"I was born and raised in Italy," he replied. "Do you trust me to order for you?"

My mouth turned upwards as I appreciated another side of Victor that I had not seen. "Sure, I guess. Nothing weird though," I warned.

"Deal."

When the waiter returned, Victor had a lengthy conversation with him in Italian. I listened closely, recognizing a few words, but mostly enjoying the foreign sounds coming from Victor's sexy lips. I heard the name Luigi several times and knew whom they were referring to, and I heard the word Pollo which I knew meant chicken, but I doubted Victor was referring to Luigi and Pollo at the same time. The waiter left, hearing all he needed in order to fill our request.

"So, what did you order for us?" I asked curiously, folding my arms on the table and leaning over the table to hear all the delicious details.

"Pollo Arrosto All'Arancia, Limone, e Zenzero. It's a chicken dish with orange, lemon and ginger. It's very good. I ordered Bruschetta for an antipasto – that means appetizer. Bruschetta is a toasted Tuscan bread that usually has olive oil on it with some chopped tomatoes and basil."

"Sounds good," I nodded in approval at his selections. "I haven't had anything like that before. So, where in Italy are you from?"

"Sicily – Catania to be exact. Lost my accent a long time ago," Victor replied, allowing his native Italian tongue to flavor his words. Hearing him speak with his natural born accent made me smile. He was so charming. I loved to discover new things about him; it made me feel closer to him.

Victor poured two more glasses of champagne. "What about you? Where are you from?"

"You're looking at it; right here. I don't have interesting stories like you do, I'm sure." I sighed, feeling grounded and dull, as though I had never grown any wings. I sipped my champagne, wondering why.

"Nothing wrong with roots, they're good to have. But I would recommend some traveling; historically the United States has nothing compared to Rome or Venice. Greece is a wonderful place to see, too. I can't imagine someone as intelligent as yourself not wanting to get away from here and see Europe."

Victor left me with the feeling he was far more sophisticated than I gave him credit for.

"I guess you've done a lot in your life. Kind of makes me feel like I could have done the same. You aren't that much older than me and you found the time and motivation to do it." I felt as if I had cheated myself the experience.

"Oh, don't feel so bad, you have plenty of time," Victor's voice was carefree. "I haven't been back to Italy in so long it would be a challenge to get around."

The waiter reappeared with our bruschetta and a silver pitcher of water; our goblets were filled and our appetizers served.

"So, any brothers or sisters?" Victor asked, placing a napkin on his lap.

"No, I mean, yes. I did." I tried to answer his question the best I could, but knew I sounded confused.

"Brother or sister?" Victor rephrased his question, looking at me while I stumbled through my initial answer.

"Brother," I replied. "But I haven't seen him in fifteen years," I added lamely. I tried a piece of the bruschetta.

"Where is he?" Victor asked, confused. "He doesn't keep in touch?" I could tell he thought the scenario was odd.

I sighed, not knowing where to begin my story. It was something I had not talked about in many years, and I still felt the uncertain emotions left over from my childhood. "My brother is about ten years older than I am, so when I was fifteen he was like twenty five. He worked as a photographer for a national magazine, and on the weekends had a garage band. His band played small clubs; he was the guitarist and the lead singer." I gave Victor a brief background. "Anyway, I remember him leaving for an assignment with the magazine; he was going to Germany to cover a story with a journalist, and he never came home."

Victor's mulled this over as he finished chewing, wiped his mouth with his napkin, took a sip of his water and candidly spoke. "No one bothered to see *why* he had not come home?"

I became a bit defensive. "I wasn't even sure how long he was supposed to be away. Kevin, my brother, wasn't living at home at the time. He had a place of his own. I just remember my parents contacting the police and it seemed to take forever to get information from the authorities in Germany," I recalled, pushing the bruschetta around on my plate with a fork. "The journalist was the last one to see him, and it was the night before he was scheduled to come home. There weren't any major events going on in Germany at the time; it was peaceful."

Victor looked closely at me. "You aren't to blame, you know. I can tell you feel some responsibility, or something. Maybe it's because there was never any closure?" He waited intently for my response, his food forgotten.

"Honestly, I don't know. I never heard the words killed or murdered or dead – just missing. You have to understand that I was not close to Kevin because of the difference in years. Maybe today we could have been closer." A memory entered my mind about Kevin that saddened me, but I shared it anyway. "I remember he wrote a song about me once; I'll never forget the one and only time I saw him sing it. It made me feel really special."

"I'm sure your brother cared about you a lot. Maybe more than you know. You may have been at that age where you didn't think he did, but I'm sure you meant a great deal to him. You were his sister." Victor shook his head as if the story still troubled him. "Seems strange though, no closure. I feel bad for you. I mean, you lose your brother at fifteen, and then fifteen years later you lose your best friend. Doesn't seem right."

I nodded. "No, it doesn't," I agreed, and added to my tale of woe. "Shortly after my brother's disappearance, my folks split up. My Dad just took off. I heard from him a few times after the divorce, but then, even that stopped, and my Mom just lost it and went over the edge. Good thing I met Sara about then. Not sure what I'd be like now if I hadn't."

"You turned out great given the circumstances. I really admire you. Look at you now, art gallery owner, radio station DJ; you're doing okay by me." Victor left me feeling encouraged about who I was. "Who knows, someday you might see your father again on good terms, and maybe your mom will come around."

I shrugged. "Time will tell. So, what about you? Let me guess, an only child."

His eyes lit up with delight that I was so perceptive. "Very good. Yes, I am." He ate his last bite of antipasto.

Images of the cocktail party for the gallery ran through my head "Since you mentioned the gallery, did you get an invitation in the mail to the opening and the cocktail party?"

"Yes, I did. I'll be there," he smiled at me.

"Would you be my date?" I asked, dropping my voice and batting my eyelashes coyly.

"Like you have to ask?" Victor was surprised. "Of course. Miss an occasion to be at the side of the *owner* of the gallery; never!"

Our conversation after that was mostly chitchat as we enjoyed our dinner. We touched base on the gallery some more, his teaching at the campus along with the Battle of The Bands promotion I was going to be part of next month. By the time our plates were cleared, I was on my fourth glass of champagne and was a little less than sober. Victor seemed just fine. But his amusement was apparent as he monitored my ebullient personality, buoyed by the champagne bubbles and the magic of the evening.

"You do have to work tomorrow, don't you?" he affirmed, sending a gentle reminder about my current state of sobriety, or rather, the lack of. He reached across the table and held my hands in his.

"Yeah. I'll be fine. I've been worse than this and managed," I giggled, remembering back to when I would bar hop with some others from the station until three in the morning and needed to be on the air at ten. I wouldn't want to relive those days, but I got by.

"Okay. Glad I'm driving though," he remarked, then slipped his hand into his jacket pocket and pulled out a small gift box. He placed it on the table in front of me. "Happy Birthday."

I looked at him, touched. "Victor, dinner was quite enough!"

"Open it," he insisted.

I picked up the gift box and untied the ribbon, removing the lid. Under a square piece of cotton was a dainty gold bangle bracelet with three oval rubies set into the gold. My birthstone. "It's lovely," I gasped. Victor reached across the table and put it on my left wrist. I admired how it sparkled, the candlelight reflecting on its surface. "Thank you." I happily and most ungracefully leaped out of my chair, running up behind him and wrapped my arms around his shoulders, kissing his cheek.

"You are very welcome," He laughed at my lack of coordination in getting over to him.

The waiter returned and asked us about dessert. Neither of us could eat another morsel, but I decided to take a slice of cheesecake home for later. After all, this was a birthday celebration; one I would remember forever. I wanted the evening to never end.

Chapter 14

Once we got back to the condo, Victor and I leisurely made our way up through the parking lot to my unit. The night was still and relatively quiet; a small warm breeze rustled through the bushes, while the sounds of the crickets making their usual chirping noises would continue into the wee morning hours. Maybe it was a certain stillness in the air despite the breeze that felt out of the ordinary to me; it was a strangeness that sobered me, cutting through the alcohol I had consumed. Physically it was still a challenge to walk in my high heels, but mentally I was totally coherent, my senses alert in a manner unknown to me, a keen acuity that felt unreal. I had somehow become more aware of what was going on in the night. I suddenly knew that things existed in the shadows that I would not have normally been able to see or hear, things that my range of human senses would not have detected. These beings carried on in their nocturnal existence, just as they had before my notice.

Even though I could not see these creatures, which apparently came in all different sizes, they were out there and they saw me. I felt like I was emitting a wave of radar that encircled me, a protective bubble that held me in relative safety. If something suddenly crossed my path I would know it, I could feel it, an internal alarm would sound that only I could hear. It was like walking with a long stick in my hand, poking blindly into the darkness, except when it struck something, I knew it; I could feel the resistance upon it. This is what I felt as I walked up the stairs to my condo with Victor's arm gently around my waist. I felt like my stick had nudged something in the darkness. Something was out there. Before putting my key into the door, I turned around on the front step to bravely look behind us, to see what my stick had hit. Initially I saw nothing, but I knew there was more in the darkness than just *nothing*. Victor was quiet, watching me as I slowly moved my eyes out over the parking lot, then the heavily treed area that bordered it, scanning carefully, my heightened vision like a searchlight. He spoke not a word but watched me intently; watching my eyes without blinking, as if he was trying to read my thoughts to find reason for what I was doing. Finally, he tugged firmly on the back of my shirt to gather my full attention, looking at me with the most puzzling and questionable stare. I returned his stare only for a moment and then unlocked the door, letting us in. Apparently my search had come up empty, although I was not the slightest bit convinced there was nothing out there.

I shut the door behind us, locked it and then kicked off my shoes, dismissing the peculiar event. Victor removed his jacket, took off his shoes and made himself comfortable on the couch, stretching out his legs and propping his feet up on the coffee table. I took a seat next to him, setting my container of cheesecake on the end table. Victor motioned for me to move closer, next to him. I slid over and under his extended arm; my head leaned against his chest, his arms wrapped around me protectively. "What was going on out there? You've done that before to me." Victor spoke in a quiet voice, almost whispering, his voice calming.

"Sometimes I just feel like there is something out there. I get these feelings. Stupid, I guess," I replied, doubting my instincts and wondering if I was just stressed out.

"Maybe not. Some people have the ability to feel certain things. It's a psychic ability," Victor explained and rubbed my arm.

"Did you feel anything out there?" I asked hopefully. I looked up at him from the comfort of his chest.

He did not answer right away.

"Did you?" I asked again, thinking that perhaps he had.

"No... no I didn't," he finally replied. "Women are supposed to have a higher level of psychic power than men anyway."

"Lucky us," I mumbled.

"How are you feeling otherwise?" Victor asked, brushing my hair back as he kissed my forehead.

"Fine... comfortable. Champagne is wearing off," I answered.

"That's good. I'm glad you enjoyed yourself tonight." He took a deep breath and sank deeper into the cushions of the couch.

"I did, very much. It was a good thirtieth birthday." I spoke into his chest, feeling very content with his company.

"You'll have plenty more to enjoy," Victor sighed. "Still oh, so young."

"You make yourself sound ancient," I slapped him on the stomach lightly.

He held my hand in his. "Sorry, feel old some days."

"Well, you don't look a day over thirty if you ask me." I leaned back to see his handsome face. "Can I ask you a question?"

"Yeah. What?" he asked, looking down at me, his dark eyes waiting for my inquiry.

"Have you ever been in a serious relationship? I find it hard to believe that someone who looks as good as you just isn't taken." It was a question that had plagued me for a while.

He squeezed my shoulder and rocked me a bit. "There have been relationships now and then, but I guess I just haven't gotten the urge to settle down completely. Always seem to be happier by myself."

"I can understand." And I could.

We sat next to one another talking for a while longer. Suddenly, I got the desire to try my cheesecake. I sat up, reaching over to the end table and opened the container, revealing a plain piece of New York style cheesecake, complete with a fresh chocolate dipped strawberry to go along with it, plastic fork included.

"Uh oh, dessert," Victor laughed.

"They have the best cheesecake," I moaned blissfully as I peered raptly into the Styrofoam carton.

"Wow." He seemed impressed with my enthusiasm over a 1200-calorie piece of cake.

"When was the last time you had cheesecake?" I asked him. I pushed his legs off the coffee table and sat directly across from him, our knees touching.

He thought a moment, staring at the ceiling. "Awhile."

"What's awhile?" I asked, sinking my fork into the cheesecake, getting ready to sample my first bite.

"I was probably a child," he recalled out loud, his eyes narrowed, thinking back.

I put the fork in my mouth, tasting the cheesecake for myself. "Oh, this is good," I groaned. "A child? You were a child the last time you had cheesecake? Children cannot appreciate cheesecake. Cupcakes are for children, cheesecake is for adults," I said, swallowing delicately.

He smiled as he watched me enjoy my dessert.

"I think you have waited far too long to have cheesecake again. Why deprive yourself?" I asked, standing over him. I boldly straddled his lap, placing a leg on either side of his thighs, sitting my rear end down on his knees facing him. I held the slice of cheesecake between us. He placed his hands on either side of me, but on the cushions of the couch, rather than my thighs. He seemed unsure of where to place them otherwise. His eyes scanned mine curiously, trying to read my intentions. I took the chocolate-dipped strawberry out, and set the container and cheesecake on the arm of the couch. I held the strawberry up for inspection. "I doubt when you were a child you had a strawberry quite like this." I placed my free hand squarely on the back of the couch behind Victor's head. I leaned forward intimately, closing in on his personal space as I nudged the strawberry seductively between his full lips. With my persuasiveness he slowly opened his mouth to accept the chocolate-coated fruit. I placed the berry between his front teeth and once the strawberry vanished inside his mouth I lowered my body towards his and kissed his lips. An array of flavors; Victor, the strawberry and chocolate blended together across my taste buds. I slid my fingers through his hair, tugging a tender handful to keep for myself. I could taste the strawberry as it crossed over his tongue; a bridge that carried his flowing juices into my yielding mouth. I had a craving for him all evening and I was searching for satisfaction. Victor finally did something useful with his hands, moving them to my rear, and clenched my backside fervently. I felt his hot breath on my face as he tipped his head, his mouth overtaking mine completely. I had not thought up to this point that Victor had overly passionate feelings for me. We had kissed before, and although the kisses had feeling they had lacked passion. I continued to return his kisses, needing to feel his lips on mine, as his soft silky tongue plunged deeply into my mouth. Images of what his naked body would feel like under my exploring hands entered my head. I caressed the side of his face with my fingers, feeling his warm and supple skin under them, my fingers marching along a chosen path, down his neck, his shoulders and rubbing his firm chest. I found myself sitting harder against his lap, closer to his groin, my short skirt rising high enough so that my black panties could be seen. I felt Victor's hands alternately stroke the sides of my thighs and then move to the small of my back, then return in a smooth rhythm. I broke our kiss for a moment, placing my hands on his torso and gripping his shirt, my chest heaving with pent up desire as I felt his doing the same. Victor's eyes were fixed on mine; there was nothing distracting him from me. I held his thoughts completely.

For a split second, an overwhelming rush of feelings and emotions erupted in my mind, but they were not my own; I felt the weight of them tangling with my own desires. The combination made me gasp and left me erotically numb. I realized in that same moment that they must be Victor's passions, very much the same as mine but different too, in a beastly, primitive way. He reached up with one hand and placed it securely on the back of my neck. He leaned forward and cradled me, rolling and pressing my backside into the couch as he ended up on top. One of my legs was between his, and I felt his weight on my legs as he kissed my neck.

"You don't know how badly I have wanted you," he growled deep in his throat. I felt his wet lips and tongue against my throat, his hands roaming my bare stomach as they crept up under my shirt and over my satin bra.

I was glad he finally said that, because I had wanted him from nearly the moment I laid eyes on him at the gallery. I was so attracted to him, much more than I had been to any man I could recall. His body was heavy on mine, but I did not mind. I knew he was there, there to stay for awhile. I ran my hands down the sides of his body, feeling the fabric of his shirt over his hard strength, teasing my senses. I wanted to feel his body and smell his skin. I tugged the back of his shirt out of the waistband of his pants and was finally able to caress his muscular back, the dip and valley where his spine was. My fingernails breezed lightly over his exposed skin. His mouth pulled away from mine; a low, throaty moan escaped his lips.

He pushed himself off me and sat up grabbing the bottom portion of his shirt and yanked it off over his head, tossing it to the floor. I watched him, my internal fire heating up as his torso appeared. I reached up, my hands trembling in eagerness, my hot palms fusing to his smooth chest, my fingers lightly flicking his nipples through soft, curling hairs. I wanted to taste the saltiness of his skin and feel his body completely naked against me. I struggled determinedly with the waistband of his pants, my knuckles brushing against the hard muscles of his stomach. My fingers skimmed over the smooth material of his pants as I separated the flap of fabric that housed the zipper. I mischievously dragged my finger up and down the nylon teeth, unfastened the button and slowly brought the zipper down. I pressed my hand on either side of the opening in his pants, probing gently. I discovered the firm hardness gratefully, and gripped it with authority. I watched Victor's eyes close as I rubbed his crotch, feeling his hardness, his undeniable excitement growing within my hand. Victor firmly covered my hand, pressing it into his body with more force than I was applying on my own. Suddenly, he stood, and with surprising ease lifted me off the couch. He looked down at me with hunger naked in his eyes and said one word. "Bed."

I pulled away from him and smiled demurely. "I guess you know what to do with me after all," I spoke softly, taking his hand in mine and guiding him through the living room, down the short hallway to the master bedroom. I opened the door and turned on the light. He sat on the edge of the bed as I lit two large pillar candles supported by tall iron candlesticks that sat on the floor. Once lit, I turned the lights off, letting my eyes adjust to the darkness. I met him on the bed. He lay down on his back and I moved next to him, draping my leg over his. I kissed his chest, smelling his natural musky scent as I climbed over him and straddled his body. Victor reached for me, pulling me close enough to him so he could slide my shirt off my body, leaving me only in my black bra and skirt, which was now hiked up around my waist. I helpfully unzipped the skirt, flinging the black garment to the bedside.

I rubbed his naked chest with my hands. "You feel so good," I groaned, falling forward to kiss him.

"You feel pretty good yourself," he responded. He placed a finger on my chest and outlined the seam of my bra; stopping at the plastic clip in the front between my breasts, he used one finger to unhook the closure. As he slipped the bra straps off my shoulders, he fondled my breasts tenderly.

I leaned forward and pressed my breasts against him, reveling in the feel of his warm skin pressed to mine. Victor put his arms around me and hugged me to him, covering my mouth with his. As our tongues entwined I could hear his erratic breathing, feel the thumping of his heart. His kisses made me feel so hot with desire, wanting his hands all over my body, making me want him inside me. I reached down to the open waistband of his pants and slid my hand over his crotch. He stopped kissing me and let me continue for a moment, eyes closed, focusing on the warmth of my touch.

We both clumsily struggled with his pants, wanting no barrier between us any longer. I stroked his body, all but naked except for a pair of steel gray silk boxers. I maneuvered my hand sideways and slithered it between his pubic area and boxers, finding and capturing his stiff penis. My desire was so intense I thought I could have an orgasm with just his body lying on top of mine. I knew that my fine-tuned senses would require little prompting!

Victor rolled on top of me; we kissed and touched each other for what seemed like hours. My body was so ready for him; I was past any coy, fair-maiden act. Finally, unable to contain myself, I moaned, "Victor, I want you, now!" I dug my fingernails into his back to underscore my desire.

He nibbled lightly on my neck and stopped. "It's been a real long time. I just want it to be right." He rolled off me and placed his caressing hand on my stomach.

"There is no way it *can't* be right tonight," I whispered looking at him. "I need you so bad. Don't tell me you don't need me."

He kissed me quickly. "I need you, I do," he confirmed.

"If you are unsure of yourself, please don't be." I could see the outline of his beautiful body traced by the flickering candles. "I really want you."

He closed his eyes upon hearing my words, they acted as an aphrodisiac on him, spurring him to further action.

I sat up and squirmed out of the last bit of clothing I was wearing; a pair of black, high cut panties. I kicked them off onto the floor and then helped Victor remove his boxers. His erect penis, free from its confines, stood up from his prone body, a glistening drop evident on its tip. I licked my lips and glanced once at Victor; not so much for permission as for acquiescence. His eyes, dusky with desire, gave me all the go-ahead I needed.

I began a path of light kisses down his torso, squeezing his firm chest and licking each nipple on my way down. Victor's hands lay next to his body on the bed, his fingers stretching and contracting with each new place I touched or kissed. By the time I got down to his crotch Victor's hands were on the back of my head, playing with my hair in anticipation. I rubbed his rigid thighs with the palms of my hands, feeling the feathery hair underneath; I dug my fingers into his skin as I slipped my body down and in between his legs. I took hold of his penis and, gripping him firmly, I moved my hand up and down, feeling his loose silky skin slide under my sensual power. My hand could barely contain his size, as his penis continued to grow larger and become extremely taut. I held him still and licked the entire length of his penis with my tongue. As the pulsing tip met my lips, I allowed it to slip in to my mouth, the rest of the shaft following. I bathed him with my tongue, all the while caressing his body with my hands. As my head moved up and down, finding a sensual pace, Victor shut his eyes tight and scrunched the comforter on the bed under his hands, gathering fistfuls of material. Tiny droplets of moisture collected on his pubic hair around the base. I rhythmically stroked him and sucked on his engorged member while Victor emitted some of the most erotic sounds I had ever heard. I wanted to jump on top of him right then and there, and feel him pump himself deep inside me. I watched his stomach and chest rise and fall with each breath he took. Reaching up with my free hand I touched the ripples of his abdomen, feeling each muscle under my finger. He began to thrust his hips slightly as he moved in time with my mouth, placing his hands on the back of my head for leverage. He began to say things that did not make sense to me, or were not loud enough or meant for me to hear. I was afraid he was getting ready to climax, so I slowed the pace down without stopping, then paused.

"Oh God, you stopped," he mumbled, brushing his hair out of his face. "You can do that all night." His voice was low as he struggled for composure. "Come here."

I quickly sat up and opened my nightstand drawer, knowing I had a condom. Retrieving it, I laid next to him with the little cellophane wrapped item in my hand. "Yes."

Victor pried the wrapper out of my hand and opened it; lying flat on his back he rolled the condom over his erection. Supporting his upper body with his arms he maneuvered on top of me. I could feel his penis solidly between us. I opened my legs for him; eager to receive the sweet gift I had been longing for. I stroked his sides, wanting to feel his body under my fingertips. Victor placed his hand on the side of my neck and brought his face to mine, kissing my lips, his warm mouth tasting sweet. My hands explored his backside from his shoulders, down his back and over his rear end. He continued to kiss me as he lowered his hips. Victor guided himself through my wettest areas; I was able to feel the tip of his penis prodding its way closer until it slipped without any resistance inside me. As he sank deep inside me, I gasped at the passion that rocked me, my excitement mounting in anticipation. I locked my legs around his hips, wiggling provocatively, letting him know that slow just would not do. I clutched him fiercely as he began to drive himself in and out of me with calculated force. I was so ready for him, needing to feel him like this and to take final control. I moaned and repeated the words 'yes, yes' over and over again. As his orgasm rocked his body, his face contorted by spasms of ecstasy. I found it extremely exciting to be able to experience my own and watch him have his. We clung to each other like jockeys in a race; our endurance and stamina tested to the limits. As I teetered on the edge of yet again another orgasm, I thought my heart would burst open with the pleasure. Finally I reached my climax and clung to his body as the wave of pleasure surged in me. I felt as if I would just spasm my way off the bed if I didn't keep a tight grip on Victor. I could hear the timbre in Victor's voice changing as he got closer to heaven, his eyelids flickered rapidly and his arms began to shake as he thrust a few more times, then letting out a throaty groan, allowing himself to stay at the deepest point within me, he came.

Slowly he lowered himself against my body, his arms spent, a thin film of sweat covering his shoulders and the slope of his back. My heart gradually slowed as a peaceful sensation filled me, a feeling as calming as it was warm. Victor groaned one last time. "Uhhhhh."

I chuckled weakly.

Victor gradually rolled off Kala onto his back, his arms extended out to both sides, crucifixion style. He was sacrificed for a good cause. A cause that had been dormant in his heart for two centuries. He lay there catching his breath, with no immediate regrets.

Chapter 15

Victor had wanted to stay the night in the worst way. He did not want to leave Kala. Their lovemaking had instilled in him a protective watchfulness, and leaving her went against his every instinct. Unfortunately, he knew that he would be of no use to her during the day, but that did not dispel his sense of guilt at her distress. He knew the flood of bewildered thoughts Kala projected were made up as much from disappointment as suspicion – her first thought was 'he must have a wife', which did not ease his departure. He knew now was not the time to tell her his true reason for leaving – someday she would know, but not now.

Victor thought about his time with Kala during his drive home. He smiled to himself when he thought about how good this young and vibrant woman made him feel; he felt almost human in many ways. Their sexual union had been mutually fulfilling; he was sure of this because of his telepathic contact with her. He had maintained a light touch on her mind with his from the moment they had begun their amorous adventure. Kala unknowingly gave Victor his biggest thrill by letting him make love to her mind. Stealing, or sharing human emotions, was something commonly done by his kind, but usually only while feeding. Being able to experience stimulation like that without feeding or risking harm to Kala made the event even more special, more than she could ever know.

Although he was able to perform any sexual act, and there was pleasure in it for him, the highest level of ecstasy came when he opened the door to her private thoughts and visions. Kala's dreams, desires, ambitions and feelings melding with his, gave him a psychological orgasm he was not prepared for. He had not realized how complicated she was.

At one point, his own passions had overcome him and had accidentally rushed back in to Kala, inundating her with so many emotions she was almost swept away. He realized that she knew the wave of alien sensations were not hers, and she could only surmise that they had to be his. Victor doubted that Kala would ever ask him about them, not knowing exactly how to express in words what she felt. He thought she would dismiss the unusual incident to the fact it was the first time they had been intimate. If some men could make the world move, then a few stray feelings should be considered a tremor.

Victor felt so close to Kala now that in many ways he would never have to ask her a question again; he knew more about her now than she herself did.

She would most definitely be angry, if she knew that Victor had invaded her most sacred inner sanctums. But, Victor found Kala irresistible. The time he had spent with her tonight had made him feel complete, satisfied, at peace, in a way he hadn't felt for a lifetime.

During several moments of passion, it was obvious to Victor that Kala's psychic capacity was increasing steadily towards a higher level of clairvoyance. The legacy from her immortal father – the non-human part of her – was budding into something fierce, something that very few would be able to tame if it went out of control. Kala's instincts were becoming powerful. They were not yet as keen as Victor's, but would give him a run for his money when fully matured.

Victor's respect for Kala's abilities had grown tonight, too, when she had paused outside the condo, sensing the unnatural being lurking nearby in the dark woods. Victor had felt it also, but he chose to ignore the intrusion. Unlike Kala, Victor did know what she was sensing. It was not a Blue Daemon, but another vampire, which meant that not only was Kala sensitive to the aura of daemons, but to the extremely mild emanations of vampires as well. Victor had mixed feelings about this; concerned for her safety he was sensitive to potential danger areas. He was worried about her ability to sense something she could not stop, something that could overpower her quickly, and was so deadly and ruthless there would be no chance for mercy. He wished she could remain unaware as long as possible, allowing her the chance to deal with her burgeoning powers. He was not confident Kala could survive an encounter with a truly hardcore killer any time soon.

Victor arrived at the Victorian and went straight to Nathan, who was up reading. Victor opened the door slowly, still lost in reflection of his erotic evening. Nathan sat on his leather couch with a book in his lap, properly dressed as always. Nathan watched his friend enter his home and shut the door almost soundlessly. Neither one said anything. Victor took a seat next to Nathan, reached over and took the book from his hands, closed it and placed it on the table. Nathan folded his hands on his lap and glared at Victor, waiting for him to speak.

"Well?" Nathan asked, breaking the silence.

"What were you doing in the woods at Kala's place tonight? And don't even think about telling me that you weren't there. You sired me; I know your scent just as well as you know mine," Victor said accusingly, trying to rein in his anger.

"I was out and about. Feeding in the neighborhood," Nathan answered squarely, as if daring Victor to tell him he was out of line for that.

"I hope it was good," Victor said sarcastically, placing a heavy hand on

Nathan's shoulder. "At least now I know that Kala can not only sense the dead, but the undead as well. I'm sure you were aware she was sensing you." Victor stared a moment more at Nathan, then removed his hand.

"She wasn't certain. She is very unsure of what she feels," Nathan argued. "All the intuitions are there, but she doesn't know how to use them."

"True, for right now. But in time, and with guidance, you know she will be like a dog; she'd sniff us out like that," Victor snapped his fingers to make the point. "Wasn't it you that told me all the things past Emissary's were able to do? Stir up weather, call upon elements, fire, spells, incantations, read minds, literally crush a living man's skeleton by looking at him a certain way? And that even the Sovereign himself fed off the Emissary to weaken her so that he would remain stronger? Is this the truth or fables?" Victor leaned over towards Nathan, pressing him for answers.

"All true," Nathan conceded.

"So why treat Kala as if she is any different? She is our next chosen Emissary and will some day be that strong."

"I just wanted to see her. I wanted to see what our next Emissary looked like. See this mortal woman who has you wrapped around her finger. *Again,*" Nathan said hotly as he stood and retrieved a pack of cigarettes from his desktop.

"And?" Victor asked, curious in spite of his anger as to Nathan's opinion.

"She is nothing special. She is human. Perhaps some day I can respectfully call her Emissary." Nathan lit his cigarette and leaned against the arm of the couch near Victor.

"Nathan, you are entitled to feel the way you do," Victor said wearily, and stood to leave. He needed rest, both physically and mentally. "I care for Kala. That never changed; you know that. I am what I am today because of a love I once had. I will hold on to what I have now, for as long as I can, no matter what."

Nathan made no reply. He just nodded; needing no reminder of the experience Victor was referring to.

It was almost three by the time I crawled into bed. I stared exhaustedly at Sara's journal on my nightstand and knew I could not read one sentence. I was far too tired and depressed, confused over Victor's abrupt departure after our wondrous evening. I did not know what to think of it. After all, he lived so close; why could he not stay? Thinking about him made my head and my heart hurt; I did not want to hurt. I wanted to welcome the oblivion of sleep to finally end the night. I was ready to start a fresh new day.

It was a cold gust of air that woke me to an almost conscious state in my dream. The same dream I had not had in many nights, and had not given a thought to before my head hit the pillow. Everything looked the same in this winter night except for one key matter; instead of being in the dream, I was watching it unravel as an outsider. When I looked down at myself I saw I was not wearing the scratchy wool coat as before, but was dressed as I would normally in the cold weather, wearing a blue ski jacket, jeans and hiking boots. I looked up and down the snowy streets; the sights were familiar, all the shops closed for the evening. I bent over and grabbed a handful of snow, packing it into my bare hands. I could feel it: cold, wet and firm. I let out a deep breath into the dark night air and watched as it plumed away in a frosty cloud. This was real; it was happening now. Then why, when I saw the young woman in the long gray wool coat walk by, could I not stop her, or touch her? It did not make sense to me. This was the same woman I had been, and I knew where she was headed; the little red house. I also knew she would never make it home. But how could I stop her?

"Hey! You!" I called, hurrying after the woman. I could only get so close to her, within several feet, but no closer. Something unseen was keeping me from contacting her. "Stop!" I shouted at her. My words had no affect on her; she continued without pause. What was the purpose of me being here, I thought desperately. I did not want to watch this woman die.

The horse drawn buggy rolled by us with the same gentleman on board. I watched the woman in wool nervously peek around just as I had done, knowing I was being followed. The woman coughed just as I had done; she was ill and her skin tone was haggard and dull. She walked further as I trailed along, watching mutely as she yelled in fear at her unseen stalker, knowing he was hidden in the night, as I had known. I remained still, wanting to see her adversary as she continued to navigate the slippery street. I saw nothing, but heard the heavy breathing of a being nearby, the same deep breaths I had heard before. The rustle of what sounded like the wings of birds were overhead, but when both of us looked up and towards a tree; again we saw only the heavenly skies.

Something reached out and touched her. It was only now when she stopped briefly that I caught a glimpse of something that came between us; when she turned quickly to try to discover for herself what it was, it was gone. I kept my eye out for it and, perhaps at the same time I figured out where *it* had been hiding; *it* made itself known from the obscurity of shadows.

If I could not prevent this woman from dying, then maybe I could see the face of her killer. "Please stop!" I begged one last time, trying to get the woman to go no further, to hear my words and obey. I reached for her several times but it was not possible to touch her; my hand kept stopping just short. My heart was pounding hard in my chest in anticipation of what I knew was coming as she walked on. Finally, I saw him. The stalker was definitely male, tall, with broad shoulders. From my vantage point I could not see his face, just the outline of his dark coat, his hands buried deep within his pockets; a manly figure. I made several steps closer, cautiously, as it appeared the woman was having a friendly conversation with this man. I did not remember having a conversation with anyone when I was her; just the shrilling tone of death in my head, drowning out the words of a voice spoken as I was lying half dead in the snow on my back. I could hear the woman and the man talking, but could not make out what they were saying; the conversation was not heated and seemed rather normal. I continued to move cautiously, unsure if at any given point they would be able to see me.

"Kala, you are dreaming again." The words came from behind me, so unexpected I froze from terror before realizing I recognized the voice.

I turned quickly and saw Victor, dressed normally in jeans, sneakers and a black T-shirt. How did he get into my dream?

"I thought I told you to try and wake yourself up if you had this dream again," he scolded, walking towards me. He seemed annoyed that I had not heeded his words.

I said nothing, shocked that I had company, someone who could see me. I glanced back at the couple, still talking, though louder now as if an argument was ensuing. I turned my back on him since he was just a figment of my dreaming state. Ignoring him I tried to listen to the words of the man who was speaking. My mission was to know how this woman died. I had hoped it was not due to an argument. Could that make this man kill her?

"Kala. I'm talking to you." Victor's voice grew louder with an edge of anger to it that I had not heard before. His footsteps crunched through the crust of the snow behind me.

I waved him off, still listening to the conversation, but not able to hear everything.

I felt Victor's hand grab my arm and wrench me around to face him. His eyes were black with anger. "Wake up!" he growled.

My own anger flared in response. He was interfering in my attempt to make sense of this dream, to perhaps unlock the mystery. Instinctively, I pressed both my hands on his chest and pushed him back with all the force that I had, wanting him to go away. When I placed my hands on his chest I felt a sudden surge of uncontrollable energy pour out of my body and into his. To my surprise, I knocked Victor nearly ten feet backward into the street, where he landed on his back. Shocked, I rubbed my hands together, feeling the residual warmth. Victor got to his feet, his shirt ruined, two charred handprints smoldering where I had touched him. I could see the skin on his chest was burned, with small blisters beginning to ooze wetly. Apparently I had more control in my dream that I had initially thought. I just wished I could have stopped the woman.

I heard a dull thud as something hit the ground. I took my eyes off Victor to see what had happened between the woman and the man. I saw the woman's body lying in the snow, face up under the tree in a pool of red, the man hovering over her. He knelt over her dying body in a manner almost reverent, saddened in a disturbing way. I still did not know how she had perished, but was sure that this man had something to do with it. I looked around, trying to locate a weapon of any sort, but without success. The man finally stood erect and backed away from the body. He lowered his head and began to walk directly towards me. I crouched down slightly, desperate to see his face, hoping the night would be generous enough to provide me with even the littlest bit of light to see any facial features. But before I could catch the barest glimpse, he took off in a blinding blur, almost as if someone had pushed the fast forward button on my dream, leaving me staring at the credits.

I stood in the cold night, my feet deep in snow, next to the body of a dead woman that I knew nothing about.

"Kala. It's over. Wake up. Please." It was Victor again, using words this time instead of brute force to reason with me.

I shook my head, knowing he was right, but was inexplicably drawn to the cooling corpse under the tree.

"Kala. Don't," Victor's voice dropped to a plea. "Wake up."

I wasn't sure I ever got to see the body because the next thing I knew the alarm clock was going off, waking me for work. I felt as if I had not gotten any sleep at all. This was going to be a long day; I knew it already.

Chapter 16

By the time my shift was over I was more than ready to come home. I needed a nap. Maybe it wasn't cool at my age to admit it, but like it or not, I needed naps. I guess my age was catching up with me, because in order to function it was a good idea that I grabbed a few zz's.

I got home about mid-afternoon, stripped out of my clothes and got into bed, exhausted. I looked over and saw Sara's journal still sitting on the nightstand. Feeling guilty I picked it up and turned to where I'd left off. *Lesson I: Moving an Object (please start small)*. I was not going to start on *any* lesson right away so I just scanned quickly through the book, noticing that she had lessons in Astral Projection, Healing Rituals, Psychic Protection, Invisibility, Bindings; the list of lessons went on and on. All of which she suggested I learn as soon as I could.

Eventually I stumbled onto something that caught my immediate interest.

The most important thing I can tell you is that some people are not what they may seem. A mirror does not lie, but it does not tell the truth, if the truth cannot be seen. There are species of beings we live and exist with that you don't know about yet, but will. Most people will never fully know about these beings; their very existence was meant to be secretive, and has been for thousands of years. Rumors of their society have always been with us, but were never taken as anything more than just that; rumors. The truth of who they are, and what they are has been concealed.

These beings once were human and have remained looking like us, talking like us, dressing like us and even working with us in our human lives since the beginning of documented time. Some of these beings have had high-level jobs in villages, towns, cities and governments worldwide. And although they are like us in many ways, the morals that make humans who we are, and make their species the way they are, is what has kept us apart all these years. Most people could probably live an entire lifetime never needing to know what I'm telling you, but you need to know.

Just as there are different races of humans, the same is true of these people and their society. One of these clans was originally known as Enforcers; guards between the gateways of several dimensions, not just the living world and the dead world – these are but two dimensions most people are familiar with. There are dozens of parallel worlds that not only mirror our own, but also produce daemons and ghost-like apparitions that people assume come from the depths of Hell, when they really are from realms we know very little about. It was the Enforcers' duty to keep the living world free from dimensional or realm floating creatures that threaten the living and to take out the corrupt humans who lived among the good. The Enforcers were to remain unsung heroes that we were never supposed to meet; dark missionaries serving a thankless job, ridding the reality we live in from hidden evils. They were exterminators of malevolent souls and wrongdoers. These Enforcers were the lesser evil; but evil never-the-less. Enforcers were killing machines, their diet consisting mainly of parallel shifting creatures and the sinners who lived among us – what the human justice system did not pick up on – Enforcers did.

Enforcers in the beginning did not live among us – they were stationed out of sight and hunted and fed in the night – they were not seen and not allowed to dwell with humans. Gradually though, the Enforcers began to go astray, they found they could live among us almost seamlessly and feed not only on the criminals and those with no morals, but also on the good, law-abiding people who lived productive and fruitful lives. Something, somewhere had gone wrong.

These beings appear to be human but are not. Please don't let their presence make you think otherwise. They can be very persuasive, cunning, charming, and usually likeable. The truth is they are savage and always have been. They are meant for a specific job – and they are good at it. They are killers. They are almost undetectably human except for one flaw – they are immortal. Their immortality can be fed only one way – by blood.

These former Enforcers dwell from dusk to dawn, and cannot appear in total day light. Immortality does have its limitations. They can be destroyed if a wooden stake is plunged into their heart, by beheading, or by being put in direct sunlight where they burst into flames or if they are prevented from feeding for a long period of time. The substance that allows these beings immortality is blood. They must kill in order to feed. If they do not kill to eat, they embrace and make more of their kind.

The overall species I have been referring to is known now as the Vampire-Enforcers are just one small sector of the populous. Yes, they exist, and they are all around the world, on every continent, on every island. Their migration has been steady. Although they live in our society they do not follow our laws; they have their own set they live by. And like the human race, they have their own rogue criminals that they must deal with.

There are a small number of people the world over who track the vampire. These hunters believe that vampires are evil parasites and need to be exterminated. The hunters' normal procedure of operating is to find vampires who sire or embrace frequently or hunt where the most unexplainable deaths to humans are or a high rate of missing people are reported. These hunters are experienced in what they do, having methods in tracking and eradicating them. The vampire hunters have little fear of the vampire, but unfortunately the vampires have little fear of the human hunter as well.

I cannot tell you how many Vampires you may have already met, or how many more you will meet. A strong mind is your greatest defense against vampires. Being able to control your thoughts, increasing your level of clairvoyance, and practicing a craft that I tried to instill upon you while I was alive is your best resistance to their powers. Vampires will always have a far superior physical strength than you, but a powerful mind will grant you your freedom.

Here is what I know about the culture of the vampire. The globe is broken up into four sectors and each sector has a High Counsel that is similar to our Congress, with a Sovereign and an Emissary who provide leadership to their people – sort of a King and Queen. (Please understand I don't have every detail to this society; I am only telling you what I know for sure.) A Sovereign is a male who was either born as a Vampire with the purest of bloodlines or is an elder in the High Counsel. The Emissary is a human born female who is chosen even before her birth to reign as an Emissary at a pre-chosen time. At that chosen time she must go through a lengthy ritual and then becomes part of their world. The Emissary is a truly powerful entity who has the physical powers of a vampire but is also immortal and has her own sorcery, since many of the chosen Emissaries in the past were practitioners of magic.

I wish I knew more about how the vampire lived, but I do not. I only know historically who some were. Most vampires today are not even versed in their own history – totally unaware of their family tree. They have no knowledge of the Enforcers and who they were. They are now bred to be survivalists in our world, and will do whatever is necessary to thrive, and if threatened will do whatever is in their power to come out the frontrunner.

Please beware once again that they are all around you. The more you learn, the higher level of protection you can give yourself and those you love around you. You are powerful, your words and thoughts are powerful... if you can think it, you can do it. Imagine it and it will happen... Auburn Starr

Not exactly the bedtime story I was looking to read. Every time I picked up Sara's journal I found out more that I did not want to know. I wondered if there were any good people left in the world. Up to this point she'd told me to be careful about everyone around me because there were many people in my life I could not trust, and now I find out that not only are there evil creatures like Blue Daemons lurking around, but vampires as well. Why could I not read something good in Sara's journal? Why was everything bad? I just felt like giving up; life was so confusing and I did not understand why I had to be involved. Could it get any more complicated? All I wanted were a few answers – like *why* I was having my dreams, and what it all meant and why I could not see the face of the killer. Why was Victor in my dream last night? That's all I really wanted to know, right now anyways.

I slept a few hours, waking and feeling a little better, refreshed from the sleep, but not from what I had read in Sara's journal. And I did not feel better about Victor, in fact, I wondered if I would even hear from him again. I cared about him more than I wanted to and I could not understand why he did not want to stay the night with me. I felt there was something wrong; maybe he was married, or involved with someone else. My imagination gave me several possible reasons, none of them reassuring.

Victor had rested during the day, but it was now evening and he was still feeling somewhat drained. Kala's dream last night had taken more of a toll on him than he had expected. Although it was to her just a dream, none of her dreams lately were *just* that. She was part of her dreams: physically, mentally and emotionally. All the feelings she thought she felt while dreaming, she did feel; it was real, as real as real could be. Victor was also very real in her dream last night. His telepathic connection to Kala had become stronger in the hours since being intimate with her; in fact, he had to struggle to sever the bond so he could allow his own mind to rest. Unfortunately, he sensed her frustrations while dreaming. He thought he could help by connecting with her so his presence would shock her psychologically into deserting the dream and waking up in her bed. It did not work the way he had planned. She dismissed him as being just a character in the dream, someone she had cast into a role. He had not anticipated that she could send him flying into the street with an electrical blast to his chest. He had underestimated her. He knew that his presence irritated her, and his constant interruptions were bothersome, but apparently he hadn't realized the extent of her irritation. He knew, though Kala did not, that knowing what happened to this dream woman would not change who she was, or who she would become. He did not feel it necessary for her to torment herself by investigating the dream any further. Victor just wished he could stop her from having the dreams... that would solve his dilemma.

From the moment he rose from his rest at dark he felt Kala's spirit within him. Her normal vibrancy was not there, and he spent a few moments linking his telekinetic powers to her, curious to find out why. He felt the uncertainties she had about him, her unhappiness regarding their encounter the night before, even an amount of regret on her part. He also detected feelings of love towards him that she had not had towards any other man, but tried to deny herself that as well. Kala's feelings saddened him. He did care for her and perhaps it was love, if that were possible for him – he had nothing to compare it to – and it had been so long since he experienced human love that the emotion was totally foreign to him. He sat on his futon with his head hanging low, hoping a phone call to Kala would ease some of her feelings about him. He wanted to visit her tonight, but was feeling a little out of sorts from her retaliation during the dream. His black T-shirt was charred and ruined, his chest and back were hurting from the open wounds received from the charge that she sent through him. It would have surely killed a mortal man. Under most circumstances, any injury Victor incurred would heal within a day, however, this one was different and he knew it. This was a wound inflicted by a power his body did not fully recognize and did not know how to mend; it would take several days to repair completely. It was Kala's power, her impending supremacy, which so deeply injured him. The quickest way to heal the wound would be to imbibe Kala's blood – the blood of an Emissary. Emissary blood was an all-purpose potion. Victor would not even think about that as an option, he would give his body the time necessary to heal itself.

There was a soft knock on Victor's door, and Nathan slowly walked in. Victor struggled to get to his feet, looking for another shirt to slip on over his hurting body to cover up his wounds. Victor held a shirt in his hands with his back turned as Nathan entered the room.

"Don't bother trying to hide them," Nathan spoke from the doorway.

Victor discarded the shirt onto the futon and turned to confront Nathan, allowing him to see the sores and blisters that would need time to heal. Victor's arms hung limply at his sides.

Nathan nodded, seeing the wounds for himself. "I knew you hurt. I could feel it. Now I know why. She did this?"

Victor slowly walked by Nathan and out into the loft area. He opened a window and pulled the blinds up on the other. "Yes, she did. I deserved it."

Nathan chuckled slightly, amused by his comment. "As mad as I have gotten at you; I have never caused you physical damage."

"You're right. You cause mental damage in me," Victor corrected him, pulling the cord on the blinds, and winced in pain. He sat down on the edge of the rocker and looked out over the city.

"So what happened?" Nathan asked, approaching Victor slowly. He knew he was hurt and sore, probably edgy as well, and he did not want to aggravate him further.

"You really want to know?" Victor asked.

"Yes. You got yourself hurt and I'm concerned. There is very little I can do to help, but I'd like to know what made her do this to you." Nathan stood across from Victor and leaned against the wall, awaiting the story.

Victor shook his head slightly. "Kala has been having a recurring nightmare. I suggested that the next time she has it to try and wake herself up by telling herself it was just a dream. Last night I knew she was having this nightmare and I thought I could snap her out of it if I walked into the dream. She was so focused on the dream, she tried to ignore me. I grabbed her arm and she forced me away; when she did, she sent this charge right through me. It was something else."

"Serves you right, interfering in someone else's dreams. I'm sure she didn't think you were actually there," Nathan scolded him.

"I agree. I thought I was doing something good," Victor insisted. "Guess I won't be doing that again." He looked down at himself.

"It's going to take some time to heal. Unless you know of another way," Nathan raised an eyebrow, knowing the only other remedy.

"Forget it," Victor growled. "I'm not using Kala for a cure-all." He looked up at Nathan disapprovingly.

"You could drop by, see her, put her in a trance, drink *only* what you need, and revive her before she even knew what hit her," Nathan suggested.

Victor shook his head adamantly. "No. I can't believe *you* even suggested that!"

"I know you slept with her," Nathan said accusingly.

"And your point?" Victor asked, brooding over his comment.

"None. I just know. Which means *they* know." Nathan planted the thought of the High Counsel back into his mind.

"I am not working for the High Counsel. I care for Kala because I care. What we do is our business, not yours or the High Counsel." Victor stood tall, his shoulders square and broad.

"If you don't think they will take her away from you if they think you are not acting in the best interest of *our* people; you are mistaken," Nathan warned, more like a democrat of the Counsel instead of his friend or Sire.

"What do you know, Nathan?" Victor asked. "If you know something you better be willing to tell me." He stared at Nathan warningly.

"I don't know anything. I just know what they *will* do," Nathan corrected himself and opened the door to exit.

"Any more information on Blue Daemons?" Victor asked his last question.

"They have some leads, and Kala is still being watched by Phillip's missionaries as far as I know," Nathan responded from the doorway.

"Well, where were they the night she had to fight one off herself?" Victor asked accusingly.

"I don't know, Victor. I am not in constant contact with the High Counsel," Nathan replied as he left. "Perhaps you should call them yourself if you are that concerned."

Victor sat alone for an hour or more when he decided he could not go an evening without speaking to Kala. Knowing how she felt about him leaving last night, and all her speculations, he just could not allow her day to end without hearing his voice. He hoped it would help, although his help lately had backfired on him.

I sat on the living room couch watching TV and nursing a beer, wondering if I should call Drew to see if he wanted to go out for the night. I was tired, but did not feel like sitting alone. I was not going to call Victor. It was not that I was mad at him, but I just felt that it was his responsibility to call me first, since we had slept together. I was not positive how he felt about me, and maybe it was an error that we had not talked about how we felt about each other before we had sex. I guess I thought he felt the same way I did about him, when I was not certain what his true feelings were. I have known my share of men in the past that dated many women and slept with them all, because that was the type of relationship *they* wanted, uncommitted to anyone for any reason. I didn't think Victor was like that, but I had that same feeling with other men in the past and was wrong.

When the phone rang I was pretty sure I knew who it would be on the other end. "Hello," I said, turning the volume down on the TV.

"Kala, it's me. How are you?" Victor asked in his usual smooth tone.

"I'm okay. Just watching some TV. You?" I asked evenly.

"Not feeling too well, tonight," Victor's voice fell a bit.

I felt bad for him. "Sorry. What's wrong? Sick?" I asked.

"Yeah. I guess I'll be better in a day or so. Maybe it's the flu or something," he sighed. "Hope you don't catch it, too."

"I'm pretty healthy; I think I'll be okay," I assured him.

There was a short silence before Victor spoke again. "I'm sorry I could not stay last night. I really wanted to. I wanted to wake up with you."

I didn't know what to say, and said nothing.

"I know it doesn't mean anything a day later. I just wanted you to know. I do care for you." His voice had a deep and convincing ring to it.

"It does mean something, and I care for you too," I replied softly, admitting to some of what I felt.

"I hope we can still keep seeing each other, you know, on nights I'm not working and you are free. I still want to be your date at the gallery opening." His voice sounded hopeful.

I did want to see him. I could not refuse. "I would like that."

"Good. So what are your plans for tonight? TV?"

"That's about it. I didn't sleep to well last night after you left," I told him.

"Sorry. Why?" he asked curiously.

"Had a lot on my mind and I had that stupid dream again, I hate it, it's so frustrating. This time it was a little different, and *you* were in it for some reason. I have no idea why. I guess you must have been on my mind." I laughed a little, trying to find some reasoning.

"I feel honored. You dream about me, too." He laughed along with me.

"I hope you feel better soon," I said. "At least for the weekend. It would be really wrong if you were sick for that."

"I'll be better. Don't worry." His voice grew stronger. "Oh, by the way, I had the radio on a little while ago and I heard your announcement for the Battle of the Bands. It sounds like it's going to be quite the event."

"Yeah, it's a big end of the summer bash. You can come with me if you'd like. It's huge. Runs all day," I explained.

"I'd like that. We can talk more about it when I see you again, tomorrow, the next night, whenever," Victor pointed out.

"Sure. I think I'll let you go. I'm going to do a few things and get ready for bed. You should think about doing the same, too." I encouraged him to rest to feel better.

"Okay. I'll talk to you tomorrow night. Sleep well. If you need me, call. I'm always here for you."

I smiled. "I will." I somehow knew he always had been.

Chapter 17

The night seemed long, like it was going to drag on forever. I had trouble sleeping and once I got to sleep staying that way was not easy. Maybe it was because I had a nap earlier in the day. Or maybe it was the disturbing feeling of not totally being alone even though the spot next to me on the bed was vacant. I had the distinct feeling of someone being with me, and no matter how many times I stretched over to turn my light on, I found the same thing; an empty room.

I had no fear tonight. I did not think I was in danger; it was just this annoying sensation of my personal space being invaded that stirred me and woke me frequently. Finally, some time in the earlier morning hours before the sky went through its change from night to dawn, I turned over in my bed and opened my eyes to see the hazy white glow of a spiritual image. I recognized it once again as being Sara, her flaming red hair giving her away. I sat up quickly, feeling the dry cool mass that surrounded her.

"Sara," I spoke softly, awed in the light of her otherworldly shimmer.

She smiled for a moment. "Please don't get discouraged."

"But I don't understand what you want of me," I pleaded. "Blue Daemons, people I can't trust, dreams; now Vampires." I sat on my knees in front of her semi-translucent appearance, needing answers.

"You have all the answers," Sara spoke gently. "It's the experience you lack."

"Experience? What experience?" I asked quickly. I felt my eyes beginning to fill with tears as my vision blurred; seeing her was agony when I could get no answers. "This is not fair, I cannot do what you ask of me."

Sara smiled serenely. "But you already are."

"I haven't done anything. I don't understand," I cried. "I need you. Or send me someone who can help me."

Sara reached out for the first time and touched my shoulder. A shock wave soared across my skin, making each hair follicle stand on end. "You have that," she stated.

"Sara, no one is helping me." I wiped some tears off my cheek. And just as I thought about asking her about my dreams and how they all fit in to the picture, the glowing sphere that surrounded Sara faded and with that so did she.

I sat in my bed crying for several moments, thinking that I must have the most dysfunctional life of anyone on earth. I did not think anyone's existence could have been quite like mine. I dared someone to compare.

I did not sleep a wink after Sara left. I lay in bed feeling sorry for myself until I got up finally to get ready for work. I was not even sure who I was any longer: DJ, art gallery owner, or wacko evil-magnet. It did not seem to matter. I was just very confused. I wanted things to go back the way they used to be, when all I worried about was how my hair looked on a Saturday night, or how I was going to lose those ten pounds I packed on over the winter months. Maybe confused was an understatement. I wish I had someone to confide in, someone I could tell this elaborate tale to, but who would believe me anyway?

"So, what are you up to tonight?" Drew asked me after my shift at the station, as he walked me out to my car in the garage.

"Not sure. I haven't really made any plans," I answered, walking beside him. I was tired.

"Did I tell you I took your advice?" Drew looked over at me as we reached my car.

"What piece of advice was that?" I asked, producing my car keys.

"I dumped Jennifer," he proudly announced, and a devilish grin spread over his boyish face.

"I don't recall telling you to dump her; I think I said something like you needed to make some choices to be happy," I said, thinking back, hoping I had not come across that way.

Drew leaned against the door of my car. "Trust me, dumping her makes me happy." He smiled. "Of course I'm on my parent's shit list now, but I think they can get over it."

"Well, I'm glad you are happy," I forced a smile. "Give yourself some time alone now; you probably need it. I know she was hard to take."

"I was kind of wondering if you and I could go out tonight," Drew said, suddenly shy, gazing at the dirty garage floor.

I knew this was coming. "Drew."

"Come on, one real date," Drew argued. "Can't you give me that? Unless you and Victor are tight." He pried for information.

"Victor and I are friendly; we do date, but..." I began to reply to his question.

"Okay then, what's the problem?" Drew interrupted, crossing his arms and facing me.

I opened my car door and flung my tote bag in. "No problem. Let me call you later on. Okay? I have a few things to do on my way home."

"So you are not saying no?" Drew asked cautiously, making sure he'd heard me right.

I sat in the car and started it. "I'm saying I will call you later on."

Drew was relentless in his quest to date me; it almost made seeing him on some days too trying on my nerves. I had never made it a practice to date more than one guy at a time, and currently I thought I was seeing Victor. My ordeal with Drew made me wonder how Victor was, and if he was still feeling ill. I had hoped in a selfish way he was feeling better so I had company tonight, or at least for part of the weekend. Come Monday I would be working at the gallery in the afternoons getting ready for the party, finishing up some last minute exhibits and deciding what kind of hours I would provide to the community. All in all, next week would be busy for me. And I still needed to find something to wear to the cocktail party.

Right around suppertime I called Victor to see how he was doing. If he was still sick I thought maybe I could drop by with some soda or soup or crackers.

"Hello?" a sleepy voice answered the phone.

"Victor, it's Kala. Did I wake you?" I asked warmly. I pictured him all cuddled up in his bed.

"Mmmm. It's okay. What time is it?" he inquired, yawning.

"A little after six. How are you feeling?" I asked.

"Um, better I think. Body hurts though. Achy," he complained.

I could hear him stretching on the other end of the phone, sighing as each joint and muscle was loosened and relaxed.

"Oh... that's too bad," I said. "Are you taking anything?"

"I'm okay. I'll be better soon."

"I guess I'll be spending tonight alone; or I'll have to find something else to do," I sighed in an effort to make him feel guilty.

"Don't make me feel worse than I do," he spoke lightly. "I wish I could spend time with you."

"I could drop by and see you," I offered brightly. "Bring you something to eat."

"I don't know if that's such a good idea. I'm still sick and I would hate for you to get sick too. I'm sure I'll be better tomorrow; we can get together then," Victor declined my offer to bring him a meal.

"All right, I understand. I'll find something to do tonight." I tried to be optimistic, thinking I could go out with Drew.

"If you end up staying in, call me later. I'm going to catch up on a little more sleep," Victor said tiredly.

"I will. Bye."

"Good bye."

After some internal debate I decided that I did not want to spend the evening alone. Being alone meant reading more of Sara's journal and I was not in the mood for reading about any more bad people or daemons or dead people. Sitting down to learn some spells and incantations was not something I had my heart set on either. I wanted to forget. I wanted to be the old me for one night. I wanted to eat, drink and be merry – and drink some more.

I think I caught Drew by surprise when I took him up on his offer of going out. I also think his version of going out and my version of the same were different. I tried to explain it was *just* for dinner, but I don't think I explained it well enough; perhaps over dinner we could chat about 'us' and what our relationship was all about.

Drew asked me to dress casual and said that he was going to make a few phone calls to get a reservation, and would pick me up at my place around 8:30 for dinner and drinks. I took a shower and put on a comfortable pair of jeans and a shirt with a pair of sneakers, waiting for his arrival.

Drew showed up dressed in jeans, a white polo shirt and boat shoes. His face, with its five-o clock shadow, looked ruggedly handsome. His brown hair was damp.

Our conversation was carefree in the car on the way to the restaurant. He had mentioned a new indoor, outdoor café bar that he wanted to try, and since the night was perfect, he thought it would be a great place to go. We were halfway through with our drinks in the bar when our table was ready, out on the stone patio. The hostess sat us at a green resin table, complete with umbrella and a flickering silver oil lamp. The restaurant was very busy, dealing with a rowdy Friday night crowd. It was difficult to hear our own conversation, even leaning across our table. Drew apologized for the excessive noise, saying if he had known we would have to put up with such a racket he would have picked another place for dinner. I assured him the noise didn't bother me; in fact, I was enjoying the boisterous atmosphere. By the time we'd had our dinner and our plates were cleared the patio area was all but vacant, with only a few other young couples finishing their dinners together, like us.

"Well, the food was good. But now I'm deaf," Drew chuckled, sipping his draft beer.

"Popular place," I added. "I think everyone moved into the bar."

"Then that's one place we won't be," Drew commented. "It's not that I don't like people, but *that* many people in a small place drives me crazy."

"I feel the same way. I was at Luigi's the other night and I could not believe how packed it was; I would hate to see how many people are stuffed in that building tonight," I rolled my eyes, recalling the feeling of being shoulder to shoulder.

"Wow, Luigi's. That's pretty ritzy," Drew's words dripped ice.

"It was the second time I was there. Quite impressive," I added, ignoring his tone.

"Let me guess. Victor?" Drew asked flatly, leaning back in his chair and holding his beer close to him. "And the bracelet?" He looked down accusingly at Victor's gift to me.

"Yes," I played with the gold bracelet, admiring the way the rubies caught the light from the oil lamp.

"Nice," Drew said, and dropped the subject.

We had a few more drinks, moving our conversation back to more neutral subjects. The summer night was quiet and we watched the cars drive by on the side street past the patio every so often. Nearby we could hear music being played from a city nightclub. I leaned back in my chair, sipping my margarita and talking to Drew about the radio business, trying to get a feel for whether he was cut out for it or not. As the time crept closer to midnight, we reluctantly decided to vacate our table and run the gauntlet through the crowded bar. Drew paid the bill and took my hand, guiding me into the café and around the mirrored bar, and out a secondary door to the sidewalk. We crossed the one-way street and walked through the parking lot to his car.

"How do you feel?" I asked Drew, rolling my window down on the passenger side of the car.

"Fine. You? Too much to drink?" he asked with a smile, putting the car into reverse and backing out of the parking space.

"Yeah. They were pretty strong," I replied, blowing my bangs off my forehead. I was sweltering and when I drank too much alcohol, my body temperature usually rose.

"Sit back and relax. I'm fine," Drew placed his hand on my shoulder and eased me back into my seat. "I can drive."

Victor was on the front porch having a late evening smoke as he often did. He sat perched on the railing, one leg extended out, the other dangling over the rail swinging back and forth leisurely. He leaned his shoulders lightly against the banister; his back was still sore from the other evening. His chest had healed slightly, but not as quickly as he was hoping it would. He did not want to put off seeing Kala another night; seeing her would make his spirits feel better. He also hated the fact that she was with Drew tonight.

He could not blame her for wanting to go out. Who would want to stay in? Who would not want her company? He could not approve or disapprove of who she went out with, but decided to tag along telepathically and see where they would end up.

He'd decided early in the evening that he did not like the way Drew looked at Kala; his look was full of adoration, like a puppy dog, yet there was something else, too. Victor could not put a finger on it. His instincts told him there was an underlying reason for Drew's attention, but Victor wasn't sure if it was his own possessiveness that was clouding his judgment. He did not have to try to figure out how just how much Drew liked her; his eyes told the entire story and Victor had become very good over the years at reading a lot about humans from their eyes. In connecting to Kala off and on through out the night, he could tell she had had to much to drink, but besides that he could also tell that she saw Drew strictly as a friend. Looking at Drew through her eyes was distinctly different from the way Drew saw Kala, which allowed Victor to breathe a small sign of relief from where he sat. Her heart for the moment was with him, which made Victor smile. He sent Kala a small psychic message on her car ride home that 'he had been thinking about her'. The thought was so tiny; she could not help but think of it as her own wishful sentiment that he was home doing the same – thinking of her.

Arriving back at the condo, I invited Drew in for a little while, trying to be hospitable. We sat next to one another on the couch and he placed a loving arm around me. I turned the TV on.

"I had a good night," Drew spoke up. "I'm glad we went out. It went well."

"We've gone out before, Drew," I reminded him. "Several times." I thought of all the places we had gone together over the last several months.

"Yeah, we have; but this was a little different," he smiled and kissed my cheek, playing with my hair.

"How was this different?" I asked, turning towards him.

"We never went out on a *date* before," he answered.

"Drew, about this date thing; I like you, I really do, and I like to go out with you, because we have fun; but as far as a relationship, I can't do it," I tried to explain.

"Why? I don't get it. I'm not seeing Jennifer any more; you said you thought of me as an equal, not younger. You still won't give me a chance?" Drew began to assume his pouty, childish manner.

"I have a lot going on in my life right now; I can't add any more confusion to it. I hate it when you do this to me. I hate it. You don't take my answers or explanations seriously. You try and make me feel guilty; it's not fair," I said angrily, and rose from the couch. "I'll date who I decide to date."

"Why won't you give me a chance?" he asked again, standing to face me.

"Drew, I think you'd better leave. I don't need this tonight. If you only knew what I have been going through." I turned my back on him and walked towards the door.

"Talk to me. Tell me what you are going through," he begged, following me.

"I can't," I opened the door wide, looking down, not wanting to look into his eyes for fear I would weaken and allow him to stay longer.

He shook his head. "I thought I understood you. I guess I don't. I have no idea what or who you are." He touched my shoulder on his way out the door.

I sat with a cup of hot tea in bed. I felt bad in a way for what I had said to Drew. But Drew did not take kindly to general hints, and for some reason he wanted to force the issue that he and I should start dating. Somehow he had in his mind that we were perfect for one another, and I could not seem to convince him otherwise. How he could think we were perfect for each other was beyond me. The feelings were very one-sided – his. I didn't like having to be so blunt with him, having to show him the door in order to make my point. Perhaps I was wrong to have gone out with him tonight; maybe I should have stayed home alone. I doubted that would have changed how Drew felt about me, and I would have had to deal with his continued pressing for a date. I only hoped that what took place between us did not destroy the friendship we had. That was up to Drew though, not to me.

I looked at the clock and thought it was far too late to call Victor, yet knew he was probably still up. He had left an open invitation to call him no matter what time, but with him being ill; I wanted him to have his time to rest. It would have been nice to talk to him, if even for a moment, before I pulled the blankets to my chin and fell asleep. I rejected the impulse to phone him. I was a big girl; I could wait another day.

Victor stood alone in his loft, resuming the painting he had started days earlier. He held his paintbrush firmly in his right hand and rolled the tip in crimson acrylic paint, saying his good nights to Kala from afar. It would have been nice to hear her voice, perhaps giving him the incentive he needed to keep working at his easel and helping him to forget his physical pain, and the twinge that tugged at his heart.

Chapter 18

I knew it was happening again. My eyes were shut; I was sleeping, but the dream was happening. The chill of the night drew me again into the dream's awful reality and I knew I was trapped. The raw coolness of the winter night enveloped me, chilling my body. I realized I was back in the body of the woman in the long gray wool coat. I felt the nasty itch of the wool against my skin, the deep ache in my lungs, the fever that meant I was ill, the coughing; I was hitching a ride again, a very temporary ride in the night.

As I began to walk down the icy, snow packed roads with no control over my legs or where I was heading, the thought of *home* filled me. I felt the need to get there, to be safe in my little red house. I walked as quickly as I had before, wanting to get out of the cold and to the relative safety of my home. The large horse drawn carriage carrying the man in black wheeled by on the dirt speckled snowy road. I began to glance behind myself, feeling as if something were closing in behind me, that I was being followed. Up to this point in my dream I had never been able to spot anyone, until last night, and by then it was too late. I reluctantly continued to play my role, checking around but seeing nothing. I could walk no faster and my lungs hurt, which seemed to have slowed me down. I still felt as if I was being stalked. I knew this feeling in my own life and I could certainly compare the feelings; I was being followed in the dream as well. My anger grew at not being able to confront the being lurking in the dark. "Who are you?" a voice from my body spoke. I was not scared; I knew that I would find nothing out of the ordinary until I reached my house. I thought ahead of the woman; I wondered if the man would return to the dream, would I be able to hear the conversation the two had? Would I finally know who killed the woman and why?

I could hear deep breathing. Not mine. I heard the rustle of birds in flight. No birds in the black night sky. "I'm warning you. Leave me alone!" I yelled. My lungs began to hurt again. "I may not know who you are, but I know what you are." Something reached out from the night and touched my long hair. I turned around, looking up into a nearby tree. Nothing, although last night I had waited long enough to be able to see something creep out of the shadows. Tonight I kept walking. The walking continued, as I knew it would, as I got closer to the end, to my destiny. It was now or never; the dream would remain the same as it had been; a cold, bloody death from an unknown killer, or I would face my killer head on and die knowing more. I heard footsteps behind me. I took two more steps, then quickly turned around, hoping to catch a glimpse of whatever it was.

"Oh my! Doctor, you scared me. I thought you were someone else," the words flowed from the mouth of woman in the long gray coat.

"Sorry Nerissa, I didn't mean to scare you. You caught me sneaking up on you," Victor smiled warmly at the woman in the wool coat, smiling just as he had to me many times.

Nerissa? The woman's name is Nerissa and Victor is a doctor? Though Victor was in my dream again I took small comfort from that knowledge. I continued to watch and listen to the two converse, not having much of a choice otherwise.

"I'm on my way in. I'm afraid I'm not feeling well tonight," she spoke softly, toying with her long dark hair. "Is there anything else you can recommend, Victor?"

He frowned. "I have done all that I can. It's tuberculosis; it's too far gone. Had I known sooner, maybe. Maybe not." He reached out with his gloved hand and stroked her face lovingly. "I would do anything for you, you know that."

She nodded, but felt her hope slipping away. It was just a matter of time before the disease took its toll and she would be dead. "I guess I can try a spell or two," she said, trying to make light of the matter.

"What if I were to tell you I had a gift for you?" Victor asked her in a cautious voice.

"A gift? What kind of gift?" Nerissa asked.

"Well, what if I told you that you and I could live together forever," Victor's voice was thick with sentiment, as if tormented by the thought of losing her soon.

Nerissa smiled. "It sounds lovely, but impossible. You know that." Nerissa had known for weeks her condition was getting worse, and realized that her time with Victor was limited.

"I have a gift that I can give to you. A gentleman I met gave it to me," Victor spoke quickly. "It is possible to live forever."

Nerissa shook her head no; she was not enjoying his game any longer. "Are you getting sick, too?" she asked sympathetically, reaching out her frail hand and touching the side of his face. "You aren't running a fever; you're stone cold!" she gasped.

Victor took her hand in his, guiding it under his coat and holding it against his chest. "Nerissa," he said softly. "My heart no longer beats on it's own."

She quickly snatched her hand from his. "Victor, what is going on?" she asked loudly, her voice cracking and congested.

"Nerissa. Please don't be scared. I have the gift of immortality. I want to give it to you. I want to live with you forever. I can't cure you. This is the only way we can be together. I did it for you. Please," Victor tried to reason with her.

I listened to the conversation and was speechless, even to my own thoughts. I watched and I listened and the more I heard, the more frightened for Nerissa I became. The more frightened I became.

"Victor, leave. I don't want to ever see you again. It is not right to live forever. You are evil. You are a monster. You are not *alive*!" Nerissa turned her back on Victor and began to walk away.

Victor grabbed her by her shoulders and turned her forcefully in his direction. "I will not go through this life by myself. I need you!" he roared at her. "It won't hurt, I promise you. You are in far less pain now than you will be later on with your diease."

She struggled with him and tried to pull away. "No, Victor! It's wrong! It's my time to die, but I will not go like this!" she screamed as he wrapped his arms around her securely and held her body close to his.

Victor said nothing more as he buried his face in her/my neck, his teeth slicing into her delicate skin. I felt the pain shoot through her body as my energy was drained out with hers. I realized she was losing blood; she was losing blood to Victor. Victor was taking her blood and drinking it. Victor – a vampire? He pulled his face away from her neck for a moment. "It's time. You must drink from me to live. If you don't you will die."

I felt her body limp in his, and although her body was dying, her mind was sharp and she refused to heed his words. I heard, *let me die,* echo inside my head.

"Nerissa, I won't let you die," Victor cried, shaking her in his arms. "You must drink from me. My blood will give you life."

Nerissa refused his dark gift once again. "Let me die," she begged weakly.

Victor sank his dagger like teeth into her one more time and drank deeply. I felt no pain; I felt nothing as I hung in Nerissa's body waiting for the conclusion.

The next thing I knew I was lying in the snow on my back, under the big oak tree. Through the branches I could see the black sky, and all the stars of the heavens; the crescent moon appeared bigger and brighter than ever. My body was cold, and a horrible migraine ricocheted in my mind, the shrilling tone that meant death to me, and a body that was paralyzed holding onto me, grounding me. Let me die already, I thought to myself. Just let it happen.

Just before Nerissa died, I found myself out of her body, not as a weightless spirit, but in full human form. In my own body. I stood soundlessly and motionlessly behind a hunched over Victor, who was kneeling in the frozen snow above Nerissa, his long shadow blanketing her in the moon's light. He was crying as he touched her still body, swearing he hadn't meant it to be like this. The last of her blood stained the snow around them. Finally, Victor stood up on his feet, swayed in grief, and backed away from Nerissa's earthly remains, his head hung low in guilt and grief. He turned and walked into me.

I gasped. I had no idea I was in the dream physically. I was not sure who was more stunned – him, or me. His eyes met mine and he looked deeply at me as if he thought he knew who I was, his eyes narrowing in thought. I held my breath, wanting to be invisible. I did not want to be seen. Without further notice Victor dropped his head back down, staring at his feet, then suddenly vanished into the darkness, leaving Nerissa and me behind.

I found myself sitting up in bed and stayed that way for the longest time, a pillow clenched to my chest as I thought again and again about what I had seen in my dream. I replayed it in my mind, and watched again as Victor took the woman's life – drank it away. Agonized, I tried to find some sort of explanation as to what it was that I saw and felt. My little voice was not so little and told me repeatedly to believe in my dream, believe in myself, and believe in what I felt. I came away from the dream knowing Victor was not what he seemed to be. The realization hit me hard – Victor was old, he was timeless, and he was a vampire. The woman in me felt cheated and lied to. Victor was someone I cared about totally. A man I made love to. How dare he even think about having any kind of relationship with me being the creature he was! How could he? What gave him the right? I re-read Sara's journal, the part about the vampires and Enforcers and how she described them as being totally human in almost every way and to not trust them; they were killers.

My anger grew as I thought about his stories of heartache and loss that he had fed me. I got dressed and, taking Sara's journal with me, drove to Victor's place, not caring it was the middle of the night. I drove past his house twice, indecisive. I held his business card in my hand, the one he'd given me the first time we met at the gallery. I was at the right house, he lived on the second floor; his car was in the driveway. I parked my car in front of the Victorian home and walked up the cement sidewalk that led directly to the wrap around porch, complete with a quaint hanging swing. The front door of the house was tall and ornate, resplendent with carvings; an oval stained glass window a majestic centerpiece. I stood there wondering when I was supposed to feel scared at confronting Victor. My heartbeat was normal, no pressure placed on me. Fear was not in me, yet. I was angry though, and betrayed. I wanted answers. I deserved answers. There were so many questions in my life and I was ready to hear answers from anyone or anything. My desperation for the truth mounted.

I opened the front door and stepped in to a large foyer. The walls were painted in burgundy and hunter green, a suspended brass lighting fixture casting a somber glow. A dark stained wood door to the left was, I assumed, Victor's downstairs neighbor. A towering staircase, poorly lit, led upstairs. I stepped slowly on each stair and quietly climbed the staircase. I don't know why I exercised such caution; I realized if Victor's senses were as good as Sara had said, he already knew I was here. By the time I reached the top steps I heard the door to Victor's loft unlatch and creak open, but no one was at the threshold to greet me. I clung to Sara's journal, feeling a sense of security with it, knowing she was with me. I pushed the door open completely with my fingertips and looked into Victor's home. Seemed ordinary.

"You could have knocked," Victor said from somewhere I could not see.

I started. "Didn't you know I was here?" I arrogantly asked, walking in, deliberately placing one foot in front of the other. I peered in one direction then the other as if looking for a train coming down the tracks, trying to follow the ring of his voice.

Victor emerged from an unlit back room with a glass of water in his hands. "Yes, I did," he replied, his tone mirroring mine. "Actually, I knew where you were and what you were doing the entire trip here. I can tell you the songs that were playing on your radio in the car. I can tell you that you passed the house twice before deciding to park, and I can even tell you that you put your shirt on backwards before you left your house."

I reached up and felt the tag of my shirt against my throat; I did have my shirt on backwards. The rash from my dream was there too, itchy and distracting. For a split second I wanted to leave. This was not a creature I was up to challenging tonight; he was superior to me; his mind and senses tuned to a degree I could not imagine. If he wanted me dead, I would surely be dead by now, but apparently he wanted me alive, at least for the moment. I held Sara's book tighter to me. "So, what are you?" I asked.

Victor stood several feet in front of me, his eyes scanning past me to something or someone behind. "Nathan, go downstairs. I'm fine," he ordered, and gestured with a slight nod to leave.

I turned my head around to discover a man standing with the utmost composure behind me. I had not heard him walk up the stairs. His eyes shone brightly, fixing me with a penetrating stare. I looked at him, noticing he was not as tall as Victor was, nor as handsome. He was dressed formally in black slacks and a button down shirt closed tightly at the neck. What I could easily tell now was he was just like Victor – a vampire. Now that I was aware of them, it was as if a switch had been turned on in me. I knew what I was dealing with; I could easily pick *them* out in a crowd. I got the distinct feeling Nathan did not like me. I could feel his animosity creeping into every corner of my body and soul. He was trying to intimidate me. I stared back at him, trying to ignore his strong psychic powers. He could just about read my mind. '*I don't like you either*,' I thought loudly in my head.

Nathan turned around without a word and began his descent to his own place at the foot of the stairs, refusing to react.

"Close the door," Victor ordered as he walked by me. He stared out the large picture window overlooking the city. "I heard what you said to Nathan, too," Victor said, raising an eyebrow and glancing at me.

I closed the door and asked my question again; this was more important to me than any non-verbal remark I had made. "So, what are you?"

Victor sipped his drink. "You know what I am." His eyes peered over his glass at me. I stood on the other side of the room; his eyes were wide and dark as they caught mine.

"I want you to tell me," I said firmly. I refused to look away from him. My handsome vampire friend.

"Are you just going to stand there, or can we sit and talk about this?" Victor asked, approaching me warily. He obviously had not been expecting me, dressed as he was in a pair of flannel boxers and a T-shirt.

"Depends. Are you going to hurt me?" I questioned as he passed by me.

His shoulders slumped as if my words had wounded him. "What do you think?"

"Victor, I don't know what to think anymore. You have no idea what my life has been like." I tried to contain my emotion as I explained, softening my defensive posture, but still clutching the book.

"I won't hurt you," Victor replied, walking into the kitchen. "Can I get you something?" He opened the refrigerator and took out a pitcher of water, refilling his tall clear glass.

"Like blood?" I asked sarcastically, taking several strides in his direction.

"Really? I wouldn't have taken you for that kind of person. It requires a certain taste," he shot back, letting the refrigerator door slam shut. "C'mon." He walked into a dimly lit room.

I followed but refused to enter without any lights. "It's too dark."

"We like it dark," Victor replied, turning a light on, but quickly softened it with a dimmer switch. "Have a seat." He motioned for me to be seated on the navy colored futon. "I promise not to bite."

I forced a smile at his comment and sat down on the edge of his couch; he sat down next to me but far enough away to not overcrowd me. For the third time I asked, "What are you?"

"I'm a vampire," he replied, sitting back, an arrogant tone in his voice as he waited for a reaction. "That is what you wanted to hear, isn't it?"

"No, what I want to hear is, how did you end up in *my* life?" I retorted. "How dare you come off being someone you aren't!"

"I never claimed to be anyone," Victor pointed out. "I'm sorry if that is the impression you got; that you think I misrepresented myself. I'm not going to apologize for who I am. I'm done with that game. I played that too long," he shook his head and closed his eyes.

"How can you possibly care? You walk into my life and pretend to be someone I can love. How can I?" I raged at him. I sat up on my knees facing him, demanding an answer.

"I ask myself that everyday. How do I care? Why do I care? There are so many of my kind that won't even share a sidewalk with a human being. They merely hunt you like deer and feed off you, thinking of you as no more than stupid animals." He shook his head, giving me no solid answers.

"What about that night we watched Interview with a Vampire together?" I asked him quickly, as it was a fresh thought in my mind. "You alluded to your kind, and you never once..."

"What would you have wanted me to say? Oh by the way Kala, Lestat and I have something in common?" Victor interrupted; he spun his glass around on the wooden arm of the couch as if amused with our conversation so far.

I bowed my head, not knowing where to take the discussion. I had so many feelings and questions swimming in my head, it was impossible to get them all out.

"Listen, I'm sorry," Victor began, softening his tone, and touching my knee. His hand was warm. "There is a lot you don't know that you probably should. It will take much more than a night for you to understand. If you ever understand."

I nodded, knowing he was probably right. "Let's start with my dream. Who is Nerissa?" I sat back down on the futon, giving my knees a break.

Victor hesitated and did not seem at all anxious to talk about her.

"You know I have been having these dreams, and you probably know what they are about," I guessed, still waiting for him to start speaking.

"Yes I do. It's a very sore subject for me. But it's something you need to know, and actually it's the very beginning of the story for you." Victor's eyes fixed on mine as he reached over and stroked my hair. "I never wanted to hurt you. Please believe me. I care for you, really, and I know that I shouldn't and that makes it even worse."

I took his hand. "Let's just try and get through this." I touched him not through affection, but to create a connection to help him tell his tale.

Victor took a long sip of water and sighed heavily before launching into his story. "I was born in 1774 into a family that already had two other boys and a girl."

I began to shake my head in disbelief as the hands of time began to rewind, trying to picture what his life was like back then.

"We weren't wealthy, but did well. When I left school I went on to practice medicine because I always had this desire to help people," Victor recalled his human life so long ago. "While I was a doctor I met Nerissa. She was a young woman like yourself whom I fell in love with while treating her for tuberculosis. After several months I realized, and so did she, that I could not help her, and her health was going down hill steadily." His voice grew quieter as the story went on. "I cared for her a great deal. She was very special to me. The thought of losing her was difficult for me. I had lost patients before and it was never easy." Victor looked in my direction sadly. "But the thought of losing her forever was too much for me." He shook his head and stopped, momentarily lost in ancient heartache. He breathed in deeply, trying to contain his emotions, and lowered his eyes to the hardwood floor in front of him. He rapped his fingers on the arm of the couch for a moment and then, without a word, he stood and walked out of the room, leaving me alone on the futon.

I wanted to believe that Victor's emotions were real and that they weren't some type of elaborate scheme to try and wiggle further into my heart, or worse, trap me and torture me for some kind of sick pleasure. I wondered while I sat by myself, if Sara could have been wrong about Victor. Not about who he was – he admitted to being a vampire – but said that he wasn't a heartless killer like many of his kind. Maybe he rode that fine line she spoke about. A fine line between good and evil, and he was the lesser evil. Maybe Victor was different. At the rate his story was unraveling it could be days before all my questions got answered. For once I called upon my inner voice, the voice I usually turned off or ignored or only heard from when I was at my wits end. I closed my eyes tightly, took a deep breath and concentrated. There was a chance I could be wrong, but at least I would know. I got up to find Victor.

I set Sara's book down on the couch, reluctant to leave it behind, but I did anyway. Quietly, I left the room and went after Victor, in the loft. I saw him sitting at the large window on the other end of the room, looking out over the city's nightly comings and goings. I approached him warily, not knowing what repercussions his temper could bring. He appeared in deep reflection. I placed a light hand on his shoulder and felt his body tremble in response, obviously startling him. I had not thought it was possible to sneak up on his kind. He turned his head towards me and looked up without a word. His eyes were deep and dark with mixed emotions: grief, anger, despair. I knelt down in front of him, not knowing what to say. He wasn't the man I thought he was; what could I say to him? Victor leaned forward in his chair and reached for me, his hands brushing through my hair, pushing it back and off my face. A chill coursed through my body as I felt his hand caress the side of my face; he was gentle and hesitant to continue for fear I might over-react to his sentiment.

"Victor, talk to me," I said gently, still feeling his fingers on my skin.

"I'm just afraid I'm going to lose you again," Victor confessed, looking down upon me. "It's been so long."

I shook my head, not understanding what he meant. "I don't follow you," I whispered.

"It's such a long story," he replied, pushing his chair back and standing, then taking several steps away from the window and me.

I stood awkwardly. "I'm sure all your stories are like that; you have lived so many life times."

"I have fears that you can't possibly understand," Victor said, taking his glass back into the kitchen.

I followed him. "I might be able to understand some. Victor, my life has been turned upside down recently; I'm finding things out daily I don't want to know about. I have a book in the other room that is an icon of horror for me." I pointed to the dimly lit room where Sara's journal was.

Victor poured himself another glass of water and took a clean glass out of the cupboard and did the same for me. I was not thirsty, but accepted it. Victor wandered back into the room and sat down heavily on the futon. I sat across from him on the other side.

"Listen," I spoke soothingly. "I know what I saw in the dream; I heard what you told Nerissa. I know what you tried to do was done out of love for her. She refused you," I recalled the dream as I remembered it. "I heard your words. I was in her body when you spoke to her."

"I became who I am today for her," Victor's voice was low and distressed. "Not only did I lose her that night but..." His voice trailed off and he did not complete his thought.

"What, what happened?" I asked him, trying to get him to proceed.

"Kala, you have to understand; I haven't talked to anyone about this in two hundred years. It's hard for me." Victor tried to make me understand how difficult it was for him to continue.

"Victor, I'm trying to understand," I pleaded with him. "I need some answers and you are the only person I know who might be able to shed any light for me." I slid over closer to him and grabbed his arm imploringly.

He took a sip of water before he spoke again. "First, let me go on record by saying I *really* did not mean to kill Nerissa. You were right by saying that she refused me; she refused the fact that I could give her immortality. But, I figured that if I just took her and forced it upon her that she would have to accept. I never dreamed that she would choose *death* over living forever. Knowing what I know now, I would not have taken the gift of immortality either. She was the smart one, always was. I was the stupid one, always thinking with my heart instead of my head," His eyes were fixed as he stared vacantly across the room.

"I'm sorry. It must be a terrible burden to carry with you." I thought about how horrible it must be to live day in and day out with regret.

He nodded. "That was only the beginning." He laughed woodenly. "As if I needed more."

"What happened after that?" I asked, still absorbing the saga.

Victor stretched out. "Well, Nerissa was more than just a woman I loved. She was supposed to be my people's next leader. I had no idea, I mean; I only had the gift a few days, I didn't know one sensation from another. I had no way of knowing what to look for or feel for. Everyone knew but me." He seemed frustrated with himself. "How was I supposed to know?"

I shook my head, confused. "What are you talking about?"

"Nerissa was someone who was pre-chosen to fulfill a role among *my* people. She had no idea she was picked; my people had not confronted her yet. It wasn't her time," Victor tried to explain. "I told you there were things you would not understand."

I thought a moment, my eyes shifting back and forth, remembering what Sara had written. "She was to be your Emissary?" I asked. .

Victor sat up. "What word did you use?" he asked quickly.

"Emissary." I replied again; he looked as if he had seen a ghost.

"How do you know that title?" Victor's voice shook slightly and his eyes were deep and dark upon me.

I picked up Sara's journal. "Sara left me this and mentioned your people. It's all in here. She warned me about you." My heart picked up its pace a little with Victor's immediate reaction to me.

"Oh... Sara," he replied softly. "I see. Then you know that an Emissary is pre-chosen, before birth, and is always a human female."

I nodded. "Nerissa was to be your next Emissary?" I asked him.

He nodded. "So, not only did I kill the woman I loved, but I also killed my people's Emissary. Emissaries are few and far between; every couple of hundred years one reigns with our Sovereign; together they lead our people. For the last two hundred years it has been just our Sovereign; so I guess you can see why my people were so angry with me. Still are," he sighed.

"But it was a mistake. You had no way of knowing," I said.

"I know. I know. But the High Counsel made its decision and that was to banish Nathan and me from our own society." Victor lifted his glass and took a long drink.

"Why Nathan?" I asked curiously.

"Nathan sired me. He gave me the gift of immortality which, according to the laws of the High Counsel, made him responsible for the demise of Nerissa, supposedly because he let me roam and run free on a killing spree," he sarcastically replied.

"Oh. So what is banishment exactly?" I asked, curious about his people.

"It means Nathan and I live in human society with virtually no contact with our own people. We have no say as to what laws are passed among our people, no privilege to vote; Nathan's political standing was stripped from him because he was an elder, and we were forbidden to Sire any others," Victor explained. "Because I only had been immortal for a few days when all this took place, it did not affect me as deeply as it did Nathan. He has been a very angry neighbor for many, many years."

"Wow ! Can you ever redeem yourself? It seems so harsh, unless I'm just not understanding your ways."

"When the next Emissary goes into power Nathan and I will have our rights restored," Victor assured me.

"That's good; any idea when?" I asked, hoping it was soon for them.

"Not sure... but one has been chosen and the High Counsel is aware of her. We will know shortly," Victor replied, suddenly sketchy with the details.

"Hmmm," I thought out loud.

"There's more," Victor offered quietly.

"What's that?" I asked, thinking, what more could these people take from him?

"Do you believe in fate?" Victor asked.

"I think it exists. Sara has referred to it often in her journal."

"And reincarnation?" he questioned.

"Oh sure, I think that's possible," I answered, thinking of the stories that supported it over the years.

"I know something about you that you need to know," Victor said bluntly. "You have to promise to hear me out."

My heart skipped a beat; I sensed I was not going to hear good news. "What?"

Victor turned to face me and cupped my hand in his. "The first time I met you at the gallery you caught me off guard. I had walked by your shop many times and never had such an odd feeling of familiarity as I did that night. I felt drawn to walk in and face whatever it was that made me feel the way I did. When you came out from the backroom, I was shocked." He recalled the evening with a bewildered spark in his eye.

"Why? I had never met you before." I remembered the evening well, thinking how handsome he was.

"That's right. You had never met me, but I had met you in a previous life – one of yours," he said pointedly, and waited, unsure of my reaction. He held my hand tightly, afraid I might get up and walk out on him.

I didn't know what to say. I sat silently, needing to hear more. I was not convinced of what he was saying and so was not as overwhelmed by his words as he probably thought I would be.

He looked at me for a moment before he continued. "I know this because of a very strong bond I once had with that person, emotionally, physically, and through blood. Seeing you made many feelings surface; ones I had put away two centuries ago; you and Nerissa share the same spirit. I am not mistaken. I confirmed that the night you cut your hand on the ladder and I tasted your blood; only I would know the taste of Nerissa's blood, and you are one and the same."

I pulled my hand out of his and nervously scratched the rash I had on my chest. I ran my fingers across the side of my neck and grimaced at an area under my ear. "I guess that would explain the dreams," I thought aloud, but was still confused over why this meant so much.

"What's wrong with your neck?" Victor asked, leaning over.

"That rash... from the wool in my dream," I replied. I touched the area near my ear again and grimaced.

Victor guided my head to the right and looked at the rash and the area under my ear that was painfully annoying. "I'm sorry that I hurt you," he replied remorsefully, staring at my neck.

"How did you hurt me?" I asked, trying to stop myself from scratching it. I put my hands in my lap.

"You have some puncture wounds on your neck, from the dream," Victor replied, looking away in guilt.

"Damn dream is very real," I muttered.

"You don't have to tell me," he said. "So now you know about your dreams and Nerissa."

I nodded. "I'm hoping the dream goes away."

"It probably will, now that the dream has been completed. I feel it's my fault you have been suffering from them. I understand why, I think." Victor scratched his head and pulled the tie out of his hair, letting it tumble wildly down.

"How is it your fault?" I inquired, not seeing the connection.

"The bond between us has gotten stronger – it started with a kiss and escalated from there..." He searched for the right words. "It has to do with bodily fluids: kisses for instance – deep kisses. An exchange of bodily fluids can be very strong, not just blood, but saliva... semen; it caries clusters of information the body processes or discards. Your body tried to process one of the quandaries I have lived with for a long time. An event that is so ingrained in my mind and spirit it *is* me."

"I see." I had a hard time dealing with everything he was throwing out at me. "There is something else, isn't there?" I felt he was keeping something from me.

"Yes."

"What is it?" I asked, wondering what on earth it could be.

"You are my people's next chosen Emissary," he answered flatly.

I scrunched my face up as if I didn't understand him.

"I say again, you and Nerissa are the same, she was to be our last Emissary; you are our next Emissary. I'm not making this up. She never served her time in power, and now you must. It's a second chance, if you will. We knew you would come. We just didn't know when." Victor tried to make me fully understand.

"I don't get it. I'm just *someone*. I had no knowledge of your people before now. I'm not some supernatural freak; I'm a DJ... an art gallery owner. What do your people want from me? This is impossible," I brooded, standing and crossing my arms. I paced. "This is ludicrous."

Victor rubbed his forehead. "I agree. You are right, but you have been chosen."

"So what does this mean? What if I refuse? What then?" I asked, firing questions at him. I felt my anger returning.

"Honestly I don't know. Please calm down," Victor asked. "I did not mean to upset you. But knowing all this will help you, I hope."

I walked out of the room, speechless. I went to the window and stared out over the city. Within a few minutes I felt Victor behind me. "I know this is hard for you to accept. But the powers you don't think you have, *you have,* and if you think about it, you'll know you have something special that other people don't have."

"Like Blue Daemons chasing me?" I asked harshly.

"I was there the night you fought the Daemon off; that was a pretty damn impressive black hole you conjured up," he said admiringly.

I shot him a dirty look. "Thanks for all the help that night. I was scared to death!"

"Your powers will continue to grow – like that hand thing you do with fire. You've got to control that. Someone is going to get hurt." Victor laughed quietly. "In time you will learn about your powers; there is help."

I began to scratch my neck again, feeling tense and nervous. "Where do the Blue Daemons come from?" I asked, turning around to face him.

"They are summoned by others with powers who control them," Victor replied.

"Who would send them after me?" I asked, continuing to rub my neck; it was so sore.

Victor grasped my hands. "Stop touching your neck. Your rash won't go away any faster and it won't make your neck feel any better either."

"I can't help it; I'm a wreck." My voice trembled as if I was going to break down any minute.

"You are safe here whether you know it or not." He continued in a softer tone, "I would never hurt you, or let anyone else hurt you; I mean that. I would sacrifice my life for yours at any time."

I looked up at him, tall, strong and immortal, and did feel a measure of security, though a little wariness as well.

"About your neck; I can help you if you want. If you trust me that is." Victor pushed some hair away from my ear and lifted it away from my neck.

"How can you make it feel better?" I asked. I wasn't sure I trusted him entirely; I searched his eyes for a sign either way.

He looked down at me while he massaged my shoulder. "The same way I did when you cut your hand on the ladder."

I was not sure I wanted his mouth anywhere near my throat. "Oh," I said quickly.

"It's up to you; it should be better tomorrow if I do nothing." He backed away, letting me decide without any pressure.

"Promise me," I asked him. "Just promise me you won't hurt me if I let you help."

He shook his head. "I won't hurt you." He reached out and drew me gently to him. "Just relax; it won't hurt at all. Put your head over to the side." He gently guided my head back and to the right, exposing my entire throat and neck. I felt incredibly vulnerable. "Close your eyes... try to relax," he urged me and combed his fingers through my hair.

I can't believe I'm letting a vampire at my neck, I thought, the pit of my stomach hopping with anxiety.

"I heard that," Victor whispered in my ear. I felt his warm moist breath against the sensitive skin of my neckline as he placed his lips delicately against the wounds that caused me such discomfort. His tongue tenderly lapped at the sores with a sensation so overwhelming I thought it would take my breath away. I gasped, not sure of what I was feeling; it was foreign to me. His hands cradled my head, and I felt his fingers manipulate my hair. He held me firmly as we sank to the floor, maneuvering so I was on my back and Victor was on top of me. I placed my arms against his sides feeling his soft cotton T-shirt underneath. Not only did he did take the pain away, but the sensation of him healing the wounds was remarkable. It felt as if he was taking *all* my pains away. I was silent and relaxed in his arms, sated to a point I had never reached before... ever. What was he doing to me?

"Take all my pains," I whispered in a voice so soft I was not sure even he could hear it. I began to think about all the things in my lifetime that had brought me agony. I thought about Victor not being human, Sara's death, my missing brother, the split of my parents and the abandonment that happened afterwards, even the loss of the family dog when I was a tiny child, everything and anything. I wanted it to all go away. I wanted to feel free from the stress and the hurt that had been with me, much of it for a very long time. My reaction to what Victor was doing was like a drug – an immediate addiction that gave me a false high. I felt a freedom I had never had with myself. Although I had a hard time understanding what was going on, I knew I enjoyed it. Victor continued his healing ritual.

I realized Victor was discovering my past, as he moved in my mind and memories; I ran into him everywhere within the confines of my head. It was frustrating until I realized he was doing some house cleaning for me and was looking for all the dirt that bothered me; he was vacuuming my subconscious of its pain and anger. This was therapy that sitting on a doctor's couch had never produced for me. Victor stopped his wet tongue from licking my neck but substituted his lips instead as he kissed me repeatedly – throat, chin, face, lips, ears, neck – all of which was extremely stimulating. My hands stroked him continuously. My inner silence was broke by Victor's voice; he did not speak verbally but sent me a mental message, "*I care for you so much, please accept me for what I am.*"

I wanted to, I really did. He was someone who made me feel good and made me feel things I had never felt before with anyone. What were the chances I'd ever find someone quite like him again – in my mortal life?

The next moment I was sitting up in my bed. How did I get home? Did I ever leave? I was fully dressed and lying on top of the bed covers with Sara's journal next to me. I looked around the room, disoriented. I checked the time – 6: 43 in the morning. I pulled my bangs away from my forehead and thought hard about the last moment I could fully remember; I touched the side of my neck. The phone rang. I nearly launched out of my skin it scared me so. I grabbed for the phone on my nightstand. "Hello."

"Hi. You okay?" Victor asked. "I didn't want you to worry."

"I was a little puzzled when I woke up," I admitted, still feeling as though my brains were scrambled.

"I just wanted to get you home before the sun came up. It wasn't a good idea for you to stay here, at least not when I wake up in the evening," Victor explained.

"How long was I out?" I asked. "What happened?"

"An hour or so. I think you just got *real* relaxed on me," he chuckled.

"Sorry," I apologized for nodding off. I stood up and walked down the hallway carrying the phone, trying to get my bearings back.

"Don't apologize. I'm actually very pleased that you are able to get that comfortable with me, knowing what you do," Victor spoke matter of factly.

Through my fog I remembered what Victor was. "Yeah... right," I replied.

"Why don't you get some sleep; I need some rest too. We can get together tonight and finish our talk. Your place is better. I have some questions for you too," Victor stated.

"That would be fine." I walked to the sliding glass door that led to the deck. I looked out over the grounds; the sun was coming up over the trees.

"Let's say seven; that should work out."

"Okay. See you then."

"Kala... thank you for handling this so well. You have a lot of special qualities I know you don't see; but I do. You have a good heart and you are very understanding. I appreciate it. I wish more people could be like you." Victor seemed sincere in his assessment.

"Thank you. Get some rest. I'll see you tonight."

I hung up knowing our story would continue, but how many chapters we would complete was still in question.

Chapter 19

I slept the better half of the day away. I was exhausted and had not rested so soundly in what seemed like a very long time. You would think, under the circumstances, that I'd be an insomniac. Once I hung up the phone with Victor and crawled under the covers I was fast asleep. It was late afternoon when I woke up; refreshed and famished. I threw a TV dinner in the microwave and then sat out on the deck having my first meal of the day. I brought my usual reading material with me – Sara's journal. I picked up where I'd left off.

Remember that everyone has a role in life, and it does not always revolve around his or her own. Each person and being has a purpose, although that purpose may not be clear; others can help guide them onto the path they were meant to walk upon.

It is sometimes easier to live your life through someone else's than it is to live the one you have, to be the person you are. In a lifetime, no matter how long or how short the path you were meant to walk can cross over others, it is normal, but in crossing over, you must eventually cross back onto your own. Crossing paths is a way of learning, developing and fulfilling the self.

As I have already mentioned, Enforcers were at one time bodied souls that guarded the realms from shifting evils. These Enforcers left their stations and crossed over to another; in doing so they created an inevitable situation that would require them to cross again – someday.

With the power of the Amulet, and the help of others who will cross into your path, you will begin to make the inevitable happen. You will know the cross has started when you begin to learn and develop a power you never had. The end result, I promise, will be fulfilling.

You need to help correct the wrong that took place so many years ago. It has taken this long, and many human lifetimes, to manifest a plan to get all the key players in place in order to correct the deterioration that occurred. Not everyone will be helpful or willing to allow the crossover to happen. Some people have used their powers in society in an abusive manner, and have altered life to the way they think best. There will be great resistance towards you, and remember, even though your path may cross another during the process of repair; you must always cross back in order to complete what you have started.

Your greatest ally will come from a being who has been misguided and exploited his entire immortal life, punished for something he did although harsh, put him on a path of learning, development and eventually with hope a fulfillment. This creature will be marked with a sign on the body, an upside down 'V' with a 'C' crossing over it. The 'V' stands for the 3 steps in a lifetime... Birth, the beginning; Life, the peak; and Death, the ending. The 'C' crossing over represents the transition from the world we live in to the after life.

As I read those words I immediately thought of Victor. It sounded like his life, as I knew it. This was something Victor needed to read. I felt as if Sara's words were not only speaking out to me but to Victor too, describing his immortal life possibly from the beginning. Maybe Victor was on my side after all. I dog-eared the page and made a mental note to show it to him tonight.

Shortly after sunset, Victor showed up at my place looking as handsome as ever. We went out on the deck so he could enjoy a cigarette; he was too polite to smoke in my house. We both sat down in deck chairs, and I placed my feet against the rail.

"I don't exactly know where to start my conversation with you tonight," I smiled uncomfortably, rocking back and forth in the chair.

Victor lit a cigarette, inhaling deeply and exhaling out his nose as he stretched out. "It's not a debate; we have all night. Can't we just enjoy each other's company and just talk about whatever comes up?"

While that suggestion made sense for two ordinary people in the beginning of a relationship, it did not fit our situation, at least as far as I was concerned. Though I wanted to trust Victor, to love him even, there was a part of me that coldly pointed out 'he is a Vampire, a creature.' I just could not quiet these feelings, which made me uncomfortable in his presence. I toyed with my birthday bracelet and wondered if he bought it for me because he wanted to, or if he felt it the 'human' thing to do for the event.

"You are full of indecisiveness tonight," Victor remarked, flicking the ash from his cigarette and putting his arms on the tempered glass table. He looked calmly at me. "I don't blame you at all for any of the feelings you have. The more I thought about you and me while I was alone and resting, the more I realized that our people don't belong together. Your feelings are normal. In many ways, thinking that what we have can continue is far beyond crazy, no matter how I feel about you."

His comment aggravated me. "I don't want some sort of trend over the last thousand years to tell me what I can and cannot have. It seems lately I am being told I can do whatever it is that I want, that I have the power and I need to believe in it. *If I can think it, I can do it. Imagine it and it will happen.* If our relationship is something I want to continue, it will." I recited one of Sara' verses from her journal to him. My tone was stubborn and sulky.

He raised his eyebrows high on his forehead. "Keep that attitude; you will need it to live among my people. Just be sure you can back it up." He relaxed back into his chair again and took a puff off his cigarette, staring up at the lavender sky.

I honestly did not know where that fierce part of me came from; it was something he said that set me off. I continued to spin my bracelet around my left arm, deep in thought.

"I bought it for you because I wanted to; not just because it was your birthday," Victor commented as he watched my fingers fondle the piece of jewelry.

Without picking up my head, I rolled my eyes in his direction, wanting to feel as comfortable with him as he did with me; but of course he was immortal and practically indestructible from where I sat. How could I feel comfortable in his presence? I felt so inferior. "I know that you know what I feel, and you think I cannot stop you from doing that."

"How do you know? Have you ever tried to stop me?" Victor asked me, not moving in his chair.

I sat up and turned my chair to face his. "You are a lot stronger than I am. I do not stand a chance against you and you know that." I was honest with my feelings. "Though I hate it, I might as well be submissive."

Victor shook his head. "Where is the person who just a moment ago told me that if she wanted the relationship to continue it would? Now you have crawled back into this shell to hide again."

I shrugged.

He sat forward. "Listen to me. If you are going to be part of my people, you are going to need to stand up for yourself. You need to stop thinking of us as powerful creatures you cannot fight; you can fight us. How do you think we got as strong as we have? People like you have allowed us to grow. We have taken your emotions and used them against you. Fear is a powerful weapon. In many ways we respect those of you who do stand up to us; it's a thrilling element to see in a life form. The difference with you is you can make things happen. Once you believe that you can, you will and I hope I'm on your good side when you get there." Victor reached out and held onto my arm, reassuring me.

"I don't know how to get there," I spoke as though I were lost. Sara's words also left me lost.

"You aren't going to 'wake up' there; it's a process, a road to follow; you must learn things. You will know when you are on the road. You will do things today you couldn't yesterday. But you have to push yourself to learn more. Like the black hole or the surge of fire, or the electricity you are able to let loose upon people; you need to work on those powers and learn to control them," Victor tried to explain. "What do you know you can do?"

"Not much," I thought aloud. "The black hole was a spell left to me by Sara to get rid of a Blue Daemon, and the fire thing only seems to happen when I get really mad or scared. I have very little control over that."

Victor scowled. "Then you need to get control quickly! Not tomorrow. Tonight! Do you have any idea what damage you can cause people with powers like that?" As he berated me, he put his cigarette between his lips and began to unbutton his denim shirt. I watched his fingers move downwards, pulling the fabric open to expose his chest; large red welts with deeper red areas and blackened scars marred his lower chest and upper abdominal area. "Remember the night I was in your dream. The night I asked you to stop dreaming and you pushed me away? Remember the surge? This is left from what you did; it looks the same on my back. It was much worse the night you did it; it takes time to heal. That's why I could not see you those few nights; I honestly was not up to the company, anyone's company." He leaned back, allowing his shirt to stay open as a reminder to me.

I didn't know what to say. I recalled the force I hit him with in the dream, but that's all I thought it was – a dream. I did not actually think I hurt him by doing it. "Victor, I'm very sorry. I had no idea that it was really you," I tried to apologize as my eyes scanned his wounded body regretfully.

He shrugged. "I know. But you could have easily killed a human. Normally I can heal within a day or so, but because of your bloodline, and your destiny as Emissary, the wound is much worse and takes much more time to heal. Punishment from an Emissary was meant to hurt, and to last as a reminder."

"What can I do? I'm very sorry," I repeated, rubbing his knee.

"I will be fine. But you can see why you need to control the powers you have. You can hurt someone badly. Anger and fear are very powerful emotions to control. You need to learn." Victor put his cigarette out in an old empty planter pot on the table.

My feelings and emotions began to merge again, and I felt an amount of love for him rekindle. I had not meant to injure Victor. I never would have done it knowingly. Even though Victor was who he was, he never deserved any attack by me; he was always the gentleman. "Victor, who are you really? I mean, the Victor I know, is that really you? An artist? A teacher? Are those just a front to cover the fact you are not human, or is that who you really are?"

"Just because I am not human now does not mean I don't carry my human characteristics with me. I was a doctor once because I cared about people. When I received the dark gift of immortality, for obvious reasons I gave medicine up. I was a rebel of my kind for many years after the banishment from my society. You might hear stories about that someday. Nathan had a huge amount of resentment towards me and we did not get along at all. For a while I even allied myself with some of the Blue Daemons – working with them and their empty cause of hurting and killing humans for a larger, more evil power. One day Nathan helped me see that what I was doing was wrong, even for our kind it was wrong, and that it was time to put the anger and loneliness behind me and start over with him. He would show me. It took a long time before I finally controlled my anger; I was mad at humanity, at Nerissa, at Nathan, at the High Counsel, and I was mad at myself. It took a long time, but I did it," Victor recalled. "I have lived all over Europe at different times; I traveled to the United States and back, and finally, about thirty years ago, Nathan and I settled here. I didn't really start picking up a trade or a hobby until the last fifty years or so; I was always creative in choosing my passions – music, playing the piano, writing for a newspaper, art, drawing, painting and now teaching. These things complete me. I have been a very empty person, Kala. I guess not being able to sire anyone over the years was harder on me than I thought. I have no family to ease the loneliness, or teach my lifestyle to," Victor said sadly, recalling the loneliness of his life. "This is me; it's too hard to be someone else, especially for as long as I have been around."

I felt his story was the truth. Maybe I could relate to the emptiness of not really having my own family, but it seemed genuine. "So, I guess the first thing you will do once you can is sire someone so you won't be alone anymore," I felt a pang of jealousy travel through me.

He shook his head. "I don't have any immediate plans to do anything. The burden of not being exiled any longer will be a relief I have never had." He took his cigarette lighter out of his pocket and tapped it on the glass table.

"Can I ask you something else?" My voice was small, unsure of his response.

He nodded. "If I know the answer I will give it to you." He played with the flame on the lighter.

"What are *they* going to do with me?" I asked, meaning the High Counsel and the position of Emissary. "If it is true that I am supposed to be this next person in power."

"What do you mean by 'do'?" Victor replied. "Are you asking how you become Emissary?"

I nodded. "Yeah, and what happens afterwards."

He sighed. "From what I have been told, when a pending Emissary has matured to a level that the High Counsel feels is appropriate, they will send for her. On her return to their Manor she will spend time honing her powers with chosen members of the High Counsel, those who have abilities like the pending Emissary. Once the High Counsel agrees that the Emissary is at her highest level of power, they will have a ritual that will bridge her over to our people. She will join the Sovereign to help him reign over the population," Victor explained the process as simply as he could.

"What kind of ritual is it?" I asked, thinking about what some of the Wiccan rituals were like, and wondered if they were the same.

"I am not certain. I know that the Sovereign himself will be the one to embrace, or sire you," Victor stated.

"I have to become one of you?" I asked in astonishment. "I have to die?"

Victor seemed taken back by my tone, and my questions. "Yes. How could a human rule over a race of people she knew nothing about; a race she wasn't a part of?" He was perplexed that I had not figured that information out on my own.

"Victor, no offense, but I don't want to die! What if I refuse to become this Emissary?" I asked desperately.

Victor placed his fingers over my lips to quiet me. "Let's talk inside," he whispered.

"But..."

"Shhh," he tried to hush me as he slid open the door and extended his hand for me to follow him. I stood reluctantly and placed my hand in his. Once inside, with the glass door shut behind us, he spoke again. "The role of Emissary is very important to my people," he said, trying to underscore the importance of his words.

"Oh is it?" I asked sarcastically. "Or is it just important to you and Nathan?" I broke free from his grip, stepping away several feet and placed my hands on my hips.

His eyes stared unflinchingly at me. "Of course it's important to Nathan and me, but our people look towards others to guide us. Like you have a Congress, a President, Governors and Mayors. You don't always like what they say, but without them your society would fall apart."

"Well, last I knew, I was an American, a human being paying taxes, and abiding laws. I am a living person and with that I have rights! I want to continue to live my life the way I want to live it, not the way a community of stiffs thinks I should and go on a liquid diet because of what these people believe to be their standards and guidelines. It's bullshit! They can't make me!" I argued. "You can't make me. If that is the only reason you continue to come around is to make sure the 'goods' get delivered, you can just leave. I'll take my chances in dark garages with more Blue Daemons. I'll practice every spell Sara left me until all I have to do is lift a finger to accomplish it. I'll find a way to fight back, even if I have to create a way to raise the sun at three AM when all you bastards least expect it. I'm not going!" I shouted at him, turning my back and walking into the kitchen. All my yelling had made me thirsty and I wanted a drink. Victor did not follow; he remained alone in the dining area where I had had my fit. I opened the refrigerator and took out a bottle of Diet Coke. I got a glass from the cabinet and poured myself a drink. My hands were trembling I was so angry with him, and with myself for letting any of this happen. I stood fuming near the sink, gulping my soda. I caught Victor out of the corner of my eye silently entering the room. I turned quickly. "Listen, I'm pissed, so stay away from my hands, okay!" I wanted to prevent what could happen otherwise; at least I was trying to be responsible.

He held his hands up in mock surrender. "I know you are mad. And when I think about where you are coming from I do understand. It's been so long since I have been like you – human, that I forget what it's like to make the change to be someone like me. I can understand your resistance." He put his hands down slowly. "It's not my place to take you to the High Counsel. Remember that I'm still banished. I am here with you because I want to be."

I spun around, still filled with anger. "But you will allow them to just take me. You will feed me to the wolves even though I don't want to go. My feelings don't count at all here, do they? I'm just a lowly human. Perhaps I should not care, since our time together is limited whether we like it or not."

"Of course your feelings count. But I have no control over what the High Counsel does," Victor tried to explain, still keeping his distance.

I walked past him into the living room. "It's obvious it will be just me alone once again. I'm the only person I can trust to try and find a way out of this. It's not like I can expect you to help, or trust you to protect me. That's obviously not your style. You have more to gain making sure I become Emissary than not." I sat on the couch and placed my drink on the table; leaning forward, I put my head in my hands. What had I gotten myself into? "I know you can't wait to get Nathan off your back and move on with your life. Even if it means an end to mine."

Victor sat down on the couch, careful not to get to close. "Let me take some time and think about what our choices are." He rubbed his head in thought. "The High Counsel will not want you right away; you are nowhere near ready with your powers. You have a lot to learn." He sighed, not knowing what else to say. "If you become Emissary, I lose you and you lose your human life. If you don't become Emissary because you refuse, they will hunt you down and make you Emissary against your will. Either way I will lose you and you will lose your human life. If I try to protect you and hide you, they will hunt us both down, and when they found us they would surely kill me and force you to be Emissary any way. So, I lose you and my life, and you lose again. Not many good options." He leaned back on the couch and tried to make himself comfortable despite his wounds.

I shook my head. "I guess I better get used to being dead." I picked up my drink, my hands still shaking, in anger or fear. I was not sure this time.

"What does Sara say in her journal about you becoming Emissary?" Victor questioned.

I looked over at him. "She never says that in her book; only tells me about your people – vampires, Enforcers and that there is an Emissary and Sovereign."

Victor raised his eyebrows. "Enforcers? What is that supposed to mean?" he asked curiously. "I have never heard that term used before in talking about my people."

I stood to retrieve the book from the dining room table. "She mentions that most of your people are not aware of what your roots are. You can read what she wrote. I have a passage that I wanted you to read any way." My trembling hands opened the book to the section on Enforcers and handed it to him, pointing out the dog-eared page.

I sat quietly, allowing Victor plenty of time to read. He read quickly, silently, and when he was done he shut the book. "I don't believe it."

"Why?" I asked, taken back at his reaction.

"It doesn't make any sense. I would have heard the word 'Enforcer' sometime in the last two hundred years from someone. The whole idea of an Enforcer between dimensions seems like something out of a super hero comic book or something," Victor scoffed. "And the part about a troubled creature being your greatest ally: although I'd like it to be true, and I know you think it's me, but I have no markings that make me that person. I'm sorry."

"Fine," I huffed. "But Sara's words are all I have to go on right now. She was right about the spell with the Blue Daemon. She also said I had powers that could be very great." I took the book back from Victor and held it in my lap. "She wrote this for me to find in case she died. Victor, she died protecting me against something. You and I both know what that something is; it is your people and this role of Emissary. There is no other explanation. She has visited me twice since her death to instruct me on these issues. I believe in her, Victor. I am sorry that you don't. It seems to me as if Sara has one road she wants me to follow, and your people have another; I will always follow Sara; I have to."

"Kala, I'm not saying Sara is a liar. What she has written may be true to an extent. I will certainly ask Nathan about the Enforcers and get his reaction. You may still meet this ally of yours as well." He never once asked me about my visit from Sara.

I set the book on the coffee table and thought about her.

"She left you many lessons to improve your psychic powers in that journal. Have you tried any of them yet?" he inquired, looking down at the book.

"Not yet. I really need to." I felt a wave of guilt run through me as if Sara herself was asking that very same question.

Victor leaned over and picked up the journal and skimmed though the pages. "Hmmm. *Lesson I: Moving an Object (please start small)*," he read out loud, then continued to read it to himself. He stood up, walked over to my mantle and plucked a green candle out of an iron candlestick, then sat down next to me, putting the candle on the table across from me. "We have all night."

"What do you know about this stuff?" I asked him, offended he would try any of Sara's lessons with me. After all, he did not believe in her.

He stopped reading. "I know as much as you do. Prove to me you want to be human. Prove to me you want to fight for your humanity. I want to see you strong!" he declared. "Mental strength. Let's work on that."

I sat next to him, feeling annoyed instead of relaxed in his presence.

"All right, I want you to get comfortable; take your time. Close your eyes, whatever," he told me, placing his finger between the pages he was reading.

"I can't relax if you are staring at me," I mumbled, looking over at him. "Tonight is not a good night. I'm too frustrated with everything. Now I know how a deer caught in the head lights feels." I brushed some hair away from my face.

"You need to start sometime," Victor said, poking me in the arm almost playfully, trying to brighten my mood.

I was silent for a few minutes; my eyes fixed on the candle on the table. "Maybe this is all a really bad dream. Tell me it is."

"I'd like to, but I can't." Victor reached over and touched my shoulder with his hand.

"Maybe you aren't really a vampire either." I glanced over at him as he watched me agonize over the ordeal again. I reached up and touched his mouth, pushing his upper lip back to see his teeth as if I were checking the jowls of a dog. "Where are they? Where are your fangs?"

"They only come out when I feed," he replied, pushing my hand away from his face, annoyed.

"Oh. So this is all real."

"Yes. This is real," Victor confirmed.

"Ok, let's work on the lesson then." I gave up thinking there was anything else I could do.

Under Victor's guidance, I tried to relax and, using Sara's instructions, tried to pick the candle up with my mind. I tried several times but it did not so much as quiver under my power. I felt frustrated, and although Sara wrote I would need to keep trying, I felt that perhaps I was one of those people who needed to experiment on my own.

"Just keep trying," Victor said. "You know you have powers. I have seen them and felt them; so have you. You just need to figure out how to channel them and work with them." He set Sara's journal on the table and rubbed my arm.

I sat silently on the couch, still looking directly at the candle, wanting something to happen. My head began to hurt I was concentrating so hard on the object. I wanted it to move so badly.

"It's okay. Give yourself a break," Victor encouraged me. "I know you are trying. Give it a rest."

Just as he finished speaking, the wick on the candle caught flame. I watched the orange and yellow fire grow and flicker. Victor, surprised at what he saw, bent over quickly and picked up the lit candle, holding it upright, admiring it.

"You did this!" His voice took on a tone of amazement. "Figures it had to be fire, but you did something. You channeled your thoughts."

I looked at the candle too, and felt a sense of accomplishment. "I did do that. I wanted it to catch fire and it did!" I smiled. I finally did something right. I leaned back on the couch, exhausted even with the smallest triumph.

Victor blew the candle out and placed it back on the table. "I think that's great!" he said admiringly, almost reverently. He moved over on the couch closer to me and put his arm around me. "I'm sorry I'm hard on you, but this whole thing with you and me is a lot to handle. I care for you and our odds aren't good. We are both going to get hurt in the end. But I can't end it, not right now."

I looked at him sympathetically, knowing exactly what he meant, but doubting that our feelings and emotions were identical – similar, maybe. I touched his face and trailed my fingers to his throat and down his open shirt, tenderly touching his chest. He pulled back, a bit skittish the closer I got to his burns. "There is a way I can help you, isn't there?" I peeked between the fabric of his shirt and studied his bare chest. I knew there had to be something I could do to ease his hurt.

"I'll be fine. Don't you worry. I feel better just being with you." He held my hand in his and kissed it delicately; his mouth curled and he smiled.

I heard the words '*your blood*' echo in my head; the voice was neither male nor female but was faint and empty, almost mechanical. There was something I could do. I realized that what Victor needed in order to be healed of his wounds was my blood. The blood of an Emissary could cure him and ease his pain. There was something special about my blood. I don't know how I knew... I just did. I stood up without a word and walked into the kitchen. I opened the silverware drawer and took out a fairly sharp filet knife. With its spiky tip and thin flexible blade, I could use this to cut myself to allow Victor to take the blood he needed to be himself again, and to make his pain go away. I held my hand over the sink, closed my eyes, and dug the point of the knife into my index finger, cutting down towards the palm of my hand. I bled immediately, feeling a little lightheaded with the realization of what I had just done. I had to call for Victor. "Victor, can you come in here please?"

I heard him get off the couch and approach the kitchen. As he caught sight of me he stopped quickly, twisting his head and body away from the scent and the sight of my blood. "What are you doing?" he asked, obviously disturbed. "Are you trying to get yourself killed?"

I continued to hold my bleeding hand over the sink. "No. I know this is what you need to be healed. I want to help you. I did that to you. The least I can do is help you feel better," I tried to explain as I placed the knife on the counter.

Victor slowly raised his head and looked into the kitchen where I stood waiting. "You really should not being putting yourself at such a risk. I will heal in time," he said thickly. The scent of my blood was driving him mad. I could see that his usual shallow breathing was more like a pant now; his body became rigid as he placed his hands on either side of the doorframe, his fingers digging in to anchor himself.

"I won't let you take too much. I won't let you kill me, if that is what you are afraid of. Just please come over here and take what you need. Or I might just bleed to death and then it would be your fault." I held my hand up, enticing him, showing the amount of blood that was dripping steadily into the sink.

Victor released himself from the doorway and slowly edged into the room, almost in a stalking manner. His eyes, large black spheres with glowing centers, were not fixed upon me, but were instead focused on my bleeding finger. I watched him intently. As he got closer to me, I could see his eyeteeth begin to protrude from his gum line, becoming just visible past his full lips. He reached over and took my bleeding hand and brought it to his mouth; he licked the blood that had run down my finger and into my palm. His tongue was wide and wet as it absorbed the entire thick red river like a sponge. I placed my cut finger into his mouth and he held onto my hand as if it were a bottle, keeping it close to him as he sucked the nourishment out, his eyes shut tightly. He took one deep breath after another, making small, animal noises as he fed. My blood. Pure enjoyment.

I could feel his tongue pulse against my finger as it pushed it against the roof of his mouth with each swallow. He sucked hard and my finger began to feel numb, as the blood drained out and down Victor's throat, soothing his ailing body. After a moment I tugged on my finger to cue Victor to remove it from his powerful jaws. "Victor, stop," I stated firmly.

His eyes opened but were still dark and glowing.

"You had enough." I looked up at him and tugged my finger again.

He held onto my hand, but allowed my finger to slip from his mouth as he licked his lips with his tongue. He stepped back against the stone counter, dazed and sated. Reluctantly, he released my hand. He continued to breathe deeply, his eyeteeth still poking out, as he tried to regain his composure. His chest heaved under his shirt. "I wish you'd warn me when you are going to do stuff like that," he growled. "It would be so easy to kill you. It's very hard for me not to. It's dangerous."

"You would not have allowed me to help if I had told you," I replied, knowing I was right. I looked at my finger which was not bleeding badly, but was not healed either.

Victor closed his eyes again and swallowed hard, extending his hand. "Let me see your finger again." He seemed to have regained some semblance of self-control.

I gave him my hand, hoping I would get it back. He opened his eyes slowly, blinking several times to clear his vision. His eyes seemed smaller, normal now, and he put my fingers to his lips, gently running the pointed tip of his tongue up and down the self-inflicted slash I had made. He kissed my fingertips gently, then pulled my hand away from his mouth, studying my finger. Nodding slightly, he released my hand. My finger was restored to the way it looked before. No blood, no pain, no signs of a wound.

Without a word, Victor turned and walked out to the deck, into the dark night, leaving the sliding door open behind him. I looked out to the edge of the wooden deck to see him leaning over the rail, still breathing deeply, trying very hard to cool down. I stood in the doorway, not sure if I should join him.

"Can I come out?" I asked, hoping he had forgiven me for being so helpfully stupid.

He took one more deep breath. "Can you get me a beer or something?"

Pleased at the normal request, I went back into the kitchen, knowing I had a few left. I reached into the refrigerator and grabbed a green bottle, wrapped a dishtowel around the cap and twisted off the aluminum top, tossing it into the sink and setting the dishtowel on the counter. I walked out to give Victor his drink, stopping to shut the door behind me.

"Here's your beer," I announced as I came up beside him.

Victor held a cigarette in his hand and took the beer appreciatively. He placed the beer to his lips and took a long sip before setting it down. "Thanks, I needed that," he winked at me.

"Do you forgive me?" I asked, rubbing his shirtsleeve.

Victor drew hard on his cigarette and exhaled the smoke smoothly through his mouth. "I forgive you. I know you were just trying to help. But you have to understand how dangerous it was. We can be very unpredictable."

I nodded. "I'm sorry. I know it was difficult for you. I won't do it again." I really had no idea what type of danger I'd been in.

"I'm glad you did though. I never would have asked for it, you know that." Victor took a seat at the table. "I feel much better. My body feels a little racy though, kind of hyper. I think it's your blood."

"That's because you haven't had the 'good' stuff in a long time," I smiled, joking with him.

"You aren't kidding. It's like running your car on high test fuel when you normally just use regular gasoline; you can feel the difference immediately." He crushed out his smoke and took another sip of his beer.

I stood in front of him and leaned over, opening the front of his shirt so that I could see for myself if his burns had healed. His chest was smooth – unblemished. I ran my hands up and down his skin without him flinching; I felt nothing out of the ordinary. "My blood did that?" I asked him, backing away; amazed a bodily fluid could be so powerful.

He looked down at himself and examined the areas of his chest that previously showed signs of my attack. "Yes. Only your blood could have healed me. Someone else's may have taken the sting out for a while, but that's it." Victor looked up at me and smiled almost in an admiring manner. "It's another attribute of you being Emissary."

"I see. You're sure of this?" I asked him again, as I sat down uninvited on his lap, facing him. I knew I was welcomed now that he felt better.

Victor placed his beer on the table and put his arms around my waist. “I’m quite sure.”

“Can’t be wrong just this once?” I asked, bracing my hands on his shoulders.

“Not this time.” Victor looked up at me, his eyes soft, no trace of the evil creature he appeared to be moments before. He reached up and brought my face to his, kissing me on the lips. “I can’t tell you how long it would have taken for me to heal on my own; I was healing on the outside quicker than I was on the inside. I have been pretty miserable,” he confessed.

“I’m glad you feel better,” I said, returning his kiss. “At least I have one power that’s always with me I can count on.”

Chapter 20

Victor stayed until I could no longer keep my eyes open. I was tired and I needed to sleep. This was one of the disadvantages of me being human: trying to keep up with the undead who didn't require as much rest. He gave me a kiss good night and left, feeling happy and healthier than he had in many days. Hopefully we would have some time to spend together before the weekend would end.

When Victor got home, he dropped in on Nathan, who was on the phone. Victor made himself comfortable; poured a drink and sat in a high-backed leather chair, casually lighting a cigarette. Victor could tell that the phone conversation was very one sided; Nathan had hardly uttered a word since Victor's arrival. Conceivably that could have been why, although he did not pick up the feeling that Nathan wanted him to leave.

When Nathan ended his conversation on the phone with a swift 'good night', he took a seat across from Victor, noticing immediately he was in better spirits than he had been in several days. Of course he could not wait to make a comment about it. "You seem to be feeling much better."

"Kala healed me. She approached me; I did not approach her." Victor made sure Nathan understood who was responsible for his well-being.

"Really. That was very charitable of her. Humans just don't offer their blood to us. And it isn't easy for us to take only what we need," Nathan said sarcastically, ridiculing the idea that Kala would just donate her services the way she did. "After all, she's the one who hurt you to begin with. How did she know her blood would help?"

Victor ignored Nathan's bad humor. "It was the Emissary in her, I'm sure, that made her aware that only her blood would help me. We have had many talks over the past day or so and she is understanding more and more about herself and about our people," Victor summarized.

Nathan was hesitant to ask. "What does she know?" He became serious.

"Most important to her was that she knew about me, my past, my involvement, and I told her about my immortality, and about Nerissa. The reoccurring dream that has haunted her nights is about Nerissa's death. Though it was a small portion of my life, it was a very important part; I felt it best to tell her everything I knew," Victor confessed without guilt, knowing in his mind he had done what was right.

"And how did she react – knowing who and what you are?" Nathan asked, crossing his legs. He seemed to enjoy probing Victor for more answers.

"She suffers through powerful mood swings; typical, human female stuff that I have to deal with. What she says and what I feel from her are two different things. I can't blame her for any of her emotions. She's strong as nails one minute and running away like a lamb the next. One moment she cares about me, the next she's not sure she trusts me. I am asking her to believe in something humans are not trained to think about or learn about... we are different, and different is scary," Victor replied. "Her biggest fear is that of Emissary. It terrifies her. I feel it in her."

Nathan's eyes widened. "She knows?" He shifted his weight, his body language as well as his words disapproving. "You had no right to tell her; it's not your place."

"I told her. She is not fully accepting yet. But I am convinced of who she is and what she was meant to be. Her blood proved it to me once again." He rubbed his chest to demonstrate there was no more pain that plagued him.

Nathan put his hand up to halt the conversation; he wanted to hear no more from Victor. "I was just on the phone with Sheldon; he and Phillip will be at Kala's cocktail party for the gallery. They apparently got a hold of an invitation and plan to attend, just to browse around."

Victor rolled his eyes and shook his head in disgust. "She'll be able to sense them. I know she will be able to. This won't work. It's not fair to her to have them just show up; this is her night. She is still human, let her have her time. I'm not sure how she will react to a pure-blood being in her gallery."

"Let's just see how things go," Nathan dismissed Victor's concern.

Victor changed topics as quickly as Nathan ended it. "What do you know about Enforcers?" He remembered his talk with Kala and what he had read in Sara's journal earlier in the night.

Nathan was silent; he did not look away but remained still and quiet. Victor's words grabbed at him like hands clenching around his throat. "What do you mean?" he finally asked, taking a cigarette out of his pocket and lighting it.

"Someone entertained me with the idea that among our people are Enforcers, ridding the world of evil realm-shifting spirits. In my two hundred years I have never heard the term used. You being more than that, I thought if anyone had, you would," Victor explained, waiting to hear Nathan's ideas on the subject. Seeing Nathan's initial reaction made Victor think he had stumbled across something. Nathan had tried too hard to cover up his response, and that was not his normal smooth style.

"I think it's folklore. I have heard stories, but that's all I believe it ever was. Our people have been the way we are now for thousands of years. We have not changed. We don't need to. We are superior." A typical Nathan answer.

"All right; I thought I would ask." Victor acted as if he believed Nathan's denial, although Nathan's body language told him otherwise.

"Who fed you this story?" Nathan asked, taking a quick drag on his cigarette and flicked some ashes into a nearby ashtray.

"Kala has a journal that her friend Sara left behind after her death. There was mention in that. The book has no value; it's sentimental to Kala only. I looked at the book myself," Victor replied. He knew the book held more wealth than that just in spells and lessons alone, but that was information Nathan did not need to know. "Well, I feel motivated to paint tonight. I'll be upstairs," Victor announced. He stood up and placed his empty glass on the table beside him, put out his cigarette and gestured a good night to Nathan, allowing the subject to rest for the moment.

Victor remained full of energy long into the night and early morning hours. He felt young, not only physically but also at heart. He contentedly worked on the painting he had started, which had given him such trouble to finish. Perhaps it was Kala's blood that gave him the boost he needed so badly. Victor sensed that Kala was pleased she could give him something he needed that would not only relieve his agony, but heal him and give him strength. Kala liked him strong and he liked being strong for her. The night before, when he was able to help Kala ease her mind by removing all the mental pain that she had stored up for so long, gave him a sense of satisfaction. He wanted to do more for her, anything. She deserved it. Anyone who thought of hurting her would have to deal with him, and that would not be a pretty sight.

As the morning sky showed the promise of dawn, Victor pulled the blinds on his windows, shading his home from the day's natural light. He was not ready to rest his body, but his mind was tired from thinking about Kala and the prospect of seeing her again. Just being in her company made him feel something he'd not felt in a very long time – affection towards someone else. When Kala returned his sentiment for the first time, words could not even describe the sensations that traveled through him. He'd been alone and unloved for so many years; looked down upon and disregarded so much, that even a touch on the arm left Victor thirsting for more. He knew that these were not normal Vampire emotions; they were apparently leftover human emotions that had not died when his body did. He was not sure if this was a blessing or another curse, feeling something he knew he could never truly have. He thought back to the night the two of them had lain in each other's arms, and held and stroked and kissed and made love. He deeply desired to share that again with her. To feel her physical presence with him, under him and be able to connect to her mind again was something Victor longed to have.

He flattened out his futon and collapsed on his stomach, his favorite way to sleep. Sleep – something Victor had not really had in days because of the burns that had scorched him from front to back. With them gone, he would surely relax well today. He sighed deeply as he positioned himself lengthwise on the bed. As he rested his head on his arm, he caught the distinct scent of Kala on his shirtsleeve, not cologne or perfume, but just her own natural pheromones. He closed his eyes peacefully and drifted off to sleep.

I woke up early on Sunday and took time to read the paper, going through all the sale circulars for the up coming week. The thought of shopping for a dress for the cocktail party seemed like something I should concentrate on. After all, it was only days away. My usual shopping partner was no longer with me, so that took the wind out of my sails. I could either go alone, or I could call someone, Addy perhaps. I had not seen or heard from her in days. I wondered if she would have the time to go and, more importantly, want to go with me.

When I got in touch with Addy later that morning she seemed eager and interested in going to the Mall with me. She said she had been meaning to call me after my birthday to see how my dinner with Victor had gone, and to find out if he would be attending the cocktail party with me. Our plans were to meet at the Mall food court around noon where we could grab a totally un-nutritious lunch and spend the rest of the afternoon poking through racks of clothes.

I arrived at the Mall a few minutes before twelve and ordered a burger, fries and a Diet Coke, waiting for Addy. Soon I saw her coming down the escalators and walking in my direction. She smiled warmly as soon as she saw that I had noticed her. When Addy got to the table, she immediately hugged me and took a seat across from me.

"Aren't you eating?" I asked, chewing on a french fry loaded with ketchup. "I thought that's why we were meeting here."

Addy shrugged and placed her oversized handbag on the floor next to her. "I had a big breakfast. I'll pass. Go ahead, finish. I'll talk." She pressed on. "So this Victor guy; he's going with you?"

I stopped eating and took a long sip of soda through my straw before I spoke. "Yes. He seemed rather anxious to attend," I smiled, playing with the plastic lid on my soda container.

"So, what's he like?" she asked, folding her arms on the table and moving in on me for the scoop, her long gray hair splashing over her shoulders.

I giggled. “He’s very nice.” I stopped, not knowing how else to describe him. Words failed me. “He’s indescribable. He’s sexy. He’s sweet. He’s romantic.” I could feel my temperature rise inside me just thinking about him.

“Wow. Sounds like you got a winner. Don’t let him go.” Addy looked envious. “Keith and I have been married so long we’re like room-mates.”

I smiled. “You must love him. Why would you be with him?” I asked, taking a bite of my burger.

“Oh, I do... I do... you just tend to lose the lusty part of your relationship after a while,” she sighed. “Oh, to be single again.”

“I’ll make sure I get lots of lust before I settle down. Promise,” I chuckled, crumpling up the wrapper to my burger and pushing it aside.

“I don’t know if that’s possible. I mean, you’re just reaching your sexual peak,” Addy smiled.

I knew I had been reaching that peak for a while, but I had never worried about whether it could be satisfied by just one man. “I guess I’ll have to keep a few guys around for back up,” I suggested teasingly.

“That’s the spirit,” Addy smiled.

After I finished my lunch, Addy and I started our shopping on the first floor. We went to a boutique that specialized in formal wear. I had a dress in mind, or should I say in Victor’s mind; something black, something little and something sexy, but not too sexy; after all, I was the owner of the gallery and I had to look suitable for the evening. Finally I found one. The woman who ran the shop referred to it as ‘the perfect little black dress’ and it was. Its silky material was form fitting, with a neckline just low enough to be suggestive while retaining a measure of decorum. I was nylons and a handbag away from a knockout look for the party. The woman suggested a black clutch purse she had on display at the register, and found a sheer pair of black nylons as well. Two hundred dollars later, I left the boutique; pleased with the attire I had bought. Shoes would be a breeze; I already had a black pair of high heel pumps that hardly got any wear. .

By late afternoon, Addy and I had gone our separate ways, promising we would see each other at the end of the week for the cocktail party and gallery opening. She was looking forward to meeting Victor and seeing all the different art that would be on exhibit.

I stopped at the grocery store on my way home and picked up the things I needed. I even felt like cooking, which was highly unusual for me. I thought that maybe I could make something simple and Victor could come over later on and join me out on the deck for dinner. I had no idea what I was going to make, so I picked up some chicken, fresh vegetables, some pasta and other versatile ingredients that would allow me to concoct something edible. I hoped. When I got home I put my provisions away and got on line to check out a few recipes that I could try for dinner tonight. I had not called to ask if Victor was available tonight. I just assumed that he would be. I thought it best to give him a call before I became Julia Child.

Victor sounded upbeat when he answered the phone. I was glad I had not awakened him. "Hello?"

"Hi there," I smiled broadly when I heard his voice. I was in the kitchen twisting the curly phone cord around my finger, eyeing my cabinets.

"Good evening. How are you?" he asked, his voice dropping to a sexy timbre.

"Ok. I was wondering what you were up to tonight."

"Not much. I have a class to teach tomorrow night," he replied.

"I was thinking about cooking something for dinner, and eating out on the deck tonight. Are you interested in joining me?" I offered my company and cooking talents. "I can't guarantee it'll be any good."

He chuckled lightly. "It's not like your cooking will kill me."

"True."

"I'd love to come by. You don't have to cook anything fancy on my behalf. I'm coming by just to see you anyway," Victor said.

My heart fluttered with his words. "That is very sweet of you. Should we skip dinner and go straight to dessert?"

"Mmm, that sounds appetizing."

I laughed at his response. "What time can you come by?" I asked

"I can get there about seven. Is that okay?"

"Yeah. Plenty of time," I answered, thinking about a dish I could prepare in time.

"Then I'll see you later on."

"I look forward to it," I grinned broadly, thinking about his handsome face, his smooth body and how good he would taste.

"Kala!" Victor teased warningly. "Control yourself. I can hear your thoughts over here!"

I laughed. "Good. At least you know my intentions ahead of time."

I could hear him take in a deep breath between his clenched teeth. "Maybe I should grab a nap."

I raised an eyebrow. "Maybe you should."

Chapter 21

I had spent the better half of the hour preparing dinner. The food smelled good and it looked good; with any luck it would taste good too.

The night was lovely, with just a threat of thunderstorms, but I did not feel my dinner plans would be hindered. A nice cool breeze had picked up which would probably move the showers in later, but it felt good for now. It was almost seven when the doorbell rang as I was out on the deck setting the table. I stopped what I was doing to answer the door, knowing that it had to be Victor.

I left the slider open and strolled through the dining area to get to the front door. "Hey there," I smiled as I opened the door, greeting my handsome dinner date, and moved aside for him to enter.

"Good evening," Victor whispered in my ear as he gave me a chaste kiss on the cheek. He took a deep breath. "Something smells good."

I shrugged. "We'll see if it tastes as good," I replied skeptically. "I'm setting the table on the deck if you want to join me."

He followed me out through the sliding door and took a seat at the table. I finished the place settings for two. Victor lit a cigarette and relaxed in his chair, stretching out and crossing his legs. "So, what's for dinner?" he asked, smiling warmly at me.

"Italian chicken," I answered, placing a drinking glass in front of each plate. "Also salad and pasta."

"Sounds good," he commented, flicking ashes off the side of the deck.

"I never claimed to be a chef. If it's edible I'll be happy," I laughed, joking at my lack of cooking skills. "I don't know what I would do without the web. That's where I got the recipes. So thank the Food Network if it's good."

"I'm sure your cooking is just fine." Not an ounce of pessimism in Victor's voice. "And dessert?" A grin gradually appeared on his face as an eyebrow lifted provocatively.

I returned his smile, feeling warm inside. "Potluck."

Halfway through dinner Victor began to ask me about the lessons in Sara's journal, and if I had had any time to practice what she wrote, or to improve on what I was already able to do. I was honest and told him 'no'. I told him about my day and that I had spent the afternoon at the Mall with Addy shopping for something to wear to the cocktail party on Friday. He suggested that after dinner we spend some time working with Sara's journal again and see if there were other spells I could learn or conform to fit my own radical style. That idea seemed to put a damper on my dessert plans, but he was probably right that I continue with Sara's lessons and try to improve my strengths the best that I could.

"Dinner was very good," Victor remarked, putting his napkin on his plate when he was through. "I mean that."

"Thanks. I don't cook too often. I forget how to sometimes," I giggled, stacking up the dirty dinner dishes.

Victor got up slowly, pushed his chair away from the table and stretched his body, reaching his hands towards the sky. He groaned in satisfaction, then walked over to the edge of the deck and leaned against the railing, taking out a cigarette. "Stop cleaning and come over here for a moment," Victor signaled with his head to join him.

I brushed my hands off on the thighs of my jeans and strolled over to his side, resting my arms on the railing near his. I looked over at him, thinking how strikingly handsome in the full moon's light he was; the cool white glow over his skin and hair made him appear like some sort of divine being sent to me from somewhere afar.

"Light my cigarette," Victor requested, holding the cigarette up in the air for me to see.

I rolled my eyes. "When did you *not* become capable of doing it for yourself?" I responded. What an odd request, I thought.

Victor smiled. "Unlike you, I can't make fire just happen. But you can. Control it. Light my cigarette." He turned to face me, holding the cigarette between his finger and thumb, waving it gently at me. "Just try."

"I don't know if I can," I mumbled uneasily, looking at the cigarette and feeling rather peculiar about his demand, as if I was being asked to perform on stage or something.

"How can you not know how? How did you make the candle catch fire? Remember back to how you made that happen and you should be able to do it again. It's all about control," Victor pointed out. He continued to hold the cigarette in my view, waiting for something to happen. "Take a deep breath and relax. It's okay."

I rubbed my forehead for a moment as I tried to recall what I was thinking when I wanted the candle to catch fire. I stared at the cigarette and thought about it as being the candle. I looked at the tip of the cigarette and studied the few tiny tobacco strands protruding past the rolled paper. I knew where the flames had to start in order for the rest of the cigarette to begin to burn. I remembered thinking about heat, a spark – not an explosion, nothing huge – just enough to light it; this is what I thought about when I successfully lit the candle. I tried this method again using the cigarette. I saw fire in my head. The colors of orange and yellow painted my conscious mind wildly and randomly, a sort of psychedelic inferno. I felt a sudden rush of warmth course through my body and, without thinking I reached out and touched the top of his cigarette. The cigarette ignited with a quick spark. I retracted my hand to my chest as if I'd been wounded, holding it close to me, astonished at what I had done, not understanding why I knew to touch the cigarette to accomplish my task. I just felt possessed to do it. Touch it.

Victor's eyes widened as he saw the cigarette smoldering in his fingertips. He placed the cigarette to his lips and took a drag off it, making the tip glow fiery orange as if testing it to make sure the fire was real. He exhaled out his nose, then reached out and examined the hand I had used. There were no signs of burns, or anything unusual. He shook his head in disbelief. "You certainly have the power. We just need to work on how you use it," he chuckled admiringly, the cigarette dangling from his lips as he spoke. "Your hand looks fine. You aren't hurt."

"Feels okay. I was scared, I guess," I confessed, feeling the shock of what I had done.

"You know what though? I'm glad you had that under control. The few times I've seen you use your hands with your powers, it's been very frightening. I know first hand how much energy and strength you have. I'm glad you didn't blow me away with it this time," he smiled.

I rubbed my hands together, feeling a tingling sensation under my skin that I was beginning to associate with this ability I had: the fire and surges of energy. "I think I know what I'm doing differently." I thought about what I had done the last two times I had used my abilities, compared to what I had done to the Blue Daemon, or to Victor. "I was thinking about the size of the flame when I lit the candle and when I lit your cigarette tonight. When I fought the Blue Daemon, I let my anger control the power and that must have controlled the size of the fire. And when I pushed you away in the dream, I let my frustration with you control my powers and did not allow myself to control it. I think that may be the key."

"I think you could be right. It makes sense. It means that no matter how hard it is for you, and no matter how mad you get, you have to control your anger. You have to. It's not an option," Victor warned. He crushed his cigarette out and tossed it over the railing to the ground. His demeanor softened and his warm manner returned. "Do you feel it is getting easier for you to use your powers?" he asked, folding his muscular arms around me and drawing me closer to him.

"I haven't tried much. You know what I can do. Certain things seem clearer to me now than they did before. I think that is a good sign," I replied, placing my hands on his sides. I loved being close to him and feeling his body near mine. I felt such a thrill when I was with Victor. It was an adventure. I had never known anyone like him before. He was a powerful creature who could take a human life in a minute, but he was also someone who had kindness and love running through his veins, even if for no one but me.

"Do you think you would be able to do something on your own if you wanted, not just something that was taught to you?" he asked.

"Oh, I don't know. I never tried," I admitted, reaching up and lightly kissing his chin and then his lips, his touch loosening me.

"Hmmm, I think you have. I can recall a few times when I am nearly certain you have unknowingly used your powers." He returned my kiss and released me from his hold, rubbing my shoulders.

My forehead wrinkled in confusion. "When?"

"How about the afternoon your answering machine began to play back your messages? You didn't get up to turn it on yourself, did you? You wanted the messages to play. And the night you and I were talking on the phone about what you should wear to your birthday dinner – the little black dress. I know for a fact that night you were tapped directly into my thoughts; I felt it, then I blocked you from continuing," Victor said, reminding me of forgotten incidents.

I lowered my eyes and thought about what he had said. Maybe he was right. I recalled both episodes, but could not remember the events well enough on a psychological level to say whether I controlled them or not, or if they were random flukes and just happened, and would never again. "I'm not sure," I replied.

"I just think you are capable of more than what Sara has left you. Obviously you are doing your own version of the lessons she wrote. I thought that you might have fully and knowingly experienced something you *willed* to happen. Try it some time. You might be pleasantly surprised," Victor encouraged, bringing me close to him again. As he pressed me against the banister I could feel the wooden slat in the small of my back. He smiled shyly, looking down at me and held my face in his hands as our lips met. I melted with his warm, soft kisses, savoring the taste of his sweet mouth on mine. His fingers combed through my hair, then gently tugged so my head turned, exposing my neck. My pulse quickened as I felt his moist breath on my skin, keenly aware of his animal tendencies and what he did to survive. Taking a life to sustain his. I wondered if he could feel my heart racing within my chest, if he understood my human emotions, and what I feared. I wondered if he could see through me, into me as if I was transparent, watching my crimson blood traveling the highways of my body deep within me. I braced myself the best I could, unsure of his intentions. I felt his lips and tongue graze the side of my neck as he traced a path over my vulnerable throat. He held my head still, fingers firmly intertwined in my hair as he buried his open mouth against the smooth skin. My body tensed as I was torn between the pleasure I felt, and the knowledge of the pain Victor could deliver so effortlessly and quickly. My hands clutched at his chest, my knuckles white, as I held on tightly as if to a lifeline. His mouth latched onto my throat, and I felt an intense sucking action, a few delicate but well placed nibbles, and then the smooth wet kisses of his lips as they journeyed up my neckline, across my flushed cheeks to my mouth.

I remember thinking how scared I was, not knowing what Victor might do to me, truly hoping that he would *not* drain me of my blood, but still not really knowing if he was capable of the feat or not. '*I would never hurt you,*' Victor sent back to me without any words, he was reading my mind and apparently I was able to at least receive the messages he wanted me to get. How strange to have a conversation without talking and still be able to kiss and fondle each other without missing a beat.

I reached my hands down between us and rubbed the thighs of his jeans with my open hands, feeling his leather belt on the way up and a small tear near one of his pockets on the way down. I blindly felt for the buckle of his belt and unfastened it by tugging the leather away from the silver tongue that locked the belt in place. I released the tension on the belt and maneuvered my fingers down into the waistband of his jeans, unbuttoned them and pulled until I heard the metal teeth of the zipper let go and sink to the lowest level.

Victor eased his hands under the front of my shirt and worked his fingers up my stomach and over my chest feeling the lace and fabric of my bra in his hands as he squeezed each breast gently.

I was about ready to either suggest we go inside or just tear our clothes off right then and there when a chilling sensation shot through my mind like an icy plunge in a lake. I pulled away from Victor, startled, trying to gather my thoughts and figure out what was going on inside me. Victor continued to caress me but recognized the fact I was preoccupied. "What's the matter?" he asked, kissing my cheek.

"I feel something," I softly replied, not sure how to convey it.

Victor's hands stopped where they were on my body and he raised his head silently, searching. "What do you feel?"

I shrugged, confused. "I don't know." I looked up into his eyes to see him scanning the backyard intently.

"Yes you do know what you feel. Tell me," Victor demanded. He took one step back and began to adjust himself and fasten up his jeans.

"There's something out there," I replied, moving my eyes to the right to signify it was somewhere behind me, out in the darkness of the yard, maybe further away than that. I was not sure.

He nodded. "I feel it too." He buckled his jeans. "What do you think it is?"

"Feels like a Blue Daemon," I answered, fairly sure of myself. I had felt the sensations before and could compare them.

Victor nodded again to confirm what I said. "That's what it is." He took me by the elbow and escorted me into the condo, locking the slider behind us. He guided me into the kitchen where he paced for several seconds before saying anything.

"Maybe it will go away," I broke the silence with naive optimism.

"Don't count on it," Victor stopped his stride. "I wish I knew why they wanted you so badly." He rubbed his chin in thought.

My heart skipped a beat as my stomach tightened. "What did I do? Why are they after me?" I asked fearfully. "I don't want to have to fight these damn things off forever!"

"The best I can figure is that there are some of my people who don't want you to become Emissary. There are many of my kind who don't like leadership, and they look upon you as being an authority figure. If they can eliminate you that would be a good for them," Victor guessed.

"What are we going to do?" I asked, grabbing his shirtsleeve.

"You aren't doing anything. I'll go find them. I'll do what I have to," Victor replied firmly, in a tone that allowed no argument.

"Alone?" I hated the pathetic whine I heard in my voice. I let go of his shirtsleeve and spun around and away from him, nervously pulling my hair away from my face.

"I'll be fine. I have had some run-ins with the Blue Daemons before," Victor assured me.

"Victor, please, that was a long time ago," I begged him to reconsider his actions.

"There is no such thing as a *long time* ago in immortal years; paths cross many times," Victor corrected me. He took me by the shoulders. "I will be fine."

"Maybe I can help," I pleaded with him, my eyes imploring his.

He shook his head.

"But I fought one off before. With you there, I will feel confident in my powers."

"I can't worry about your safety. If you were with me it would be a distraction." Victor shook his head again and stood his ground, not allowing me to leave the house with him.

"But what if things don't work out as you have planned? What if you get hurt? What then?" I asked him, fear in my expression.

Victor stood in front of my refrigerator, took a black marker off an erasable magnetic white board and jotted a phone number down. "If I am not back here in fifteen minutes, call this number; it's Nathan; tell him about the Blue Daemons and have him come here to help me. Do not, and I repeat, do not, come out to help me."

I lowered my eyes, understanding what he said, but not liking it. I for sure did not like having to call Nathan; I knew he didn't like me and I didn't like thinking I might need to call him for help.

"How are you going to fight these things?" I searched my mind wondering what type of device he could use.

"With everything I have."

I closed my eyes; not liking what was happening and having little control over the situation. I had no choice as I watched Victor walk back out to the deck, straddle the railing and leap off into the darkness.

Chapter 22

I never knew fifteen minutes could be so long. I stood anxiously looking out the sliding door, trying to see anything that would give me a clue as to what was happening out in the darkness. The wind had risen in strength since dinner, the gusts whipping the trees as the storm approached. The distant rumble of thunder reached my ears as sporadic flashes of lightning slashed through the starless sky. The full moon that had shone on us earlier had vanished behind the ominous clouds, gone with no trace as if it had been stolen from under Mother Earth's nose. I wanted desperately to know that Victor was not hurt, that he had been unable to find the Blue Daemons and would return to me unharmed. I would think no less of him for not being able to find them, or for not fighting.

Finally, in desperation, I unlocked the glass door and slid it open, poking my head out into the dark and peering in all directions, listening attentively for any noise or voice that would put my mind to rest. From deep within the wooded area behind my building came the shrieking sounds of something abominable, rising over the wind and the thunder. I was so frightened my body trembled and shook. I slid the door shut and somehow latched the lock with trembling fingers. My mind spun wildly out of control, unable to process what I heard. I only knew it was not human and it sounded like no animal I was familiar with.

A rush of adrenaline sent me running into the kitchen, still shaking in fright, to check the time on the microwave. More than fifteen minutes had passed and there was no sign of Victor. I wanted to be with him. I was more scared for him now, out there alone, than if we were standing together, facing a pack of Blue Daemons. Not knowing, being helpless; this was a far worse terror for me.

The mere thought of calling Nathan tied my stomach into knots, but how could I not call him? He was the only person I knew who could help, the person Victor left me orders to contact. What if Victor's life depended on Nathan? I had to make the call. I had to. I darted into the living room and plucked the cordless phone out of the cradle from the desk near the front door, and sprinted back into the kitchen to dial Nathan's number. I took a deep breath as I dialed the phone, not knowing how I would explain the situation to him.

"Hello?" a voice spoke. He didn't sound like a vampire.

"Is Nathan there?" I asked timidly, trying to level my voice and cover up some of my fears.

He paused before he replied. "Speaking." His voice was smooth and calm, with little inflection.

"Nathan... You don't know me. This is Kala. Victor asked me to call you," I stammered, hoping he would listen to me and not want to hang up after knowing who I was. The thought of my someday becoming his Emissary never crossed my mind; though that perhaps was the only reason he stayed on the line.

"What is it, Kala?" he asked, addressing me politely.

"There are Blue Daemons here, outside my home. Victor went out to try and deal with them on his own, without me. It's been awhile and he told me to call you for help if he did not come back," I explained, trying to sound calm.

"I see. How many Blue Daemons are there?" Nathan asked thoughtfully.

"I'm not sure. I'm just very worried. Please help him. I know you don't like me, but please, for Victor?"

"I will see what I can do. I suggest, since you are the future Emissary, you stay in doors where you are safe. I'm on the way, " Nathan said as he hung up the phone.

I replaced the receiver, my heart pounding with my pent up fears. Oh, how I wished for the light of day!

The minutes passed, and still I heard nothing from Victor, or even Nathan for that matter. I planted myself in front of the sliding glass door; it had become my crystal ball gazing into the night. I watched the bad weather continue to roll in, unable to discern what might be happening outside my refuge. My fears gradually turned to frustration as the time dragged on with no news. After all, it was *me* Victor was trying to protect, and I didn't know if he was alive, so to speak, or not. It was *me* the Blue Daemons wanted, and here I sat, like a coward, as someone I cared for bravely shielded *me* from harm. Maybe I could help. What if Nathan never came? I wasn't sure I could live with myself, knowing Victor might be hurt and I had done nothing to help. I remembered the stern look and the tone in Victor's voice as he told me 'Do not, and I repeat, do not come out to help me.' Listening and taking direct orders was something I rarely did. I decided to do what my little voice told me to do, find Victor and help him.

I walked out the front door, holding on tightly to the doorknob and struggled to slam it shut, fighting the weather every step of the way. The wind was gusting and seemed to hold me back as if warning me not to go any further. I fought the blowing force as I went down the cement stairs to the parking lot. The wind was deafening as it howled through the leaves in the trees, bending each branch and shaking it violently, angrily, at me. I wasn't even sure I could hear a voice; the sound would just get carried away. I struggled to keep my balance, fighting the wind as I jogged around the side of my complex where I thought the Daemons had been earlier. I stopped for a moment to get my bearings, and pulled my wind-whipped hair out of my face; it was tangled and snarled and looked like a cheap Halloween wig. I had to concentrate, but fear and frustration was making it difficult. I had to calm down, gather my thoughts and, for the sake of Victor and myself, manage and work with my powers; allow them to come to me, *want* them to come to me. I remembered what Victor had said before about 'willing' something to happen, to see if by wanting something badly enough I could make *something* happen. What I wanted to know most right now was where Victor was, and that was all I thought about, it was like I was in a trance; my thoughts were focused on wanting to know where he was. I concentrated so hard on Victor's whereabouts that for a moment I stopped hearing the wind, and the thunder; all noise stopped.

Someone grabbed me by the arm. I whipped around, adrenaline flaring, prepared to do battle. I recognized Nathan as I spun like a top into his arms. He was dressed totally in black from head to toe. I was glad he was not a Blue Daemon, disappointed he was not Victor, and scared to be so close to him, knowing I was not his favorite human.

"Nathan," I yelled over the wind's fury. "I can't find Victor!" Saying the words out loud made me sick to my stomach and my heart began to take off again, beating at a high rate of speed as the shock began to engulf me.

"I can't either," Nathan shouted back. His voice was barely audible.

"I'm scared," I confessed, looking around as the lightening flashed several times, making the night appear bright as day for brief moments.

An earth-shaking clap of thunder boomed, followed by noises that were shockingly loud, loud enough to be heard over the storm. It was not a voice or a cry; it was something totally foreign to my ears. Nathan's nostrils flared as he picked up on the sound. He yanked me by my arm, dragging me into a thick patch of trees and brush towards where the sounds had come from. The night got darker, the trees shading any possible light that might have gotten through. I had no choice but to be towed along by Nathan, who moved quickly, gliding through the forest with hardly any effort. The lack of light, the storm's fury, and lugging me behind did not seem to hinder Nathan's ability to navigate in the slightest. We heard the strange noise again, and still couldn't identify it. Nathan stopped suddenly, jerking me to a halt, my chest slamming into his shoulder blades. I could see an eerie glow ahead of us. It was a glow I had seen before. The grayish blue hue of a Blue Daemon. My heart raced, dreading another confrontation. Nathan's company did not exactly comfort me; I did not know what kind of ally he would make. I tried to move around Nathan, to catch a glimpse of what this Blue Daemon looked like; big, small, tall, short, but Nathan would not allow me to come out front and see for myself. He extended his arms to block me, and would not permit me to pass or get a good view of what was ahead. The more I struggled the more Nathan attempted to restrict me.

"Damn it Nathan!" I shouted. I sensed the Blue Daemon knew we were there, but for some reason it did not care. There was something else that I could sense, but I could not put my finger on it. The Daemons were busy doing something else. I needed to *look.*

Nathan turned around quickly, his body rigid and he grabbed my shoulders with more authority than Victor ever had. "Stop fighting me." His eyes glared at me in anger. His anger was not geared towards me, but the Daemons. As I looked into his dark, deep-set eyes I was startled to see a vision – I was never able to do this before! Nathan's eyes were telling me a visual story; it was clear but confusing. My senses told me it had to do with Victor. It was about Victor.

"Victor!" I yelled. "What about Victor?" I watched his eyes as if they were tiny TVs. Nathan was protecting me not only from the Blue Daemons but also from seeing what *they* had done to Victor. I again tried to fight Nathan for just a glimpse of what was ahead of me in the path. The Blue Daemon had made no attempt to approach us, apparently preoccupied with something. Victor.

"Kala. There is nothing I can do," Nathan spoke loudly.

My heart skipped a beat and my body ached with his words. What did he mean? Victor. I could feel my emotions begin to take control of me instead of me taking control of them. I needed to see what was going on. Where were the noises coming from and what was making them? If Victor was hurt I needed to know; I needed to help if I could. The wave of energy that had caused me so much trouble in the past began to build within me. I let it grow in intensity, thinking I might need a little extra. "Nathan! Let me by!" I yelled. My anger was getting the best of me.

"You can't. They will hurt you, too," Nathan warned and he locked his elbows, gripped his hands around my biceps and kept me several feet away from him securely. He was strong.

I lunged at him, feeling my hands tingle, and pushed him away by his shoulders. A surge of energy shot out of me, not like the one that injured Victor but a swell of force that sent Nathan staggering back, shocked and off balance.

I got a full view of one Blue Daemon and saw possibly two others behind him, but there was another figure that I saw with them. A figure I recognized, wearing blue jeans and dark sneakers, lying on the ground amongst the evil. It was Victor. I could not tell if he were alive or dead. Nathan advanced towards me and I held up my hand warningly.

"There is nothing we can do right now," Nathan yelled at me over the storm. "We have to wait." Nathan tried unsuccessfully to reason with me.

"There has to be something," I screamed back. "He's your blood, for God sakes!" My words wounded Nathan. After all, Nathan was his Sire. I had not thought it possible to hurt him, given his hard-nosed exterior.

"They have his strength; they are too strong for you and I," Nathan explained hotly, approaching me again.

I thought quickly, but tried to be rational at the same time. The pressure was on me from all sides. I had Nathan coming at me again, Blue Daemons in my path, the raging winds, a rain that had begun to fall, deafening thunder and blinding lightening. Yet I simply made myself think, 'If I were a bag of bones, what would I fear most?' I closed my eyes, clutched my Amulet in one hand and made a fist with the other, focusing harder than I ever had on making *something* happen.

"What are you doing? We have to get out of here," Nathan growled. He stood near me but did not dare lay a finger on my body.

I opened my eyes and looked at him. "I hope it worked," I said. I was skeptical about what I had tried to summon.

"What did you just do?" Nathan demanded.

I shook my head. "If it works, grab Victor and run like Hell!"

A few seconds went by and then we heard the sound of barking in the distance, rapidly drawing closer.

"Holy shit!" I gasped. "It worked!" I grabbed Nathan's arm.

"What the Hell is it? Sounds like dogs..." Nathan looked around quickly, trying to locate the source of the barking.

"We have to get Victor!" I exclaimed.

The resonance of barking was closer now, sounding like a stampede of cattle, even the ground shook. The Blue Daemons immediately turned their attention away from what had held them so intently and turned towards the sound. Immediately one good-sized Daemon saw me and I became its next target. It knew who I was and remembered its mission. The Blue Daemon zeroed in on me, traveling quicker than I had seen it move in the past; it was not clumsy but rather agile and overtook me rapidly. Nathan reached for my arm, dragging me out of the Daemon's reach. The barking and growling rose in crescendo, as the pack reached the treed area we were hidden in. The Blue

Daemons milled in confusion, attempting to locate and identify the source of the barking. Nathan and I dashed past the trio of Daemons and to a tiny clearing in the path where I had seen Victor's body. Nathan pushed me on down the path and leaned over, scooping Victor up and effortlessly tossing his limp body over his shoulder, fireman style. "Keep going!" Nathan yelled at me. I ran. I could hear the growls, and snarls of the beasts behind us; I imagined their huge mouths dripping with saliva, crammed with sharp triangle shaped teeth. The pack had reached the Daemons and had begun their mission; they were carrying out the command I had summoned them for; *dispose* of the Daemons, devour their bony bodies until only shreds of cloth and specks of their flesh were left to be washed back into the Earth.

We continued to run as fast as we could back to the well-lit and manicured grounds of the complex and continued towards the front of the building. The rain hammered down upon us as we found ourselves sprinting for the door. I could hear Nathan's footsteps splashing in the soaked grass behind me as I climbed the stairs to the condo and threw the door open wide, allowing Nathan and Victor access into my home. I shut the door behind us and watched as Nathan laid Victor's wet body on my living room floor.

Victor did not move. I dropped to my knees beside him. Nathan stood towering over both of us. I looked up. "Is he..."

Nathan shook his head. "He's hurt in a way you can't know, not yet any way."

I touched Victor's chest. His shirt was drenched and stuck to his body. "What can we do?" I asked.

. Nathan sighed and crouched down on the other side of Victor and brushed some hair out of his face. "Not too much right now. This isn't the first time this has happened to him with the Blue Daemons."

"This has happened before?" I asked, stunned, picking up Victor's cold hand in mine.

Nathan rubbed his temples hard and stood up. "Yes. A long time ago."

I looked at Victor again who remained motionless. "What happened to him? What can we do?"

Nathan walked around the living room with his hands behind his back and his head down in thought.

"Nathan. If there is something that you or I can do, let's do it." I watched him as he slowly circled the room. "I know you don't much care for me..."

Nathan looked at me. "Whether I like you or not has no bearing on what we do or don't do for Victor. I always have his best interest in mind." He stopped walking and placed his hands on his hips, looking down upon Victor. "Serves him right. How he thought he could take on more than two of those

Daemons I'll never know. I don't know what he felt he had to prove."

I suddenly was overcome with guilt and lowered my eyes over Victor's body. "I didn't want this to happen to him," I said remorsefully.

"Victor is stubborn," Nathan said, sitting on the arm of the couch. He put his hands on his knees, leaning forward, thinking about Victor. "He's not even stubborn in an obvious way. He doesn't talk about what he plans to do; he just goes off and does it. That's what gets him into trouble. He hates confrontation and knows that if he told anyone half of what he had planned, someone might actually try and talk him out of it."

"You have known him longer than I have. I'm sure you know him better than me." I sat flat on the floor and faced Nathan. I was going to be blunt with him. I had been warding off his feelings of hate for nearly an hour. "Okay, so we don't like each other. I feel it; I feel it now. You resent me, you resent me for Victor laying here on the floor, but the fact is he needs help and maybe we are the only two who can. So I ask again, what happened to him and what can we do?" I refused to back down; knowing Victor would probably get no better unless Nathan and I worked together.

Nathan rubbed his chin. "You don't know much about Blue Daemons, do you?" he asked.

"No, tell me." I drew my knees up to my chest and wrapped my arms tightly around them.

"Blue Daemons are warriors, for a lack of a better word. They are the muscles behind the brains. Blue Daemons do not think for themselves; they have very limited capabilities. They do not permanently reside in our world. They stay until their job is done or until they are called upon to return to the realm that they live in."

"Victor mentioned something about the Blue Daemons being after me and that it could be some of your people who sent them." I expressed my concern over what Victor had told me earlier in the night.

Nathan nodded in agreement. "Oh, I'm sure that's what the case is. They have no reason to be after Victor, and in his earlier years he even worked with them for a while."

"So he said."

"Basically, these Blue Daemons travel in two's or three's and are sent by someone who is powerful enough to call them up. The Daemons are instructed by that person to fulfill a job. That is the job they are meant to do and no other, and they do not rebel or disobey, because they don't know how to." Nathan paused and looked down at Victor who still had not moved. "In the case of the Blue Daemons looking for you; I know they have been around. I know you have felt them. I know you fought one off. I also know that some of my people have been tracking them in order to keep them away from you. I believe the ones that have pursued you have been sent by the same person or people. Initially I think it was to eliminate you, but now with what has happened to Victor, I know that that is not the case any longer."

I shrugged and let my legs stretch out in front of me. "What do they want then? I don't have anything of value." I was confused, what I could offer?

Nathan chuckled sardonically. "What about your powers? My word, you challenged the strength of an old vampire tonight." He raised his eyebrows, referring to himself. "I saw the burns you left on Victor. Now, be honest with me; how hard did you have to try to push me away?"

I remembered back to the surge that I used to push Nathan back and realized that even though I was angry and frustrated I still had control over my powers, and had not used them full force against him. "Not too hard," I finally replied.

"I see. And the dogs; how hard was that for you to pull together tonight?"

"They were wolves," I corrected him. "I had never tried before. I was desperate, though."

"Good first try," Nathan said, but his words chilled me. "I don't know you well... but I can tell as I sit here with you now that you do have great powers and you have only hit the tip of the iceberg. Whether you like it or not, your powers will continue to surface and you will be faced with learning how to use them, control and sharpen them."

I thought out loud. "So the Blue Daemons are after me for my powers? What do they plan on doing with me? Taking me back to where they came from?"

"I doubt it," Nathan answered quickly. "They have ways of only extracting what they want and leaving the rest, sort of a shell, behind." Nathan looked down at Victor who was just that – a shell.

I looked at Victor, tasting my fear. "What exactly did they do to him?"

"They drained him of all his powers, strengths and knowledge, the knowledge that he carried about you." Nathan sat down on the floor near Victor's body. "The Daemons could not reach you, so they took what they could from him."

"If they were after me, and could not get me, and are only programmed to do a job, how did they know to attack Victor?" I asked in bewilderment, looking at Nathan.

"Apparently, whoever has called for these Daemons knows that you and Victor are connected. So if they are unable to get to you directly they will use Victor against you to find out all they can about you. They want your powers."

"But what will they do with me once they find me?" I asked.

He shrugged. "I don't know. It would seem that they could take you alive or they could drain you of all your powers and leave you for dead. The Blue Daemons would then take your raw powers back to whoever called upon them and deliver the powers to that person to use themselves." Nathan's eyes scanned me briefly. "And the Amulet would go, too." He pointed at the Amulet I was wearing. "I know it means something; I'm just not sure what. I've seen it before. It's old, very, very old." His eyes narrowed as he studied the pendent hanging around my neck.

I sighed and touched Victor's arm. "So these Blue Daemons drained Victor of his powers and knowledge and left him for dead?"

"Not for dead; that's not really possible. Mentally he is drained; he needs time to recharge. He will. It will take many days before he is well again," Nathan explained. "That's why I tried to tell you out in the woods that there is nothing we could do right then and there; we could only wait. I was trying to think of the safety of the Emissary, get you back indoors and go back for Victor."

I shuddered at the word Emissary but allowed it to pass. "My blood, will it help him?" I asked. I had shared before with Victor and I was willing to share again.

"Not this time. Not now. He is not physically hurt, as you can see. Once his strength improves your blood will assist in his recovery, but right now, time and darkness is all he needs."

I nodded. "How do we get him back home?"

"I think it best that for the first few days he stay right where he is. Do you have a dark area that he can rest in without disruption?" Nathan inquired. "I will come by at night and check on him."

I did not mind Victor recuperating in my home, but I remembered his warning about me being around him when he woke up from a long rest. "Will I be safe here with him? Is there any danger to me here with him?"

Nathan considered this. "He won't be going anywhere for a few days. Once he starts to regain some consciousness, I will take him home. It would be best that way for all of us."

"I have a spare room that I don't use. There is just a bed in there. The blinds are usually always pulled and the room doesn't get a lot of light," I offered.

"It's better than the futon he sleeps on now," Nathan conceded. He lifted Victor easily and cradled him in his arms.

I walked down the hallway and opened the door to the spare room, turning on the bedside lamp; it had a low wattage bulb that gave off a dim glow. All the blinds were down and the room was fairly dark. Nathan followed me in and set Victor on the bed.

"Help me get him out of these wet clothes," I asked Nathan.

It took several minutes but we finally got Victor stripped down to a pair of boxers and under the covers to rest. I took Victor's clothes and tossed them into the laundry. He would need something to wear that was clean and dry eventually.

Before Nathan left, he instructed me on what to expect from Victor in the next few days. He explained that Victor might appear to be somewhat responsive to words and movement in the room, but said he wouldn't really be coherent, or able to converse with me. Nathan warned me that Victor's first instinctive response when he was feeling better would be to feed, and that's when there could be trouble. He also added that this stage was quick to pass but wanted Victor out of my home, to avoid any danger to me and any more life-long regrets for him.

Chapter 23

After Nathan left, I spent some time with Victor, although, according to Nathan, he could not hear me. I wasn't sure in my heart if he could or couldn't. I guess I thought about all the accounts of people who had come out of a coma recounting conversations that had happened around them. I wanted Victor to know that I was there if he could hear me. If he couldn't, well, I guess it didn't matter what I said. I finally left him in the comfort and safety of the darkened room to rest. The best medicine I could provide for him right now, so I was told.

It was getting late and I needed to go to work the next day as well as stop by the gallery. Before I went to bed, I cleaned up the dinner dishes, forgotten out on the deck during the chaotic evening. The rain had done a good job of washing them clean. The weather had finally broken and the skies were clearing; the air was thick and heavy, humid and uncomfortable to me. I could feel the weight of baleful stares coming from the trees, zeroing in on my back as I cleared the table. It was the most disconcerting feeling. I could hear movement coming from the trees and panic filled my body as I thought about what kind of nighttime creature might be out there. I forced my feet to move towards the railing, closer to the sounds of rustling of leaves and brush, struggling against my will that told me to ignore it and just walk away. A part of me needed a glimpse; it was pure curiosity, the kind that killed the cat.

A statuesque white and silver wolf sat halfway between the safety of the edge of the woods and the openness of the grassy backyard. He was so still, he could have been mistaken for a statue. He calmly looked at me, clearly waiting for an acknowledgement of some sort. I was shocked by its beauty and returned its stare, realizing that he was one of the wolves that I had called upon to aid me in saving Victor from the Blue Daemons. He had come to tell me that he and the others had completed their jobs; – the Blue Daemons were gone.

"Good boy," I called softly down to the yard. "So brave."

The wolf stood on all fours as I spoke to him, waited a moment after my praise, then turned and trotted like a miniature pony back in to the woods.

Such a magnificent animal, I thought to myself as I loaded the dishwasher, and so obedient. I had not expected to see any of the wolves I called upon again. It was a pleasant surprise to see a creature that, for once, was not after me.

I slept well, given the type of night I had, and my concern over Victor who lay silent across the hall from me. Before work I looked in on him and was not surprised to see he was in the same position Nathan and I had placed him the night before. I left home hoping I would not be out too late after work, and could sit with Victor for a moment before Nathan came by to check on him.

On my way to work I thought about what my Monday would bring me – Drew. I had not heard from him all weekend. Not since our little falling out on Friday; it seemed so long ago, when I reflected back through the entire weekend. I stopped to think about what I knew on Friday about Victor, Nathan, the Blue Daemons and even myself and what I knew now driving into work. Wow, who would have ever guessed life could get more complicated for me? No wonder I hadn't had any time to think about Drew, or anything else for that matter, over the past few days.

As I walked into the station and past Sue the receptionist, I began to feel the pressure of the day ahead, more specifically facing Drew and seeing how he was going to treat me. I worried about it. I probably shouldn't have. But I did like Drew and I cared about what he thought of me. So, at ten when I started my air shift and he had not shown yet, I presumed that he had decided to take the day off or he quit his internship, one or the other; the thought of either left me distressed and feeling a little guilty.

By the time I got off the air I had forgotten about Drew, not totally, but realized my mind was partially preoccupied with the gallery and the opening and cocktail party on Friday. It suddenly occurred to me that even if Victor had a miraculous recovery this week that he would most likely be in no shape to accompany me on Friday as planned. More distress and disappointment in my life.

I could not remember when I picked up my mail last at the gallery, which could explain why the box was overflowing. I opened up the shop and dumped the pile of envelopes and packages on my desk. The answering machine was flashing away, the red beacon flickering off and on as if pleading with me to take notice. I sighed, not knowing where to start first, mail or messages. I pulled out the black leather swivel chair from my desk and sat down with a dejected thump. My eyes were fixed on the clutter in front of me, a mountainous pile of mail. I began to shuffle through it, finding more advertisements than pertinent information, filling my trash can before I reached the surface of my desk. Cracking open a can of Diet Coke, I began to sort through what mail I felt was important enough to take home and what I thought could stay in a drawer at the shop to be gone over at a later date.

The front door of the shop opened, the heavy creaking sound on the hinges alerting me to look up from my duties.

"Hi, sorry I missed you today," Drew spoke, allowing the door to close behind him. He punched his hands deep into his wide jean pockets and, obviously uncomfortable, approached my desk.

I rolled my chair back and against the wall, crossing my legs. "It was slow. Got to start working on The Battle of the Bands thing soon."

"Yeah, coming up sooner than we think," Drew added, and pulled up a chair on the other side of the desk. He sat stiffly but made an effort to appear composed.

"I've got a busy week otherwise," I rolled my eyes and blew a lock of hair out of my face. "Friday is the big night." I tried to be casual, knowing he did not feel at ease with me.

Drew leaned over my messy desk. "I need to talk to you."

I nodded. "We can talk."

Drew folded his hands on top of some flyers on the desk. "I realized over the weekend that I have been a little pushy with you. My priorities are off and I have not been thinking straight. I have to finish up school in the next month or so; I have my internship with you that I am grateful for and I need to find a job. I have really been blowing it lately because all I want is to have a great time – all the time, and I wanted to spend time with you outside of work."

"Nothing wrong with wanting to have fun as long as you keep the rest of the stuff in mind too. As far you and I..."

"Yeah, I need to talk to you about that." He sighed as if it were something he would rather not bring up. "I have been a little over-ambitious when it comes to you and me. I'm sorry."

A kind smile crossed my face. "Listen, it's like I've been saying: I do like you, and I do like to go out with you. We have a great time together."

"Yes, we do have a great time. And I figured that we could step our relationship up and I forced that on you; I shouldn't have," Drew mumbled looking across the desk at me, his eyes round and sad. "I don't want to ruin our friendship, because relationships come and go but good friendships can last forever."

"I worried about how this would all turn out. I didn't want to lose you," I said. "I do care about you." I reached forward and placed my hand on top of his. "I get bored at work without you."

Drew laughed a little and sat back in his chair. "But you care about Victor more than me, right?"

I only had to think a second about what he said and I nodded. "Yes."

"Lucky guy."

I determined it was a good time to change the subject for all parties involved. “So, you coming to my opening on Friday so I can introduce you to some culture?”

“I don’t know. I’m pretty resistant to that kind of stuff. Culture scares me.” He laughed and stood, sliding his chair back to where it came from.

“Oh come on, free booze and food,” I said persuasively.

He thought for a moment before replying. “I’ll let you know. We’ll be seeing each other before then.”

“All right. You get your butt into work tomorrow,” I ordered him. “Don’t make me mark you out again.”

He slowly walked to the door as I teased him; his head tipped back looking up at the tall ceiling. “I’ll be there, I’ll be there; hazelnut with sweet-n-low and cream, don’t worry.” He let himself out of the shop and waved a goodbye as he passed the storefront window.

I was glad that was behind me. I was glad Drew was still part of my life.

I returned a few phone calls, gathered up some of the mail I wanted to bring home with me by packing up my tote bag, straightened up my desk and locked up shop on my way out. It was around dinnertime when I stumbled into the condo with all my belongings, allowing them to flow out of my arms into a heap on my desk near the door. I was exhausted.

After kicking off my sneakers my first priority was Victor. I walked down the short hallway to the quiet room where Victor lay. I stopped outside the door and pressed my ear close to see if I could hear any movement or noises from within. I could not but remained cautious while I slowly turned the knob and opened the door silently by pressing my shoulder against it. I opened it just a crack, enough to slide my body through. The room was very dark, warm and stuffy, almost stagnant due to the lack of circulating air. I wanted to open a window but did not dare for fear even the smallest ray of sunshine could seep into Victor’s tomb. I reached for the small table lamp and turned the switch once, illuminating him with a faint glow. Victor had repositioned himself and was lying on his stomach; the covers down around his waist and his arms sprawled out on either side of him. He looked quite content. I noticed immediately that his long beautiful hair was a snarled, ratty mess. I took a hairbrush out of the bathroom and returned, sitting gently next to him on the bed. He looked so peaceful sleeping; I wondered if he was or if he was in any pain or some type of discomfort that I could not fathom. I removed the tie from his hair as gently as I could, hoping I wasn’t yanking any strands of hair with it. I placed the coiled up tie on the nightstand and carefully began to brush Victor’s hair. I smiled as I groomed him, feeling like a little girl playing with a doll; only Victor had much nicer hair than any doll I’d ever had. I brushed his hair into my hands, feeling how silky and smooth it was;

it flowed through my fingers like the finest silk. I ran my hands down his back caressing his skin; it was dry and cool to the touch. My fingers followed the curves of the muscles on his arms, down over his biceps. I rested my hand on his, wanting him to feel me with him.

The door to the room opened silently. I turned my head quickly, alerted by the puff of cooler air from the hallway. My contentment vanished as I saw Nathan standing in the open doorway, a somber square-like image with his arms to his side. Once he was sure I saw him, he spoke. "Your front door was unlocked. Now it's not."

"I wish you would have knocked," I whispered.

Nathan stepped into Victor's room and approached the side of the bed I sat on. The lack of light in the room made Nathan look more ominous than usual, his gloomy demeanor magnified. Thankfully, I did not detect the immediate vibes of his disinterest or dislike in me tonight.

"Did you turn him?" Nathan asked, looking into Victor's face, obviously amused with how he was resting. "He likes to sleep like this."

"No... he was like this when I came in to see him," I replied. "Is that strange that he moved on his own?"

"A little," Nathan replied cautiously. "I take it he's not talking yet." Nathan circled the bed. "Each recovery is a little different."

"Not yet." I watched him walk around the foot of the bed. "If he's progressing quickly, should you take him home soon?"

"We'll see how he is tomorrow night. If you start seeing some activity coming from him, let me know. You have my number."

I ran my fingers through Victor's hair lovingly. "So I just leave him here like this?"

"For now... I really don't think there is anything anyone can do. The last time this happened it took about a week – maybe a little less for him to feel well. Once he wants to feed, his recovery time should be quick," Nathan explained, recalling back god knows how many years.

"There goes my date on Friday night for the opening of the gallery," I laughed dryly, confirming my suspicions I'd be going solo.

Nathan switched gears. "I have been asked by the High Counsel to invite you to their Manor on Saturday night." He spoke as a diplomat for the counsel. I half expected to hear a trumpet and see Nathan pull a scroll out of his jacket pocket with an official declaration of the event and cordially requesting my presence.

"What for?" I asked nervously, wondering what they wanted of me.

Nathan came close to me. "I believe it so the Counsel can meet their next Emissary."

I did not know what to say. I felt flushed, almost faint and strangely unable to move.

"It's just a meeting. They have no plans on doing anything with you on Saturday night. I can assure you that," Nathan further clarified after seeing my initial reaction to his invitation.

"I see," I managed to say flatly, as if I had watched my life flash before my eyes without any way to retrieve it.

"We can talk more about it later on in the week," he suggested. "If you think Victor needs me, or if you have anything to report, call me," Nathan added as he walked out of the room, leaving me alone with Victor once again.

I left Victor while I made something for dinner and did some laundry. It was strange how even though I could not see Victor I felt his presence all through my home. Perhaps I was just overly conscious of him because he was near, or maybe it was because I knew he was not well and my heightened senses were acting like a baby monitor. I didn't want to be too far away in case Victor needed me, although if he did need me, I didn't know what I could do.

I was rinsing off my dinner dishes in the kitchen sink when I heard Victor's voice. '*Hot*'. I turned the water off. "Victor?" I said aloud. There was no immediate response. I set the dishes into the sink and wiped my hands on a dishtowel. '*Hot*,' I heard again, the sound coming from Victor's room. I walked out of the kitchen and into the living room, my suspicions aroused, thinking that it was not possible for Victor to have gotten out of bed. Was I hearing Victor in my head? Maybe he was trying to tell me something. I approached his bedroom door and again listened carefully from outside to see if I could hear anything. It was quiet. I opened the door slowly, peering into the blackness, waiting for my eyes to adjust to the gloom. Victor had managed to change positions in bed again. He was now lying on his back, as he was when Nathan and I first put him there.

I cautiously made my way to the edge of the bed and looked down at him. He was perspiring badly and had kicked his covers nearly off. I sat next to him and felt his forehead; I wasn't sure if it was possible for him to run a fever, but something surely was pushing his body temperature up. Victor moved his head in my direction and slowly opened his eyes; he blinked several times. I smiled at him as he continued to stare at me. "I don't even know if you understand me, but I'm here for you," I spoke softly.

His lips didn't move, yet I heard again, '*Hot*'.

"Yes you are, you are running a fever," I said to him as I brushed his hair away from his face. "Let me see if I can help." I walked into the kitchen and poured a chilled glass of water from out of the refrigerator and then found a plastic container in the cabinet and ran some luke-warm tap water into it grabbing a clean face cloth from the bathroom on my way back. I entered the room and set the container of warm water and the face cloth on the nightstand. I wasn't sure if I could get Victor to drink or not, but I knew he had to have water. I held the glass in front of him. "It's cold," I spoke gently, as if talking to a child. I propped Victor's head up and placed the glass to his lips. He seemed to understand what I was doing and struggled to drink, managing to swallow some of the water. He fell back exhausted on his pillow and closed his eyes. "I know you must be tired," I said, placing the glass of water out of reach on the nightstand.

I set the container of water and the washcloth on my lap. "Still hot?" I asked him, not expecting an answer. I wrung the terry cloth out and then folded it in half, placing it gently on Victor's forehead. His eyes opened wide. "I'm sorry," I apologized, but kept the cool cloth pressed to his hot skin. His eyes rolled in my direction following my voice. "I did not mean to startle you," I soothed. "I'm trying to help." I picked up his hand and placed the damp cloth on it. I smoothed it over his skin he watched my every move, his eyes tired and unfocused. "I bet this feels good," I said, trailing the cloth up his arm slowly as he watched and then to his neck. He closed his eyes and appeared to relax under my touch. I dunked the cloth back into the water, squeezed out the excess and patted his chest, soaking up his sweat. I thought I heard him sigh in contentment. Without me saying another word verbally I decided that maybe I could communicate with him the way he had with me, telepathically. I had never tried it on my own except for the time I was at Victor's place and gave Nathan a piece of my mind. I looked at Victor, whose eyes were still shut. I continued to wipe off his chest. '*How are you feeling*?' I asked in my mind. Victor opened his eyes sleepily and let his head loll in my direction. '*Tired*,' he responded. I smiled because I had finally gotten through to him and felt reconnected in a way. '*I'm here for you*.' A ghost of a smile touched his lips. '*I know*.' I opened up the face cloth and laid it on his stomach. He shivered a bit. '*Nathan was here tonight*,' I commented. Victor nodded slightly. I removed the cloth from his stomach. '*Maybe you can go home tomorrow night*'. Victor made no response, but just watched me sleepily. I reached down to the foot of the bed and pulled the covers up to his waist. '*Can I open the window a little for you? I'll close it before I go to sleep – promise.*' He blinked his eyes contentedly and sighed, '*Yes*'. I stretched my body over the nightstand and reached under the blinds, unlatching the window and raising it several inches. I could feel a night breeze blow in right away. '*I'll let you get some rest. Be back before I go to sleep.*' I bent down and kissed his cheek. Victor smiled slightly again and shut his eyes to rest. I gathered up what I had brought in, shut off the light and closed the door behind me.

I called Nathan after I left Victor's room. I knew he was not expecting me. I told him that Victor was running a fever, and explained what I'd done to help. Nathan said that the sweats are sometimes brought on by the need to feed, but thought they had occurred far to soon in his recovery. I also told him that I was able to talk to him for a while telepathically. Nathan was surprised and wanted me to keep him updated, saying he might have to take him home sooner if his progress didn't slow down. I said I was going to check on him one more time before I went to sleep and would call him back if there were any other changes. Nathan reminded me be careful.

Before I retired for the night I checked on Victor one last time. He was resting quietly and did not stir when I passed the bed to shut the window. I did not want to disturb him so I said nothing verbally or telepathically while I was there. I allowed his sleep to be uninterrupted.

Chapter 24

The next day, as promised, Drew was at the station. He waited, coffee in hand, as I walked into the reception area. I smiled, glad to see him, and told him we had lots of work to do when I got off the air. The Battle of the Bands concert was only a few weeks away and it seemed I would be having meetings with the staff, other department heads and station management up until the day before the event. Drew appeared to be back to his usual self – vulgar, entertaining and carefree, which made me feel like *me* again, at least for a little while, until I thought about Victor recuperating at home alone. How I wished I could be with him, even though I knew I could do nothing to speed his recovery. I wanted to know how he was, to ease the anxiety I felt.

After I got off the air, Drew and I worked on some production together in the studio. The head of our Promotion Department barged in to ask Drew if he was interested in taking the station van downtown to some of the local bars and hang-outs, and give tickets away to promote the end of the summer bash we were all working so hard on. Drew being Drew could hardly say no; it gave him a chance to be *someone* – have chicks hang all over him, eat and drink for free and do some live phone-ins with the night-time jock. Drew was experiencing a slice of heaven. He needed very little encouragement from me to accept the offer, and snatched the keys to the van from my hands, joyfully leaving the station and feeling on top of the world. I was happy for him.

I realized I had little need to be at the gallery today, since I just wanted to call the caterer one more time. I had been feeling a little nervous about Friday and needed to assure myself everything would go smoothly, at least on their part. The woman confirmed again that she and her staff would be at the gallery an hour before the party, and would stay up to an hour afterwards to break down and clean up. Much to her reluctance, we went over the entire appetizer selections again as she tried to assure me that everything would go just fine, she did this for a living, not to worry. I told her I would try *not* to think too much more about it between now and then. After all, I had other things to think about.

The threat of thunderstorms made me want to get home quickly. It was getting dark; the gunmetal gray clouds funneling in around me meant Victor was probably stirring in his bed. I wondered how his healing was progressing, and tried not to think too much about what Nathan had warned me about, that his time to feed would surely come. The more rapidly Victor improved, the faster the threat to fulfill his craving to feed. I guess I never looked upon Victor as being a true danger to my existence; I knew he was a creature, a killer, but I never felt *I* was ever at a great risk. Perhaps I felt most of the time I was above all that. The worst I'd felt around Victor, when his intentions were unclear, was a sort of tension, the kind that teeters between the thrill of the moment and the possible regret afterwards.

The sound of thunder rumbled in the distance as I unlocked the door. I unloaded my tote bag at the desk and wondered when I'd be seeing Nathan tonight, especially with the thunderstorms approaching. I decided to check on Victor before attending to my evening chores. As I started down the hall I could tell almost immediately that something was not right. Victor's bedroom door was open. Cautiously, I peeked into his room. The bed was empty, the sheets rumpled and tossed back in disarray. Surprised, I didn't know if I should be alarmed, frightened or just pleased that he was well enough to get himself out of bed. Where had he gone? I turned to check my room and saw that the door was shut. I never leave the door that way unless *I* am the one sleeping. I took hold of the doorknob, twisted it quietly and walked in. Victor was asleep in my bed. The bed was in shambles, looking as if some life or death struggle had taken place, separating the mattress from the foundation. The comforter, blankets and sheets were twisted and knotted in between all the bedding layers. Victor lay across the mattress diagonally, his face buried in my pillow that he had clutched in his arms and pulled intimately against his body.

He appeared dead to the world, as if not even a sonic blast could rouse him. I still was not sure what his intent was for abandoning his bed for mine. I sat on the edge of the bed, picked up the phone and dialed Nathan's number to give him an early evening update.

"Hello."

"Nathan, it's Kala," I said, looking over in Victor's direction. He had not moved.

"How is Victor?" Nathan asked apprehensively, as if he knew I was going to tell him something different tonight.

"He's sleeping, but somehow got out of his bed and is now in mine," I spoke wonderingly, as if I was giving the details of a child's first steps.

"Hmmm," was all Nathan said.

"Did you want to take him with you tonight? It seems like he needs more supervision than I can give," I admitted. I didn't want anything to happen to him while he was under my care.

"Let me come by and see how he is. I think I know what he's going through. I've been getting strange messages from him all day," Nathan told me. He added, with some certainty, that he could answer most of my questions tonight.

"All right. I'll be here," I replied.

Just as I hung up the phone I noticed out of the corner of my eye Victor peering over the pillow with the most devilish look in his eyes. He continued to hang on to the big green feather bundle, his arm wrapped around it, snuggling it against his chest. His look made me smile, as if he was playing hide and seek with me, with only a portion of his face showing behind the fluffy obstacle. "What are you doing?" I asked softly, reaching my hand to push the pillow away from his face.

Victor made no reply. He let go of the pillow and abruptly slid his body closer to me. He was focused totally on me; his big brown eyes looking so inquisitive yet also appeared to be smiling in my direction. He reached over and touched my body for the first time in days, placing his hand on my side, rubbing firmly up and down.

"You must be feeling better," I remarked, watching his expressions.

Victor moved closer, invading my territory on the bed. His body was like the ideal all-terrain vehicle, climbing over everything in his way, including me. He swiftly rolled me over onto my back and maneuvered himself to straddle my thighs. He placed a hand on either side of my head as he held himself up on all fours looking down upon me. His dark hair fell forward around his face and cascaded along his bare shoulders.

"Victor?" I said, looking up at him. I reached to touch his chest and with that he quickly pinned my hands down to the bed in one motion, not allowing me to move. "What's up?" I tried to laugh but the serious, intent look on his face was beginning to unnerve me. I thought that maybe I could connect telepathically to him although he had not tried yet with me. '*Victor – what are you doing*?' I asked, staring at him, wanting answers. '*What do you want?*'

Victor, who was still wearing only the pair of boxers Nathan and I had stripped him down to, lowered his body onto mine, rubbing his crotch against my fully dressed body. I could feel the stiffness of his penis press into my thigh. '*You,*' was all Victor uttered in his mind. He continued to look down upon me, holding his body above mine.

"Victor, now is not a good time. Nathan is on his way," I warned him. I don't think Victor understood what I was trying to tell him, or I accidentally sent him the wrong message because he didn't release me. He lowered his arms and brought his face to mine, taking some of his weight off my restrained wrists and hands. I felt his hot breath against my face as our lips touched. His hands snuck under my backside and he drew me tightly to his chest as he continued to kiss me. "I want you," Victor finally whispered in my ear. It was good to hear his voice. "Need you." A low guttural moan came from deep within him as he made an effort to control his desires. His hands slid down over my rear end and along the outer curves of my thighs as he dug his fingers deeply into my jeans.

"Victor. Get off her," Nathan's firm voice cut through the pressure of the moment.

Victor lifted his face away from mine and then up to the voice, acknowledging the source.

"You heard me," Nathan ordered. "Let her up."

Victor glanced back down at me, his eyes saddened by the turn of events, crushed and disappointed. With his spirit extinguished, I was able to struggle and worm my way out of his grasp, finally standing next to Nathan.

"Victor, let's get you back to your room," Nathan extended his arm out and reached for him to come closer. Without much resistance Victor followed his Sire's instructions and rolled out of bed, still clutching my pillow, hugging it under his arm. Nathan took hold of Victor's arm, but had trouble pulling him in the direction he wanted. Victor held the pillow to himself and looked back at me, refusing to leave. "Kala, will you please go into the other room? Perhaps he will follow you." Nathan asked for my assistance, frustrated at dealing with Victor's childish antics.

I quickly scooted by both men without a word and crossed the hallway into what was now Victor's room. Nathan seemed to have an easier time getting him to vacate and go back to his own room using me as the bait. Once Nathan and Victor entered, I dropped back away from the bed, and Nathan persuaded Victor to lie down, although he was reluctant.

"Victor, I want you to stay right here. We will be back in a minute," Nathan spoke slowly, hoping he would fully comprehend his command. Nathan escorted me out of the room and closed the door behind us.

I walked into the living room and took a deep breath. "Well, that was interesting."

Nathan crossed his arms. "He can be so human at times, it's infuriating!" He ground his teeth in displeasure, his face flush with anger.

"What is that supposed to mean?" I asked, feeling slightly insulted by his remark as my eyes followed him.

Nathan shook his head as he spoke. "There are two primal emotions humans have – to survive and to mate. We have one – survive. We feed to survive. That's it. Very few of us have a second primal emotion which is as strong as the first, in fact, it is extremely rare for it to surface..."

"Nathan, what are you talking about?" I asked, confused.

"I assumed by now Victor's primary instinct to feed would be evident, but the instinct he is following now is mating. That's your fault," Nathan huffed.

I wrinkled my forehead and looked up at him. "Excuse me?" How was I to blame?

"I should have known. Leaving him here was not a good idea. He can pick your scent up everywhere in this place," Nathan snapped. "Why do you think he is carrying around your stupid pillow? It reeks of your scent. That's why you found him in your bed. He's looking for you, he wants to, you know, with you..." He struggled to explain in the most tactful manner he could that Victor wanted to have sex with me. He paced the floor like a parent in distress.

"I'm sorry." Even as I apologized, I was thinking how exciting it was for Victor to have such a strong will and desire to want to me. I tingled with the thought of having Victor that way, primal and uninhibited. "What about his need to feed?" I forced a more appropriate question, trying to push the thought of Victor's naked body out of my mind.

"That still must come. Soon," Nathan sighed, rubbing his chin. "Although he is persistent, annoying and bothersome, he is no danger to himself tonight, or to you. I can't think of a way to keep him put. He apparently has the strength to be mobile now, and the strength of a vampire, whether he thinks he is one or not at this point. It's not like we can tie him up; that unfortunately would not be right," Nathan thought out loud.

"I have a spell that was left to me for 'bindings'. I could try it. I'm not promising anything," I offered, remembering seeing it in Sara's journal. "But that is cruel too... isn't it? He would still be restrained. Can't you just take him home with you?"

"Honestly, I don't want him home like *this*," Nathan was appalled with Victor's natural desires shining through. "He'd be unbearable. *All* I've been doing *all* day is trying to tune him out; he's been tossing and turning and dreaming and thinking *all* day about *sex*. If he and I were under the same roof he'd deafen me with all his chatter. It's hard enough to block him at a distance." Nathan had reached his wits end with Victor and his sexual thoughts. Perhaps Nathan was hot and bothered too, though he'd never admit it. "I can deal with the need to feed and the continuous hunt of the night. I can relate to that."

"So you are just going to abandon him until he reaches a point where you can deal with him?" I asked, shocked he could turn his back on one of his own. "What happened the last time he went through this? Isn't this the same?"

"I'm not abandoning him. This time it's different. Last time he didn't have feelings for a female. Nerissa was long gone and it was just the two of us, so he didn't have any reproductive urges." Nathan's body language was beginning to get defensive. "He shouldn't have them to begin with. They are futile in most of us. Only a chosen few are able to reproduce. Victor is not one of them," Nathan barked in irritation, with me, and the entire situation. He slowly walked to the sliding glass door and looked up at the storm clouds moving in, disinterested in me.

I went after him, livid with his lack of understanding to what Victor was going through. "Well, maybe if he had been allowed over the last two hundred years to sire and love someone himself he wouldn't be like this today. If you want to hold anyone to blame, make it your own people. For God sakes – he'd been embraced but a few short days before his own people cast him away. He was forced to live like a human in a human world when he wasn't; he had no willing role model in you because you hated him for what he did to Nerissa, even though he knew no better. You hated him for what you lost in your life. He had no one to turn to; no others like him to confide in, so he rebelled against you and your people and began to work with the Blue Daemons. He was angry at the world he lived in, though eventually in time he changed and was able to turn to people like me, keeping his identity a secret but still able to befriend us because that was all he knew – to be human and turn towards humans. What a horrible life he must have lived. You should be ashamed of yourself!" I hollered at him, not able to understand why he was so unsympathetic to Victor and what he had to endure over the years.

It was so obvious to me why Victor was who he was today because of the actions that took place so soon after his gift of immortality, his birth into the night. Victor might be a vampire in regards to needing blood to sustain his life and not being able to tolerate the day's light, but everything else about him that I felt counted was human to me. What a good person he must have been when he was alive; I wish I knew him then, or at least remembered him from my past.

Nathan apparently was not pleased with the tone in my voice or what I had said to him and retaliated by promptly clasping his hand around my throat and squeezing firmly. His eyes lit up in fury at me. "You don't know anything about my people. Emissary or not I could crush you to death right now!"

I said nothing because I was unable to. I could only feel Nathan's large and powerful hand around my throat compressing my windpipe, making it extremely difficult to breathe. I wheezed each time I tried to inhale. I stared at him, knowing he would not dare kill me. He would not allow himself to do it. He had waited too long to regain his freedom among his people and would not let the big mouth of a human stand in his way.

"No," Victor's voice called out from behind me.

My ears began to ring as my blood flow was constricted, and I could feel the tension in my head mount. Nathan did not respond to Victor's voice and continued to look upon me as I tried not to struggle in his grip.

"Nathan. No," Victor said loudly, as I heard him come up on us.

Nathan released his grip and threw me away as if I were trash being disposed of. I doubled over and breathed in as deep as I could, swallowing, trying to reopen my airway where the muscles had contracted in on themselves.

Victor approached Nathan angrily. Even though Victor was still not feeling one hundred percent, he stood his ground, refusing to back down. I heard nothing verbal take place between the two of them, but my head swam in a sea of ferocity as they traded evil sentiments to one another over what had happened with me. Little by little I hoisted myself to a standing position, finally getting enough oxygen into my system to clear the ringing in my ears. Still lightheaded, I braced myself, holding onto the back of a dining room chair several feet away from Victor and Nathan.

"Enough," I exhaled sharply. "It's not worth it." I began to walk away from them into the kitchen for a needed drink. I opened the refrigerator and took out a can of soda, slamming the door shut.

Victor came close to me and combed his fingers through my hair soothingly, then placed his hand under my chin and tipped my head up. He looked into my eyes, concern on his face, and then scanned my neck and throat quickly for any injuries I might have sustained from Nathan's brutal force. "Are you okay?"

I nodded and pulled away from him, uncomfortable with Nathan being close by. I glared in Nathan's direction and walked by him without a word. I sat on the couch and picked up Sara's journal, and began to thumb through it. Although they did not know it, I could pick up pieces of their private conversations in the other room. They were arguing over what Nathan had done to me. I sat back, a telepathic eavesdropper to the exchange of psychic interjections, until its conclusion. I looked up from my book as they entered.

"Victor refuses to come home with me tonight," Nathan said in disgust. "But, he has agreed to let you use your 'binding' spell on him to insure you will be safe here in the event his mood changes. Tomorrow night Victor will come back with me."

"I see." I looked up at both parties. "What if I feel Victor should leave with you tonight?" I asked, placing the book on my lap.

"He would rather not. But if you can talk him into it, I will take him with me," Nathan bargained.

Victor sat next to me on the arm of the couch saying nothing, but I could feel within him that he was happier with me than with Nathan at this point in his recuperation, needing more understanding and consoling than Nathan could ever dream of giving him. Without consulting Victor, I allowed him to stay. "I'll do it for Victor."

I searched Sara's journal for the 'binding' spell I had come across earlier and when I found it read it through. It seemed simple enough. I had the words, all I needed was two black ribbons, one longer than the other. I went through one of the boxes that I had packed up with her belongings and found a small spool of black silk cording. I cut it in two lengths – one shorter size representing the arms, the other the legs, and put them in the journal as a bookmark to easily find the 'binding' spell again. When Nathan was ready to leave for the evening we ushered Victor into his room and got him situated for the night in bed. I was not sure exactly how tight to make the 'binding' spell. I did not want him to be uncomfortable, yet I did not want him to get free. The spell's strength supposedly was determined by how tight the knots were tied, so I wanted to do it correctly. Apprehensively, I cleared my mind and tried to focus.

The spell needed to be read twice, once for the arms and once for the legs, tying knots in between readings. Victor got as comfortable as possible before I started the binding spell for his arms. I took the shorter of the black cords and held it up as I read the following: *"A spell to bind. A spell to confine. I work my art of magic on you tonight. Lend me your power to make it right. By all the elements of the land, the sea and the sky I summon your power to bind my spell. I call on you to bind him well."* I tied the shorter black cord loosely, slipping the knot near the center.

"Okay Victor, try and move your arms," Nathan ordered, walking around to the side of the bed.

Victor's arms lay at the side of his body. He tried several times to move them. "I can't," Victor replied and laughed a little.

Nathan attempted to lift Victor's arms but could not. "Seems to be holding," Nathan confirmed.

I walked over to Victor and took his hand, expecting not to be able to lift it either, but I could with ease. "C'mon you guys, it didn't work," I sighed.

"Kala, I could not lift his arm. I'm telling you he is bound down," Nathan argued with me and tried unsuccessfully once again to lift Victor's arm.

Victor tried again as well. "I can't. Only Kala can. It's her spell," Victor announced.

Uncertain, I read the spell again and tied the longer cord to bind Victor's legs. Once again neither Victor nor Nathan could move a leg, but I could. Just to prove to myself once and for all that the spell did hold I began to tickle Victor, running and poking my fingers erratically up and down his sides and under his arms. He wiggled and laughed on the bed and pleaded for me to stop because he could not fight back. Apparently the spell held. To reverse the spell, all I had to do was untie the black cords and say, *"Reverse the spell that bound so well, unbind, unconfine."*

I walked Nathan to the front door, eager to see him leave. "Good night," I said unenthusiastically as I opened the door.

"Victor will need to feed soon," Nathan said, standing in the doorway. "Before you come home tomorrow night I'd like you to stop by and pick me up at the house, so I can get Victor and make sure you are safe. It's for your own good."

"Don't worry about me," I muttered, as if I didn't have a care in the world. "I'll be just fine."

"Kala, I'm serious. Even Victor thought it a good idea. He feels it coming upon him, that's why we decided the bindings had to go on tonight," Nathan tried to reason with me.

"I'll call you tomorrow," I offered. "Before I come home." I wanted him to leave. I would have said anything.

That seemed good enough for Nathan at the moment. He knew he was not my favorite person. People who try to kill me usually aren't.

Chapter 25

It was still early when I put on my nightshirt to lounge around the house. I turned the TV on and tried to make myself comfortable in the living room even though I knew Victor was in the next room by himself. I felt a little guilty knowing Victor was alone and bound to the bed by my spell with no radio, TV, or even a book to keep him company. Maybe he didn't require it, but I sure as hell would. Maybe he was content laying in the dark resting and thinking. I wondered what he was thinking about. Did he need my company? Would it help or hinder him not knowing his current frame of mind. Would it be torture to him for me to sit next to him on the bed? Would I just be stirring up emotions that could become volatile?

I thought about Victor *with* me, needing me and wanting no other – the way he moved over the bed and onto my body in the most domineering manner. How he took control, held and restrained me. Not like the first time we were together sexually. Our first encounter, I chose the pace and made the rules that we played by, but today it was clearly his game; he knew what he wanted and if Nathan had not been there, Victor would have gotten it. I could not have fought him off; his strength was too great and I would not have been able to resist his sexual chemistry. It was much too strong. So was there anything wrong with thinking of going in to see Victor, knowing I still had pent up passion? Maybe continuing where we left off earlier? Was it wrong of me to openly offer myself to him if it was something I was craving as well? Was it wrong to leave him bound and just *take him* the way he was? Would my boldness satisfy his need and desire or would he need more? All questions I had no answers for.

I sat in silence, brooding, waiting to see if Victor would try and contact me from his bed. He had to be aware of my inner turmoil, and I knew his desire for me had to be rising. I heard nothing and felt the same. My sizzling desires eventually became too tempting, and watching TV and sitting in comfort was nearly impossible. I needed to see Victor; see what was brewing in his mind and through his body tonight.

Collecting myself I knocked lightly on Victor's door and let myself in. Victor looked in my direction as I entered the dimly lit room. He appeared comfortable and smiled a little as I approached him. Sitting on the bed I picked up his arm, because only I could, and placed his hand in mine. I played with his long fingers. "How are you feeling?" I asked, caressing the top of his hand, my eyes refusing to meet his.

He shrugged. "Okay. Getting closer to being me, hopefully." Victor watched his hand in mine, not being able to withdraw it but being able to arrange his fingers between mine.

"Is it easier for you to talk like this or in my head?" I asked, not wanting to drain his energy; my eyes still focused on our hands.

"Doesn't matter," he replied, watching me, his head cradled in the thick goose feather pillow.

I finally raised my eyes; I wanted to see his face. Victor's brown eyes were dark, wide and alertly on me.

"I wish I could touch you," Victor sighed miserably, still watching me with the most captivating stare, as if drunk with my vision.

A small smile grew on my face. "I wish you could, too." The thought of his touch anywhere on me made my skin feel alive.

He closed his eyes and breathed in deeply, as if putting himself into a trance, trying to make all his feeling, desires and emotions go dormant.

"Maybe I should leave." I felt a little naughty, knowing my intentions for the visit were making him fight for composure, even though they were the same urges I let foster within me.

"No," he spoke firmly, opening his eyes, agitated at the thought of me leaving.

"All right. Do you want to talk? Would it help?" I asked, not knowing if in his circumstances it truly would or not. I was desperate to find a common ground for us to start on.

"What? Tell you that if I weren't bound down to the bed I'd be humping you like a dog?" he said bitterly, very unlike the Victor I knew. "I've been like this all day." His voice filled with frustration, referring to the itch of desire he could not scratch. His eyes rolled back into his head as if trying to think about something else, anything else.

A small blossom of desire kindled itself in my groin at his words. I stood up and looked at him sympathetically.

"Where are you going?" His eyes followed me.

"Who said I was going any where?" I answered coyly, placing a knee down on the bed, poised over his body. "Do you want me to stay or go?"

He swallowed hard and closed his eyes for more than a moment then forced a reply. "I *want* you to stay, but..."

"But what?" I asked slowly, balancing myself on both knees next to him.

"Why are you doing this to me?" he asked quietly, his voice sounding low and wounded.

I sat astride his lap. "Doing what?" I asked, playing dumb. I lowered my eyes to his smooth and unclothed stomach, then back up to his face.

Victor tried to keep himself calm as his eagerness grew and with that his aggravation with me did, too; I sensed his utter frustration with the situation. "Kala, damn it! This is not fair! Why are you doing this to me?" His pupils enlarged as he demanded answers.

I leaned forward on my hands and knees and inched myself up the bed over him. I looked in his eyes for a long moment, then bowed down and kissed him lightly in a teasing manner, breathing delicately onto his firm chin and jaw line. He made no response other than grinding his teeth together. Sitting upright, I straddled his waist, placing my hands on his chest, touching the soft wisps of hair beneath my palms as I seductively gazed upon him.

"Take the spell off, or call Nathan to come get me," Victor barked in irritation.

I refused to let the tone in his voice dissuade me. I smiled and bent down to kiss him again, this time being a bit more persuasive. My tongue separated his lips as I exhaled deeply, fueled by my own desires for him, wanting him to surrender and let me pleasure him. I moved my hand to the side of his face, a gesture of benevolence, feeling his hair sweep across my hand and winding his dark locks around my fingers. Victor's lips and tongue began to respond, working in perfect rhythm with mine. My brain was flashing visual fantasies of Victor and I that ran continuously like a slideshow in my mind. I felt the jarring sensations of Victor's own fantasies flash periodically through my mind's eye, but I wasn't sure if he was projecting them at me, or if I was stealing those sensations too. His kisses developed into long passionate ones that pierced me to the inner recesses of my being. Even without the use of his arms or hands I found myself securely united with his body, unwilling to remove my body from his.

"Break the spell! Break it, please," Victor implored, his voice spilling against my skin.

"I can't, it could be dangerous," I whispered, pulling away with resistance. I affectionately palmed his face.

"Just my arms, please, I need to touch you, to hold you." His eyes searched mine. "I won't be able to get free. You know that." He struggled to speak with me, to find a way to reason.

I pushed myself off of his body, climbing from the bed to the floor. I backed up several feet, contemplating his request for limited freedom, to break part of my spell. I felt torn by desire and sanity. I blinked hard several times in an effort to clear my mind and avoid the influences that tried to overload me. I wanted to do what was best for both of us and putting me in danger was something that I knew Victor would not allow in his proper frame of mind. But if Victor were unable to move his legs to get out of bed perhaps he would not be a threat to me. However, without his arms in bindings, his upper body strength could easily crush me and kill me. I knew that because of his unpredictable mood swings, his craving for blood would be soon be as strong, if not stronger, than his current longing for sex. The debate ate at my conscience. It didn't matter what I decided, nothing was going to satisfy Victor at this point, at least, as long as he was bound. Either my safety or his satisfaction would be compromised. The whole thing was frustrating. Maybe the best thing I could have done tonight was to have stayed on the couch watching TV by myself and permit the mood to pass; it would have in time.

"Kala." Victor tried to get my attention from the bed.

His voice jerked me from my train of thought. I looked down Victor, still restrained, eager for me to return to bed with him. I did not know how high the odds were that he could become unstable and I could be in danger if I released a portion of the spell. I was not a gambler. A coin toss could have made my decision for me; I just did not know what to do.

"Kala," Victor spoke again, louder this time.

"Victor, I don't know what to do," I said dejectedly.

He wiggled his body against the sheets of the bed. "That's all I can move. Please. I need you but I need to be able to move."

I sighed in confusion and lowered my head in a brief moment of thought before I took Sara's journal from the nightstand and opened the book where the black cords marked the binding spell. I removed the shorter of the black cords from the page that would release the spell on his arms. I hoped I was doing the right thing in the long run, not just the right thing for the passion of the moment.

I slowly untied the black cord as I watched Victor's anticipation grow for his limited and partial freedom to be given back to him. *"Reverse the spell that bound so well, unbind, unconfine."* With those words I placed the cord back into Sara's journal – my job was done. I shut the book. Victor shook his arms out to regain feeling and rubbed his hands up and down them vigorously to start a more rapid blood flow. The spell was broken. His mood changed almost immediately as he retook control over a portion of his body. I put the book back onto the nightstand, and continued to stay a safe distance from Victor, knowing the strongest portion of his body had been released and he was now a potential danger to me.

"What's wrong?" Victor asked as he sat upright in bed, watching me with some confusion.

"I'm not sure I did the right thing." I was being honest as I shifted my weight away from him.

"Then why did you break the spell?" Victor asked, extending his arm in my direction. He reached for my hand, wanting me to join him on the bed.

"Probably for selfish reasons, maybe hoping I was doing something good for you. I don't know," I replied, not moving to take his hand.

He retracted his hand and rolled the covers from the bed down his legs, watching my expression warily. "Come here. Please," Victor spoke softly. "It's very hard for me to stay level-headed right now. Work with me." He reached for me again.

I knew this was true. I had seen his fuse get shorter and shorter in the last hours. I let him take me by the hand and draw me closer. I faced him but did not look directly into his eyes, afraid I'd see someone I did not want to see or recognize, not wanting the other Victor to surface, the one who would need to feed and could be a danger to anyone's existence, even mine. I wanted to be above it all, but the problem was at this moment I felt as vulnerable as anyone else. I also did not want to have to explain to Nathan any ill-fated happenings that might have occurred with my poor judgment call and releasing part of my spell from Victor.

Victor guided my face so he could see me. "You released me because you want this as badly as I do. I could feel it in you." He pulled close, placing a hand on the back of my neck, and kissed me.

I finally let my eyes meet his; the same Victor for the most part, the one I had come to love. "I need to put the spell back, later," I mumbled, needing for him to understand. "It's best for both of us. Please understand." We sat forehead to forehead, his hand still clutching the nape of my neck, keeping me within arms reach.

Victor said nothing but nodded in comprehension, pulling me on top of him and draping his arms around my backside as he held me snuggly against his body. I could feel his hands rummaging for the bottom of my cotton nightshirt that hung loosely at my thighs. As his lips pressed firmly against mine, I could feel him exhaling quickly and trying to catch his breath. He let his head fall back onto the pillow and closed his eyes as he blindly continued to raise his hands under my nightshirt, his warm fingers tracing my spine. I propped myself up on my hands and permitted Victor's bare thigh to separate mine as I lowered myself against him. He wrapped his arms around me firmly, petting me gently and cradling my head to his neck. I lifted my torso over his and moved further up his body until we were face to face. His eyes flickered open and he looked up at me in uncertainty as I lowered my lips to his for a kiss. He returned the kiss immediately, his tongue charging into my mouth and sweeping in all directions. My fingertips grazed his sides, feeling his hard rib area, then locating the soft pliable skin of his belly. My fingers groped at the hollow pit sandwiched between his rib cage and his navel. He reached his hand down between us, found the opening in his boxers and freed his erect penis from the confines of his shorts. I felt the heat of his penis penetrate through my nightshirt against the crease of my thigh as his body temperature inched higher and higher.

I sat upright on Victor's body, leaning back to remove my nightshirt over my head. He stopped me suddenly by grabbing both wrists and yanked me down to his chest so quickly I thought I suffered a case of whiplash. My body came to a jarring halt as it slammed into his. Our eyes met. Victor's glare stunned me, his eyes dark pits that sucked my strength from me. I remember thinking that now I knew how others felt, the unfortunate ones that met Victor under the worst of all circumstances, the times he needed to feed. My body was paralyzed as I looked down upon him, my eyes fixed on his; I did not want to continue to stare at him but I had no choice. He wanted it.

"Release the spell. Totally," Victor growled as his eyes burned deeply into mine. He was taking me over, trying to command me.

"Victor," was all I was able to utter, still stunned that he had turned on me.

"Get the book," Victor snapped. "Release me. I can't stand it any longer." He held onto my wrists with his vampire strength. I thought he might break them into splinters.

I could not respond. I could not speak. Victor overwhelmed my mind. I was not able to think for myself although I wanted to. I was sure if I had even a few seconds to think, without Victor's manipulation, I could find a way to free myself from his grip and flee to safety.

Victor sat up in bed, still keeping me in custody. His eyes grew larger, darker – meaner. "Listen to me! Get the book. Reverse the spell," he snarled, letting a wrist go and grabbing a handful of hair from the back of my head. Victor pulled at my hair in anger, and then pushed me off of him onto the floor, discarding me. I fell awkwardly to the carpet onto my back. I allowed myself a moment before I sat up, hoping it was all a dream; that Victor was not hostile and vicious and fighting me. "The book!" Victor yelled.

I shuddered with his words. His voice curdled the blood in my veins, a cold wave swept through my body. I had no choice but to obey his request, get the book, reverse the spell. I was unable to think for myself. I felt like a marionette as I struggled to stand, wobbling to and fro. I saw Sara's journal on the nightstand, my hand trembled as I reached for it; I knew better. I knew that I should not break the spell, but I had no control; Victor was my master and I was nothing but a submissive slave to him. My fingers fumbled to the marked page with the spell and the last black cord with a knot. I labored to untie the cord, my fingers refusing to work together; finally it loosened and the black cord was free from any knots. *"Reverse the spell that bound so well, unbind, unconfine,"* I spoke with a trembling voice, afraid of what would happen once Victor was responsible for his own actions. I realized just how scary he could be, especially not knowing his next move. Perhaps I had not really thought about what Victor was, who he was and the fine line that allowed us to live in harmony... under his terms. I dropped to the floor in fear, clutching Sara's journal to my chest and making a compact tiny package of myself, hoping to hide. I shuddered as I heard him spring up from the bed; he was free. I refused to watch his actions. If death was imminent for me, please take me quickly.

I could hear him move quickly around the room looking for something. I soon realized he was putting on the clothes I had laundered for him after his duel with the Blue Daemons. I could hear him putting on his pants, his legs gliding into his jeans, the sound of the zipper. He sat back onto the bed and donned his sneakers before buttoning up his shirt. I continued to stay huddled in a ball, my head against my knees. I wept tears of fear, frustration and betrayal. I wanted him to leave. I wanted him to forget I was in the room with him. I remained quiet, hoping he would not notice me, hoping he would follow his instincts that would, with any luck, send him out into the night. I heard Victor rise to his feet. I took a deep breath, hoping he would leave my home and never come back.

"You," Victor said sharply, suddenly.

I felt him grab me by the hair again and haul me off the floor. I did not fight him, allowing myself to be pulled up. I wiped away the few tears that coursed down my flushed cheeks. Victor grabbed my shoulders and held me forcefully in front of him. I closed my eyes; not wanting to remember Victor looking like a heartless, soulless beast before he killed me, hurt me or, if fortune was on my side, walked out on me.

"Look at me," Victor ordered, the voice of a parent in control dishing punishment out to an offspring.

Like a child I refused to look at him. My eyes were glued shut. I shook my head adamantly.

The next thing I remember was coming to, my legs sprawled out on the floor, arms and head on the bed as if I had collapsed and was left where I had fallen. I held my head up off the mattress, feeling dizzy immediately. I pulled my hair away from my face and looked around, briefly disoriented to where I was. A vision of Victor's fierce vampire visage entered my mind and a sobering thought it was. I looked around apprehensively, seeing no trace of him. I did not feel his eerie presence. I tried to get up but couldn't. Still unstable, I got to my knees and reached for the phone that sat on the nightstand. I needed to make Nathan aware; no matter how badly I didn't want to, what had happened with Victor. I could hardly remember his number as I punched keys on the phone.

Nathan answered the phone almost immediately. "Hello."

"Nathan," I mumbled.

"Kala? What's wrong?"

"Umm, Victor is gone. He went berserk," I tried to explain, hoisting myself unsteadily on to the bed.

"What happened?" Nathan asked, concern in his voice.

"I was stupid. I removed part of the spell, and then he demanded the other part be removed. He got hostile with me. When I woke up he was gone," I tried to explain. "I'm sorry." Tears began to flow down my face.

"Victor will be just fine. I'm not too concerned about his well-being. He's doing what comes natural to him right now. He knows where he lives – I hope. That is to say I hope he doesn't try to return to your place, since that was the last place he was." Nathan was quiet as if he were weighing all the options. "Are you okay?"

"I'm a little dizzy. I'm sitting up," I replied, trying to get my bearings.

"I cannot pick up any signals from Victor right now. Let me come by and stay with you until morning, just to make sure Victor does not come back to your place. If he does, I will take him back with me. It will be safer that way. I wish you had left the spell on him, Kala, though I'm sure Victor persuaded you to remove it. I know you would not have done it on your own. Now you see how *we* can be; we are dangerous. Don't forget that."

"Nathan, right now I hate him for what he did," I cried, thinking back to the abuse I took. I tried to stand and held onto the nightstand.

"He is what he is," Nathan replied. "He may look human and even act human, but he is not. We are not. We have survived over the years because of what we are. We are keen hunters, we have extraordinary strength, better than perfect vision, superb hearing skills, mind-altering abilities; we are the ultimate living creature."

"So I found out," I replied in a whisper. I knew another side of Victor I could have gone a lifetime not knowing about. Bastard.

Chapter 26

A few moments later I found myself putting on a pair of sweatpants under my nightshirt. I certainly had no one to impress, least of all Nathan. He was just babysitting the Emissary – a thankless job I'm sure he wished he did not have. But protecting my well-being had its perks in the end: reinstatement to his society was closer for Nathan than it ever had been. Maybe I was worth something to Nathan despite his attempt to choke the life out me.

Nathan arrived with reading material in hand; dressed casually in a pair of Dockers, a crisp white button down shirt under a dark knit vest. He always looked presentable and ready for any occasion. I allowed him in and directed him to the living room. I wasn't all that happy to have him over, all things considered. It was more than apparent that he felt my current state – being human – was beneath him. And although I was just a human, I thought I deserved to be treated better than he had been treating me.

The fact was, he was in my home. "Make yourself comfortable," I pointed towards the couch where there was enough light for him to read if that's how he decided to bide his time

Nathan nodded, acknowledging my offer, and took a seat on the far end of the sofa. He crossed his legs, took his glasses off and rubbing his eyes wearily. "How do you feel?"

I hesitated before answering his question, taking a seat on the arm of the couch furthest from him. "Well... pretty good, I guess, considering I had two vampires try to kill me today."

Nathan slowly placed his glasses back on his face and looked steadily at me. "I see. So, what do you last remember about Victor before he left here?" Nathan asked, ignoring my comment and trying to get as much information from me regarding Victor's quick departure as he could.

I thought about the last few moments I could remember. "I recall him shaking me by my shoulders. I was afraid, so I kept my eyes closed and refused to look at him. And then that was it; I woke up and called you," I said, giving him the short version.

Nathan stood up and set his book on the coffee table. He walked towards me, a grim look on his face. I cringed as he got close to me, more afraid than I had ever been of his kind. "I'm not going to hurt you," Nathan promised, seeing my fear. I looked up at him skeptically as he stopped in front of me. He placed his hands on the side of my face and examined me, turning my head side to side and lifting my chin to see my neck and throat.

"What are you doing?" I asked him, annoyed, as he manipulated me.

"I want to see if Victor hurt you at all," Nathan explained with a stern and serious tone in his voice. "See if he bit you, bruised you..."

I interrupted his assessment. "I'll probably be full of bruises tomorrow," I snapped, pulling away. "I don't think he bit me." I rubbed my neck, scowling at the horrible thought of him sinking his teeth into me. "My body aches. I've been tossed around, shook, grabbed, manhandled... and for what?"

Nathan continued his examination by taking hold of my hand and turning my wrist, rotating it clockwise, then gently rubbing his hand up and down my arm from wrist to shoulder. "Does this hurt?" Nathan asked, looking for any marks on my limbs.

"A little. But I will live," I replied, taking my arm back. I did not want to be touched. "I just want you and your people to leave me alone," I said bitterly, turning my body and sliding off the arm of the couch past him.

"I understand. But don't be angry at me for who you are and who you are meant to be," Nathan said. "On Saturday, the High Counsel will meet with you."

I had forgotten about Saturday night with everything else that had been happening. I sighed and my shoulders fell. "Nathan, I'm not up for it. Please postpone this. I am not ready."

"There is no postponement. The arrangements have been made," Nathan said coldly, taking a seat back on the couch and retrieving his book from the table.

I turned around to face him. "Why is this so important? Why now?" I failed to understand the urgency of making this appointment happen so soon.

"I believe they would like to evaluate your abilities," Nathan answered briefly. He crossed his legs, only half interested in me now.

"Evaluate my abilities?" I asked him. "Like what?" I walked back to the couch wanting him to pay attention to me, to answer my questions.

Nathan shut his book again and rolled his eyes in my direction. "Every Emissary has powers, specialties – spells and incantations. The High Counsel and the future Sovereign would like to speak to you, learn more about you."

I shook my head in frustration. "I have no specialties. I am not particularly good at anything," I grumbled.

"Sit down," Nathan sighed as he patted the seat next to him on the couch, as if he had something profound to tell me, like it might really change my life.

I did not want to hear any long drawn out explanation. I reluctantly sat down. "What?"

"The High Counsel knows that you have powers and that they will grow. The more you use them, the more control you will have over them and they will help you. I'm sure you know that a spell does not need to be sophisticated to work. Look at your binding spell, just black string and a few words. It worked, though. How about the pack of wolves – a mere thought produced them. The charge of fire and electricity you are able to release onto people. These are all abilities that you have, you use and you need to control. I'm sure there are more, but for someone to pick up a book and read a passage to a spell and make it happen, first time without error, says a lot to the Counsel. For someone who can think quickly enough in an intimidating situation and call upon elements of the wild – your wolves for instance – tells them you have the ability to think quickly under duress. Your ability to manifest fire and electrical charges tells us you have a vicious temper that needs to be controlled. The High Counsel needs to be prepared to deal with these issues; ultimately, they will be the people you will guide and work with very closely."

"I think you are wrong," I came back sharply. "If I could think so quickly, why did I not find a way to fight off Victor? His mind overpowered mine; I didn't stand a chance. Not just once but several times he took hold of me and I was not capable of defending myself. I was scared. I was not able to reason or rationalize anything. I had no time; I didn't have the strength." I was discouraged thinking back to my failures.

"Because you love him," Nathan flatly responded. "Love can make you very strong or it can make you very weak. You did not see Victor as a vampire tonight. If you had, you could have fought him off more than likely, but you saw him as human, the way you want to see him, the way you want to love him."

I had nothing to say in return. I was angry with Victor for mistreating me – or was it just the vampire part I was angry with?

I allowed Nathan some peace and quiet to read and make sure that Victor did not return. I needed to get some rest but before I could even think about that I had two bedrooms to put back together. Victor had made near disasters of them. After I finished straightening out the spare room, I walked across the hall to reassemble my bed and get ready to sleep. While I was tossing the last pillow on the bed and aching to rest my body I heard a light rap on the doorframe. I turned around.

"I just wanted to let you know that Victor is at the house. I have picked up his vibe. I'm going to head back and make sure he does not endanger you. I would think he should be himself in the next few days and should not be a threat to you after that. I'll let you know."

I blew my bangs out of my eyes and sat on the bed. "All right. Thanks for your help... I guess."

Nathan left to return home to deal with the recent instabilities of Victor, his mood swings and his yearning to feed from the innocence in the night.

Victor lay face up on his futon, staring at the swirling stucco pattern on the ceiling above him. His body felt warm and satisfied with the amount of blood that surged through him; his mood was placid as he recalled some of the events that had transpired over the past few days. Recalling most of them left him feeling rather guilt-ridden since he had not been himself lately, although he did not seem to think it was an excuse for his actions. He lay still as his mind teemed with images that tried to relay a tale, an explanation as to why he was experiencing such disturbing mood swings and episodes of aggressive behavior. He thought back to the last time he was in this much psychological chaos; it was a falling out with the Daemons that left him in a state of oblivion for many days; a state that took many more days before he felt himself again. He could not remember when his head got all mixed up, but he could feel it start to level out, and was relieved to know that his right frame of mind would soon return. He hoped that he had not caused any hard feelings among the few he cared about, although he knew there was an amount of damage he could not repair.

The heavy door to Victor's rooms opened slowly with a high-pitched creak. Nathan wove a course in the dark to the spot Victor liked to rest, the room where his futon was. Nathan saw his friend lying in silence and was able to sense his aggravation with the gaps in his memory over the past several days, the agony of guilt, irritability, tension and confusion. He pulled a small side chair close.

"And how are you feeling my friend?" Nathan asked quietly. "You seem content. You fed well?" Nathan could feel the fresh blood circulating within Victor's body, giving and sustaining him his life.

"All right," Victor answered in a monotone, putting his folded arms behind his head.

"Whatever you are feeling, it will pass," Nathan pointed out. He had no idea exactly what was going on in Victor's head; his thought pattern was extremely erratic.

"All right," Victor replied again. "What happened?" He turned to face Nathan, waiting for the details as to why he felt the way he did.

Nathan paused. "Well, apparently it was the Blue Daemons again. You just have real bad luck with them."

"Yeah, I guess," Victor replied softly. "I did some bad things, didn't I?"

Nathan not feeling like diving into that topic so he answered in an evasive manner. "No. You did what you were supposed to do."

"Why do I feel so strange? So bad?" Victor asked tiredly, looking at Nathan for the answers.

"I don't know. I can tell you more later, when you are feeling better. Do you need to feed again?" Nathan asked as he stood. "I could join you if you want the company. It's been a long time since we have killed together."

"I'm fine now. Tired," Victor muttered, rolling over to his side.

"I'll let you rest. If you need me I'll be downstairs. I need to make a few phone calls," Nathan announced as he departed, allowing Victor the rest he needed to recover.

Nathan wanted to update Phillip and Sheldon of the progress he had seen in Kala recently. He thought they would be pleased. Nathan also thought it best to forewarn them of some of her more damaging talents – fire and electrical charges – that could certainly injure even someone with the purest bloodlines.

"Sheldon, it's Nathan, I'd like a moment to speak to you about Kala." His voice was smooth and pleasant, well mannered.

"Of course. I hope everything is all right," Sheldon replied, mirroring his tone.

"Oh yes... just a few bumps in the road," Nathan answered. "Ever since Kala found out she is traveling a path to be Emissary things have been quite exciting. Her abilities are budding."

"That's wonderful news. How does she feel about coming here on Saturday?" Sheldon asked.

"Well, honestly, it's a little over-whelming for her, I think. But I will make sure she gets there," Nathan was upbeat in his response. "I'm sure she will come around. No need to use force."

"Excellent. So what kind of powers is she exhibiting?" Sheldon asked curiously. "I have heard some interesting stories through the grapevine."

"I'm sure the Counsel has. Her spells are coming along well. I've seen her conduct a binding spell that worked. I know that she has telepathic links regularly with Victor and they seem to be strong. We had the misfortune again of having to deal with some Blue Daemons, and this time they got a hold of Victor. I would appreciate it if Phillip could look into that. They are quite a bother."

"I will speak to Phillip; I know he has some people on it. Is Victor all right?" Sheldon asked with some concern in his voice, although Nathan was fairly certain it was far from sincere.

"Recovering. It was a rough one on him. It was the night Victor had a run in with the Daemons that she did pull off a miraculous stunt though. Kala summoned a pack of wolves to distract the Daemons while I got Victor away from them. It worked, and I believe the wolves destroyed the Daemons. I can't image there could have been much left to them, seeing the size of the pack." Nathan seemed impressed in spite of himself.

"Well, that sounds impressive!" Sheldon said. "She can command animals?"

"I can only tell you what I witnessed," Nathan stated.

"What else?" Sheldon asked, musing over her powers.

"We do have a small problem with one of her talents; she has the ability to release fire or electrical currents through her hands when she is scared or angry. She has been working on controlling it, but I know it's hard for her. She hurt Victor quite severely with it, and I got a jolt once, too," Nathan explained. "Extremely powerful, painful – deadly."

"That is a problem. We will work on that with her. I have seen powers like hers before. She was born under a fire sign. It makes all the difference in the world. Fire signs have hot tempers and when they don't vent regularly, or as needed, and they finally blow – look out!" Sheldon seemed to have some past experience.

"Other than that I think things are progressing fine. Will Stuart be there on Saturday night?" Nathan asked, wondering who the invited people were.

"Yes. Phillip and myself, you, Kala, and Victor if he is well enough to join us. I think it's time Kala and her father get reunited."

"It will be good to see everyone. What about our Sovereign; will he be with us?" Nathan asked curiously.

Sheldon paused. "Teague has been letting me assume some of his responsibilities lately. He is old and tired; he is looking forward to stepping down and relinquishing the title of Sovereign to me. He is in need of a rest. It's been a very long and lonely two hundred years for him. I look forward to taking over, meeting my Emissary, getting to know her and enjoying my reign. Teague may be around; he may not. I'm not sure lately."

"I see. It would be good to talk to him again," Nathan sighed and remembered the old days when he knew Teague well.

"Perhaps. I will pass on your sentiments to Teague when I see him. I must go now. Phillip is here; I will mention your concerns regarding the Daemons to him."

"Thank you. We will see you on Saturday," Nathan said. "Good night."

The next few days were quiet. I made them that way. After my battles with Nathan and Victor I was just tired, tired of everything. I think I was depressed but didn't really know why. Drew even asked if I was feeling okay; I told him I was suffering from PMS. I didn't want to go into detail about the rocky road Victor and I were on. Drew didn't push the issue; he needed no more detail.

I thought I felt Victor over the next several days try to contact me telepathically, but his signal was either too weak or I maybe I was just mistaken. I knew I was not going to pick up the phone and call him myself to find out. And I was not going to try to telepathically connect with him in case he *wasn't* trying to reach me. I know it sounds immature, but I had no idea who Victor was any longer. I felt like calling him was like dialing a wrong number.

I could not figure out for the life of me if he was Victor the human, or Victor the vampire. One I could love, the other I loathed. It was like a Jeckyl and Hyde movie come to life. Maybe that was what was depressing me so, knowing that I could not truly have Victor. He could never be mine, ever.

When Friday night rolled around I tried to make myself feel bubbly, professional, successful and beautiful. I stood at the bathroom sink putting my makeup on and fixing my hair. I avoided looking in my own eyes, not wanting to see the nervousness there. I felt cold inside, but tried to ignore the feeling.

I was pacing the living room floor, going over the entire evening in my mind. My stomach felt sick with trepidation, my head was swimming with all the things that could possibly go wrong through the entire party. My only hope was that if the food was good and there was plenty of alcohol, no one would have a chance to notice. Once again I was more than likely blowing what could go wrong way out of proportion. I wanted to be optimistic, but it did not come easily. The phone rang. I immediately thought the worst – the caterer could not make it. I lunged for the phone on the desk.

"Hello?" I tried to remain calm, hoping it was a telemarketer I could easily hang up on and not give a second thought to.

"Kala."

"Yes. Hi." I was taken back. It was Victor. He was the last person I expected to hear from. I hadn't heard his voice in days. I wasn't sure I wanted to, not with the party already on my mind.

"You must be getting ready for your cocktail party," he asked softly, awkwardly.

"Yes. I'll be leaving in a few minutes," I replied, looking at the clock. I continued to pace up and down the room in front of the coffee table.

"I just wanted to wish you well. I'm sure everything will be great," Victor's voice brightened a little with encouragement.

"Thanks. Let's hope so," I sighed, unsure of myself. I crossed my arms and cradled the phone against my shoulder.

"I can tell you are nervous. Please don't be. Things will be fine. I'm sorry I can't be there, I'm still... I'm doing better," Victor tried his best to explain his feelings and situation.

"I'm glad you feel better." I forced myself to say something nice.

"I'd like to talk to you; I need to. It's important to me."

"I can't even think about it right now Victor. I'm not sure I want to think about it," I told him, a tinge of anger in my speech.

I could hear him sigh before he spoke again. "I know. I do, really. But please allow me to talk to you about it. Tomorrow night we are all going to the Manor where the High Counsel resides. I want us to be at peace with each other before we get there."

"Do you think it will be that easy? We can just talk and make everything okay?" My fuse was short with him.

"We need to start somewhere," Victor argued. "I'm feeling better. I want to talk to you. I have avoided you over the last day or so because I wasn't sure I could talk to you without making matters worse. Please. I feel bad."

"You feel bad?" I huffed. "Why, it's just your normal instincts taking over. Why apologize for it?" I was being sarcastic.

"Kala, I care about you. I feel very badly about what happened. I keep remembering more and more about how I was and what I did. It bothers me. I don't want to go another night like this. Can I at least call you later on tonight, once your party is over and you are home?" He seemed anxious and eager to finish our talk when time was on our side.

"All right, all right. I should be home no later than 11:30," I caved in to his request, knowing that meeting the High Counsel would be stressful enough for me without adding the pressure of a distraught vampire on top of it, too.

"I'll call you then. Have a good time; things will be fine," Victor seemed happier or perhaps more relieved that I was willing to converse with him.

"Thanks. I'll talk to you later on. I have to get going now." I forced a rapid end to the phone call.

"Good luck. Bye."

"Bye." I replied.

Chapter 27

I arrived at the gallery a few minutes before the caterer, unlocking doors, turning on lights, emptying the mailbox and taking a seat at my desk to try and relax. To keep my mind off the party I opened the mail I had received over the last few days. When the caterer arrived she parked her van in the alleyway and used the back door to move her equipment in. She seemed very pleasant, as did her helpers; they worked quietly and quickly together like they had done hundreds of jobs just like mine before. The food smelled great and I watched the wait staff roll in carts of alcohol and ice. Maybe tonight would not be a disaster after all.

The time on the invitations I had sent out read 7:00 PM so I glanced up at the clock on the wall every few moments until my first guests arrived. It was Addy and Keith, her husband, and Melinda the interior decorator; people I could greet quickly and walk around the gallery with very little effort on my part, since I knew them well. Shortly after Addy, Keith and Melinda made their way around the gallery more guests began to filter in. I smiled warmly, waiting at the door and shook hands while keeping an eye about the room to make sure everyone seemed to enjoy themselves. Most of the artists had found time to come to the opening as well and were stationed next to their exhibits to personally show off their work and speak to those who might be interested in purchasing. I watched from a distance as the wait staff walked around with trays of bubbly drinks and appetizers. I held a drink in my hand to loosen up; it gave me something to fidget with and the coolness against my fingers felt good. I was beginning to feel like a piece of art myself, as I stood like a sentry at the door with a smile plastered on my face.

One of the local television news crews showed up, which put more pressure on me. I watched them park their large white van in the street with their network affiliation displayed proudly on the side, then a camera guy piled out along with a reporter. I sighed, prepared to smile and act happy in order to pull off a flawless interview.

"Oh look – a news truck!" Addy pointed with excitement behind me as she watched the street over my shoulder.

I smiled. "How about that? Stress," I chuckled.

"Oh... come now. You do that kind of work every day. Only difference is you are heard and not seen. This is a good thing for you and the gallery," Addy said, taking great joy in sharing her opinion with me.

"You're right. It will be fine." I turned around to agree with her, since I was in no mood to argue.

"By the way, where is your date? Mr. Wonderful. Victor?" Addy asked, looking around the crowded floor, thinking perhaps she had missed him. "I saw his work. Very nice."

I had been so busy I had not even thought to tell her I had come alone. "Victor hasn't been feeling well. He's home tonight. He wished he could have come though." A small part of me wondered what Victor was doing home by himself tonight; maybe he wasn't home alone. Maybe he wasn't even home. Perhaps he was out and about in the night; sucking the fluid of life out of every day ordinary people – people like me.

I had no sooner finished the particulars regarding my missing companion then I felt the strangest draining sensation take me over. A frosty shiver surged up my spine that branched out to my limbs; my blood thickened in my veins as my body stiffened up completely as if I was grounded in a corpse with rigor mortis. I helplessly watched as two well-dressed young men approached the front door of the gallery that was opened wide in welcome to the street. It was something about these two men: a handsome blond and a muscular brunette, that turned me into a piece of garden statuary. My eyes watched vigilantly as the men entered the threshold of the gallery. They stopped for only a moment to examine me by glaring up and down my body in the most mortifying manner. I could somewhat hear their thoughts. Vampires, I thought to myself. A bell rang loudly in my head as if to alert me to the finding. Even though these two were vampires, there was something still different about them, or at least one of them. They felt like everything Victor and Nathan were to me, only more – stronger, sharper, bigger and deadlier. I had not expected any vampires to attend my party – other than Victor. I knew they were out there of course; I was sure of it after the facade Victor and Nathan had was uncovered. I was not sure how to handle my unexpected guests, especially knowing there was a powerful difference that radiated from them. They apparently knew who I was, or was to be. I could easily gather that information from them as they scoped me out and spoke without any words to each other. I tried to not allow them to intimidate me into hiding in a shell. I had a potentially long night ahead of me and a room full of guests that required my attention, not to mention the television crew that was setting up outside in the street.

I narrowed my eyes in displeasure as they sauntered by me into the gallery as if I was nothing but a minor and insignificant obstacle. I breathed deeply and willed my body to relax, trying to recover as quickly as possible from the shock of my unexpected visitors.

I could tell where my undead guests were all night; it was like sonar, and the closer they got to me the louder the signal played in my head. I watched them cautiously as they paraded between art displays and socialized with others. They made me feel extremely uncomfortable as I worried for my safety as well as my gallery full of unsuspecting humans. They never bothered to introduce themselves to me and I wondered why. The three of us knew *we* existed. I knew who *they* were and they knew *me*. Every time I thought about approaching them and attempting to make civilized contact, I got distracted by a guest or a waiter or the reporter who finally made her way into the gallery for a quick look around. I spent a few moments in the street under the hot lights of the camera, answering some questions for the late night news. One of the questions that the reporter had asked was my shop hours. It was something I had put a lot of thought into and told her that due to my first career as a radio disc jockey, the only time I could find to dedicate to the gallery right now was Friday evenings and Saturday and Sunday. All other hours would be by appointment only.

During the last hour of the party the crowd started to thin out and I noticed that the vampire interlopers had left. I searched the entire gallery and did not find any signs of them. I was glad they had left but wondered who they were, where they came from and if I would ever meet up with them again. It was the most unsettling feeling. I suppose I could have called Victor and asked that he drop by to escort me home, but my pride got in the way and I quickly dismissed that idea. Contacting Nathan didn't seem feasible either, for obvious reasons. I guess I would have to hope for the best and handle any unfavorable situations like the Emissary would; however that would be. My last guests to leave were the first that showed – Addy, Keith and Melinda. I thanked them for coming and told them I'd be leaving soon myself, right after the caterers broke down their equipment and cleaned up. We all felt that the night was a success.

I breathed a huge sigh of relief as I gave the caterer her check for a job well done, walked her out the back door into the alley where her truck was parked and said good night. The evening was over and I'd survived. It hadn't been as bad as I thought it would be. I turned back into the gallery and dead-bolted the lock to the heavy back door. I slowly made my way into the front of the shop to take a few moments to wind down, finish any straightening up and turn the lights off for the night.

As I entered the main gallery my sonar kicked in again and I felt the same disquieting sensation I had earlier. A chill spread through me and goose bumps erupted all over my arms. *They* were back. I stopped walking, the muscles in my legs refusing to operate at will. I brought my eyes from the stone floor that I had been concentrating on up into what I wanted to see – an empty room – but instead saw the two distinguished looking men; the vampires were back and waiting for me. Their hands were deep in their trouser pockets, suit jackets buttoned and positioned like GQ models. We stared at each other to see who would speak first. A stand off.

"What do you want?" I boldly spoke first.

They watched my moves like predators hunting their evening prey. The blond loosened up first and took his hands out of his pockets and a step towards me. "Kala," Sheldon spoke softly, almost affectionately. "I just came by to see *you*."

"Why? Who are you?" I asked, a slight edge to my voice. My body stiffened the closer he got to me.

Wordlessly, he approached me, his eyes looking me up and down as if I was a piece of merchandise he was thinking of purchasing. He noticed the Amulet that dangled from my neck and glanced at it curiously, but continued to browse the rest of the package. "My, you are very fine," he whispered as he positioned himself behind me. I felt his hand brush the small of my back as he came full circle and ended up in front of me.

"What do you want?" I asked again, annoyed with how I was being treated. I held onto the Amulet and let it slip nervously through my fingers. I looked past the blond to where the other vampire had been standing. He was gone.

"I told you. I came by to see you. My Emissary," Sheldon repeated, his eyes on mine.

I tried not to look at him very long. I had been captured that way before and did not want to be that easily misguided again. "Okay... you've seen me. Please leave now," I asked firmly.

"Is that any way to treat your Sovereign?" a voice behind me asked in disappointment over the tone that I taken.

I turned quickly to see the brunette had reappeared and was several feet behind me. "Sovereign?" I asked.

The blond took two steps towards me. "Yes. You and I – Sovereign and Emissary." He smiled in the most evil manner. "What a couple we will make." He extended his hand out and brushed some hair away from the side of my face and then ran his fingertips past my ear and down the side of my neck as he admired me.

I took a half step backwards and bumped into Phillip. I felt his arms wrap around my waist as he held me motionless.

"Watch out for her hands," the blond warned his male companion. "I've heard about the things she has done." His eyes fixed on mine knowingly.

I huffed. "What do you want?" I wiggled to get free.

Phillip took my wrists in his hands and pulled them behind my back in handcuff fashion. I winced at the tugging on the muscles in my shoulders.

"Kala. I just wanted to meet you. See you," Sheldon spoke softly as he touched my arms.

"How did you get in here?" I asked angrily, still struggling.

The blond laughed. "What could stop us?"

"All right. You've seen me. Now let me go," I spoke bitterly.

Phillip tugged on my arms harder to get me to stop resisting him. I cringed again.

Sheldon combed his fingers through my hair and cradled my face in his hands gently. "Shhhhh."

I felt him trying to take control over my mind, poking and prying at me. I refused it. I did my best to shut him out. When he could not easily conquer me with plan A he moved onto plan B and somehow disabled my body from responding to me. My legs gave out from under me as if I had been shot. I couldn't feel my legs at all. I felt as if I my body had died and all that remained inside me was my common sense. Phillip held my body upright, supporting me against his. He finally let my arms go and they hung motionless at my side, useless to me. My neck fell forward, unable to hold up the weight of my head. Sheldon tipped my chin up to look into my eyes and smiled wildly. "What's wrong, my Emissary? You don't seem so strong and powerful right now," he taunted me, allowing my head to fall back and to the left, giving him time to study the Amulet that swayed at the bottom of my throat. "Before we leave, get a good look at this Amulet, Phillip. I've seen this somewhere before." Phillip acknowledged the order and held my arms out at my side so my body was shaped like a limp 'T', displaying me like a trophy to the pending Sovereign. Sheldon ran his hands over my hips and lightly breezed them up my torso, finally caressing my throat and neck. He spoke to Phillip. "Where to start. Such an appetizing dish." His eyeteeth had begun to extrude from his mouth.

Phillip turned my weakened arm in Sheldon's direction. "A wrist?" he offered his friend.

Sheldon's eyes glowed at the sight of my blue veins that lay very close to the top layer of my skin on my arms and wrists. Those veins made donating blood easy when I chose to donate, not when it was just raped from my body.

Although I was cognizant to what was going on between Sheldon and Phillip I could do nothing to stop them from physically taking whatever they wanted from me, like my blood. I feared that if they took too much I could lose consciousness and then what? What would prevent them from doing whatever they wanted, not that they couldn't now? What if I suffered pain;

how would my body react to that? "*Please don't*," I spoke without moving my lips. I caught the blond's eye. I hoped I could reason with him.

A raw smile over took his face, his fangs more prominent now than they had been. "Ahhh, she speaks. Telepathic connection established. Very good." He kissed my wrist and manipulated my fingers in his hands in a toying manner. "It won't work; but thanks for making the effort." He moved the soft underside of my arm upward towards his mouth like a piece of ripe fruit and punched his fangs deeply into my skin. I could hear the membranes break under the pressure of his jaw as his long sharp teeth severed the main arteries that fed my hand. The initial pain was abrupt and a cold shiver shot through my body as he sucked the fluid from my limb. I felt weaker. Pulling away he breathed in deep, allowing air to fill his lungs as Phillip watched. "So sweet. It's no wonder Victor killed the last Emissary. Who could stop?" Sheldon lapped at the blood that continued to flow out of the gaping wound. He dropped my arm and let it swing at my side.

"You taste so good, Love." Sheldon crept close to my face. I could feel his breath against my cheek; smell my blood on his lips. "Where to sample from now?" he thought aloud as his eyes scanned my body again. He grasped my left breast in his hand and squeezed firmly, pushing it up in my bra so the fullness rose out of the dip in the front of my black dress. I could feel his teeth tear into the skin of my breast over my pounding heart as he bit down hard and wrapped his arms around me, pulling me uncomfortably close, tugging my body out of Phillip's grasp and clutching me to him. I remained loose and limp as the pain bounced all around inside my body so quickly I was not sure where it began and where it ended. My entire body burned in pain.

"*Please stop*," I pleaded with Sheldon again in my mind. "Don't." I spoke in a whisper, my mouth hardly able to form the words. I could feel my heart racing inside me as he sucked my life out through my chest. I struggled and was able to raise a hand up and grabbed the sleeve of his jacket. Breaking his jaws free from his meal he tossed my nearly lifeless body back at Phillip as if I weighed nothing. Phillip gazed down at me in his arms and looked at the Amulet hanging around my neck. He looked at it for a moment as if it was somehow familiar to him, but then turned his attention to the fleshy tear in my chest and siphoned the blood that had pooled in the cavity of the wound for himself like a scavenger.

"She is very good. Thick, sweet blood." Phillip smiled at Sheldon, now understanding why he craved me so badly and continued to feed from me even when he knew he should not. Phillip positioned me and pulled my body back against his chest and found the bottom of my dress that clung to my thighs. He slid the dress up so that the crotch of my panties could be seen. "Sheldon – your favorite spot to feed." Phillip enticed the to be Sovereign with the sight of two bare thighs knowing the largest arteries in the body were here. Large rivers of red blood that flowed heavy and hard through the body.

Sheldon followed Phillip's voice, partially in a daze from the blood he had consumed; drunk on the potency that ran rampant in his body. He fell to his knees on the floor in front of my unresponsive body. Sheldon dug his fingers in my thighs, putting large holes in my sheer black nylons and tearing a section away large enough to place his mouth over the skin and sink his sharp eyeteeth into. He lifted my leg slightly, high enough to lock his mouth on and sink his fangs into me again – this time deeper than he had before. My body jarred with the pain as he hit a nerve or muscle. I could hear a crushing noise, something that made me react involuntarily. The pain was horrible. I began to sweat. My leg ached under his mouth as it drained more of my existence from me. I was light-headed and floated in and out of consciousness, scared I would die. I was even more scared I'd become one of *them* tonight. I was not sure which was worse. I finally felt Sheldon release my leg from his grasp and he staggered to his feet. Groping at my body, he turned my face towards his. I looked him squarely in the eye, knowing I had little at this point to lose. His eyes were glassy and he was not mentally astute. "I look forward to embracing you. What a night we will have," he smiled. "To drain you completely and fill you with me; you will be my creation." His voice sounded airy, out of breath. "I can't leave you tonight without giving you a little something from me." He smiled as if possessed by something wicked. I watched him as he bit his own wrist and pried my mouth open to accept the red secretions from his own body. I felt his blood roll down the back of my throat as I groaned with displeasure and turned my head. He laughed as he removed his wrist from my mouth. "Someday soon you will love me for it," Sheldon spoke softly. "You will want me – and my blood." Sheldon allowed Phillip to dump my bleeding body in a heap on the stone floor. "Someday."

Chapter 28

It was getting much too late. Victor had not been able to reach Kala. He tried calling her at the house. No answer. He tried calling her at the shop, but still no answer. Since his battle with the Blue Daemons, any contact he made with Kala telepathically was totally by accident, or a fluke. Truth was he couldn't do it; not at a distance like he used to; he would need her blood to reestablish a bond as strong as the one he had. He missed the link he had with her. It had quickly become a part of him and he felt less complete without it. Even though he did not have the link to support how he felt, he knew that something was wrong. It was past midnight and she was not at home or at the gallery. Maybe for some reason, she wasn't able to get to the phone. It wasn't like her not to answer, even if she had been less than pleased with him lately. He could tell she enjoyed the confrontations they had on occasions; they lit her fire and she liked to vent.

On his way out, Victor stopped to tell Nathan that he was worried about Kala. He said that she was overdue getting home from the gallery, and that he was going to stop by her place and make sure she was okay. Nathan understood Victor's concerns but offered little consoling. Nathan remembered that Sheldon and Phillip from the High Counsel were going to be at her party tonight. Victor apparently, in all the confusion of the week, had forgotten. Nathan did not bother to remind Victor of this; he just hoped that nothing transpired at the party that would cause her to be too late; or get herself hurt. Nathan thought about Sheldon or Phillip harming Kala, but the idea didn't make any sense. She was their Emissary, Sheldon's Emissary, his companion for many years to come. Harming her would serve no benefit, as he would be many times stronger with her by his side than feeding from her once and discarding her. After all, killing a future Emissary was a punishable crime among his people. Victor and Nathan were proof of that.

Victor arrived at Kala's place and saw her convertible right away. He felt some relief; at least she was home. The top on the car was down, but that was normal for her. He parked his car and ran up the cement stairs to the door. He hesitated before knocking, wondering what he would say. Perhaps he would just smile and give her a kiss. He hoped she would allow that. He had been craving her lips and wanting to feel her body near his for days. He rapped on the steel gray door and waited for Kala to greet him. Several seconds passed and she did not answer. He knocked again, louder and backed up on the landing to see if there were lights on in the living room. Still no response. He got that funny feeling again, like something was wrong.

He quickly returned to the parking lot and approached Kala's car. He placed his hand on the center of the hood. It was still warm; it had not been parked too long. Without delay he glanced inside the car and initially saw nothing unusual, but then he picked up a familiar scent. The scent of blood; Kala's blood. Victor made himself snap out of the trance the smell had put him in; his willpower over blood or the sight of blood was very low since his fight with the Daemons. He touched the steering wheel. His hand came back sticky with coagulating red fluid – her blood; he could taste it without even placing his tacky fingers to his lips. Leaning deeper into the car, he patted the cloth driver's seat and felt the fabric was beginning to crust over with dried fluid – blood.

Without delay, he ran back up the stairs to her condo, calling her name loudly as he reached for the doorknob, hoping it was not locked. He turned the brass knob to the right and it moved without resistance. It was unlocked. He threw the door open and bolted into the entryway. "Kala!" he called, moving swiftly from the living room to the kitchen. Within a moment he found her in a jumbled pile on the bathroom floor, huddled near the tub. He stopped abruptly in the doorway as the perfume of her blood swept over him again. He knew there was a lot of it. "Kala," he said softly, not sure whether she was conscious or not. He knew she wasn't dead. The smell of death was something he could not confuse with any other scent he had ever run into over his two hundred years.

Victor dropped to his knees and slowly reached for her, taking a deep breath to contain his emotions. Then anger began to slowly fill him. He would make Kala tell him who did this to her, find him and kill him! Tonight! Victor placed a hand on her shoulder and cautiously rolled her into his arms.

He was sickened with what he saw; she had been attacked by one of *his* kind. She held Sara's journal tightly against her chest. The book was covered in blood. Her face had traces of blood as well – her lips and tongue – he could see it and smell it on her. He set her down on the bathroom floor and removed the journal from her limp fingers, uncovering a large, gaping bite wound on her left breast. The pages of the journal had absorbed some of the blood and were dried and stuck together. He held her wilted arm to see yet another puncture wound on her wrist and, gazing further down her body, saw that her black nylons were torn. He lifted the skirt of her dress only an inch or so and saw another wound – this one the worst on her body. Large slashes, obviously made by fangs, were still open and weeping blood.

"Kala," Victor murmured, his mind racing in several directions, not sure what to do with her next. "Kala! Wake up!" He grabbed a wet cloth from the sink and began wiping the blood from her face.

My body hurt. No. My body sobbed tears of blood. I was in so much pain. I had no idea what was wrong with me other than the pain was indescribable. I moved my head away from the wet washcloth Victor was patting my face with. I did not want to be touched. I wanted to die.

"Kala," he said again as I stirred under him.

I could see an overhead light shining through my eyelids, the orange glow guiding me to a firmer reality. My eyes slowly opened; even they hurt. I blinked and Victor's concerned face swam into focus.

"Kala. It's me, Victor."

I was dizzy just lying where I was, probably from the loss of blood. The room spun wildly. My stomach was nauseous and I had very little control over my body. Moving my arm took every ounce of energy I had. Victor took my hand in his.

"Do you know what happened to you?" he asked quietly, trying to remain calm for my sake.

I closed my eyes to think but could not. The pain was too great.

"I need to call Nathan. I need his help to help you," Victor tried to explain while he blotted my sweaty skin, neck, chest, shoulders.

"I hate you," I mumbled to Victor. "Go away." I wanted him nowhere near me. "Let me die."

"I know you don't mean that," Victor said, although the hurt was evident in his voice. "I won't let you die. I have to reach Nathan."

A voice spoke from the bathroom doorway. It was Nathan. "I'm here." He looked down upon the bloody mess with Victor poised over my hurting body.

Victor shook his head in disbelief over what had happened to me, what his people had done. "Nathan," he said as he pointed at my wounds. "They're bad."

Nathan knelt on the floor and took my hand. He examined the wound on my wrist, gently poked at the punctures on my chest and hiked up my dress to see the awful gaping wound on my thigh. His mouth tightened but he made no comment.

"Let me die," I pleaded again through dry lips. Death was the quickest way to end my pain.

Nathan set my arm on my stomach softly and brushed some hair out of my eyes. "We won't let you die," he said in a no-nonsense tone. "I can help you. Victor isn't well enough yet."

"I want to help," I heard Victor say.

"Victor, it's too early for you. I'm surprised you can even resist the sight of all this." Nathan touched my shoulder and shook his head.

"There must be something I can do!" Victor said. He continued to blot the sweat from my body.

"I need some room and some quiet so I can work with Kala. This is not going to be easy. These are large wounds. She is in pain and in no mood to deal with *things* right now," Nathan said bluntly. "Go have a cigarette; I'll come and get you as soon as I can." He sat flat on the bathroom floor, leaned against the half-tiled wall and scooped me up into his arms. "Hand me a towel on your way out."

Victor silently handed Nathan a towel and left. I watched as Nathan stared at me for what seemed like the longest time. His eyes were focused on my face, mouth, cheeks and eyes, perhaps wondering if he were doing the right thing by helping me. He cradled me in his arms, wrapped in the large towel. I returned his stare although mine, I'm sure, was blanker than his was. "Can you help me?" I asked in a whisper. He was close enough to hear my weak voice.

A rare smile crossed his face. "I have to, or nothing will ever be right again."

I wasn't sure exactly what he meant, but it was a positive response never the less.

"If I hurt you any more than you do already, I apologize in advance."

I nodded numbly.

"We need to get the bleeding to stop first, before you go into shock," he explained, stretching out my arm and examining the oozing wrist closely. He picked up the washcloth and gently wiped away the old blood to reveal a set of fang marks that dug deeply into my wrist and tore back some surface flesh.

"I don't feel good," I said faintly, turning my head in towards his chest; the light over the sink was bothering my eyes too.

"Whoever did this to you fed you their blood. It's making you sick. It's like poison to you," Nathan told me. "The less you move around, the slower it will circulate in your system."

I nodded faintly.

Nathan firmly took my arm and bent it so that my wrist was lightly touching his lips. I watched him, anticipating his next move and squinting with the light in my eyes. I felt his other arm come around the back of my neck slowly and his hand gently shielded my eyes from the brightness of the light. It also effectively kept me from seeing what he was doing. I felt the warmth and wet of his mouth and tongue over my skin, his breath hot. My skin instantly cooled as he pulled his mouth away from the wound. His strong hand encompassed my thin wrist and I could feel his thumb massage the palm of my hand, flexing it, working it, and moving it around. His mouth latched back onto the wound and I could feel the light sucking sensation against the open flesh. Over the next several minutes I felt the wound begin to seal, tugging and twitching as if it were being pulled tightly together with needle and thread, tugging the tear together. It was a feeling that made my body shrink with hurt.

Nathan took his hand away from my face, allowing me to see him, possibly as a sign of reassurance that he did not mean to hurt, but was trying to help. I blinked several times as I watched without a sound. He removed my wrist from his mouth; the skin was in one piece, though badly bruised and discolored. Nathan took a deep breath and sighed out loud. "That's the best I can do given the circumstances. It's closed and healing on its own now. The bruises will go away in time and so will the pain."

I nodded again, glad that one of my injuries was taken care of.

Nathan shifted my body closer to his, placing an arm around my back and gripping my shoulder tightly as he held me so my chest was facing him. With care he pulled the narrow strap of my dress off my shoulder and edged the blood stained black fabric down to expose my bra. He cupped my breast and lifted it delicately higher on my chest, relieving some of the tension on the skin. Dipping his head to my upper body his tongue lapped at the wound that had continued to bleed steadily. My heart beat faster, feeling the burn of the assailant's damage as the salt in Nathan's saliva poured into the open wound. I gasped and closed my eyes tightly. I reached up with my hand and grabbed his arm; he allowed this as I buried my fingers deep into his biceps. Tears began to roll down my flushed cheeks and continue down my neck. I bit my lip and groaned in extreme distress. Nathan pulled away, hearing the torment in my voice; he noticed the river of tears that had made tracks down my face. "I'm sorry," he said gently.

I just sobbed in his arms and said nothing. I thought how I wanted to die; nothing was worth going through this. I hated his people and what they had done to me.

"I know you hate us," he said, looking down upon my wounded breast. He slowly licked the area that had been ripped wide open with the soft flat portion of his tongue. My body pulsed under him as if moving in time with the throbbing pain that had seized me. I trembled in his arms.

"Close your eyes and breathe deep," Nathan instructed.

I did. I breathed deep and waited for Nathan to continue where he left off.

The next thing I recall was the feeling of being rocked like a child, embraced in someone's arms in a soothing fashion. My body still ached but not as badly as I remembered it; in comparison the pain was now tolerable for me but still very much evident. I felt the large fluffy towel blanketed around my body and sturdy arms holding me tightly against theirs.

"Nathan," I whispered.

"How are you feeling?" he inquired softly, still rocking me.

I swallowed, my throat dry. "Sick, but better," I replied.

Nathan nodded. "Your leg has stopped bleeding but I have not had the chance to work with it yet."

I stared down at my thigh for the first time to see the horrible sight of blood and loosened flesh. The gruesome sight made me sick. My body was still feeling pain and now I knew where it was coming from.

"I want to talk to Victor for a moment," Nathan said. "I want you to rest quietly until I return."

I nodded weakly and closed my eyes.

Nathan walked outside on the deck to join Victor, sitting silently in the dark, the tip of his glowing cigarette a tiny beacon. Nathan leaned against the railing and stared at his friend.

"You are going to have to make amends with Kala," he began. "There is so much uncertainty in her it is inhibiting her healing process."

"What are you talking about?" asked Victor.

"What happened between the two of you; it hurt her. You need to repair that damage so she can get better."

"I haven't hurt her," Victor protested. What he meant was, he hadn't meant to.

"But you have. You have hurt her," Nathan interrupted, pushing himself away from the edge of the deck towards Victor.

Victor frowned. "I didn't mean to."

Nathan put his hands in his pockets as he paced the wooden deck, trying to find the right words. "Victor, you knowingly went into a relationship with Kala. She rightfully thought you were human. You try to be human. You live and work with humans. She finds out you're not. A level of trust is broken. A big level of trust; you weren't who you portrayed yourself to be. Your relationship never should have happened with her. She was able to somehow regain some trust only to have you mentally and physically abuse her and take advantage of her while you are were staying here struggling with your recovery after the Daemons got a hold of you. More trust is broken. I know that you did not mean it. I do know that, because I know you. But Kala has always seen you in her eyes as being human... she has no concept of the fact that you aren't. You are a vampire. She got her first dose of how devious and conniving we can be the night you attacked her. You were being you – the vampire in you. Something that does not require an apology. But because of the way Kala was introduced to you, and because of what you pretend to be most of the time – human – there are some areas that may not ever get resolved. You need to see that before you go and try to talk to her. Reason it out with *yourself* before you try and reason it out with her. Know where she is coming from."

Victor hopped out of his chair. "Did she tell you this?" Victor asked curiously, as if Kala had been confiding her deepest secrets to Nathan all this time. "That I hurt her this way?"

"I felt it in her. It hurts her. Blood is a wonderful book," Nathan replied. "I'm not saying this to anger you. I'm telling you so you know in your own mind where to take this with her, if you plan on talking to her at all about it."

"I need to talk to her about it. I need to voice my feelings of how I feel about her; if for nothing else it will make me feel better," Victor mumbled, grasping at his shirt, where his beating human heart should have been.

I lay on the floor for a while, allowing the worst of the pain to subside and the queasiness to recede. I tried not to think of the wounds; the reason I was prone on my own bathroom floor, waiting for a vampire to return and nurse me back to health. After a moment, I decided to try and clean my self up, without waiting for Nathan. Shakily, I struggled to sit upright, bracing myself against the cool wall. Taking the washcloth from the sink, I wiped my face clean. I hesitated, then peered down at my thighs; the right one was raw and bloody and looked more like a small section of hamburger than human anatomy. Sickened, I did my best to clean up the area around the gashes, though even the slightest touch sent pain through me in all directions. Carefully, I put my nightshirt on over my head so it didn't touch the blood and ooze that still seeped from my leg.

I felt a little better, clothed and cleaner, but knew I was still in bad shape. I pulled myself up, panting short breaths through clenched teeth. Once on my feet, I allowed myself time to let my head catch up with my body, still not feeling entirely attached. I used the hallway as a support to get to where Nathan and Victor were. When I reached the dining area, I saw them out on the deck, deep in conversation. Using each chair at the dining room table I hobbled to the screen door. I felt as if I had traveled a million miles. My body had broken out in a cold sweat. "I made it," I announced, but the pain in my leg was starting to get the best of me with the flow of blood that was now surfacing out of the wound again.

Nathan and Victor walked into the dining area. "You should have called for us," Nathan scolded me. "I don't want you up on your feet."

I was about to apologize for my stupidity when Victor picked me up without warning. Giving me no time to protest, he carried me in his arms past Nathan and down the short dark hallway to my bedroom. Nathan entered the room behind us and spread the towel out on the bed for me to lie on to avoid getting my bed nasty with blood.

"Can I have something to drink?" I requested meekly, looking up at Victor and Nathan. My throat was so parched from crying and sobbing and deep breathing I could not even swallow any longer.

Victor smiled. "I'll get you something."

"Thank you," I replied.

Once Victor returned with a glass of ice water, he departed quickly but reluctantly as requested by Nathan, shutting the door behind him. Nathan circled the bed observing me, then took a seat on the opposite side. "How's the pain? You don't seem to be hurting as much."

I sipped my water. "It hurts, but it feels funny – sort of numb right now," I replied.

Nathan nodded as if in thought.

"Not good, right?" I added softly. I could tell by the look on his face something wasn't.

"When I looked at it initially I thought it was bad. I thought there might even be damage I could not repair, like a nerve or something was crushed or severed. That would explain your lack of pain, the numbness. But I don't know for sure. It looks as though whoever did this to you did not get as much blood as they wanted out of your leg, just a big bite. Poor aim. Consumed too much blood already and didn't know what they were doing," Nathan speculated, feeling the area on my thigh surrounding the bite marks with his fingertips. "You didn't lose as much blood as I thought. You were lucky."

"Either way I know it's going to hurt me whatever you do to it," I frowned, looking at my leg and then at him.

"You just lay back and get as comfortable as you can."

I lay back and placed my arms at my side. Closing my eyes for a moment I began to try and relax. Then a notion entered my mind. A thought. Nathan's thought. I opened my eyes quickly. "You were thinking about embracing me," I sat up quickly, alarmed with the idea, even jarring Nathan with the statement.

He frowned and removed his glasses. "The thought entered my mind for a moment," he confessed.

"When you held me in your arms in the bathroom and stared at me, and I asked you if you could help me, you actually thought about embracing me!" I stammered, glaring at him.

"Lower your voice," he requested calmly. "I didn't know what was best. Let you die, try and do what I could or just embrace you. I did the right thing."

I fell back down into the pillows, my stomach feeling sick again.

"I guess I'll have to be more careful about what I think or don't think when I'm around you," Nathan mused.

I broke out in a sweat. "Let's hurry before I get ill. My stomach again," I explained, turning my head and looking over at him.

He nodded. "Relax and try not to think," he suggested as his mouth got close to my thigh. I could feel his words flow against the tiny hairs on my skin.

Nathan gripped my thigh and dealt with the smaller gash first, licking the flesh gently. I felt a scalding burn each time his tongue swept into the opening. My fingers dug into the towel beneath me as the burning torture heightened. Closing my eyes did not seem to work any longer, and I found the need to focus on something other than the black nothingness that engulfed my mind.

"Are you okay?" Nathan asked, interrupting me.

I gulped, my stomach still queasy. "Go on." The quicker he finished the sooner I could throw up if need be.

Nathan did not resume; he sat upright on the bed and swung his legs over the side. "Let me get Victor. I think he can assist." Nathan stood and headed for the door.

"What can he do?" I asked faintly from my pillows as I watched him open the door.

"Relieve some of your pain perhap, he's good that way. I had forgotten he could," Nathan said as he walked out of the room.

I sighed, wanting the night to be over. I had been right. The evening was a disaster, at least for me. Thank goodness for small miracles. My guests had a good time, though.

Nathan returned with Victor. They were both silent and serious as they took separate seats on the bed. "So?" I asked.

"I want Victor here for you, to make you comfortable. He is much better at it than I ever will be," Nathan said as he moved towards my right leg.

Victor took me by the arms and sat me upright. He removed the pillows behind my head and took a seat behind me, resting my body against his so that my back was pressed against his chest. "Is this okay for you?" Victor asked softly.

"I think so," I answered, although Nathan had not started up again; only time would tell whether Victor could help at all or just be a piece of furniture for me to lounge on.

Nathan got down between my spread legs to work on the other side of the wound, the larger area on my inner thigh. It looked very awkward to see Nathan in such a sexually oriented position. I closed my eyes to try and put *that* out of my mind. Nathan was too scary to think about *that* way.

I leaned my weight against Victor, allowing him to brace me up. I did not have the strength to sit there, tolerate pain and try to think about something else. It wasn't possible. I felt Victor encouraging me to lean back into his arms; he wanted to hold me. I slowly let my body recline; he hugged me against his body and stroked me. I heard his voice in my ear. "Remember the night I took all your pains away? The night you let me in your mind and I got rid of all the hurt you had pent up? Let me do it again. Let me take the pain away."

"How?" I asked softly, fighting the pain that radiated from my leg into the rest of my body.

"Trust me," Victor said. "Just trust what I do. That's all I ask of you." He brushed my hair back and kissed my forehead.

The pain was getting more intense and with it my stomach churned and my body broke out in a chilling sweat. I had more to gain by allowing Victor to try and help. I was fairly certain Nathan would not let anything bad happen to me under his watchful eye and he was the one who suggested that Victor could help me. "Okay. I'll trust you," I mumbled.

As the pain deepened, my body became more rigid. I could feel Victor's soft lips touch my face, his kisses just grazing my skin. I was in no mood for romance and wished that he would stop, but to make him would require that I use energy that I did not have. I could feel Nathan's tongue probing at the ragged flesh that surrounded my wounds. I held my breath and clenched my teeth as the piercing pain continued. Victor brushed my hair back off my face and stroked me like a wounded animal. I felt him draw me closer to his body, his face nearer to mine, his warm breath bonding to the beads of agony on my face and neck as he kissed me. I did not want this, I batted at him with my arm to stop. He pulled away far enough to whisper in my ear, "You were going to trust me. Please. Trust me." His voice was smooth and audibly soothing to my head.

I lowered my arm to my side, allowing him to continue, giving him my consent. I had promised him that. Once again I felt Victor's lip press against mine softly, calmly; they eased against mine, his tongue nudged at the separation between my lips, trying to gain access to my mouth. I opened it far enough to feel Victor's tongue slide in. He lowered his body closer to mine, curling around me. His arms reached around my back and held me firmly. I could feel Victor's kisses become deeper with Nathan still positioned between my legs. I could not escape the sexual connotations of this tableau; having two men so close to me. Not even two men – two vampires; two deadly creatures so entwined in my body that escape was not possible. My life hung in their hands; their most powerful weapons poised and lapping at my body. If death was meant to be, it could easily happen to me tonight.

As Victor became more involved, his lips and tongue getting reacquainted with me, I began to feel my body slip into a state of relaxation similar to but not quite like the night Victor had reminded me of. I could sense his existence with me, not just physically but also in my mind as he became part of me mentally; he was with me and shared my thoughts. He felt my pain and began to channel the sensations away, blocking me from feeling anything hurtful or negative. 'How can you do this?' I asked him.

'Your body fluids. I told you how strong they could be,' Victor reminded me.

I had forgotten. It was his bodily fluids that caused me the reoccurring nightmares. Now Victor was using this method to benefit me and attach himself to my mind and help to eliminate the physical pain I had been enduring all night.

In the process he flooded me with his own thoughts, ones he had caged up and was unable to share with me. '*I have missed you, I have been so worried about you,*' He relayed to me. '*I'm sorry I hurt you. So sorry. I never meant to. I love you.*'

I could feel his sincerity and the resentment he had towards himself for being something he did not want to be, and how arrogant his species had become over the years. He was angry for living so many lifetimes alone, the unfairness of it . He did not want to endure another day the way he was. If the one he loved could not accept him for the momentary lapse of reason he once had, the one that made him the creature he was today, then how could he continue.

I lay in his affectionately smothering hold, locked in a kiss of compassion, steeped in generations of a vampire's loneliness and desire of wanting to be accepted and forgiven for a mistake he made that altered his life forever.

I must have slept, because I woke from my state of relaxation to find Victor lying beside me on the bed, watching me attentively. I didn't say anything at first; letting my mind collect all the information it could about the evening and trying to process it before I asked any questions. I looked down at the foot of the bed. Nathan was gone.

"Nathan's gone. He went home," Victor offered an answer to my obvious question.

"Oh! Why are you still here?" I asked.

Victor rolled over on his side and propped up his head on his arm, fondly admiring me from where he was without touching me. "I wanted to make sure you were okay."

"What more can happen?" I asked lightly.

"That's just it, I don't want anything else to happen, nothing," Victor quickly replied.

I could feel my body ache, my stomach was still unsettled.

"You're going to hurt for a few days. You were really messed up. Nathan did a good job on you," Victor said, praising Nathan's hard work.

"I know. I need to thank him," I mumbled. How strange it felt to want to thank Nathan for something he did.

"If you don't want to talk about it we don't have to, but do you remember who attacked you?" Victor asked softly. "It's very important that I find out."

"Why? So you can kill them?" I asked, sitting up and trying to make myself feel better. I looked down at my thigh, noticing several areas that would most likely be dark thick scar tissue, even when fully healed.

"Yes," Victor answered shortly.

I shook my head. "I don't remember. I wish that I could," I sighed. "I'm sure they made me forget"

"It's a method vampires use. I just thought perhaps it didn't work with you. I guess it did. Nathan and I talked about this. He could not find any answers in your blood and I got no answers either when I was sharing your thoughts. You've been wiped clean." He sighed in defeat, as if he would never get a chance to vent his wrath.

I put my feet on the bedroom floor and pushed myself off the bed to stand. My right leg had feeling to it, only a slight bit of numbness like pins and needles as I put pressure on it. I limped as I took a few steps under my own power, still feeling lightheaded and sick to my stomach.

"You really should rest," I heard Victor's voice from behind me on the bed. "Try in the morning."

I blew some hair out of my eyes and jacked my nightshirt up high enough to see the remnants of the bite. The fresh scar was terrible to look at – long, discolored and disfiguring. I let my nightshirt fall back into place and hobbled to the edge of the bed. Dispiritedly, I sat back down.

"It's really not too bad. It's still healing."

"I don't know why I'm worried; I'll be dead soon anyways. Right?" I asked, lying back down and pushing my pillows up against the headboard.

"How do you mean?" Victor asked, moving closer to me.

"Dead, like you," I replied. "This whole Emissary thing. We have to go to the Manor tomorrow night; meet the whole family."

"That's right. Nathan must be in his glory, rubbing elbows with purebloods and other counsel members. I'll be the misfit – the black sheep, the wallflower."

"I don't even know if I'll be able to make it myself. If I don't feel well enough the last place I want to be is in the company of..." I stopped what I was going to say, not wanting to be offensive to Victor after being privy to his thoughts and how much he hated who he was.

"Just let me take care of you for a while." Victor crawled closer and looked down upon me, his hair loose against his shoulders and handsome as always.

"I think I want to be alone," I softly said, looking at the clock on my nightstand. It was very late and if he stayed any longer he would be staying the night.

"Do you? Or if I were human, would it be okay for me to stay the night?" My words saddened him.

I thought a moment. "I'm skittish right now. Tomorrow night will be very hard on me. I still don't know who hurt me, who would want to. First Blue Daemons sent to get me, and they get you instead, and now I'm being stalked by the night frights." I shook my head. "I guess I'm not strong enough to fight you guys off yet. I have a lot of learning left in me."

"I can easily understand your reluctance to be in my company after what happened tonight, and after what I did to you recently. I cannot apologize enough for what I did. It's so unlike me." He struggled to make me understand how badly he felt, knowing he could not take it back.

"I don't know what is real any more," I sighed, looking over at him. "I wanted you to be real, but you aren't."

Victor took my hand in his. "I'm real. Just because I'm different doesn't mean I don't exist. I'm not perfect and I don't pretend to be. I'm here with you now because I care about you. The Victor you know would never harm you. He couldn't. The creature you had to contend with recently is the primal element that makes the vampire in me live. I don't like that part of me, but it's there. I deal with it because I have to, because I need to. It's that part of me, and my kind, that I want to protect you from; but I can only go so far with it." He leaned over and kissed me gently on the lips. "I love you and Nathan can't understand that. I have always loved you. Maybe that's what kept me going over the last two hundred years when I had no one else in my life but Nathan. When we fought and could not even stand to be in the same room as one another; I thought that someday I would have you again."

"I just feel my whole life is spinning and that I have no control over it at all. I just want to live day to day. I don't want to think about anyone else but me, don't want to think about who is lurking in the shadows, who wants me dead; it's not fair," I mumbled, lost in my misery.

Victor touched my face. "Let me share your screwed up life with you. Maybe between the two of us we can balance each other's lives out." He smiled at his suggestion, leaning over and kissing me again.

"No one has a life like mine; I'm sure of it." I returned his kiss slowly, enjoying his lips on mine.

Victor's face nudged down into where my shoulder blade met my neck and nuzzled his nose up near my ear. "Hey, when you are feeling better; can you try that binding spell on me again?" his voice low and throaty with built-up desires. "I think that could be fun."

I laughed a little because his nose was tickling my ear and I had not expected Victor to mention the binding spell ever again. "This time no matter how much you beg, I'm not letting you go," I warned in a whisper.

"That's what I'm counting on," he growled, nibbling on my neck lightly.

Chapter 29

Victor left shortly before dawn. With the impending day's light less than an hour or so away he was fairly certain I would be safe from others like him, until dusk that is. Victor needed a good rest; he was more than tired and his mood was rather listless. At least he felt he would sleep well knowing he was back on my good side.

I had a hard time clearing my head with all that had happened in such a short amount of time. The cocktail party seemed days ago, although the wounds of my attack were very fresh in my memory. The stiffness and soreness within my body remained a constant reminder as I tossed and turned in my bed, trying to get comfortable. I could not clear my mind. I wanted to remember who harmed me, how many of them, what they looked like, their motives, but nothing came to me, not even the smallest detail. Perhaps that was the frustration that did not let me sleep for several hours as I lay awake staring at the ceiling, wanting to either remember *everything* or let my body shut down and doze off. I might just have to surrender to the fact that I would never know what happened and I would have to live with it. The meeting with the Counsel scheduled for later in the day was weighing heavy on me too. I had no idea what to expect – purebloods, High Counsel Members, all vampires. My mind swirled with all kinds of thoughts of *who* these creatures were and how I would be treated. Would they be like Nathan, snooty and sophisticated scholars, or would they be like Victor, handsome, down-to-earth creative spirits? I had very little to compare my run-ins with vampires to. I had the feeling that even vampires, although the same in many ways to one another, were also very different; similar to humans in personalities, perhaps. Whether good or bad, I would not have to wait all that long to find out any of this. I just needed the time to sleep to bridge me over to that point. Exhaustion must have taken over eventually because when I woke up it was late. Apparently I had slept solidly through the entire day.

The first thing I wanted to do as soon as I could was *stand.* I did not want to feel like my attacker had won. I wanted to be as good as new. I wanted to be able to walk or run if I wanted to or had to. I cautiously swung my legs off the bed and firmly planted my feet onto the floor. I pushed myself up quickly to stand, staying in one spot for several seconds before I got the courage to take a step. Surprisingly my injured leg did not feel that bad. I had the strange sensations of a muscle spasm in my upper thigh, although it did not hurt. It only seemed slightly irritating and it only happened intermittently, so perhaps in time it would go away entirely. I was optimistic as I pulled my nightshirt up so I could see what kind of healing, if any, had occurred while I was sleeping. The scarring still remained as I remembered it, but the colors appeared more fleshy and less gray or blue. I seemed to be making slow progress.

I studied my injured wrist. In the day's light, it looked almost healed. While I was in the shower I examined the leftover gash marks on my left breast. That also appeared to be mending nicely. The jagged tears in the skin were still evident but seemed to be fading. There was still some pain when I pressed my fingers or a facecloth against it but it was obvious that I would live – a while longer any way.

The only pants I could manage to put on were a pair of black leggings. I added a T-shirt; this would have to do for my meeting with the Counsel. Under the circumstances, I would hope they'd understand. Victor called me shortly after dark and wanted to know if it was okay if he picked me up. He thought it better if I were not alone. Bringing me back to his place was his temporary plan until he and Nathan heard from the High Counsel as to when the car was being sent for us to attend the meeting. I agreed, still feeling troubled from the recent attack on me.

Some time later I heard a soft knock at the front door. I answered it, greeting Victor. He was dressed casually as usual, in a pair of black faded jeans, black short-sleeved shirt and his black sneakers.

"You're awfully dark tonight," I noticed out loud with regards to his attire. Victor didn't dress totally in black as a rule; he loved colors and enjoyed wearing them.

He walked past me, took a seat on the couch and replied, "I figure I won't fit in no matter what I do, so I could make things a *little* easier on myself by dressing more their part." Victor watched my achy gait as I came to meet him on the sofa.

"I see," I said through gritted teeth, sitting slowly on the edge of the couch.

"Your leg is bothering you, isn't it?" Victor asked.

"A little. I believe it will get better." I tried to smile. "I couldn't wear jeans though; couldn't stand the fabric rubbing against my thigh. I hope they understand." I looked down at my casual garments, feeling underdressed for the occasion.

"I'm sure it will all be explained. They will understand." Victor reached out and stroked my arm affectionately.

My eyes caught his unexpectedly and I grinned. "Well, it's not like I have to make an impression on anyone; I already have the job, right?" I giggled at my poor sense of humor.

Victor smiled back. "It's not what's on the outside that matters; after you live as long as I have you really do realize that. It's so true."

"Maybe someday we can philosophize about that, when I have some experience," I replied, thinking about the years he had on me.

Victor took my hand in his and examined my wrist. "Looks good," he commented, searching to see where the marks once were.

"Yes."

"How is your chest?" Victor questioned, letting my hand go and leaned back on the couch crossing his legs.

"Hurts a bit but doesn't look half as bad as it did," I answered, pulling the neck of my T-shirt out so I could glance down at whatever markings were left.

"Well, that's good. I just wish I knew who did this to you," Victor turned serious.

"If I knew, I would tell you. But you know, the more I thought about the attack, the more I realized that the only reason why it's *wrong* to you is because it happened to *me.* If it were anyone else it wouldn't bother you. You might even claim it to be natural."

"In some ways you are right – but, it's not natural for *us* to maim and leave a body to eventually bleed to death and die if not found. Even the most brutal attacks mean certain death. The human is drained of blood and already dead before we leave them behind. You were not drained of all your blood, and you may not have died if you were not found. We have no way of truly knowing. Plus, whoever attacked you was not a new vampire. It was skilled and therefore *knew* who you were, who you are meant to be. This was a hate crime, a rebellion to our society. That's what disturbs me so much about it," Victor explained with anger in his voice.

It was a disconcerting feeling to think someone could hate me for no reason; they did not even know me. It was like being in grammar school again where kids could hate you with no explanation. Usually it was just out of immaturity, and it was considered okay because someday they would grow up and know better. Apparently this was not the case in vampires who forgot all they were ever taught in their human lives.

"Rebels are not uncommon with my kind, especially if they are angry with the person who sired them or are just bad in nature. They are looking to take their hostilities out on anyone. Don't take it too personally." He took my hand and pulled me close to him, putting his arm around me and embracing me to his warm body.

"I'll never be able to get off the couch now that you got me all cozy," I huffed jokingly, glancing up at Victor from under his arm.

"We'll get you up, don't you worry," he spoke softly in my ear, then kissed my cheek.

Victor and I did not stay at my place long; he wanted to get me back to the Victorian. He felt that safety in numbers was important since neither he nor Nathan knew how many vampires had attacked me the night before, or if they would strike again. While Victor was retrieving me, Nathan was going to try to find out what time we were supposed to be at the Manor. He was also going to brief them on the attack and prepare them for my potential frailty.

Victor put the car into park and shut the engine off. I said, "Victor, if you don't mind, I'd like to talk to Nathan alone to thank him for last night." I waited, unsure of how he would respond.

He seemed perturbed with my request but finally agreed, saying, "All right. Knock. Let him answer the door. Don't let him push you around and don't forget to ask him what time the car will be here to pick us up for the meeting before you come upstairs."

"Okay."

We walked up the cement path to the porch, his arm around my shoulder. He unlocked the catch and opened the old heavy stained glass door to the foyer. I entered first, as Victor shut the door quietly. He stopped with me outside Nathan's door and kissed me on the forehead, then climbed the stairs to his place, silently ascending into the darkness at the top.

When Victor was out of sight, I knocked twice on Nathan's door, waiting for him to respond. I heard footsteps from the other side, then the deadbolt was unlocked and the door opened wide.

"Hello," I smiled nervously. "Can I come in a minute?"

Without a word he backed out of the doorway that led into his home and allowed me admittance to the living area – a mausoleum of darkness. As the door closed behind me, my eyes scanned the room rapidly, noticing the built-in cherry bookcases that held thousands of hard covered books. I'm sure in all Nathan's years he had read each one of them, maybe twice. Between the bookcases were tall windows dressed with heavy thick drapes that blocked all light from the outside ever coming in. "I just wanted to thank you for last night. You didn't have to do what you did." My voice was steady. I watched him move around me and take a seat at a desk near the back corner of the room.

"You are welcome. I did it for many reasons," Nathan declared, sitting back in his leather chair and pulling a cigarette out of his gray jacket pocket. He lit it with his gold plated lighter and placed the cigarette loosely between his thin lips. He appeared extremely sophisticated, even for someone who'd been around for as long has he had.

I got a sensation from him I had never felt before. It puzzled me. "Whatever your reasons were, they make no difference now. I just didn't want you to think I was some ungrateful human who took advantage of you because you had the power to make a difference in my life." I forced a smile as I spoke.

He pointed to a leather chair in front of his desk, cigarette in hand. "Have a seat." His voice was smooth and to the point.

I hesitated before I hobbled over to where he wanted me to join him. I slid the chair out from the desk and sat down slowly, using the arms of the antique to guide me down onto the smooth leather seat.

"Last night, I never would have helped you except for Victor's plea to me and due to the fact that you will someday be my Emissary. I did what I thought was best. In helping you, I consumed some of your blood, unavoidably. I learned much about you, about who you are and what you will become. There was a great influence in your life, someone who is no longer around to guide you daily, but someone you look up to for direction." He put his burning cigarette down into an ashtray and opened up the top drawer to his desk and removed a bloodstained book. I recognized it immediately as Sara's Journal. My eyes grew wide and I felt violated again. How did he get it? Nathan held up his hand in a gesture to ask me to stop whatever I was thinking and allow him to finish.

"Last night, when Victor found you, this book was clutched to your chest, thus the blood stains. I thought the book must be something very important to you for you to instinctively find it and want it with you while you were losing blood and being so close to losing consciousness. In spending as much time as I did with you last night, and being able to feel so many of your emotions and thoughts, this book cropped up several times. I was eager to learn more about this influence in your life because of that. I apologize for just taking it, but I knew asking you would not give me the response I wanted. I took it. I read it. I read a lot. It's a passion of mine." His eyes scanned the walls of the room that surrounded him with books. "I hope you understand. It's the only thing I truly enjoy anymore." Nathan leaned over the desk holding the red-stained journal out for me to take back. I snatched it up quickly, wanting it back in *my* possession. "Sara was a very knowledgeable person. If you have not finished reading her book to you, please do. I think it will be a growing experience for you. You will find it extremely helpful, especially in what's to come."

I was speechless. I did not know what to say to him that would not result with Nathan's hands clutched around my throat again. I got to my feet and limped to the door. "What time is the car coming?" I asked flatly, my back to him. I did not turn around to get his response.

"Ten," he replied from his desk, puffing on his cigarette. I could hear him inhale.

I opened the door without another word, leaving and feeling as if Nathan knew Sara better than he ever should have. I had not even finished reading her journal to *me* yet. How unfair. It hurt me deeply to think someone else had personal knowledge that was meant for me. Nathan's news to me had brought my mood down. I felt more than obligated to Sara to read her journal entirely now, if for no other reason than to see what Nathan knew that I did not.

I climbed up the dark staircase to Victor's and opened the door without knocking. Victor's place was much brighter in color and lighting than Nathan's was, truly day and night personalities. It was hard to believe at times that had Nathan sired Victor, they were so different from one another.

As soon as Victor heard the door close, he appeared from the back room to greet me. "So... was he civilized with you?" Victor asked, placing his hands on his hips and slipping a finger into his belt loop.

I looked up at him, mystified with his body language. What did he think I was at Nathan's place for? "He was fine. Quiet," I replied. "Why, has he been in a bad mood tonight?" I held Sara's journal close to my chest and took a step back from him. He felt overpowering to me.

"No, not really. Just curious." He returned and looked down at the bloodstained book. "I didn't see you bring that with you when we left your place." He pointed out my book with a motion of his head.

I took a deep breath. "Nathan took it before he left us last night. He read it. Now he's returning it," I answered, still angry over the violation. "He said he didn't ask, because he knew I'd say no. So he took it. Victor, I haven't even finished reading it yet. He knows more than I do." I shook the stained book in front of him. "I have no idea what Sara said in here. I have no idea what statements she made towards your people, or any other for that matter."

Victor stalked to the door and opened it. "There is soda in the fridge. Make yourself comfortable. I need to have a few words with the bookworm downstairs."

"Let's not get into a big fight tonight. The car is coming by at ten to pick us up and I would really hate for us all to be at each other's throats." My arms hung limply next to my sides as if I did not have the will to continue with any hostilities right now.

"There will be no fights. I just need to iron out a few things before we leave," Victor said and shut the door firmly behind him. I could hear his determined trot down the stairs, heading towards Nathan's. I wondered how many times in the years they lived together that Victor had made that same route, for the same reasons, to iron a few things out. Probably quite a few.

I went in to Victor's kitchen. Bachelors' kitchens truly amaze me, the scarceness of nutritional foods, utensils, and the abundance of junk cuisine from famous chefs like Little Debbie, Hostess and Bryers. But, a bachelor vampire's kitchen; I was not sure what to expect. Blood flavored jell-o, blood preserves, a can of blood drippings on the stove. I opened a cabinet to find it full of clean glasses and a stack of plain white dishes. I took a glass for soda. I opened the refrigerator next and saw it not was quite as empty as I had supposed. There was some food – a loaf of bread, a six-pack of beer, a bottle of Coke and a bottle of Diet Coke and a lonely stick of butter. I took the bottle of diet soda out and poured a glass, returning the bottle back to the refrigerator when I was done. I wandered through his loft with my glass of soda in hand and gravitated towards the area where he worked on his paintings. Victor kept it so clean; his paintbrushes all lined up, his paint tubes all capped, even paper towels close at hand. Sighing, I waited for him to return

Victor entered Nathan's home without warning. He flung the heavy wooden door shut behind him, making his presence known, if Nathan had not sensed it prior to that. Nathan sauntered into the living room, emerging from an area near the back of the house. Unperturbed from the slamming door, he appeared calm and collected. As he buttoned up a dark dress shirt he noticed Victor waiting menacingly for confrontation. "Shouldn't you be getting ready for the conference at the Manor?" Nathan asked, continuing to button his shirt and trying to distract Victor.

"Why did you take the book?" Victor asked Nathan angrily. "You have *no* idea what that book, or Sara, means to Kala." He ignored Nathan's initial comment.

"I don't often apologize, but I did. I'm sorry I took it without asking. I'm *not* sorry I read it. And I do know how important both are to Kala," Nathan retaliated, straightening his collar. Having had a taste of Kala's blood had made him aware of things he had not known before about her.

"I am afraid knowing you the way I do that whatever you now know about Kala, Sara, and the journal will go straight to the Counsel. You want to be with them *so* badly at times I think you'd do just about anything, including betraying us!" Victor hurled his accusations at Nathan. "I know very little of what is in that book. I only know what Kala has wanted to share with me, and no more. I don't want that kind of knowledge to leave this room."

Nathan put his hands on his hips and tapped his foot impatiently on the hard wood floor. "Is that what this is all about? You think I'm going to turn Kala in to the Counsel? Maybe last week I would have..." his voice tapered off as he moved over to the bar cart and poured himself a strong drink. "I won't, don't worry about it. I won't offer any information and I am powerful enough to keep my thoughts to myself." He sipped his drink.

"Why the sudden change?" Victor asked, confused with the abrupt transformation in Nathan's character. "Why do you care about her? You must. The Nathan I know would not allow such leverage to go to waste." Victor approached him, his eyes narrowed in thought. "That book either contains totally useless information or something *so* big..."

"Victor, quit while you are ahead. I told you I wouldn't share any of the information I know. I meant that. Drop it," Nathan advised him, taking another sip of his drink to calm his irritability.

"What is it about her?" Victor asked, pressing the subject and testing his ground. "I have never known you to..." his voice trailed off as he sensed something different about Nathan.

"Victor. Drop it!" Nathan said sharply.

Victor knew he was pushing Nathan to the limit, but he persisted with his ideas. "You had her blood..." He shook his head, trying to understand what was going on with his friend, refusing to pay attention to any warnings to halt his questioning. "I know how I felt when I had it – the bond. Christ, I'd give up just about anything to have that back again, to feel her with me; her constant companionship. Is that what it is? You feel her with you; your Emissary is with you? That's it, isn't it? I bet Kala has no idea she even has a power like this. It must affect each of our kind differently; it's a fulltime soul mate for me; it's a type of conscious guardian angel for you. You even apologized to her, for God's sake..." Victor's thoughts flew out loud. "What would her blood do for her Sovereign? Or a pureblood, or another Counsel member; maybe her attackers last night knew her blood could do something special for them. That's why they did not kill her?"

"Victor, get ready. The car will be here soon. I don't have time right now to deal with you. I give you my word I will not speak of the book, or Sara." Nathan left Victor alone in the living room, his final words hanging in the air.

As Victor left, his stomach twisted with jealousy. Nathan had Kala's blood in him, not by his choice but by his healing her wounds, and it had established a connection to her. Victor had lost his when the Blue Daemons attacked him and stripped him down to bare circuitry, requiring him to rest and allow his body to replenish itself over a week's worth of time. Now even though he was well, he was missing something he had prior to that night, a blood link that let him speak telepathically to Kala. It didn't matter if it was from a distance; it was at least a signal that let him know when she was in danger. It was also a companion for him and a comfort knowing she was deep inside him, traveling within his veins. Nothing could be closer or more intimate to him. Their telepathic connections currently were frustrating. Even in the same room he had trouble reaching her. It wasn't her lack of powers, it was his. She was perfectly capable of receiving a signal if only he could send one. Victor could continue to send telepathic messages to his own kind, and sense other vampires around him, but Kala was out of his loop and that bothered him. Perhaps when Kala was stronger and felt more herself she would allow him the bond back, the smallest drop of her blood could make him very happy again.

I sat on Victor's futon skimming through Sara's journal, still plagued by guilt for letting the book out of my sight. I was trying to keep myself preoccupied, since it would be nearly two hours before the car that the Counsel was sending would arrive to pick us up. I wondered how much longer Victor would be with Nathan and what was transpiring between the two. I wondered how much longer I would be by myself. I heard the front door open. I stopped my mind from wandering further and continued to browse the journal, waiting for Victor to find me.

I listened for him, hearing the refrigerator open, and the sounds of him pouring a glass of soda, then the refrigerator door closing. His light footsteps grew closer upon the wood flooring. He stopped and stood silently in the doorway of the room, staring at me. I felt his eyes on me. I glanced up, trying to read his mood. He smiled and took a sip of his drink.

"Everything turn out okay?" I asked, flipping the book over and placing it in my lap.

He shrugged. "Like any conversation with Nathan," he replied vaguely. He walked over to the futon and took a seat next to me, placing his drink on the floor.

"Well," I prodded, "Things are okay between you two; it didn't come to blows, I hope?" I turned to face him.

"It's been many years since that has happened," Victor chuckled at my comment. "He's very strong-willed – strong-minded. His age I guess." He reached over and put an arm around me.

"Guess he has the right." I agreed and snuggled closer under Victor's welcoming arm.

"Just think of all he knows and all he has seen," Victor said, awed over his Sire's experience.

"Think how I feel looking at you," I laughed, patting him affectionately. "God-like."

"Hardly God-like," Victor mocked me, leaning his head against mine. "Most humans would look upon me as the Devil himself. Only in your eyes would I look like a God."

"Most people don't know you, the *good* you; let's not talk about that *other* thing that surfaces," I mumbled, placing a hand against his stomach and curling into his body.

"Kala, you do realize I'm one and the same, although I try and keep them separate. I am who I am. I am a vampire; I'm not human. How does that make you feel? That you care about something that is not human and has not been in many life times?" Victor asked, pulling away to see my face, waiting for an answer.

"I try and not think about it. You seem very human to me. More human than Nathan. More human than many humans I have known and loved. I don't like to think about the bad in something that is so good," I answered quietly. I knew deep down inside he was a vampire. I knew first hand. I just refused to think of Victor and the other creature as being one and the same.

Victor looked very thoughtful before he spoke. "Until you can understand and take me for who I am and what I am, I risk hurting you unintentionally, every day. That's hard for me to accept because I am allowing you to continue to see me in a way that is fictitious. You need to come to recognize that I cannot offer you a normal relationship, or a life style that you deserve with a lifetime commitment. We are different."

"But I do understand most of that," I admitted. "Maybe I am avoiding some of what you are because in time it won't matter," I sighed. "Won't I be just like you? If I have no way of *not* being Emissary and I will be forced to assume this task whether I like it or not, won't I *be* like you, a vampire? Yes, as I sit here now I don't want you to be the creature you are, but can you blame me? There is so much good in you."

"Nathan was right," Victor sighed. "I'm glad in many ways you see me the way you do. I wish the world saw me like you do through your eyes. But you are not the world; you are more important to me than that. I need for you to see me honestly and that means taking the good with the bad." Victor stroked my hair lovingly. "No matter how long it's for."

"I know what you are. I may not understand it, but I know about it. I don't like it; does that count as taking the bad with the good?" I asked, softly caressing his chest with my hand.

He grinned slightly. "Not really, but maybe we can work on it. Maybe the more of us you meet, the more accepting you will be. There are more of us in this city than you would ever think."

"Great. How am I supposed to walk the streets now? I'll feel like fast food. Take-out, even," I frowned. "After last night I'm pretty nervous about meeting any more of you; that means tonight, too."

"I think you will be safe tonight. I won't let anything happen to you and I know Nathan won't. The High Counsel is just that, the highest echelon in my society. Purebloods, elders, a future Sovereign, and possibly *the* Sovereign himself will be there. Politically, the room will never get any larger. You will be well protected." Victor hugged me and rubbed his hands up and down my back.

I held my breath as he held me, wanting to believe everything would be okay.

"Let's just sit here like this; holding each other until we have to leave. I could do this all night," he spoke softly, nuzzling his face into my clean hair.

I moved closer, feeling his body against mine. I wished we didn't have to go to the stupid meeting. I didn't want to go. I was very content not moving a muscle and spending hours right where I was with him.

"Will you stay the night?" Victor asked, his voice floating over my head as his hands gently kneaded my tired muscles.

I raised my head up. "Stay? With Nathan below us? Won't that be kind of weird for you?"

"I don't know; I've never had a woman stay with me while I have..." his voice stopped with this train of thought. "Come to think of it, I have never had a woman over in the years I have known Nathan."

"Active sex life." My eyebrow rose, teasing him. "Gigolo."

Victor smiled. "Sex for a vampire is not the same as sex for a human. They are interchangeable but very different and although I do enjoy sex the way you do, there is more to it." He spoke rather fondly of the subject, perhaps remembering back to some memorable experiences of his own.

I pursed my lips trying to follow him. "So what is it that vampires enjoy? What is this type of sex you speak of?" I tilted my head to watch his facial expressions. Any information he had on the subject would be worth hearing for sure.

Victor's grin never left his face. "It's hard to explain to someone who has not experienced it themselves. With *us* it's more about emotional pleasure than it is physical pleasure. The sharing of thoughts, erotic or otherwise, with someone you care about, connecting in a way that is so intense you actually seem as one being for a time." He shook his head slightly, frustrated with his statement. "There is physical pleasure involved with the emotional pleasure;

it's all kind of one package, but not."

To some extent I understood. "Some sort of telepathic connection?" I asked in wonder.

He struggled with an answer. "Yes, but no." He looked down upon me with a look of uncertainty on his face.

"It sounds telepathic to me. We already have that; why can't we have sex the way you want then? A little for you, a little more for me; we could both be happy." I ran my index finger up and down the side of his neck persuasively.

He laughed a little. "We don't have a telepathic connection any more, and it's not quite that easy for someone who is human to have an experience like I described with a vampire."

"Sure we do. We've shared thoughts before. I know we have," I argued with him stretching myself up to kiss the side of his mouth.

Victor shook his head no. "Not since the Daemons. I lost it." It brought his mood down a notch although he tried not to let it show.

"How? Why?" I asked surprised. "They took it away from you?"

He shrugged gently. "Yes, it was taken," he replied lightly.

I frowned. I had come to like being able to communicate without having to think about it or having to say anything.

"We can talk about all that later. It was not a good idea to ask you to stay. It would probably be more uncomfortable for you than on me anyway." He sighed loudly.

"If you want me to, I will," I responded. "I am not that worried about Nathan."

"Don't dismiss him so lightly," Victor warned kindheartedly.

He was right. Nathan was a powerful individual who continued to surprise me with his words, actions and his wealth of knowledge. He had a level of experience in his lifetime that I was sure many would never meet or come close to. Being in his presence was like touring a museum. Only Nathan himself could have been an artifact.

Chapter 30

I could tell when the car arrived to pick the three of us up because Victor's eyes became very round and dark and his disposition grew solemn. "What's wrong?" I implored. He looked so distant.

"They're here."

I pushed myself off his futon, stretched my legs and anxiously paced the room for a moment. I needed him to be strong – for me. I needed him to get me through this event tonight. "Victor... Please." I reached my arms out to him.

His eyes stared at me blankly. Reluctantly, he stood. I put my arms around his waist, taking hold of him securely. "I thought I was going to look to you for strength and courage tonight." I leaned my head back to see his handsome face. I knew he was strong. I didn't need to be reminded, but I thought he did.

Victor shifted his weight back and forth for a moment, as he appeared to be lost in thought, maybe anticipating what the night would be like for us. He captured me in his arms and looked down at me with the start of a consoling smile. "I'll be there for you," he promised. He kissed me lightly on the lips, then confessed his apprehensions about the night. "I just don't know my people. Don't forget, I have been more a part of your world than their world over the last two hundred years. It's very hard for me to go to the Manor tonight and not feel some resentment towards them."

"I don't think anyone could look down upon you for feeling the way you do," I said honestly. "You know," I added, thinking out loud, "Maybe this will be a chance for us both to get to know your people better, since you have not been privileged to be in their company, either. It'll be like the first day of school for us; we'll ride there together; we can sit together; we can make fun of them together; it will be all right." I smiled, trying to make him feel better. How I ever ended up being part of the cheering up committee I will never know; after all, it was *me* who was going to be different than the rest tonight, and whom all eyes would be upon.

Victor shook his head, but smiled with me. "Maybe we can just skip." He planted a firm kiss on my forehead.

The car waited out front as Victor and I gathered our composure and met Nathan in the foyer. Victor and Nathan looked at each other for a moment, sharing some final private communication that I was not meant to hear. Nathan opened the front door and we filed out onto the porch. A fine rain had started. The wipers of the car swiped across the windshield of the ominous black limousine that was parked, taking up the entire driveway. '*What the neighbors must think*,' I thought to myself as I followed Nathan, my eyes on the black car with dark tinted windows and gold-lighted trim down the side. '*They think we have a black limo in our yard*,' Nathan replied back in thought to me. It was the first time I had ever gotten any messages from him; his voice sounded strange as it echoed in my head. I wanted *his* voice to be Victor's. I did miss that more than I had thought.

A youthful driver, dressed quite formally in a hat, gloves and black, form fitting uniform with shiny silver buttons running down the front, waited by the side of the limo clutching an oversized umbrella, shielding himself from the mist of rain. His skin was pale and his eyes small, round and beady like a nighttime animal; when his eyes caught the light I could see flecks of red. He looked unnatural to me, like some sort of monster.

The driver mechanically approached us like a toy soldier and held the umbrella up in one hand high enough to prevent a soaking; with the other hand he opened the car door, allowing Nathan to climb in the limousine first. I walked by the driver next, vampire, I reminded myself as I got closer to him. I ignored the sensation because it was beginning to be a common feeling hanging around Victor and Nathan as much as I did. I was careful to keep the thought to myself as I slide in next to Nathan. I had a difficult time with my aching leg, trying to get into the car. Victor helped the best he could as he got in last behind me.

As soon as I took a seat I felt the presence of another being, even before I visually made contact with it. Vampire. He sat across from the three of us; a blond young-looking male dressed in black, stretched out alone on what was his side of the limo. The lighting inside was muted, a soft radiance like an early evening moon giving off just enough light to make out his strong features. He admired us, his company, as he sipped a glass of red wine. I stared at him for a moment, knowing he was a vampire, but also knowing that everyone else I met tonight would most likely be, too.

This vampire was different; he made me feel peculiar in an eerie way. The sensation was very near crippling as it sent nervous impulses like a caffeine rush through me. When he returned my glance, I looked away uncomfortably. The car door shut and there was silence for a moment until the driver began to back the large vehicle out into the street.

"Welcome." The blond smiled warmly as he raised his glass of wine.

"Good to see you, Sheldon," Nathan replied, crossing his legs and trying to seem as casual as possible.

"Nathan, Victor," Sheldon acknowledged cordially. "Glad you are feeling better. I heard about the Blue Daemons. Such vile creatures they are."

"Thanks," Victor was slow to reply, careful to keep his voice emotionless.

"You must be Kala," Sheldon said, dropping his voice and his eyes as he started to introduce himself. "I am Sheldon, the future Sovereign."

My heart skipped a beat and I involuntarily gasped as I was confronted with the creature that would someday be my mortal killer and father of darkness. I swallowed hard before I spoke. "Pleased to meet you," I responded, as coolly as possible.

"I heard what happened to you last night. I want to apologize for my people. I hope you are feeling better," Sheldon spoke as he slid himself across the leather seat to the mirrored bar that extended the length of the car's interior. He uncorked a dark glass bottle and poured three glasses of wine.

"I'm feeling better, thanks to Nathan and Victor." I gave credit where credit was due, my eyes shifting from right to left.

Sheldon returned a small smile and offered a glass to Nathan, who accepted, then one to me. I looked down at the glass; my eyes followed his hand, to his arm and up to his face. I could not extend my arm to take the glass.

"Kala will pass," Nathan spoke in my behalf and took the glass of wine from Sheldon. He handed it over to Victor who unenthusiastically accepted it.

Sheldon frowned. "A little blood wine never hurt anyone." He sat back effortlessly on his leather seat, crossing his legs and gazed in our direction in the most elegant way.

I clasped my hands in my lap tensely, took a deep breath and thought how awful their drinks sounded. Blood wine. Even the name... icky.

Sheldon took a long savoring sip of his drink enjoying the flavor as it filled his mouth, his taste buds rising to the occasion. '*Some day you will love it as we do.*' I heard him tell me. He watched me intently as the last drop rolled across his tongue and down his throat.

He had a way of communicating with me like Nathan did, or like Victor had been able to. I did not like Sheldon so close to me; he was a stranger and I did not like him being able to communicate with me without my permission. I thought of it as an invasion.

I turned my head towards Victor, only to be surprised to see he was *actually* drinking his wine. My face wrinkled and I grimaced as I observed Victor consume half the glass. It was painful to think about ingesting such a foul beverage. Victor's eyes rolled away from mine when he saw the expression on my face. I did not mean to make him feel embarrassed; the last thing I wanted was to isolate him further from his kind on account of my feelings. Of course I had no way to convey this to him... he could pick up none of my thoughts and I did not want to ask Nathan to tell him. I was sure my message would get screwed up somewhere in translation. I sat in silence, hoping I'd have time later to say I was sorry for making him feel normal.

I had only been chauffeured in a limo a few times and each time I had enjoyed it, yet this time the ride was too stressful for me and I couldn't relax. Although we were probably only penned up together for thirty minutes it felt like forever. I sat stiffly between Victor and Nathan, refusing to allow myself to make any type of contact with Sheldon. I was sure he was just waiting for the chance to catch my eye. I was trying to deal with the thought of being the only *living* life form in the car, surrounded by three dead men who were capable of draining my body of blood and tossing me on the roadside as a corpse. Occasionally I amazed myself with the way I thought, how totally gruesome it was. I continued to sit very quietly, feeling very vulnerable. I wondered if any of them missed being like me, human, that is, and if they even remembered what it was like. Would any of them, if given the chance, go back to being a human again? Could they cope and manage after so many life times of being immortal? Victor, I was certain, would jump at the chance to be totally human and stop being what he hated. I found it hard to imagine what it would be like for me to be like them. Sleeping days, waking nights, never being ill, never worrying about death or dying, living a false life in society to fit in, having superior senses, an appetite for blood, it was hard to imagine. '*You get used to it. We all do. Unless you are like me – born into this life knowing no other. It's very normal for me.*' Sheldon spoke silently from across the car. I cringed at hearing his voice resonate in my head. The sad truth was; it was something I needed to start to think about. My life after death.

When the limo finally stopped, I felt a rush of mixed emotions. I desperately needed to get out of the car, get some fresh air, and perhaps receive some sort of reassurance from Victor that everything would be all right. On the other hand, I knew I was about to embark on what was possibly the most important thing to ever happen to me, not to mention that I would be surrounded by a room full of vampires; High Counsel Members whose cold stares would burn like icicles. I did not anticipate these people being friendly; I expected the worst.

Victor got out of the car first and assisted me in climbing out with my bum leg. I stood very close to him as Nathan and Sheldon exited next. A degree of calmness flowed into me as I brushed my hand against Victor's arm. He looked down at me and smiled grimly; I knew he was not happy being here and neither was I, but at least he was with me. I would be in pure terror otherwise.

The limo was parked on a circular limestone driveway that curved in front of a magnificent home. The imposing structure towered on a bluff overlooking the ocean. I could hear the surf beating against the rocky breakwater, the sea breeze carrying both the sounds and the scent of the salty foam. The smell of the salt water reawakened me; I felt almost fresh and clean. The ocean winds poured up the cliff and caressed my skin, riffling through my hair and lifting my spirits for the moment. How I loved the sea.

The home was an architectural beauty, built of tan stucco and wood. It appeared to be old, but certainly not forgotten as it was scrupulously taken care of. The center island in the driveway was packed with flowering foliage, trees, and large granite statues. I figured the house was old, perhaps several hundred years. In the darkness of the night, even though the property was well lit, nothing could be taken for granted.

I stood very close to Victor. Sheldon and Nathan were standing nearby chatting in a very low secretive tone that my mortal ears couldn't hear. I nudged Victor and he leaned closer to me. "What do you think they are talking about?" I asked, trying not to draw too much attention in our direction.

He shrugged. "Nothing too important I'm sure. They would not be talking out loud if it were."

"Oh," I sighed.

The night was quiet since the rain had stopped and the skies had begun to clear. The thick stormy clouds from earlier in the night were parting to let the moon and the stars shine through. Subtle breezes drifting up the land made me close my eyes as I listened to the ocean again, relaxing. My reverie was interrupted when I sensed Sheldon approaching. My eyes snapped open like shades on a window and I felt the tension mount in my body. Sheldon put his hands behind his back and took a few more strides in our direction, making his advance more personable than business-like. "If you are ready we can enter." He motioned towards the house with a nod of his head.

The front doors were wide open and I could see partially into the entry way where a large stone fountain filled with cascading falls and plant life thrust up through the floor. Victor and I followed Sheldon as we climbed the wide granite steps to the threshold of the Manor. Nathan had already gone inside. Sheldon entered first and was greeted by a woman dressed in service attire. She was a tall, redheaded female, attractive and very fair skinned with orange freckles over her nose and cheeks. Irish, I thought, in her human life. She smiled at Victor as if she knew him somehow; it was not the smile of a first encounter. Her eyes watched him affectionately as he and I entered the

Manor together. Victor went out of his way to ignore her, to not notice her. His avoidance was obvious, because she was quite stunning. I immediately went on the defense. He was mine – okay, not technically, but it was a rush of female hormones that made me think otherwise. If I asked Victor about her later on, maybe he would not feel I was crazy in my assumption that they knew each other. I would have to wait and see; there were other, more pressing things to worry about now.

As I dismissed the woman from my mind I became instantly overwhelmed with the massiveness of the home. The entryway was floor and ceiling, nothing in between but air and some highly placed windows and skylights. The sounds of the water fountain echoed pleasingly against the marble tiled floors. I steadily made my way to the great fountain, admiring the green plant life cascading out of it on all sides. It was etched and detailed with a gothic theme: gargoyles and cherubs. A large winged gargoyle sat perched on the top of the fountain, a powerful spray of fresh water coming out of its mouth that poured into the basin many feet below. The closer I got to the fountain, the more the atmosphere changed. The air was damp and cool as it rose out of the stone fountain in a frothy mist. I could hear many voices coming from a room off the entryway but I tried to disregard them by dangling my arms into the large stone basin, reveling in the coolness on my skin. I wanted to put off the inevitable – the meeting of the High Counsel.

I remained at the water fountain, feeling a sense of security with its size and the fact that I could see the entire open room from where I was. My eyes looked back at the redhead still near the doors. She was conversing in low tones with another servant. I had not seen a female vampire before, which she obviously was. I did not mean to stare but the thought of a woman being a vampire had not crossed my mind. I felt sexist and discriminating for a moment. Then I wondered how many more there were, females that is. Would I see any more tonight? The redhead must have felt my intrusive stare and, still talking, slowly looked in my direction. Her bright blue eyes looked at me with interest as we locked stares. I could certainly see why men would be interested in her. She smiled at me and I returned the same with a bit of reticence.

I tried to find other objects in the vicinity to keep my interest and slowly wondered away from the focal point of the room, the fountain, but not too far away from Victor. He had not moved since we'd entered the house and remained standing still on one of the black marble floor tiles. I looked around like a child trying to absorb all the colors, textures and smells at once, but it was impossible to do. The walls soared straight up, their height papered in a light green pinstripe. Two thirds of the way up, the paper stopped at a cherry trim-rail, and the rest of the wall was painted a lighter shade of green to the ceiling. An exquisite antique armoire stood grandly against the wall closest to the main doors, away from the voices I still heard rattling away. I walked over to it, admiring the detail in the wood and the carvings. I felt the grain, cool and smooth under my fingertips, a highly varnished surface polished to reflect a gloss ordinary furniture could never attain. I delicately trailed my sensitive fingertips over the elaborate carvings in the matching chair as I peeked back in Victor's direction. He was watching the redhead. I wondered how Victor saw her, and what he thought. Was he curious because he lacked experience in being with his kind? Was it all in wonderment? Did he look at her like any other vampire, as a female vampire, beautiful, average? Did he compare her to me? Did he see her differently than he saw me? Or was she a fallen lover from many years past? I was thinking all the things a suspicious human female would think. My envious meditation was rudely broken as Sheldon walked up to me.

"I think you are very attractive," Sheldon said bluntly, not bothering with any preliminaries.

I refused to acknowledge his comment or his presence, although I did keep a wary note of his body, so close to mine. I did not trust him one bit.

Sheldon poised himself arrogantly at my side. I could feel his arm against mine as the vibrations of his aura beat against me like a hammer. He looked towards the front doors of the house as the redhead closed them tightly together and locked them into place. "Lyla is beautiful, don't you think?" Sheldon asked me, admiring her from afar. "She has been on our staff for years."

"Pretty," I muttered under my breath, glancing at her again. Victor was now cautiously observing my one-sided conversation with Sheldon. He watched with irritation growing in his eyes.

"I hope you like the Manor. It will be your home as well," Sheldon said, his head moving in all directions, taking in the sights and sounds of the room as if pleased by his royal surrounding.

I spun to face him, feeling a shooting pain up my thigh with the abrupt movement. "What?" I blurted out.

Sheldon faced me; our eyes met. "As Emissary you will live here, at the Manor. This will be our home. Many of the High Counsel Members and staff reside here as well. I assure you the house is plenty big enough for us all to live happily without being in each other's way." He smugly clasped his fingers together and looked quite pleased with himself as he delivered this bit of news to me.

I felt waves of heat begin to kindle in my body as my anger and resentment grew. Who does he think he is, I thought to myself, telling me where to live. The Manor was lovely, but not *my* home. As my fury mounted, I placed my hands behind my back, mindful of the damage they could cause.

Sheldon leaned closer to me and in a placating voice said, "I did not mean to anger you. Please compose yourself. We have much to do tonight, and getting you upset is not part of the plan."

Just as I was about to spit a retort at him, I saw Victor approach us. I was glad that he had noticed our little confrontation because I was badly in need of at least a semblance of support.

Sheldon stepped away from me. "I should get into the conference room," he announced as he retreated. "Victor, I'd like you to take a seat next to Nathan. He's waiting for you in the room. Kala, please stay here; I will send Lyla to get you momentarily." Sheldon walked off, casually commanding, "Victor, please join me."

My body heat remained way above normal as I listened to his speech. His words entered my head and circled around but made little sense; my anger still getting the best of me. Victor halted at my side like a guardian angel, refusing to take another step in Sheldon's direction. Victor glanced down at me; his eyes full of concern, feeling the heat of my body radiate over to him. He knew it meant I was enraged. I bit my bottom lip, gathering my thoughts and trying to control the one emotion I could never quite get a handle on – anger.

"Victor. Please come." Sheldon motioned for him again with a wave of his hand. "It has to be done this way. Kala is safe here. She will join us shortly."

I looked at Victor calmly. "Go ahead. See you soon. I'll be fine." I did not want him worried about me. I just wanted to get the night started, so it would finish.

Victor nodded and touched my arm. "Cool off. It's not good for you." He followed Sheldon's lead. I watched them depart into a room located on the other side of the fountain. Once they'd entered, Lyla shut the doors from outside the conference room and stood guard in the entryway with a short well-built brunette male.

I sighed deeply and knew all I could do was wait; five minutes, twenty-five minutes, an hour; I had no idea. I ran my fingers through my wind blown hair and made my way back to the water fountain. I brushed my hands over the stone, savoring the coolness on my warm palms that had held so much heat with my pent up fury. They cooled quickly.

I admired the flowers and the plants, feeling the soft greenery between my thumb and fingers, wondering if they were real or fake. The leaves had a waxy texture to them, yet they were real. I wondered what else was real and what was not in this house.

I never wore a watch, depending on others for the time of day, so time was never all that important to me, until now. I waited for what seemed like the better half of an hour. I finally heard the doors of the conference room open, getting Lyla's attention and mine, but as quickly as they opened they sealed back up with a heavy thud. I could see her walking my way. My heartbeat picked up and my stomach began to twist in my gut. I watched her hips sway back and forth under her gray dress. "Kala, the Counsel will see you, now." I was right. She was Irish; her brogue was thick but clear.

I nodded slightly and proceeded to walk in her direction, following her with my obvious limp. She led me to the conference room door. The male had not moved from his post as if a Centurion Solider, although I could feel his stare on me the closer I got to the doors.

Lyla twisted the handles to the right and released the door so it swung silently open into the conference area. I felt my chest tighten with anxiety. The room's light was subdued with a golden luminosity that came from a sizeable antique chandelier suspended over a long lacquer table. Counsel Members sat silently with their eyes shut in meditation, hand joined to hand, together for some purpose I was not aware of. I felt Lyla place her hand on my back and gently push me through the doorway and into the darkness of the room. The sound of the door closing broke the quiet in the room, but no one's concentration at the table. I did not know what to do or say since no one was acknowledging my presence. Not even Victor or Nathan, who were also seated at the large table in silence, eyes shut, hand in hand, bothered to look at me.

I reached up and uneasily stroked the Amulet around my neck. My heart began to race as the tension grew within me; soon even involuntary actions like breathing became difficult as my lungs labored somewhere between inhale and exhale. My hand slipped down from my Amulet to my chest as I tried to relax enough to remember to breathe in and breathe out. I clutched the front of my shirt in frustration, then realized that I was really having trouble breathing. I staggered a little on my feet as my light-headedness grew. I began to hear what sounded like a horn and many voices amplifying quickly inside my head. The horn was a constant penetrating blare like a school fire alarm, one tone that pierced through a student's brain telling them to exit the building, only I could not. The voices were looping and never ending, uttering and chanting and talking all at once, the horn and the voices together swelled in my head. The cacophony seemed able to split my cranium in half, projecting brain matter out into the room, on the walls, on the ceiling, table, everywhere. Tears filled my eyes. The pain no longer allowed me to stand. I plummeted to my knees onto the swirling pattern of the carpeted floor, my hands still gripping the front of my shirt, head hanging over my body in a fetal position so it nearly touched the floor. I rocked myself, trying to ease the discomfort; but the pain that throbbed and boomed in my head was too much and I could hardly capture enough air to sustain awareness.

I felt myself hoisted off the floor in one quick motion, noticing for the first time the horn and the voices had stopped. I struggled to regain a regular rhythmic breathing pattern, huffing and puffing, hyperventilating, as the pounding in my head continued. My legs refused to support my weight beneath me and I hung limply, dimly aware of my surroundings. There was a ringing in my ears that reminded me of the aftermath of a very loud concert, the level of deafness or audible numbness that could take several hours to fade away.

"She needs some air. Take her outside," I heard a voice bark out.

I felt what seemed to be at least two sets of hands pull at me to stand and when I could not I was simply scooped up and carried away. "Kala." I heard a voice speak to me. I heard more voices, arguing people and then a rush of cool air hit my body, my hair streamed over my face. I could smell the ocean and the salt, hear the waves and the white water. I felt myself lowered back onto my feet. "Kala, open your eyes." My head fell to the side and I did not respond to the voice although I wanted to.

'*Kala, tell me how you feel.*' It was Nathan.

'*Oh God Nathan. What happened?*' I asked him, most of my energy fizzling and sparking trying to re-ignite my spirit and strength.

'*It will all be explained. Victor and I are here with you. Open your eyes.*'

"Kala, come around." Victor spoke audibly as he shook me carefully, trying to rouse me.

"Trying," I spoke softly, taking a deep breath of sea air. Firm hands turned me and propped me against a stone railing to brace me in a standing position. "Why?" I asked faintly. "What did you and Nathan do to me?" My eyelids hovered on the horizon, half slits straining to stay open.

I could feel Victor's hands comb gently through my wind-blown hair, moving it out of my face. He lightly wiped away the tears that trickled out the corners of my eyes. "I'm so sorry. I did not know what was happening. No one told me you would get hurt," he whispered, looking at me with pity in his eyes.

I reached out and grabbed his shoulders to help myself stand. Leaning forward, I put my head against his chest, still not able to hold it upright without dizziness.

'*Hold your Amulet. Request it to regain your strength,*' Nathan telepathically suggested to me. '*Do it... quickly.*'

I shook my head and took a deep cleansing breath to clear my mind, blindly reaching for the Amulet. I thought repeatedly to myself – give me back my strength, give me my strength back. I felt Victor's hands on me, caressing my arms with his reassuring touch. I slowly raised my head off of Victor's chest and let my eyes open gradually, fighting the desire to curl up and drop off into a long sleep. Victor massaged my shoulders vigorously when he realized I was regaining some of my strength, trying to pull me back into the game.

'*Good,*' Nathan's voice echoed in my head. '*Again. Keep it up.*'

I held the Amulet in my hand tightly and continued concentrating. I was soon standing on my own, requesting a glass of water and some aspirin to make my headache go away. I waited on the balcony alone for Victor or Nathan to return with a drink and the medication I asked for.

I leaned against the stone railing that framed the balcony overlooking the little quiet harbor area the house sat on. The ocean breezes blowing off the water onto me soaked into my skin and tangled into my hair, although I did not care what I looked like; I was more concerned with how I felt. The evening sky calmed me and I drank in the sight of the shimmering pallid moon and twinkling stars. At last, a measure of tranquility filled me. I closed my eyes, feeling a gust of wind travel up the beach and blow around me. I wrapped my arms around myself with a sudden outbreak of goose bumps.

"Here is your water and aspirin."

I turned around quickly to see Sheldon with me, the reason for my goose bumps. I said nothing to him and just glared in hostile silence.

Sheldon extended one hand with the pills and the other with a wine goblet filled with water.

His presence angered me. I blamed him completely for the entire attack I had just suffered through, the migraine and the breathing difficulties. I turned my back on him and continued to gaze out at the ocean.

"Kala, please stop playing games with me," he said petulantly, almost like a child.

I turned to confront him. "Games? What do you call what happened to me in there?" I snapped. "If we are going to play games, let's have some rules, okay!"

"What happened inside will be explained to you. It was an accident," Sheldon said defensively.

The sound of his voice made my stomach clench. There was something about him I didn't like. He was appealing to look at from a distance: clean cut, blond, blue eyes, attractive, but something about him rubbed me wrong. Conversing with him made me see red; being in his company annoyed me. I did not like him and it was a far greater dislike than I initially had for Nathan. My feelings towards Sheldon bordered on hate, although I had no idea why. Possibly it was just this prearranged merger of Sovereign and Emissary; a merger that I had no say in whatsoever, that fueled my resentment, but I wondered if my feelings ran deeper than that.

"Take your aspirin and water so we can go back inside," Sheldon requested reasonably.

I turned to face him and looked at the glass of water he held in his hand. He stretched his arm out to try and offer it to me once again. Suddenly, the goblet shattered in his hand and water splattered with fragmented pieces of glass that tumbled to the stone patio floor. I looked down at the debris.

"Well, I guess you really didn't want it after all." Sheldon tossed the aspirins out into the blackness over the balcony and patted his hands dry on the seat of his pants.

I shrugged. "Sorry." The polite thing to say but not said in the most sincere tone of voice.

"One way or another, your temper will be controlled," Sheldon stated as if the event did not matter to him. "We need to go back into the conference room; the night is still young."

I did not want to go back in. I did not want to be with him.

"Nathan and Victor have already assumed their seats at the table." Sheldon stepped back and extended his arm to accompany her into the Manor.

I shuddered at the thought of touching him.

"Please don't make them wait. The Counsel really hates to wait," Sheldon warned lightly.

Just as his words finished the blasting tone and voices started to play again in my head, the same ones that sent me crumpling to my knees gasping for air. Sheldon knew when he warned me that *it* would happen again; he even had an evil smile on his face; his way of retaliating. I winced and leaned heavily against the stone rail, the initial shock causing me to go weak at the knees and fear tumbling to the floor again. The pounding in my head increased. Sheldon watched as all the fight went out of me, leaving me submissive and allowing him to take my hand and tow me back into the Manor, leading me to the conference room to continue what was started.

Before entering the room where the Counsel Members sat, Sheldon grabbed me by the shoulders and firmly explained what he expected of me, as if I was the defiant offspring and he an overstressed parent. "You will control yourself, answer our questions the best you can; do what we ask of you and you should be fine. If you don't I'm not going to take responsibility for what might happen."

I rubbed my temples as he spoke, his voice salting my wounds. The tones had stopped the moment Sheldon dragged me into the Manor and I had given up my struggle, but my head still throbbed in pain.

"I'm going to open the door. I want you to walk in first and go to the open chair at the table – don't sit in it, just stand by it." Sheldon removed his hands from my shoulders. "Understand?" he demanded.

I nodded, still too shaken to argue.

Sheldon reached forward and opened the door to the room. I walked in slowly as he'd asked me to, my eyes scanning the faces around the table cautiously. I had not had the chance to get a good look the first time I walked in. I recognized no one except for Nathan and Victor who sat together on the far end of the table. They both appeared expressionless as they watched me enter and approach the empty chair in the middle of the table. I guessed there to be about twenty Counsel Members gathered at the long black lacquer table. Each member was dressed in black and all appeared solemn and dignified. The exception was Victor who, although dressed in black too, had a more casual air about him. I could not help but notice that three of the Counsel Members were women – all brunettes, appearing less than middle-aged. I stood silently looking down at the smooth black leather that covered the chair; I placed my hand on the back of it, waiting for instructions. I heard the door shut securely and felt Sheldon's aura getting stronger the closer he got to me, until he was directly behind me. I could tell without turning around. He placed his hands on my shoulders, easing me away from his chair so he could sit. I cringed with the weight of his hands on my body. He rolled the chair towards the table, leaving me standing behind him off to his right.

"I take it everyone is now convinced that Kala is our next chosen Emissary?" Sheldon said pointedly, directing his question at those members of the Counsel who had not believed him.

The Counsel Members at the table all appeared to be in agreement, with nods and yes's all the way around.

"I think we owe an apology to Kala. The calling we placed to her tonight was far too intense. It usually must travel over hundreds or thousands of miles in order for it to reach an intended party or, in the case of Kala, get *through* someone to reach her. We have become so accustomed to sending powerful signals because of the blockade, we did not think to send a weaker signal. Kala was right here in the room with us and there was no obstruction tonight. That was eliminated a short time ago. Perhaps an individual call from select members would have been enough to convince those of you who were skeptical. Kala, please accept the apology from the Counsel for the pain and suffering we delivered upon you." Sheldon spoke conclusively, as if my acceptance would bury the hatchet with his people.

"How long have you been sending out a signal like that?" I asked quietly, but loud enough so that all the members in the room could hear. I was sure I would have noticed a signal like that if I had heard one in the past

There was no response to my question.

"Am I not allowed to ask questions?" I inquired a little louder this time. I looked at the silent Counsel and felt a little bit of courage returning to me.

'*Kala, be careful.*' Nathan looked at me in warning.

"Yes, you can ask questions," Sheldon finally replied. I could hear the strain in his voice, which only served as encouragement for me.

"How long has the Counsel been trying to reach me?" I asked again, stepping back from Sheldon's chair.

"Well, perhaps ten years now," Sheldon replied, thinking out loud.

"Hmm." I could feel eyes upon me, cold, unfriendly eyes, as if I were wasting their time with questions that had no importance to them. "If your call tonight blew me away, what in the world would prevent me from hearing that signal some twenty miles into town? I have lived in this city for more than fifteen years. I probably could have felt a signal like tonight's on the moon."

'*You are trying my patience*,' Sheldon told me, his voice resounding in my head.

"And you are trying mine," I responded verbally.

Sheldon suddenly pushed his chair back from the table and stood to face me – Sovereign to Emissary. "Let's talk about it." He glared at me, wheeling his chair out for legroom.

"Let's," I repeated defiantly, crossing my arms. I didn't bother to watch the faces of the Counsel Members. Honestly, I did not care what they thought of me at this moment. If I was Emissary I deserved answers.

"Yes, my Emissary, you do deserve answers," Sheldon spoke my thoughts. "But can you accept the answers?"

"Don't you worry about what I can accept or not," I shot back, rubbing the Amulet in my fingers.

Sheldon watched me fondle the pendant before he continued. "Where did you get that Amulet?" he asked, walking around the table and waiting for my answer.

I let the Amulet fall to my chest. "A friend," I replied briefly.

Sheldon accepted the answer and took several more steps, then turned his back on me. "Would her name be Sara?" The tone in his voice was almost playful as he waited patiently for my answer

I swallowed hard hearing her name roll off his lips. "Yes." I tried to appear unconcerned.

"How long did you know Sara? I understand she passed away recently," Sheldon said as he continued walking by a few more chairs, then stopped behind Victor and Nathan.

"Fifteen years or so," I replied slowly. I knew Sheldon was building up to something.

"That was just about the time your parents split up, isn't that right? And your brother disappeared." Sheldon recited the facts as if he was a defense attorney trying to break down the witness.

How did he know all this? My stomach twitched inside. I had started this confrontation not knowing he would pry so deep into areas he should not be in. I could not back down; it was not possible. There was no apology big enough on my part that could take back my heated war of words that started all of this. I answered his question with little enthusiasm. "About that time," I admitted.

"Didn't you spend a lot of your time with Sara from that point on? She was a witch; yes?" he asked, his mouth contorting on the word witch.

I crossed my arms at my chest. "Yes and yes." I wished he'd move right onto the point, but vampires appreciated a pursuit. I guessed I would have to go along with his game for now.

Sheldon began to make his way back to my side of the table. "Didn't you ever get the feeling that Sara was trying to shelter you from something or someone, protect you from something? Didn't she always try and make you stronger, even practice her crafts?"

I thought a moment. "She was my friend. She did what friends do for friends. I never practiced her crafts," I answered, annoyed with his questions. "I didn't practice anything witchcraft related until recently."

Sheldon chuckled a little, amused by the statement. "So I've heard; fire, electrical charges, wolves, breaking glass, very amateurish." He smiled shortly at me. "What if I were to tell you that your friend Sara *was* trying to protect you from someone?" He toyed with me some more.

"Like you?" I said pointedly.

Sheldon stood directly in front of me, his body language totally challenging and confrontational as he replied. "Exactly."

"I'm not surprised," I said, looking him boldly in the eye, refusing to be cowed. "She was very smart."

Sheldon shook his head. "Not smart enough." He walked around me as if a piece of furniture and took his seat back at the table, dismissing me.

"How so?" I asked from behind him. Again I could feel the temperature in my body climb. My hands tingled and I rubbed them together instinctively.

"Death is so permanent," Sheldon sighed. "Don't you agree?" He pushed his chair back so he could get my facial reaction to the word *death.*

I was hoping I was not going to hear what I thought this was leading up to. "Usually. Unless you have a strong spirit."

"Apparently your friend Sara chose death over several choices that could have granted her life, or better," Sheldon said smugly, leaning back in the comfort of his cushy chair.

My eyes scanned the faces of the other vampires, all sitting quietly through our verbal sparring. Their eyes were on me; no one at the table seemed annoyed any longer with the game of questions and answers. I think they found entertainment in the volley of words.

"Thus her mysterious death?" I replied. I clenched my fists behind my back, feeling the friction under my skin building and burning, the palms of my hands like hot plates.

"Thus," Sheldon spoke. "For some ten years she blocked our signal to you; a calling to be our Emissary. When asked to step aside and let fate happen she refused. Now that she is gone, the signal was placed and the transmission was received. You, my sweet Kala, are to be Emissary."

His words only fanned the burning fire building within me. I faced Sheldon, bracing myself with both hands on the table. Through clenched teeth, the fury evident in my voice, I growled, "If you knew where I was, and you knew who I was, why did you just not take me? Why?" I felt the layers of the table under my hands start to give way. I looked down at my hands; the heat that emanated from them was melting through the paint and the lacquer on the tabletop.

Sheldon glared down at his black table without blinking an eye, watching the hard shiny black coating melt, bubble and ripple under my power. "We have procedures that need to be followed. The Book of Jorn is very specific and our people follow it to a T. We only knew Sara was protecting someone; we were not sure who it was until recently, when Victor rediscovered you."

"No wonder none of the detectives can find any clues..." I thought out loud, referring to Sara's murder.

"She had a choice; don't blame my people for her death," Sheldon said.

"I'm not blaming your people; I'm blaming you!" I spat at him angrily. I pulled away from the table leaving two very large handprints that had burned through all the coats of lacquer and into the wood, singeing the area around them as well. "How dare you try and put the fault on Sara!" I rubbed my soiled hands on the thighs of my black leggings. "She did what she felt was right for me and I'm not so sure she didn't make the right decision. After all, I've seen her several times since her death. She guides me better than you ever will, my darling Sovereign!" I snapped, and with that a large cut crystal pitcher split, cracked and fell into fragments, flooding the table in ice and water.

Sheldon bolted from his chair again. "The temper tantrum starts!" He looked at me in displeasure, knowing he could not touch me, then stared in rage at the pool of fluid and ice that covered the table.

"It's your job. Control me," I taunted him. "Not doing too well, are you?" I stood at the head of the table rubbing my Amulet in my hand. I was so angry with Sheldon and the people of the Counsel, now that I knew they were responsible for Sara's death. They had killed my best friend and no justice would ever be served.

The chandelier overhead began to sway back and forth as I thought about throwing the largest object in the room at Sheldon.

Smoothly, quietly, an older-looking vampire stood up from his place near the far end of the table. He had graying hair and ashen skin, but had a certain authoritative air about him. He released the one button that fastened his dark suit jacket and placed his hands into his trouser pockets, standing calmly but apparently bored with the rivalry between Sheldon and me. "I'd like a moment to say something," he announced firmly. He had a deep voice with a European accent that sounded polite and full of etiquette.

Sheldon pounded a fist on the table, venting his anger. "What? What do you have to say?" He leaned over the table, supporting himself on his hands, furious face reflected in the polished tabletop, his arms trembling with pent up rage.

"It would seem that *our* job here is done. Our mission tonight was to verify the legitimacy of the woman you claimed to be our next Emissary by sending out a calling, and to put to rest any skepticism around it. The call was placed and Kala proved to be the woman Nathan, Victor and you declared her to be. There is nothing the Counsel can do now but wait. Kala's time will come. Until that time it is the job of our current Sovereign, Teague, you and appointed Counsel Members to ready Kala for the change that will take her from her mortal life to her new life as Emissary. How you decide to do that is your decision; the Counsel has no influence until Teague and you feel she is ready to take on her responsibilities. Then and only then can we vote on it as a Counsel to proceed with the ritual, or wait and allow her more time. This meeting should adjourn."

Several other members nodded in agreement with the well-spoken man.

I too wanted the meeting to end. I wanted to go home and fall asleep in Victor's arms.

Sheldon stood abruptly. "Perhaps you are right. What is happening now is something Kala and I will need to work through on our own; you should not be part of it. Meeting adjourned." He rolled his angry eyes at me and then up at the heavy swinging chandelier. "Make it stop."

The Counsel Members began to disperse. One of the women members pushed her chair in and spoke loudly. "Sheldon, looks like you have your work cut out for you. She's a live one. Maybe that's what we need in our next Emissary, a spark to liven us all up." She smiled broadly, obviously enjoying his discomfiture.

Sheldon tried to roll with it. "We will see." He forced a smile in return but I could tell it was difficult for him to manage. He combed his fingers through his hair and sat sullenly in his chair showing signs of exhaustion. Victor and Nathan remained seated and silent, perhaps wary of saying anything, this being their first night at the table. I was still standing at the head of the room fingering my pendent and watching the chandelier continue to sway.

The room cleared quickly and with it came a heavy stillness. Lyla shut the doors behind the last Counsel Member, leaving the four of us alone. Sheldon leaned back in his chair and put his feet up onto the damaged area of the table. He folded his hands on his stomach and stared at the ceiling. Victor pushed himself away from the table far enough to cross his legs and get comfortable, not knowing how much longer he would be cooped up. Nathan sat quietly at the table with hands resting on the arms of his chair.

"Kala, sit down, just not near me please," Sheldon ordered and he breathed a strong sigh, trying to keep his irritations within him.

I slowly moved to the opposite side of the table from Sheldon, feeling his eyes follow me every step of the way. I pulled a chair out next to Victor and sat down. I wished fervently that he and I were anywhere but here. I wanted to forget the pains and the trials of the night; I wanted him to take them all away; to feel his lips on mine and let the passion of the night take us to whatever level it may. I wished I could tell Victor how I felt, but I could not. I settled for eyeing him as seductively as possible under the circumstances. He returned my stare, the naked desire shining in his eyes. Although he and I had only had that one beautiful night together, the memory remained fresh and tantalizing to both of us, the present situation only serving to amplify our emotions. As incongruous as it seemed, I wanted him now, tonight, as soon as possible, and it was obvious he felt the same.

"Kala." Sheldon broke the heavy silence. His voice was soft and calm again as he reclined in his chair. "What went wrong tonight?"

"Are you serious?" I replied quickly, but with no disrespect in my voice. "You assumed that I would go along with everything, not ask questions, just be a good little girl and follow your little script. Well, Sheldon, in case you didn't realize, I'm not that kind of person. I'm not stupid. If I don't understand something or I feel something is wrong, I don't just sit there. I question it."

Both Nathan and Victor glanced over at me as I replied, listening expressionlessly.

Sheldon straightened in his chair. "It's not your place to question our motives or plans," he snapped in irritation.

"Then maybe I'm not the woman for the job," I replied, standing my ground. "I am who I am."

"That can all be changed," he pointed out warningly.

"Let me ask you something. I really don't want to be talking to you at all right now, but..." I paused, trying to formulate my thoughts. "If I am the *chosen* one, don't you feel that perhaps I was chosen because of who I am? If you can mold anyone the way you want them to be, couldn't you grab any female off the street and modify her? Isn't it reasonable to think that there is something about *me*, something special you all need, which is why I was picked, and not Lyla or another woman? Don't you think it has something to do with who I was created to be? Who my mother and father were? Don't you think there is a bigger picture here than what *you* want? If your Book of Jorn is so particular about people and events and times; it would seem to me that I was chosen because of who I am." I tried to remain calm as I finished, but the sight of Sheldon's smug face was making it difficult.

"Don't preach about something you know nothing about," Sheldon responded. "And speaking of who you are and the whole creation thing, I have a surprise for you. It's on the way in." He leaned back again and swiveled his chair to face the door.

The large doors opened wide as Lyla walked into the room, followed by a middle-aged man. He was dressed in a blue suit, light colored shirt and tie and appeared composed as he entered. With despair, I recognized him as my father. I closed my eyes, remembering the last moment I had laid eyes on him as a teenager, remembering my confusion and sadness when he disappeared, never to be heard from again. My heart sank. I felt the uncanny vibes only a vampire emitted. My own father – a vampire. He stood at the head of the table, arms at his side, gazing calmly at me. I looked down into my lap, not knowing what to say, confused over what was taking place.

"I did bring in the right man... didn't I?" Sheldon asked, looking at my father and then at me. "I see some resemblance, I think."

I swallowed hard and looked at my father again.

"Well, Dad, don't you have a hug or something human to give her?" Sheldon asked sarcastically. "C'mon; after all, it's a reunion." He glanced from my father to me, obviously enjoying the moment and his own warped sense of humor, as Lyla backed silently from the room, shutting the doors behind her.

"Don't bother," I said directly to my father. His touch was the last thing I wanted at this point.

"It *is* good to see you Kala," My father finally spoke as he sat near Sheldon towards the front of the room.

"What is the whole point of tonight?" I asked to the room at large. "You've made your case as far as me being the Emissary. You've told me that you all murdered my best friend. The same people who want me in power. I've been told I'm to spend my time with someone I can not stand," I glared pointedly at Sheldon, "and that my *father* is a vampire. Am I missing anything?" I finished sarcastically, leaning over the table in exasperation.

"No, that's about it for now," Sheldon smiled broadly. "I think you should get to know your father again. Once you become one of *us* you will understand more than you do now. Your mind will change. Not because *I* want it to... it just will."

"I don't think it's a very good idea right now," I sighed, having reached my limits for the night. I could feel exhaustion begin to settle in. "I need some time." I looked at Victor again, his eyes full of sympathy now, having watched my emotional turmoil.

Sheldon tactfully agreed. "Tonight did not unfold as I had planned. As pending Sovereign, I want us to all be in accordance. My people deserve that at least. There is no point in beginning our alliance on a foundation of hate. I will make arrangements for us to meet here again soon – all of us."

Chapter 31

The limo ride back to Victor's left me uneasy. Sheldon had seen us off, telling Nathan he would be in touch over the next week or so. I sat beside Victor, mulling over the night and all that had happened. When I thought about what I had experienced over the past several hours, I realized what disturbed me the most was seeing my dad after so many years. Why was it so important for him to reappear in my life right now? Was it just Sheldon's idea of a sick joke, or was it a subtle reminder that I actually had roots in the vampire society? Over the years I had come to accept the story that my dad was trash for divorcing his wife and leaving his children behind. I was not ready or willing to change fifteen years of belief. I had made it half my life without him and I wasn't keen on the idea of taking him back, vampire or not. The truth was hard for me to endure. He had always been a vampire. I knew that now. The knowledge helped explain the inexplicable sensations that periodically coursed through my body. I had felt them all my life, but dismissed them as just part of a woman's hormones and sensitive emotions. His return had changed something in me – but what was it? Maybe it just made me more aware.

I struggled with another hit I had taken tonight; finding out that Sara's murderer would never be punished. There was never going to be any arrest and there never would be retribution for it. I knew more now than Detective Drake did – no wonder her death had been labeled suspicious. It wasn't like I could pick up the phone, call Drake, and rat off a bunch of vampires! He'd have me locked up! What about Addy? How could I ever tell her? I couldn't – she'd think I was crazy! This whole vampire thing had held me back from getting too close to her. I didn't think there was any way she could deal with this nightmare I was living; after all, I was barely making it myself! So what I knew would have to stay with me – forever. It did not comfort me in knowing how she died and who was responsible for it; there was no closure. I thought with knowing I could put it behind me... but now I knew it would never truly go away.

It was very late when we arrived at the Victorian. The silence that had filled the limo during the ride home continued as we entered the foyer. Nathan went directly to his quarters, and the slam of his door as he closed it on us left no doubt of his take on the entire evening.

Victor and I climbed the stairs to the second floor and walked into his loft, together, yet very separate. We had not said a word to each other in almost an hour. The night had placed a great deal of stress on him and me; the combination was stifling. Victor headed for the kitchen. "Can I get you anything?" he yawned, opening the refrigerator, disappearing behind the door and taking out a green bottle of beer.

"Beer," I faintly replied. "Tylenol." I walked over next to him.

Victor took a glass from one cabinet and opened another, retrieving a bottle of painkillers. "Check the date. I don't get aches and pains that often," he said as he handed me the bottle of pills.

I looked the label over and the expiration date was still good. I popped open the bottle and took two tablets, then placed the rest of the medication on the counter. Victor poured my beer and passed me the glass. Thankfully, I washed the pills down. Victor walked by me, his weariness apparent as he headed towards the dark back room with the futon. Looking over his shoulder at me, he raised a questioning eyebrow. "Are you coming?" he asked.

I shrugged. "Do you want me to?" I tapped my fingers against the side of my glass, nervously waiting for his answer.

He sighed with fatigue. "Please." He walked over to the futon and sat down, leaning his head back and sighing deeply. As he closed his eyes, I sat down next to him, just far enough away so we each could keep our space. I watched him as he sat quietly, and soon began to feel a small measure of peace myself. At last he opened his eyes and turned to look at me.

"The quiet is nice," he remarked.

"Yes, it is," I replied, placing my drink on the floor.

Victor tipped his head upright and took a swig of his beer. "I'm just glad it's over."

I nodded. "The night may be over, but it's not over," I sighed, playing with the silver rings on my hand.

Victor reached over and touched my cheek and tucked some hair behind my ear. It was gentle. "Tough chick."

I rolled my eyes in his direction. "How so?"

"Hon, if you don't know by now..." he shook his head. "I just want you to know that I'm glad you don't roll over and play dead. I'm glad you're a fighter." He smiled in appreciation.

"Doesn't mean I'm a winner," I replied with a slight frown.

"It means you stand a chance."

"Nathan must be beside himself over what happened tonight," I laughed, thinking about how stuffy he normally was and how the conference room had turned into a circus or some sort of romper room for unsupervised children.

Victor took another sip of his beer, his eyes widening as he replied, "He was a little surprised tonight, not just at how you acted but at Sheldon as well. Don't worry too much about him; he takes everything very seriously. I, for one, thought my first counsel meeting was rather interesting."

"They made you a member?"

Victor hesitated before he answered. "Yes and no. Let's call it a trial membership." He seemed confused with the honor or maybe it was doubt in his voice.

"Does that mean your liberties have been restored to you and Nathan?" I questioned, turning to face him head on, knowing how important it was, at least to one of them.

Victor balanced his beer on his stomach and looked up at the ceiling as he spoke. "It appears that way, if everything goes all right, although I have no idea what those rights are. I mean, I have lived the way I have for so long, I don't think I can change, or want to change. It's not like they have a Human Resource Department I can check with, or a handbook to read."

"I *like* who you are; I don't want you to change," I said fondly, touching his leg and sliding closer to him. "But I want you to be *what* you are; I'm sorry I made you feel uncomfortable tonight with the blood-wine thing in the limo. It was wrong of me."

Victor dismissed it. "Don't worry; I'm sure there is stuff you eat I'd be sick about."

"Like pickled eggs?"

"Tell me you don't," he laughed, his head falling in my direction, waiting for my answer.

"Not me," I smiled.

Victor climbed to his feet with his empty beer bottle in hand. "Make yourself comfortable; I need to see Nathan. He's been calling me. I should see what he wants. Be back in a minute." He grabbed my shoulder and squeezed tenderly as if assuring me his good-bye would be very brief. He set his beer bottle on the counter and left, allowing the door to shut on its own behind him. I wondered why Nathan needed to see Victor after such a long and seemingly painful night for all of us.

I stretched out on the futon, feeling abandoned by Victor and nursing my beer. I thought about ending the night for good and going home, climbing into bed and shutting my eyes and mind to all I had seen. The thing was, I did not want to be alone. I did not want to go home and be by myself, even if all I did was sleep.

I noticed a pile of folded laundry on a small tan wicker table near a sliding closet door in the room. I wondered what Victor's reaction would be if he came back and found me in his bed, wearing only one of his clean shirts. We had talked about it earlier, but had made no decision one way or the other. I wanted to stay. I wanted to fall asleep in *his* bed, with him.

Sorting through some of his garments I found a large gray T-shirt with the college logo on it. Trying to work as quickly as I could with my ailing leg, I hurriedly stripped my clothes from my body, folded and placed them next to his stack and slipped Victor's T-shirt on over my head just as I heard the front door opening with his return.

I approached the doorway casually, not wanting to draw too much attention to the fact that I had rushed my change of clothes while he was gone, that I was out of breath. I wanted him to think that I just slipped into something more comfortable while he was away. Just as I reached the doorway, Victor appeared in front of me. I froze as he looked at me, his eyes sliding up and down my body as he noticed my change of attire. I stepped forward and boldly placed my hands on his chest, caressing his firm body as I whispered, "I don't want to be alone tonight."

The flush slowly rising on Victor's cheeks was answer enough to me, at least as far as the physical question went. The lust shone in his eyes, but I knew he was struggling with more than just the thought of being with me again. Only a Sire and his progeny or immortal companion ever spent resting times together; mortals were never supposed to stay anywhere near the sleeping areas. In many ways I felt as if I were Victor's fledgling, through chance and not by blood, since I had learned about his kind with his guidance, evolving my abilities and powers to a higher level with his encouragement, and being his lover through past and current lives. Two hundred years of lonely nights had gotten to him; the isolation was too much. I was the rising sun in his dark world; a sun he had not seen in many lifetimes, one that was finally awakening him from his nocturnal sleep. He studied my face intently, scanning my eyes, still not saying a word but hearing my affirmation echo in his head.

I ran my hand slowly over his chest. I let my fingers roam the outline of his neck and throat, then reached around and loosened his hair from the elastic that held it away from his face. His long silky mane fell around his shoulders, outlining the definition of his muscles. With a groan, Victor encircled me with his arms and pulled me hard against him. He kissed my parted lips deeply, our mouths meeting in a rush of wet velvet softness. My fingertips grazed the sides of his face, tracing the outline of his jaw as we kissed. His mouth left mine and he raised my hand to his lips. As he delicately kissed each finger and the palm of my hand, I could feel the heat of his breath, the fire I knew was contained inside.

"I wish I knew what you were thinking," he said softly as he moved his kisses along the side of my face and close to my ear.

I dug my fingers into the solid muscles above his waist, clinging to the soft cotton of his shirt. "I want to share all my thoughts with you again," I whispered, weak with desire as his tongue caressed my ear.

My words had the effect of a bucket of water. Victor straightened and ceased caressing me, although his hands did not leave my body. He looked intently at me, obviously wanting to tell me something, but not quite able to get the words out.

"What?" I asked gently, lightly kissing him.

"I want it too much," he said. "You don't know what it's like."

I reached up and wrapped my arms loosely around his neck, feeling his hair cushion beneath them. "Is this how we are different?"

"Very," Victor said simply.

"It's the blood, isn't it?" I somehow knew it was the bond of blood he had with me that up until recently let him enjoy my intimate company without frustration, to share my thoughts and passions and allow his to flourish as well. It was my blood he needed; just enough to allow us to safely share our passions. Without that bond, there was no guarantee he would not hurt me, or worse, during our times together.

"Yes. Your blood," he replied, his voice straining for a level of self-control.

I kissed his lips. "Then you know what you need to do." I let my fingers weave between the strands of his hair. I watched his eyes closely, waiting for a reaction or a sign of some kind. He and I both knew that consuming some of my blood was the only answer if we wanted to continue our intimacy.

He shook his head in disapproval.

"Victor. It's something you need; we both need," I argued. I didn't mind shedding blood for him. Especially if it was something we both wanted and would get mutual enjoyment out of in the end.

Victor lowered his eyes. "You have lost so much blood in the last day..." his voice trailed off.

I opened my mouth to console him, to let him know that, other than the occasional twinge, I was doing pretty well, when suddenly he lunged at me. A quick abrupt pounce that sent the two of us tumbling over each other and onto the hard wood floor. Victor landed on his back with me securely in his arms on top of him. He rolled all his weight over onto me, pinning my arms over my head. His eyes were large and round. I had seen him like this before and not all that long ago. He scared me. I didn't know if he was still rational, or completely overcome by the creature within him.

"Victor!" I called loudly, my eyes rapidly scanning his face. He leaned over my body and breathed heavily against my neck, sending shivers up and down my spine. The sensation was both erotic and terrifying at the same time, since I had an idea of what Victor was capable of.

"I want you," he spoke softly, in a tone that was very much like the normal Victor I knew, but I could hear in his voice the struggle he was having with the vampire inside.

"Victor, look at me. Please!" I asked, still unable to move with his weight holding me down, my arms pinned to the cold wood floor. I remembered Nathan's advice from the last time Victor had dominated me in this manner – to treat him as the vampire he was, not the human I wanted him to be. I was *trying* to treat him as the vampire he was, I argued with my conscience; *I* offered him *me*; I was sacrificing my blood for him.

"I need you. Your blood," Victor said thickly in my ear. His mouth hovered over my neck and I could feel his lips gently making contact with my skin as his fangs begin to enlarge. "Please..."

"Yes. I know." I swallowed hard as a lump formed in my throat. "Be gentle, please." Before now I had never been able to think about Victor feeding from me, at least from my neck. I had healed him with a cut from my finger; a cut that was self-inflicted. This was different.

With my consent, Victor locked his mouth over my throat. I braced myself for the pain I anticipated would come when his sharp teeth broke through the skin. He released my arms and took hold of my body, then firmly plunged his fangs into my throat. I trembled with the initial sharp sting and my heart raced frantically. I gasped, holding my breath against the sensation. His mouth created a tight seal over my throat, allowing my blood to flow from the gashes he'd made straight down his throat. I let my hands caress his sides and felt his body heat up with the passions of my blood.

As the initial shock passed, I was almost amused with the fact that I felt an element of gratification lying beneath Victor as he sucked the blood from my neck. A dark force deep within me brought forth an intense desire to bite Victor's throat, that I latch my own jaws upon it and bite down and drink from him as if I were starving. Where this desire sprang from, I had no idea. I certainly did not need his blood in order to live; in fact I knew from Nathan it was rather poisonous to me. Nevertheless, I felt the need to reciprocate. Victor fed vigorously, taking only a moment to catch his breath still lapping up the blood that continued to flow from the artery on my neck. I lay motionless under him, waiting for the moment to end, the moment that would send the creature back to where it came from and my handsome Victor back to me. My eyes remained closed as I waited, willing myself to submit. I felt his tongue press against the wounds he had inflicted upon me, healing them, and leaving me pain free.

Victor lifted himself from me, rolling to a seated position on the floor. He gently nudged my arm to get my attention. "Kala," he spoke softly.

My eyes fluttered open even before he called my name. With his body weight off of me, I knew that he had completed what he needed to. He helped me up to my feet and took me in his arms. "I hope you still want to stay with me tonight," he whispered, rocking me in his hold. "I want you to."

"I do want to stay," I replied quickly, swaying in his arms. I wasn't sure how the rest of the night would turn out, but I would be in his bed and that was all that mattered to me right now.

He flattened out the futon and took a blanket and a few pillows out of the closet. I helped him make the bed up for us. "I apologize for the sleeping conditions," he said. "I just usually crash – no blanket or quilts, no nothing." He tossed a pillow on each side of the bed.

"No problem," I smiled, spreading the blanket over the flat futon mattress and climbing onto the bed.

Victor stood at the foot of the bed, kicked off his sneakers, removed his socks and then tugged his shirt off over his head, letting it fall to the floor in a heap. Seeing his body always kindled a fire in me. I waited patiently for him to join me under the covers, watching as he unbuckled his black leather belt and unfastened his pants. He let them fall to the floor in a pile with the rest of his garments. He stood tall, clad only in a pair of dark green long legged briefs, a picture perfect specimen of what a man should be – almost. He walked around to his side of the bed and yanked the covers back, allowing himself to roll in close to me.

"Why do you normally sleep without a pillow or blanket?" I asked him curiously, since he looked so comfortable with them tonight.

He shrugged. "I guess I don't sleep to sleep, I just rest. I need darkness and quiet. That's all I really need. Nathan likes his bed, and sheets and pillows and all that fancy stuff, but I never needed it," Victor replied. "But maybe it's time for a change." He smiled as he pulled the soft blue blanket up to his chin.

"It's never too late, especially in your case," I smiled, moving my body closer to his. He put his arm over me and kissed me on the lips. "I'm glad you are here tonight. You don't know how many times I thought what we had was over. But here you are."

"Is this odd for you? Me being here? With Nathan downstairs?" I asked, laying my leg on his and watching him rest comfortably next to me.

"I can block him out, unless he really wants to be persistent. What about you? He has a blood bond with you now as well, but you must know that already," Victor spoke with a yawn.

"I noticed. It was strange for me to hear his voice for the first time in my head. I was so used to hearing just yours; then it went away." I thought a moment more about the voices in my head. "I hear lots of voices now and again. Is that normal? It's hard to explain."

Victor did not reply at first. "I think what you are hearing off and on are vampires in the area, the waves we emit. I'm so used to hearing them I don't even notice them anymore, unless I'm looking for one in particular. I'm sure you can feel the difference between direct contact and just background noise."

I nodded. "But it drives me crazy. I can't turn it off."

"You'll learn. It just takes time," Victor replied.

The two of us lay on our sides, facing one another in silence for several minutes. I had started to think about my dad again, then Sara, wondering when I could begin to finally put it behind me, or if I were ready to move on and accept everything the way it was. I looked at Victor and wondered what was running through his mind, his first High Counsel meeting, how my blood felt in him, Lyla...

"I'm thinking about you," he smiled warmly, touching my face, running his finger down my nose lightly.

I felt a little funny; he had been reading my thoughts. "I've been thinking about something, but then again you probably already know."

He shrugged. "Not really. What?"

"What am I?" I became serious.

"What do you mean?" he asked.

I sighed. "I mean, my father is like you and my mother is human. They had me. So what does that make me? What did that make my brother, Kevin?" I questioned, my face showing signs of my confusion.

Victor put an arm behind his head in obvious thought. "It's not very common; as a matter of fact it's very rare that one of my kind is able to bear children at all. I have heard of very few cases in my lifetime. Let's put it this way; there is not enough of you to start up a support group."

I pulled the covers up to my chest. "But what does it make me? Am I entirely human? Mortal? What?"

He quietly looked up at me. "You're human, most definitely. But because of your father you share traits of the vampire. Your strong telepathic skills for instance."

"I see." I thought about Victor feeding from me. "What about this strange feeling I had to bite you just a few minutes ago? And the fact that I think I enjoyed you drinking from me. That's not normal. Not human normal anyway."

Victor positioned himself on his elbows. “I don’t know. But please don’t over think some of these changes you are going through, or these feelings and thoughts that pop up. Don’t forget, you have many more of them that will happen to you.”

I bowed my head, not getting the answers I needed or wanted. I knew I was going through changes. It was obvious. But what I wanted to know was what I was changing into. Who I was changing into?

Chapter 32

I fell asleep in Victor's arms, but not before he passed on a request that came from Nathan. Stop in and see him on my way home, because he wanted to ask me a few questions. But when I asked Victor what Nathan needed to see me for, he just rolled over, put his arm around me, spooning me close to his body and said, "Go to sleep. Nathan will be there when you wake up."

I slept well, but was barraged with strange short dreams throughout the duration of my sleep. The dreams were the kind that you remember only in little snips when you are awake, little bursts and bits and pieces for no apparent reason. They made no sense while I was dreaming and made less sense to me as I tried to recall them, to understand them. It was early afternoon when I woke for good in Victor's bed. I lay next to him, watching him sleep, his breathing shallow, and body still-life beautiful. I wanted to run my hands over his smooth back and curl close, making a cozy spot under his arm to cuddle into, but instead I got up quietly and put on my clothes, careful not to wake him.

I was silent as a mouse while I tiptoed around Victor's loft. I searched quietly for his car keys and found them in his pants pocket. I glanced up, noticing Victor had not moved since I had slid out of bed. He was asleep on his stomach, his arms wrapped around his pillow with his face pressed into it contentedly.

I tied my sneakers, picked up Sara's journal, and left his rooms quietly, gently shutting the door behind me. I wondered as I carefully descended the dark stairwell if Nathan was awake himself since Victor was not, and, if he was awake, was it a good time to drop in on him.

'*I'm awake... come on in,*' Nathan's greeting startled me, his words echoing in my head.

When I reached the landing at the bottom of the staircase I opened the door and let myself in to Nathan's place. "Nathan," I called out, shutting the door behind me. The living room was as I remembered it, depressingly dark. It was mid-afternoon but you certainly could not tell in here. I stood in the center of the room with Sara's journal tucked under my arm. "Nathan?" I said again. I knew he knew I was there.

"Have a seat," Nathan's voice came from down a long hallway towards the back of the room.

I sat on the edge of the long leather couch, waiting uncomfortably. He finally entered the room, buttoning the cuffs to his white shirtsleeves as he walked past me and sat down in a winged back chair.

"You don't sleep much, do you?" I asked, looking at him as he ran his fingers through his damp hair. It was evident I had caught him just getting dressed after his shower.

"No," Nathan replied shortly, crossing his legs and relaxing back in his chair. He seemed annoyed already with my company.

I decided to cut to the chase since Nathan did not seem very talkative. "Victor said you wanted to ask me something." I waited, balancing Sara's journal on my lap.

Nathan leaned forward in his seat as if he was going to spring at me. "Have you been able to remember anything about the other night when you were attacked? Before you say no, please take a moment and think about it." He reached for a pack of cigarettes on the table next to him; his voice was level and serious.

I closed my eyes and took a deep breath. "I really haven't stopped to think about it again. I wasn't able to remember any of it yesterday. Why should I be able to remember any of it today?" I rubbed my forehead, thinking back to Friday night. As much as I wanted to remember the event; I didn't want to.

Nathan lit a cigarette, taking a long drag off it, savoring the taste. "I know. It's important that you try and remember as much as you can. Any of it," he asked patiently.

I recalled getting ready for the cocktail party at the condo, arriving at the shop and meeting Addy, Keith and Melinda. I remembered shaking lots of hands, talking to prospective clients and giving the interview with the news station. I remembered walking the caterer to her truck and closing up the store for the night, but had no recollection of ever meeting any vampires. I didn't remember feeling the presence of any vampires; it was as if the attack never took place, although *we* all knew that it had.

"I understand," Nathan replied, disheartened as he listened to me describe as much of the night as I could. "I only have one last question then," he said, exhaling a steady flow of smoke through his nostrils and crushing out his cigarette in a nearby ashtray. "Have you, willingly or not, let any vampires feed off you recently?"

I was startled by the question and said nothing; I didn't know why he would ask such a thing. I stared at Nathan, narrowing my eyes, trying to figure out where he was coming from; what *that* had to do with anything.

"I can tell my question puzzles you. I apologize. Trust me when I say it's important. I need to know if you did. Was it willingly or not, and when?" Nathan pushed himself to stand and rose above me, waiting for my answer.

I tipped my head up to face him. "Don't you think I would have mentioned something like that to you or Victor if one of your kind had drunk my blood? That's quite a violation. Not to mention I don't know many of your kind to begin with."

"I would hope you would have reported such an act against you. So?" Nathan placed his hands in his pant pockets and slouched slightly, still waiting for a direct answer to his very direct question.

I hesitated before giving my reply, not wanting to cause any friction between Victor and Nathan. I was not sure how Nathan would react to the fact that I very willingly allowed Victor to drink from me. I had no choice but to tell him; I'm sure he already knew, or it would be more than possible for him to find out whether I wanted to share the information or not. "Last night, I let Victor. That's it. Why the questions?"

Nathan seemed unfazed by my answer and walked to his desk. He took a seat behind it, pulled a pad of paper across his blotter and picked up a black pen. He began to write. "I am investigating your attack; who your attackers might have been." Nathan peered over his glasses at me as he jotted down some notes.

I got up from the couch and made my way to his desk, standing on the other side across from him. "I see. I wish I could tell you more. I do. I'd like to know who hurt me." I looked down at myself, knowing my scars were nearly gone. I looked okay, but my leg still ached and probably would for a time to come. The emotional scars of the attack were still ingrained in my mind. Not the actual attack, because I could not remember any of those details, but the hours after that which left me in pain and bleeding. I didn't think I would ever forget any of that or the help Nathan was to me, for not letting me die.

Nathan put his pen down on his desk. "If I find out anything for certain I will let you know. You have my word on it."

"I would appreciate it. I'm sorry I can't help you further. But I just don't remember," I sighed.

"If you find yourself remembering anything unusual about the night of the gallery opening that you think I should know, call me." Nathan took his glasses off and placed them on his desk, rubbing his eyes with his knuckles until they were red.

"How come you don't need as much rest as Victor? You do sleep, don't you?" I asked curiously. "You look tired."

Nathan stopped rubbing his eyes and put his glasses back on his face, blinking several times as he said, "Yes, I sleep. I don't require as much rest as Victor. The older our kind becomes, the less sleep we need, and the less we need to feed. The more perfect we become."

"Being able to go without any rest or food makes you perfect? I find that rather odd," I said.

"At *that* point we are considered perfect. Think about it for a moment..." Nathan placed his folded hands on the desk and leaned forward. "A being that walks the earth and requires nothing to maintain its existence. Is *that* not perfect?"

"Yes, I suppose that is *near* perfect, with the exception of sunlight, wooden stakes and that kind of stuff." I sighed, realizing that Nathan's comment about his people was right on the mark. By the point in their lives he spoke about they were like machines. As long as there was an area of darkness, they would survive forever. "Nathan, do you ever miss being human?"

Nathan fell back in his chair and glared in my direction as if he could not believe that I would ask such a question. "No," he answered gruffly.

I nodded, hearing the hostility in his voice. "Of course you don't. How stupid of me. You don't even like to be *with* humans." I stood up. It was time for me to leave.

Nathan added to his answer. "I don't even remember being human like you any more, it's been so long. But I am what I am now, a far better being in my book. I have no cares or worries, time means nothing to me; I live my life the way I choose." He looked very noble as he spoke behind his large desk, holding his head high as if balancing a heavy gold crown of jewels.

"Must be nice," I mumbled, backing away from his desk with Sara's journal in my arms, feeling the need to leave. "I've got to go. I'm taking Victor's car; I'll meet up with him later on."

Nathan dismissed me with a wave of his hand, watching in silence as I left.

On my way back to the condo I decided at the last moment to stop by the gallery to take a look around, to see if I could remember anything about the night of the cocktail party that I could not remember before. I hoped seeing the gallery might bring back some suppressed memories that might help Nathan find out who my attackers were. I parked Victor's car on the street and went in through the front door of the shop. Nothing looked unusual at first as I walked the perimeter, inspecting all the artwork on the walls and remembering the events of Friday night. I spiraled my way in towards the middle of the shop, checking on the sculptures and other pieces of art displayed on pedestals and podiums. Everything seemed okay.

Suddenly, as I got closer to my desk, an indescribable feeling swept over my body, causing me to instantly be on alert. Something was different about the atmosphere here; it was almost as if I'd walked into a physical wall of emotion. I froze where the feeling was the strongest and looked down upon the stone floor. I bent down and examined a pattern on the stones which did not seem to belong. The irregular patterns were dark splotches tinged brownish red. I was not a detective, but it appeared to be blood. I was surprised at the small amount on the floor, considering I had suffered three large wounds that had bled so copiously they'd ruined my black dress and the towels Nathan and Victor used to staunch the flow. Other than the bloodstain, I didn't notice anything unusual, at least, nothing that seemed to cause the intense feeling that still held me in its grip. I was not sure where the actual attack took place, but every time I moved away from the blood stained area and back again that same oddness plagued me. For a split second I recalled something – a memory perhaps – but it wouldn't come clear. Frustrated, I walked away from the spot and let the feeling subside. I left the shop and continued home, unsettled.

It was early evening when I heard from Victor. I explained to him that I had been to the gallery on my way home from his place and wanted to meet him there as soon as he could make it. Victor agreed, saying he would walk over, since I had his car.

I arrived at the gallery to find Victor already waiting in front of the store, leaning casually against the lamppost. He was as handsome as ever in the night's light, dressed in his usual attire of jeans and a T-shirt, long hair pulled neatly back. I parked his car in the street and welcomed him with an embrace, slipping his keys into his front jeans pocket and squeezing his thigh with good cheer. He returned my playful gesture with a smile and a quick kiss on the lips. I unlocked the shop and let us in, locking the door behind us and flipping on some overhead lighting.

"So this is it, all ready for business," Victor said admiringly as he walked over to a large black and white photo collage that hung boldly on the wall. "Looks different from the last time I was in here."

"I hope so," I replied.

"Now, what is so important that you wanted to tell me?" Victor turned to face me, curiosity in his voice.

"Follow me." I moved towards my desk to show Victor the area on the floor that I had wanted positively identified, the marks that I assumed were my blood. I pointed. "What do you make of it?" I backed away so he could easily see what I was gesturing to.

Victor knelt down over the stains. Without pause he looked up at me. "Blood. Your blood," he answered, looking confused at having to state the obvious.

"I figured it was. Nathan had some questions for me this afternoon. He was trying to get to the bottom of who assaulted me and I wasn't too helpful. I thought that maybe if I came here and walked around, I could jar myself to remember more." I leaned against my desk.

Victor stood and took a step closer to me. "You were attacked in here?" he asked, looking around the gallery.

"I don't know where the incident took place. I thought I had a flashback this afternoon when I was here, but it faded." I tried to act like it did not bother me, but it did. He knew it did.

"My kind has a very powerful way to block or erase memories when we want to; but with your strong telepathic skills, I would think you could break through it. If you had what you think was a flashback you can force yourself to remember more."

I scowled at what seemed impossible for me to do. I did not think my extrasensory skills were strong enough to help me remember the events that occurred several nights before. I didn't even want to try, so I looked at Victor mutely and shook my head.

He approached me slowly and took me by the shoulders, shaking me gently. "Kala," he said quietly. "Please stop selling yourself short. I mean it. Nathan would tell you the same thing. Our senses are much stronger than yours are; if we feel something *we know it;* it's unmistakable to us, to me, to Nathan – all of us. Nathan would not waste his breath talking to you, if he thought you weren't strong, a force to reckon with. If you were *just* a human, he would have nothing to do with you... nothing. Ask yourself why Sheldon didn't *push* you. Even *he* knows. Find it in yourself to use the powers and skills that you have. Don't ignore them."

I heard his words but remained unconvinced, still filled with trepidation. Victor released me and walked away. "I have your blood in me," he spoke, his back facing me. "I know what I feel in me. After two hundred years I should hope I know my own limitations. Now, I know what you are. Who you are. If you don't believe in yourself, then believe in me, and if not me, Nathan. I would hope that our experience would convince you that we know what we are talking about. I'm not bullshitting you. Really."

"Then tell me what it is that I have to do to make it all work; I truly don't know," I sighed, my shoulders slumped in acceptance.

"We can find a way that works for you," Victor replied.

Nathan had spent the afternoon making phone calls. One of his phone calls was to the Sovereign, Teague. Nathan had known him for many years; theirs was a strong bond through blood, and it was only since Nathan's abolishment from his people that he had lost contact with him. Nathan wanted to meet with him at the Manor alone so that they could talk face to face. Teague agreed, saying cryptically there was no time like now to rekindle an old friendship and perhaps talk about current issues that Nathan thought might be important enough to bring to his attention. In fact, there was something that Teague himself wanted to talk to Nathan about, so perhaps a meeting in person was best for both parties. The conversation left Nathan feeling uneasy, nervous in a way he had not been in more years than he could remember.

Nathan arrived at the Manor in the limo that had been sent by Teague. Lyla met him at the grand entrance of the home. She escorted Nathan through the halls, ending up in a room that was obviously a den, complete with large marble desk and green velvet Queen Anne chairs. It was a small room compared to the rest of the ones Nathan had seen. The ceiling was much lower here than in the other areas of the home, making it a more comfortable and intimate atmosphere, less stark, with some very old paintings mounted in fancy gold frames centered on the walls. The windows were multi-paned and tall, opening onto stone terraces, their heavy drapes pulled back. Nathan took a seat in one of the two chairs and waited as calmly as he could for Teague to join him.

Within a few moments a gentleman older than Nathan entered, closing the door behind him. Nathan watched him silently as he glided into place in front of the other chair, looking as imperial as he always had. Teague smiled for his company and held a bottle of wine up for the two to share. “It has been too long,” Teague stated as he crossed Nathan’s path, opened up a wooden cabinet and retrieved two glasses. Sitting down across from Nathan, Teague breathed a sigh. “Just how long has it been?”

Nathan tipped his head as he replied, looking at Teague fondly. “Nearly two hundred years I’m sure.” He spoke quietly as if the memory pained him. “I have missed your company,” Nathan admitted.

Teague finished uncorking the bottle and filled the two glasses. He nodded in understanding. Nathan’s exile had not been easy on him either. Teague had been the one to enforce the order voted by the Counsel to ban Nathan, not only from his seat on the Counsel, but as a citizen among his own people, people he had served well. When Teague heard that the new Emissary had been found, a great weight was lifted from his shoulders. He realized that soon his child would return – to him, to his people and to his seat on the Counsel. “Yes, blood bonds are hard to overlook; they always seem to be there. They pull at you constantly. I do know the feeling.” Teague lifted his arm and offered Nathan a glass of blood wine.

Nathan took the glass from him. Teague smiled as he sipped his drink. In his mortal years he might have been forty years old, tall, with black impeccably kept hair, dark skin and eyes with long feathery lashes that took the edge off his hard features. Greek perhaps. He dressed as Nathan did; a mix of formal and casual that caused you to blend in the public's eye; to look like someone you could bring home to your parents and even *they* would approve of.

Nathan took a drink of his blood wine and swallowed. "It is good to be here again."

"And it is good to have you here. I wish I could have joined you last night; I hear it was quite the event," His eyes twinkled with merriment.

"I'm not sure what happened last night. It sure wasn't like the Counsel Meetings as I remember them to be," Nathan replied, thinking back to when he used to sit at the table; he could clearly recall the serious, silent meetings.

Teague chuckled. "It's not the Counsel it used to be. Things have changed, Nathan. In big ways." He held his goblet between his thumb and first finger, moving it in a circular motion and watching the wine spin about, his eyes intently following the ripples of burgundy.

"How so? I know there are new faces, but..."

Teague interrupted him. "Finish your drink and we can talk; I can't say anymore right now." His teeth bared in a smile that did not reach his eyes as he stared at Nathan.

In one long gulp, Nathan downed his drink, then set the glass on the side table. He needed to get down to business; the tension of the night was wearing thin on him.

Teague nodded approvingly and did the same. Two empty glasses sat on the table.

"What's going on?" Nathan asked, shaking his head in confusion and trying to be respectful to his Sovereign and Sire while still getting answers all the same.

"The wine is special. There is a spell on it. I can't tell you where I got it, or who made it. I can only tell you that it will make our minds unreachable to those in this house who like to eavesdrop. Trust me; there are many ears here that do," Teague finished, apparently unmoved by the fact there were people in his home he couldn't trust.

Nathan stood and took several paces towards the large doors that led out; he fingered the soft, dark fabric drapes that hung around them. Being at the Manor brought him comfort, and to be with his Sire once again; the most powerful man he knew. But it also brought him anxiety; the distant past was not so distant and he had trouble thinking about the here and now, to not allow history to overwhelm him with anger. "Teague, talk to me. I feel funny.

I feel like something has happened, or is happening. I can't even put my finger on it. It's like I don't belong any more. What's wrong?" Nathan looked out over the terrace.

"Nathan, it's a new generation taking over; they want to make the world their world. They are manipulating everything we were ever taught and believed in to suit them, bending and twisting every rule and value. It's not just here. It's all over the globe. This new generation is bastardizing The Book of Jorn; they claim to be reading from it when what they are doing is interpreting the writings the way they see fit to make our society the society they want – good, bad or otherwise. It's been going on for a while now. It was a slow change, but for you it must feel very abrupt and foreign." Teague had not moved from his chair as he spoke in an even voice, as if he had come to accept the changes over the years and wanted Nathan to as well. "I feel your uncertainty. Your blood is with me as well. But I am Sovereign first, your Sire second. I must work with the entire Counsel. You know that. I can respect your opinions; I might even agree with some of them, but our blood cannot come between our people. What happens here, privately, between you and me, is just that – between you and me. Outside of here I am a leader and I must act that way. Try to understand my position."

Nathan shook his head violently. "I do understand your position. I would never risk the Counsel knowing that you sired me. But it's not supposed to be this way. Who are *they*? You keep referring to *they*." He turned to face the Sovereign.

"The people I am referring to are the Counsel Members. The faces have changed; only two have remained the same over the course of time, not including myself. As you know, I am not the sole ruler; the Counsel votes and I have final say, but I cannot rule against an entire table of Counsel Members; they would kill me," he said matter-of-factly.

Nathan took his seat again in the chair facing Teague. "What about this Sheldon? Your replacement. What do you know about him?"

Teague poured another glass of wine for himself before replying to Nathan's question. "He's young. He's a purebred. His parents are from a good bloodline. I've let him take over some of my duties, get his feet wet. He's got a long way to go, just as this Kala I have heard about does as well. As it stands now, they would tear each other apart, there is so much hostility between the two of them, and I can't have that." He sipped from his glass, watching Nathan absorb his every word.

"What have you heard about Kala?" Nathan asked, trying to relax as he took a cigarette from his shirt pocket.

"Not too much. I understand it was Victor who found her. That was frightening to hear at first, I must admit. He seems to have a nose for detecting Emissaries." Teague stared off, reflecting back on Nerissa, his chosen companion, someone he would have grown to love over the years. Teague felt cheated of that experience and would always hold an amount of resentment towards Victor for that. "I heard Kala is a little spitfire; her father is one of us, her mother is human. That is an interesting mix for an Emissary to have – the traits of both races. It will be amusing to see how an embrace turns out and which of her strengths will be dominant. You are familiar with her; what are her strengths now?" Teague's curiosity was peaked as he thought about an Emissary finally returning to the Manor.

"She's a fighter. I mean that she is fighting the fact she has powers, so when they surface she doesn't know how to control them. Anger is a big problem; she does not know how to channel it. She has a minor background in witchcraft – spells, incantations. I have seen her work with these. Telepathically, I think she's good. Victor communicates with her through a blood bond, and I do as well, so she receives and sends messages clearly," Nathan reported, lighting his cigarette, then leaning back and inhaling deeply.

"Blood bond? You and Victor both have Kala's blood within you?" Teague was confused with the sketchy details. "No one should be consuming her blood. Certainly not Victor, at least, not after..."

"Teague, I know. No one is more aware than me," Nathan said, now uncomfortable with the direction the conversation had turned. "Victor's relationship with Kala is unique and yet similar to the one he had with Nerissa, except he knew Nerissa while he was human, before the embrace. He was confused, and you know the rest. He has been very cautious with Kala, protective; they have found a way to share common interests and be together, for the time being." Nathan told Teague only what he needed to know and knew no matter how he tried to explain the situation there would be no approval. Even Nathan himself did not approve for the most part.

"Unacceptable," Teague's eyes glowed with hostility. "And you – how do you explain your bond to Kala?" He placed his goblet down next to him and folded his hands together, clenching them until his knuckles gleamed white.

"Did you not hear about the attack on Kala's life the other night?" Nathan responded. "It was one of our kind. She was bitten; someone drank from her, wounded her in not one, not two, but three different areas on her body. Victor found her bleeding; she could have died. I sat with her all night, healing her. I consumed her blood for medicinal purposes only. I did not feed from her. I don't feed often any more; I'm not as young as I used to be."

"We cannot afford to lose another Emissary. Does Kala know who assaulted her?" Teague asked, anger building in his voice, his fingers sinking into the plush green velvet of the chair's arms.

Nathan shook his head. "No, she tried to recall but couldn't. I asked her to keep trying. But I think I know who did, and you must hear me out before you go off defending him."

"Present me with facts; that's all I ask. You know me to be fair." Teague spoke as a true Sovereign now.

"The only way someone like Kala can be truly telepathically connected to one of us, prior to her being one of us, is through a blood bond. She may be able to pick up mixed signals from us but it's the consumption of blood that makes the link. In doing that, there is the ability to communicate. This is the only way. Correct?" Nathan asked Teague, knowing he was correct but deferring to him regardless.

Teague nodded. "As far as I know."

"During the Counsel meeting last night, while Kala and Sheldon were arguing; Kala responded to Sheldon verbally by saying something like 'you are testing my patience as well.' However, Sheldon had said nothing out loud. Therefore, she was responding to something he said to her telepathically. I asked Kala point blank today if she willingly or unwillingly allowed any vampires to feed from her recently and she said no. Since she has no memory of the attack, she believes what she says to be true; she does not know the ins and outs of our kind and what we can do or have to do to perform some of our normal functions. Speaking to Victor and me telepathically is beginning to be normal for her and hearing Sheldon the other night must not have seemed odd, although she should not be hearing his voice unless he had established a blood bond with her. I also know that he and Phillip planned on attending Kala's gallery opening, which was the same night as the attack. Sheldon claimed he wanted to get a look at his future Emissary. We know Kala was there, there was blood in her car and she somehow made it home. That is where Victor found her," Nathan recounted, watching for a reaction from Teague. "I don't quite know what his motive was. Seems risky if he just wanted to feed off her for the rush. She could have died, and even *I* know that is a very serious crime among our people. At least, it always was, unless that has changed, too."

Teague sat quietly in contemplation, staring at an oil painting across the room. "A crime is a crime. There are no exceptions," he finally spoke, not taking his eyes from the artwork on the wall. "What *is* happening with our people? If what you say is true and I'm not saying it is or isn't, this is a very serious problem. How many followers does he have? How many bad seeds? The Book of Jorn talks about something like this, you know that..." Teague's voice trailed off and he fixed his gaze on Nathan.

"I don't remember what the Book says. What does it say?" Nathan asked.

"It makes mention of a fox in the hen house, a passage that reads something like 'and so your friends are now enemies, your children turn against you, bringing a new darkness to the night'. It may be nothing; it may be something. The Book of Jorn has never been wrong yet," Teague answered.

"But it also says Jorn will rise from his resting place, reuniting his family to preside over his children again. Perhaps the passage you refer to happens after he assumes power. You did say the word 'child' and technically we are all his children," Nathan gave his interpretation of the passage.

"Unfortunately, this prophecy comes before yours. When Jorn returns, and I know he will someday, it will be because our society is in dire straits and only his power can pull us back together. It will be a reunion of *all* people, the way it used to be. He would insist on nothing less." Teague was all too familiar with The Book of Jorn; he knew it by heart and at times it scared him to think of Jorn returning, knowing that his anger was something none of his people would be prepared to deal with. Teague knew that many of his kind would die. The young, the stubborn, the misguided would go first, followed by all the non-believers of Jorn's divine powers. Teague sometimes wondered that if Jorn ever returned during his reign, whether he himself would be blamed for the decline of the precious society Jorn had fathered so many centuries ago. He felt he would probably be one of the first to go – start at the top and work his way to the bottom – eventually Jorn would have a pure culture to call his own again.

"The best we can do is to keep our ideals and rules in place for our people, whether they follow them or not. It will all work out one way or the other in the end," Teague said with finality.

Nathan nodded in understanding. He changed the subject. "You had mentioned on the phone that you had something important to tell me. It sounded that way." He was impatient to find out why Teague had been so secretive.

Teague's face became grim. "More Counsel issues, I'm sorry to say. This concerns you and Victor."

"I'm listening," Nathan said flatly.

"There is some opposition to you taking your rightful seat back in the Counsel and Victor assuming his. The Council voted almost unanimously that you and Victor renounce your seats on the Counsel," Teague said emotionlessly. "As your Sire, I will share with you that three members were in favor of you staying. One of them was me."

Nathan twisted the buttons on the sleeves of his shirt as he asked, "And their reason for our dismissal?"

"They feel they are a *new* Counsel; they don't want to look back; they don't want any bad blood among them," Teague explained the reasons behind the call for their resignation. He edged himself to the corner of his chair. "If you want to stay on the Counsel, they have given you an ultimatum."

"I can hardly wait to hear this," Nathan muttered. "What?"

"A blood-cleansing ritual."

"What are the rules and who must be present?" Nathan asked.

"You must ask one of your peers to join you in the ritual, but they have the right to decline. You may then ask one other. If they both decline, you have no choice but to give up your seat on the Counsel and Victor must as well. If one accepts, you must feed from your peer, consuming what would be considered clean blood. Once you have consumed, you will re-embrace Victor to pass on the good blood. I warn you though. You may ask only two members and one cannot be me. It may not be Victor either since his membership with the Counsel is not solid yet. The ritual must take place here at the Manor, and your request for a donor must be made at the Counsel table. Victor must be present for the ritual."

"I may ask anyone at the table, excluding you and Victor, and can only ask twice?" Nathan made sure he understood the rules of the ritual.

Teague nodded.

"I approve; when do we begin?" Nathan asked, already anticipating the challenge.

Chapter 33

Before we left the gallery, Victor called for some Chinese take-out from a tiny restaurant a block from Spellbound. He suggested we eat it in the park like we did the first time, the first time we enjoyed each other's company, which seemed so long ago. Victor and I had a leisurely stroll to and from the restaurant, holding hands and taking in the sights and the sounds of a quiet Sunday night in the city. We found a picnic table close to the street and unpacked our dinner, relaxed in each other's company and conversing quietly. I can't recall the last time we sat to talk about *whatever* and not about what crisis was happening next. It felt good to just chat and eat, like two normal people on a date, with the exception that nothing about either one of us was terribly normal. For a brief moment it did though; it felt normal, until the black limo came into view, its stretched length creeping slowly down the street. I could see the scarlet eyes of the pale driver as he pulled even with us and stopped, the engine idling ominously. Eyeing the driver warily I glanced at Victor. I was not up to another trip to sit with Sheldon and the Counsel, the people responsible for Sara's death. A slow burning anger kindled within me and I could feel that Victor's emotions matched mine. He did not want to go back; there was something about the Manor that did not sit well with him and it wasn't just the Counsel Members. The tinted driver's side window slowly opened and the pasty complexion of the creature behind the wheel emerged. Victor looked in his direction and their eyes met, but only for a moment before the window rose back to blackness.

"We have to go. Nathan's at the Manor." Victor stood and began to pack up the Styrofoam containers and packaging; there was some urgency to his brisk movements.

"Is there a problem?" I asked in concern, looking back at the limo as I helped Victor gather up the rubbish.

"I don't know. The limo will take us to the Manor. We won't know until we get there." He threw the trash in a garbage can. "Come on." He wiped his hands on the seat of his blue jeans and headed for the long black car.

I followed without a word, watching the driver climb out of the car and open the passenger door near the back. He held the door wide as Victor disappeared into the limo. I stared at the driver; he was the same one from the night before. I tried not to think about his ghoulish appearance as I forced a small smile and edged my way onto the leather bench seat next to Victor. The door closed solidly behind me.

Once the car got rolling I was aware of the anxiety building within Victor. I placed my hand on his and squeezed gently to get his attention. "Why do you think we were sent for?" I asked in a whisper.

Victor's face was blank. "I really don't know. The driver was told to get us. Nathan knew I was with you at the gallery. I saw him on my way out this evening and mentioned it. This was the first place he looked for us. It sounds critical that we get there as soon as we can."

"I hate not knowing, especially with your people. I really hate surprises like this." I was aggravated and he knew it. I continued to think about what Sheldon had said the night before – about Sara – and his virtual confession of being responsible for her death; and being proud of it, proud that he could stir up emotions in me I didn't want to feel again. The truth was I really hated him. I was in no hurry to meet up with him now or any time in the near future. But I was equally plagued by curiosity as to why Victor and I had been sent for; it was an interruption to a fairly peaceful evening between us.

We arrived at the Manor and waited as the driver opened the limo door, allowing us to exit. Looking up the wide stone stairs to the home's entrance, I saw Lyla with her long, wavy flowing red hair, standing on the threshold awaiting us. I followed Victor's long strides as he made his way up, filled with dread and anticipation at the same time.

"I really hate being here," Victor muttered under his breath to me as I caught up and stood next to him.

"Why?" I asked.

"Long story. Let's get this over with." He continued to ascend with me at his side.

"I've been waiting for you, Victor," Lyla's Irish accent could be heard clearly in our silence as we reached the top, her voice soft and sweet.

"I'm here. Take me where I need to be," Victor answered shortly, not playing her game, his body showing no evident emotions.

She smiled widely. "No need to take a tone like that with me just because *she* is with you." Lyla placed her hand on his back and guided him into the Manor, leaving me to follow. "We should meet up some time again, soon," she told Victor, deliberately loud enough for me to hear. She walked him back to the conference room door. Behind the heavy entrance was the room we had all spent time in the night before. "Counsel is waiting for you." Lyla opened the painted door slowly, letting Victor see in. "Kala must stay out here with me until the Sovereign sanctions her to enter."

Victor glanced back; assuring me it would be soon. "See you in a few."

I nodded. I had to wait just as I had the night before until everyone was ready for me.

I paced the entry way and finally settled into my spot by the fountain. I wondered again how Victor and Lyla knew each other; it bothered me that there was obviously some history between them. Maybe that was why Victor didn't like to come back to the Manor; it was something about Lyla. A long story was what Victor said. Bad memories? Hurt? I felt funny on the inside as I watched her. She was so tall and pretty; no wonder they'd gotten together. I watched the water trickle down the rock formation into the stone basin and thought about Victor's reaction to Lyla. It was as if Victor was pushing her away, not just physically, because it certainly seemed as if her nearness did nothing for him, but verbally as well; dismissing her remarks and wanting her to *just do her job* and escort him to where he needed to be. For some reason though, until Victor and I talked about Lyla and I understood what had happened between the two, if anything, no matter what I thought did not matter. I needed to hear Victor's explanation straight from him.

I hadn't been waiting too long before Lyla and a servant approached me briskly. My eyes scanned both of their faces and I knew it was show time. The Counsel Members were ready to see me. Lyla took me roughly by the arm and tugged me to follow. I snatched my arm away and gave her a dirty look instead.

"Follow Lyla," the man said, pushing me gruffly by the shoulders in her direction.

"Okay, okay!" I shot back. "All you have to do is ask. You don't have to get all hostile on me!" I squared my shoulders and took a deep breath, then followed Lyla to the conference room door. She opened it and held it wide for me. With a last baleful stare at her, I walked in.

The room was bright. The crystal chandelier overhead sparkled with radiance instead of the eerie glow it had on the previous evening. The Counsel Members weren't hand in hand as before, but instead sat almost casually in their black leather chairs, all eyes fixed on me. I stood at the front of the room, the door to my back. I saw Sheldon right away, his smug face looking at me as he reclined easily in his seat, legs crossed comfortably. I scowled at him fiercely, letting him know in no uncertain terms that I was not here to see him. Make no mistake, this was *not* a friendly visit.

A stylish gentleman who sat to the right of Sheldon rose from his chair and faced me. His broad shoulders and muscular physique demanded immediate respect, but there was something about him – a power he held, that showed he was larger than Sheldon, not just in body but in character too. His olive green jacket complemented his dark hair and skin, making him very distinguished looking.

"Kala, come to me," the well-dressed man spoke clearly, his voice smooth and deep; he extended his hand in my direction.

I awkwardly limped towards him, self-conscious of my current disability. I stood before him and looked up in his eyes. I did not speak. For some reason, I felt his power and bowed to his obvious dominance.

"I am Teague, Sovereign. While I know you are not Emissary yet, I will allow you to sit at our table as a guest of Nathan and Victor's. You must be silent unless spoken to. I will sit between you and Sheldon to avoid any scenes like last night. Please be seated." He indicated the chair next to him. "I believe this spot is yours." He smiled slightly as we both looked at the bubbled black lacquer handprints I had left behind on the table top in my fit of anger from the night before.

I smiled weakly in return. "Thank you." It seemed fitting he was Sovereign. It was easy for me to see the qualities that made him who he was. I could never see Sheldon filling his shoes. I pulled my chair out and sat quietly, folding my hands on the table over my personal markings.

The Sovereign took his seat and returned to the business at hand. "A vote was taken as to whether Nathan may continue to sit among his peers at the Counsel table. According to his punishment, which is coming to an end, he has the right to take his seat back at the Counsel, but the Counsel also has a right to vote him out. However, Nathan may keep his seat *if* he is able to perform a blood cleansing ritual using the rules that have already been established by the Counsel. The rules are as follows: Nathan can select up to two of his peers to take part in the ritual. One of the two must accept. If both decline then Nathan must give up his seat, which will automatically preclude Victor of ever having a seat at the Counsel. Furthermore no one sired by Nathan or Victor will ever sit as a Counsel Member here or at any other Counsel table from that point on. No fledglings of their fledglings may sit at the Counsel and so on and so on. Nathan may ask any of his peers at the table – with the exception of *me,* Sovereign, and Victor, who share's Nathan's blood line – who is not by our rules a full Counsel member yet." Teague's eyes ran up and down the table as he spoke. "Are these rules understood?"

A chorus of yes's was uttered.

I felt bad for Nathan, which was a first. I knew though, from what Victor had said, that rejoining his people was something Nathan had waited a very long time to do. Of course that meant being on the Counsel, because without that he would feel less than adequate. For Victor, not being on the Counsel meant very little to him; he would just carry on the way he always had and had always managed. But for Nathan, this was a way of life he expected to have returned to him and looked forward to taking back. I could not understand why they no longer wanted him.

"Fine," Teague said, and then directed his conversation to Nathan. "Do you understand the rules, Nathan?"

"Yes, I understand," Nathan answered and looked at me intently as he did.

"Remember, no matter how this turns out, your rights within our society have been restored to you and Victor. Please begin."

Nathan stood, trying not to let the fact that most of the people in the room did not like him or want him around affect him. He pushed his chair away from him and the table as his eyes scanned the Counsel Members before settling on me. "I chose Kala."

My eyes widened at hearing my name. I was ordered to silence and so could not respond, not unless the Sovereign gave me leave. I had no idea what kind of ritual Nathan wanted me to take place in. By the sounds coming from the Counsel Members it seemed as though I was off limits. I heard a low murmur of "she's human, she's not a peer, no," which was suddenly disrupted by Sheldon who jumped violently up from his chair. He angrily shouted, "I forbid it! No one will drink the blood of my Emissary! No one but me!"

"And how was she?" Nathan immediately snapped at him, his eyes boring through Sheldon as he slammed his hands on the table.

"Enough!" Teague shouted. "Enough! Both of you sit! I will make a ruling on this, not either of you!" Teague remained sitting, but was intimidating all the same. He waited for Nathan and Sheldon to be reseated and the room to quiet. I remained silent, curious to hear Teague's thoughts on the matter.

'Trust me Kala, just trust me,' Nathan looked me square in the face and spoke within my mind.

I nodded slightly, afraid even a telepathic signal would be considered talking.

"Kala is our guest tonight and although she is *not* one of us yet, she will be. She will be your Emissary. Don't begin your relationship with her by being totally disrespectful. Most of you were human once, as vile a thought as it may be to some. I don't know if you are aware of this or not, but Kala is not 100% human. Her father is like us; her mother is mortal. I find that interesting." He paused in reflection, then continued on. "The real reason we are here tonight stems from a mishap that occurred over two hundred years ago. I'd like you all to remember back to when Nerissa was taken from us. She was still human, but a chosen Emissary never the less. The incident involved her, Victor, who was just a fledgling vampire at the time, and his Sire, Nathan. They ended up paying a *very* high price for the damage done to our people. Nerissa was in a class of her own because of her future role with our people. She was to be untouchable. If she had been just a simple human, not a pending Emissary, her death would have provoked no response from the Counsel. Unfortunately, because of her distinction, the crimes against her were punishable. As I sit here tonight I can tell you that if the same were to happen to Kala, the people responsible would receive the same punishment Nathan and Victor were given because of *who* she will be for us. Kala *must* be considered at least a peer – if not higher." Teague's voice rang out in the room's silence. "Sheldon, if someone murdered Kala tomorrow, and the killer was one of us, would you not want to see that person punished? Would you not seek justice? Would you not be as bitter as I was to have your chosen companion taken from you? That's all I ask you to consider."

I tried to lean around Teague to see the reaction on Sheldon's face as he asked him to think about what he was saying. I was sure Sheldon wanted me dead.

Sheldon's face was expressionless as if he was holding back his true feeling about me. A muscle in his jaw jumped as he spoke. "I understand."

"Good, that's all I ask." The Sovereign accepted his response. Teague swiveled his chair back to face me "Kala, you do not have to accept what Nathan has asked of you. You can decline. No one will force a decision from you. It is your choice."

'*Don't you dare say yes. I won't allow it*!' Sheldon's growl rang in my head as he tried to coerce me into doing what he wanted.

I was not overly concerned with how I looked in the eyes of the Counsel. It was obvious that even though my status was a pending Emissary, in their eyes I was still just a human. A weak, feeble creature. "I accept," I spoke loudly. I wanted to make sure Sheldon heard the eagerness in my voice. After all Nathan had saved my life. I owed him one.

A spiteful look passed between Nathan and Sheldon as I answered. Victor looked down at the table, obviously displeased with my decision to help Nathan. I did not know why; I was securing his future by helping Nathan, whether it was something he wanted today or not, plus it was for future generations to come.

"You accept," Teague said in surprise. "That's very admirable. How do you know this is something you even want to take part in? It's a ritual to my people, but something you know nothing about."

"Nathan would not ask me to take part in your ritual if he knew I could be permanently injured," I explained confidently.

Teague nodded as I spoke. "I see a lot of Nerissa in you – heart, compassion, kindness – all the things that got her killed. Be careful;

sometimes too much of a good thing is bad."

Lyla entered the room quietly. I could feel her aura drift by me as she slipped in virtually unnoticed, situating herself in a corner near the front of the room. I glanced in her direction to see what she was up to. She looked slowly around the table, her vivid blue eyes missing nothing. She looked at Victor, her face unreadable as she studied him.

"Nathan; Victor; Kala; Lyla will escort you to the North Wing where the ritual will take place. The rest of us need to determine which two of the Counsel Members will witness the ritual to make sure it happens correctly." Teague motioned us to follow Lyla.

Victor left the room first, followed by Nathan, then me. Once the conference room door had shut, Lyla immediately linked her arm to Victor's, acting more like *he* was escorting her instead of the other way around. She smiled broadly and whispered something in his ear, giggling as they walked by the fountain towards a long, dimly lit corridor.

'*Bitch.*' I thought to myself as I followed along. Nathan, walking slowly in front of me, turned and allowed me to catch up to him.

"Problem?" he asked quizzically.

Lyla and Victor continued arm in arm through the Manor.

"You heard me?" I said with a frown.

"Yes. I know what you were referring to." He looked after Lyla's retreating form. "I know humans have a tendency to be jealous, but you have no reason to be. Believe me on this." Nathan was obviously referring to Lyla and Victor's relationship.

"What's it all about?" I asked.

Nathan paused before replying rather cryptically. "Talk to Victor about it. I'm sure he would tell you. Lyla is a little too late; let's just say that." He started in the direction they had gone. After a pause, I followed. Then Nathan stopped and turned abruptly, looking as if something else was on his mind that he needed to share with me.

"I appreciate you saying 'yes,' you know." His eyes met mine as he awkwardly conveyed his thanks.

"I know it's important to you, and future generations too," I told him, shifting my weight off my aching leg and leaning up against the wall to help support me. "It's important to Victor as well, although I don't think he sees that."

He nodded in agreement. "Generations." He seemed awed. "It's been so long since I could even think about anything except Victor and me. And who knows how many more there will be. I certainly don't. I am pleased that you trusted me enough to accept my plea."

"I owe you one anyway," I said softly, thinking back about how Nathan had spent countless hours nursing me back to health.

"How's that?" he asked in confusion.

"You saved my life," I answered, surprised that he could have forgotten what he had done.

Nathan shrugged and looked almost human as he replied, "I never told you that you owed me one." He couldn't grasp the concept I was using.

"Friends don't have to."

I don't think Nathan knew quite what to say in response to my comment. I had not said it to deliberately make him uncomfortable. Perhaps it was the thought of *friendship* that left him wordless, or the thought of befriending a human. He remained silent as he began to follow the voices at the end of the dim corridor. As I again started after him, he said, "I believe you will make a good Emissary." Without another word, we continued on towards the ritual.

The room at the end of the hallway was extraordinary, a solarium, full of flourishing plant life, trees and flowers of all sizes and colors. Soft lighting set the mood, glowing warmly from small fixtures scattered amongst the greenery, and falling from a skylight above. This was where the ritual would take place.

I thought it odd for a culture of people who survived by night to love and want such vibrant living things around them. The lack of color at night had made me wonder if some, with their human heritage, missed that – living by day, bright colors, sunrises – and others, like Nathan, hid from it. Each plant needed the sun in order to survive, the very element that would end their existence. It seemed funny in a twisted way. Most of the Manor was painted, papered and decorated in somber tones and colors that made this corner of the house all the more vibrant and alive.

I looked straight up to see a galaxy of lights strung over me. I could easily pick out the moon and the stars through the glass roof as I peeked between the burgundy leaves of a beautiful tree towering above me. I could hear the voices of Victor and Nathan. They seemed irritated with each other and it became more evident as I got closer by following a stone path in between some giant hibiscus plants. When they saw me approach, their heated voices dropped to whispers, then to silence. Nathan abruptly excused himself as I took a place beside Victor, who pretended to be engrossed in the details of a yellow tea rose.

I sat upon a stone bench amidst the dark green ivy vines and kept a watchful eye on Victor, as I thought about Lyla and what the saga was between the two of them. I let my legs swing back and forth and marveled at the beauty surrounding us.

"Don't ask," Victor's voice broke through the quiet.

I turned to face him, not sure what he was talking about. "What?"

"What you are thinking, don't ask," he replied again, leaning back against the smooth silver bark of a sapling and fixing his eyes on the vegetation.

"Why you and Nathan are mad at each other?" I questioned, pushing myself to stand.

"No, the other," he said, as he crossed his arms at his chest.

"You and Lyla?" I offered my most recent thought to him.

"Yes. That's what I was referring to," he spoke sharply.

"All right. I won't ask. Not now anyway." I dropped the subject. "What's on your mind? You seem like you are preoccupied with something."

He stared at me. I could feel the anger within him building. "I can't believe you would even consider taking part in this stupid ritual. That's all it is, stupid." He glared heatedly at me.

"How could I not? Do you understand what will happen if I don't? None of your generations will ever be able to make a difference with your people. They will have rights but never be able to work towards sitting on a Counsel that makes decisions in your society. All I have to do is take part in this ritual to make sure that doesn't happen. I am paying a small price for what could be thousands of years and generations."

"It really doesn't matter though. I'm sure you can see that. The Counsel is a farce. I don't care whether I sit at that table or not," Victor retorted.

"What about Nathan?" I asked. "Why is he not opposed?"

"Nathan needs to see beyond that. He sees this Counsel the way it *used* to be. It's changed. I can see that, and I never was part of it. They are self-serving; they don't work for the majority of us." His eyes darkened with anger.

"Maybe he thinks he can make a difference, turn things around. I'm sorry you don't approve of what I'm doing, but I have to. Plus it really pisses Sheldon off."

Victor sat back down on the stone bench. "After two hundred years I feel like it's all starting over again." His body was stiff as he spoke, every muscle tensing with the stress of the night.

"This is it. This is the end, right? It can't go on forever. You were tried, convicted, paid your dues. It's over now." I sat next to him.

"It has to be. What more can they want? What more can they find?" he asked quickly as if he had been pushed too far already. "I have kept to myself for the better part of two hundred years. My associations with any of these people were rare and it was usually quite by accident or by chance. My knowledge from Nathan is all I know." His temper continued to flare.

"Let's take that last small step. After tonight, no more. They took all they could and you gave what they asked for. It's over. Give Nathan back the rights he wants, what he had before you and he were chastised. Then you will have yours whether you choose to exercise them or not; they are there for you. You have a long life to live. Don't think for today. Think as a Sire. Think for the tomorrows."

Chapter 34

Quite a while had gone by before the three of us were joined by the two Counsel Members who would witness the ritual take place between Nathan, Victor and myself. I guess I was not too surprised to see that Sheldon was one of the Counsel Members. The other was a female who I had seen at the table but knew nothing about. Her name was Nadia; short and just shy of middle age by a few years, dressed smartly in a maroon suit with a form fitting skirt and tailored jacket. Her complexion was very pale, but her eyes were a strange shade of emerald green that grabbed my attention, the color was so striking. Her brown shoulder-length hair was swept to one side and she constantly ran her fingers through it to keep it out of her eyes. I watched Sheldon and Nadia engage Nathan in conversation; it was rather brief and lacking any emotion. I figured they must have been going over any last minute rules.

Nathan made his way in my direction. "It's about time to start," he informed me, placing his hands on my shoulders and getting my full attention. "Here is how this works. There is a stone altar; you will be seated on it. In this ritual I am to consume untainted blood; because of that I cannot puncture your skin with my teeth. Sheldon will use a device that looks like a thimble. It fits over his thumb and has a very sharp point at the end. It will make a very clean incision on your wrist; once that is done I can drink your blood. Because I can not interrupt the ritual to stop your wrist from bleeding I want you to wrap it in this." Nathan reached into his jacket pocket and pulled out a white cotton handkerchief. "Use it. Don't let Sheldon try and prevent you. I already warned him not to. Once I drink your blood, I will offer my clean blood to Victor. When he drinks from me the ritual is complete. I will return to you and heal your wound."

I held his handkerchief in my hand, winding it around my fingers as I listened to him explain what I could expect. "I understand. How is Victor taking this?" I asked.

Nathan sighed heavily as he answered. "He's okay. I know he's going through with it for me." Nathan began to take off his dark blazer; folding it neatly he set it on the stone bench in the ivy. He rolled his shirtsleeves up to his elbows. "Follow me; I'll show you to the altar. Victor is waiting for us."

Deeper into the solarium we walked, as if on some sort of safari, ducking and dodging vines and branches to a location that boasted a large uniquely shaped pond with trickling fresh water, bursting with lovely, elegant floating plants and flowers. I could see huge gold fish swimming and feeding below the surface. A stone altar was situated on the other side of the pond with a thick green fabric draped over it.

Victor stood silently on the right side of the altar. Nathan motioned for me to take my place, so I slowly walked to it. Victor helped boost me up so that I could sit comfortably on the flat stone. I waited, my legs swinging freely over the edge. I felt as if I was on display; a rare creature perched on a pedestal, alone in strange surroundings. Sheldon, my natural predator, lurked close by, trying to get my attention by creeping into my mind, a constant interruption of my own thoughts. I finally looked at him in repulsion, acknowledging his unwanted persistence. He grinned coldly and held up his hand, allowing me to see the silver object secure on his thumb, its razor sharp tip ready to score my wrist. The anticipation was evident on his face as he waited for the chance to cut me and watch me bleed. It was not going to be hard for him to smell my blood or watch it flow as it might be for others like him; his delight was in hurting me and watching me suffer.

Nathan proceeded to the altar, passing Nadia and Sheldon without giving them a second look. He was focused on one thing and that was to complete the ritual that would allow him his seat back on the High Counsel.

Nathan stood directly in front of me. From where I sat, my height was just about even with his. Our eyes met and he stared at me intently, making me feel ill at ease. His eyes held unfathomable mysteries, knowledge and horrors so profound I could not hold his gaze. Perhaps it was the weak, human side of me, but I could not continue looking at him. I felt as if I would drown in those dark eyes, lost forever. I turned my head slightly towards Victor, seeking a measure of safety, of comfort. Nathan's mysteries were not something I was prepared to deal with right now.

"You may begin anytime," Nadia said, her voice rising over the trickling water in the pond.

Nathan reached out and gently took my left arm, drawing it close to him. He pushed the sleeve of my shirt up past my elbow and rotated my arm so my wrist was exposed. He looked at Sheldon, standing next to us. An unspoken message passed between them – a warning or a challenge – it wasn't clear, but before I had a chance to think about it, Nathan had relinquished his hold and allowed Sheldon to hold my arm. My instinctive reaction was to pull away, but before I could do so, Nathan firmly turned my face towards Victor, not allowing me to watch Sheldon and his grim task.

'There is no need to watch,' Nathan told me. "Keep your eyes on Victor only."

Before I could reply, I felt Sheldon give my arm a firm jerk as he made a quick incision in my wrist. I jumped at the fiery pain, which was suddenly replaced by a bone-freezing chill. Nathan's mouth latched on my wrist, his tongue pressed tightly against the wound as he received the gush of ritual cleansing blood surging into his thirsting body. He had not tasted blood for quite some time and now my blood, not just any blood but the blood of an Emissary, was a gift from me to him, whether I knew it or not. It not only thawed him but also gave him back some of the strength he had unknowingly lost over time. Nathan had recently tasted my blood through weeping wounds that oozed – but this was different, this was how it was supposed to be – warm, clean and pure.

Feeling lightheaded, I tried to turn and see what was happening. Nathan had regained possession of my arm from Sheldon as he consumed the blood needed to finish the ritual. His hand was soft on mine as he moved his thumb rhythmically in my palm in a calming motion. Finally, Nathan's eyes opened wide. He reached into my lap for the white handkerchief he had given me to use for a tourniquet, then unclamped his mouth from my wrist and pressed the handkerchief securely to the wound. He wrapped it tightly around my arm to staunch the flow of blood, all the while looking reassuringly at me. I nodded slightly in response, then turned my gaze to Victor.

It was obvious he was uncomfortable, but with himself or the entire process I couldn't tell. He remained silent as Nathan carefully bit a small opening in his own wrist, then offered it to Victor, the blood beginning to flow out heavily. Victor's eyes became dark and round, a sight I remembered vividly. He stepped forward, placed his mouth over the wound and began to drink. My stomach tumbled and flopped as I watched Nathan, his eyes closed, offer his blood to Victor. I wondered briefly what they might be thinking, Sire and offspring, as one took and the other nourished. Finally, Victor removed his mouth and stepped back, watching as Nathan licked the wound, healing the puncture marks rapidly. Without looking at me, Victor turned away and walked down the stone path. No one said anything.

I wanted to join Victor but I was still bleeding and waiting for Nathan to fix me up.

"I think we have fulfilled your requirements for the ritual," Nathan told Sheldon quietly.

"For now," Sheldon snapped. "But I'd watch who you befriend." He stepped down and gestured for Nadia to follow him. "After all, I will be *your* Sovereign."

"And I will be *his* Emissary," I spoke up, not liking Sheldon's threatening tone.

"I am not going to argue again with you tonight, Kala. We have many years to work our differences out. Your Hell could be my Heaven." He smiled coolly as he placed an arm around Nadia. With a last pointed look at us, he pushed the large glass door open into the Manor and they left together.

I narrowed my eyes as I watched them leave. Nathan removed the bandage from my wrist and I tried not to look at the bloody wound, still painful and fresh.

"Don't watch," Nathan told me as he raised my wrist to his mouth. It fascinated me how he and Victor were able to heal and cure; that creatures so deadly could do such good – when they wanted to. Our eyes met and I felt a rush of emotion pass between us. His deep black eyes appeared bottomless, deep pools of mystery I could never plumb. He licked at the blood that flowed intensely from the cut. For a moment I was not sure if he had begun to feed from me again or if he was actually mending the wound. Unexpectedly he dropped to his knees in front of me. He knelt upon the slate step of the altar keeping my wrist at his lips, his eyes large and sad. '*Forgive me,*' his voice echoed in my head.

This was totally unpredicted. In confusion I replied, '*What for?*'

'*I could not help myself,*' he said softly. '*Your blood. It's been so long.*'

It was then that I realized that he *was* feeding from me and not healing me; maybe he was not even aware until my thoughts united with his. The knowledge visibly shook him. I'm not sure if it was because it was *me*, someone he now knew, or if it was because I was Emissary, and he knew he had to stop. I swallowed hard, knowing I was not in any *real* danger; Nathan had his wits about him again, and Victor was no more than a scream away, but it gave me a brief scare. I forced a smile, aware that just like Victor, even Nathan tried to keep his monster buried deep within. '*It's okay. Please fix my wrist.*' I held my wrist out to him, distracting and focusing at the same time.

Silently, he dropped his mouth to my arm and continued the healing. It only took him a moment to finish. He then cleaned my arm with his handkerchief that he had dipped in the cool pond water. Finally he excused himself back to the Manor, stating he still had business with the Sovereign.

When the large glass doors closed behind Nathan, I went looking for Victor. I didn't want to think any more about Nathan and what had happened. I hobbled slowly down a stone path, the one I'd last seen Victor wander away on. When I came upon him among a patch of tall green flowering bushes I slowed my pace even more. As I drew near, he began to speak, his back to me. "I really should try my hand at painting nature again, flowers, leaves, trees," he said, his voice soft and emotionless. "I always get so discouraged with myself though; nothing looks right. My night vision, I guess." He reached out and yanked a budding leaf from the bush and held it up, studying it in the glow of artificial light. "I know colors look different in the day's light. They have to. I can't remember, but they must. Maybe some day."

I came up behind him and wrapped my arms around his stomach, squeezing gently and resting my face against his back between his shoulder blades; the sweet smell of his cologne seeping through the fabric of his cotton shirt. "Perhaps some day you should take your paint and brushes and a canvas and come to the solarium and paint, try it again, now that you are welcomed."

Victor tossed the leaf away and covered my hands with his. "Hmmm, I don't know," he said uncertainly. "I could paint you." He broke free from my hold and turned to face me. His arms snaked around my waist as he held me close, looking down upon me as if he had already started a visual painting in his mind.

"I'm sure you could find a better subject," I smiled.

"I doubt it. I'd love to spend time, a lot of time, working on a project like that." He leaned his head back, staring up into the night sky with a vision in mind. "Of course it would have to be a nude, and then I'd never get any work done at all. " He laughed a little, looking back down at me.

"Why even bother to bring the paint?" I smiled broadly. "Just throw a sheet on the floor and ... "

"Well, because I'm a professional," he interrupted. "I'd paint you eventually; even if it took a hundred years."

I giggled. "I guess I better get used to you being around."

Victor and I hitched a ride in the limo back to the gallery where his car was located. It was late and, although I really wasn't ready to end it, I had to work in the morning. The thought of crawling into bed and shutting my eyes to sleep left me feeling restless. I knew I'd toss and turn for hours. Victor gave me a lift back home, parking his car next to mine in front of the condo. He sighed heavily and tilted his bucket seat back, stretching his legs and closing his eyes as if he was finally able to relax for a moment.

"Would you like to stay awhile?" I whispered, leaning over the center console and touching him lightly.

A smile turned the corners of his mouth up as his eyes opened slowly. "I'd love to, but I'm teaching a class tomorrow night. I need to get things together. I'll never make it if I wait and do it tomorrow before I leave for campus."

"I understand," I said as I straightened up in my seat. I did. Although I wanted him to stay. "Can you at least walk me to the door?"

"I'll even walk you inside. Make sure you are safe," he offered as he opened his door and got out.

I got out of the car and met him on the sidewalk. He placed his arm around my back and we walked in companionable silence to my front door. I placed my key in the lock, turned and pushed the door in and open. "No boogie men waiting for me," I said as I peered into the entryway before crossing the threshold. Victor followed me in and leaned against the wall.

Looking around my silent condo, I turned my gaze beseechingly to Victor. I wanted him to stay the night. My body needed him to stay the night. I stretched up and kissed him, feeling him soften and melt against me as his arms reached around me. *'Stay with me tonight,'* I asked him, as we continued our kiss.

'I can't, love, I have a class,' he responded, pulling me tighter against his chest.

'I want you. It's been so long,' I urged as his lips moved softly down my neck.

I heard Victor sigh in frustration in my ear. "I know our timing has been off," he said out loud and kissed my cheek, trying to console me. "Soon."

"Can you stay *a little* while?" My voice pleaded with him as I rubbed suggestively against his body. I began to kiss him again. I wanted to be as persuasive as I could. I thought of an erotic fantasy for him to stumble upon in my mind. I knew he was aware; I could feel him there. It was easy. Being able to think out a fantasy, see it play out in your head and have someone else share it with you without saying a word, understanding and feeling exactly what you do is incredible.

"That's not fair," he mumbled, breaking his lips free from mine, arms loosening from my body. "I can't." His voice was harsher than I needed to hear.

I pushed myself free from him. "Okay, fine, I understand," I snapped. "Apparently this is only one-sided. I get it. I'm not stupid." I turned away from him and petulantly kicked my shoes off under the desk.

"That's not it and you know it. I can share your thoughts just as easy as you can share mine; you should *know* how I feel by now. You just never try. If it doesn't jump out at you, you don't see it or feel it," he retorted.

"Maybe I don't want to feel," I spoke loudly. "I can barely handle my own emotions, let alone someone else's. And I have shared yours before," I reminded him.

"Tonight is just not good," his voice dropped and his arms hung at his side.

"I got that impression," I said frostily.

"I'm sorry."

Even though I had told Victor that I did not want to feel, that was not the truth. I liked to know what made him say and do the things he did, but the problem with knowing is finding out things you don't want to know. That was what scared me the most about sharing thoughts. And that was probably why my heart fell when I read some of Victor's thoughts, as I stood there facing him. Looking deeply into his eyes and without a doubt, I knew he felt what I felt. "It's Lyla, isn't it?" My voice was low and steady as I contained my hurt.

He did not try to protest at my accusation, but instead simply replied, "It's a long story."

I ground my teeth. "Well, it's after midnight. We'll talk about it when you have time. You have your class to get ready for. Good night." I wanted to hear no more. I turned and headed for the kitchen. I stood in front of the refrigerator door but had no strength to open it. As I stood there, Victor came in to the kitchen. Ignoring him, I tugged the door open and reached for a cold beer.

"You are blowing this way out of proportion." Victor's voice was calm. He crossed his arms and leaned against the entry.

"Am I?"

He nodded. "Yes. I have a lot on my mind. Not being able to stay tonight has nothing to do with Lyla – really."

"I won't call you a liar, but I don't believe you. I mean, I understand you not being able to stay; that's fair because you have a class to get ready for. But not being able to be intimate with me? That's because she's on your mind! Ask me how I know! Ask!" I angrily pulled the dishtowel off the counter and wrapped it around the top of my beer, cracked the cap off and flung both into the sink.

"I know how you know," he said evenly. "But there is a lot you don't know. And perhaps I am thinking about her, a little. But it's not because I care for her, not now. It's hard to describe. I said it's a long story."

I shrugged and gulped my beer. "Nathan seemed to think you'd be willing to talk to me about Lyla. I guess he was wrong."

"Nathan..." Victor sighed. "What did he tell you?"

I walked past Victor to the sliding door that led to the deck. "Not much. Just that I should not worry about her and that you would be pretty open to talk about Lyla." I slid the door open and walked out, taking an abrupt seat at the table.

Victor followed and pulled a chair up next to me. "Listen. Here are the facts about my love life and me; Nerissa was my one and only true human love. I wanted to marry her, live happily ever after, have a big family, and grow old with her. That was my plan. I knew it the day I met her. Except, things could not have gone more wrong." Victor's face showed the strain of his memories. "Lyla was my first immortal love and I use the word love loosely. It was brief, torrid – and hurtful. Over the past two hundred years I have had my share of infatuations with human females and immortals, but nothing serious. I never allowed it."

Victor's voice trailed off and he sat quietly for a moment. Without looking up he spoke again. "I've told you this before and I will tell you again. I knew someday that you would come back. I felt it, but could never explain it. I never stopped loving Nerissa. Not one day. And when I met you, it wasn't like I needed to be introduced to you. I knew who you were, and I loved you already. I didn't have to fall in love, I already was. I will tell you about Lyla; I will. I have nothing to hide but the pain of the relationship, and what you feel is that. There is no love for her. You are strong enough to read me. Do it and you will see the pain I have is not from *missing* her all these years, but because I have *seen* her after all these years. I think that's the emotion you are sensing. For someone like yourself, who is not familiar with picking up feelings, I can understand the mix-up. Emotional pain is not like physical pain; there are differences." Victor finished, his eyes never leaving my face. I was silent, watching him from my seat as I rolled the cool bottle of beer between my hands, weighing his story.

As I sat there in my chair, I thought about just how easy it would be to read Victor, to walk into his mind and look around, to ask questions and find answers. With Victor's invitation for me to try, I thought I might. I had felt a flash of Victor's thoughts and emotions on other occasions although I had not gone into his mind probing for them. They had come to me in the excitement of our passionate embraces. I studied Victor and wondered what I would look for. How would I spot deception, or lies?

Before I knew it, it was apparent that I was *in*. Perhaps the most noticeable aspect of Victor's mind was that it was dark. The color black repeated constantly in my head. His memories surfaced easily, appearing and dissolving simultaneously and constantly around me. Victor's human recollections melted flawlessly into his more recent ones. He had many fond memories of Nerissa, her beauty, thoughtfulness, style and uniqueness. Accompanying her visions were obvious changes in his mood that altered the blackness into shades of green and blue, showing the calming effect they had on him. His thoughts of Nerissa were strong, and his feelings were too, He still loved her, there was no mistaking that.

A kaleidoscope of people, faces, events and eras filled me, leaving my head spinning as I tried to place people in history back into his life and figure out what they meant to him. Thousands of people zoomed by me at a rate of speed I could not keep up with. Abruptly, the chilling realization came to me that these faces were Victor's victims over the years – all of them – dead by his hand. He remembered each one in his own special way, a memorial in his fight for survival in a society of people who were ignorant to the creatures who shared their world. I absorbed centuries of his memories, but could not find the one thing I wanted most – his thoughts and feelings of Lyla. I did not feel Victor was hiding anything; I never sensed diversions or deceptions to push me off track, or make me believe something that was not true. I gave up my hunt willingly, hoping Victor would tell me his story of Lyla. Maybe not tonight, but soon. Victor was aware I had given up on the search and exited his mind as I returned to my own thoughts. He sat calmly in his chair, alone with his.

"Well?" he asked, waiting for my reaction.

I sipped my beer before I replied. "I didn't find what I was looking for. It's like hunting through an archive and I don't know your filing system."

"I'm sure it must seem that way," he sighed, as if even he was overwhelmed at times with the amount of life history he had stored within him. "I promise that I will tell you about Lyla. I can't right now. It's too hard for me. It's devastating. I know you can't imagine how that can be, but you will understand. Just please trust me. I have no reason to lie."

"I hope you don't," I said coolly, trying to quell my jealousy.

Chapter 35

Victor did not stay much longer. There was still tension between us, an uncomfortable, unspoken hurt on my part that I know he felt. I just could not help dwelling on how *one* woman could cause Victor so much anguish, that so much emotion could be left, even from a woman such as Lyla. My bitterness stemmed in part from not knowing the entire story. Since time healed all wounds, I would think two hundred years of time would have certainly done the job for Victor.

As I lay in bed alone, I struggled with many thoughts. I knew Victor handled his emotions differently and opening himself up to me as far as his life story was concerned would be difficult, at best. Still, I desperately needed to hear, from him, the events that had made him who he was, that had brought Nathan and Lyla in to his life, that had brought us to this point in time.

'Stop doing this to yourself,' I heard Victor's voice loud and clear, interrupting my inner conflict.

I sighed out loud.

'Are you listening to me? I know you can hear me.'

I tugged my feather pillow out from under my head and flopped it over my face to try and stop his voice from coming through. *'Not listening.'*

The phone rang, shrill and persistent. I knew it was Victor even as I threw the pillow off and reached clumsily over the bed to the nightstand for the phone. "Hello," I grumbled.

"Why aren't you answering me?" Victor asked.

"Because I am trying to sleep," I replied curtly, sitting up and trying to straighten my bedding and pillows around me.

"No, you aren't. You are still thinking about Lyla and me. Please. Stop it. It's bothering *me* now," Victor said, his voice strong and not sympathetic. "I have work to do here."

"I'm sorry. I will try and *think* about something else," I snapped, laying back down and yanking the covers over my chest.

"I love you. Just stop this," he pleaded with me. "Give me at least a week to work this out myself and I promise I will enlighten you. Just know this. Lyla is a thing of the past. She and I are no more. Okay?"

A week, I thought to myself, a week until I might fully understand what this woman had meant to Victor. "I guess," I answered morosely. It wasn't like I had a choice.

"Go to sleep. I'll see you or call after class. Good night," he whispered, his voice suddenly tender.

"All right," I mumbled. "Good night."

I tossed and turned, unable to let the evening go. Victor made no further attempts to talk to me, maybe knowing I was at least trying to let it go for now. By morning I was exhausted, the hours wasted. As tired as I was, I had to get up. I forced myself to rise and get ready for work, not waiting for the annoying sound of the alarm clock rudely proclaiming it was time to get the day started.

I decided during my drive to work that I would see if I could get the next few days off before the Battle of the Bands concert on the weekend. I had plenty of vacation time coming to me and with the way my life had been going, I could use some time to myself to read, relax, think. I struck an easy deal with management to take Wednesday, Thursday and Friday off. They knew that Saturday, the day of the Battle of the Bands, would be a long one, what with the entire concert schedule, the live, on-air coverage, as well as meeting listeners and introducing bands as they hit the stage. Besides, it kept them from having to pay me over-time. The time off gave me some needed enthusiasm and energy to make it through the next two days knowing I had a few days of vacation to look forward to.

Victor and I did not see each other until Tuesday night after his class. His schedule had become rather full lately, as he was taking over for another teacher who was away on leave. I was happy for him, since he was able to do more of the teaching he loved.

Victor and I sat with a bottle of wine and a pizza in my living room, celebrating his new job with the college and my mini-vacation that I was just getting into. Our last conversation was tacitly ignored, although I was still uncomfortable with the situation. I just could not put Lyla completely out of my mind, and the wine was not helping matters.

"I didn't realize how badly all this bothered you," Victor said softly, referring to my inner conflict. He poured himself another glass of wine as he leaned forward on the couch, the liquid splashing into his glass. "I would think that it would get easier as the night dragged on, but it's getting worse, isn't it?" He leaned back slowly into the cushions next to me and took a measured sip from his glass.

He knew me well and could effortlessly read me. I nodded as I set my glass down on the table. "It's hard to put it out of my mind. The harder I try the worse it is."

"I have tried to comfort you all that I can. I ask that you believe me when I say there are no good feelings towards her on my part. I know you are confused as to what I do feel, but surely you can compare how I feel for her with how I feel for you. The feelings are not even similar," Victor patiently explained as he curled his arm around my shoulder and dropped his head closer to my ear. "Let yourself feel the truth. You are not allowing your psychic abilities the room they need to grow. Stop pushing them aside. Feel it! It's right in front of you."

"It's too frustrating," I sighed. "I can't sort out what I feel when I try what you ask. I'm not sure if it's me or you or someone else."

Victor leaned his head back on the couch and closed his eyes for a moment. "I know you don't think I understand, but I do. Can you relax? It would help."

"Of course I can," I replied defensively.

"I don't say that you can't," he soothed. "I just wonder if maybe you aren't as relaxed as you think you are."

I shrugged. "I think I'm relaxed just fine."

Victor slowly drew me against his body. "I mean very relaxed, like when I have taken your pain and disenchantments away. Remember how that felt. You can make yourself that relaxed without me. It's possible. You just need to work at it a little."

"Really?" I asked in surprise. "I thought that was only something you could do."

He began to smile. "Of course not. You can too. I can for myself when I need to. I actually find it easier doing it for me than doing it for someone else because when it's not *me* I have to set *me* aside and that can be hard, sometimes too hard."

"I guess I can understand that," I mused, pulling my legs up onto the couch and nuzzling my face against his chest. I rested my open hand on his stomach.

"Maybe over the next few days you should use your free time to relax. Practice; it will do you good," Victor suggested. "This weekend will be hectic for you."

"I will, and I want to finish reading Sara's journal, since Nathan already has. I have so much to catch up on," I added.

"Sounds like you are stressed out already," Victor said pointedly. "Take your time."

I smiled; he was right. I was packing my days full of things to do before the sun even rose.

I suppose it was too much to expect that I would sleep soundly the first night of my mini-vacation. I certainly did not imagine I would be seeing a most welcome apparition – Sara. I hadn't thought about her in some time, yet she always remained in the back of my mind. This time, she appeared at the foot of my bed in her usual fashion, so life-like, but then again, not quite. There was a glowing aura surrounding her that caught my eye; I was glad to see her, but I confess to some nervousness too; in anticipation of what her appearance meant, what evil she might be warning me about.

"Sara, what? What's wrong?" I asked, sitting up quickly. I rubbed my tired eyes with the back of my hand.

"You must learn the strength behind the Amulet soon. You will need the Amulet to guide you," Sara spoke slowly, making sure I heard and understood her words perfectly.

I touched the Amulet that I had been wearing since the day I found it. "I'm wearing it. What kind of powers?" I asked her.

"*All* the powers. It will guide you. You *must* let it. The Amulet is not from your world. You will need to return it to where it came from, but have no fear; it will come back to you, and when it does, you will know who the Enforcer is. You will know who will work for you, with you, protect you and help rid the evils that could harm not only you, but also the rest of the people around you. Do not fight the call to return it. So much depends on you," Sara explained.

"Return it to where? How do I return it?" I inquired quickly; fearful she would vanish before answering.

"The answers are in my book. Read. It's all in my book," she spoke softly.

"Sara; I just have not had time. I swear; life is very strange right now." My throat caught and I felt tears begin to well as I spoke.

Sara smiled lightly as she gave her advice. "Be strong, and don't be afraid when you return to the Old Maple Forest."

"The Old Maple Forest? Why? Why do I have to go there? Is that where I have to return the Amulet? How will I know?" I jumped out of my bed to meet her face to face. Before my feet even hit the floor, Sara was gone. I pounded my fists on the bed in anger and aggravation. What I would not have given at that moment to have all the answers, and stop guessing at what could be.

When I woke up in the morning, I was still frustrated by my brief encounter with Sara. I sat with a large cup of coffee on the deck, her journal in my lap. I pried open the pages, stiff with my dried blood, and remembered the night I lay helpless in Nathan's arms, hurt and bleeding. I forced those memories quickly out of my mind; I was better and didn't need to agonize over the events any more. I skimmed many pages in the book, hearing Sara's words about the Old Maple Forest and her admonition to not be afraid. I found it hard to concentrate on what I was looking for in her journal, the words fading in and out of focus, trying to look for answers to her comments regarding the Amulet and its power, and the return of it to the world in which it belonged.

Truth was I had no immediate plans to ever return to the Old Maple Forest. I had been there for Sara's funeral and not since. Now that I knew it was technically haunted by at least one spirit who had touched me the last time I was there; it gave me the creeps to ever think of going back. How many more spirits were there? I'd be a paranoid wreck, constantly looking over my shoulder to see if any ghosts or spooks were following me. And if the Amulet needed to return to the Old Maple Forest, what was this place all about if the Amulet did not come from my world? Was the Old Maple Forest not what it seemed? Maybe the weird stories around the Old Maple Forest had some truth after all.

It wasn't long before I found a few pages that spoke specifically about the Amulet and some of its history. According to what Sara had written, the Amulet had been discovered prior to the 16th century in France, making its way to England during the time of the Windsor Witch Trials. Though those poor women were innocent, and wrongfully accused; the Amulet did belong to a true witch named Lady Avery, who lived around the same time period in a nearby town. Although Lady Avery was a good witch who practiced white magic, she still felt it prudent to hide the Amulet until it could be used by a witch or chosen person without fear of being arrested, tried and prosecuted. Lady Avery disappeared a short time after; and no one was quite sure of where she went or what ever happened to her. The Amulet found its way to the United States sometime in the 19th century where it was passed secretly among selective Wiccans until it reached Sara, who was to hold it for me. Even though there was no danger in being known as a witch, the Amulet's identity was still kept quiet as it made its way to Sara. Apparently, even though the Amulet was only used by a small number of witches before Lady Avery, only Sara and myself had the privilege to display it after her.

The journal warned that the Amulet held powers that in the wrong hands could be devastating, which was the primary reason for keeping it under wraps. For more than two hundred years many had searched for the Amulet to make it theirs. Daemons of all kinds, practitioners of both white and black magic, self-proclaimed Devil worshippers, the undead – Vampires, even hired thugs like pirates – all wanted to find or use the Amulet to benefit their self-serving causes.

Protecting the Amulet had been the highest priority. Now it was rightfully mine; a mighty piece of jewelry people were willing to kill for, draped delicately around my neck.

No one is quite sure who made the Amulet and where it originated. The only thing Sara was sure of was that it was not constructed of any earthly metals and was not forged by any man-made machines. What she did know was that the person who gave it to her some fifteen years ago retrieved it in the Old Maple Forest, near the natural altar, in the full moon's light. It had not been purchased at an estate sale as I had thought, that was just a front, the day Sara took possession of it for me.

You will know when to return the Amulet to the Old Maple Forest, Sara wrote, with no further explanation or instruction. *When that time arrives, you will go to the altar, which will be prepared for ritual and you must read the following, the Amulet in hand:*

I hold the power before you –

I request you allow me to keep it

I am strong, I am faithful, and I am bound to the goodness that surrounds you.

I give you the Amulet as an act of conviction that I am who I say I am –

Return the Amulet to me if you find I am worthy

for I have a job to be done... show me the way.

Once you have read the verse you will be prompted to send the Amulet back. On its return you will clearly know who the Enforcer is.

I was a little confused as to why Sara did not come out and name Victor as my Enforcer. I was still convinced it was Victor, even though he claimed not to have the markings of an Enforcer. It was true that I had not seen them either, but I couldn't envision anyone else I could possibly trust, especially among the handful of vampires I'd met. It had to be Victor; it just had to be.

As usual, the journal left me with many questions, like how would I be summoned to return the Amulet? Where would I be and what would I be doing when the call arrived? I hoped it would come at an opportune time.

I spent the rest of the day the lazy way, trying to relax. Victor called me later on that night after his class. He was still at the school, with a small group of his students who were staying late to finish a project. He asked what I had been up to all day. I just sighed and truthfully told him, "Nothing."

"That's good to hear, I guess. You sound bored," Victor pointed out. I could hear laughter in the background. "Hey guys, I'm on the phone. Keep it down, okay? We're here to get this done," Victor belted out away from the mouthpiece.

I giggled a little at his effort to keep the students in line. " I am bored," I replied to his comment. "First day of vacation and I'm climbing the walls. Not used to sitting around, I guess. I never even left here today."

"Excellent. You need a few days like that. Do you feel stressed out?" he asked, pleased with hearing how insignificant the events of my day were.

"Not stressed, just restless. Do you think you'll be able to drop by later? I'm kind of feeling, well, you know. I thought maybe we could; I mean, you and me..." I stammered, not sure how to let him know how vulnerable I was feeling.

"Well..." he stumbled over the idea at first, but then caught himself. "That would be nice. I'm not sure when I'm getting out of here, especially at the pace these guys are working."

"I figured as much," I said, my disappointment showing.

"Now, don't get upset; I'm just busy here at school. I'm picking up all these projects in the middle and trying to get the students on track. It's taking more time than I thought," Victor explained, trying to keep his tone mild.

"I know. I hear the rowdy group of scholars behind you," I said, my voice light.

"Listen Kala; we are bound to end up together this weekend, after your Battle of the Bands. You can come to my place or I'll stay at yours – deal?" he bargained, quickly planning our rendezvous.

"Okay, I can wait," I agreed to his proposal.

"All right. Let me go. I need to help finish here and clean up. I'll talk to you soon, I promise," Victor spoke quickly, preoccupied with the voices in the classroom calling his name behind him.

I smiled. He was needed by others too, not just me. "Okay, take care."

"Good night," he whispered, in a way that made me think he really did want to be with me tonight.

Chapter 36

It's funny how when there is nothing to do, you resort to sleep. It's not like I needed it; I felt fully rested from doing nothing all day. I thought of other things that I could have been doing, but then again I did not want to do them alone. So sleep it was, something you could do by yourself and not even know it.

I must have been sleeping soundly because my awakening was abrupt. I'm not even sure why I woke up. I just know that suddenly I was sitting bolt up right in bed, overwhelmed with a sense of foreboding; a feeling of anxiousness, like when you've overslept and missed something important. I had an unmistakable sensation of obligation, that I needed to be doing something other than sleeping, something productive and necessary. I sat silent and still in the dark, waiting for the feeling to subside. I told myself it was late and I had the day off, go back to sleep, it was okay, but no amount of mental talk helped. Every time I placed my head on the pillow I found myself back in a sitting position, beyond my physical control, like a field mouse going for the cheese each time I set off the trap, snapping me back to attention.

Okay, I thought to myself. I will stop fighting *it*. This must be *the sign*. The Amulet was trying to tell me something. If not the Amulet, well, something wants to be noticed. It was not Sara. This was something new.

As I got dressed I glanced down at my chest where the Amulet dangled on its chain. The center stone pulsed and faded from its natural dark color to a dull grayish tone. When I tried to resist the feeling of leaving my home the stone's colors changed rapidly – dark, light, dark, light. When I acknowledged the Amulet and allowed myself to feel its power, and the urgency to return to the Old Maple Forest, the Amulet's stone went dark and quiet. It was obvious what I had to do; just as Sara stated; the Amulet was directing me to return to the Old Maple Forest. Against my better judgment, I grabbed Sara's journal and left.

It wasn't long before I was driving in the main entrance of the Old Maple Forest. The parking lot was dark and empty, with just an inadequate halogen fixture throwing a ghastly yellow light over part of the lot, and a pay phone over in the far corner. I was not sure how I'd make it into the woods without tripping over my own two feet or anything else that crossed my path, even with the flashlight I found in my glove box. "This is crazy," I mumbled to myself as I opened the car door, plucking the journal off the seat next to me.

I reluctantly slammed the door shut, the noise deafening in the quiet night. It sent a shiver up my spine. I was already full of jitters and anxiety. I tried to shake it off, needing to keep my mind focused. I had to enter the forest and make my way to the natural altar as quickly as possible, for the sooner I completed my unknown task, the sooner I could go home. Clutching the journal to my chest, I started out.

Once I entered the forest, every disturbing thought, experience and story I had ever heard about the Forest sprang to mind. I wondered briefly if it was my sensitive state of mind that gave the stories a knee-weakening power over me, or whether a higher power was doing it to sabotage what composure I was able to put together. It was difficult to fight the thoughts and concentrate on my footing. Blue Daemons were the first thought that entered my head; their bluish aura could be spotted at a distance, especially in darkness like tonight. I wondered if any would show up while I was here alone all by myself. At least I had the spell with me to get rid of them; it worked before. It would more than likely work again.

In the next few moments as I slowly made my way forward, I noticed how quiet the night had become. I looked up towards the sky a few times seeing only blackness with no significant signs of light at all. It gave me a feeling of disorientation, perhaps what pilots might feel when they get caught in a fog and can not distinguish sky from ground without properly reading their instrument panels, a horrible feeling, I'm sure.

I began to question whether I was walking on soil or not. I know that sounds stupid; where else would I be walking? If I had any instruments to consult I would have done so just to prove to myself I knew up from down. I fought the sensation of being suspended in mid air like a bat hanging from a branch. I would have given just about anything to have been that bat as I struggled through the darkness, to be able to see as well, and hear as well. It was probably all in my head but it made my journey just that more difficult. The dark tunnel I was navigating finally ended and I could see some signs of evening light, the moon and the stars, penetrating the leaves that hung thick and high above me. Their light shown down with an eerie, silvery-blue hue which made the warm and humid night appear to be cold and raw. With the solid darkness of the night behind me I could see a slight clearing ahead – the Natural Altar.

I sighed loudly; relieved I'd made it this far and not thinking of the return trek home. As I approached the area of the altar I noticed some flickering golden lights that lent a warm visual glow to the clearing. I saw that someone, or something, had been there before me. There were several large bamboo torches that surrounded both altars. The large altar was covered with a purple cloth; a pentacle, cup, bell, crystal and cauldron placed on it. In the cauldron some herbs were burning; the sweet smoke drifted lazily by me. The smaller altar had a white cloth over it, with some leaves, twigs and feathers scattered on top. I walked behind the larger altar so I was facing the North and set Sara's Journal on it, opening it up to the pages I would need to read to perform the ceremony that the Amulet had brought me here for.

I let myself stand at the altar for several moments feeling safe. It was a pleasant feeling after my fearful, confusing walk through the darkness. Finally, I felt as prepared as I ever would to begin the ritual; the ritual that would send the Amulet back to its world and show me who the Enforcer was.

I read the following phrase out of the journal as Sara had instructed, while removing the Amulet from my neck and keeping it in my closed hand. "*I hold the power before you. I request you allow me to keep it, I am strong, I am faithful, and I am bound to the goodness that surrounds you. I give you the Amulet as an act of conviction that I am who I say I am. Return the Amulet to me if you find I am worthy for I have a job to be done – show me the way.*"

I continued to hold the Amulet, unwilling to release it, yet unsure of how it would make the transition back to where it had come from. Suddenly, the surface of the altar collapsed into nothingness, taking with it all the things that had been lying on top. Fortunately, I had kept a hand on the journal, so I was able to snatch it back quickly. I looked down into what now appeared to be a black hole that led down to – what? I carefully set Sara's Journal down on the second altar and gently placed my free hand above the blackness in the center of the large altar. The air that rose out of the darkness was cool and damp. Turning the palm of my hand over I could see a fine layer of moisture had adhered to it. I poked my finger gingerly into the hole, then pulled back. I still had five fingers – what was this all about? I opened my other hand that had been clenched shut to take a thoughtful look at the Amulet, to see if it had any guiding wisdom. As I opened my fingers the Amulet nearly leapt out on its own. I caught it just shy of dropping into the dark hole. My heart beat quickly as my fingers curled firmly around the Amulet. "That was close," I mumbled, my heart still up around my throat.

From within my hand I could feel the Amulet begin to pulsate like a pager that was set to vibrate. I was being called; something wanted my attention. Perhaps the Amulet's way home was the black hole and I was preventing it from returning. I carefully opened my hand again, this time allowing the chain to stay securely in my palm and letting only the Amulet loose. I held the Amulet over the altar and felt a steady pull from beneath, coming from the hole of darkness. Something definitely wanted possession of the Amulet. But was it the Amulet that wanted to go into the hole or was it something in the black hole that wanted *it*? I could not tell. I wasn't sure I ever could.

I took a deep breath and made my final decision; I would let the Amulet go, let it plummet into the dark hole, not knowing if it would return or not. I closed my eyes tightly and allowed the Amulet to hang freely from my fingers, feeling the energy of the hole pull at it, then finally let it silently drop out of sight. My immediate reaction was to dive in after it; I had made a terrible mistake; I never should have let it go, but it was too late.

Several moments passed. I held the journal in my hand, flipping pages and trying to make more sense out of what was still to come. The journal did not say how the Amulet would return to me. I looked around the clearing, at the burning torches, for an answer I knew I would not find. Would the Amulet drop out of the sky? Would it come back through the black hole to my world? How would I know the Enforcer if it weren't Victor? I had no way of knowing, and I had too many questions.

"Looking for something?" A man's voice, clear and sudden, came out of the darkness, startling me so badly I stumbled backwards, away from the altar. I placed my hand against my chest, feeling my heart thundering wildly. I had been so engrossed on the Amulet that I had not been unaware of his approach. It took me a moment to realize the voice was familiar – Nathan.

"What are you doing here?" I gasped as I regained my balance and returned to the altar, blocking his view of the black hole.

"What are *you* doing here?" he repeated coldly, taking several stiff strides in my direction.

I had never seen him dressed so casually before. I didn't think he even owned a pair of jeans, let alone a pair of very worn ones, faded almost white. My eyes scanned his appearance from head to toe again, intrigued by his new look. I saw immediately that he was not wearing his wire framed glasses; without them he looked so – so *average.* Even his shirt wasn't tucked in, but instead hung loosely around his hips. I wasn't sure if it was his clothes, the light, or what, but Nathan looked *different*, younger, perhaps, but I just wasn't sure.

"So, what are you doing?" Nathan asked again, glancing at me, to the altar, and back again.

"Nothing, really," I replied quickly. I had no idea why he was here. I wondered if he had followed me. "Am I in danger or something? Why are you here?" Nervously, I looked around the clearing, anxiously scanning for signs of Blue Daemons – or worse.

"You really have no idea, do you?" he asked in astonishment, taking his hands out of his pockets and walking closer to me.

I stiffened defensively at his approach. Of course I had no idea what he was doing here – in the middle of a forest during the darkest part of night. Obviously he must have followed me. Why? I asked myself. An answer suddenly occurred to me; but no, that couldn't be it.

"No," I finally spoke aloud. "No."

"Why? Why no?" Nathan asked steadily, planting himself in front of me.

I looked deeply into his eyes and mutely shook my head at what I saw in them. Without another word he opened his hand to show me the Amulet nestled snuggly in his palm. "You are here for this," he said. "I'm bringing it to you."

I gawked at the Amulet in his hand. "How did you get that? Where did you find it?" I asked accusingly, as if he had stolen my property.

"Let's just say *it* found me," Nathan replied, closing his long fingers around the Amulet securely.

"So, what does this mean?" I inquired. "You can't be..." I left my words hanging in the air, unspoken, although my meaning was clear.

"I can't be what? Say it. An Enforcer?" Nathan snapped. "It's not like I want to be here tonight with you."

"I'm sure. So why are you?" I retorted.

"Because I was chosen. Like you; I was chosen. Not much of a choice." His irritation was evident in the tone of his voice.

"What about Victor?" I asked challengingly. I was convinced Victor was my Enforcer; he would be my ally and my protector; he would bring me back my Amulet, not Nathan. I did not want it to be Nathan. How horrible.

"What about Victor?" Nathan asked crossly.

"He is the Enforcer – not you!" I shot at him.

My comment made Nathan chuckle faintly. "Victor – why him?" he asked in amusement.

I sighed, distraught. "You read what Sara wrote in her journal about the Enforcers, and how the one that would help me had such an awful existence from the moment he took the dark gift, how damned he was. It was Victor; when I read it all I could think about was Victor," I tried to explain, frustrated at the change in events.

"It's not Victor. How can I make you believe otherwise?" Nathan asked, looking up into the night's sky as if searching the heavens for the indisputable answer. He lowered his eyes and walked over to the altar, stopping only momentarily to show me the Amulet, which hung freely from his fingers, then let it plunge back into the void where I'd sent it originally.

I took two quick steps to the side of the altar and looked in. The blackness was total and I saw no sign of the Amulet. "What did you go and do that for?" I barked. "I don't know how to get it back!" I glared at him angrily.

Nathan looked at me and calmly replied, "Me, neither."

"Idiot."

"Just shut up and watch," Nathan spoke shortly and raised his hands so that they were cupped open and empty under the night sky. I watched his hands as he stood there, motionless. There was no sound except our breathing, which sounded harsh to my ears. Suddenly, soundlessly, the Amulet was back in Nathan's hands, secure once more.

"Do you believe me now?" he asked expressionlessly.

"But all that Sara wrote; it sounded like Victor," I stammered in disbelief. I had believed for so long it was him and had not even seriously considered it to be any one else.

"It probably does describe Victor's life; probably others, even mine," Nathan agreed, thinking back to what he read and how he interpreted Sara's words.

I went back to shaking my head 'no' again. "What about the markings?" I asked suddenly, remembering each Enforcer had a special mark, somewhere on their body.

Nathan nodded knowingly. "The inverted V with the crossing C. Yes. As Emissary, if you want to see it, all you have to do is ask and I have to willingly show it to you."

"Show me," I demanded, my voice suddenly hard.

"Very well," he acquiesced and handed the Amulet back to me.

He turned around and tugged his shirt over his head, exposing his slender back. He stood patiently for my inspection, clearly comfortable with the situation. "I take it you see it clearly," Nathan said dryly, referring to the brand of the Enforcer.

He was right. The markings Sara spoke of were very obvious to me – to anyone who saw it. Perhaps this explained why he wore mostly dark colors for fear any light colors pressed against his body would give him away. I approached Nathan slowly and touched the smooth pale skin where the markings were; they resembled tattoos and were perfectly located between his shoulder blades. Wondering if it was some sort of hoax, and they had perhaps been recently placed on him with magic marker, I pressed my fingertips firmly against the dark lines of the V and C, checking my skin to see if the ink had smeared. It did not appear to be magic marker or anything freshly added to Nathan's body these identifiable shapes; the inverted V with a C crossing through it had been with him for a long time. He was an Enforcer.

"I see," I said lightly. He was who he was. I had to accept that now, I guessed.

"You must do something now that you have seen the mark of the Enforcer," Nathan said, looking back over his shoulder at me.

"What?"

"You must take the Amulet and place it on my back between the inverted V so the Amulet fits wholly inside it. Once you do, hold the Amulet by the stone only," he instructed, then turned his face away. "Stone only," he repeated.

"Why?" I asked curiously.

"Just do it," he ordered without further explanation.

It was a simple request and I only needed to take a step towards him to place the Amulet against his back and maneuver it so that it fit within the inverted V. I did so, then pressed the piece firmly against his skin. Once I had the Amulet in place, holding it by the stone, it began to singe and burn itself into Nathan's back. "Oh my God!" I gasped and tried desperately to pry the Amulet off of him, burning my own fingertips in the process. The Amulet was so hot it smoked against Nathan's white skin like ember shot from a bonfire. "Nathan! Nathan! I'm sorry!" I gasped as I tried to pull the Amulet from his skin. Finally the Amulet fell loose and tumbled to the ground at my feet. I bent down and picked it up by the chain, which was cool to the touch, although the Amulet was still glowing with amber heat.

"Nathan, are you okay? I'm so sorry. What happened?" I was so concerned about his injury my anger was forgotten. I draped the chain of the Amulet around my wrist.

"Just give me a minute! Just back off!" His voice was tight with pain as he struggled to regain his composure. Not only could I hear the agony in his voice, but I could also feel a swell of pure pain escape him. It passed through me like a blast of cold air, stirring my consciousness and awakening my senses. I remembered my talent for healing those I'd inflicted pain upon. Would it work now with Nathan?

I gently touched Nathan's shoulder as I slowly moved behind him. I saw the impression the Amulet had left on his back, the edges curled and red, the center still smoking slightly. I winced thinking about the level of agony he must be in.

I placed my hands on either side of his rib cage; his skin felt cool and clammy. I leaned forward and placed my lips on his shoulder blade and began slowly tracing a path towards the terrible wound.

"Kala, don't." I heard his voice say weakly.

Ignoring him, I continued my slow kiss. As I felt the edge of the wound pass my lips, I opened my mouth and allowed my tongue to gently lick the heat and pain away. Nathan's body trembled slightly with the sudden sensation of his hot-blistered skin cooling so rapidly. I calmly ran my hands from his sides around to his stomach feeling the tightness of his abdominal muscles contract in apprehension under my touch. My fingers grazed over the line of fine body hair that ran from his navel to his chest.

"Kala," he moaned, but didn't stop my hands. He kept his eyes closed.

I continued to lick his burns, the warm wetness of my tongue making short work of his pain. Nathan did not fight me as I worked; he knew my ability to heal was a natural one, but he instinctively struggled with my physical human presence, not wanting me near him, touching him, feeling him. I could sense an uneasiness that I had not felt from him before, as if I had found and seen his weaker side. A side that was vulnerable, that hurt. A more human side than he may have thought he had. As much as he hated my touch, my soft hands upon his body, he could not remember the last time he had felt something like that.

"Finish," he hissed warningly between clenched teeth, my touch finally too much to take.

I rubbed his stomach softly, paying no attention to him or the creature that resided within. His burn was gone, but the scar of the Amulet would remain forever embedded on his back, entwined with the mark of the Enforcer.

I had just decided to let Nathan be, to allow his temper to simmer down as his burn had. But before I could release him, he attacked. His threshold of pain, annoyance, and anger had reached its peak. In lashing out, I was the first solid object he found. I could feel his body quickly jerk and twist to the left, raising his right arm to strike me. I dropped to my knees, holding my left arm up to block his blow. I bowed my body and turned my head, waiting for the impact that never came. I slowly looked up, uncertain what the next move should be.

"Nathan," I spoke softly with my left arm still raised defensively above me. I was afraid to lower it as I could see Nathan had stopped his attack in mid-stride, and now stood over me with his right arm frozen in a striking manner.

"I should have known," he growled under his breath, his eyes hot with anger.

I staggered to my feet and timidly rose in front of him, lowering my left arm and feeling the chain of the Amulet slip down around my wrist again. I had forgotten I still had it.

"What?" My voice shook nervously as I watched his curled fist.

"I can't touch you," he said bitterly, withdrawing.

"Why?" I questioned, watching him put his shirt back on.

He pointed irritably at my arm with the Amulet swaying from it as his head poked out of the collar of the shirt. “The Amulet. I can’t hurt you. It won’t allow me to.”

I took the Amulet from my arm and held it up. The stone was a bright green. “It changed colors. Why?” I asked looking at Nathan who was straightening himself up from his fit of anger.

“Just put it back on. We have to get out of here,” Nathan spoke shortly.

I did as he asked. “But I want to talk to you,” I pleaded.

Nathan grabbed me by the arm. “We aren’t safe here any more. We need to leave.” He tugged me to follow him.

I grabbed Sara’s Journal off the smaller altar. I needed to put the torches out and clean up. “But what about all this –“

”It will be taken care of. Come on. Follow me. I’ll get you out of here,” Nathan snapped. He seemed anxious to leave and wanted no resistance.

With Nathan’s nocturnal eyesight, our progress out of the forest was rapid. We reached the parking lot in only a few moments.

“I have so many questions to ask you,” I gasped, out of breath but still walking to the car. Nathan was now several paces in front of me. “Are we safe now?”

Nathan turned to me. “Safer,” he replied.

“Let me ask you something then.” I jogged up even with him. He turned around and continued to walk towards my car. “Nathan, can we talk?” I asked.

Ignoring me, Nathan kept walking as I followed. He opened up the driver’s side door – a hint for me to leave.

“I can’t. Not yet,” I begged him.

“You are right. We must talk. But not here. Not tonight. Soon.” He was curt and eager to send me on my way. “Leave now. Please.” He guided me around the car door and pushed me in. “You will be safe if you leave now.”

“What about you?” I asked, starting the car and looking up in his direction.

“I’ll be fine.” He shut my door and backed away. “Go. Now.”

I frowned and tossed Sara’s Journal on the passenger seat. I put the car in gear and drove away, thinking there was no sense in arguing with a Vampire; they would always live long enough to prove you wrong.

Chapter 37

I could not believe Nathan sent me on my way without filling me in. I knew nothing, nothing other than he was the Enforcer that Sara spoke of. What was Victor, then? I couldn't picture him as having no major role in this storyline that was playing out. After all, he knew me even before *I* knew me. He found *me* – in a world of countless people, he found *me* – that must account for something, doesn't it? It couldn't have been an accident, could it?

I had so many questions for Nathan about me, about what was happening, and what he knew about Sara and all she represented that I even began to wonder about Nathan himself. After all, I had never really given a second thought to him. His life interested me now, where it hadn't before. He was such a mystery that I knew there had to be some sort of phenomenal story behind him, how he came to be, all he had done and seen – his life as an Enforcer.

What I did know was that I needed to see Nathan, to talk with him, and I wasn't up to explaining why to Victor. I just couldn't deal with his questions or any type of attitude right now. Since he was away in the evenings with his classes, I figured I could take a chance and go directly to the lion's den, Nathan's home. I had no idea how he would react to my arrival, but I felt I had no choice. We needed to meet, and tonight I would make it happen. I waited impatiently for the day to end, the sunlight to fade from the sky. As night descended, I drove to meet my Enforcer.

I parked on the street and slowly walked up the sidewalk to the house. My nerves were jangling, and I took a deep breath of the thick, humid air, trying to calm myself. As I reached the porch of the Victorian the distant but distinct sound of thunder rolled from miles away, warning inclement weather was coming.

I stood silently outside the front door, trying to determine that the only person home was Nathan. I was fairly certain the only presence I felt came from the first floor of the house. I pushed open the door, then shut it behind me, hearing the solid click of its closing echo softly off the dark walls. I took several steps towards Nathan's door and hesitated, uncertain about how to make my approach. I decided to reach out with my mind and contact him before knocking on his door, whether to show respect or put us on an even playing field, I wasn't sure. I just thought it was the right thing to do, at least, I hoped it was the right thing to do.

'Nathan – it's Kala. Can we talk?' I sent my message as clearly as I

could, staring at the dark piece of lumber that stood in the way of my answers.

The door quietly opened, although no one was there. I walked in, trying to appear calm; feeling little jolts of fear in the pit of my stomach, a feeling Nathan often left me with. "Nathan!" I called loudly; the room was much too quiet for me.

'When I said we had to talk soon, I didn't mean this soon,' Nathan's voice rang in my head laced with irritation.

"I'm sorry," I responded. "I have so many questions." I closed the door behind me and waited.

'Have a seat,' Nathan ordered tersely.

I did. I sat on the edge of the leather couch near the center of the room with my arms crossed nervously, my uneasiness overpowering me. My eyes scanned the room, adjusting to the dim lighting and absorbing all the little details I had not noticed before. His reading materials, magazines, books and newspapers, were piled on the floor next to his chair. His cigarettes were spilled carelessly on the end table, and there was an open bottle of some type of liqueur out on the bar, with an empty glass next to it.

I heard footsteps approaching from the back hallway and straightened instinctively as I turned to face the door. Nathan entered the room and our eyes met, his unreadable and mine fearful. He was buttoning the cuffs of his shirtsleeves and tucking the hem into dark blue pants, his hair still wet from a shower. His face showed no expression as he walked by me to the bar.

"I was expecting you," he said. "I knew you did not have the patience to wait for long." He poured himself a glass of the liqueur, then turned to me inquiringly. "Would you care for a drink? I have wine, or diet soda if you prefer."

"A glass of wine would be fine, thank you," I answered politely.

Nathan filled a crystal glass with a dark red wine, then handed it to me. As I accepted it, he moved to the chair opposite me. He set his drink on the small antique table next to him and reached for his cigarettes. Wordlessly, he lit one, then sat back and inhaled. He crossed one leg over his knee, then exhaled two streams of blue smoke from his nostrils, all the while looking steadily at me. I felt the tension rising in me as I endured his perusal. Finally, I had had enough.

"This has to stop," I said forcefully, refusing to let his silence intimidate me.

He raised an eyebrow but remained docile as he reached for his drink. "Really? And what would that be?"

"This stress between us. It should not be. I don't want to fear you, to be so nervous around you," I said honestly. I tried to make my voice calm.

"Well then, why do you fear me?" Nathan asked, his tone mild. "Did I do something to make you fear me?"

"Oh, no, just the usual," I replied sarcastically. "Like trying to take my head off last night at the altar."

Nathan sipped his beverage and shrugged. "I tried to warn you last night, but it's funny how humans never listen when they are spoken to. I was very clear with you. You chose not to listen."

"I was only trying to help," I snapped defensively. "I don't even know why I did. You are habitually nasty."

"Was I so nasty the night I held your dying body in my arms? Was that what you thought then?" Nathan asked, sitting up in his chair and stabbing his cigarette out in the ashtray.

I narrowed my eyes, remembering the pain and terror of that night. It seemed so long ago. So much had happened since. "I remember how you helped me. I'm grateful you let me live instead of going with your alternate plan," I conceded.

"Not much of a plan if you remember," Nathan sighed, thinking back to the night in question. A flash of lightening blazed outside the heavily draped window beside us, illuminating the edges of the fabric.

"Let's just forget the past," I suggested quietly. "We can't let what's done get in our way now. If I'm correct in my thinking, there is a lot ahead of us and we can't afford to have any animosity between us. That is why I'm here."

"You are correct," Nathan affirmed. "There is much ahead of us. I know you came here seeking answers. I have some, but others we will learn together."

"Then all I ask is that you tell me what you can. It must be more than I know now," I asked plaintively.

"Yes, I would think that would be so. But you also have to do the same for me if I ask you a question," Nathan responded quickly.

"I'll answer if I can," I replied truthfully, wondering what kind of information I could have that would be of any use to him. He had already read Sara's journal and in my mind that put him light years ahead of me.

He nodded. "Good."

"So where do we start?" I asked, taking a deep breath and clicking my fingernails against the side of my glass thoughtfully.

"Let me start by saying you are still in danger, maybe more so than ever before," Nathan warned.

"Well, that's nothing new," I sighed, although my heart fluttered at his words.

"I'm quite serious," Nathan said. "I am not confident you are safe at all any more and I am not sure what I can do about it, if anything."

"Why do you think this?" I asked; swallowing hard and trying to keep the fear inside me smothered.

"Your name has come up in conversation recently, and it concerns the Amulet. You know from Sara's journal that there is a lot of power that comes with it, power that many people covet and have been trying to possess for years. Since the Amulet has surfaced again, there are those who would stop at nothing to get it. Though possession is no guarantee the power will follow the wearer," Nathan said solemnly.

"What do you mean? Why?" I asked, trying to follow him.

"The Amulet is a power in its own right. But it's also a piece to a puzzle, if you will, and when the pieces to the puzzle are put together the power of the Amulet grows. Whoever is wearing the Amulet becomes the universe for that power; all power is channeled from the Amulet to that person. I know it's hard for you to imagine how much power that can be, but it's a lot. If the person who has the Amulet is skilled in using their power and the power of the Amulet together, then literal Hell can, and will, break loose," Nathan paused and sipped his drink, then continued. "You noticed last night the stone of the Amulet had changed colors. That is natural when the Amulet has been *charged.* The charge happened when you placed the Amulet against my back on the symbol of the Enforcer. I am a piece of the puzzle just as you are and last night those two pieces were united. The Amulet rose to another level last night. Many who are watching *you* from a distance have been waiting for the change in the Amulet to take place. Now that it has happened, I fear that you are in a greater danger than before. The problem is that the Amulet can be taken from you only with your permission or by me physically removing it from you. The Amulet will protect itself from anyone else who tries to remove it from your neck. No one must know that *I* have that power to be able to remove the Amulet from you. No one must know that *I* am the one who charged the Amulet either, for if people find out, too many other things are at risk, including lives. We do not want this to happen. I must not be connected yet."

"Then how do I protect myself from these people who want it?" I asked him. My words were almost drowned out in a crescendo of thunder as the storm's intensity grew.

"The Amulet will protect itself, and you to a degree, until *you* learn how to control the Amulet. Our concern is to keep you from getting into a situation where these people might try to hurt you and cause you to use the Amulet for their designs," Nathan said. "This is not going to be easy. But if they know I am also involved they will try to use me against you, and that's not good. A unification of sorts took place last night when you branded me with the Amulet; now my job is to safeguard you at all costs."

"I can't imagine how happy that must make you," I said sarcastically, trying to make light of his words.

He ignored my poor attempt at humor. "Victor may feel he needs to protect you. He wants to protect you. I on the other hand *have* to protect you. It's not a choice I have, it's my obligation," Nathan said flatly.

"Why are you obligated? Why should you even care about what happens to me? Can't someone like Victor, who does care, protect me? I'd sure feel safer with someone who cares about *me*, rather than someone who could care less, someone who's just doing their *job!"* I said hotly. "Don't do me any favors!"

"Don't consider this a favor. As I said, it's an obligation. Just like you have no obvious choice other than to accept your role as Emissary, some day I will have no other choice but to protect you the best that I can. Your destiny is entwined with mine," Nathan spoke as if my words hadn't affected him. "I have the blood line of the original Enforcers in my veins, beings who were reborn to kill and fight and survive any way they could in conditions most people could never conceive possible. I am at least three times the warrior Victor could ever hope to be. I taught him all I know. He's good, he's strong and he's bigger than I am but I have a proficiency that he will never have."

"If you have this blood of the Enforcer, and you are so strong, why is Victor not as strong as you?" I couldn't understand why Victor wasn't more important than Nathan was saying. After all, he'd become important to *me.*

Nathan looked at me silently, as if deciding something. He stood and picked his glass up, then wordlessly reached out for mine. I gave it to him and watched as he went to the bar, refilled our glasses and returned. I thanked him and waited as he sat back down. He looked at me with tired eyes as he sipped his drink. I almost felt sympathy for him, a human emotion for an inhuman being.

"What's wrong?" I asked quietly.

He sipped from his glass again before speaking. "Perhaps you should go now," he said expressionlessly.

"Why?" I prodded. "Obviously you have something to tell me. I know it's important, otherwise you wouldn't bother. Why are you afraid to tell me?" Nathan remained tight-lipped, staring down at his fingers as they cradled his drink. "Please, Nathan," I pleaded. "Don't hold back on me. I don't care what it concerns. Just tell me. I have a right to know, especially if it has to do with Victor!"

His dark eyes turned to mine and he looked steadily at me, taking in my distress as he made up his mind. He reached for his cigarettes, lit another and finally said, "What I am about to tell you must never go any further than you. Only one other person knows what I am going to recount to you. As I am bound to you; you must do the same for me and you must respect my wish to never repeat what I will say to you."

I nodded. "Of course."

Nathan continued seriously, "You must also use your skill to put what I will tell you as far and as deep out of your conscious mind as possible so that no one will find it. No one, especially not Victor." His eyes flashed a warning I could not ignore.

"Yes. I will," I replied sincerely.

The steady roar of the storm outside filled the room. Rain beat brutally against the windowpanes as if discharged from a fire hose. The noise of the downpour distracted Nathan for a moment, but by the time he finished his cigarette he appeared focused again, eager to tell his story now that he'd made the decision to do so.

"Perhaps things that did not make sense to you before will make sense to you now," he began. He stubbed out his cigarette and sipped his drink thoughtfully. "I know Victor has had lengthy talks with you about his life, his human one, and the one after. Rest assured his stories are all true. His stories are just has he remembers them to be, but I have stories too. I have stories of Victor as a human, and after the dark gift; not just my side of his stories, but elements to his stories that he is not even aware he has missed. There is no way for him to know because he knows no better; he has no recollection."

"You mean he has no memory of events?" I asked curiously. "His stories seem to be seamless. There are no gaps. He has no trouble telling them." I held my wine glass but was too intent on Nathan to drink.

"For lack of a better explanation that's correct. He has no memory of *one* particular event that took place in his life, and that is my fault," Nathan confessed.

"What event is that?" I asked.

"For you to understand completely I need to explain some things that led up to the event," Nathan said evenly. The howl of the wind outside and the electrifying snap of the lightening gave an eerie emphasis to his words. His eyes grew narrow in thought and distant memories. For a moment he looked younger than I'd ever seen, the look of a confessor again touching him with human qualities. I had began to suspect the story revolved around his role in Victor's change, and realized that Nathan carried a burden of guilt for some reason, and had for over two hundred years.

"You can tell me, Nathan," I assured him quietly. "If you can tell anybody, surely you can trust me."

He nodded slightly as I spoke. "I knew someday I would be telling this to you. My worry is that the story will get to Victor, and it must not. At all costs, it must not. You care for him, I know, and I fear your human emotions will be transparent to him."

I looked down into my lap as I answered. "Nathan, I can't help who I am or what I will become. I also can't help whom I love, but if you and I are supposed to be united and work together, what good does it do either of us if we can't trust the other? Whatever Sara has planned for me apparently involves you, and in order for her plan to work you need to tell me these truths. You must!" As I finished, I looked directly at him. He was staring at me in the strangest way, as if he was not just looking at me, but looking into me. I could feel the icy tendrils of his intrusion within my mind, a sensation that was becoming all too familiar to me. A chill went up my back.

"Why are you doing this?" I asked him. "What are you looking for?" A deafening clap of thunder shook the floor under my body and with it a bright white burst of lightening that touched down somewhere close by. The house went black. Electricity was lost. I sat in the darkness with Nathan, still upset with his action.

Nathan warned flatly, "Stay where you are. I'll light some candles."

I could hear him get up and rise to his feet, brushing by me as he went to the bar. "You can see in this, can't you?" I asked suddenly.

"Yes," he said shortly, his voice floating over from behind me.

"Figures," I muttered, more to myself than to him.

I heard the unmistakable strike of a kitchen match followed by the orange flame that danced on the tip of the stick. Nathan lit a large green candle and brought it back, setting it on the table next to me. Its warm glow seemed so small in the dark room and the flame sputtered fitfully now and then, as if overwhelmed by the storms both outside and in. He sat back down and resumed his conversation as if we'd not been interrupted.

"You think you are so strong, Kala. So strong and capable and you have no idea what you are up against. You are going to have to build a wall in your mind, one that you can hide behind in times of trouble. Make no mistake, there will be trouble. Hear what I have to say, and you will understand." The icy sensation returned as he reiterated his warning in my mind, as if to underscore his words. '*Listen to me now Kala – you will understand.*'

I sat in the glow of the candle, trying not to let Nathan see he'd scared me. I hated the effect his words had on me, hated the way he'd warned me. I was so tired of being scared and uncertain, and I knew I had to hear his story if I was to have a chance at all. I waited, grimly determined to get what I'd come for.

"I met Victor when he was human," Nathan began. "I had settled for a short time in his town. It was small and quiet, which is just what I needed at the time. I would see him in the distance at night at the local Pub where all humans of the time would gather and talk and socialize. He was an attractive man, just as he is now, always with people around him, his good looks grabbing the women's attention. One night while I was sitting alone, Victor came to my table, offered me a drink and sat with me. I had always sat alone, and he knew that. He said he thought I could use the company, that I had been in the Pub alone too long, and it didn't look right. Everyone needs a friend. That's what he told me. So we spent the evening talking and drinking." Nathan's eyes brightened as he relived that evening. "I had never made it a practice to befriend humans as you know, but given the size of the town, and the fact that I still consumed human blood regularly, I thought it best to make at least *one* friend, and a doctor was a figure to befriend. Victor and I would meet nightly at the Pub, have dinner and drink, talk. He is wonderful with conversation, very open and easy to talk to, even with me." Nathan seemed mystified with the fact that Victor had such a gift. "One night he surprised me by asking to turn him into what I was! I asked him 'And what would that be?' He replied quite seriously, 'A vampire."

Nathan shook his head as he recalled the night, still bemused at Victor's words, even after all this time. "I was floored! I listened to him tell me in exact detail what I would have to do to him in order to make *him* like *me*." Nathan tugged at his chin in thought. "Victor told me that he knew I was different. He said he was not sure how at first, but he was curious enough to pull out some old books and do some research in his free time. It took him many weeks before he was certain, but once he was he confronted me. Of course I denied the accusations. I told him he had had too much to drink; he was not thinking clearly, and that he needed to go home and get to bed."

"But he didn't let it drop, did he?" I asked, sipping my wine.

"No. Not Victor. He would meet up with me nightly, no matter where I was. He would hunt *me* down like I was the prey. He would find me and hound me. He never stopped. It became an obsession for him. Naturally, I continued to deny his allegations. But one night, he came to my house, something he had never dared before. He was upset and crying. He told me that Nerissa, his love, was dying and nothing could save her. He said he wanted the gift of eternal life so he could pass it on to her, and he needed it right *then*, or she would not even have strength to feed from him to complete the rebirth." Nathan shifted in the chair and continued. "Perhaps I was softer then than I am now, but I could see the desperation in his eyes and I knew how deeply he loved her. He wanted nothing more than to give her life, and when being a doctor was not good enough, he began to search elsewhere for possibilities. I guess I admired that in him, that unselfishness."

I nodded in understanding. That fit with the Victor I knew.

"Although I continued to deny the fact I was a Vampire, I told Victor to come back later in the night to my home and he and I would talk some more," Nathan paused as he lit another cigarette and sipped his drink.

"And he came back to see you," I said.

"Yes," Nathan said quietly, studying the smoldering end of his cigarette. "He came knocking. When I answered the door he looked scared. I'll share that with you, he looked like a man who was staring death in the eyes – and he was. But he walked right in, said hello, and suggested we get started. He didn't want to talk. He had come for a reason. He was sure of what I was." Nathan went silent for a moment and his face looked tired. "I tried to talk him out of what he wanted, what he thought he wanted. He was too stubborn to listen to reason; he wanted that one thing too badly."

"Why did you try and talk him out of it? I would think that you would want what Victor asked of you," I said in confusion, staring at him in the candle's flickering glow.

"Perhaps in most cases. I only tried to talk Victor out of it because even though I knew he loved Nerissa and her time was growing near, he would eventually get past her death. He would mourn of course, but whether it took six months, a year or maybe longer, he would move on. He was a doctor. He understood death. His life would continue. I tried to make Victor see that. I failed." Nathan's voice was almost a whisper, as if he was making a confession about something that was his fault alone.

"So you did what he asked of you; you made him what he is now," I stated.

Nathan took a puff on his cigarette then rolled the ashes around in the ashtray. "No, no I didn't." His eyes watched me, waiting for a response.

"You didn't what? Make him what he is?" I asked, my confusion growing.

"I did not," he replied shortly, his eyes never leaving mine. He laid his cigarette in the ashtray and ran his fingers through his hair wearily. "I was not the only Vampire in town."

"Another Vampire did this to Victor? You let that happen? I don't understand. You are Victor's Sire, aren't you?" I struggled to comprehend what I thought Nathan was trying to tell me.

"I am not Victor's Sire – and I did allow another to embrace Victor,"

Nathan confessed quietly.

"But Victor thinks you are his Sire. He knows you are..."

"The mind is a very powerful object. You should know that by now, Kala..."

"You have some sort of mind control over Victor?" I asked abruptly, thinking what an awful thing for even Nathan to do.

"Let me finish the story so you understand. Don't accuse me of things I have not done. Listen and you will understand why I did what I did," Nathan said firmly. "When Victor came to my home to be embraced, he saw *me.* The last thing his human eyes saw was *me*, and when he awoke the first thing his new Vampire eyes saw was *me*. Thus his very powerful assumption that *I* was the one who sired him. I admit I let him believe this."

"But why? Why did you not just embrace him yourself? I don't get it."

Nathan shook his head vigorously. "No, I wouldn't do it. I won't do it ever. I have the blood of the Enforcer in me and that bloodline will be passed down to anyone that I embrace. As you know, the true life of an Enforcer is not supposed to be a glorified one. Eternal life as an Enforcer is a curse, not a gift at all, and I refuse to pass a lifestyle like that to anyone. Victor just wanted eternal life for Nerissa and himself, not the markings and the job of the Enforcer to hide from for the rest of eternity. No one should have to do that! No one!" Nathan said bitterly.

"If you didn't sire Victor, who did? If the connection of blood in your people is so strong then why has he not sensed you are not his sire yet? I thought..."

Nathan interrupted me. "It's not important who embraced Victor. I got him what he wanted." He was terse with his admission.

I walked to Nathan's chair and knelt on the floor next to him. "But it is important. You know that. If you did not embrace Victor and someone else did, then you took responsibility and punishment for Victor when he accidentally killed Nerissa. You didn't have to, so why?" I knew there was more to what he was not telling me.

Nathan looked down at me. "You know all you need to know." He waved me off as if I were a hovering mosquito.

"Not true," I snapped. "We agreed there would be no secrets between us. You have your reasons for not telling Victor, I suppose, even after all this time, but those reasons are not mine. I have the right to know about anything that may affect me as the Emissary."

Nathan's tone was stony as he answered. "His Sire is dead. I made sure of that. Stupidity on my part or I might not have had to live the last two hundred years in this lie. It's all a lie!"

I pursed my lips as I sat in thought. I could feel Nathan's guilt, anger and despair burning inside him. I decided to soften my tone, but continue the conversation. "Why did you kill Victor's maker?" I asked softly.

"What difference does it make now?" Nathan growled. "I can not change what I did, or the choices that I made. I can not change that fact that I have lived the past two hundred years as a pariah, punished for a crime I didn't commit, for a being I did not create."

I saw a muscle jump in Nathan's cheek as he held himself in check. "Nathan, I am not here to fight with you. I am here for answers. I have questions, but I don't want to upset you."

"If you don't want to upset me, go home," Nathan barked.

I ignored his retort. I stood up, retrieved my wine and took my seat back on the couch.

"Well, leave." Nathan motioned to the door.

I shook my head. "I want to finish talking. It's important. You can't go throwing me out every time we hit an obstacle." I sipped my wine calmly.

"Yes I can."

I sighed, not wanting to irritate him further. I wondered if I just sat in silence long enough if he would give in. We did not have long, though, because Victor's classes would end in a couple of hours. I sipped my wine, trying not to grip the slender glass stem too tightly. I willed myself to appear tranquil and calm, and not let Nathan's anger affect me. I let myself feel his emotional turmoil again, and sadness filled me. He was suffering from years of mental pain and anguish, but suddenly, something else was also clear to me.

"You killed Victor's creator because you wanted Victor to be yours," I said in astonishment. "You wanted him to be your blood, only yours, but you wouldn't allow yourself to take him." I was almost breathless at the realization.

Nathan's eyes burned holes in me as he answered. "So, now you know why I had to take the blame. Denying I was Victor's Sire would lead to questions as to *who was* and then more investigations as to *why I wasn't*. Killing one of our own is a crime, but being an Enforcer, well, that is punishment enough, especially being disclosed as one." He thought a moment. "An Enforcer had not been seen in years. Many thought we had all died off or got stuck in a dimension we could not escape from. We became a myth. Some believed we existed, others didn't."

Nathan stood and kept talking. "No matter what I decided to do I was faced with retribution. Declaring the fact that I was an Enforcer in a world I didn't belong in brought punishment and witch hunts. Admitting to a murderous crime I committed to cover my tracks was also punishable. I had nowhere to turn. The road has been long; very, very long and I am very, very tired." Nathan's voice was hollow, as if in speaking he had drained himself of all the poison permeating him. I actually felt sorry for him. He walked to the window and pulled back the heavy drapes to see out into the storm. "You have no idea what I have seen in my life and what I have gone through. The initial years with Victor were Hell. We fought constantly, until one day he left."

He let the drapes fall back into place and turned around to look at me. "Even though Victor and I have had our differences, when he left, I let him go. Getting him back was another story altogether. He was full of hate and that took many years to work out of him, but I finally did. After all this time, he *is* mine, regardless of the bloodline, even though we are as opposite as opposite can be at times."

"Nathan, do you know who made you?" I questioned.

"Of course. Why do you ask?" Nathan walked past the candle, his shadow preceding him along the wall.

"I was just curious. Do you see your Sire?"

"I have," Nathan said expressionlessly.

"Who is your Sire?" My eyes locked on his. "I feel inside me that your Sire lives."

"I can not say. You know too much now. Information like that does not get told. There is too much at risk. I will not risk my Sire." He shook his head firmly.

I shrugged, conceding this point at least. "So why are we together in this? I don't get it. We are like oil and water."

Nathan smiled at that. "Kala, I honestly don't know. That is something we will both have to figure out together. Your friend Sara never alluded in her book as to why. I do not have the answers to give you, but I know we are stuck working on this."

"What is *this*? What are we trying to do, or fix?" I asked in bafflement, setting my glass on the table.

"My feeling is this," he put his hands on his knees and bit his lip, weighing his words. "Something has gone wrong, in my world, the world of realms and dimensions, in Sara's mystic world and in the Vampire's world. Somewhere, somehow, something got messed up. I cannot tell you for certain what it is. It is a feeling that is growing inside me. I see people in the Manor and I know they don't belong; things happen and they should not, things go unexplained. I am not the only person to feel this way. But no one is certain what has happened, or how to correct it if it even can be. I don't know if one entity is responsible or many." He scratched his head in confusion. "Every time I think about it, I feel all confused and confounded and I have to shake myself loose from it. Never in all my years have I had that sensation."

"I don't feel what you do," I replied from the couch.

"Maybe you can't. Maybe the Amulet won't allow you to feel the confusion for a reason. Maybe you need a clear mind," Nathan guessed.

"Do you think all this strangeness revolves around the Amulet?" I asked, stroking the pendant around my neck.

He watched me handle the Amulet thoughtfully. "It definitely has something to do with it. People want it for a reason. You must take very good care of it, and yourself. Be very cautious – of everyone – day and night. I will be able to tell when you are in danger, but I can't guarantee I'll be there quick enough to help."

"Yes. I know." I stood up and put my hands on my hips. "Well, I guess I should leave. I won't burden you with any more questions tonight."

"Yes, Victor will be home soon. Be careful going home in the dark. By the way, I will be leaving for a day or more. I need to check on a few things. No one knows that I am leaving, not even Victor. He won't be concerned if it is only for a day, but if it's longer he will start to ask questions. Pretend you know nothing."

"Then why tell me?" I asked, walking to the door. "If I need you, can I reach you?"

"Although I will not be *here,* I can still sense you if you are in trouble. Yes, you can still reach me."

"Is this Enforcer business you are on? Is that why you are being vague?" I asked, turning around at the door.

"Yes, in a way," he answered shortly.

"All right. Good luck," I said, and turned to leave.

"Oh, Kala," Nathan added unexpectedly. "Remember when you asked me if I missed being human, and I said no, I did not even recall being human?"

"Yeah."

"Well, I remembered something last night." He hesitated before continuing as if he felt he should not have started. "I remembered the feeling of being loved by another." He sounded both embarrassed and defiant as he confessed to me.

I felt a flutter of sorrow in my heart. I could not imagine how difficult it must have been for Nathan to admit that to me, how much he must have felt it in his heart to need to verbalize it. I looked at him – this creature of the dark – and wondered at his complexities.

"Nathan," I gently smiled. "That is the best memory to have."

Chapter 38

The big day was finally here. The Battle of the Bands would consume most of my Saturday and I hoped I was ready for it. The few days off I'd enjoyed (hah!) had contributed to an almost lethargic attitude towards work. I hoped I could get a grip on myself and pull it off.

Drew had called me at home early in the morning to make sure I would not be late and to let me know where he would be waiting for me at the club when I did arrive. It was good to hear his voice after so many days. Even though he understood we were not dating he was still friendly and I appreciated that. I had packed a change of clothes to leave in the car, not really knowing how the day would go, and perhaps I was looking forward to staying with Victor, even though I did not allow myself to dwell long on that.

When I arrived at the club, I could see people wheeling in the amps and sound equipment in preparation for the concert. I was glad it was not my responsibility to make sure all that electrical stuff got brought in and connected up right. Most of the equipment weighed in at one hundred pounds or more.

I saw Drew working with some of the recording system and walked over to him. "Hi there," I greeted him cheerfully.

"Hi yourself," he smiled back. "Hey, have you seen the program?"

"Nope, just got here. What's up?" I asked him, pushing my sunglasses up on top of my head.

He straightened up from his task and took some papers out of his back pocket. "Look it over; somehow another band got added." Drew shoved the paperwork out for me to take a look at.

I shuffled the papers in my hands and scanned them quickly. "Eleven bands in twelve hours!" I exclaimed, examining the schedule for the day. "How do they think we are going to pull this off with set changes and stuff?" I asked in exasperation.

Drew sat down on the crate he had been standing on. "The eleventh band must know somebody at the station. There is no other way they would have been added with the time restraints we have today."

I turned the paper over, looking for more information on the newly listed band. "There isn't even a band name. You think it's a major act stopping by? Is that possible? Who is touring the area?" I asked out loud, although I was running down a list of possibilities myself. I took my sunglasses off my head and bit the earpiece, forcing myself to concentrate.

"No. Some of us already thought of that. Management says no big name, just a band." Drew crossed his arms and shrugged, dismissing that possibility. "Just have to see how the day goes. Maybe there will be a band that might not make it. Maybe they are a fill-in. Who knows?"

I nodded. Anything was possible in situations like this and I was most likely looking too deeply into one extra band. The world would not end. "You're right. Well, I better find out where I'm broadcasting from and see what kind of radio station goodies I have to give away today. I hope it's good stuff or it will make for a very long day."

The doors opened an hour before the first band took stage and although the club was not even half full we expected the bigger crowds to show up sometime after dinner. That was the typical club hopping time even for an all day event like we had planned. The best that I could do as a radio personality working for not only the station, but for our client who owned the club, was hype the Battle of the Bands as best as I could on the air and try to get as many people into the club as possible. Enticing the listeners with free radio station merchandise usually helped too.

By nightfall, I wondered how I would make it through several more hours of noise, handing out station paraphernalia, forcing toothy smiles, tiptoeing across the beer soaked bar room floor and breathing in cigarette smoke by the lung full. I was starting to get a horrible headache. I sent Drew in search of Tylenol while I kicked back on a soft leather couch for a few minutes in the sound room with the volume down and the lights low. I closed my eyes and after a few moments I began to nod off, but was startled awake by a pair of warm hands that gripped my shoulders gently.

"Put the Tylenol on the table. I'll get a drink in a minute," I murmured with my eyes still shut, allowing the tender fingers to work my tense shoulders.

"If I knew you had a headache I would have brought some," I heard Victor whisper in my ear, and he kissed my cheek softly.

I giggled a little for mistaking him for Drew. "Sorry, Drew went to get me some. I thought you were him," I replied, opening my eyes and smiling at him.

"You didn't feel me when I walked in?" Victor asked with a surprised look on his cleanly shaven face.

"Honestly I didn't. I was just about asleep. I'm glad you woke me; it would have been embarrassing to sleep through the next act and never even introduce them." I pushed myself to stand and peered out the studio window and down a flight of stairs into the club to see what was happening.

"How are things otherwise?" Victor asked, sitting down on the couch.

"Okay. Just a very long day," I sighed, looking warmly at him.

The studio door opened suddenly and Drew marched in. A barrage of music swept in behind him, then was silenced with a hefty slam of the steel door.

"I got your Tylenol," Drew announced as he looked at Victor with hostility.

I ignored his obvious pique. "So how is it out there?" I asked him, looking back out the window.

Drew pulled up a well-worn wooden director's chair and parked himself. "There's a mosh pit that broke out near the stage and more beer on the floor than floor – oh yeah and there is a pretty good looking girl outside the door with no shirt on who puked all over herself..."

"Ah, a normal club night," I chuckled and opened the bottle of pain tablets. "Do we know anything more about this last band tonight? Seems like all the bands who should have showed today did." I removed the cotton from the bottle and shook two tablets into my hand.

"Not a word. Guess they go on last," Drew answered.

I shrugged as I reached for my soda. "Oh well," I said, and sipped and swallowed the tablets hoping they would start to work fast. "If I know nothing more than I know now when it's their turn to go on, what am I supposed to do? Stand on stage and act stupid because no one bothered to inform me?"

"By midnight you think anyone will care?" Drew laughed. "There isn't a sober person in the building now."

"What's with the last band?" Victor asked.

"The line-up was for ten bands, and someone added an eleventh, but no one knows the band's name or anything else," I briefly explained.

"Oh, is that a problem?" Victor asked.

I sat next to Victor and looked over at Drew. "Time is tight," I replied. "But they will get squeezed in somehow."

Drew nodded.

As the midnight hour approached I knew no more than I had earlier in the day about this added band. Drew told me he had seen one of the band members backstage, but when he tried to engage him in conversation, the guy had rudely brushed him off. Drew claimed the guy gave him the creeps so he decided to back off. He was apparently one of those weird Marilyn Manson types, pale, long dark stringy hair and hollow eyes – daemon-like.

"Looks like your mystery band is taking the stage," Victor called to me from the sound room window as he leaned casually against the wide sill.

I fell onto the cushions of the couch with the can of soda in my hands.

"Let them." The stage volume was turned down low in the room but I could hear the band begin the first few notes to their opening song. Drew had started to pack up the radio station van, coming and going with boxes in his arms and helping the street team who usually drove from event to event and were accustomed to setting up and breaking down. I closed my eyes in exhaustion.

"You going to make it to midnight?" Victor asked from his seat at the window. "You look really tired."

"I am tired," I admitted.

"Am I going to have to carry you home, get you undressed and tuck you to bed?" Victor asked teasingly.

"Would you do that for me?" I bantered back, a yawn escaping my mouth, although I tried to force it back.

"Anything," he replied quite seriously.

The music grew louder in the club and I found myself humming involuntarily to the song that I could barely hear. I was surprised at that, because I had heard a lot of music over the day, but nothing that moved me enough to even tap my foot.

The music blew into the studio in a wave as the door opened and Drew walked in. "Okay, the van is packed," he said, shutting the door quickly. "You got anything you want put in your car, Kala, before I leave?"

I stopped humming the song. "No thanks, all set," I replied, trying to sound vibrant and awake, all of which I was not. "Why do I know this song?" I asked suddenly.

"Maybe it's a popular one," Victor suggested.

"Can't be. Rules for the event state all music must be original," Drew explained.

I sat up tiredly on the couch. "I just know that I know this song," I insisted as I finished the last of my soda, thinking about the melody and the lyrics.

I was not sure why all of a sudden I knew where I had heard the song before, but I did. I leaped to my feet and charged past Victor to the studio window, focusing my eyes onto the stage. My eyes could not believe what they saw even as my heart swelled at the sight. How could it be, how was it possible? Where had he been and what had brought him back? Kevin, my brother, alive and breathing, singing the song he had written for me so many years ago. That's why I knew I had heard the song before. Because I had – it was my song. My eyes filled with tears and I covered my mouth with a trembling hand as I stared in disbelief.

"What's wrong?" Drew asked, coming up behind Victor and me

Victor ignored Drew and cautiously reached out and placed a gentle hand on my shoulder. “Don’t cry,” he whispered softly.

All I could do *was* cry. I wept as I pointed down onto the stage, unable to speak.

“Kala?” I heard Drew’s concerned voice ask again.

“Drew, leave, it’s okay,” Victor said as he looked at him. “Go.”

“But –“

”Go!” Victor’s voice did not allow Drew to argue any more. He did what Victor ordered him to do; his footsteps were hasty, but led him out the door. As it slammed, Victor and I were alone.

I couldn’t take my eyes off my brother. He looked so well. I wanted to hug him and touch him to know he was real, and once I knew that he was, punch him square in the jaw and ask him why he left and never came back. Why he’d left *me*. I let my tears run down my face unchecked, to be absorbed in the collar of my cotton shirt. I sobbed.

“I can’t believe it,” I finally was able to gasp between my tears.

Victor hugged me tightly. “When you told me Kevin had vanished with out a trace I did some investigating. I tried to find him, to get him to come here to see you. I hope you aren’t mad at me, “ he finished.

I shook my head. Of course I wasn’t mad, but why would Kevin have to be coerced into coming back? Didn’t he want to see me?

Kevin continued to belt out his song on stage as I watched silently from the sound booth. Suddenly, I *knew* that Kevin knew I was nearby. A connection between sister and brother perhaps? I watched as his eyes wandered the room and then finally looked up where Victor and I stood. His eyes met mine and a small smile crossed his face.

“He knows you are here,” Victor remarked.

I nodded quickly. I knew as well. I backed away from Victor and the glass window that separated me from fifteen years of pain. I headed impulsively for the studio door. I hurried out the door and into the smoke filled club. Victor shouted something after me as I bolted out of the room, but I was not sure what his message was and I was not turning back to find out. I crossed the crowded floor to the stage, all the while keeping my eyes on Kevin. Two very large bouncers approached me brusquely as I stood close to the corner of the black painted stairs that lead to the small stage.

“Stop,” bellowed the larger of the two men over the music,,his multiple facial piercing’ and tattoos intimidating in the dim light.

“That’s my brother up there,” I pointed tearfully to the stage behind the bouncer’s formidable bulk.

“Wait here,” the bouncer insisted, extending his arm like a bar and pushing me back several feet.

I did not protest, for I was now alarmed to feel a familiar sensation starting up in my hands. I could feel the tingling in my finger tips begin to surge and charge surely due to the fact that I was so excited by seeing Kevin after so many years. I found my powers controllable for now as long as I concentrated on Kevin's face. I tried not to take my eyes off him.

As soon as Kevin finished the song, the crowd erupted in applause. One by one each band member left the stage and came down the side stairs. They were all clad alike in black leather boots and jackets, and faded jeans. I recognized the band member who had scared Drew back stage and felt a cold chill course up my spine.

Kevin was the last one off stage, disappearing in a sea of bodies as he reached the floor. I tried to move closer to reach him.

"Kevin!" I called out, trying desperately to get a closer glimpse of him over the heads and shoulders of others much taller than me.

My voice caught Kevin's attention and I saw his eyes pan the crowd for me. My voice also caught the alertness of the creepy band member with the pale skin, awful long hair, and wicked eyes. He glared back in my direction with an empty dark stare that sent a deeper chill through me. I tried to ignore the stranger and shoved my way through the dense swarm of people towards Kevin. Once I was face to face with my brother I could do nothing more than throw my arms around his neck and squeeze his body to mine. I could hardly breathe. "Oh Kevin," I sobbed.

I felt his hands tighten against me. "It's been a long time." His voice was so familiar after all these years. It brought back memories that had lain dormant in my mind since I was a child. I had forgotten them because I could no longer recall his voice, or his face.

" I missed you. It's so good to see you," I cried again, not wanting to let go. I closed my eyes tightly. I loved him more right then than anyone else in the world.

All at once, I felt a jolt inside me as if something or someone had flipped my *switch* back on – a swell of energy detonated within my core making my body stiffen in a higher level of consciousness. It shook me with its unexpected emanation. My little voice was screaming a warning at me. Something about Kevin felt wrong now. 'He's not alive,' my inner voice declared. 'There is nothing to feel because he's not alive.' My eyes widened in shock as I pulled away from Kevin awkwardly. I stared at his smooth youthful face. He was young and perfect – not a day over twenty-five. He had not aged at all since I saw him last. He was forty but he looked no older than I did. I placed my hand against his face in wonderment. He drew back, but not before I had felt the unreal coolness of his skin. Kevin was not real. Oh he *was* real; he just wasn't the Kevin I remembered – not *my* brother. He was another part of the world of the un-dead.

"You're..." my voice stuttered over my thoughts and words. How stupid I was, following my heart instead of allowing my brain to sort out all the facts that lay before me. I knew enough about the culture of the un-dead to realize the reality of his disappearance fifteen years ago. How naïve I was. It was so obvious now as to why Kevin never came home. How could he?

Out of the corner of my eye I could see Victor next to me as I stared into the hollowness of Kevin's vampire eyes. Victor tugged on my arm slightly, perhaps anticipating my reaction in knowing what Kevin was.

"Kevin," I began, but words failed me as the realization hit me. All those years of pain and sorrow, missing Kevin and living with a broken heart. All that was swept away as the truth sunk in. Kevin had the dark gift. He either took it or it was given to him, but either way his existence had always continued, but in a way that I could only understand now through knowing Victor and Nathan.

"Kala, come with me. We'll see Kevin in a little while," Victor said as he took me by the elbow forcefully.

"No," I cried loudly. "No! I want to talk to him now!" My outburst began to draw the attention of the crowd around us, but I did not care.

"Kala, stop it!" Victor ordered as he powerfully dragged me out of the club, careful not to grasp my hands. He knew better. "Kevin, meet us back at the Victorian. I'll take Kala now." Victor barked out his commands over the noise of the crowd and continued to ignore my resistance.

Kevin nodded in Victor's direction and walked away backstage without any further comment. He never even gave me a second look. My heart was broken. I was crushed. He wasn't the brother I remembered; he only looked like him, and that wasn't enough. I felt robbed. Kevin did die. He died fifteen years ago and seeing him again now only made me miss him more.

Chapter 39

Victor drove us back to his place, as I was in no state to drive. My mind whirled with conflicting emotions, fueled with the heat of anger. More deceit, materializing from the depths of the un-dead world once again. I sat mutely in the car for most of the ride as Victor also maintained his silence. He made no attempt to console or counsel me, nor did he touch me telepathically.

"Why?" My voice cut the silence.

Victor had just parked the car outside the Victorian. "Why what?" he asked quietly, as if he had no idea what I was referring to. He removed the car keys and handed them to me.

I snatched the keys from him and angrily said, "Why didn't you tell me he was coming? Why didn't you tell me what he *was*?"

Victor leaned his head back against the top of the driver's seat and stared out the front windshield past the nose of the car and down the vacant dimly lit street. He seemed frustrated but resigned; he knew I'd be asking him questions. He thought for a moment and began carefully. "It took time to find Kevin," he said quietly. "I had a hunch over dinner the night you told me about Kevin and what had happened to him in Germany. People who go away and don't come back and whose bodies are not found..." he hesitated, shaking his head, then continued. "It's not just a simple death. In most cases it usually means they have become *one of us,* not always, but enough of the time. Trust me when I say a majority of missing persons are not really missing, at least, not in the sense that their families think anyway."

"So..." I prodded him to continue.

He looked out onto the street as he gathered his thoughts. "When I found out about Kevin and what he was, it wasn't through Kevin at all. It was a person who knew a person who knew a person. That wasn't good enough for me to go back to you and tell you. If I was going to tell you about Kevin at all I wanted to know first hand. I wanted to hear Kevin's story from him."

"And?"

"Well, I pressed on and continued to hear about his whereabouts; in Paris for a while, Rome for a while, and the stories kept mounting, but no Kevin. I never even spoke to Kevin from a distance. I told the people in Europe why I was looking for Kevin, and that the Battle of the Bands show would be an opportune time to make himself known to you again and still be able to blend in with the crowd without really even trying. Music is still a big part of his life, I was told." Victor placed his hands on the steering wheel, his fingers playing with the leather trim. "It wasn't until last night that I actually met and spoke with him for the first time. He came by here; he was waiting for me after my class. I had very little time to talk to him, get his story and pull some strings to get him into the Battle of the Bands today. I didn't have time to think how all this would affect you. I really didn't believe he would come here. I was almost as surprised as you,"

I sighed and picked the keys up out of my lap. "Is anyone in my life alive?" I opened the car door and let myself out onto the sidewalk. "I'm beginning to understand why my mother is the way she is," I said flatly.

Victor got out of the car and quickly caught up with me in the driveway. "I can't say I know *exactly* how you feel, but I was only trying to help. I wanted you to either put Kevin totally behind you in the event he was actually dead, or know what *really* happened. As Emissary, some day you would have had that knowledge and maybe then it would not matter, but today it does." He put his arm around my shoulder as we walked onto the porch. He stopped at the wooden swing and drew me down next to him as we sat.

"Why didn't he come back? How come he could not have tried to explain it to me before now; before someone like you went looking for him?" I asked in confusion.

Victor kissed my forehead and softly squeezed me closer to him. "Kevin is coming by tonight. Let him tell you his story. I think your questions need to go to him, not me."

I bit my lip in despair. "I don't know how I can sit in the same room with him; ask him questions I needed answers to a long time ago." Tears began to build in my eyes again.

"He expects questions," Victor assured me quickly. He gripped my shoulder more firmly. "That was the *one* thing I made sure he knew last night. If he stayed in town to do this show, it meant he would be meeting up with you at some point and that you *would* have questions. He had to be prepared to answer them, all of them. If he could not meet the demands I put on him I told him to leave town right then and there. Kevin's decision to stay here, do the show and meet with you was a choice he made knowing the stipulation I put on him. Ask him whatever you feel you have to. This might be your only chance."

"Only chance? Why only chance?" I asked breathlessly, as if something bad was going to happen to me or to Kevin.

"It's just that Kevin has a very low profile; he leads a very private life. His preference I guess. I had a very hard time finding him so I would assume anyone else would too, especially a human like you, regardless of your future standing in our society," Victor clarified and took a cigarette out of his shirt pocket.

"What if Kevin wants to stay in contact?" I was angered at the thought that after so many years he could just walk back out of my life and never speak to me again.

Victor struck a match and lit up, tossing the smoldering matchstick into a large stone ashtray on the porch floor. "We'll see. I can't speak for Kevin." He took a drag off his cigarette and leaned back, trying to unwind from the night.

"You're right. You don't even know Kevin. I don't even know Kevin any more. How can either of us answer for him?" I resigned myself to the fact that I would have to wait and have that brother to sister talk that was some fifteen years overdue.

When Victor finished his cigarette, he and I walked into the house. He paused momentarily in front of Nathan's door as if he had forgotten something, but then walked on without comment.

"Were you going to see Nathan?" I asked, hiking the stairs behind him in near darkness.

"I usually stop in and see him on my way out at night and on my way back in, but he's been gone since last night and I am not sure where he went off to," Victor replied in annoyance.

"Oh. Is it odd that Nathan left without telling you?" I inquired, remembering Nathan's parting words to me from the night before about not being around for a few days. I pushed them deeply inside me before Victor picked up on them.

Victor opened the door to his loft. "Well..." he paused, letting the door swing open. "When he knows he is going to be going away he tells me. It's the unannounced trips that make me worry." Victor continued into the loft and headed for the kitchen.

"I take it this is an unannounced absence?" I closed the door behind me and followed Victor to the kitchen. I dropped my keys on the breakfast bar and leaned against it.

Victor switched on the light over the stove. "Yes. When I got home from class last night he was already gone. Kevin was here, but I haven't seen Nathan since." Victor opened the refrigerator and took out two cold bottles of beer.

"Maybe you will hear from him," I suggested, trying to be more upbeat than he was.

Victor twisted the cap off his beer and took a sip, then flipped the top into the sink. It rolled around the stainless steel, making a tinking noise until it fell to rest. "I won't know he's back until he's back. Nathan's weird that way."

"Are you worried?" I asked, trying to figure out what Victor was thinking about Nathan's disappearance.

Victor opened my bottle and handed it to me. "No, not really. I just wonder what it is that makes him leave at times without telling me, especially because he does it so infrequently. When he returns he never quite seems himself. It's odd." He sighed and shut the refrigerator door on the way out of the kitchen.

"Maybe he has a girl friend," I suggested with a smile.

"Right," Victor scoffed. He walked out of the kitchen as I trailed behind him.

"Mid-life crisis?" I guessed.

"Very mid," Victor laughed and sat down on the futon in the backroom.

I smiled and sat next to him, sipping my beer.

"I'm not going to worry about Nathan or talk about him any more tonight. He's more than capable of taking care of himself. Besides, I want to spend time with you." Victor leaned over and kissed me on the lips. "You look so tired."

I yawned. "A little."

"Why don't you rest for a bit? I'll let you know when Kevin is here; I have some papers to grade in the mean time." He stroked the side of my face with his hand.

Although I didn't think I could nap with Kevin on his way over; I could not think about staying awake all night to visit either. "I don't know," I said uncertainly, rubbing my eyes with the back of my hands.

Victor stood up and yanked a blanket from over the back of the futon. "Lay down, get comfortable," he ordered. "Do you want one of my tee shirts?"

"I have a bag in the car," I replied, putting my beer on the floor and kicking my sneakers off. They flopped onto the hardwood floor with a dense thud. I wiggled myself flat on the lumpy mattress and put my arm behind my head as Victor spread the blanket over me.

"I'll get your bag later on. Even if you don't sleep right now, the rest won't kill you; it's been a long day for you. Mine has just started," Victor said as he covered up my feet with the big blanket.

"All right, I'll lay here." I tugged the blanket up to my chin.

Victor smiled. "Good. I'll be in the other room doing some paperwork."

I nodded and watched him leave the room to attend to his schoolwork.

I lay in the faintly lit room staring up at the ceiling for several moments, trying to empty my mind just for a *little* while. It would be enough time to restore some of my energy and give me the strength to sit with Kevin calmly, to talk, to reason and to try and understand what happened fifteen years ago. In draining my mind, the stillness in the room put me to sleep or into such a restful state that I thought I was sleeping.

I had become familiar with dreams recently and how real they could feel, but what I experienced next was not a dream, or anything I found easy to explain to myself. I had cleared my mind in order to rest and in doing so allowed an unfamiliar sense to take over my consciousness. It was so unusual and difficult to describe that I can only call it an out of body experience. There is no reasonable explanation for what I was able to do, and for what I saw, since I knew my body was relaxed and physically powerless on the futon. I must admit I felt quite alive though.

Victor sat at the big window in the living room area in his rocker, reading a report in one hand and a red marker in the other. I watched him from a distance, at first thinking, *he must know I'm here,* he always knows when I'm around, but he never acknowledged me. I moved in closer; I was very near to him, yet he didn't know I was there. How was this possible? I could see him, but he could not see me? I could even smell the light scent of his cologne and feel the cool night breeze sweeping through the wide-open windows. I circled him, admiring his level of concentration, the thin lines furrowed in his high forehead and how he twirled his red marker in between his fingers as he read. I looked over his left shoulder as I saw him pen a big read *B* on the cover of a report entitled: "*Realism, Impressionism and Expressionism 1850-1910.*" He capped his pen and gently tossed the report to the floor by the side of his chair. He picked up his beer and took a long drink. I saw the large pile of ungraded papers next to him and knew he had a long way to go.

Suddenly, I felt myself being pulled away from Victor as if someone had turned on a powerful vacuum. I was helplessly swept from his loft and launched down the dark staircase towards Nathan's place, although I never opened the door to leave on my own. I almost instantly appeared on the porch in front of the hanging swing. I stood looking out over the lawn in the silence of the darkness. Only the chirp of crickets echoed as I watched the moths swarm around the streetlight anchored at the curb.

My quick but abrupt trip from Victor's loft to the yard had startled me, but I forced myself to focus intently on a car that was coming up the street. I heard the tires upon the tarred pavement crushing the tiny granules of sand as the car approached. I knew it must be Kevin. I dreaded facing him and looking into the vacant eyes of a stranger I thought I once knew.

Out of the parked car emerged three people – two men and a woman. One of the two men I immediately recognized as Kevin, and my heart wavered. I had to remind myself he wasn't the human brother I once had; he was a different Kevin. His changes were not ones that someone would expect over time. Time in the case of Kevin had no bearing as life, as he knew it would forever continue. The other male with him was the tall and ominous guitar player in the band; the one who disturbed Drew backstage and made me feel so uneasy after the show. I remembered his eyes cutting through me, looking at me in a way that made me feel as if I had done something awful to him, sending me intimations of revenge. The woman I had not seen before, but she was a vampire, there was no mistaking that. I knew the feeling too well, that sense of swimming with sharks and hoping they were well fed and would ignore you. The other creature that traveled with them I was not sure of. He certainly gave off an odd feeling, like a vampire, but not exactly. Perhaps he was a daemon of sorts. I wondered if it would be rude to ask.

The three gathered by the driver's side of the car and began to talk amongst themselves, voices whispering in sync with the crickets. I could not hear what they were saying to each other. Maybe if I truly wanted to I could have gotten closer. I could have gotten closer to check out that *thing* that traveled with Kevin. I wondered if he had ever been human.

I realized as I watched them that none of them could see me. They weren't even sensing me. My body was still up in Victor's place and it was only my consciousness that was here on the porch. I supposed this was a form of astral projection. I had never tried it; I'd only read a little about it from time to time. I knew Sara had been able to project herself out of her body, but she'd never taught me herself. I had discovered some lessons in her journal I had skimmed over, but I had not tried them. Perhaps I had found one of my gifts without realizing it.

In a breath I was back. I lay quietly with my eyes shut on the futon, still relaxed. I could feel Victor nearby, as close as being in the same room. I was back in my body and knew he was near enough to hear me speak.

"Kevin's here," I mumbled as I rolled over on my side sleepily, struggling to open my eyes.

Victor smiled. "You say that like you're sure."

"He is here. I know he is." I curled my arm under my head and looked up at Victor, admiring his handsome features. I yawned and continued. "But, he's not alone – there's a woman and a very strange looking guy as well." I sat up and swung my feet onto the floor.

Victor sat on the edge of the cushion where I was. "How did you know that? Are you sensing these things now?"

I ran my fingers through my hair as I answered, "Not really, but sort of. I'll have to tell you about it later on." I saw Victor glance at the Amulet. Watching his face, I knew he had seen something different about it – the color. I looked down and saw the stone, too. Maybe the Amulet's power had something to do with my newfound ability to roam outside my body. I did not know for sure but the possibility was there. I ignored Victor's questioning stare and reached for my bottle of beer on the floor. I took a drink. "It's strange," I added.

Victor raised his eyebrows. "I bet. I look forward to hearing about it. But until then, let me get our guests situated at Nathan's and then you can come on down." He stood and walked to the doorway of the room. "Give me a few minutes to talk to them, okay?"

I nodded in agreement. "Okay, I'll be down in a while."

"Thanks."

While I waited I freshened up in the bathroom by splashing some cool water on my face and blotting it dry with a fluffy towel. Brushing my hair free of snarls, I looked at myself in the mirror and noticed the stone on the Amulet was slowly pulsing. The stone's deep emerald green color fluctuated to a brighter green in its core. I tapped it with my finger, then tugged the neck of my shirt over the Amulet and adjusted the chain to keep it hidden.

I went back to the futon and finished my beer, thinking about Kevin somewhere below me in Nathan's home and wondering what he was saying to Victor. I envisioned myself opening up the front door to Nathan's gloomy rooms and not knowing what to say as I found myself in the presence of three new vampires, or at least two. Was I their Emissary or just a human? What was Kevin *really* to me? I waited for my summons nervously, wondering what I could expect.

Chapter 40

I composed myself as best I could. I finally found the strength to face Kevin, my lost brother who appeared to have escaped death in a way I could never have foreseen. I knew I needed to hear his story, no matter how nightmarish I might find it.

I must have stood outside Nathan's door for a full minute, knowing full well that they must know I was standing there. How comical this must all seem to them, my humanity paralyzing me, making me look weak and insecure. My hands flared with pins and needles, a sure sign the stress of the night was taking its toll on me. This was the last thing I needed. This could be nothing but trouble.

I hesitated before I reached for the tarnished brass doorknob, feeling another stream of tension rush beneath my skin, flowing from my fingertips up my arms, across my shoulders and leaving me almost weak in its wake. Mustering my courage, I opened the door and entered Nathan's dark chambers.

I did not know what to expect, and at first stood still, my hand lingering on the doorknob as if clinging to my last avenue of escape. My heart hammered in my chest as I anticipated my first words with Kevin, and I swallowed hard, trying to loosen the knot in my throat. My eyes scanned the dim room, looking for Nathan's familiar figure, but the only presence visible in the shadows was the female Kevin had brought with him.

The vampire woman sat alone on the couch, her only company a tall drinking glass filled with ice and amber colored liquid in her thin hand. There was no sign of the others. The woman stared at me, studying me, her oval face tipped sideways, allowing her ashen blond hair to flow alluringly across her arm.

I rubbed my hands together tensely. "Where is everyone?" I asked, careful to conceal the nervousness my voice.

She pointed vaguely in the air, gesturing somewhere in front of her. "Outside," she replied shortly and sipped her drink.

I stood for a moment, uncertain, then went and sat in Nathan's favorite chair. I crossed my legs and pretended to be comfortable.

I looked casually at the blond, wondering if she was the one who made Kevin what he was; if she had sucked the life from him. She was pretty in a way. She could have seduced him I supposed. I could tell even though she was sitting that she was extremely tall; her legs were crossed and both feet nearly touched the floor. Her body was incredibly slender; her blue shirt hung loosely off one shoulder, collarbones protruding significantly. She lacked the soft fleshiness of a well-nourished human woman, the rounded contours of the shoulders, neck and chest. She gave a new meaning to the term "stick thin."

My curiosity finally got the better of me as the two of us sat in silence broken only by the tinkling of the ice in her drink.

"I know you know who I am," I began. "What is your name?" It felt funny to be so polite, under the circumstances.

"Citrina," she replied, uncrossing her legs and stretching them out. Her voice was strong. "Some people call me City."

'Did you do that to Kevin?*'* I thought at her. "Did you do that to Kevin?" I repeated aloud, unflinchingly. My eyes did not leave her.

She chuckled slightly as though my question was funny to her. "No. Not me. I have known Kevin only a few years." She placed her drink on the table next to her and looked directly at me. "I advise you to compose yourself before you ask Kevin any questions like that, especially in that tone of voice. I can see that you are on edge and you will get nowhere with him like that."

"He and I have a lot to talk about," I snapped, suddenly irritated by her words. Who was she to give me advice on how to speak to my own brother? "You have no idea what it has been like. Not to know. And *now* to know..." my voice trailed off. "No idea," I repeated, leaning deeper into the soft leather.

"Understood. Kevin is not heartless. But he does not like to be pushed. He does not like to feel cornered or trapped. Those are feelings he has left behind. You cannot treat him as a human. You can't treat *any* of us as if we were human like yourself, because we are not. You may see some of yourself in Kevin, being born of the same blood, having the same immortal father; you might see a little of it, if he allows." City's voice had a certainty to it as if Kevin had already made up his mind and shared with her how much he would tell me.

"What is that supposed to mean? 'If he allows it'?" I repeated belligerently.

City reached for her drink. "All I am saying is that Kevin broke his ties with you and the rest of his mortal family years ago. He is not one of you anymore. In my opinion he never should have come back to see you. I'm still not quite sure why he did." She balanced her glass on her knee.

"Maybe he came back because he cares. After all, *I am* his sister," I snapped.

She shook her head and drank from her glass. My tone of voice had not stirred her. "When the Kevin you knew left fifteen years ago, he never came back because *that* Kevin died. Your human brother no longer exists. If you continue to think of him as he once was, your experience with him now will be deplorable. It's been my experience that humans hold on to their memories dearly; they cherish them. It gives them a reason to live and something to reflect on, I suppose, but I'm here to tell you now that if you don't put those feelings aside, the only thing you will walk away from this reunion with is misery."

"Thanks for the advice," I retorted, getting up and heading for the door. I did not want to believe that Kevin was as she described him. He could not be *that* different, could he? Did my memory fail me as to how I remembered him or did his new life produce a whole *new* being and the brother I loved was really dead? If Victor could be warm and sensitive was it too much to expect the same from Kevin? I left City sitting in the darkness of the room by herself. I could not stand to be confined any longer.

Reaching the entryway I darted out the front door. I stopped on the porch and took a deep breath of the fresh night air when I realized I was not alone. Victor was leaning against the railing, smoking a cigarette and casually chatting with Kevin.

Victor raised an eyebrow in amusement at my reaction. "Where you going in such a hurry?" he smiled. His smile faded as he felt the residual heat from my hands radiating like the hot metal surface of an iron. I quickly placed my hands behind my back; aware of the latent power I possessed. I certainly did not want to injure Victor again.

Victor frowned at me in concern. "What's going on?"

I wanted to apologize. I had not meant to interrupt their peaceful conversation. "I'm sorry. I just wanted to get out. I needed to clear my mind, get some air. Sorry," I repeated, my eyes flicking to Kevin who had not said a word. I noticed the odd looking creature was missing from his side.

Victor took me by the arm and gently led me away to the end of the porch. "What's wrong?" he asked softly as he looked first at me, then at my clenched fists.

I looked up at him beseechingly. "I'm really stressed about all this. I don't know how much more I can handle."

"Kala, you are strong," Victor began. "I know you must be feeling overwhelmed, but just clear your mind of the things people have told you and trust your instincts. You have the right to know certain things. Kevin may not be happy being here, but that's his problem. Obviously he must feel some sense of obligation or he never would have come all this way." Victor looked back at Kevin, who had taken a seat on the porch railing. "I'm going inside now; I'll let you and Kevin talk. I'll be close enough so that if you need me, I will hear you." His face became stern and his tone serious. "Kala, try not to touch anything."

I nodded slowly in understanding, my hands hanging innocently by my sides. "Okay."

Victor put his hand against the small of my back and drew me close to him. "You'll do fine." He kissed my forehead. "Good luck." And with that he left me alone.

Victor stared hard at Kevin as he passed. He said something to him and their eyes locked. I couldn't hear what he said, but I imagined it was a warning of sorts. I saw Kevin give a shrug of his shoulders in acknowledgement. Victor opened the front door and disappeared inside, leaving us alone on the porch.

I remained at the end of the porch, uncertain what to do, or how to approach him. I had no idea how he felt about me, since Citrina's allegations had raised too many doubts. Kevin sat silently, nursing his beer and acting as if he was alone.

I swallowed hard, forcing a wave of emotion back into the pit of my stomach. "I never forgot you," I began. "I just never knew what happened."

Kevin stiffened slightly, then relaxed and stood up off the railing. "That was a long time ago," he replied softly. His voice was as I remembered it.

"I need to know what happened, Kevin. I have to know why you left, and why you've been gone all these years." I did not even mention the fact that he was now a member of the undead.

Kevin looked at me, then quickly looked away. "There's nothing to tell. You know what I am. Nothing else matters."

"I know what you are. But how can you say nothing else matters? How did it all come to be? Who did it to you? Where have you been? Why couldn't you tell me?" I fired my questions at him, my voice rising with emotion.

"It makes no difference now. I am not that person you once knew. I am not your brother; I only resemble him." Kevin spoke clearly and with finality.

"You'll always be my brother," I insisted stubbornly. "No matter who or what you are, you will always be my brother."

"But you have not been my sister in many years," he said, his eyes boring into me. I refused to look away, and instead met his gaze defiantly.

"Then why are you here? Victor was only trying to do me a favor by following a hunch he had on you; he said he never even spoke with you until last night. Somehow word got to you about me, so you came here. Why? If I'm nothing to you, why did you return?" I put my hands on my hips demanding answers

"Don't get all sentimental on me. I'm only here for a little while and then I'm gone," Kevin retorted. He must have seen the anguish on my face because he relented and softened his tone. "Okay, Okay!" He shifted his weight from foot to foot uncomfortably. "Go ahead and ask your questions. Let's get it over with."

"Can't you be civil? Can't we sit and talk about things? Catch up on fifteen years? Can't we get to know each other again?" I implored him.

"I knew this would happen!" he exclaimed suddenly, his anger belying his conciliatory words the moment before. "I knew I should not have come! I should have listened to City, but, no! Stuart calls and convinces me to come all the way here from Switzerland..."

"Why would you need convincing?" I asked in confusion, approaching him.

Kevin backed away from me, keeping space between us. "Damn it! He just thought it was a good idea; that maybe if I saw you and then you became Emissary, I would lead a better life." He shook his head. "I didn't want to come! I can't take this human shit! I can't stand to have a warm-blooded person this close to me unless I'm in it for the hunt. Drives me crazy!" Kevin appeared shaken as he spoke, as if even now my human presence was disturbing him. "Maybe in time things will change. I won't thirst as often as I do..." His words trailed off as he collected himself. He continued, "I don't know how Victor does it. He claims to love you, but I don't know how he can kiss you or share a bed with you. I can't stand to be in the same room with you! I'd rather kill you than look at you!"

My heart broke hearing Kevin talk about me the way he did. To him I was just a human canteen he could sink his fangs into and drink from when the need arose. I tried not to let him see how his words had wounded me. I tried to heed his warning and think of him as an adversary instead of the brother I'd missed for so long. "I'm sorry," I said. "I've been in the company of many vampires and never had them act like you." I remembered each of my encounters and how every vampire was composed and collected, almost divine in spirit. I had rarely seen any of their kind lose their cool with me just because I was human, with a heartbeat and warm blood. I had been looked down upon for being human, and therefore less than perfect, but I had never been treated as Kevin was doing.

He shuddered in disgust. "I should not have to talk to you about these things. You are human. You cannot possibly understand. I'm different than you."

"And I am not different than other humans?" I asked sarcastically. I hated

Kevin at this moment, mostly for thinking I could not understand his pain. "Ever since Sara died, my whole existence has changed! She was protecting me from everyone and everything!" I shouted at him. "I've just found out that I was born to rule a culture of clinically dead people, and that my father was a vampire and my brother is a vampire, and I will be a vampire one day! And guess what? I have no choice! None at all! I have these abilities and powers that are *bursting* to get out of me, like electrical charges that make my hands hot enough to burn the flesh from a person's body. And I don't know how to control it or use it. But I know I can really hurt people if I don't learn how to use it soon. I have no idea *where* these powers came from or *who* gave them to me. I just know that I struggle everyday hoping to learn more." I stamped my foot in frustration and glared at him. "Ever been chased by Blue Daemons? I have! Ever been drained of *most* of your blood? Left to die and then live to tell about it? I have!"

"Not the same!" he protested. "Our worlds are very different."

"You're right. Our worlds are very different. I may not be *like* you yet, but I travel the same road you do. I can hear thoughts like you can, but not always as clearly. I spend countless hours a week in the company of your people. So I may not be like you now, but I soon will be even though I don't want to. I'm in limbo, which is worse than being one of you because I am stuck waiting. Just waiting! I'm tired of the wait, the suspense! Just take me! I am a human only until I get some sort of okay to be Emissary. So I wait. I cannot lead a totally human life because I don't know how much longer I have. I can't get involved in a human relationship; I can never expect to marry and have children; I can never be normal!"

I burst into tears. He balled his fists and turned his back on me, his tense arms quivering at his sides, his body shaking as I continued. "I cannot lead the life you have because I am not one of you. I am not accepted yet for who I *will be.* Tell me again how different you are! You know what you are! I don't! What am I? And on top of all this, you pop into my life *now*? After fifteen years you are back, because you think you can live the good life once I become Emissary, even though you can't stand to look at me, or talk to me, or even answer my questions now? You make me sick!" I screeched at him through my tears. "All I wanted to do was care about you and I still do, even now!"

I could feel Kevin's anger building in his body. There was nothing he could say to me. I don't think he could have formed words to speak even if he could think of any. We were both too charged with emotion to trust ourselves, him with his thirst and me with my fists of fire.

Kevin's madness was deeper than just his resentment in seeing Kala after so many years. He wanted no part of this. He'd left her at the tender age of fifteen with a promise to himself that he would never return. Up until now he had kept that promise. He'd always thought it would be best if she never knew what had become of him. What he hadn't known at the time was that the little girl he left behind would some day be the woman, the Emissary, who would assist in governing the people of his world.

Kevin still had strong memories of his father during his mortal years, and remembered him constantly referring to Kala as special, as being 'one of a kind'. He always said, 'you just wait until she is all grown up' and Kevin heard in his voice the belief that some day Kala would be a force to reckon with. What Kevin hadn't known at the time was that his father *knew* what Kala would become – the Emissary – because he had planted the seed himself.

Kevin's return to the town he had grown up in to visit a sister he had long since deserted but never forgotten was forced upon him. His instructions came from powers higher up, and left him little choice but to comply. The order that came from the High Counsel was simply stated: make yourself known to Kala; put to rest any reluctances she might have in becoming part of our society. Reunite yourself with Kala and your father, and do whatever it takes to make Kala come willingly to the side of Sheldon, to make her use her powers in the best interest of the Counsel. And, lastly, make this happen as soon as possible.

Kevin's inability to cope with Kala's emotional outburst stemmed from his hunger for blood. Under normal circumstances, his tolerance would be much higher. Human blood mellowed his spirit and made him easier to deal with, but he had starved himself of blood during travel and now was thirsting ravenously. As a rule, feeding was somthing he did nightly, without thought. It was a process he carried out to keep himself living and breathing, and he did so with some enjoyment. When he'd been ordered to return to the sister he'd abandoned so long ago, a small part of him had quailed at the thought of her seeing his present state. He had refrained from feeding in the mistaken hope he could present a normal appearance to her. Unfortunately, his idea had failed and the situation now had gotten out of hand. As usual, he thought, he'd failed miserably.

We stood on the porch facing each other but not saying a word. I was searching for some words, for a gesture even, when I noticed an abrupt movement out of the corner of my eye. I saw Kevin's cohort cautiously coming up the steps, silent and deadly, his beastly countenance fixed steadily upon us. Like a shadow he moved, quietly and effortlessly. He was taller than I remembered, and his tiny glowing eyes made me shudder. A low growl escaped from his thin lips, drawn back to expose dirty jagged fangs. I had no idea what the sound meant, if it was a signal to Kevin, a greeting, or a warning to me, but it scared me anyway.

My eyes flickered from Kevin to his friend and back, trying to gauge the depth of their communication. I certainly did not want to be attacked, but I also did not want to have to defend myself. I was afraid of the results if my anger or fear caused me to use my power. My hands throbbed and I could feel the Amulet around my throat pulsing with a steady beat.

Without delay, in response to our screams of anger at each other, City and Victor rushed out the front door onto the porch.

"Are you all right?" Victor asked me, his voice strained. As I nodded mutely he glared at Kevin.

City had her arm around Kevin's shoulder in a calming manner. "I told him this was a bad idea. I did." City spoke up looking at Kevin who was still full of fury.

"If his temper is a problem and he can't seem to control it, he should not have come. He knows that and so do you," Victor snapped.

"He's doing very well, considering what his thirst must be like. We traveled a long time to get here and he has not fed in days," City fiercely defended him.

"And that's our fault? He knows what he has to do; waiting until you're blood-blind does no one any good, not him, not us, not his kill, " Victor retorted.

Kevin pushed City away from him and straightened, trying to compose himself. "I have to go," he said flatly. He turned and walked down the steps toward his car. "Gage," Kevin said shortly, and the creature instantly fell in behind him like a well-trained dog. They got into the car and drove off. We were left alone,City, Victor and I.

Without looking at us, City abruptly went into the house, slamming the heavy door behind her. Victor gently took my arm and led me to the swing, where we swung quietly in the cool night's silence. The night was more than half-gone and the heavens were making their change from intense navy-colored sky to the soft sponging of lavender on the horizon. I leaned against Victor's strong shoulder tiredly, his quietness helping to ease me. I felt the built up emotions slowly cease and the pressure inside me drop. I did not know what to say; the whole day had left me numb. I probably wouldn't make sense anyway.

Victor began. "It's okay, Kala," he said softly. "You had no idea what would happen. It's my fault for bringing him here in the first place."

"No," I protested. "You had no idea what he'd be like. I thought I would, but he's not like I remember him. He's changed." I sighed, thinking about him leaving with Gage and not being able to finish the talk I so badly wanted to have. I had thought for sure that I could convince him to sit down and talk with me when the night began, and now with the night almost over I knew that I was wrong. "Is he a *normal* vampire? I mean, he seems edgy. You aren't like that. Are you the exception?" I asked curling in towards Victor's body affectionately and placing my hand on his chest.

He laughed a little and put his hand over mine, massaging soothingly. "Age has a lot to do with it. The thirst for blood is great at a young age. You can't *not* feed yourself. It's horrible, it's like a drug addict or an alcoholic not sustaining their habit, except blood is not a habit for us, it's a way of life. When you don't nourish yourself you start to break down; you become irritable, distant, fidgety, even violent. Deprivation altogether means death. When you get older you start to level out; you don't need blood as often, but you always have the craving for it. Your temper is much easier to control. Look at Nathan. You'll know what I mean. Even in his worst rages he is so cool and calm that that in itself is scary."

I remembered Nathan with his hands around my throat in a fit of anger, no words, no sound, just his eyes burning through me. I nodded in agreement.

Changing the subject, Victor informed me of our plans for Sunday. "We have to go back to the Manor tomorrow night," Victor said softly. "Sheldon called while you were out here talking to Kevin."

I raised my head and stared at him in distress. "Why?"

"Sheldon knows that Kevin is in town. He is going to get us all together." Victor's voice was tired at the thought of returning to the Manor. "I hope Nathan will be back; otherwise I'm not sure how to explain his absence."

"I suppose I have to go?" I asked, knowing the answer to my question already.

"Yes," Victor said. He squeezed my arm. "But don't worry. We will stay together."

The night ended quietly with no further chaotic events breaking into dawn. I had lived the night of the dead. I had remained awake the entire night just as Victor had done since his birth into immortality. I wondered where Nathan was. He was still missing and none of us had seen or heard from him. With the sun sneaking over the distant horizon, I was certain Nathan was escaping the world of daylight for some needed darkness.

I sat alone on the porch swing, my eyelids heavy with lack of sleep. I kept nodding off, but stirred with each fresh noise of the new day. Victor had gone up to his loft to retire, but I refused to follow, wanting to be awake for Kevin's return. If he returned.

Just moments shy of the sun's first warming rays, Kevin and Gage returned to the Victorian. I heard the car's doors slam shut, the sound rudely jarring me awake. I blinked several times and wiped the corners of my eyes with my knuckles. I sat upright, my drowsy eyes following their approach to the house. When they reached the porch, Kevin motioned to Gage to go inside the house. We looked at each other for a moment and then Kevin broke the silence. "I'm sorry about last night." His voice was tired, but he appeared sincere.

I nodded. I heard what he had said, but was too tired to respond with words.

"Maybe we can try again, to talk, I mean, later on tonight," Kevin suggested.

"Alone?" I asked.

"Whatever," he replied with a shrug.

"All right," I agreed. I stood up but did not move closer to him. "I'm going home. If you see Victor, would you tell him that?"

Kevin nodded. His mouth opened, then closed, as if he wanted to say more. Finally, uncharacteristically, he said a nice thing as he fled the morning light into the dark seclusion of the house. "Drive careful."

I nodded. I would try.

Chapter 41

I was asleep almost before my head hit the pillow. I hadn't even had the strength to undress myself and pull the covers back. I simply collapsed and fell off into a long and mostly undisturbed sleep.

I remember dreaming about Kevin at one point and feeling very frustrated that I could not make him understand how much I cared for him. I suppose this was residual disappointment from our earlier confrontation. I recall crying and pleading with him to hear my voice, to listen to my sincerity. The entire time I was trying to convince him of how important he was to me, City was telling him how inferior and how pathetic and weak I was, that he did not need my company, he deserved so much more. The angrier I got with the situation between Kevin, City and myself, the more I heard the unseen Gage growl and howl. With each octave, my voice climbed until I could hear nothing, not even my own voice. Just the ear-piercing cry of Gage's wailing.

I'm not sure what it was that woke me. I just remember the beastly screaming ended and I felt the bed beneath my body. As the dream faded, I became more aware and alert to my surroundings. I hoped this was not a sign of what was to come tonight, when Kevin and I had the chance to speak again, together – alone.

It was late afternoon when I finally got myself into the shower and dressed for what was left of the day, although I felt rather guilty for sleeping most of it away.

I started to fret over my return to the Manor, not knowing who would be there; what kind of surprises were in store; seeing Sheldon again, seeing Lyla. That reminded me, Victor still owed me an explanation regarding Lyla, and how they came to know each other so many years ago. I was still troubled about their unknown relationship. Victor had asked that I give him the time he needed to come around and tell me his story on his own, all the while stating how he loved me and always had. Tonight was the deadline that he himself had set to enlighten me. Tonight I'd be reminding him that I hadn't forgotten.

I was a bit disoriented at seeing the dusk instead of daylight so soon after waking. Now I knew what the workers on the nightshift were always complaining about. How strange it was to be sitting down for breakfast while everybody else was tossing back their evening beers!

I made a full pot of coffee and had a seat out on the deck to relax. I thought about the assembly at the Manor that Sheldon had thrown together at the last minute, ostensibly to celebrate my small family reunion. I decided to give Victor a call after my first cup of coffee and find out what time Sheldon was expecting all of us. I had been thinking about Victor, about being with him again, and hoping that tonight would not be a fiasco, when I got the distinct feeling Victor was with me. I sensed him. I continued to sip my coffee and look out over the yard into the darkness. The feeling was strong – a vampire's strength, although no blood lust tainted the sensation. I was not scared. I set my ceramic mug on the table and, without turning around, broke the silence.

"Are you there?" I asked quietly, with a half smile.

"Mmm, " Victor purred in acknowledgement. His voice was close, but did not startle me. A few steps brought him to my side and he touched my shoulder affectionately.

I tipped my head back to look up at him, smiling into his eyes. "How did you get up here, anyway?"

"I'm very agile," he whispered in my ear. "What took you so long to speak? I didn't know how much longer I could stand quietly waiting." He leaned over my right shoulder and brushed his lips over mine, then moved to my neck with a quick little nibble.

I shuddered, feeling his warm lips on my skin. "I wanted to make sure," I replied.

"When you sense me, is it the same sensation you feel with Kevin, City and Gage, like last night?" Victor asked seriously.

I shook my head. "Not even close."

"There's a lot going on in your life right now; things are changing, aren't they?" he asked sympathetically.

"No more than the usual, I guess," I replied. I leaned back in my chair and took my coffee mug from the tabletop. I cradled it in my hands.

"So, how did you know Kevin and his friends had arrived last night if you did not sense them like you just sensed me?" Victor had a seat and removed a pack of cigarettes from his shirt pocket and shuffled it back and forth from hand to hand like a deck of playing cards while staring intently at me.

I shrugged, not sure how to explain the event. "Do you believe in out-of-body experiences?" I asked, sipping my coffee.

"I've heard of them," he said as he lit a cigarette and put the pack back in his shirt pocket. "Describe what you mean."

"Well, like have part of you leave your body and be able to check things out somewhere else without your body having to be there." I struggled to clarify what I meant.

"I have heard of the experience, though I've never tried it myself or known of anyone who has. What was it like?"

I smiled. "It was almost like being in a dream, but different somehow."

"How do you know it wasn't a dream?" Victor asked curiously.

"Because of the detail, I guess. Because I know what I saw," I replied, remembering how I felt like I was right there in the room with Victor last night, watching him grade his papers.

"You and I both know that your dreams are very real." He cocked an eyebrow, intentionally signaling me to think about the similarities between the two events.

I nodded. "You are right, except I saw things as they happened last night, and I was there. Not in my body though. I had no body, but I was there. I floated sort of." I finished my explanation, realizing how lame it sounded, even to my own ears.

Victor dipped his head in thought. "Could still have been a dream," he said, unconvinced.

I removed my feet from the edge of the chair he sat in and straightened up. "I watched you grade a report last night," I insisted.

Victor stood up and took a few strides to the edge of the deck and leaned on the railing, gazing into the woods. "But I told you I was doing some paperwork." His cigarette dangled from his lips as he spoke. "It still could have been a dream."

"I know – but I watched you put a big red B on a report entitled '*Realism, Impressionism and Expressionism... 1850*', or something like that." I tried to recall what I had seen on the cover of the report. I put my coffee mug down on the table and joined him at the edge of the deck.

Victor looked down at me with an unreadable expression. "Really?"

I knew I had caught him by surprise with that little detail. "Yes. I watched you read it for a while, then grade the paper. At first I wondered why you had not sensed me, even though I felt as if I was right there watching you with my own eyes. You never knew I was there. I got very close and watched you over your own shoulder. That was when I saw you put the B on the report."

Victor tossed his cigarette out in to the darkness and turned to face me. "Odd. I did not feel you. But I did grade that report with a B." His voice was thoughtful as he reflected back "It was a good report."

"Do you believe me?" I asked mildly. This, to me, was far less strange than some of the things that had occurred lately.

"Just because I don't understand it doesn't mean I don't believe you. After all, I know you are capable of many things. This may be just one more." He reached out and encircled my waist, pulling me close. "How did you know about Kevin?"

"Same way really. I went from watching you in the loft to being on the porch watching Kevin pulling his car into the driveway and seeing City and Gage get out with him." I curled my arms around his neck and studied his face as I continued my story.

"Fascinating," was all Victor said as he leaned forward and kissed my lips slowly.

I felt his mouth open on mine and his tongue tease my lips, encouraging them to open. His mouth was warm and sweet in a way I had not tasted before, a taste that was unknown to me, though not unpleasant. He wound his arms around my body and pulled me snugly against him. I felt his heat radiating through his clothing. Brief but graphic images flashed into my head, a movie trailer of what must have been events from Victor's early evening hunt to drink blood and give back to his body what it had been craving.

"Maybe you are right. We do need to spend some time together," Victor whispered. His eyes were luminous and I felt myself longing to swim in their depths. His hands caressed my body intimately. "We have some time before we need to leave," he suggested.

I touched his lips with my fingertips. His tongue gently licked at each one. "It was a woman, a middle aged woman..." I spoke softly.

His eyes narrowed at my words. He gathered my hand in his, drawing my palm close to his lips and kissing it softly.

"You fed from her, tonight, before you came here," I continued, not taking my eyes off of his, concentrating on what I had only momentarily seen play out in my head. With a touch of surprise I told him, "You spared her. She begged for her life." I touched his fevered cheek. "How good of you to let her live; that's why you are so warm against me – her blood."

"What's happening to you?" Victor said in wonderment, his eyes searching mine. "What are you becoming?" His gaze dropped to the Amulet on my neck.

"I tasted blood in your kiss," I replied nervously. "I've never tasted that before." I pushed a few stray locks of hair away from his eyes. "It just happened. I saw it; I'm sorry." I lowered my eyes, feeling like a voyeur caught in the act. "Sorry," I mumbled again and pushed myself a safe distance away from him before turning and taking my seat at the table.

Victor stood alone for a moment, perhaps feeling guilty for making me feel so ashamed and then in turn making himself feel guilty for doing only what came naturally for him. "I was cold. I have been. I did not even want to share my bed with you last night if you had stayed; my skin has been so ice-cold. I have not fed since before your birthday. It was time. I had to be close to you again, to be intimate – but be safe." His voice was thick with emotion.

"I know. I know why you need to," I said, looking over at him. "I just did not think you let them live. I have heard that you can, but usually don't. That was what surprised me, not that you had fed." I stopped talking for a moment, then asked, "Why? Why did you let her live?"

Victor shrugged as he returned to his chair next to me. "I picked her to feed from because she reminded me of someone, and then once I remembered who, it was too late to stop. She had the courage to look me in the eye as I held her in my arms and ask me to let her live, that she had her first grandchild on the way. I did. I had to. I could not take her. She reminded me of my mother."

"Were you close to your mom?" I asked curiously. I was always envious of anyone who was close to their parents, since I never was.

He nodded slowly. "I still remember her sometimes, but I have to think hard. It's been so long. She died under my care; when I was still human and still a doctor. It was very hard on all of us at the time. I think my grandfather blamed me for her death. He blamed me for a lot back then." Victor stretched out his legs and leaned back in his chair, looking up into the star flecked sky. "They are all long gone. Everyone I once cared about, gone."

I remembered a saying, something along the lines of, 'it was better to have loved and lost then never to have loved at all', or something like that, and wondered if it applied to familial love. I was not sure what was worse – to have loved and lost your family or to never have been loved by your family. "I would think that someone who has gone through what you have would be irritable and grumpy like Nathan, disliking everything and everyone. But you aren't. You are different." I smiled in admiration. I moved from my chair to a seat on his lap and draped my arms around his neck. "You're understanding, loving, attentive, a protector. What more could a girl ask for?" I said cheerfully, hugging him.

His mouth curled with repressed laughter. "Gee, thanks." He squeezed me close to him.

I kissed his cheek. "I've been dying to spend time with you." I let one of my hands travel down his chest.

"What I wouldn't give to spend one night with you – alone," he sighed. He leaned his head back; our eyes met. "I have a new semester starting soon, and I have so little time."

"I know," I said wistfully. "We are both busy people. I work during the day and have the gallery too, plus all the other unusual things that seem to take place."

I looked at Victor's handsome face as I finished, and felt a rush of warmth. I leaned forward and kissed him deeply, urgently. I felt his hand caress the top of my thighs, then slip down between my legs, squeezing the fabric of my jeans against my inner thighs. I touched the side of his smooth face with my fingers and traced the contours of his jaw and neckline, then trailed my fingers down over his firm chest to his hard, flat stomach. I broke our kiss and allowed my mouth to follow the path my fingers had taken, stopping at the top of his jeans. I raised my eyes to his and smiled shyly. His hands moved lightly over my back and caressed the back of my head as he wordlessly allowed me to continue. I turned back the front of his jeans and released his stiff penis. As I bent my head forward I glanced quickly up at him. The look of naked desire on his face felt like the heat of the sun to me; an irresistible expression that made my stomach tighten and my legs turn weak with passion.

I took him in my mouth then, our groans of ecstasy mingling. I could feel his muscles tightening as I closed my eyes and concentrated on his sweet taste. "Feels so good," he muttered thickly, his fingers twisting in my hair. Abruptly, he lifted my head away from him, freeing his erect member from my mouth. "Take your jeans off," he ordered, his voice gruff.

Quickly, I obeyed, allowing my jeans to fall to the floor and meet his in a rumpled pile. He grabbed me and turned me around, grinding himself roughly against my backside. I gasped and reached out to a chair for balance as he entered me quickly. He hung on to my hips firmly, plunging himself into me forcefully time and time again. I dug my fingers into the arms of the chair, his size filling me, stabbing me, almost more than I could handle. Wild sensations flowed through me as he continued, my body teetering on the edge, pain and passion mixed together. I gasped out loud, unable to speak even his name.

Victor continued pounding himself in and out of me, his hands kneading the flesh above my hips. His breathing was shallow and I could tell he was trying to keep his passionate utterances low, aware neighbors could hear us, if not see us. My endurance was being tested; my strength began to fail, my knees to weaken under his onslaught. I slowly maneuvered to a standing position.

"Wait, wait," he gasped as he knotted his arms around my waist and drove his groin one last time at me. His body froze in orgasm as a steady stream of satisfied moans flowed from his open mouth against my perspiring back. He slowly lifted my body back against his, still staying securely within me. "Sorry," he whispered, pulling my hair away from my ear and neck gently. "Did I hurt you?" His arms wrapped around me tightly.

"I'm okay," I replied weakly. I knew if he let go I would fall to the floor.

Victor licked at my neck and bit it softly. "I want to make you feel good.

If I keep doing this, will I?" Victor trailed one of his hands over my pubic hair and lightly dipped his fingers, searching for the source of my pleasure.

"Maybe," I sighed, feeling his mouth on my throat. I moved my legs apart slightly, letting him access me in any way he wanted.

Victor continued to kiss my neck and throat while teasing my clitoris. His other hand moved to my breast, squeezing and stroking firmly. I leaned against his sweaty chest and relaxed. Within a few moments I began to feel the slow but steady climb towards my own climax. I sighed loudly, letting Victor know that what he was doing was working and not to stop. He pulled even closer and fingered me steadily; my legs began to weaken again the closer I got. I could feel Victor growing hard again as he worked my body.

"I'm so close," I moaned, kissing the side of his face, his long hair a tasseled woven mess with mine.

Suddenly, at the moment that of my climax, Victor latched his mouth securely onto my throat and bit down hard, breaking my skin. His blood lust had re-emerged in the heat of his own rekindled passion. I cried out and squirmed in Victor's arms, almost overcome with the sensations from both ends of my body.

As Victor buried his teeth in my neck and sucked, my knees buckled in exhaustion. My arms hung limply at my sides. I was unable to fend him off; I just hoped he knew when to stop. '*Victor*,' I let my inner voice ring in his head, as my body grew weaker.

Victor quickly pulled his mouth back and moaned with satisfaction, my blood still spilling down his throat. "Kala," he mumbled, turning me to face him. He shook his head as if to clear his mind. "Kala – I'm sorry," he spoke with the realization of what he had done.

I looked at Victor, shaken, my eyes fixed in shock on him. His teeth were stained crimson from my blood. I rubbed the side of my face in confusion. "Why?"

Victor gripped me by my shoulders. "I got excited. I'm sorry. Let me fix you, please." He put an arm around me and looked at the wound on my throat. He touched it with his fingers and drew away some of the blood that had collected around the gashes.

As Victor attended to the damage he'd inflicted, I stood numbly in a foggy daze. The after-glow of my sexual heat slowly faded and I dreamily re-played my role in his pleasure. A half-smile crossed my lips as I thought about the mix of sensations we had both just experienced. I wondered if he'd liked it. I know I did.

Chapter 42

We were offered a ride to the Manor in the limousine, but passed in favor of taking my car. We wanted the convenience of leaving when we wanted to, not just when Sheldon's driver was available.

"Are you mad?" Victor asked from the passenger seat of the car. He appeared to be full of nervous energy.

"No," I replied quickly. I didn't think that I was.

"You are very quiet," he insisted, rolling the window down a crack for some fresh air.

"Well, why don't you do the talking," I suggested, looking over at him. "You were going to tell me about Lyla. I think today was the day?"

Victor leaned back in his seat, an almost sour look on his face. "Yes, I know today was the day. And I do owe you some sort of explanation behind Lyla and me."

I nodded in agreement. "And?" I prodded, helping him continue on.

"Can we make it through this bash first? Then I *promise* on the way home I will spell it out for you," Victor bargained. "I'd rather go into it at the end of the night, not now. I'd just rather not think about it now."

I shrugged, keeping my eyes on the road. "That's fine. Any particular reason as to why later is better than now? Are you afraid of how I might react to you or to Lyla when I see her tonight?" I was curious as to his motives.

"I just want to give myself enough time to tell you the story and answer any questions you might have. I would hate for us to be in the driveway at the Manor and still be discussing this."

I concurred with him. "All right, fair enough. So, is Nathan back?" I wondered if he had returned from his impromptu trip and would be part of the company at the party.

"No, " he replied. It was obvious that Victor was still peeved at Nathan's disappearance.

"I see," I said quietly. I was now concerned as to what Nathan was off doing and where he was doing it. After all, I was the last one to see him. I was wondering now if I was going to be the last to have *ever* seen him.

We arrived at the Manor, pulling onto the grounds and down the circular driveway, parking behind the big black limo near the front steps that led to the double doors and the grand entrance of the mansion. I shut the car off and glanced at Victor. He stared straight ahead, his attention focused on nothing in particular and appearing none too thrilled at being here.

"Nathan's here," Victor abruptly announced as he rolled his window up. I could hear the anger in his voice.

"Okay, take it easy. Let's not cause a scene." I grabbed Victor's arm to make my point. "Give Nathan a chance to answer your questions, okay?" I looked him straight in the eye. We didn't need any more emotional outbursts at the Manor. I knew that from experience.

Victor closed his eyes. "I will be on my best behavior," he ground his teeth between his lips. "I can control my anger – really. Nathan already knows that I'm here and that I'm not pleased with him."

"Okay. Let's go; the sooner we get in there the sooner we can leave. I'm not exactly thrilled to be here either."

My plan for the night was to stay as far away from Sheldon as I could, even if it meant mingling with those I did not know. Aside from that I was eager to have a few private words with Nathan; to see where he'd been and what he'd been doing. I'm not sure what made me think he'd actually tell me, but it was worth a try. I guess I felt that now we had some sort of bond, that maybe I was special. I also anticipated seeing Kevin again. My stomach was full of butterflies when I thought about it, but I remained optimistic.

Victor and I walked up the broad stairs to the Manor. As we approached the tall doors at the top they silently opened inward, allowing us admittance. We could hear the soft tinkle of distant piano music and a multitude of voices coming from the back terrace. It sounded like the party was in full swing. Victor and I stopped near the waterfall in the vestibule and he reached out and took me by my arms. "They know we are here; Sheldon is on his way to greet us," Victor said. "He wants us to wait here for him."

Just then the French doors at the far end of the room opened, their lace panels dancing with the slight movement. A formally dressed Sheldon entered and stood for a moment looking at us.

"So good to see you both again," Sheldon said as he closed the doors behind him. He held a glass of wine in his hand and sipped it in the most debonair manner.

Victor put his arm around my back as we walked towards Sheldon. "Kevin and his friends are here as well?" Victor asked.

"Oh yes. I invited them to stay here at the Manor while they are in town. No sense in putting you and Nathan out. We have plenty of room here." Sheldon's eyes roamed the great room. "Kevin is quite interesting; he's done much in his travels. I can tell Kala is eager to meet up with him again. This is good."

"I guess Kala and I will go outside and *meet up with him then*." Victor mocked Sheldon and pushed me along, his hand pressing firmly into my back. I was ready to cut my encounter with Sheldon short and promptly followed Victor's unspoken urging to get us to the party.

"Why don't you join everyone outside, Victor. I would like to speak with Kala for a moment, take her on a little tour of the mansion. She's in good hands. Don't worry, I'll return her to you unharmed. Promise." Sheldon produced a big toothy smile and his eyes sparkled with amusement at me.

Victor did not utter a sound at first, already pissed off over the reappearance of Nathan. He finally spoke, looking directly at Sheldon as he did so. "I'd better not find out you crossed over any lines while you are with her."

"I would not even think about it, " Sheldon scoffed at Victor's threat. "My Sovereign is here tonight and my future Emissary as well." His eyes locked upon mine. "I will be a gentleman."

I swallowed hard, feeling a large lump tightening in my throat. I did not want to be left alone with him.

"Make it quick. I will come looking for you if I think you are trying to pull something," Victor warned him as he gently brushed my shoulder with his hand and took steps to the exit. He looked back once, hesitantly, before letting himself out, the piano music rising and falling with the opening and closing of the doors. He was gone. Victor surely would find Nathan, given the mood he was in. He had things he wanted to say.

"He's very protective of you," Sheldon sighed, as if Victor's actions were foolish and totally unnecessary.

"He cares about me," I said.

"That much is obvious, to all of us." Sheldon laughed lightly. "Enough of all that; I thought tonight we could be civil to each other. Start over. I'd like to show you around." He motioned up the stairs with his glass of wine. "Come. One day you will share in all this." He slowly began to climb the stairs, waiting for me to follow. Having little choice, but knowing Victor and Nathan were within screaming distance, I did.

Sheldon stayed several steps in front of me as I followed him slowly and reluctantly to the top. I had little interest in seeing much more of the home. Fact was I did not really care. What I had seen up to this point was beautiful and in some ways eccentrically designed; I was sure I'd see more of the same going from room to room. This was not my home and never would be. Knowing my brother was nearby clouded my mind as I scaled the stairs. I wanted to see him again, much more than I wanted to see this house. Even if we could not talk freely right away, just being able to cast my eyes on him would please my heart.

"Kevin will still be here when we are done," Sheldon read into my thoughts, turning and chivalrously offering me his hand.

"I hate it when you do that," I muttered, irritated with his uninvited intrusion. I accepted his hand and stood next to him on the landing at the top.

"Hate what?" Sheldon seemed confused with my comment but began his tour anyway, walking down the short hallway. He felt as if he had done nothing wrong.

"You know, when you read my thoughts. I don't like people in my head," I said as I walked by his side.

The hall was short but wide with ivory wall coverings and large tightly loomed tapestries done in muted tones. Very Victorian, they hung to the floor. The house felt old to me now, as if I could finally sense its age. It wasn't so much how it was decorated or any mustiness or staleness in the air; it was more a feeling I got as I walked down the hallway; as if I had done it before, sometime in history. I didn't think it was possible, but then again maybe it was Nerissa who walked this hallway so many years ago. What would she have been doing here? She knew nothing of her position as Emissary and therefore would have no purpose to be in this house. I was puzzled. The feeling was strong.

I remembered back to the first night I was here at the Manor with Victor and Nathan. How I admired the structure from the driveway, and thought the home had to be several hundred years old. I was fairly certain now that it was. My soul dated it.

"I don't mean to intrude by reading your mind. That is one of the ways my kind communicate," Sheldon explained, stopping directly in front of a white door. He set his wineglass on a small olive colored, marble-topped table and reached for the jewel-toned doorknob. "I will try to not read your thoughts," Sheldon added, pushing the door open.

I was impressed with Sheldon's composure with me tonight, and the fact that he was acting as classy as he was dressed just made me wonder what he was up to. I hated to think so cynically of him, but Sheldon did not seem the type to be genuinely nice to someone he did not like, and I knew he had little tolerance for me – and I for him – which made our little sightseeing trip seem like a sham. We were acting two-faced towards one another and neither one of us would end the charade. What was he up to?

"This is one of our spare living quarters; Kevin, City and Gage will be staying here in the main house. This will be one of their rooms," Sheldon explained, turning on an overhead light so that I could see the room fully with my human eyes. "Everything is antique of course, English, Victorian."

I nodded, feeling as if I was in a museum and wondering where the red velvet rails were to keep me away from the furniture and on track to the next exhibit. “Looks very expensive,” I said, running my hand down the polished maple footboard of a queen-sized sleigh bed dressed in pale pink chenille and lace pillows of all shapes and sizes.

“I’m sure if it were for sale it would be,” Sheldon agreed quickly with my comment, proud he could show such items to me. “Come, I’ll show you the others.” He awkwardly placed his hand on my arm to guide me out of the room and shut the door behind us. “I don’t live in this section of the house. I stay in a section that is newer – over looks the harbor, very nice. You would like it. I know how much you love the ocean air.” Sheldon made small talk as we approached the next door on the opposite side of the hallway.

The moment Sheldon opened up the door to the room, which looked identical to the last, I stepped backwards instead of forward. My little voice, silent all evening, had kicked in, causing me to take several steps away from Sheldon. A distinct voice within my head screamed ‘*don’t go in*!’ I was reminded of the night I stood at my own front door paralyzed in fright while the Blue Daemon lurked nearby. How determined my little voice was to make me do what it wanted me to. It was difficult to ignore.

There was something about this room that wasn’t right; something my inner spirit picked up. It was an oddness I could not describe. I watched as Sheldon entered the room, unaware that I was no longer behind him. He flipped the light on. I was able to look in at him nervously but did not make any effort to follow him. I began to feel very cool; it was drafty where I stood, as if I were standing in front of a blowing fan or under an air conditioning duct, but I wasn’t.

“What’s wrong?” Sheldon asked from the middle of the vacant room. He stared perplexed at me.

“I don’t want to go in there. I can’t.” I shook my head vigorously and jammed my hands in my front pockets.

Sheldon glanced around the bedroom, puzzled. “This is an exquisite room.” He opened his arms up and turned around to admire the design and decoration.

I shook my head, still feeling the chill and then looked behind me, feeling as if I was being watched. The feeling grew to an almost physical sensation, as if I was being touched in a way. “I’m going downstairs,” I announced and promptly took off for the staircase that would lead me down and out to the party where Victor and my safety were.

“Wait!” Sheldon called from the room. “I don’t understand.”

I heard his cry of bewilderment, but by that time I was halfway down the stairs. I was out the French doors and amongst the party crowd, breathing heavily, before Sheldon reached the railing.

I had not known so many people would be here tonight, vampires of all different mortal ages circulating at once. I finally caught a glimpse of Nathan and Victor in the corner of the patio near a flowering trellis. They were talking somewhat heatedly; at least, Victor seemed rather animated with his hand gestures towards Nathan. I did not care what they were talking about or what I interrupted; I required their company. I hurriedly made my way through a small crowd of females to where Victor and Nathan bickered, facing one another with drinks in hand. They became silent as I joined them.

"Kala," Nathan acknowledged me shortly.

"Hello," I snapped back. I spotted Kevin with City on the terrace as well, near the baby grand piano. They were engaged in conversation with Sheldon, who had just made his way back to the party.

"What's wrong?" Victor asked me, watching my expression.

I shrugged and peered around me again. I didn't know how to describe what I had felt.

Then I heard it. An unnatural voice, echoing in the distance. I heard it clearly and turned about to see the source. The voice sounded as if it was coming from far away, eerie and high as if it were pitched and propelled at me through a tunnel. "Did you hear that?"

"Hear what?" Nathan asked, sipping his drink and looking at me over the top of his eyeglasses as if wondering how much I already had to drink.

"I heard something. A voice. And, I've been feeling things..." my voice trailed off and I crossed my arms in discomfort, my uneasiness keeping me on the edge.

"Voices? You mean like we talked about not too long ago – background noise?" Victor questioned, attempting to get to the bottom of my apparent anxiety. "There are a lot of people here tonight."

"No. Not at all," I replied, watching Sheldon from where I stood. He was still addressing Kevin. I wanted it to be me; I wanted to talk to Kevin, too.

"Did Sheldon do something to you?" Victor asked, watching me watch Sheldon.

"He wouldn't dare," Nathan said in astonishment and poked Victor's arm with his index finger. "Even *he* knows better than that."

The three of us stood making small chat for several minutes, looking like any other group. I tried to forget my bizarre experience with the unknown – the voices, the cold chills – and joined in with the discussion at hand. My attention was broken every few moments by the voice in my head, or was it coming from somewhere nearby? I could not tell any longer; it was all around me. I had no idea what it was saying. Each time I heard the voice, I concentrated harder and harder, trying to catch the message. I became oblivious to the goings on around me and stood there, focusing inward, ignoring Victor, Nathan, and the party. Then Lyla came by, distracting me as she wrapped her long slender pale arm around Victor's waist and cuddled up against his strong body. She coyly told Victor that they were opening up a vintage bottle of blood wine and he had to join her in a glass. Poof, they were gone.

I looked at Nathan, unsure how to act now that he and I were alone. But were we? The voice still filled my head, though it had lessened in volume. I struggled to decipher the words; I could not. I thought the voice might be male, but that was all I could tell. I was becoming frustrated again. I tried to push the voice away.

A waiter approached offering Nathan and me drinks; we both gratefully accepted. I held mine close, admiring the color of the wine as it spun like a mini whirlpool in my glass as I swirled it.

"Just get back?" I asked, breaking the uneasy silence between us. My eyes left the glass and fell upon his stony face. I wondered if he could hear the voice I heard too, but had found a way to ignore it, or maybe the voice didn't bother him at all. I wondered.

Nathan nodded. "Tonight." He lit a cigarette.

"Victor was upset," I chuckled a little, thinking Nathan would find some amusement in it. I chuckled trying to drown out the voice that would not leave me.

"So he told me." Nathan did not seem to want my company. His coldness blocked my friendliness like an Arctic front. Just when I thought I had gotten used to his abrupt manner, I realized I never would.

"I see," I mumbled and let the subject of his disappearance and Victor's resentment lie. I had to take advantage of the few moments we had to speak somewhat freely. The voice in my mind was driving me crazy. "Nathan, I'm hearing voices..." I began as yet another wave of voices wheeled about in my head. My shaking hands brought the drink to my lips and I sipped slowly, waiting for any words from him that might make me feel better.

"What kind of voices?" Nathan looked at me clearly for the first time as he pressed his cigarette to his lips.

"I think it's just one voice, but I can't tell anymore. I don't know if it's all in my head or if it's something near by – a ghost, or spirit – even one of your kind playing with me. I just don't know. Can you hear it?" I could not explain it any better.

"I hear nothing unusual. I can tell you it's not one of us. I would know. It's not our style." He exhaled a stream of pale gray smoke out his nose.

The voice became louder in my head now and it was obviously male.

There seemed to be urgency for me to understand what it was that he was trying to convey. I heard it by the tone, not by content. The language was not English and I spoke nothing other. Hearing the voice echo in my head made me shake as it hammered relentlessly again and again, picking away at my nerves. I held my drink out in front of me, not saying anything yet, hoping Nathan would understand that I needed him to take the glass away from me before I dropped it, thereby breaking it and causing a scene. I did not feel I could hold onto it any longer as the resonance in my head had started to make my body tremor involuntarily.

"What's wrong?" Nathan asked now aware that I was in distress. He had no idea what was causing me to act so strangely. He watched me closely, his eyes narrowing.

I stared down at the stone floor, trying to focus on it. I felt lightheaded and needed to fix on something I knew did not move. I tried to rationalize that my feet were planted firmly on the earth; I was not walking; I was not moving, but the sensation continued on. "Take it," I mumbled, still holding my drink out and hoping he'd understand me.

I could see and feel Nathan move in on me, but he made no attempt to take the glass. "I can't," he said slowly. "The glass – look at the glass."

I looked. The glass was melting in my grasp, slumping and roiling like hot wax. Pieces of the liquid glass fell splattering to the patio floor, mixing in with the red wine. The glass got so hot I had to let it go; it burnt my fingers as they sunk into the gelatinous mass. Startled and confused, I stared at the puddle of glossy pink tinged debris that began to harden on the cool rocks, oblivious to the crowd that had gathered around.

"Kala," Nathan's voice spoke softly. "What's wrong? What are you hearing?"

The crowd around me had now spilled further out onto the patio, catching the attention of Victor who was trying to cut his encounter with Lyla short. He knew that something was not right with me; he knew that only a human could draw a swarm so quickly in a party of Vampires.

"Is there a basement to this house?" I asked out loud, drawing my arm close to my body and feeling the pain of the burns. I tried to breathe slowly and evenly and not give in to the hysteria that was welling up inside.

Victor appeared in front of me, his mere presence calming. "No basement here, just a wine cellar," Victor replied evenly. "Why? What's going on?"

"I need to get there," I insisted. "Victor, there is someone in the wine cellar who needs to speak with you. Take me there." I left no room for argument. I had no idea who was in the wine cellar, or why I knew they needed to speak to Victor, but I felt it deep inside me, the voice's effort to communicate with me. Since I could not understand the vocal pleas I had been hearing all night the voice had found another way to reach me; my own little voice interpreting and translating the desperate need, making me understand.

"What do you mean?" Victor asked.

"Just take her there," Nathan commanded.

Victor turned and cut through the crowd with no further words, leaving room for me to follow. I did so, with Nathan close behind. We entered the house together and Victor led us behind the main staircase. He indicated a door that lay flush with the wall. He depressed something and the door sprung open to reveal a deep dark stairwell leading sharply down. Losing your footing on these steps could be, at the least, a broken neck. Victor reached into the blackness and flipped a switch. The dim light that flickered on did a less than adequate job, but would work with Victor's keen eyes leading first.

"Yes! This is it!" I said, as I smelled the air drifting up from the damp quarters below us. "Take me down!" I pressed my sore hand against Victor's back, encouraging him to lead on.

"All right, but be careful," Victor cautioned as he took the first step onto the aged tread. He reached back and took me by the wrist, wrapping his fingers securely around it and squeezing tightly. I followed him down, Nathan close on my heels.

"How deep is this cellar?" I asked Victor, looking nervously around, seeing only dark patches and tall shadows in each direction.

"Not too deep," he answered, his voice echoing softly in the blackness. "It was used for some storage and wine, that's about it."

I could see old timber crates and moldy unmarked cardboard boxes stacked very high against the walls and piled about. There were some antique wooden barrels that had seen better times scattered through out, with remnants of yellowing newspaper covering much of the flooring. "Take me that way." I pointed down a dark path where some dusty, opaque bottles, festooned in cobwebs, lay unbroken on the ground.

"What's back there?" Victor asked, as if even *he* did not want to go that far.

I had no answer for him. "I don't really know. I only know that *someone* is here for you. This person *must* speak to you. We don't have much time." I spoke from intuition only.

Victor's eyes left mine and met Nathan's, who stood silently behind us, observing only. He shrugged in a manner that suggested he was leaving all decisions to Victor. It was up to Victor to resume the journey, which was the only way any of us would truly know who waited.

Victor led me down the path I had chosen as I slowly allowed my eyes to adjust to the dimness. "How much further?" Victor inquired, ducking his tall frame under a hefty sized beam that had started to separate from the ceiling above.

"Right there! Right there! He's there!" I exclaimed in excitement. I was thrilled that I had found the source of the voice and that my intuition had been right. "That man – that's him." I said. I pointed at an old man sitting dejectedly on a metal container in the corner, his wrinkled face looking sad and weary.

"Where? What are you looking at?" Victor looked in all directions. "I don't sense or see anyone else here."

My eyesight could not have been failing me and I knew Victor's was much better than mine. Why did he not see what I did? "Right there!" I said again, stretching my arm forward and extending my index finger to point out the man who had come to see Victor. "Can't you see him?" I took a step past Victor and stood closer to the old man. He looked directly at me and began to speak to me in a language I still could not understand, his eyes pleading for comprehension.

"I see nothing!" Victor said in frustration.

"Victor; he's a elderly man, short, wearing a tan cap and a tan jacket. He looks very sad." I tried to describe what I was seeing to him. I continued to look at the man as I spoke. "He's here to see you, and I don't know what he's saying. It's not English." I watched the old man speak. I could see how intent he was that I understand what he was saying. I felt horrible that I could not.

"Well, tell me what he is saying," Victor said. "Try and speak back his words."

I listened to the man articulate his feelings and watched him move his hands about vigorously trying to make his position clear to me. "I can't. I can't. He's speaking much too fast," I said in anguish.

"Try!" Victor bellowed, forcing me closer to the old man.

I suddenly realized there was no way for me to accurately unravel what was being said to me. With my little voice hammering insistently, I grabbed Victor by his arm and tugged him to me. "Look into my eyes," I ordered without explanation and directed his face in line with mine by placing my hands on the side of his head tightly and angling it just so. I then slipped my hands over Victor's ears like a pair of headphones. I knew by getting Victor to look into my eyes he could see the old man as I saw him, frail, dismal, but determined to speak what was on his mind. By putting my hands over Victor's ears I could enable him to hear the man as I did, in the foreign language that I heard but could not translate.

I could see by the change in Victor's face that he was able to understand the language and what was being said to him. He recognized the visitor even though I did not, and though he could not see the man with his own eyes, by borrowing mine he could. He seemed pleased to be in the old man's company.

It would seem I was some sort of medium – that the man I saw, only I could see; the man I heard, only I could hear. The man was apparently a spirit, although he looked and seemed very alive to me. He was someone from Victor's past who needed to reach him in the present and used me in order to do so.

Nathan had quietly left before Victor and I were ready to leave the cellar. Victor sat silently on a pile of bundled up old newspapers, his hands clasped loosely in his lap, lost in thought. His experience with the spirit was over. I stood next to him silently.

"Thank you," Victor said finally, rubbing his hands on the thighs of his jeans. He looked at me and smiled.

"For what?" I asked, confused

"For what you did," he replied lightly. "Letting my Grandfather speak to me. He's been waiting so long to talk to me."

"Your Grandfather?" I asked in astonishment. I tried to grasp the whole idea of reuniting Victor with his Grandfather; allowing a spirit that had been dead some two hundred years to communicate with someone in the here and now. But why?

"Yes. The man that I had just told you about tonight who I thought blamed me for my Mother's death. Only he doesn't. He was just sad like we all were that she had died so young. He did not blame me, not for that, not for anything that happened after that," Victor recounted with a cleansing sigh as if he could finally let some guilt and ill memories go.

"He came back to tell you all that?" I asked, running my fingers through his hair, tracing his ear.

Victor slid off his newspaper stool and stood next to me. He draped his arms around my waist and hugged me tightly. "I have much to tell you about my past. I owe you this story. Let's get out of here and find a place to talk."

Chapter 43

Victor and I managed to escape the party by ducking out the front door of the Manor while all the guests were still out back socializing. We did not know how long we could remain absent before people would begin to search for us, Sheldon particularly, since he would be wondering where we had gone and what we were up to. Victor needed to talk to me; he had some explaining to do and wanted to find a place he could do it without interruption. He guided me down a steep bank on the far side of the house that led to the beach. It was difficult to see the ground and maneuver through the tall sea grass over the loose and rocky terrain, but once at the bottom of the sharp hill the earth flattened out to the soft sands of the quiet inlet.

We silently walked along the beach under the star filled sky. The surf curled and crashed next to us. I relished hearing and feeling the white water snap and crackle, the mist on my skin, the salt tang in the breeze. I could feel much of Victor's tensions vanish with each step we took together and I felt myself relaxing too. We stopped a distance down the beach, not so far away that the huge house, balanced on the cliff above us, was out of sight. We sat on some boulders near the water's edge, listening to the gentle winds that swept off the surface of the ocean mix with the elegant tones of piano music drifting down from the party.

"I used to love to come here," Victor said, as he lay flat on his back on top of a cool stone; he placed his hands on his stomach and breathed deeply, smelling the clean salt in the night air.

I climbed onto the boulder next to his, letting my legs hang over the sides. "When did you come here?"

"A lot when I was a kid – when I was human," he said. "I would lay on this rock just like I am now, during the day or at night, thinking, dreaming; I just loved to be here." Victor seemed happy with his ancient memories.

"Why here? How did you know this place as a child?" I asked curiously, knowing the home up above us was occupied with undead tenants and had been for a long time.

"That is where my story begins, just about the time I became what I am today," Victor said somberly. "This house – oh, this house." He shook his head sadly.

"How's that?" I asked, leaning back on my elbows and hearing some very loud laughter come from the party on the patio up at the house. I guess we were not missed yet.

"This house did not always belong to the people I refer to as *my* people now. It once belonged to my family, *my* human family, a long, long time ago," Victor began quietly. He picked his head up and folded his arms beneath like a pillow. "So much went wrong and I blame myself for it."

"I guess that explains why you knew your way around the house and how you knew about the cellar when others may not have known, especially since you were never really welcomed in the house."

"Yes. My Grandfather owned this house. He built this house – the original part of it anyway. My Grandmother died before I was born and before the house was complete, but my mother lived here with him for many years, until she married. When us kids were born we would come and visit my Grandfather often, spend summers here. It was great! One of the paintings in your gallery is of this harbor. The way I remember the ships coming and going in the night when I would watch them from my bedroom window."

I recalled the painting of the tall ships under the moon in a tiny harbor that hung on the wall next to my desk. "Yes. It does look like that," I agreed, looking out over the inlet and seeing a small ship anchored in place.

"When I took the dark gift, it was a few years after my mother had passed on and my relationship with my grandfather was very not good. My brothers and sisters and I would see each other occasionally, but they were all married and had families of their own so there was no one I was close to. I worked a lot. I spent time with Nerissa. Thinking I would spend the rest of eternity with her was the best thing I could have done at the time, so I thought. But of course *that,* as you know, did not work out as planned. After the trial Nathan and I went through due to Nerissa's death, we were banished and all alone. But some people in the High Counsel still had some unsettled business with me, I guess. They felt it was not enough to just be cast out of society."

"What do you mean? What more could they do to you?" I asked him.

"You'd be surprised," Victor laughed hollowly. "We can be ruthless parasites."

"What kind of unsettled business did the High Counsel have with you?" I slid off my rock and stood near Victor's shoulders. He continued to lay flat, staring up at the night sky.

He turned his head. "Well, a short time after my banishment I met up with a woman – my kind. I had little dealings with any of my people up to that point, just Nathan and the members of the Counsel who hated me. So, I was eager and interested in many ways to get to know this woman. She was tall, she was beautiful and she seemed sympathetic to what I had gone through. She was a light in my life at the time when I had none and I really needed someone."

"Lyla," I interjected flatly. It was clear to me who that light was.

"Lyla. Yes. Only she was never what she appeared to be. I spent some time with her and we got to know each other. Then, all that she learned about me and about who I was she took back to the members of the High Counsel. They used that information to hurt me some more, not just me, but my human family this time." The tone in Victor's voice was deeper, this memory was painful to recall.

"She was a spy?" I asked.

"Whatever you want to call it. She turned on me. The Counsel must have promised her something as a reward. It was a job to betray me. That's the way I look at it. Shortly after Lyla broke away from me, the High Counsel took over my grandfather's home. They don't ask you nicely to leave when they invade a home, they just take. The Counsel wanted the property, so they took it. They killed everyone in the house that night – my grandfather, some workers and a cousin and an aunt. Murdered."

I did not know how to respond. Saying I was sorry after hearing about a two hundred-year-old loss didn't seem to make sense. I just rubbed his chest gently with my hand and allowed him to continue his story.

"So, you can see why I hate to come here. You can see why I don't want to be here with Lyla. I had not seen her in many years and did not expect to see her the first night we were all back here together. Who would think she'd still be here? I was quite surprised and not in a good way either."

"How can you even stand her to touch you? To take hold of you as she does and drag you off somewhere with her?"

"I'm numb after so many years. I have no feelings about the past unless I want to remember it. It's very hard to explain to someone like you. I was human once, but not any longer. Lyla has no place in my heart. She lost that spot. I tolerate her right now because of all that is going on around you."

"What did your grandfather have to say to you tonight?" I asked.

"He told me that he did not blame me for my mother's death. He knew she was sick; he was devastated when his daughter died and said that he knew I did all I could as a doctor. He also wanted to let me know that he did not hold me responsible for the massacre that took place in the house the night he was killed. He knows *what* and *who* I am now – a vampire with eternal life – and why I took the dark gift to begin with. It was my love for Nerissa that started the entire events that led to my Grandfather's death. He knows all about it. He understands. He forgives me. They all forgive me."

"How does he know all this? He just does? Or when you die you become all knowing? Is he watching you? " I inquired. I was intrigued, momentarily obsessed with the dead.

"Nerissa told him," he replied reverently. "He told me that everyone is waiting for me, whenever I am ready to die. My mother, all my brothers and sisters, my grandfather, even Nerissa is waiting for the day I decide – you know. Nerissa still loves me. They still love me and understand why I did what I did. They forgive me." Victor's voice was as light as a whisper when he spoke to me, as if what his grandfather had told him tonight was the most delicate and fragile of all memories he would ever have.

I swallowed hard, hearing him tell me about people waiting on the other side for him. I thought about Sara and hoped that someday she would be there for me, on the other side. "That's incredible. I can't imagine what must be going through your mind."

Victor sat up, towering over me. "It's all good, I assure you. I always wondered what would happen when and if I died. Now I know. It gives me something else to think about."

"You aren't thinking about ... "

Victor interrupted me immediately. "No, no, please don't think like that. I have no plans to end my life soon. But when you have lived as long as I have and know you can live forever, it's a new thought to think there is some way to end it all, to know someone will be waiting for you. It's almost like being human, you know. I'm not so invincible after all."

"Yes, I guess I can understand it. You, who have lived forever, know you don't have to, that you can die if you choose."

Victor nodded. "It's almost humbling."

As we walked back along the beach, I realized I did not know how I would react to seeing Lyla again. I knew I would run into her a few more times tonight. Her beauty infuriated me. How could she strut about light-heartedly as if she had done no wrong, to clutch Victor like a new or rekindled lover? How arrogant.

Slipping back into the party was harder than sneaking out. Perhaps it was the scent of me being human that drew attention to Victor and me as we rejoined the social gathering. The crowd had thinned out slightly and that could have been another reason our return was more noticeable. It was easy for me to spot Kevin and City. They were sitting together on a wrought iron bench. Gage was missing; I had not seen him all night. Nathan was still part of the celebration, a drink in one hand and a cigarette in the other, conversing with the current Sovereign Teague while Sheldon stood nearby and observed everyone's actions.

I was dying to walk up to Kevin and City, to take a seat next to my brother and talk with anticipation about meeting up with him later. Somehow I just couldn't find the courage to do it. I couldn't face being rejected again for being personable, for acting like a sister. I knew he was willing to speak to me privately, later on tonight after the party. I would have to leave it at that and hope for the best.

A short time later Nathan nonchalantly approached me. Victor had left briefly to get some cigarettes from the car, so for the moment I was vulnerable and alone.

"We need to talk," Nathan said. He was always so business-like. Never a friendly hello, or a forced welcoming gesture, just always the stern face and affairs at hand.

"Okay. When?" I asked with a shrug.

"Later. After the party," Nathan said.

"My brother Kevin and I are getting together sometime tonight. To talk. It's very important to me."

"All right. Make sure you don't talk here. Find a place to go away from the Manor. There are too many ears here," Nathan warned. "It's best."

"We can do that," I agreed.

"But you and I need to meet before dawn. Don't be surprised to see me at some point later tonight."

"What's wrong?" I asked, knowing by Nathan's determination that something of magnitude was waiting.

"Not here; not now," Nathan frowned. "Let me see your Amulet. Be casual about it. Don't draw attention."

I slowly drew the chain out of my collar and allowed the stone to lie flat against my shirt. "See it?" I asked quietly.

"Put it back, hide it, leave it there – don't let anyone else see it," Nathan ordered harshly.

I glanced down at the pendent in my fingers and noticed it had changed colors again. It was now white. My eyes widened and flew up to meet Nathan's. "What does this mean?" I asked, hurriedly tucking it back into my shirt and feeling it rest against my bare skin.

"Later. We will talk later." His voiced trailed off as he started to walk away from me. I saw Victor return through the double doors and smiled as he joined me on the patio.

Victor placed his arm around me and gave me a quick squeeze. "Nathan was chatting with you," Victor commented. "What about?"

"Not a whole lot. You know Nathan would rather kill me than talk to me. I think he was just being diplomatic, for the Counsel," I replied, resting my tired head on his shoulder. "Nights are so long." I sighed heavily.

"Not really. But you have your human life you live by day, and your secret life you live by night, and very little time for you to rest. It's catching up to you."

He was right. I had been living both night and day for a while and giving myself very little sleep time. It appeared tonight would not be any different.

Chapter 44

I left the Manor with Kevin – alone. It had been Nathan's suggestion, and one I eagerly accepted. We needed the opportunity to finally be alone and talk. Victor and Nathan left in the limousine provided by the Manor, while Kevin and I took off in my car.

Our ride was quiet, broken only by polite comments about the party and trivial things like that. As we chatted, I thought about where we could go, a place where we wouldn't be bothered by over-zealous cops checking all the lovers' lanes and that type of thing.

The destination I chose was the parking lot at the Old Maple Forest. I didn't have a specific reason, I just remembered it as a fairly remote, quiet spot. I felt safe with Kevin; I knew he would protect me if trouble arose. I did not dwell on if he'd do this because I was his sister, or because one day I would be his Emissary.

When we arrived at the lot I parked under the one and only overhead light. I put the convertible top down, partly to enjoy the balmy night air and partly to increase our ability to spot any potential danger signs. I shut the engine off and turned in my seat to face Kevin – to face I knew not what.

"Did you really think it crucial to drive this far away from the Manor?" Kevin asked bluntly, breaking the silence.

"Well yes, actually, I did," I replied quietly.

"All right. I think you're being a little paranoid, but whatever," he said in annoyance. "What would you like to talk about?"

I tensed up at his tone, at the overt hostility. This was not how I wanted to begin. "Listen, if you don't want to be here there is no sense in putting us both through this. I'll take you back." I straightened and reached for the key in the ignition.

"Look," Kevin said. " It's not that I don't want to talk to you. It's just that I don't want to talk about what you want to talk about. You can see I exist. Now, why can't you just let the rest go? Forget who I was. Just know me as I am now."

"How do you know what I want to talk about?" I said irritably.

"I know you want to talk about the past. I'm just not in the mood for it."

"Fine," I snapped. "Then I won't talk about all that. Just answer me one thing, okay?"

"What's that?"

"Tell me whether it was your choice to become what you are today or if it was forced upon you unwillingly. That's what I want to know."

"Why do you need to know?" Kevin asked.

"I know you have not been human for a while now. If you wanted to be this way – to be what you are – then I guess you got what you wanted, good, bad or otherwise. It was your life to do as you wanted and that was what you chose. I can accept that. If on the other hand it were forced upon you – well, then I would feel bad for you. I might even be able to understand your attitude towards me – being human and all – something you are not any longer. Maybe that's another reason why you've been avoiding me as long as you have. Please answer the question. Then I promise – no more questions about the past." I waited.

"It was my choice and I'm not just saying that to take the easy way out of this conversation," Kevin replied with a sigh. "Listen; you were just a kid when I left. You didn't know some things about me. I was not perfect. My health was not the greatest. I was a diabetic and I hated the injections. I hated the diets; I hated all of it. I could not even look at a needle any more without getting sick to my stomach. I knew the disease would get worse when I got older, so I just didn't get older. It was easy," Kevin explained, no remorse or regret in his voice.

"I might have been just a kid, but I knew you were diabetic. It couldn't have been that bad that you felt like killing yourself," I said. "And when did you find out about our dad – that he was, you know – like you are now?"

"A short time after. It was no big deal then. Still isn't," Kevin answered flatly.

I wished I had the same attitude about our father that he did. "Are you happy now?" I prodded.

"I look good; I feel good. That's all that matters. Someday you will understand what I mean."

"Maybe," I said doubtfully. "What about your friends, City and Gage? How do you feel about them?"

Kevin did not respond right away. "Feel? These are all human emotions. I can't relate."

"I don't understand. Victor can feel, he can love; what's the deal with you?"

"Victor is a mystery to me. It must be in his bloodline to have as many human traits as he does. His emotions are considered a weakness to our people. Feelings and emotions are what get you into trouble. If we feel anything, it's immediately suppressed. If you don't have emotions to get in your way, your reaction time to a situation is instantaneous. We operate off instinct – act fast and for yourself. That is *our* way."

"I'm glad Victor is the way he is," I said heatedly. "I don't see him as weak."

"You are not one of us. You would see the failings if you were."

This still wasn't working out the way I had hoped. Our talks now seemed to be more like a debate, but at least we were communicating, although agreeing on nothing. "So, where has Gage been all night?" I changed the topic carefully.

"Out and about. He doesn't like to be in one spot for long," Kevin replied distantly as if he wanted to be somewhere else, perhaps with Gage.

"He's odd. He gives me the creeps." I didn't care if my comments showed my human emotions. "I know he's your friend and all, but what's up with him? He's different, kind of like you, but not. I can't explain it."

"Gage is not what he seems; let's just leave it at that." Kevin smiled as if amused by my observation and opened up the car door to get out.

"Where are you going?" I asked. I got out of the car as well.

"I can't stay here. I need to get going, really. I'm going to find Gage or something," Kevin said, suddenly full of nervous energy. "It's night time – my time to live."

"At least let me drive –"

Kevin stopped me. "No, it's okay. Really. I'll walk or something. You should get home. It's late. You'll be safer at home." He shoved his hands in his pockets as he finished, turned and began to walk away from the car and me.

"Are you sure?" I asked in confusion, closing the car door and standing next to it. I couldn't decide if I should go after him or let him leave. I didn't understand his sudden change of mood.

"Yes."

"When are you leaving town?" I asked in desperation. I felt as if I would never see him again as I watched him walk away.

"I will let you know before I go," he answered without turning around. He continued to walk further away and into the darkest portion of the parking lot, headed away from the main road. I let him go. I didn't have the nerve to stop him.

I stood there in the quiet parking lot, my head down, as I thought about our meeting. While it hadn't gone as I'd hoped – I still had many unanswered questions – at least I felt that we had communicated and that he now thought of me as a person again – not an enemy to be avoided. Sadness filled me as I remembered the young girl and boy so many years ago. A brother and sister in memories only.

On the bright side I was still breathing. I had made it through the entire evening at a social gathering for the dead and managed to stay alive. Of course there was still the question as to why my Amulet changed colors tonight; this time from green to white, and what that all meant. I figured Nathan knew and that was why he needed to speak to me so urgently. That worried me. Nathan worried me.

I reflected back on the night once more and sighed. I was ready to head home. My questions would eventually get answered and a new week was ready to blossom. Work for me was less than ten hours away. I was tired and needed sleep. I felt like I could sleep one hundred years if nobody interrupted me. Fat chance.

I went to open my car door and the oddest thing happened. As I went through the motions I noticed there was no sound – no squeak of handle or hinges, no rustle of my clothing, nothing at all. I thought for a moment I had gone deaf as I glanced around me in the total silence, a silence so unexpected it was vociferous. No rustle of gentle winds through the trees; no animals creeping through the brush; no evening crickets chirping in the undergrowth; just stillness as if something with ultimate power over *all* had commanded the quiet and every element and being obeyed. I recalled again the stories I had heard about the Old Maple Forest and how pockets of a frightening silence had been reported by many who entered. There was never an explanation either.

Bemused, I stood still and looked around me. I wasn't actually *in* the forest, but the silence still enveloped me. A flicker of light caught my eye and I looked in the direction of the altars. A faint golden light shone through the trees and I studied it carefully. I remembered the last time I'd been here, with Nathan, when my Amulet had reacted so strangely, and I thought about Sara. After all, her ashes were scattered around here. Maybe this was another sign from her?

I reached into the glove box of the car and fumbled for my little flashlight. Straightening, I flicked it on and followed its feeble light into the forest and headed towards the altars. The unnatural silence continued to surround me.

When I arrived at the small clearing, I saw the tall bamboo torches were lit as they had been the last time I was here. Three torches blazed brightly under the cover of the soaring maples and pines in unruffled tranquility. I watched the orange glow of the flames bounce atop their fiber wicks silently, as silent as everything else around me. I tried to yawn and pop my ears to get them to operate, although I did not think the phenomenon was just happening to *me*. I felt the silence was everywhere.

I shut my flashlight off and felt the heat of the torches warming my skin. I walked slowly around the clearing. There was no sign of anybody, nothing except the torches – no decorations on the altars, no footprints, nothing.

"I'm glad you could make it." A voice behind me broke the silence, its complete unexpectedness caused my body to jump. I whirled around. Nathan.

"What are you doing here?" I asked in surprise.

"I told you that I needed to speak with you tonight," Nathan replied, walking by me and casually taking a seat on the smaller of the two altars.

"How did you know I'd be here?" I asked mistrustfully. "Were you following me?"

"I did not follow you," he answered with a sigh. "I don't have to."

I stood stiffly on one side of the altar. "What do you mean?" I asked.

"Forget all that for now," Nathan dismissed my question. "We have other things to talk about. Important things." He looked down at me. "Let me see the Amulet again."

I removed the chain from beneath my shirt and let the Amulet fall against my chest. "Why did the stone change colors?" I asked, wondering what this new phase meant. He was right. This was more important than some creepy silence.

Nathan reached out and slipped his fingers under the white stone. He examined it closely, not saying a word at first. "It looks as if the stone was charged again. That's stage two." He released the Amulet, allowing it to lie back upon my chest.

"Stage two? When?" I asked, looking down at the piece myself.

"Earlier tonight. A doorway opened for you when the spirit of Victor's grandfather came to you and you were able to acknowledge it. You were a medium between Victor and his grandfather's spirit. Currently, you sit on the threshold of three worlds: the living, human world in which we all live right now, vampires included; the portal to the spirit world where Sara and souls like Victor's grandfather continue living, and the Realm of Imprisonment where many of the Enforcers were stationed, myself included. The Realm of Imprisonment is just one of many realms that I know exist. I have the ability to travel from this world into The Realm of Imprisonment when I wish to. Someday when you have mastered all your skills and powers I would think you too will be able to cross over from one world to another – one dimension to another – one realm to another. The possibilities are endless. This world is full of gateways into other worlds, other places. You will know where they are and will be able to use them whenever you want." Nathan's voice was tinged with excitement as he spoke, the first time I'd heard real emotion from him.

"How do you know this? What does it all mean?" I asked.

"The Amulet has been three distinct colors thus far: black when you first found it and placed it around your neck. You are from *this* world – black is the signifying color. Once the Amulet was charged by placing it into the sign of the Enforcer, it turned green. I am from The Realm of Imprisonment and that color is green. And then it turned white when you encountered the spirit of Victor's grandfather. That is the world of spirits, apparitions; that color is white. You are becoming more sensitive to paranormal events. Your abilities, the ones Sara saw, are becoming more apparent everyday. This is why you are so sought after. It is now a race to see who will claim you."

"Claim me? Who wants to claim me?" I scratched my head in total bewilderment.

"Kala," Nathan said gently. "The situation is far more perilous than you could imagine. You know my people claim you, but there are other realms as well who covet you and will stop at nothing to attain you and your power. Sara and the Amulet are just a small sign of all that is out there. The problem for you right now is this: if you don't go willingly to the High Counsel when your time has come my people will force you, most likely causing you much harm in the process. This is true of the others; they will force you to win you."

I thought out loud. "Sara's book tells of a 'reunion', something about people coming together for the first time in a very long time. Am *I* the reunion? Am I the link – the center – bringing everyone together from everywhere? If I am in the middle of all these worlds, realms and dimensions it would seem that no society should claim me. There must be a way for me to do whatever I'm supposed to do – or be – without being a 'prize' to claim!"

"I don't really know," Nathan said. "I don't have the answers. Remember I told you when all this started that some answers I would have, some answers you would have and some we would have to figure out together. In the end it may just be what you want." Nathan removed his glasses and set them on his lap, rubbing his eyes with his fingers.

"Nathan, what do you think I should do?" I asked taking a seat next to him on the altar.

"What do you mean?" He looked at me

"Where should my loyalties go? What is your opinion?"

"I believe I will lose no matter what happens," he answered, skirting my question.

"Why will you lose?" I asked.

"The Enforcers that are left, including me, have been in hiding for a long time. Now that our rumored existence has been confirmed, we will be systematically hunted down and killed or sent back to another realm. Either way, our enemies are determined to remove us from this world. Those of us who remain have vowed to never create any more of us; we refuse to sire, so that eventually in time we will all die off – ending all of this."

Hearing Nathan speak the way he did was sad. "Well, when I become Emissary, perhaps I can make some changes," I said brightly. I didn't *like* the idea of becoming Emissary, but somehow it didn't seem so far fetched any more. I just didn't know the why's and how's yet, but I knew I would someday. I realized there would be many perils ahead of me – the Amulet was itself a sign – and I hoped I would be up to the tasks.

"I can not predict the future. We will have to wait and see how this unfolds," Nathan replied, putting his glasses back on his face.

"Is that all you wanted to talk to me about tonight? The Amulet? Not your trip or anything else?" I asked.

Nathan sighed loudly and hopped off the altar. "Nothing else. That was it."

"Are you sure?" I asked skeptically. I felt there was more; I just did not know what.

"That was it," Nathan insisted firmly.

I knew he was holding something back, but I did not push it. I knew better than to do that with Nathan. The right time would present itself – I hoped.

Although Nathan's meeting with Kala was over, he was far from done for the night. He'd had so much more to say to her, but had held back for fear of burdening her with too much. He knew she was in danger constantly now, and he feared a time would come when he would not be able to protect her. If the attack were to occur during the daylight hours, he would be powerless to help, and he knew no one he could call upon who was able to walk in the light of day.

Victor was the only person Nathan knew who actually knew humans and co-existed with them. He was Nathan's only chance to help Kala. Nathan had a feeling that now was not the time for Kala to become Emissary – maybe not ever... something was wrong. The timing was wrong. Nathan knew Kala was being hunted – she was a prize and many cultures wanted her.

Sheldon and his followers' had been patiently waiting for Teague to fall out of political power, allowing Sheldon to take over – they waited for an Emissary and now they had thought they found one in Kala. The political fall of Teague was going to happen with a shove – if Sheldon had any say. Sheldon had tasted Kala's blood – nearly drained her empty with blinding desire – he knew he needed her, *now*. Sheldon was ready to take over.

Nathan was obligated to help Teague remain in power; after all, he was his friend, his Sovereign, his Sire and a fellow Enforcer. Teague needed Nathan whether he knew it or not. Nathan was also bound by the Amulet to keep Kala safe. To accomplish all this, Nathan needed Victor. With this on his mind, he resolutely approached Victor's loft, determined to enlist his aid. He knocked once and entered without waiting for a response.

"Where've you been?" Victor asked dryly, turning away from the painting he'd been working on. If he was surprised at Nathan's abrupt entrance he didn't show it.

"I've been around," he said. "I had some things to take care of."

"So you said earlier tonight." Victor dropped his paintbrush in a jar of turpentine, then began roughly cleaning his paint-spattered hands on an oily rag. "To what do I owe this visit?"

"I need to talk to you about Kala. There are things I need to do, and I need your help. I can't be specific, however, so you are going to have to trust me. I know you care for her – she needs your help." Nathan walked slowly past his friend and leaned against the frame of the large window looking out over the street.

Victor stared at Nathan's back. His mind raced. What had happened? "What's wrong?" he asked.

Nathan got right to the point. "I believe there are members of the High Counsel and others who support Sheldon in his pursuit to seize Kala prematurely and make her Emissary. I believe that there is a conspiracy to overthrow Teague and begin a new parliament with Sheldon in definitive command. I also think that *all* of this is wrong somehow..."

"How do you know? What have you heard?" Victor asked. How could he watch out for her well being if he was kept in the dark? "She isn't ready – she can't control the powers she has. Sheldon would be stealing her powers and using them himself somehow."

"Yes. No matter what, it would be a difficult adjustment for her and certainly not a safe one," Nathan added. "I'm sure you must have seen the pendant Kala wears – the Amulet."

"Yes, I've seen it. I've asked her about it but she doesn't say much."

"I can't add much either. What I can tell you is that the Amulet has a big impact on this entire situation." Nathan began to pace back and forth.

"Why?" Victor inquired, his eyes following Nathan.

"It's a source of power – a very special power. Different things raise the levels of its power – all kinds of things. Here is our problem and why I need you to help ensure Kala's safety, at least until she is ready to make the step to Emissary, if that is what is meant to be." Nathan stopped pacing and looked squarely at Victor. "I understand that our people have enlisted humans to pursue Kala during the day. They are to bring her to them by night with the hopes they can make Kala Emissary soon. Very soon."

Victor shook his head. "They must be pretty desperate."

"Sheldon is ready; he wants his power. I am also reasonably certain that he is the one who attacked Kala at the gallery that night and drank her blood. He wants her – it's deep in his veins now. Kala's blood in his veins – it's a good feeling. You should know that." Nathan spoke from experience; even he had some of Kala's blood in him.

Victor nodded.

"We need to find a way to keep Kala safe. What do we do during the day?" Nathan asked. "Any ideas?"

"I have one. You must let me handle it the way I see fit," Victor said. "I swear I will keep her best interest in mind – not mine, not yours, not our peoples'."

"What I want you to keep *in mind* is that we need leadership. Teague should remain in power for now. Teague may not be the most dominant ruler our people have ever had, but he has been fair. You may not think so, but he could have had you and I killed two hundred years ago for what happened and he didn't. I owe him for that. So do you."

"I understand," Victor replied. "I can't do anything until tomorrow evening; will that be too late?"

"Your plan is our only plan at the moment; it will have to be," Nathan replied. "Can you give me a clue as to what this idea of yours is?"

"As soon as I line it up, and I hope that I can, I will let you know. I will not allow Sheldon to just take Kala like this. I don't care who he is."

"All right. Is your plan something radical?" Nathan asked.

"Very," Victor said briefly as he began cleaning up his brushes and paints.

"Thought so. Just tell me later." Nathan shut the door behind him, knowing that however radical Victor's plan was, Kala would be as safe as anyone could hope for.

Chapter 45

I returned to work on Monday and heard the praises of the concert over the weekend, how all in all it went off without too many problems. The sponsors were happy; the crowds were happy; the bands were happy, which left station management happy. Drew wasn't there, though; I thought for sure that he would have come in to bask in the glory since everything had gone so smoothly. Strange. He loved the spotlight.

By late afternoon I was in one of the studios catching up on some commercial production I had put off in my rush to leave for the weekend. I heard a light rap on the door. I looked up just as Drew poked his head in.

"You busy?" he asked, looking around to make sure I was alone.

"Come on in. I missed you earlier," I smiled and leaned away from the production board and back in my chair.

Drew shut the door behind him and pulled out a chair next to me. "Sorry. Should have called to let you know I was not coming in," he apologized. "I was worried about you all weekend. I figured if I stopped by to see you, Victor would kick my ass or something."

"Worried?" I asked, picking up my ballpoint pen and tapping it on the counter.

"Yeah. You were a mess Saturday night. That last band took the stage and you lost it. I mean really lost it!" Drew exclaimed.

I reflected back on my reaction when I'd first seen Kevin. Yes, I must have looked like a mental case blubbering away for no apparent reason, or none that Drew was privy to. "Well, it was late and I was tired," I began, trying to think of a convincing explanation. "I recognized an old friend in the band; it had been a long time. I don't normally react that way." I continued to smile, still tapping the pen rhythmically.

"Friend? Not with the way you were carrying on." Drew did not swallow my story. "And Victor – well, he just played the valiant boyfriend. He would not even answer me – he stood between you and me so that I could not even speak with you. A friend?" Drew repeated.

"A very close friend that I had not seen in many years. I did not know if he was alive or dead. No one did. Then... there he was. It was surprise. That's the best way I can describe it. I was shocked."

Drew was quiet. He did not totally buy the tale. I could see it in his eyes. "I wish I had known *then* and not today," he finally said. "Seeing you so upset bothered me. Really. I wanted to call you, but I didn't. I wanted to come by, but didn't dare. I was so glad to hear you on the air this morning. I don't know what I would have done if someone else were filling in for you." There was no denying that Drew cared about what was happening to me. I just could not be totally honest with him. I was not able to be honest with anyone any more, at least, not as honest as I would have liked to be.

"I'm sorry. Really. I know you care. I appreciate it," I smiled.

"What are you doing after you finish up here?" Drew asked, trying to change the mood; he spun from side to side freely in his chair, apparently feeling assured about my health and welfare.

"Oh, I don't know. I hadn't thought that far yet." I sat up and started to sort through the paperwork I had completed and the work I still needed to do.

"Why don't we grab a pizza and a few beers? As friends, like it used to be." Drew tried to persuade me by throwing one of the spongy foam spit guards from one of the microphones at me.

I laughed a little, enjoying the feeling. It had been a while since I'd felt like laughing. "Sure, why not. Let me finish up and we can go."

Drew left. A short time later I caught up with him at the boardroom door in conversation with the promotions manager about the concert over the weekend. I could tell by the smiles on both of their faces that each was pleased with the outcome of the event.

"Ready to go?" I asked.

"Yeah. I'm starved," Drew replied and ended his talk with the promotions manager with a handshake who then headed into the boardroom. "Let's try that new place, the one near where you live."

"Okay. Let's take separate cars; that way I can just go home afterwards," I suggested, throwing my tote bag over my shoulder.

"Sure; we'll meet up at the pizza place in, say, ten minutes." He pulled his keys from his pocket. "I need to stop and get gas and a six pack for later."

"All right; I'll order us beers and wait for you," I said agreeably and headed out the door.

It was just before five when I arrived at the pizza restaurant. The place was already becoming crowded, attesting to its popularity. A cute teenaged waitress seated me at one of the first booths closest to the door. I faced a long wall of plate glass windows that overlooked the main street. The walls were crowded with neon beer signs, all promoting the newest and hippest adult beverages in blazing colors. Vivid café style curtains hung at seated head height, giving the patron some privacy from the action of the city but allowing a quick peek now and then to see what was happening outside. I ordered two draft beers and waited patiently for Drew's arrival. I hadn't been waiting long before he entered the restaurant, spotted me, and took his seat.

"This place is hopping," Drew said as he slid down the length of the vinyl-covered bench.

"Sure is," I agreed, taking a sip of beer.

Drew reached for his beer. "Let's get a large cheese pizza with loads of onions and peppers." He groaned in mock food-related bliss.

"Well, you won't be kissing me good night," I joked with him.

One large pizza and four beers later, Drew walked Kala to her car. He had enjoyed her company and for the most part ignored the fact that she was not interested in him romantically. Victor's name did not come up once, which was fine as far as he was concerned.

After bidding Kala good night, Drew left for his apartment near the campus. He went up his two flights of stairs with his six-pack of beer and the day's mail. Time to unwind. He unlocked the deadbolt and pushed the door open with his shoulder, whistling under his breath as he reached for the light switch. He flicked the switch on and kicked the door closed with a thrust of his boot heel. He tossed his mail on his blue recliner and continued into the kitchen to put five of the six beers into the fridge. One he uncapped immediately and returned to his chair to stretch out and sort through his bills and other junk mail.

"You should really make sure you lock your door. You never know who might walk in off the street," Victor announced, slamming Drew's front door and getting his immediate attention

Drew leaped out of his chair, startled and scared, and pissed off at the unwelcome intrusion. Worse than that, it was the man he'd just been brooding about. "Where the hell did you come from! You always just barge right in like this?" he shouted angrily. He stared as Victor continued walking in. "Hey, if this is about Kala, we just had beers and pizza. I swear it!" Drew sputtered, sure that was why Victor was here.

"I know," Victor said lightly as he looked around the apartment. "I'm not here because of that."

Drew narrowed his eyes and blew out a deep breath. "Then what? I don't owe you anything. I don't even like you." His indignation grew as he watched Victor coolly take a seat on the arm of his couch.

"Boy, you are bad," Victor chuckled softly. "Real bad."

"What are you talking about?" Drew asked angrily.

Victor shook his head in disbelief. "I knew you were different the first time I met you. I also know I didn't much care for you. The other night I finally realized why."

"You're nuts! I'm calling the cops," Drew shouted and stomped into the kitchen to get the phone.

"Oh come on. A jail cell isn't going to hold me. You know that. You must be new, very new, at this." Victor laughed out loud and followed Drew into the kitchen.

"What are you talking about?" Drew turned around quickly to face Victor.

"Look at me. Look into my eyes," Victor ordered and grabbed Drew by his shoulders, holding him firmly. "The hunter and the prey. You people think you are such great killers and stalkers. Ha! I could end it all right now if I wanted to and you know it! Now, you ask yourself why I'm here!"

Drew tried to maintain his fierce look, locking eyes with Victor. Finally, he broke eye contact, looking down at the floor in embarrassment as his shoulders slumped. He knew he could have been dead fifteen minutes ago if Victor wanted him that way. Drew swallowed hard. "Okay," he admitted. "It's obvious to me now. Want to kill me?"

Victor pushed him aside disdainfully. He opened the refrigerator and helped himself to a beer. "If I wanted you dead you would be. I want to talk."

"Talk? What do you and I have to talk about? We are enemies and always will be."

Victor ignored him and made his way back into the living room. "We need to talk," he tossed over his shoulder as he sat back down, waiting for Drew to join him.

Drew bit his bottom lip, then sighed again and followed Victor. He knew there was little he could do at this point. Victor was obviously toying with him and, vampire hunter or not, Drew had never been alone with one before. "So talk," Drew said as he dropped down on the sofa and chugged his beer, trying to appear nonchalant.

"I know you are a hunter. You must be new. I know you don't run this killing group by yourself. You aren't good enough. So, I want to meet with your leader. It's important." Victor looked calmly at Drew as he spoke.

"No way. We don't meet with you. That doesn't really serve our purpose," Drew replied. "I don't know what your game is but I'm not playing."

"How long you been doing this?" Victor asked curiously.

Drew was hesitant to answer; he didn't want to provide Victor with too much information. "Less than a year." Drew's eyes fell to the floor. "I'm not good, I know." He sighed.

"Consider tonight a lesson; another vampire might not have been so generous with your life. Actually, I can't think of any other who would have spared you," Victor said honestly as he finished his beer.

"Then why let me live?" Drew asked. He was puzzled. He knew about

Victor's kind and how they showed no emotion. He knew Victor could kill him instantly if he chose.

"I need you; I need you to go to your leader. I need to meet with him," Victor repeated.

Drew shook his head no. "I can't."

"It's about Kala. I hope you'll reconsider," Victor said using her name as leverage to get what he needed – to get what she needed.

"What about her? Does she know about you? About your kind?" Drew asked quickly.

"She knows. I am here because I need your help. I need assistance in an area I cannot get involved in. It's not that I don't want to, it's that physically I can't."

"Why did you go and get Kala involved with your people? That's crazy. You should have left her alone," Drew said heatedly. "I'll see what I can do. I can't promise anything."

"No. Here is what you *will* do. Bring your leader to the diner at eleven-o-clock tonight. Sit in a booth near the back. I will meet you there. I don't have to remind you what will happen if you don't do this," Victor warned. "And don't call Kala or anyone else to tell them I was here, just your leader." With those instructions he got up abruptly and left without even glancing at Drew again.

"I'll see what I can do," Drew said, trying to preserve what was left of his dignity. He made a face at Victor's retreating back and drained the rest of his beer in one angry swallow.

The earliest part of the night seemed the longest for Victor; it was the wait that was driving him crazy. He avoided Kala, although he did not want to. It was just that he could not afford the distraction. He didn't want to deal with her inevitable questions when it was time for him to go to the meeting.

Victor had no idea who Drew's leader was. He knew nothing about how deep-seated his desire was to kill his kind. He might be nothing more than novice like Drew, someone who had minimal experience in hunting the vampire and even less in the actual way of killing it. Either way, Victor had to meet him and put aside his own personal feelings, his dislike for Drew for instance. It wasn't just that they competed for Kala's affections; it was more than that. The first few times he had met Drew he knew there was something odd about him that he could not place. He hadn't known then that Drew was a hunter. He hadn't really been on the alert so perhaps he'd just missed the telltale signs.

Victor knew that many hunters were extremely knowledgeable regarding his kind. They made it their life's work to know everything they possibly could about their quarry. There were quite a few hunters too and they could be quite bothersome to vampires such as Victor, who were trying to live a low-key existence. These hunters did not fix on a specific target, but rather killed indiscriminately as they discovered one. Other hunters who had stayed in vampire-plagued areas for a long time became experts and knew each vampire they killed by name, knew them intimately; who they hung around with, where they lived, who they sired and even who sired them. It was an obsession for some hunters to continue to kill until the entire clan was eliminated.

How would Victor explain to this leader that he needed to hire one of his people's biggest foes to help him out with an extraordinary set of circumstances? Would Drew or his leader even believe his story? Would they even show for the meeting?

As Victor waited in the parking lot in his car across the street from the diner, he hoped that Drew and his friend would arrive on time. Leaving Kala by herself was something he did not want to think about, even though Nathan himself had offered to keep a watchful but distant eye on her. Nathan was still oblivious to the fact that Victor's radical plan to help maintain Kala's safety involved vampire hunters. Victor was sure the look on Nathan's face when the words rolled off his tongue would be priceless. But what else could Victor do? Not only did Kala need protecting during the dark hours of the day, but also now even during the time when she'd been the safest. Truth was the only qualified candidates for this job were the vampire hunters, humans familiar with the creatures of the night. The key to making Kala safe was finding a hunter Victor could rely on, one who was strong enough physically and mentally to deal with all the inherent hazards.

The problem was compounded now by a select group of Victor's kind that had only one thing on their mind; to capture Kala and bring her to Sheldon to complete the ritual that would make her his Emissary and begin the act of mutiny over Teague. And if that wasn't bad enough there was a new enemy for Kala – those humans who sought to be eternal and were willing to do anything in order to become a vampire, young, beautiful, invincible and immortal. To attain this, all they had to do was bring Sheldon his treasured prize – Kala. Sheldon didn't care how she came to him, as long as it was very soon and she had a pulse. He would do the rest.

As the hour reached eleven Victor watched two cars pull into the diner parking lot. Drew and another man were in one. The other, a van, parked a little way off and remained motionless. Victor could not see the driver, nor could he tell if there were others in it, although he assumed so. He was amused at the idea that a van full of hunters would sit outside the diner, watching and waiting, while he carried on a presumably civilized conversation with their leader.

At eleven, Victor left his car and walked across the lot to the diner. He ignored the van as he passed it, although he could *feel* the anger and hatred directed at him from those inside it. He opened the front door and the big silver bell that was mounted on a piece of red cording bounced against the lowest pane, announcing his arrival to all. He casually walked into the restaurant and past a rack of free reading material, seeing only a handful of people at the counter having a late night bite as they read the newspaper. Drew and his companion were seated at a booth near the back.

"Good evening," Victor greeted them cordially as he slid in next to Drew. "Thanks for coming."

"Didn't leave us much of a choice, did you?" Drew's boss answered for them. His voice was deep and serious and he stared boldly at Victor as he sipped his black coffee.

"This is important. You know it must be, if I am taking the chance of meeting with people like *you*." Victor leaned back in his seat and stated the obvious fact about the meeting. "I know about your little squad outside in the van," he added.

"It's pretty standard that we travel this way when we are hunting or plan to be in an area where we know vampires exist. As you know not much remains safe in your company," Drew's boss said calmly.

Victor nodded in acknowledgement. "I didn't catch your name."

"Detective Jeffery Drake. I'm a cop," he replied clearly. By his tone alone Victor knew he was a man of authority and would not allow himself to be bullied. Drake pushed his coffee cup away to the center of the table. It was time to talk business.

"You know my name. I'm sure Drew has enlightened you with as much as he knows. I'll get right to the point. There is a human woman who needs protection from some of *my* people. They have recruited some humans to seek her out during the day when they cannot. Some of us have been protecting her, and it's those of us who are safeguarding her who are looking for help." Victor stated the facts simply.

"From what? Why are your people seeking her? There is a city full of females; why her?" Drake questioned. "We're speaking about Kala, right?"

"Yes, Kala," Victor replied, knowing Drew must have prepped Drake with the information. "She's special and my people realize that," Victor finished ambiguously.

"Drew tells me you are romantically involved with this human woman.

Are you sure you are asking for her welfare, and not because of some jealous rivalry?"

Victor shook his head. "No, not even close. She is in danger. I don't know how much you two know about my people but trust me when I say that she is in danger. I am not saying this lightly. She is alone now even as we speak because I am here with you. She should not be alone. I need you to understand."

"I'm not seeing the big picture here," Drake said. "You are asking us to hunt your own kind to protect Kala because she is 'special'?"

"Pretty much," Victor agreed.

"Well, I'd like to hear the *more* of the story because what you've told me is not going to win me over. You want to give me names; I'll look into things. I know people who know people who know your kind," Drake bartered. "I'll see what I can find out."

"Not good enough," Victor argued, his body beginning to tense; they did not understand the urgency or level of danger.

Drew remained tight-lipped and silent during this exchange. Victor supposed Drake had instructed him to keep quiet.

"Victor, if you want our help – and I'm not promising anything – you have to be honest with me. I have met a few of your kind before and I know you have a real problem with being honest. It's just not in your vocabulary. Your people are hostile, erratic, self-righteous, self-serving and demean everything else that is not like you. That is why I despise your kind. That is why I hunt your kind. You kill and murder and cause pain; that's all you know how to do. Now all of a sudden I find myself sitting across from one the killers I've sworn to destroy, listening to a plea for *help*? I'm supposed to *believe* this story? You're going to have to do a better job convincing me!" Drake's face burned with hostility as he struggled to keep a lid on his temper.

"I will not argue the fact with you that most of my kind is as you state. No matter what we look like on the outside we are cold and care for no one, not even others like us. I could say the same about you humans, being human at one time myself. There are those of you who are good and those of you who are not. Although you humans are not like us, we do share many of the same traits; the capability of lying, being deceitful, of being cold-blooded killers. Yet, you are a cop. I would hope your eyes are open wide enough to see our similarities. I can understand your resistance to help me, but I am *not* like my brethren. Yes, I feed on the blood of humans. Yes, I am immortal. Yes, I can only go out in darkness. The difference is that I still have human emotions. Why, I don't know. I have always been the way I am now. It's as if I have two very distinct people living in me; one a human who needs and wants things as any other human wants and then this beast who can be conniving, and ruthless. I am human in many respects and looked down on it for being that way within the company of my people. They don't understand me. But I can be just as scary as any of my kind you have met before," Victor spoke hotly. Taking a deep breath he continued on. "I know it is very difficult for you to rethink the way I am, but I am probably the most human vampire you will ever meet."

"Then be honest with me. Let me see some of this humanity you have. Tell me more about Kala." Drake reached for his coffee cup.

"I am not going to bore you with the politics of my people. I will assume that you have been in the business of hunting for a while and are familiar with the structure of my society," Victor began.

"You mean the legislative body that dictates? The High Counsel, your Sovereign, that sort of thing?" Drake asked.

"Exactly. Since you already know, I will not bore you with explanations as to what their roles are. How long have you been doing this anyway?" Victor asked out of curiosity.

"Fifteen years."

Victor thought for a moment before he began. "Every so many years an Emissary takes power and rules with the Sovereign. Kala is to be that next Emissary someday most believe, but she is not ready now. There are people within my government who are looking to overthrow the current Sovereign, place a new Sovereign in power and make Kala Emissary at the same time, and do this immediately. This cannot happen. It's wrong, and there are those of us who are trying to stop it from happening. But the group of my people who are adamant to make this change happen now have enlisted humans to help out by day and bring Kala to them. Their reward is to be immortal. I ask that you do whatever it is that you can to ensure Kala's safety."

A middle-aged waitress approached the booth to refill Drake's coffee and ask Victor if he wanted anything. He declined politely.

"Your people have not had an Emissary in many years from what I have heard. There is quite a story that revolves around that, if I am not mistaken. Your people must be very excited to make this happen, and sooner rather than later," Drake said, still absorbing Victor's story. "Of course, you have to understand that I don't feel it's right for Kala to ever be Emissary, to even have ever been approached by you or your people. To have ever known *about* your people." Drake never took his eyes off Victor. "Allowing that to happen is not what I am about."

"I can understand your position," Victor acquiesced. After all, Drake was a protector of humans; to save her now only for her to become one of them later seemed a conflict to his profession.

"Are you sure Kala is the next Emissary?" Drew asked in disbelief, unable to remain silent any longer. "I read that –"

Victor looked over at him sternly. "It's been confirmed."

"Then it is *all* true," Drake sighed.

"Of course it's true," Victor said, puzzled at Drake's tone. "I spoke the truth."

"I guess you did. And I know a little more about this topic than you think I do." Drake rubbed his unshaven chin with a thoughtful look about him. "I met Kala a few times. I met her right in this diner as a matter of fact." He tapped the tabletop with his index finger. "Not too long ago I was here with her when I was on a homicide case – her friend Sara who was killed. I'm sure that name must ring a bell with you."

"Yes, but I did not kill Sara, if that is what you are getting at."

"I know it wasn't you. I have heard names of who might be responsible, not that it makes a difference in my world," Drake said. "Sara was very concerned about Kala. She came to me months before her death, looking for help."

"Why did you not help her?" Victor asked surprised. "Sara was human."

"Don't think that I didn't! I did help her, until she no longer wanted my help," Drake explained regretfully. "She just gave up, I think."

"Gave up what?" Victor asked.

"Sara came to me because she had heard I handle the *unusual* cases down at the police department. Not just homicides, but bizarre events, the unexplainable. She asked me to meet with her, said she had something to talk to me about. I did meet her at her shop where she explained her concerns about Kala. One of the problems was the one you just talked about; Kala being 'special' – this Emissary you speak of. Sara told me what she knew about your people. Much of it I already knew of course. She told me of her growing concerns about *who* Kala was becoming, not just in title among your people but as a *being*. At first I thought her story was way out there, I mean even for me. Kala was this *special* person, the core to many worlds, whatever that meant. But I was able to confirm some of what she told me about the level of powers that was building within her, about the people who would help her, things like that. Some things she told me, like there is a source of power Kala could tap into, I could not confirm or deny. That was when she told me I just had to believe her, that all this would happen over time. Kala needed time." Drake recalled his conversation with Sara.

"So what did you do to protect Kala and Sara?"

"Well, at first Sara asked me not to do anything with Kala. Sara had been handling the situation up till that point and felt she still could. She told me that she had found a way through her magic to block the signal your people had been sending to locate Kala and pull her to them. She felt confident that she could continue to impede it, but one day she called me and told me *they* had somehow found out about Kala. She wanted me to think about how I could protect Kala. She did not feel she could continue to guard her own safety as well as Kala's. Basically, she was afraid."

"And what did you do?" Victor asked.

"Well," Drake continued and looked over at Drew. "I knew someone who I thought I could place into Kala's life fairly inconspicuously to watch her and to get close to her, possibly get involved with her on a personal level."

Victor looked over at Drew disapprovingly. "Really."

Drew responded defensively. "Listen, it was for her own good. I do like her – a lot. I thought I was in... I really did. We saw each other during the day, I'd hook up with her at night and it was becoming pretty steady, but then you stepped into the picture. Hard to compete with tall, good looking and undead," he finished sarcastically.

"All right, so you put Drew into her life. What about Sara?"

"Sara became rather distant with me after that. She would not return my calls, she avoided meeting me, until one day I popped in unannounced and asked her what the problem was. She didn't have much to say to me other than she didn't want anyone else hurt. She was thankful that I was looking after Kala and Drew was now doing the same, but the further *I* was away from her, the safer I would be. I asked her from what – vampires? I felt confident that I could take care of her and myself if I had to. But she just ignored my questions about her own protection and insisted I make sure Kala was all right. I could not force myself or my protection upon her, so I had officers make a few extra trips down the block every day, plus I'd check on her without her knowing it. Then I got the murder call – it was Sara. In retrospect I think Sara knew she was going to die but didn't know when, and did not want anyone she knew or cared about with her when it happened. She feared for *their* safety, not her own. I think she knew Kala was a very special person, not just to your people, Victor, but also to many people. I wish I could recall what she had said to me to make me believe that. Maybe it's just a feeling I have. I don't remember now."

"If you believe me then tell me how we make sure Kala stays safe. I am open to suggestions. You can do whatever you feel you have to. If someone is posing a threat to Kala, kill him. I will, if I find Kala in danger, and I don't care if they're my kind or human."

"Isn't it a crime to kill your own kind?" Drew asked.

"Yes, it is. I've been in my own share of trouble with my people in the past; what's a little more?" Victor was not thinking about the ramifications of his actions; his prime objective was to ensure Kala's safety.

"I will need some time to think about all this, Victor. I cannot give you an answer tonight. Let me weigh what our options are and I will get back to you. This is a huge task at hand."

"I don't know if we even have a day's worth of time," Victor retorted. "This is something we need to act on now!"

Drake reached down to his belt and removed his pager, looking at the LED screen. "I need to make a phone call. I'll be back in a moment." He stood and walked towards the back of the restaurant where the pay phones were.

Victor ran his fingers through his loose hair, exhausted from conversation and stress. He could not understand why Drake had to think things over. After all, Drake did say he believed him; he knew Sara and had been helping her out until her death, and even knew that Kala was special. It dawned on Victor finally what the hunters could be up against in their pursuit to make sure she remained safe. The war between his people and the hunters would be fierce and bloody and, no matter how experienced Drake's crew were, they'd lose against the vampires' superior strength, powers and numbers.

"I tell you what," Drew interrupted Victor's train of thought unexpectedly. "No matter what Drake tells you, whether he will or will not help you and Kala, I will. I promise to do a better job than I have in the past, especially now that I know how serious all this."

"Why?" Victor asked.

"Because I want to help Kala. But you have to do something for me," Drew added.

Victor tugged on his chin and narrowed his eyes thoughtfully. "And that would that be?"

"I want what you have," Drew whispered.

"You want Kala?" Victor asked as if they were haggling over an item and not a life.

Drew pursed his lips. "No, not that. I want to be immortal. I want you to make me like you. I know you can."

Victor went cold as the words registered. No one had ever asked *him* to be like him. "You can't be serious. You are on the other side, Drew. You fight for humanity. And we don't even like each other!" He could not understand why he would ask for such a thing.

"I am willing to put *my* life on the line for Kala. I will watch her all day. How many people do you know who can do that for you? How many humans do you know, or who even know who you are?" Drew pointed out. "I will make myself available at night if that's what you need. How long can all this last?"

Victor clenched his fists as he answered. "Those of us who don't agree with this whole situation need to find a way to remove certain people from power and restore positive leadership to our current Sovereign. I really don't know how long it will take."

Drew's words still resounded in his head. Victor had never sired anyone. He couldn't up until recently, because of his punishment, and now that he could, he hadn't given it a thought. If he had, it certainly would not be male and he never would have thought it to be Drew. Victor would rather bleed Drew dry then to sire him. Give Drew some of his blood? Have a connection to him that he did not want? Why was he even thinking about it?

"Let me take this job on. After all, I am already involved. I will report *everything* I see or hear to you. I ask for no money, just my compensation to be like you. It is not an unusual request; your kind do it all the time!" Drew pressed on. "You aren't like the others I have heard about, the few I have seen. You blend with humans. I want that and it's in your blood. I want the immortality you have." Drew looked at Victor with shining eyes as if he was some sort of divine God. "It's a pretty good deal. Take time to think about it."

Victor hated Drew even more now. How dare he ask for something in return for Kala's safety! That was so hypocritical. How dare he want to be like him – forever young and immortal – and how dare he change his tune the moment his boss left the table. Victor did not want Drew to live forever; he would rather just kill him now and get it over with.

But as much as Victor did not want to acknowledge it, Drew was right. Unfortunately he already *was* involved in this mess. Drew knew Kala, he knew Victor, and he knew of Victor's people, not to mention he was a hunter and human. He fit all the criteria except for the fact that Victor did not like him. But if Victor did not promise Drew what he wanted in return for Kala's safety, would he betray her? Would Drew get what he thought he wanted, immortality, a life longer than he could possibly imagine – from another source, by taking Kala straight into the lion's den?

Just how badly did Drew *think* he wanted the gift? Victor knew how badly he thought he wanted it so many years ago and he'd *thought* he wanted it for the right reasons. Victor could find no obvious *wrong* reasons – Drew was the good guy – he was on the right side of the law.

Victor left the diner abruptly before Drake even returned to the table. Victor was appalled with Drew's actions. Perhaps the only reason Drew was a hunter was to hunt for his eternal source of life. Maybe his motives to hunt vampires wasn't the same as Detective Drake's, who obviously, through out his years of law enforcement and hunting the vampire on a serious level, showed a true desire to rid the world of Victor's kind. Victor wondered how Drew fit into the picture – why Drake found him useful at all.

Victor got in his car and headed out of town to less busy roads, where he could drive and think at the same time. He did not dare go home, for fear Nathan would ask him how his plans to protect Kala were coming along. Victor's one and only plan was fizzling out with each moment that ticked by. In many ways he felt he had made the situation worse by telling Drew and Drake about how badly some of his kind wanted Kala – how even humans were involved and how they were being repaid. If Drew wanted immortality it could be easily attained. Perhaps there was nothing anyone could do to protect Kala. Maybe no matter what, fate would take over and Kala would become Emissary now – whether it was right or wrong. Maybe that was the way it was supposed to happen. Victor wondered if he was now tampering in an area that was sealed – a chapter written that could not be rewritten.

Suddenly, he remembered Kala and that he was to have called her a long time ago. He wondered how angry she must be with him. It was going on one in the morning. He pulled into an empty parking lot and tugged his cell phone out of its holder. As he dialed her number, he tried to think of what he could say to appease her. The phone rang but only twice.

"Hello?" I mumbled in the receiver. I struggled to open my eyes. I had dozed off on the couch. My leg was numb underneath me.

"Kala... it's Victor. I woke you." His voice was low and apologetic.

I sat up and shook out my left leg that had been wedged between a cushion and the back of the couch. "I fell asleep on the couch. I was waiting for a call from you. I was worried," I said, still groggy.

"I'm sorry. I'm fine. I had class, and then a few students who are not doing well in my course asked if there was something they could do for some extra credit. So, I sent them to the back of the classroom to the closet. You remember, the one with the paintings stored in it?" Victor voice sounded tired to my ears.

"You made your students clean that closet?" I asked, surprised. "Were they doing that badly?"

"Well, it was the only thing I could think of at the time. They accepted so I stuck around and graded some papers while they camped out in the closet. Before I knew it was after midnight," Victor embellished his lie.

"Oh, did they finish?" I asked, pushing myself off the couch and walking into the kitchen.

"No way; they have a lot left to do. I finally called it quits and told them they could finish it another night." Victor took a drag on his cigarette and rolled his window down, allowing the exhaled smoke to escape.

"I'm glad you are okay. I had called Nathan earlier and he said he thought you might still be on campus." I opened the refrigerator and took out a soda.

"I did not mean to make you worry, and I'm sorry I woke you. I'm heading home myself. Getting gas and smokes first," Victor felt better now that he was back on truthful ground.

"Yeah, I should get to bed soon myself," I yawned, pulling the tab on the soda.

"Are you busy tomorrow night?" Victor inquired, crushing out his cigarette.

"Not really. I'd like to stop by the gallery after work and get my mail and messages. I have been avoiding that place again; I can't help it. After that, nothing. Why?" I asked, sipping my soda and heading back to the couch.

"I thought maybe I would make reservations at Luigi's for us," Victor said with a smile. What he would not have given to have things as they were when he'd taken Kala there for her birthday, her still unknowing of him and his people.

"What's the occasion?" I asked brightly.

"I don't know. I just thought since we had such a good time on your birthday – and a really special time after that at your place – we should go back. Okay?" Victor explained, fondly recalling the date, the details still vivid in his mind.

"Sure. Sounds wonderful." I felt butterflies in my stomach like I did the first time he'd asked me out.

Victor hoped the night would be equally as nice as the first. "I'll give you a call tomorrow and let you know what time I'll pick you up."

"Great. I'll talk to you tomorrow then." I beamed from ear to ear.

"You get some sleep." Victor said. "Good night."

"Night. Take care." It was good to hear from Victor before I turned in for the night. I smiled to myself, feeling cheerful. I wished I always felt like this.

Victor could not even think about going home. He wanted to. He wanted to relax, maybe paint a while before sunrise, but he couldn't. He needed a plan. He could not just let Kala sit helplessly by and be hurt. He decided he would not allow fate, or anything else stand in his way of at least trying to prevent Kala from being plucked out of her human life before her time. He'd never forgive himself if anything happened to her and he'd had the chance to prevent it. It was beginning to look like his options were exhausted; he saw no other way but to swallow his dislike and let Drew help. What more could he do?

It was a thunderous knock at the door that roused Drew from a deep sleep. He had dozed off in his lazy boy while finishing his beer and going through his mail. He heard the knock again. He struggled up and staggered to the front door. Fumbling, he slid back the chain on the lock and turned the doorknob.

The instant the lock freed, the door slammed open, knocking Drew back several steps and leaving him stunned. Victor filled the doorway; his blazing eyes boring in on Drew like red-hot laser beams. In two quick steps, Victor had Drew by the throat and slammed him against the wall. Brutally, Victor twisted Drew's neck and plunged his fangs deep in his exposed jugular vein. He savagely sucked two huge mouthfuls of hot blood, swallowed, then threw Drew aside. Gagging and choking, his hands covering the bleeding wound, Drew stumbled over to his chair and fell into it.

"Consider yourself hired!" Victor growled in Drew's direction then loomed menacingly over him. "Now I *will* know everything you see and hear. If you even think about betraying me or Kala I will hunt you down myself and kill you."

Fearfully, Drew forced himself to look up at Victor, shock in his eyes. "I wouldn't."

Victor turned and started towards the open doorway, then turned to address Drew one more time. "You start at sunrise. Don't be late." How would Victor ever tell Nathan what he had done?

Chapter 46

When Victor arrived home, Nathan was waiting on the porch, a drink in one hand and a cigarette in the other. As Victor slowly approached him, his shoulders slumped with weariness, Nathan sipped his drink and watched him with measuring eyes. He could see the depression and fatigue etched on Victor's face.

"Kala called here earlier looking for you," Nathan broke the silence. His voice was steady and even. "I told her you were at the college. But I'm not sure where you were, honestly."

Victor leaned against the railing across from where Nathan sat. "Taking care of business," he replied softly.

"Business? Does this have anything to do with Kala?" Nathan asked.

"Yes," Victor replied unemotionally. "But you aren't going to like it." He frowned as he admitted it – he was disappointed in himself as much as at the outcome.

"Oh?" Nathan's voice rose. "Why is that?"

"I hired a vampire hunter," Victor confessed. There was no way to sugarcoat it. Nathan would just have to deal with it.

Nathan scratched his head, frowned, but at first said nothing. "I see," he finally commented. "And you did this why?" It was clear Nathan was reining in a building anger.

"Because truthfully I had no choice. We have to have a human; there's no way around that. This one is the best I could come up with. Kala's safety demands we ignore our natural resistance towards humans. I know I certainly had to," Victor ended sarcastically.

"I hope we all don't wind up dead," Nathan said through gritted teeth. "This could turn into a bloody massacre! We'll all need protection, not just Kala!"

"We'll just have to watch ourselves and hope for the best," Victor said slowly – his energy spent. He turned and went into the house, thinking about Drew's conditional cooperation. Now was definitely not the time to tell Nathan about that!

Victor was just as unhappy as Nathan was with the plan, but he'd been honest; he really felt there was no choice. What Nathan didn't realize was that Victor would be living with far greater consequences than just enlisting a human's aid; he'd now be responsible for Drew being one of them. Of course, Victor could still refuse to give Drew the gift of eternal life, but then he'd be risking Drew's anger at being denied what he coveted. Drew could compound their problems by focusing the vampire hunters' attention on them. At this point there were only two choices: go through with Drew's demand, or kill him.

As Victor readied himself for sleep, he wished he knew for sure that Drew was with Kala, protecting her. He fretted about his lack of control over the situation and worried even more about Nathan's anger. Restlessly he tossed, unable to close his eyes in the safe darkness of his shuttered room, replaying his conversation with Drake, and Drew's smug insistence on the deadly reward.

When I arrived just before nine at the radio station, I saw that Drew had arrived first and was already parked in his usual spot. I pulled in next to him and caught his eye. He was on his phone. Drew smiled and waved and motioned for me to wait for him. I gathered up my belongings and stood outside his car waiting for him to end his phone call.

"Sorry about that," Drew said as he got out of his car. He folded his tiny cell phone and slid it into his pant's pocket.

"No problem. You're early today," I pointed out. "What's up with that?"

"Nothing. My first class was cancelled. I was already awake; so I just came here," he said.

"It's just I normally only see you this early when we have a meeting. We don't, do we?" I asked anxiously.

"Nope. Just your typical day. Nothing happening now, nothing on the horizon," Drew replied, smiling at me.

He was right. The day was pretty typical. I did my shift, with Drew's help of course, and then cut a few spots in production afterwards. I was ready to leave the station just before four and head over to the gallery to catch up on the work I had been avoiding. I would have to speak to Addy soon. I needed some guiding words; the gallery just wasn't working for me. It was too much. I mean, maybe someday it would be a great career for me, but my heart just wasn't in it right now with the way my life was. I had no time or energy left to put into making it work. I felt exhausted and guilty; my guilt stemming from knowing how disappointed Sara would be in me.

I don't think I was at the gallery more than forty minutes when I heard a knock at the shop's front door. I was not expecting anyone. I got up from my desk where I had been sorting mail and went to the door. I could see Drew outside on the street. Unlocking the deadbolt I said, "Don't you have a life anymore?"

He walked in with a leather portfolio under his arm. "Well, yes. I have something to show you though. I had to run home to get it."

I relocked the door and escorted Drew to a chair at my desk. "Have a seat. I have some bills to go through before they disconnect my phone and I have no electricity." I flopped down into my chair on the other side of the desk.

"If you are busy I can come back," Drew offered.

"No, stay. I'll take the bills home and do them with my own," I replied. "What have you got to show me?"

"Well..." Drew paused as he unzipped his black leather case. "I photograph things as a hobby. I wanted you to look at some of my pictures."

"Are you thinking about doing something with them?" I asked in surprise. I couldn't imagine Drew in the world of art; he had avoided my grand opening party at the gallery, claiming to be afraid of culture.

Drew replied shyly, "Yes. I want you to tell me what you think. I thought maybe I could matte them and frame them, then maybe you could, you know, display them here."

"How come you didn't tell me this earlier? I mean, you acted as if art was something you could not relate to." I was curious to see what that case held for my eyes to judge.

"I don't know. I apologize. I meant to. When you said you were going to be here today I thought I would just do it. Show you." Drew spun his portfolio in my direction. "I have some favorites."

"That's all that matters then," I said. "Take what you like out and show me. I always have room for stuff here. Problem is, I need to have hours for the public to see what I currently have on display. I was going to dedicate weekends. I need to get my shit together and start doing it, or hire someone to do it for me."

I looked over what Drew had brought me. Much of his work was landscapes, the ocean and mountain vistas. He said he had taken many of his photos while on weekends and day trips over the last few years. I thought he did a wonderful job and had a good eye for natural beauty. I suggested that we select a few of his favorites and get them matted and framed; we could do this together.

When Drew and I had his batch of photos narrowed down to a half a dozen, the gallery phone rang. "Out of the Shadows, may I help you?" I greeted my caller.

"Kala, it's Victor."

"Hi. Kind of early for you isn't it?" I asked, checking the time. I leaned back in my chair and watched Drew continue to thumb through his portfolio.

"A little. I tried you at home and when I got your machine I figured you must still be at the gallery. Are you alone?" Victor asked.

"Actually no. Drew is here. Believe it or not, you two have something in common," I laughed. Drew rolled his eyes up at me from the pile of photos.

"Really? I can't possibly imagine what that is," Victor's voice was slightly chilly, as if I'd just told an offensive joke.

"Yes. Seems you both have a talent for art." I ignored his tone.

"You have to be kidding me. He doesn't paint, does he?" Victor asked, curious in spite of himself.

I laughed out loud. "No, he doesn't paint. He's a photographer. His work is very nice." Drew smiled at my praise and shut the leather portfolio; he had made his choice of what pictures he wanted displayed.

"Oh. Pictures. Okay." He changed the subject back to why he'd called. "I got us a table at Luigi's at eight-o-clock."

I checked the time again. "Oh, I guess I better leave here soon then, give myself enough time to shower and change."

"Yeah. I'll be over around seven, a little before maybe. it's getting darker earlier now." He dropped his voice a little. "I really want to see you tonight."

I smiled. "I look forward to it." I did not want to say too much with Drew listening to my every word. "I'll see you around seven."

I helped Drew set aside the photos he and I would work on together and packed up the rest. I locked up shop and Drew walked me out to my car. He wished me good night and added a grudging, "Have a nice dinner." I smiled as I drove away. Maybe Drew was mellowing after all. Now, if only Victor would follow suit.

Drew followed Kala at a safe distance. He had to keep an eye on her. Victor would have his head otherwise. He doubted Kala even knew he was behind her. The way she was engrossed in her thoughts of the evening, he could have hung on her bumper the whole way home and she wouldn't have noticed. As trivial as he was to her now, he knew that someday he *would* be a somebody and she'd have to take notice.

I arrived home a little after six and knew I had only a short time to get ready for Victor. That was fine. If he came to the house and I was only half-dressed, well, that would be fine, too. I raced up the stairs outside the condo, unlocked my door and darted inside, throwing all my belongings on the table near the door. I kicked off my shoes and tore off my clothes as I raced to the shower. I wasn't even sure I could find something nice enough to wear on such short notice. Women have that problem even with a month's notice so the dilemma was always there. I started my shower and began to dig frantically in my closet.

Drew cruised slowly by Kala's condo and saw that she had made it safely inside. He continued driving through the complex and out to the main street. He pulled out his cell phone and hit redial.

"Hello," Victor answered quickly.

"It's Drew. She's home. Do you want me to park somewhere near by and wait for you to get here? Your call. I'm still on the clock."

"I'll be leaving here in about half an hour. Stick around another fifteen minutes, then head home. She should be okay. I'll call her before I leave here," Victor finished his instructions.

"All right. Will do. I won't talk to you again then until tomorrow, unless there is a problem."

"Nothing out of the ordinary happened today then?" Victor asked.

"Nothing. Very quiet," Drew said wearily. He was becoming bored with the secret squirrel stuff and at times wondered if Kala really was in danger.

"Good. That's the way I want it," Victor said. "I'll talk to you tomorrow."

I took out my black skirt and set it on the bed and found a dark green shirt sandwiched between some winter clothes I had totally forgotten about. Nice surprise, it went well with the skirt; I had my outfit for the night. Just as I was getting ready to head in for my shower the phone rang. I almost decided not to answer it, but then at the last possible second I did. It could have been Victor – but it wasn't.

"Hello," I said, focused more on my shower than my caller.

"Kala... it's Addy." She sounded very upset. I could hear it in her voice; fear, bordering on hysteria.

"Addy! What's wrong?"

"I've been robbed!" she cried into the phone. "It was horrible! They had guns!"

"Oh no! Are you okay? Did you call the police?" I walked with the cordless phone into the bathroom and shut off the shower. I felt terrible; I hadn't called her in awhile, and now this.

"Yes. The police are here now." Addy sobbed uncontrollably.

My heart flopped. I could not imagine being held up at gunpoint. What must go through a victim's mind, knowing that no matter what you do and how quick you are to follow their commands they could still blow you away in cold blood. "Calm down. It's over." I tried to comfort her as I walked back into the living room.

"Kala; I really need you right now. Can you come by the store, just for a little while?" Addy pleaded. "Keith is away on a business trip and I have been all alone since last week. I'm scared."

How could I say no? My dinner plans would just have to wait. "I'll leave now, be there in a few," I assured her as began to redress myself and shove my feet back into the shoes I had tossed off on my way in. I would get to Spellbound and call Victor from there. I knew he would understand.

Normally my drive into town took only a few minutes, but tonight it seemed like it took forever. I hit every traffic light on my way to Spellbound and then when I got to the street it was partially blocked off, not because of the robbery but because of a sewer problem or something that was going on underground. I had to drive two more streets over to come up in the opposite direction to park in front of the shop as I had planned. I ran up the sidewalk and bolted into Spellbound. There were no lights on; the overhead fluorescent lights had been shut off. The only illumination came from the natural light of the fast fading evening that bled through the multi-paned front window. Maybe Addy was ready to go home. Maybe she'd waited so I could follow her and make sure she was safe.

"Addy?" I called loudly as the door shut behind me. I took a few long strides into the store and looked around worriedly for my friend. "Addy?"

"Kala!" I heard Addy's voice from the back room.

"Are you okay?" I asked, following her voice.

Addy appeared from the back room. She looked terrible, pale, haggard – as if she were at the end of her rope. "Glad you could make it." She tried to smile, but it was forced.

"I got here as quickly as I could," I said and stepped forward to hug her. We wrapped our arms around each other and stood motionless. For once, I was the strength, the rock. I was happy that I could finally be there for my friend.

Suddenly I felt an intense pinch and burning sensation in my abdomen that made me pull away from Addy instantly. A bee sting, I thought stupidly. I backed away far enough to look down at my stomach and see a hypodermic needle sticking out of my white T-shirt. What is this? I thought to myself. Stunned, I looked up at Addy who had taken several steps back and away from me. "Addy?" I asked, my eyes searching her face. What had she done? I reached down and batted the needle out of my stomach; I was shocked. "What's this?" I repeated slowly, gesturing to my lower region. "I thought you were robbed. I don't..."

"I *was* robbed!" Addy yelled at me in a tone I had never heard come from her before. "Sara robbed me! You robbed me!"

I began to feel weak in the knees. Whatever was in the needle was now hitting me; it took hold fast, gripping like gravity as it tugged me to the floor. I had to fight it. "I don't understand." I had tears forming in my eyes. I had never robbed or crossed Addy as far as I knew, and what did she plan on doing, killing me? What was in the needle?

"Beautiful Sara! Always Sara – and you always here because of her. You never cared for me! You didn't even know I existed until she died, when you had no one!" Addy spoke bitterly. She approached me, hostility etched on her face.

"No," I mumbled. "It's not like that." I staggered away from her. My legs began to go numb underneath me; the sensation was creeping steadily through my body.

The front door to the shop opened. I heard the bell ring against the glass and felt a night breeze roll in with the company. I turned feebly, knowing by the unique aura that the visitors were not human. Vampires. Not just any vampires either. There was a dark haired one I recognized from the Manor. He was the one who I had heard addressed as Phillip, and there was Lyla. I wanted them nowhere near me; especially not Lyla, not after all I knew about her now and all she had done to Victor in his lifetime. Lyla grabbed my left arm and Phillip took me by the right. Together, they jerked me roughly in their direction. My legs fell out from under me and I landed on my knees. Nothing good would transpire from this.

"Such a *special child*; that's all I ever heard about you from the day you walked in here. You were going to change things, Sara would say. One day you would be powerful and make a difference in our lives. The chosen one. You don't look so powerful now! Miss Goody Sara always looking out for you! Not any more, huh? You're all alone now." Addy grinned like a wild woman possessed with making me pay for whatever I had done – whatever Sara had done. "It gave me so much pleasure to put Sara out of my life, and now your fate is up to someone with a higher power."

I could not believe what I was hearing as I hung limply between Phillip and Lyla, with no other choice but listen to all the hate that poured out of Addy.

"You did it? You killed Sara?" I cried.

Addy laughed. "No, I didn't kill her. I simply *had* her killed. After all, I had the knowledge of knowing who you are; you have been great leverage in getting me what I want."

"You're sick," I sobbed. I couldn't talk to her anymore, or stand to look at her. I bowed my head. The combination of Addy's betrayal and the drug was too much for me to bear. I lost my will to fight and began to succumb to the rising darkness, almost welcoming the oblivion I knew was coming. I was fading fast.

"Well, well," I heard a male voice utter cheerfully. "Look at you now."

Sheldon! I struggled to raise my chin off my chest. The voice belonged to Sheldon. The attack made some sense to me now. This had everything to do with my becoming Emissary and the Amulet that hung from my neck. There was no question in my mind. I remained silent, refusing to acknowledge him. He came close and reached out to stroke my face as I hung limply between Lyla and Phillip.

“Watch her hands; she will hurt you,” Sheldon warned my captors who still had me by the elbows. “You can try and fight all you want,” Sheldon whispered in my ear. “I have all the time in the world; I will wait for you.”

Weakly, I tried to straighten, but I couldn’t muster the strength. I glared impotently at him, fueled by a burst of anger.

“Go ahead; try and fight it. There was enough sedative in that needle to slow down a race horse. I’ll wait.” Sheldon’s voice sang as if he was the happiest bird in the cage, but I knew his type – a vulture.

Chapter 47

Something was wrong. Victor knew it. He felt it, or rather, he *didn't* feel it. There was a sense of awareness he had with Kala. She was with him, in thought and deep in his veins, in his blood – she swam within him. The emptiness slapped him with bewilderment; one moment he was looking at himself in the mirror, getting ready to meet Kala; he was thinking about her, his desire to spend the evening with her was swelling inside him, the next moment, blankness rushed through him. Before he could fully identify what caused the episode, he lost it. It was gone, out of his reach, leaving him with a vague impression of what it *might* have been and even that was evaporating with each second that elapsed.

Victor immediately tried to call Kala. Even as he listened to her phone ring he knew she wouldn't be answering. His instinct told him something was wrong – terribly wrong. Frustrated, he hung up. *Drew,* he thought. He dialed Drew's number from memory.

"Hello," Drew answered. He had only been home a few moments when the phone rang.

"Where is she?" Victor barked roughly. "Where is Kala?"

" I told you she got home safe. I waited the fifteen minutes and left. Why? What's wrong?" Drew asked, startled by the concern and anger in Victor's voice.

"Something is wrong. I called and she's not home. I feel nothing – not anything," Victor answered. "I swear, if you had any..."

Drew quickly interrupted. "Listen, I did nothing! I did only as you asked. You bit me, you know. I'm working for you."

"Then get back out in your car and look for her. Call me; I want to hear from you every fifteen minutes!" Victor snapped. He hung up, not allowing Drew to respond.

There was only one other who had the same blood connection to Kala as Victor did... Nathan. Victor wondered what, if anything, was he feeling?

Nathan's gut was churning. He, too, had a brief spell that was out of the ordinary. He knew something was wrong concerning Kala. Unlike Victor, Nathan's bond to Kala was even stronger. The power of the Amulet enabled Nathan to be aware of Kala's danger the moment that the tranquilizer tainted her blood. The problem was Nathan was in no immediate position to come to Kala's rescue. He knew that there must have been a concerted attack; a well-thought-out plan, in order to bring her down without a fight. This foretold the start of something big.

Nathan decided to call Teague. As his Sire, his Sovereign and a fellow Enforcer, Teague was one of the few vampires Nathan felt he could trust. He knew his life was safe in Teague's hands. He knew he would get the advice he needed from him.

Victor barged into Nathan's home unannounced as he frequently did to find Nathan in thought, standing at the small bar with a drink in his hands.

"Something is wrong." That was all that Victor said as he approached Nathan.

Nathan nodded. "Yes. How many people can we get together and how fast?"

"I'm not sure. What do you know?" Victor asked.

"Teague says Sheldon has been gone for several hours. There are no Counsel members left in the Manor. They're all gone." Nathan left his glass on the bar and slowly walked over to his desk in the back of the room. "It must be time; Sheldon is pushing for it." He rubbed the side of his face with a sigh.

"Sheldon is crazy; he's hungry for power, that's all. Why can't he be happy knowing we have found the Emissary?" Victor shouted out furiously

"Or maybe we haven't. I have been thinking... when was the last time an Emissary owned a powerful Amulet? They never have. Nerissa never had one..." Nathan's voice trailed off as he took a seat. "I've had bad feelings about this – but haven't been able to figure out what's going on. I understand Kala answered her calling – a calling only an Emissary should have been able to hear but..." Nathan was clearly mystified – this puzzle concerning Kala was giving him trouble. "It seems as if Sheldon is hell bent to go on with the ritual to make Kala Emissary – whether she is supposed to be one or not. All signs point to this happening now – tonight." Nathan's eyes darted up quickly to Victor who was hanging on his words. "Sheldon would have to pick a place that is special to Kala as the pending Emissary and at least six High Counsel members will need to be present to partake in the ritual – it needs to be complete before midnight."

Victor's cell phone, buried in his jacket pocket, rang suddenly. He fumbled for it, anticipating Drew's call. "Yes," Victor answered tersely.

"You're right; she's not home. I drove by, I knocked, no answer. I'm down around the gallery now driving around. I spotted her car at Spellbound but the shop was closed up. I don't know where else to look. Something made her leave home after I made sure she was safe there. She came here and now she's gone. Maybe she's okay; I mean, she's been part of Spellbound for years. She has friends here," Drew said as he stopped for a red light several streets over from where he'd spotted Kala's convertible.

Victor cursed and swiped angrily at the hair that hung over his forehead. "I know what it is that I feel. Don't question me. Keep looking. I'm trying to get to the bottom of things here."

"Okay. I'll check in with you soon." Drew replied and ended the call.

Nathan continued his conversation with Victor. "I think we need to get to the Old Maple Forest. That's where they are taking her. It's a sacred area. Or it always was for Sara. She referred to it in her journal many times. I know there is some attachment there for Kala as well. It's a powerful place." Nathan felt fairly sure of himself. Although he had the same emptiness Victor had regarding Kala, he knew she was still alive. He knew no ritual had taken place yet. She was not un-dead, not yet. "We won't be able to sneak up on Sheldon and his followers. Our scents will be just as strong as theirs are to us. If they are there we will know and they will know the same of us. There will be many of Sheldon's followers in attendance; you can count on that. They will be willing to die for this cause."

"I think they just might." Victor gnashed his teeth in anger. He had not killed his kind in many years. At this moment though, he would have gladly annihilated his race to save Kala.

Working together, Nathan and Victor quickly enlisted the aid of a sizeable group of Vampires sympathetic to their goal of thwarting Sheldon and rescuing Kala. The threat of an immense power fueling the impending battle spurred them on. They would need as many allies as they could possibly muster.

The next time Drew called Victor; he still had no more information than before. Victor instructed him to contact Drake and apprise him of their suspicions that tonight would be the night, and that the Old Maple Forest would be the place. If Drake's hunters were as good as their reputation they would find themselves with a massacre on hand. This would possibly be the largest gathering of Vampires in years and would include members of the highest ranking too. Victor doubted that Drake would pass up the opportunity.

After they had assembled enough members to give them a fighting chance, Victor laid out the plan of action. He instructed everyone that they would meet near the Old Maple Forest, everyone arriving on foot so as to stay unnoticed for as long as possible. Victor knew that Sheldon would know they were there at some point, but he hoped to delay that moment for as long as possible. He reminded them all that their main objective was to follow the timeline set by The Book of Jorn, preserve Kala as she was – human – until it was her time to assume her role among Victor's people – as Emissary, or as something else.

Of course, Victor had his own private reasons for fighting for Kala. He loved her. She was human and he loved that part about her, but if ever there came a day when she no longer wanted to be human, when she wanted to spend eternity with Victor; he wanted to be the one to Sire her. This secret he kept deep within him, not wanting to open himself up to accusations of personal interests.

Later that night, Victor and Nathan stood silently at the side of the road not far from the Forest, listening for the sound of their support to arrive. Victor smoked a cigarette with nervous movements – sucking the smoke in deep and blowing it out forcefully, the red tip glowing like a baleful eye in the shadows. They were still not completely sure who would show up to help them. Nathan raised his head suddenly and his nostrils flared. Teague was here. That was good. Drew would arrive soon, hopefully with Drake and his hunters in tow. They still were not sure about Kevin, City and Gage – were they collaborators with Sheldon? Where was Stuart, Kala's father? Where did his loyalties lie?

Nathan remained quiet and stoic, ignoring Victor's nervous pacing. He knew that tonight, no matter what; he would be at Kala's side, fighting the way he had been bred to. He had no doubt about it and no qualms either. He would do what he had to do to protect her. He felt a little easier though, knowing Teague was here, fulfilling his position of Enforcer even as he ruled as Sovereign. His quiet strength and presence soothed Nathan like a balm, allowing his mind and senses to remain clear and focused.

If Kala did survive the night and found out her father and brother were behind the task force that wanted to thrust her into Sheldon's arms; Victor did not know how she would react. He was sure her initial reaction would be hurt, not fully understanding his people's ways. To them, blood meant nothing unless it was being consumed. Her assumption that they would defend her because they were *family* was dangerous to the extreme. They would betray or kill her in a heartbeat in response to Sheldon's commands.

When it finally came time to move, Victor and Nathan's army was lacking. There was Teague as expected; Drew, who swore to help out in order to be rewarded in the end and Drake, who showed up alone, armed with a crossbow. He assured them that more hunters were coming; that they were just readying themselves for what promised to be a bloody battle. Drake had trained his men himself. They were the Navy Seals of dry land, the proclaimed killers of those who live in the night. They thrived on the heat of battle.

By the time the small group had reached the parking lot, Nathan and Victor knew the vampires had gathered. "They are here," Nathan uttered. "There are many. Kala is here as well."

Victor had no reply and he had to take him at his word, for he still had not regained his connection to Kala.

As they crossed the vacant lot, Kevin and Gage joined them. Gage was probably just following Kevin along like a dog out for his nightly walk, but even so his presence, if nothing else, was menacing. No one was positive of Gage's fighting skills, but he was ugly; that was his strength for sure.

Nathan stopped just shy of the path that would lead them into the Old Maple Forest. He turned to face them all. Calmly, he said, "Our objective is to get Kala out of here. I need a path cleared and I need it done fast. I don't care how much fighting takes place behind me, but we need to get in and then get Kala out. I don't want any of you to risk getting hurt and then not being able to pull this off, understand?"

They were silent as they listened, just nodding in acknowledgement. There were to be no heroes – just get the job done.

I lay helpless, still immobilized by the drug, on a fabric-covered piece of plywood that was stretched across both altars. Although I could not move, I was conscious of what was happening around me. Through my closed eyelids I could see the bright orange glow of fire. I felt the heat of the flames warm my body and heard the low murmur of voices. A soft breeze ruffled my hair as it slipped through the rutted trunks of the trees, bringing with it the delicate scent of the evergreen pines and the omnipresent maples.

The pressure of a touch startled me. "Kala, are you with me?" Sheldon asked as he shook my shoulder roughly.

I nodded groggily. My body was heavy; I had no energy, but I was aware.

"Good. It's almost time. We must hurry the ritual and you will need to drink from me quickly. Understand?" Sheldon whispered urgently in my ear. I sensed an uneasiness about him, but I could not figure out its cause.

The High Counsel members began to gather around the transformed altars where I lay. A low guttural chant began that rumbled within me like a bass drum. It was similar to the calling I had heard at the Manor the first night I was asked to attend. A female voice began to read a passage from a book – The Book of Jorn. I recognized the accent as Irish and knew it to be Lyla right away. Anger flared deep within me, but on the outside I remained motionless.

Someone grasped my arms and yanked me to a sitting position. My head flopped back weakly, exposing my throat. I heard Sheldon's voice, thick with eagerness, close to my ear.

"You must find the strength to drink from me," he said. "You will die otherwise." And with those words he bent forward and clamped his mouth on my neck, careful to stay clear of the Amulet. I felt the unmistakable sting of his fangs as they broke my skin and buried deep in my throat. With no strength to resist, I helplessly lay there as he drained me. My heart beat furiously, frantically as my life's blood left me. I knew I was dying; I could feel more and more of myself leave my body, my essence and my life, all that I was vanishing until the balmy sweat on my skin turned cold with my own death. My body was dead.

Sheldon backed away, swallowing one last time as he left Kala's body on the altar. He had drained her. His own body warmed as her blood coursed through his veins. Now, he waited; waited for the inevitable – the power of the change – when she would awake to take back what he'd stolen. The blood. Her blood, combined with his.

Cautiously, the group of vampires made their way through the forest, Drew and Drake following as best as they could. Their human eyesight paled in comparison with the vampires' nocturnal vision and there was no moonlight to help. Nathan was the first to see the burning glow of light around the altar, although he could not see what was happening inside the circle of vampires. He could feel Kala slipping away and knew he had very little time to succeed in saving her. Six Counsel members stood around the altar, joined by hands, ready to welcome their new Emissary. Lyla, her long red hair blazing in the reflected glow of the fire, held The Book of Jorn tight to her chest. Addy stood next to her and together they recited the ritual passages. When the night was over, Addy would receive her reward from Sheldon, eternal life, a seat on the Counsel, a home within the Manor, wealth and eventually, with any luck, the Amulet. Her ultimate plan was to convince Sheldon she was more powerful than Kala and could bring him more supremacy if it were placed around her neck. Addy felt this was all well worth the wait.

Half a dozen members stood in protective stances around the Counsel. They were prepared to do battle tonight and knew the pending conflict was moments away. The scent of Nathan, Victor and the rest was now overpowering; the scent of humans sweetened the bouquet. There were more onlookers who stood outside the circle, watching the ceremony continue even with the threat of disruption looming. Nathan did not have time to study all the faces but he did recognize one. Stuart, Kala's father, was waiting in anticipation to see his little girl become his bragging rights – the next Emissary. Drake armed himself with his first arrow, pulling his bow back and locking it into place. Slowly Nathan's squad came out of the darkness and became visible to all.

The brightness was blinding; a white light that burned with its intensity. I put up my arm and shaded my eyes with my hand as if blocking a blazing sun. I felt I was being watched, felt the weight of judging stares. I tried to see through the brightness, through the barren glare. I knew I was not truly alone, but I could also feel the surprise of those who remained unseen. It seemed I was an unexpected visitor. It took me a moment to gather my thoughts and understand what it was I was looking at or looking into. They were souls; the essence of those passed on. Their heavenly eyes gazed at me. I was frightened, but calm at the same time. I understood then that I had gone through my own death. It was the only possible explanation as to what I was witnessing now and how I could be.

"*Kala,*" I heard a woman's voice. "*You must leave.*"

I knew the voice well. I felt as if I was in a dream. "*Sara?*" I asked. "*Sara, where are you?*"

Out of the brightness, my Sara appeared. She looked as lovely as I remembered her, long wavy auburn hair electrified in pure energy, wearing the same diaphanous blue gown she'd worn when she visited me in my home. She floated effortlessly in front of me. "*You can't stay. You must go back. This was not part of the plan,*" she said.

Not only could I hear her words, but I could feel them touch me and filter into each fiber of my being. "*I must be dead,*" I told her. "*That's why I am here.*"

"*You can't die. We cannot allow it. You must go back,*" she insisted. I could feel her delicate hands push me away from her.

"*No. I don't want to go back. I will be one of them*!" I cried. "*Let me stay. I miss you, Sara.*" I tried to touch her, to hold her sleeve, but I couldn't.

"*You are our last chance. You must go back.*"

"*What am I supposed to be?*" I implored her. "*Why am I so important? Please help me understand.*"

"*You are unique; the only one of your kind. You can help so many. Believe me when I say you must go back. You are the link.*" She pushed me away again, harder this time.

"*What link? Help who*?"

"*You are wasting time. Just know that help is on the way. Now trust me and go!*"

Sara shoved me without any physical contact; she used a power that she had within her; a beam of concentrated strength that pushed me so far out of the bright white light that I landed back in my cold, dead body. Instantly I sat up, propelled by forces beyond my control. I was still dead; there was no doubt about that. My veins were dried up riverbeds, lacking the life fluid. My heart lay dormant in my chest and my lungs were deflated and unable to take on air. It was as if I was a zombie, a puppet, my movements orchestrated by a force that had no name. The horrible truth was that I was aware of the state I was in and powerless to do anything about it.

A battle raged around me; one that had begun while I was with Sara. Drake had fired two arrows before he had totally come out of the obscurity of darkness. He'd hit two vampires, shocking them enough to allow Drew to plunge a sharp pine stake through the chest of one and turn to gouge the chest of the other. Gage had managed to overpower Lyla; his hands were full with her spitting, clawing strength. Victor and Kevin were violently fighting off attack after attack. Teague and Sheldon were standing face to face, staring each other down – Teague full of anger at Sheldon's betrayal – Sheldon, his veins flowing with Kala's blood, arrogantly standing his ground.

Nathan saw Kala suddenly sit upright on the altar, her face beyond pale, her eyes empty. He knew she was in the throes of the ritual but ran to her anyway. He held her slumping body in one arm as he tore and shredded a fellow Counsel member to death with the other. Nathan's unbound strength flowed easy from him. Drake's squad finally arrived. They were fighters, but the one who needed to fight the most was Kala. She was in a fight for her life and she was losing the battle. Nathan could feel her crossing back over. He knew she wanted to die and he was not sure he could stop it from happening. He tore the Amulet from Kala's neck and threw it to the ground, causing the crystal to break into several large pieces. Nathan knew this endeavor could only be used once. He hoped this was the time *and* the place to call upon such a power – if not, Nathan would surely pay with his life. He was calling upon a force that was legend; a supernatural being that had been latent for many, many years – the creator of their kind. Jorn, housed at rest in the Amulet until now.

The instant the crystal broke, an eerie silence dropped like a heavy cloak upon the forest. All fighting ceased as the combatants, both vampire and human, realized what had happened. They all froze and stared at the Amulet, lying broken on the ground. Nathan fastened both arms protectively around Kala. "Stay, Kala. Stay," he whispered softly in her ear.

The ground beneath their feet trembled as if an earthquake had started somewhere deep within the earth's crust. Teague turned and shot Nathan a look of complete horror; he knew what Nathan had done. He knew the broken crystal had unleashed the power of Jorn. Somewhere below the altars a power of mystical proportions was building. The energy that seeped up through the ground was charged with a powerful electrical current that snapped and crackled. As the power grew, a continuous humming tone began, rising in intensity and volume until Nathan's very teeth ached.

Suddenly a dynamic blast from deep underground blew a hole in the soil between both altars, pitching the fabric-covered plywood slab directly up in the air. It smashed to the ground several yards away, sending deadly splinters of wood in every direction. Another explosion shot out of the crater, spewing a thick cloud of dirt and smoke. As the debris settled, a figure remained standing where a moment before there had been nothing. It was Jorn. He stood silently, a long black cloak covering dark and heavy woven clothing from years gone by. His face was pale, his lips thin, and his dark eyes showed no emotion as he gazed out over the silent gathering. He brought his arms up and clasped his hands together in front of him as he silently looked at them – vampires and humans alike. Finally Jorn's eyes rested on Nathan and the limp woman he held in his arms. An unspoken question passed between them.

"I broke the crystal on the Amulet," Nathan said. " There was a ceremony to make this woman, Kala, Emissary. We were able to stop it, but I must get her to a hospital before her human body dies. I am her protector; you must let me leave."

"Sovereign, stand forward," Jorn commanded. His voice was deep and, though audible, sounded as if it was coming from far away.

Teague took a deep breath and stepped forward from the crowd. "Jorn – Master," Teague said and bowed his head.

"What has happened here?" Jorn inquired sternly.

"There was an attempt to overthrow me and make this woman Emissary. Her powers, combined with the next Sovereign, would conquer me," Teague explained without pointing fingers. He wanted to take care of Sheldon himself.

Jorn looked upon Kala thoughtfully. "She *is* the chosen one," he agreed.

He turned to look at Teague and then his eyes narrowed, his head turned and he looked directly at Sheldon. The blood of a betrayer would always call out to him. "I tell you all now – she is chosen, but *not* to be Emissary. Her task is much larger than that. It is so written in the book. You demean her and yourselves with your actions." His words were caustic, laced with anger. He looked around again and saw the Amulet on the ground. Instantly it was in his hand, though he made no movement. He raised it up to Kala's face and touched her with it. She stirred in Nathan's arms, but did not awaken. "Take her now, while you have the time. She will live if you go now." He handed the Amulet to Nathan. Nathan bowed his head slightly, turned and sprinted into the darkness with Kala to safety.

"Master Jorn," Teague began. "We have anticipated an Emissary for so long. All signs made us think she was it."

"Teague is right," Sheldon said as he took a position next to his Sovereign. Perhaps now was the only time he would have to save himself. "It was part of my understanding as well. She answered the calling. I felt her power."

"Of course you felt her power. She is special. A chosen one; if called upon she will answer!" Jorn said scornfully. "There will be no more Emissaries in your world. She is *your* liaison; she is *your* link; she is the past, the present and the future. She has such a long way still to grow and you nearly ended all that. Without a link there is nothing!" Jorn roared. "Are you all so caught up in yourselves that you cannot see? The punishment will be severe to those of you who wronged The Book of Jorn and to those of you who betrayed the existence that I permit you to have. You will all rue your actions this day!"

Chapter 48

Nathan had done all that he could. He'd rescued her and brought her to the only place where her human body could be saved. Her life was in the hands of the doctors now. He paced restlessly, torn between waiting for word on her and what was possibly going on back in the Forest. He was not worried about his friends; he'd sensed that Jorn knew who was right and who was wrong. He did not even dwell on the fact that his status as an Enforcer was now out in the open. There was too much else going on. Things were happening fast.

Nathan stopped and stared down the long white hallway. Victor was coming. He had survived. Nathan breathed a small sign of relief. Victor gave a slight smile and took a seat next to Nathan wearily. "Well?" Victor asked.

"I think she will be okay. I haven't heard from anyone for sure yet. But things *feel* better. Can you tell?

"I feel her. It's weak, but it's there," Victor confirmed. She was back inside him.

"What happened out there?" Nathan asked.

Victor was silent for a moment as he thought back. "I think Jorn is here to stay for a while. He knows that things are not right. But we already know that"

"Maybe that's for the best. He will find the truth. Nothing can be hidden. Now, what about Teague? Sheldon? The rest?"

Victor shrugged. "Jorn told the humans he'd give them one minute to leave his sights before he would bleed them all dry – a long sleep had made him hungry." Victor chuckled. "The humans left – quickly. Drake took Addy into custody after that for Sara's murder. Lyla, Phillip and the remaining security members were exiled, like we were so many years ago, only they did not leave on their own as you and I did. One moment they were there with us, the next, gone. Who knows where they are? Stuart was spared since he is Kala's father, but Jorn told him not to interfere anymore. I don't think Stuart will be a problem."

"Teague? Sheldon? What about you?" Nathan asked again.

"Jorn told Teague that he would be disciplined with the *others* – whatever and whoever he meant I'm not sure. As far as Sheldon – well, Jorn was furious. He said he was appalled that someone with blood so pure could do so wrong, and then Sheldon just vanished. He disappeared and I didn't ask where he was. I'm just glad he's out of the picture." As far as he was concerned, Sheldon could stay wherever he was for a long time.

"And your punishment?" Nathan asked.

"Kevin and I got off okay. I was warned; he knew I had fed from Kala. He knew her blood was within me." Victor shook his head. "I have nothing to hide from him anymore; I can tell you that. He knows me better than I do, or you ever thought you could."

"I'd like to say it's all over but I know it's not," Nathan said with a sigh. "There will be changes. They will be happening."

"I don't know what to make of it," Victor said. He stood up and walked over to the large window on the other side of the couch. Dawn would be breaking soon. He could see it in the barely perceptible lightening on the horizon and could feel it in his tired body. "At least Kala is safe now. I don't think anyone will dare lay a finger on her with Jorn here. "

"I'm sure you're right about that," Nathan agreed. "Why don't you go have a cigarette and I'll see if I can get some news on Kala. You look like you need a few minutes to yourself." Nathan stood up and stretched; he was exhausted, too, and the urge to feed was beginning to blossom in him as well. It had been a long time since he'd fed well.

Victor nodded. "Yeah, sounds good. I'll meet you back here in a few minutes." He was already reaching into his shirt pocket for a cigarette and a lighter. "I'll be outside."

Nathan watched Victor leave and then went to Kala's room. The station nurse had told him he'd find her in the Intensive Care Unit, but he knew that she was going to be all right. He did not need a doctor or nurse to tell him what he already knew. As he approached the door, he sensed she was alone. Just one simple human heartbeat, beating slowly and rhythmically. As he entered the room quietly he could hear the beeps and tones of the machines monitoring her heart, her pulse; an IV hung in a clear bag on the far side of the bed. It was attached to her arm by yards of tubing. She lay soundlessly in her clean bed, white cotton sheets pulled up and folded over a light blue blanket at her chest. Her right arm was lying on her stomach and her head was softly cradled on a small pillow in a nest of her dark hair. Her skin was ashen and there were blue shadows beneath her closed eyes.

Nathan pulled a chair up next to her and watched her breathe for a moment; the rise and fall of her chest comforting to him. He picked up her right hand from its resting spot and held it tenderly in his.

I stirred, feeling a chill in my hand. I opened my eyes and turned my head to the right to see Nathan holding my hand in his. He looked so sad and so serious. I lay quietly, remembering what had transpired. My heart ached at

Addy's betrayal. I shuddered suddenly, remembering Sheldon as he sucked the life out of me. He had taken every thought, every attribute, every secret I had and made it his own. I realized that every secret Nathan had entrusted me with was now in the hands of a renegade. No wonder he looked so serious.

"Sorry," I whispered hoarsely as the tears streamed down my face. I had failed him.

Nathan blinked and looked at me as he realized I was awake. "Sorry for what?" he inquired softly, still holding my hand.

"Everyone knows now. You told me things about you and Victor and now everyone knows because of me." I quietly cried as I condemned myself. "You were right; I can't keep a secret."

Nathan shook his head as I spoke. "No, no. You did nothing wrong. You were very strong," Nathan assured me and squeezed my hand. He reached out and gently wiped the tears from my cheeks.

I sniffed, knowing Nathan would not sugarcoat my blunders if I had made any. "Okay." I reached up with my left hand and patted my chest where the Amulet should have been. It was gone. I looked down at the hospital gown I was wearing, feeling the tears well up again. "I lost the Amulet. I'm so sorry," I gasped and then began to cry again. Now I knew why Nathan was upset; I lost something as valuable as the Amulet.

He shook his head again. "No. You didn't lose it. I have it; I took it from you for safekeeping. Please stop crying. I'm not supposed to be here and if a nurse walks in and sees you upset, they'll throw me out." Nathan forced a smile to try and get me to calm down a little.

I rubbed my eyes with my IV hand. "Okay. I'm sorry," I whispered. I was still not thinking clearly. "Victor!" I asked suddenly.

"Out having a cigarette. He's fine," Nathan answered, keeping his smile.

I sighed in relief. "Is it over?" I asked him.

As far as Nathan was concerned, things were over *right now* for Kala. Whatever was in store for her would eventually make itself known. Whatever her role was among his people was far greater than he and many others had ever suspected. Kala would need to be patient and allow her life to fall into place as it was meant to do. With Jorn around there was no doubt in Nathan's mind that her life would go on with little interference from anyone. "We're all set for now," Nathan finally replied and he kissed Kala's warm hand, still resting in his. Many other journeys had just begun.

* * *

Printed in the United States
18342LVS00001B/204